DAVID

THE CLOTH ELEPHANT

WHEN WAR SHATTERS A YOUNG SOLDIER'S LIFE, CAN LOVE AND LOYALTY SURVIVE?

MEREO
Cirencester

Mereo Books

1A The Wool Market Dyer Street Cirencester Gloucestershire GL7 2PR
An imprint of Memoirs Publishing www.mereobooks.com

The cloth elephant: 978-1-86151-148-5

Printed and bound in Great Britain by
Marston Book Services Limited, Oxfordshire

A CIP catalogue record for this book is available from the British Library.

The address for Memoirs Publishing Group Limited can be found at
www.memoirspublishing.com

The Memoirs Publishing Group Ltd Reg. No. 7834348

The Memoirs Publishing Group supports both The Forest Stewardship Council® (FSC®) and the PEFC® leading international forest-certification organisations. Our books carrying both the FSC label and the PEFC® and are printed on FSC®-certified paper. FSC® is the only forest-certification scheme supported by the leading environmental organisations including Greenpeace. Our paper procurement policy can be found at
www.memoirspublishing.com/environment

Cover design - Ray Lipscombe

Typeset in 9/12pt Bembo
by Wiltshire Associates Publisher Services Ltd. Printed and bound in Great Britain by
Printondemand-Worldwide, Peterborough PE2 6XD

Acknowledgements

I would like to acknowledge two sources:
The Bomber Command War Diaries, edited by Martin Middlebrook, and *The Last Battle* by Cornelius Ryan.

Dedication

To my wife for her eternal patience, and to my family and friends for their unflagging encouragement.

Prologue

On a windy September day in 1985 in the city of Bonn, a black Mercedes saloon, flying the flag of the People's Republic of China, turned into a secluded square and stopped in front of a three-storey glass-fronted building which had risen from the ashes of the Second World War.

The driver opened the rear passenger door and a tall, well-built man in his late sixties stepped out. He wore a black fedora hat and a long waistless coat. He had a short well-trimmed grey beard and a small grey moustache. His skin was a little pitted and showed two scars, one on the forehead, the other on the left cheek.

The man walked to the entrance and the automatic doors opened noiselessly. He mounted the marble stairs, trying to ignore the stiffness in his left leg. His discomfort caused him to remember another September day a long time ago. His left hand slipped backwards on the metal banister as the memory of the shame of that day returned. He regained his composure.

His secretary, Katerina Lindemann, was waiting at the head of the stairs. She was in her early forties, with a shock of curly blond hair.

The name-plate on the door of the man's office read, 'Kurt Vietinghoff, Professor of Oriental Studies.' Katerina had been his secretary for twenty years and loved him to distraction. He wanted to know every facet of her life, but he did not return her feelings. His behaviour triggered attacks of depression in her.

Arno Kreuzfeld, the Professor's deputy, worshipped Katerina as fervently as Katerina worshipped Kurt. He had taken her to the opera, but she had felt faint and fled from the theatre. His enquiries led him to Katerina's childhood nurse, who told him Kurt was aware of her problems.

Arno saw Kurt wince with pain and persuaded him to see his doctor, who referred him to a hospital for tests. He kept the results a secret and no one saw him for days. Katerina phoned Kurt's doctor, who announced that he was in hospital and would see her.

On her way to the hospital, Katerina remembered the advertisement for the post of secretary to a distinguished academic, and how her flatmate Philomena had challenged her to apply for it. Her old School Principal, Frau Ackerman, had written her a glowing reference and come to the interview to support her. No one else was called and she was offered the post. She had not considered this unusual, until now.

One day Kurt had left, saying he was meeting a Chinese official, and Katerina had dashed off after him with his briefcase, assuming he had forgotten it. She had found him having lunch with Frau Ackerman, and realised they were lovers. That seemed to explain how she had got the job all those years ago. She was jealous, but felt they deserved each other, and Katerina was aware that Frau Ackerman was a remarkable and beautiful woman.

The hospital was a modern two-storey building partially hidden behind cleverly-planted trees and shrubs. Outside the main doors was a statue of the Virgin Mary and child. The doors parted noiselessly. The receptionist led her to the specialist's room.

He asked Katerina to sit down, peering briefly at a computer screen. "I understand you are very close to Professor Vietinghoff," he began. "He speaks very highly of you. Fräulein. I'm afraid you must prepare yourself for bad news. The cancers are aggressive. There is little we can do beyond making him as comfortable as possible."

She didn't want to believe him, and fought back tears. "Surely you can do something?" she said. The specialist shook his head. He asked only to see you, Fräulein," said the doctor.

Kurt smiled broadly and held out both arms. She embraced him and burst into tears. He showed no sign of fear and behaved as if Katerina was the patient.

"I believe you know the worst", he began. Then he took both her hands in his. "You must understand I have lived a good life. I've lived only as long as I deserve." A familiar look told her not to ask any questions. A half-smile crossed his face. "You must really look after Arno now. He's going to be your new boss."

He produced two telephone numbers, one for her old school, the other a Berlin number. "Please tell them what has happened, Katerina" he instructed her. "Only you can take care of my funeral arrangements" he added solemnly.

She broke down and threw her arms round his neck. "How can you treat all this like a military operation?" she asked him in despair.

His attitude changed as if it had been a charade. He grasped her hand and tears streamed down his face. She was frightened because she had never seen him like this before. "Please, please come and see me every day," he whispered. He still possessed great strength and he was hurting her arm. "Please!" he implored her. She couldn't accept that this authoritative man, so much larger than life, had been reduced to such a helpless figure.

Kurt deteriorated quickly. Finally the specialist advised that the end was not far off and urged Katerina and Arno to visit as soon as possible. Frau Ackerman respected her lover's wish that Katerina should not see her at the hospital.

"I have a strong feeling that you should be alone with him at the end," Arno told Katerina. "Please say I'm thinking of him."

The priest was already there to administer the last rites. "The end is not far away," he said. "If you need me, you know where I am."

The priest made his way down the corridor aided by a walking stick and clutching a bible in his right hand. She saw that Kurt was asleep and tiptoed in, afraid he might wake. His face was thin and pallid.

She stroked his head, listened to his laboured breathing, and watched the lifelines disappear. The nurse took her arm. "I will take care of everything, Fräulein Lindemann," she promised.

Katerina sat in the hospital gardens feeling emotionally drained. She remembered Agnes Felsen's words; Katerina must telephone if ever she lost her boss. Within an hour of receiving the call, Agnes was with her in her apartment. She stayed until Katerina was asleep.

Frau Ackerman organized a memorial service in the cemetery after the funeral service. Katerina was not consulted about the details, but Frau Ackerman insisted she must be there. She looked for a space at the back of the church, which was full to overflowing. The priest led them to two seats usually reserved for relatives. On Katerina's seat were a name card and yellow flowers.

She knew none of the group gathered round the memorial stone except Frau Ackerman, and no names were mentioned. One of the men was tall, with features like a boxer. His companion's face was brown and weatherbeaten. Their wreath was made of oak leaves. A tall blonde woman, consumed with grief, had sat behind Katerina during the service. The centrepiece of her wreath was a photograph of a dignified old lady.

The other man was elderly and Chinese. He draped a white scarf of mourning over the stone and placed a wooden box inscribed with Chinese characters at its foot. They all knew Frau Ackerman except for the Chinese man, and embraced her warmly.

Frau Ackerman had commissioned the memorial stone. On it was inscribed 'A great man and a great German.' There was no name, and it was only then that Katerina realized that the name Kurt Vietinghoff was probably an alias.

Within a week, Arno had moved into Kurt's office. The Bursar gave him a set of keys. Arno unlocked the cupboards and showed Katerina his discoveries. A battered straw lay on a green cheongsam, made for someone quite young and decorated with a golden dragon.

A long box attached to the underside of the table contained a broadsword with jade set into the hilt. With it was a small silver ingot. Arno was sure the sword had once belonged to a Chinese warlord.

"Why would he keep these things here?" asked Katerina.

"Because he knew I would show them to you, Katy," said Arno.

"The priest thought I ought to have this," she said, producing the wooden box left at the memorial. She opened it and withdrew a model soldier. "It must belong with all these things, don't you think Arno?"

They were interrupted by a call from Berlin. Johannes Berger, one of Kurt's lawyers, thought Katerina should attend the reading of Kurt's will. "It's to do with your work on the University Trust," suggested Arno.

Her train arrived on time and she took a taxi to Wilmersdorf. She tipped the driver and walked towards the steps of the main entrance to the lawyers' offices. "They're all waiting for you, Fräulein," said the chief clerk.

Kurt had left money to the University Trust and an ex-servicemen's association. He left the bulk of his fortune and his baroque family home near Berlin to Katerina. She was to allow the present incumbents of the house to live there as long as they wished.

She had telephoned ahead to tell Arno there were financial matters requiring her attention. Her door was half open, although she knew she had locked it. She pushed it open cautiously. "Please close the door," said Arno firmly.

Ten minutes later, Arno had proposed to her and she had accepted. The day's experiences had left her light-headed.

"Is this the end of Kurt's story?" she asked Arno.

"I fear it's only the beginning, Katy," he replied. "This came for you." He handed her an envelope. It was a letter inviting Katerina to Father Meinecke's residence.

She arrived exactly on time. The priest opened the heavy wooden door and ushered her in out of the cold evening air.

His indulgent manner suddenly changed. He gently withdrew a cardboard box from a safe and laid it on the table. Then he produced a duplicate of the cremation urn Katerina had seen at the memorial service. It contained Kurt's ashes. The explanation lay in a letter for Katerina. He wanted her to take them to Holland, and she was to go alone.

The three-hour journey felt like the longest in her life. Police searched the train for drugs and inspected the holdall containing the ashes. The weather worsened and a helpful attendant said she would soon be at Arnhem. Her instructions were to meet two men in the hospitality suite. She went to the information office and it was clear she was expected. "Please wait in there," said a woman in the office.

The train was due to return to Bonn in ten minutes. She decided to wait another five and then leave. She was just about to abandon the mission when the woman from the office stuck her head round the door.

"Don't worry," she began. "They're running late. They're on their way."

Five more minutes passed and Katerina heard the train leaving for Bonn. Two men in their sixties walked in. Both wore leather jackets, and she recognised them as the men from the graveside.

"We cannot introduce ourselves, Fräulein," said the smaller man. "Please trust us for the sake of Kurt, and please don't be scared of us."

"This won't take long" said his companion. You will be in plenty of time to catch your next train to Bonn. You have the ashes of course?"

She nodded. "Don't you think I deserve some answers?"

"The Professor cannot lie in peace unless this mission is carried out," the smaller man explained. They led Katerina to the station concourse. She thought the fog a fitting cloak for their activities. She fastened the top button of her coat and shivered.

The bigger man waved to his right and a black saloon glided into the taxi rank. The driver knew the two men and shook hands with them. Katerina sat in a rear seat with the smaller man. "You know the way, Wolters," the bigger man said to the driver.

They drove West of Oosterbeek through the rain and the fog for two or three kilometers. The car turned onto a rough track and stopped. The smaller man took Katerina's arm and led her through a picket fence, painted a mottled green and brown and surrounded by oak trees. In the gloom were rows of graves; she read the name 'Karl Eberhardt' on one of them. Three lions had been carved below the name.

A man appeared holding a spade. "You've brought him?" he asked, pointing to the hold all. He removed the urn and placed it reverently in a newly dug grave.

The three occupants of the car stood in a line and remained motionless for two minutes. Then each of them threw a handful of earth over the urn. The Dutchman filled in the grave and laid the stone slab to rest. The slab also bore the three lions and read, 'A Panzer Grenadier of the Third Reich. "Unknown"'. The three men stiffened and gave a half-Roman salute.

"This is not right," said the big man. "There should be a name."

"I know", said his companion. but there is nothing we can do. You must know that."

Katerina felt she had been plunged into the centre of a web of lies. Her companions felt she deserved to know something.

"Please try to understand Fraulein. This is our world, our other life" said the big man. He pointed to the grave behind her. The stone had been laid before the others and bore the marks of constant attempts to keep it clean. The script was still readable and she knelt down, not noticing that two of her companions had melted away. The gravedigger used a stiff brush to make the script clearer. Katerina read it slowly:

Untersturmführer Bruno Grabowsky
Reconnaissance Company, 9th SS Panzer division
Hohenstaufen. Arnhem 1944.

She read it over and over again, as if she hoped it would make the soldier rise from the dead and resolve the mystery surrounding Kurt. The others had gone. She heard the crunch of car tyres on the gravel as they left.

"It's all arranged. I am to drive you to the station," said the gravedigger. The Dutchman said nothing until they reached the station.

"Auf wiedersehen, Fräulein," he said. "Good men. I knew them all a long time ago."

"We have work to do," she announced to Arno on her return. "We must consult military records. I want to know everything about the Hohenstaufen Division in the war."

She knew the SS had been involved in war crimes and dreaded the thought that Kurt and those other men had been involved.

Arno found the Hohenstaufen had a blameless record, and did a little research of his own. "Liu Chen's translated the characters on the scarf, my love" he said. "It says, 'Goodbye Little Big Head'."

Chapter 1

Dawn was breaking in the South China Sea on a late autumn day in 1927. The *Derfligger*, a white-painted 15,000 ton passenger steamer of the Hamburg-East Asia line, was bound for Shanghai.

The radio operator ran to the bridge, clutching a message from the German Foreign Ministry. The ship was to make an unscheduled call at Whampoa Island at the mouth of the Pearl River Delta. On board was a young diplomat and his family. Peter von Saloman already possessed sealed orders. He and his wife and son were to be disembarked at Whampoa Island as quickly as possible. They were to transfer to a riverboat which would take them the last thirty kilometers to the city of Canton, where he was to promote German business interests. That really meant selling arms to the Chinese Nationalists. Concealed in the hold of the *Derfligger* were padlocked crates to be offloaded at Whampoa Island, containing rifles and machine guns.

His cabin door opened abruptly and a five-year-old boy, dressed in white trousers and a naval jacket, rushed to the port rails holding an old naval telescope. "Papa, Mama come quickly!" he called as a school of dolphins broke the surface of the sea and joined the ship. His mother appeared first, as she was always the first to answer her son's call.

Käthe von Saloman was tall, slim and elegantly dressed. Her auburn hair set off her pale skin and deep brown eyes. Her distant and confident bearing concealed a warm nature and a sharp sense of humour. She placed her arm on her son's shoulder. He gave her the telescope and she bent down and kissed him on the forehead. She produced a handkerchief and wiped her brow. Even at this early hour, the air was hot and oppressive.

"Can you see our destination?" said Peter, joining them. He was of medium height and square shouldered. His hair was cropped short and he wore a military moustache. He was dressed formally in a tropical suit. Alongside his wife and son Adam, he seemed stiff and ill at ease.

CHAPTER ONE

"Papa – look, we are coming to the river, the ship's turning!" said an excited Adam.

There were three other occupants of the first class cabins, and they stood apart from the family at a discreet distance. One had a distinct military bearing. He and his companions gazed intently at the shoreline. This man knew Peter's identity but had been ordered to conceal the fact. He was bound for Shanghai to talk to friends of General Chiang Kai-shek.

"Good morning sir," said Adam, saluting the man, who was taken aback, given the arrangement with Peter von Saloman. "Good morning young man," he replied, casting reproving glances at the boy's parents. Käthe hurried over to drag Adam away and apologized to him. He thanked her and forced a smile. "He has the right instincts, madam," he said curtly, turning away. The conversation was at an end.

Peter was embarrassed. "You must ask permission before approaching strangers, Adam," he said.

"You are right," said Käthe, squeezing her husband's arm. "But how else can he advance his military ambitions?"

Peter's stiffness was an outward sign of his shyness, but he managed a smile. Then he relaxed and laughed quietly. Adam held his hand as the ship turned towards the river. Even at his age, he had become expert at healing even the slightest rift between his parents. Peter had learned that Adam was allowed to do as he wished, and that was not too much of a risk because he was mature beyond his years. The encounter with the passenger showed Adam's fearlessness, but Peter feared an excess of that in his son.

He looked adoringly at the wife he believed he didn't deserve. He had seen widespread service in the Great War in Russia, Poland and finally in France. As victory was snatched from Germany in 1918, he had been seriously wounded near Albert on the Western Front. He had developed pneumonia and been given little chance of survival. As he lay, barely conscious, in a Berlin hospital, he felt a hand stroke his forehead. As he opened his eyes fully, the first person he saw was Nurse Käthe Holman.

Within a few weeks, they were deeply in love. Peter recovered and they were married in 1921. He left the war as a decorated Lieutenant, but there was no military future for him.

Peter's father Gustav used his contacts in the diplomatic service to secure his son a junior post in the Foreign Ministry in Berlin. During the next few years he did well and became an expert in communications. One morning he was called into the office of the Principal Secretary, who handed him a small pile of Chinese textbooks. He was given the telephone number of the Chinese Consulate in Berlin and instructed to use any means possible to learn rudimentary Chinese in the next six months.

He was informed that Käthe and Adam were also to learn the language. Peter was pleased that they took up the challenge, but envious when he heard the laughter behind closed doors. This was not the first time he had felt excluded.

Then he received a letter appointing him Deputy Consul to Karl Weidling in the southern Chinese city of Canton. Passage had been booked and he was to take up the appointment forthwith. The news received a mixed reception. Adam was excited, but his mother was deeply disappointed. Gustav, Peter's father, had taken to her immediately, but his wife Frieda was much more reserved and regarded Käthe as a social upstart.

The newcomer was patient. She was attractive and intelligent, and her patience was rewarded when Frieda introduced her to her glittering social contacts in Berlin.

Her new mother-in-law regularly invited her to Horcher's restaurant in Berlin for lunch, and slowly Käthe was accepted into Frieda's social circle. Frieda had found a new friend and now Käthe was expected to abandon her new life. Her own parents in Hamburg expressed reservations, but she dutifully made preparations for the sake of the one good chance Peter had to make a name for himself.

Adam made a show of enthusiasm, but he did not want to leave his grandfather Gustav, who doted on him. The little boy carried a small battered brown suitcase his grandfather had given him and inside were several toy soldiers his favourite relation had made for him in a wooden shed behind a magnificent baroque house beside the Wannsee. They were the symbols of the military career Gustav expected Adam to follow. But for the moment he forgot his grandfather in his excitement. The family peered through the late morning haze as the ship slowed and there was a clatter as the anchor was paid out.

Out of the morning mist came a small pilot boat, flying the flag of the People's Republic of China and crammed to the gunwales with soldiers. The pilot climbed a rope ladder into the waist of the ship. Two small tugs approached the ship and guided her towards a long wooden wharf, on the end of which was a solitary unloading crane.

Behind the wharf was a collection of wooden buildings, some built on stilts over the water. The wharf teemed with people and Peter and his family watched them as the ship was secured.

Most of the men wore little else but a sleeveless canvas vest, a loin cloth and reed sandals. The women wore long canvas dresses, their heads covered in turbans or wide-brimmed conical hats. They, not the men, carried the goods, which included black long-beaked birds in wooden cages and poultry, still alive, carried upside down in threes.

Beyond the people on the dockside was a rusting twin-funnelled river steamer and by the gangplank a detachment of soldiers. A crane moved on rails to the foredeck of the *Derfligger*. There, secured under a tarpaulin, was a new Mercedes saloon intended for the use of the Consulate in Canton.

Peter ordered his family into their cabin as the crane dipped and secured the car. It looked as if it might plummet into the river as it was swung onto the foredeck of the river steamer.

Four of the Chinese soldiers, led by an officer with a gleaming sword, marched at the double to the companionway of the *Derfligger* as the captain conducted the von Saloman family to the quayside. The officer welcomed them in halting German and then offered to escort them to the riverboat which was to take them the remaining thirty kilometers to Canton.

The throng of people were not interested in the foreign visitors. They surged towards the gangplank but were driven back by rifle butts to make way for them. As the family reached the riverboat, an immaculately-dressed waiter carrying a silver tray met them and bowed.

They were conducted to a canvas awning by the side of the now-secured Mercedes. Iced lemon drinks waited for them on a small collapsible table covered with a lace cloth, under a sun umbrella. When they had made themselves comfortable, the usual passengers were allowed to board. Peter watched with alarm as the boat settled in the water, carrying far beyond its capacity. The Mercedes lurched forward, severely testing the chains securing it.

He removed his hat and wiped the sweat from his forehead. The crowd surged up to the ropes which separated them from the German visitors. Two soldiers stood by the ropes; they would stay there for the entire journey.

The riverboat's engines coughed into life and clouds of blue smoke came from the funnels. It changed colour to a dirty white and the breeze blew its acrid fumes onto the decks. The boat followed a series of buoys into a central channel and set off northwards down the Pearl.

Käthe leaned over a rusty hand rail to look in the direction of the *Derfligger*. She felt a deep sadness as she saw the only link with her life in Germany disappearing into a yellow haze. She wondered how she would ever get used to her new life.

The throng of people behind them became quiet for ten minutes, many of them glaring suspiciously at the wealthy passengers. Suddenly several of them burst into a babble of excited chatter. There was even loud laughter, and the guards wondered at the source of the amusement.

Adam was seated on his old brown suitcase, peering down the river through his father's telescope. He saw the joke, jumped up from the suitcase and waved it at them.

"Please Adam," said Peter stiffly. "Remember who you are." The little boy sat down glumly on his suitcase and the laughter continued, making Peter uncomfortable. Käthe squeezed his arm. "It's all right my darling. They mean us no harm."

Two of the Chinese women pointed to Adam's straw hat. Then they pointed at their own conical hats and made signs that they would like to try his. Adam thought this great fun and exchanged hats, to the consternation of his parents. He walked up and down the ropes extending his small hand. He looked at a sullen man holding three chickens. Adam held out his hand and the man smiled. Peter was furious.

"Shake hands with them, Peter. We must make friends with these poor people," suggested Käthe. Peter regretted not having given his wife lessons in protocol. He kept his distance and went no further than smiling indulgently at the crowd. He continued to sip his lemonade in a dignified manner and retreated into his shyness.

The three Germans gazed at the scenery around them. The river banks, barely distinguishable from the many small islands, were nearly half a kilometer away.

Brilliantly-coloured fish and dolphins followed the boat. A large black and white crane surveyed the ferry from its vantage point on a large sandbank and a long yellow shape slithered into the water from a sandbank.

CHAPTER ONE

Adam seized his father's hand, dragging him to the rail. "Here, Papa" he said, handing him the telescope. "It's your turn. It's an alligator."

Peter and his son scanned the riverbanks. Villages had been built over the water. Fields lay behind them. He placed his arm round his son's shoulders. The boat fought the current and at one point it seemed to stand still.

Peter and Käthe settled into their deckchairs and fell asleep, and the crowd behind them became quiet as the foreigners were no longer a novelty. Adam thought of his grandfather, picked up his suitcase and sat on a deckchair. He opened the suitcase watched by the woman who had tried his straw hat. One by one he took out four toy soldiers and arranged them in a line looking upriver. His grandfather had told him, "You can be like them and ride to victory for Germany." He lovingly replaced them in the suitcase.

Adam gently shook his parents. Somewhere in the distance he had heard a clap of thunder. The city of Canton, for one hundred and fifty years the only city in China open to foreigners, materialized out of the mist. Peter's map of Canton was nearly a century old and clearly much had changed. He trained the telescope on the town.

The riverboat shook as the engines slowed and Peter could just distinguish Shamian Island, where most of the foreign concessions were to be found. Hundreds of interlinked wooden houses gave way to two-storey brick buildings. Small craft obscured the water in front of the wooden dwellings and scores of fishing nets hung on poles. Small junks were tethered on their own wooden jetties. The riverboat was swallowed up by the seething mass of activity on the riverfront. The air was yellow.

Peter scanned the waterfront on the mainland – and saw a European Church spire. He gave the telescope to Käthe and her spirits rose. "It must be the Catholic Church of the Sacred Heart, Peter," she said. Both were grateful to see a European sanctuary in this alien land. "We must go to confession there as soon as possible," added Käthe.

The riverboat slowed even more and the crew stood by as they approached a long wooden jetty. The Chinese passengers began to push and jostle, but once more they were made to wait.

The jetty teemed with at least twenty heavily armed soldiers and a machine gun on the end of the jetty was sited to sweep the waterfront with fire. In their midst stood a tall bespectacled European wearing a broad brimmed white hat, immaculate in a tropical suit. He stood quite still with his hands behind his back. Sergeants barked orders and the soldiers stood to attention. The boat was secured and once again a crane appeared and the Mercedes was hoisted onto the jetty. One of the soldiers immediately climbed into the car and started it. Two soldiers rested their rifles on the bonnet pointing them towards the waterfront. Adam was excited, but Peter and Käthe were worried. "Why all these soldiers, Peter?" she asked; he confessed he didn't know.

The companionway was extended to the jetty. Peter led his family onto the waterfront and approached the tall European.

"I am Karl Weidling and you are all most welcome to Canton," he said. Adam saluted again.

"This must be your son, Herr Von Salomon? I think he will fit in well here," he said with a smile. Weidling's first words to Adam had just fuelled one of his greatest hopes; that there might be someone of his own age at their new home.

The sergeant of the guard walked over smartly and spoke in Weidling's ear. It was clear he wanted the small party to leave the waterfront, as soon as possible. "You must be careful," said Consul Weidling. "Do not think for one moment we are popular here among the poorer people. Our best friend, Chiang Kai-shek, is thirty kilometers away on Whampoa Island."

He could see that Peter deserved an explanation, and promised one. The driver opened the car doors for the new arrivals and the soldiers closed round the car. A motorcycle escort of two men appeared.

To Peter's surprise, the car moved off in an easterly direction, not towards a waterfront ferry. It entered a maze of narrow streets and was forced to stop on several occasions as their escort cleared the way. Käthe drew Peter's attention to the number of men, young and old, sitting outside doors apparently in a stupor. She was already reverting to her role as a nurse. "What are they doing, Mama?" asked Adam. She was just as puzzled.

Peter opened a window and the driver was alarmed. A sickly smell entered the car and Adam covered his face with his sleeve. Käthe recognized the smell of opium.

The car reached a hidden exit at crawling speed, but three men wearing wooden armour stood in their way, all carrying rifles and bandoliers of ammunition. The man in the middle had a long pointed beard. He had tired but threatening eyes and carried a wicked-looking broad sword. Their soldier escort bowed to him.

Weidling knew him. They acknowledged each other and the car was allowed to pass, but not before the man had cast a predatory glance at Käthe. Weidling explained.

"That man is a warlord opium dealer. He is called Huang Lin Hui. He is evil and unpredictable, but he is a friend of Chiang Kai-shek. Therefore he must be our friend. I realize you must find that disturbing, Frau von Saloman," he said.

Peter grasped her hand. He was beginning to regret bringing his family to such a dangerous place. Even the usually fearless Adam was not comfortable.

They emerged from the narrow streets onto the business area of Canton controlled almost exclusively by Europeans. A large sign announced they had passed a light engineering factory owned by Siemens and Peter felt proud. "Look, a famous German company," he said, trying to make his family feel more at home.

The car turned left down the old main street for a short while. Up until now theirs was the only car they had seen. Now they ran into a small traffic jam as other cars tried to make their way through the press of local people.

The car turned right and began to climb, emerging after a few minutes near a collection of traditional Chinese houses. Adam saw the consulate first, and his doubts disappeared. It was a white building on a rise partly obscured by an avenue of trees which led to iron gates. It was completely alone and looked across the roofs of many of the Cantonese houses towards the riverfront.

"Please stay in the car until we have passed through the gates," ordered Weidling.

Adam stared at the two soldiers who opened the gates and he noticed that, unlike some of the soldiers at the dock, they wore brand new uniforms with shining knee-length leather boots.

After the gates had been opened, they presented arms and Adam saluted them from inside the car. The taller of the two smiled and returned Adam's salute.

Weidling was reluctant even now to explain the security displayed ever since the family had disembarked. But as Consulate staff helped to carry luggage from the trunk to the Von Salomon's new house, he took Peter aside. When he heard what the Consul had to say, Peter began to regret ever having to come to China. Chiang had suppressed a Communist uprising in Canton only a few weeks before. Nationalist soldiers had beheaded their prisoners openly in the streets, and for days afterwards the heads of some of the victims, skewered on wooden stakes, had gazed down at passers-by as a grim warning. Chiang claimed he had finally defeated the Communists, but Weidling expressed doubts.

Chiang wanted to unite China, which suited the German purpose, but there was the problem of several warlords who didn't want this. Weidling explained that they all wanted German guns, and some were bitter enemies. "So you see von Saloman, we have a diplomatic problem which should test our ingenuity," he said regretfully.

The gates closed and the car stopped within a few yards. Chinese servants appeared and opened the doors, fixing their eyes firmly on the ground. The family had been used to bustle and noise for the previous two hours. Now there was silence except for the sound of running water.

Peter and Käthe stood either side of Adam protectively and they looked around them. The apartments and offices were set in a huge cloister two stories high. Each office displayed a small brass nameplate announcing its function and the name of the official. The largest office was at the head of the quadrangle, at the top of a small slope. The flag of the Republic of Germany flew outside its large panelled door and the nameplate bore Karl Weidling's name.

Adam ran to an adjacent office and pointed to a brass plate bearing Peter's name. "This young man is doing my job for me," said the Consul.

Each office and each apartment had a small well-tended garden connected to a pathway stretching the whole length of the inner perimeter. The rest of the space was taken up by a large pool with a circle of six fountains. Adam was already staring at the koi carp lazily moving in the pool, surrounded by a large close-cropped lawn with circular flower beds. The fountains gently lapped the water. There was no sign of anyone else except the servants.

"You are impressed, my friends?" asked Weidling.

"Indeed we are," answered Käthe politely.

"I noticed you seemed surprised when the car turned away from the waterfront," he added. Peter's training led him to expect a vague explanation of the Consulate's location.

"We felt we wished to be away from the other foreign concessions on Shamian Island." He looked directly at Peter. "Because, perhaps of our, what you might call broader approach to diplomacy. But let me show you your apartment. Please follow me."

As they approached their new home, Käthe noticed it was next door to the surgery. A cheerful-looking figure wearing large horn-rimmed spectacles, bounced down the steps to meet them. He stretched out his hand enthusiastically to all three of them in turn.

"This is Dr Jacob Meissner, and I think he is about to request in the friendliest terms that you attend his surgery for a medical as soon as possible," said Weidling.

"Indeed," said the doctor, beaming. "I believe I am in the company of the former Sister Käthe Holman?" Jacob Meissner had the gift of engaging the interest and attention of almost everyone at once, and the family took to him immediately.

"Perhaps I may borrow Frau von Saloman from time to time?" he asked hopefully. Käthe looked equally hopefully at Peter. "Perhaps, perhaps, but my wife will be principally concerned with our son's education" he reminded Käthe.

"Of course," replied Dr Meissner, concealing his disappointment. "Perhaps I may be able to help in that area," he added hopefully.

"We have a surprise for you and your son, madam. It is to do with other skills I have heard you possess," said Karl Weidling with a broad smile. "I shall leave you now. The servants and Jacob will take care of you and I shall expect you all to join the doctor and myself for dinner this evening at eight o'clock."

The servants waited dutifully with the luggage, but Adam hung on grimly to his little brown suitcase. Peter opened the front door which led to a small vestibule, which in turn led to the entrance hall.

Käthe and Peter held hands and stepped onto a deep red carpet. Dark oak panels had been let into the walls, and overhead were two silver chandeliers. There were two rooms either side of the entrance hall and one other at the end, which covered the whole width of the apartment. Its door was closed, although muffled sounds emerged from it.

Adam opened the door. Standing at a cooking range holding a large onion was a small rotund Chinese cook wearing a chef's hat. He had a smile nearly as broad as his corpulent body. He bowed to Adam who bowed and hurriedly retreated.

The two rooms on the left were a reception room and lounge equipped with a clever mix of Chinese and European antique furniture. The first room on the right was a study designed for Peter. The second was locked. Adam loved the mystery, but it was resolved when the cook appeared with a key once again bowing and grinning. He pushed the door open. The carpet was white and on it in the centre of the room was Weidling's surprise, a Steinway grand piano.

Käthe almost forgot her doubts about moving to China as she sat at the piano and played a few notes to check that it had been tuned. "This will soon be your seat, my darling," she said to her son.

The servants waited patiently beside the luggage as Käthe directed each suitcase to its destination. The family unpacked and for the moment ignored the surroundings on the first floor settling in the lounge. They looked at each other as if they could hardly believe they were there.

Chinese paintings adorned the walls. The days were gone when a diplomat's living area was dominated by a portrait of Kaiser Wilhelm II. Peter wondered whose portrait might replace some of the Chinese pictures in the future.

That evening, Karl Weidling hosted a candlelit dinner. Peter and Käthe were introduced to Peter's new colleagues and the wives of those who were married. Adam seemed comfortable in the company of older people. That had been his lot so far. He had begun to think he would never find friends of his own age.

The gathering was supposed to support the new German Republic, but the interest generated by Adam's revelation of his military ambition suggested otherwise. One Under Secretary was not ashamed to proclaim his support for an up-and-coming right wing party called the National Socialists, led by an obscure Austrian called Adolf Hitler.

Adam looked round the table. There were no children, almost as if the officials of the Consulate had been chosen for being childless. He decided to put on a brave face.

"You must miss your friends," said Frau Keller, a kindly-looking lady in her fifties.

"My parents are my friends," answered Adam. "Oh I see" said Frau Keller, who spent the rest of the evening trying to make Adam feel more comfortable. She felt she was being politely rebuffed.

As Adam prepared for sleep at an hour late for him, he went through his usual routine. His mother had laid out his nightshirt on the bed. He unpacked his brown suitcase. He took out his four Uhlan cavalry men and photographs of his grandparents and arranged them on the dressing table in a protective arc facing his bed. He repeated his grandfather Gustav's words over and over again: "You will receive the approval of your family one day, when you ride to victory for Germany."

Flushed with pride, the lonely little boy fell asleep.

Chapter 2

Early next morning the new lives of the von Saloman family began to take shape. At eight o'clock there was a sharp rap at the front door of the apartment and Peter answered the door. It was Weidling's adjutant.

"Please wear military uniform," he advised. "Chiang and his German advisers will be here soon."

Peter changed accordingly, but felt uncomfortable. He looked in a mirror and thought it was not possible to look more unmilitary. Käthe came to his rescue, accompanied by Adam and the cook, who showed Peter how to bow.

"Remember who we are, Papa," Adam reminded his father. Adam saluted Peter, who sallied forth to his first major engagement. Ten minutes later the quadrangle echoed with the sounds of barked orders as the gates were opened. Twenty immaculately uniformed Chinese soldiers escorted a large American saloon car into the Consulate.

Out of it stepped the trim figure of General Chiang Kai-shek. He was met by Peter and the Consul, who shook hands and saluted. Peter was inwardly quaking in his boots, but he needn't have worried. The General took to Peter immediately and Weidling was delighted. It seemed that Peter had discovered a hidden talent.

They all disappeared into Weidling's office for the first of many military conferences. In the coming weeks, Peter couldn't wait to make his mark.

Adam loved the idea of his father strutting about with powerful men, and quizzed him as soon as he returned from each mission. He missed his father, whose repeated absences drew them closer together. Even so, Peter knew their relationship could never rival that between Adam and his mother.

Käthe's attitude to her husband's achievements rarely exceeded politeness, something which Peter failed to notice at first. He was happy so long as her first concern was Adam's welfare. Dr Meissner had to deal with an outbreak of food poisoning in the Consulate and again asked for Käthe's help. Peter's attitude was almost condescending. "Those days are over my dear," he announced. "You must now carry out the duties of a mother and a diplomat's wife."

Peter failed to see how annoyed his wife was. For the moment, she decided to busy herself with Adam's education.

The Industrial Revolution came to China at a snail's pace, barely noticed by most Chinese. A new single-tracked railway snaked its way northwards to join the Trans-Siberian railway far to the North at Mukden, but for now, it had only reached Wuhan. An airstrip was quickly built there and a complementary one at Canton. Soon Chinese Nationalist forces would strike north, and it became clear that they depended on their German friends for arms and advice.

Peter bombarded Käthe with his enthusiasm, to no avail. What was worse, she had no female friends and was unlikely to make any, as Peter insisted that the female staff were all of a lower class.

Dr Jacob Meissner became her devoted friend. He behaved like a considerate uncle who believed his charge should be indulged, and constantly made a fuss of her. Peter's absences were frequent and Käthe began to feel other longings. Always her loyalty to Peter enabled her to suppress them, for now.

Peter had already made an impression, but only in the company of Karl Weidling. Now he was to strike out on his own, and Weidling gave him a personal aide.

The Chinese Nationalists were ready to strike northwards from Canton, but they were as yet unsure of the attitudes of some of the warlords. Peter was to journey north to conduct negotiations with possible allies. His task would be difficult, and he was to be absent from the Consulate for long periods. Weidling told Peter he was part of the new grand purpose of the German Republic. The consul could be complacent and didn't tell Peter he might be journeying into danger.

Peter left his wife with instructions to busy herself with Adam's education, with strict instructions to remain inside the Consulate. At first she played the role of the dutiful wife. Peter and Käthe were both devout Catholics and she attended daily prayers with Adam in one of the two chapels in the Consulate. Each day he accompanied his mother to the chapel, clutching the prayer book he had been given emblazoned with an imperial German eagle.

The grand piano was in good condition, and Käthe was a better than average pianist. Adam was an eager pupil and practised regularly. His mathematics teacher was Dr Meissner, who was surprised at the speed of Adam's progress, but dismayed at his apparent unconcern at the lack of young people of his own age in the Consulate. Adam gave the impression that he preferred the friendship of older people, and soon grew close to "Uncle Jacob."

Käthe soon realised that Jacob Meissner had a great deal of influence on Karl Weidling. Once Peter had left for the north, she began to work on him. He had no answer to Käthe's charms. When she offered help in the Consulate surgery, despite Peter's strictures, Meissner had no hesitation in persuading Karl Weidling that Käthe and Adam would be quite safe in Canton under military escort.

Käthe had a powerful argument. She and Adam needed to take communion at the Church of the Sacred Heart in Canton. Käthe was fortified by Adam's confidence and couldn't wait to visit the town. Their plans didn't include a visit to the church, to begin with, and Adam enjoyed the deception.

Two days after Chiang Kai-shek's visit, Peter left for the north on the new railway line to Wuhan. He shelved any doubts he had had about moving to China and accepted Chiang's assurance that the Communists had been expelled from Canton. He now almost believed his family to be safe, and his determination to do his duty became a minor obsession overcoming any of his doubts.

He didn't allow Käthe and Adam to see him off at the makeshift railway station, because Karl Weidling persuaded him there was a slight risk. Käthe clung to Peter as they said goodbye at the iron gates. He possessed the reserve of many upper middle-class Germans, but not towards Adam.

Peter hugged his son tightly and instructed him to look after his mother. Unlike Käthe, Adam was confident that they would soon see his father again, but he found it difficult to choke back tears. He clutched his mother's arm as they watched the smoke from Peter's train disappear into the Chinese countryside.

The great oil-fired locomotive pulled one carriage only and on the side were the crossed flags of the new Nationalist China and the German Republic. The only passengers were Peter and his aide, Ehrich. Neither of them expected to negotiate as early as they did and certainly not for their lives, as well as for the prestige of Germany. Four hours into the journey to the north, as the train travelled through the endless paddy fields of Eastern China, Peter heard a volley of shots. The train stopped slowly, almost as if by arrangement. The driver appeared and suggested that Peter and his aide Conrad Ehrlich get off the train. They naturally behaved as if it were beneath their dignity to do so.

They changed their attitude when they saw the scene outside the train. Lined up in perfect order were about one hundred heavily armed horsemen, wearing long padded belted coats. The brigands parted to allow their leader through.

"Your Excellency. This is the Warlord of this Province. He extends his greetings," announced the driver, who hardly dared lift his head. Peter nodded condescendingly.

"It is the custom, Your Excellency," continued the driver, "To pay a toll when crossing the Warlords' territory."

Peter glanced at the weapons carried by the brigands; many of them were antiquated. A few of the horsemen had no firearms. All the modern weapons were German. Peter's aide reminded him they were negotiating for their lives. He nodded, but ignored the advice. He was resplendent in uniform and had discovered his old regimental spirit, and he knew the bargaining power of the silver ingots locked in his safe on the train.

"Tell His Excellency," began Peter, "That if there has been no prior agreement, the German Government will not pay such a toll." His aide froze and the train driver began to foam at the mouth. The Brigands shifted threateningly. Peter pointed to the German flag on the train and then to the Mauser rifle carried by the Warlord.

"Please inform His Excellency," said Peter, "That if the train is allowed to continue without payment of a toll, then His Excellency will soon be provided with more German weapons."

Peter waited. The Warlord dismounted and saluted him. Ehrlich breathed a sigh of relief and the private army escorted the train for the next thirty kilometres.

Peter had now established himself in the local fiefdom as the most respected of the German contingent in Southern China. He felt self-satisfied as they met the military escort at Wuhan. He would not have felt so pleased with himself had he known of the events which were already unfolding in Canton.

Chapter 3

Käthe told Jacob she would not be happy for her son's future unless they were both allowed to visit Canton. She knew there might be little time before Peter's return, and she kept up the pressure. A Lutheran pastor visited the consulate, but there was no Catholic chaplain. Käthe told the doctor it was vital for her to go to confession and the best place was the Church of the Sacred Heart in the city. She gave the impression that she was in religious turmoil. Jacob pleaded with Karl Weidling to allow them to go, and it worked.

The consulate car was escorted by two armed motor cyclists to take them the short distance into the city. Two more soldiers were to meet them on foot. The doctor thought they would be quite inconspicuous among the other Europeans, but Weidling insisted they be an advertisement for the German Republic. Adam dressed like a diplomat and Käthe a representative of high fashion.

The car stopped on the waterfront and the driver gave them three hours. The pair should have been afraid, but Käthe's son was her prize asset. He believed he could protect his mother whatever happened.

The two walked down one narrow street after another and Adam tried out his Chinese and was largely ignored. They stumbled across the Church of the Sacred Heart hidden between the commercial district and the waterfront. The priest was French and was delighted that Käthe spoke his language. Mother and son took confession and the priest introduced some of his Chinese flock. They left him to look for the main attraction, the Qing Ping market. Käthe intended to buy and had come equipped with American dollars.

The noise of the market was deafening. A stall holder waved a bamboo cane at a man who was refusing to pay him. A crowd gathered round. The man handed over some money, then snatched a figurine from the stall and ran off towards the narrow streets.

Wizened old women manned isolated stalls. One of them plucked Käthe by the sleeve. She recoiled, but Adam rescued the situation by bowing to the old lady. There were more and more stalls, until it became difficult to walk down the streets.

The sun beat down on the market and the air was yellow and oppressive. An old man with a long silver beard offered Käthe a wooden bowl containing water. She took it gratefully.

The stalls were status symbols. Some stood behind mock-ups of pagodas, some behind a few planks. Others arranged reed baskets and sandals on the open ground. The air crackled with the cooking of street food. An old man offered Adam a small fish on the end of a stick. He tried it eagerly, but the old man laughed at his attempts to speak Chinese. Hens clucked, pigs squealed. Occasionally money changed hands, but many bartered. One dignified old man was surrounded by dried fish, snake and alligator skins for medicinal purposes. Wooden and paper lanterns, some containing lighted candles, hung from rails. The smell of tallow filled the air.

Käthe produced a few dollars and the atmosphere instantly changed. She bought silk, drapes and a lantern, all carried by the soldiers, to the delight of the stallholders. The three hours had nearly passed and their escort begged the pair to leave immediately, as the soldiers feared terrible punishment if anything should happen to their charges.

The press of people continued as the small party elbowed their way through the narrow streets on the way to the waterfront. Suddenly the chattering crowd melted away and there was an ominous silence. Adam took his mother's arm and hurried her along. The soldiers urged them on, aware of how common kidnappings were in Canton. They came to an abrupt halt. Their way was blocked by three fearsome-looking men. They stood stock still, hands resting on the hilts of their huge broadswords. The leader's right hand rested on a partially-drawn Luger pistol.

"Madame or Frau?" he asked in a high pitched voice.

The two soldiers by now were on their knees, their rifles lying uselessly on the cobblestones. Käthe was sick with fear, but Adam held on to her hand tightly and stared defiantly at the Warlord.

To the horror of their escort, Käthe found the courage to announce that she was the wife of one of the most important Germans in Canton and this young man was her son. She was barely understood, and the warlord looked her up and down with a leer. "You are in my kingdom here, dear lady," he said.

CHAPTER THREE

As he moved closer to Käthe, she was aware of the sickly smell of opium. Adam drew himself up and stood directly in front of her. The two bodyguards laughed. One of the soldiers raised his head and was struck senseless by a blow to the head from a rifle butt. Adam shouted, "Stop that!" The Warlord grinned and held up a restraining hand. By now his pale, sinister face had adopted a half smile.

"Welcome to Canton," he said. "You are now under my protection." He spoke slowly so the two could understand. "But I see you already have a protector, dear lady," he added, looking at Adam. One of the bodyguards laughed, but was silenced by a withering look from the Warlord, who introduced himself as Huang Lin Hui. "I will remember you," he said to Adam and turned to leave. Then as a parting remark, he added, "Der Deutsche Junge." The three men disappeared into the narrow streets. Their escort's face was covered in blood and they helped him to the rendezvous on the waterfront.

The soldier was hurried to the surgery, where Dr Meissner bandaged his wound and forbade any more visits to the town. Karl Weidling interrupted to ask about the expedition, but Käthe could hardly face him. The purchased goods now seemed like useless baubles.

To the doctor's amazement, Adam told Karl Weidling, "Today was good sir. The Warlord is now our friend." Weidling's political brain now worked overtime. Perhaps another expedition might be allowed, he thought. If only this little boy was a few years older, how useful he could be.

Käthe took a few days to recover, but she didn't intend to be trapped in the consulate. The doctor warned her that Peter might return soon but she seemed deaf to his warning, determined not be intimidated by these three men on the waterfront. Besides, she had heard about the little Opera House and the department store in the Waterfrontbund.

Then came a message delivered by hand to the consulate gates. A frightened young fisherman announced that the Warlord had guaranteed Käthe and Adam safe passage in future. Weidling breathed a sigh of relief and thought another expedition would help relations with him, although he held the man in the highest contempt.

Other hostile eyes who were not followers of the Warlord had watched the foreigners on the waterfront. Their comrades had been slaughtered by Chiang in the communist uprising and they planned revenge on the hated foreigners who had supported him.

Käthe's main diversion was dinner in the evening with either Jacob Meissner or Karl Weidling. The doctor was a live wire and shared his professional experience with her. He always involved Adam, which pleased her. Karl Weidling mistakenly believed that Käthe wanted to hear the story of his unfulfilled life repeated over and over again. She had no choice but to listen, longing for Peter's return. She knew she must cultivate favour with him to be allowed outside the consulate.

Adam noticed that the two soldiers they had first seen at the gates were always there at the same time each week. Celebrations were in order in the Nationalist community because Chiang had acquired a new wife. On this October day, the two guards wore their best uniforms. Karl Weidling let it be known that the German community would like to formally offer their congratulations.

At noon, the gates opened to allow Chiang's personal aid through and the two guards snapped to attention. The gates closed and they relaxed, chatting to each other. The younger of the two noticed they had company. Standing on guard with them was a model soldier. They turned round to see a small boy clutching the gates.

"Hello, I am Adam von Saloman," he announced. They turned round and pretended to ignore this self-important young man. They both stared down the walnut grove for a few seconds, trying not to laugh. The younger brother turned and saluted the model lancer, and Adam smiled with relief.

Karl Weidling took pity on Adam as he saw him clutching the gates. He saw the lancer and reached inside a metal box attached to an inner wall, taking out a large key. He unlocked the gates and was deferential towards the two guards, knowing they were the sons of one of Chiang's influential supporters. "Gentlemen," he began, "look after this young man." He told Adam he was allowed one hour outside.

The relief guard took over and the brothers invited Adam to sit on a concrete pillar. The younger of the two brothers gave him the lancer and they sat cross-legged on the grass. Karl Weidling and his guests withdrew to the poolside, leaving Adam alone with them.

The brothers pretended not to relax. "Do you have anything else to say young man?" asked the older one.

"My father is very important" said Adam, a little lost for words. The younger brother replied "Isn't your mother important?" Lines crossed Adam's face. Then the elder brother laughed and held out his hand.

CHAPTER THREE

"We are brothers," he began. "I am Bing Wen and this is Bing Wu, and our father is very important too."

The brothers continued to enjoy the young foreigner's embarrassment as they slowly relaxed. They said they lived in a village forty kilometres north of Canton and had been soldiers for nearly two years. Their father, Huang Yuxiang, owned a lot of land and wanted his sons to help Chiang and the Nationalists. Adam gained confidence and asked if he might visit their house, quickly adding that they could come to Germany and visit his family home near Berlin, 'Die Schwanen'. Adam knew nothing of Chinese custom and did not realise that such a visit was unlikely.

Over the next few weeks, the friendship grew. Adam always sat on the concrete pillar clutching his model soldier who, he believed was the go-between in the friendship. Bing Wen and his brother told their young friend about the beautiful sub-tropical countryside and their life on the river. They described the huge granite karsts, outcrops of rock, which looked over the land. To Adam, it was the backdrop of a fairytale.

He told Käthe every detail. She listened attentively and it refuelled her desire to go on another expedition. He told his new friend of his mother's ambitions, but Bing Wu became very serious and advised Adam to be careful. "We'll choose the soldiers who'll go with you," he said.

The day out was more like a royal procession, and nearly all the consulate staff turned out to wave them off. Their cheerful Chinese cook had prepared a picnic hamper which was stowed in the boot of the Mercedes. Käthe insisted on travelling in an open car. She dressed elegantly, and Adam was resplendent in white tropical trousers and a straw boater. He had persuaded his mother to see the Chinese countryside for the first time because the brothers had talked about it so much.

The roar of motor-cycle engines told Käthe and Adam that the time for departure was close. They were watched by one of the Chinese servants, who was satisfied he had played his part. His comrades in the city knew the Germans were coming.

The car forced its way through the press of people to the waterfront and Käthe was in her seventh heaven as she spent lavishly in the department store in the Waterfrontbund. They were given a conducted tour of the small opera house and visited the French priest at the church once more.

Adam reminded his mother of her promise to visit the countryside. They found the car and travelled down the main city street, dodging the throngs in the daily markets.

The car left the city of Canton behind and the road gave way to an earthen track.

"Are you sure you wish to go on, my darling?" she asked. The brothers said the countryside was beautiful. Therefore he owed it to his new friends to see it.

"Of course, Mama," he replied.

The car jolted violently as it hit deep ruts and the driver suggested they stop as soon as possible. One of their motorcycle escorts had fallen off his machine and their Chinese escorts wanted to go back.

Adam saw houses in the distance, and the driver was persuaded to go a little further. The car stopped at a crossroads, the soft red soil still wet from the last storm. The path to the left disappeared into fields of tall maize.

Adam and Käthe stared out of the open-topped car into the shimmering midday heat. The tiny houses were made of bamboo and adobe and each had a small pond. Stretching in to the distance until they disappeared into the heat haze were endless paddy fields. There was no bustle here. There was a sense of urgency, but it was disguised by the slow movements of the people, almost all of them in the paddy fields. No one looked at them.

The car moved closer and Adam stared at a bamboo enclosure occupied by black pot-bellied pigs. He watched the water wheel, worked by mules. Some of the figures moved up and down the tracks, burdened by heavy reed baskets on carrying poles. Adam's ambition did not drown his compassion.

"Are Grandfather's farmers like this Mama?" he asked.

"I'm afraid they might be, Adam," she replied, equally affected.

The driver unloaded the picnic hamper and the table and chairs were set out. Käthe felt ridiculous dressed as she was and Adam had long since shed his jacket. They soon began to lose interest in a picnic, which was beyond the wildest dreams of the people whose privacy they felt they had invaded. Their escort and the driver tried not to watch them eating, but it was too much for Käthe.

"Please ask them to join us, Adam," she asked.

The driver was reluctant, but Adam took his arm and led him to his own seat. The couple watched the blue-green horizon grow darker as the sun began to sink and the driver insisted they return. The motor-cycles were restarted in clouds of exhaust smoke.

The car jolted once again in the ruts, but soon reached the outskirts of Canton. Adam was disappointed because he had seen nothing he could describe as spectacular and was afraid he would disappoint his new friends. Both were tired and Adam fell asleep on his mother's shoulder. Käthe herself could hardly stay awake. She saw nothing of the movements in the half-light around them.

The streets were strangely deserted and Adam briefly awoke as if he sensed danger. Faces appeared in alleyways and then suddenly disappeared. "Should we go faster, Mama?" he asked.

"It's all right my darling," she replied, but she wasn't so sure. Adam cast a glance behind them and was sure he saw shadowy figures following the car. Their escort seemed unconcerned. Adam waved to the motor cyclists. They waved back and he felt better. The car reached the walnut grove.

Five men were using the trees and nearby scrub to hide their movements. All carried rifles and bandoliers of ammunition. They'd waited for this moment ever since the hated general had slaughtered so many of their comrades on a September day in 1927. One man carried a knapsack and was wrapping his fingers gently round a grenade. All wore reed sandals and a khaki field cap displaying a red star and kept in touch with pre-arranged signals.

As the car approached the gates, Käthe gently shook Adam so that he might greet his new friends. Half a kilometer away, the last army patrol of the day remounted their old American lorry and adjusted the nationalist flag on the bonnet. Each day in the late afternoon, they drove past the end of the walnut grove to do a cursory check on the hidden German consulate on their way back to the barracks. The five men expected it and didn't expect to live.

Adam got out of the car and approached Bing Wen, who smiled. His expression suddenly changed when he looked over the young German's shoulder. A man was kneeling down a hundred meters away, aiming a rifle. Bing Wen threw himself at Adam, shouting, "Down!"

The bullet missed Adam and tore into Bing Wen's left thigh, but he managed to drag Adam behind a concrete pillar. More shots rang out as their attacker was joined by his comrades and bullets ricocheted off the consulate walls.

Käthe screamed and tried to get out of the car. The driver restrained her; a bullet tore through the car's rear window and hit him in the neck.

Shouts mingled with Käthe's screams. The driver looked at her wide-eyed as his blood covered her clothing. By now one of the motor-cycle escorts had dismounted and returned fire with Bing Wu, but his comrade was not so lucky, a bullet puncturing his petrol tank. Flames shot in the air and ignited his uniform, his screams filling the air with Käthe's. Bing Wu shouted to the consulate staff at the gates to keep down.

The patrol arrived. The soldiers jumped off the lorry and advanced, firing on the five men. The attackers had expected to die, and four of them did. Käthe shouted to Adam, "Get back in the car now!" as the firing died down.

"Do it!" said the injured Bing Wui, trying to stem the flow of blood from his leg.

Adam ran to the car but slipped on a piece of chain attached to the concrete pillar. He recovered and grabbed Käthe's out-stretched hand. The remaining fighter reached inside his knapsack, withdrew a grenade and primed it. He ran towards the car, his arm drawn back, and before his body was torn by gunfire, threw the grenade at the car. It exploded and Bing Wen was hit by some of the splinters.

The car body was thick enough to protect Käthe and the driver but a large metal splinter tore into Adam's left leg. She dragged him into the car, screaming "Open the gates!"

Despite his injury, the driver managed to drive away and get the car to Dr. Meissner's surgery. Käthe got out of the car, screaming for help. Nurse Lisa Müller helped Käthe to carry Adam to the surgery.

"Make a tourniquet, we must stop the bleeding!" shouted Käthe.

"Leave this to us," ordered the doctor, but she refused to leave. "Get hold of yourself Käthe," shouted the doctor. She looked at him in amazement. "Tend to the other wounded now. You are the only one who can," he ordered. Karl Weidling took her by the arm. "I will help," he said.

Käthe left her son and tended to Bing Wen and the driver, but neither were badly injured. "Go back to your boy," said Bing Wen.

Adam lost consciousness. The doctor extracted the grenade splinter, which had partially severed a main artery and tendons in his leg. Jacob hastily stitched the wound and worked through the night to save him. It was touch and go near midnight when a blood transfusion saved the little boy. Nurse Lisa took turns with Käthe and the doctor to watch over him.

As dawn broke, Dr Meissner, his face drawn and tired, looked through the shutters of the surgery window. The entire staff were waiting there for news of Adam. Nurse Lisa sent them back to their lodgings, promising to keep them informed. They reappeared at seven o'clock, desperate for news. Käthe had not slept. She had fainted with exhaustion and was lying by the side of her only child.

Jacob Meissner appeared at the surgery door. There was a murmur from the crowd. "Adam will live," he announced. He turned back into the surgery, sat on a waiting room seat and fell asleep.

The doctor knew that Adam's problems were only just beginning. There was a danger of infection. He couldn't bring himself to prepare Käthe for the worst. She insisted Jacob tell her the truth, but he remained evasive, hoping he might be wrong.

"We must be patient," said Jacob. "Adam must remain here for weeks, perhaps. Only then will we be able to tell." She was not reassured. She had seen similar wounds during the war. In many cases, they had led to amputations.

As she walked back to her apartment, Käthe had a horrible thought. Peter would be home soon and she would have to explain her defiance of his orders not to leave the consulate.

Peter's legacy from the war was sudden eruptions of violent temper which up to then had not been turned on her, and as a result she almost wished she'd died in the attack. She had become selfish since her marriage and she would change, she promised herself. She remembered she had not enquired after the health of the two brothers or the driver.

Chapter 4

The farmers of Jiangxi province looked up at the silver aircraft several thousand feet above them as it lost height in its descent towards Canton. Peter was returning from the first round of serious negotiations with the warlords of the East and was chatting amiably with his co-negotiator, who had left his seat. "I'll leave you to prepare your report, von Saloman," he said. The aircraft was running into turbulence, and he lurched his way to the pilot's cabin.

Peter could think of nothing but Käthe and Adam. He knew he had condemned them to a gentle imprisonment, and decided there and then to show them the sights of Canton, no matter what it took. He had deliberately shown little interest in his son's military ambitions and resented his father's encouragement of Adam. Now he softened and decided to use his influence to ask for a visit to the Nationalist forces for Adam as a Christmas present.

As a privileged passenger, Peter was quickly passed through all the official channels. An armed policeman escorted the passengers to the consulate Mercedes waiting in the car park. Peter's colleague politely refused a lift and was met by his own car. He would continue from here to see Chiang on Whampoa Island.

Peter saw the dressing on the back of the driver's neck immediately, but the driver had been told to say nothing and evaded Peter's enquiries. The returning diplomat had also noticed the smell of fresh paint on the car, but was too impatient to see his family to enquire further.

There was no sign of them. Peter got out of the car and walked towards their apartment. He didn't see Käthe watching anxiously from an upstairs window.

The first familiar figure to appear was Jacob Meissner. He assumed the news had been telegraphed to Peter, and looked solemn. "I trust you had a good flight, Peter," he began. "I will not detain you. Please feel free to visit the surgery at any time."

"What do you mean, Jacob?" asked Peter, perplexed. The doctor's jaw dropped as he realised Peter did not know what had happened. "Käthe is waiting for you, Peter. I must return to my duties," he said hurriedly. As he retreated to the surgery, Jacob Meissner wondered if he should shoulder part of the blame for what had happened.

Käthe flung open the front door and threw her arms around Peter's neck. She kissed him repeatedly in a public display which embarrassed him. Then she drew him inside and closed the door. Before she could say anything else, he asked "What did Jacob mean by inviting me to the hospital, my love?"

She let go of Peter. Her hands shook as she stuttered details of the attack on the car. She tried to describe Adam's injuries, but broke down sobbing. Peter said ominously, "We will speak of this later."

As Peter entered the surgery, nurse Lisa Müller was changing Adam's dressing. "Please, this is not a good time Peter," said the doctor.

"I won't wait," said Peter. He saw the extent of Adam's wound and watched his son crying with pain. Peter kissed his son.

"Where's Mama?" the little boy asked. When his father didn't answer, Adam knew the whole episode would be blamed on his mother. He did his best to make matters easier for her.

"It was all my fault, Papa," he began. "We should have stayed here and waited for you. My friend Bing Wen was hurt too, but I think he's all right now."

"Please Peter, let him rest," pleaded Jacob. "Come to my office please."

Jacob Meissner closed the door of his office. "I have removed the metal fragment," began Jacob. "There is now no further risk of blood loss and I believe the wound will heal." He paused and looked downwards. "I cannot discount the possibility that your son will be disabled. I have no way for now of assessing the long-term damage to the nerves surrounding the wound." He tried to smile. "But his life has not ended, Peter. There are things we can do for him, and he has such great courage."

If the doctor believed his prognosis would diffuse some of Peter's anger, he was sadly mistaken. Peter felt that both he and his son had been betrayed. He thanked the doctor and marched back to his apartment.

Käthe met him in the entrance hall, hoping that Adam's injury would unite them. She was equally mistaken.

"Please explain yourself," he began coldly. Käthe had never seen him like this before. She said there was every reason to believe that the Communists had been driven out. Karl Weidling thought that was the case. The attempt to share the blame infuriated him even more.

"Why? Why?" he shouted. "After everything we have been told! You knew that Chiang still had enemies here. Weidling's behaviour must have made that clear to you! Have you lost your wits?"

She sat down, covered her face with her hands and begged for his forgiveness.

"Ever since I've known you, you've been irresponsible," he shouted. "I have tolerated it in the past. This is too much. You have toyed with our son's life!"

His face reddened and he stood over her. It was too much for Käthe. "What did you expect us to do, Peter?" she asked. "Sit here and never see Canton?"

She realised her mistake and tried to stutter an apology, but it was too late. He picked up a mahogany chair and hurled it at her treasured Meissen figures, shattering several of them. She sank to her knees sobbing. Peter collapsed into a chair, gasping for breath. Käthe walked towards him on her knees and looked at him imploringly, laying her head on his lap.

There was a delicate footfall behind them and the sharp sound of wood on wood. The couple turned to see Adam framed in the doorway, supporting himself on crutches, tears streaming down his face. Nurse Lisa had left him for just enough time for him to confront his parents. Both Lisa and Jacob appeared behind Adam, who had turned pale and expressionless and was staggering forward. Käthe caught him by one arm and Peter by the other. A deeply embarrassed Peter asked if he might conduct his son back to the surgery.

Jacob Meissner surveyed the broken crockery and the upturned chair. He cast a reproving glance at the couple. "Nurse Müller and I will take care of Adam," he said sharply. They returned Adam to his bed, leaving Peter and Käthe feeling flustered and irrelevant.

Karl Weidling appeared and asked if everything was all right. He crossed his hands in front of him. "I hope you will both forgive me," he said. "The fault is entirely mine."

Käthe wiped away her tears and took pity on this harmless man. She touched him on the arm. "We know where the blame lies, Your Excellency," she said and grasped Peter's hand. "It has little to do with you." Weidling gratefully half smiled and left them.

Before dinner that evening, Weidling had read Peter's report on his mission. The Consul now knew that the success of the German mission to China in the south was due to his deputy's work. He treated Peter accordingly. Weidling watched them approach his quarters in the evening and breathed a sigh of relief to see Peter and Käthe were arm in arm with Käthe leaning on her husband and laughing.

The dinner was lavish. Weidling was a good listener, and Käthe was the centre of attention. She was sensible enough to let Peter describe his escapades, and for now the cracks in their relationship seemed to have been papered over. The consul bade them goodnight and prayed there would be no investigation by his superiors.

Käthe went slightly ahead of Peter, who had lingered to accept further thanks from Weidling. When he arrived, he heard the strains of a Viennese waltz on the phonograph. Käthe stood with open arms. She had dressed carefully to accentuate her perfect figure. They danced for a few minutes and both made no secret of their needs. The phonograph played into silence and Käthe led Peter up the stairs. They collapsed into each other's arms. "Do your duty, lieutenant," she whispered as her hand drifted downwards.

In the morning, they woke together. Käthe stroked Peter's body and they made love again. "Tell me about Adam's new friends," said Peter, and she told him almost everything she knew. He had often watched Adam and Käthe together and was sure Adam told her much more than she told him. The euphoria of the night slowly wore off.

Peter asked Karl Weidling how they might enquire after the health of Huang Bing Wen and the consul sent a radio message on their secret frequency to Whampoa Island. Chiang Kai-shek personally answered the enquiry, adding his good wishes for Adam's speedy recovery. He sent a courier upriver to Bing Wen's family house, on the Si-kiang river.

Within a week, Bing Wu brought the reply. It came in the form of a rice paper parcel sealed with red ribbons and beeswax. "I think this is very unusual," said the doctor. "I am excited. Please open it."

Käthe carefully removed the paper to find inside a scroll tied with another red ribbon, which she carefully untied. As Peter prepared to read the letter, a sepia-brown photograph fell from it. The letter was edged with the signs for honesty, wealth and good fortune.

"Wait," said Jacob, as Peter was about to read the Chinese script. He examined the box. "I know this sign Peter," said Jacob examining the characters. "It shows steam rising from a cooking pot. It's the sign for the energy of life itself. What does it say Peter?"

Käthe gazed at the photograph of a family group and recognised the two brothers in shining military uniforms. The head of the family in the centre was like an eighteenth century statue come to life, with a long thin face and a pointed beard. His hair was silver and tied in a traditional pigtail. He wore a cheongsam decorated with a dragon. His half-smile combined humour and firmness, but his face was pale and the expression distant. Jacob thought he might be in his seventies.

His wife seemed a complete contrast. She was round-faced and younger than Huang Yuxiang and her smile was welcoming. Any attempt at gravity might have been spoilt by her protruding teeth. Her hands seemed tiny and she seemed to be trying to hide them in the folds of her qipao.

They turned their attention to the box. "May I?" asked Jacob. He opened it; inside, wrapped in rice paper, were two toffee apples for the patient.

"This is very special," said Jacob. "This is an unusual display by a Chinese family towards Westerners. I'm sure we'll hear more."

Weeks passed. Käthe was worried when Adam removed his soldiers from the chest of drawers and packed them away in his suitcase, and stopped making enquiries about the two brothers. Käthe asked him why, and Adam replied that he couldn't face seeing Bing Wen and Bing Wu on crutches.

Jacob looked for improvement in the leg. Adam began to complain of lack of sensation and the doctor feared the worst. It was possible now that poor circulation might turn the leg gangrenous. The little boy began to walk quite well on crutches, but as time went on his efforts were more laboured. Peter and Käthe put on a brave face as they celebrated his seventh birthday in late spring.

The pressure on Käthe increased with Peter's continued absences, and to make matters worse, a letter arrived from Frieda and Gustav. They tried to extract a promise that Adam, Peter and Käthe would come home for the next Christmas. They were not told of Adam's injury.

Käthe discovered a diversion during Peter's absences. She shared Adam's education with Jacob, who discovered another of her talents. Peter had told Weidling that she was a competent pianist, but no one had heard her play. A resumption would bring back unwelcome memories of the time when her parents said they couldn't afford lessons for her. Adam knew his mother could play and embarrassed her by telling Jacob Meissner, who gently insisted she play one evening over coffee in the von Saloman apartment. "I am out of practice," she objected, but he was persistent. "Play a simple opening," he suggested.

Käthe flexed her fingers and lifted her head. She played a little Rachmaninoff, and it was clear she had more than an ordinary talent.

Jacob was overcome. "I have a recording of that," he said. "You are very impressive. May I make a suggestion? Why don't you teach Adam to play like that?"

Here was a chance to divert Adam from his military ambition and his terrible injury, but it had a negative effect. One evening when Adam had finished a lesson and gone to bed, she looked in the Louis XVI mirror by the side of the piano and tried to remember how she had looked when she was thirteen years old. Back then, she had believed her nose to be too big, and she laughed at the memory. Then Käthe remembered when her father had told her they could not afford to send her to music school. Tears came to her eyes as she thought of what might have been. The conspiracy to stop her personal development seemed to be continuing out here. She read Gustav's and Frieda's letters again and longed to return to Germany.

Without warning, Bing Wen and his brother resumed guard duty, but Adam had mixed feelings about their return. He couldn't talk about the attack, and their conversation became awkward until Bing Wu asked, "Where is your lancer, Adam?"

Adam admitted he had packed the four soldiers in his suitcase. He didn't need them any more, he said. But Bing Wu smiled and replied "Unpack them Adam, and always bring one to our talks." Even the brothers had begun to believe that the model soldier was a talisman, and they knew of other plans for him.

Bing Wen asked if he might take tea with Adam's parents and Doctor Meissner together. One week after the request, the meeting took place in the von Saloman apartment. The brothers arrived in Chinese traditional dress, escorted by two soldiers from the Warlord's army. Jacob knew how to brew tea in traditional fashion and after a few pleasantries, the brothers came to the point of their visit.

"We understand you are very concerned about the health of your son," Bing Wen said to Peter and Käthe. "Are you satisfied that everything possible has been done?"

Jacob nodded. Bing Wen then directed his attention to Käthe. He displayed an authority none of them had suspected.

"The leg can be restored, Frau von Saloman," he said firmly. "My father is prepared to treat Adam."

There was a stunned silence. Peter thought it a ridiculous proposal, but turned to Jacob. The doctor surprised the couple. "I have conducted studies," he began. "And it is clear that Chinese medicine can succeed where Western medicine has failed. I feel we have little choice."

"Please let him go, my darling," whispered Käthe to Peter hopefully.

"What must we do, gentlemen?" Peter asked the two brothers, without hesitation.

"We would like Adam to be our guest for two weeks," said Bing Wen. "Please leave all the arrangements to us. Our parents are preparing a welcome as we speak. Adam is expected at the end of next week."

Then he made an unwelcome announcement. "We realise that neither of you could be released from your responsibilities here for such a period," added Bing Wu. Käthe and Peter were being told that Adam must go without them. Bing Wen assured them that their son would be in the care of troops for the whole forty kilometres of the journey.

Peter asked what gift would be appropriate for Yuxiang and his wife. None would be expected, the brothers said. Their father considered it a privilege to treat the son of such distinguished parents.

Events moved quickly as the acceptance of Yuxiang's offer was conveyed upstream. The brothers neglected to say exactly how messages were conveyed upriver. Adam was soon to find out.

CHAPTER FOUR

The family and Doctor Meissner waited at the gates at nine o'clock on the pre-arranged day. Peter insisted that Adam dress as if he was the son of a diplomat. He was allowed his straw hat and tried to insist he wouldn't need his crutches, but Jacob said he must use them. Yuxiang insisted that no pain-killing injections be given.

The morning sun was already hot and had started to clear the ground mist. A cloud of dust and the roar of an engine told them Adam's transport was coming. As the dust cleared, an old American army lorry appeared packed with soldiers. It stopped, turned round and reversed up to the gates. The soldiers smoked, laughed and shouted.

Peter was not impressed by the motley appearance of Chiang's regular troops. Käthe looked equally worried. When a young soldier threw a cigarette end out of the back of the lorry, Bing Wen snapped at him. The young soldier was afraid of the landowner's son and picked up his litter.

One of the men pushed a ladder out and invited Adam to climb it, and Käthe watched, her heart in her mouth. Adam winced with pain as he mounted the bottom rung. Another soldier jumped out and threw Adam's brown suitcase and crutches into the back of the lorry. A hand grabbed his shoulder and hauled the boy into his seat to loud cheers, the brothers looking embarrassed.

Adam leaned outwards as Käthe climbed the ladder and kissed him. Peter and the Doctor did the same. Then Adam said quietly to the doctor, "Please may I call you Uncle Jacob?" Jacob grasped Adam's hand and smiled. "Of course you may," he replied.

"Don't forget this," said Peter, handing his son the old naval telescope.

With a grinding of gears, the lorry moved down the walnut grove. Bing Wu tapped his brother's arm. Lying against one of the trees was the canvas knapsack from that fateful day.

The lorry's suspension was in need of repair and it lurched alarmingly from side to side. It wasn't long before Adam was in pain, but he didn't betray his discomfort. The soldiers chatted to him in local dialect. He pretended to understand and shook hands with each of them.

Chapter 5

The lorry took the same route out of Canton as on the day of the attack. As the metalled road gave way to an earthen track, Adam's leg began to hurt him terribly. He was close to tears as Bing Wu grasped his arm. "Remember your men in the suitcase," he reminded Adam.

One by one the soldiers left the lorry as they reached the villages along the river. Each of them shouted an enthusiastic farewell to his comrades in the lorry and then disappeared into the fields of maize. Soon only the three of them were left.

The lorry bumped to a halt and turned round and the driver jumped from the cab, bowed to the brothers and lowered the ladder. Adam struggled down, into the heat of the midday sun. The lorry turned and trundled back to the barracks, leaving the three of them standing on a dusty crossroads watched by a few villagers.

"We didn't tell your parents about this part of the journey," admitted Bing Wen. "They might have been worried." The two brothers thought it all amusing.

Adam looked round and saw the village which had pricked his and his mother's conscience. This time he could see the jagged, blue-black granite karsts rising out of the earth to the north. To his left, maize and bean plants waved gently in the breeze.

His leg began to hurt. He felt alone and was beginning to wonder if the brothers had played a cruel trick on him.

Adam put his right foot in a rut and fell over in pain, refusing help and glaring at his companions. They just smiled. "Will you walk a short distance, my little friend?" asked Bing Wen. Adam proudly said he would. Bing Wu picked up the suitcase and Bing Wen carried the crutches and threaded them through his army pack. He stepped into a wall of maize which was taller that Adam.

"Come little one. It's all right," he said as an old and well-worn path appeared. The crickets chattered and the only other sound in the heat was the breeze rustling the maize. Bing Wen produced his army water bottle and gave Adam a drink.

They walked for ten minutes, but to Adam it seemed like half an hour. The path twisted and turned and slowly grew wider as the three emerged from the maize into a copse of mulberry trees. There, glistening in front of them, was the Pearl River.

Adam could walk no further and was failing to fight back his tears. "Be brave, little one," said Bing Wen. "Soon you will rest." But Adam refused help and used his crutches to go on. They stopped at the top of some stone steps leading down to a wooden platform. The brothers helped Adam down, sat on their packs and waited.

An hour passed and the sun began to fall in the sky. Adam passed the time by scanning the river with his telescope. He became bored and sat on his suitcase, and his head fell forwards as exhaustion caught up with him. He was roused by the sound of an engine, and trained his telescope on the deep channel to the north. A small battered steamer was chugging towards them. Its long smokestack in front of a huge copper boiler billowed blue-black smoke.

A lone figure stood in the stern, holding a huge wooden tiller. He waved to the brothers, and they seemed amused at the prospect of meeting him.

Adam had dozed off again, the telescope slipping from his fingers. Bing Wu gently shook him. "Your way to the north is here, little friend." he said. The lone sailor reversed the engine, drew alongside the jetty and threw a rope to the brothers. He was much older than the brothers. As the sailor wiped away the sweat with his forearm, Adam saw he had lost most of his hair. What remained were a few graying wisps, hanging over his ears. Most of his teeth were missing, which didn't spoil the broad, cheerful grin. He wore a sleeveless cotton shirt and a long cotton loincloth, both oil stained. He seemed to belong among the petrol drums scattered about the boat.

The boat deck was a metre below the wooden jetty and the old man produced a wooden ladder which the brothers secured to the landing stage. Bing Wen passed Adam's crutches and suitcase reverently to the boat owner, who laughed and unceremoniously threw them into the bottom of the boat.

The young German was carefully fed down the ladder and conducted to a wooden cross member in the bow of the boat. A large silk cushion with the image of a yellow dragon had been placed on it. "The cushion has been specially sent for you," said Bing Wu.

The boatman stood squarely in front of Adam in mock confrontation. The brothers laughed. "This is Luang Guang Csai," said Bing Wen and from that moment the old boatman behaved as if he was Adam's long lost uncle.

"Sit on this," he said. "It's the most expensive cushion on the Pearl River." He waved a piece of dried fish on a stick in front of Adam's nose, and Adam took it and ate it as a gesture of politeness. The boatman became more serious, banging the tiller and seizing a spanner to adjust a valve. "Get that tiller, your lordship," he shouted at Bing Wen. Water was seeping through some of the boat's seams, and Bing Wu calmly bailed it out with his tin army cup.

Adam's fear had gone now that he had started an adventure. He tried to stand up and help at the tiller, but the old man told him to stay where he was. Blue-black smoke poured into the boat as it followed the deeper channels a few meters from the riverbank.

Adam steadied himself and looked over the side. The water was teeming with fish of all colours. Occasionally a lifeless-looking cormorant perched on a sandbar came to life, took off, dived into the river and reappeared holding a struggling, gleaming fish.

Several villages, the houses in a state of collapse, now appeared on the riverbank. Their landing stages, victims of frequent typhoons, were now tangled heaps of splintered wood. The riverside crops gave way to wild ground cover and then to the beginnings of the forest. Thick groups of cypress trees appeared. Just visible inland were the upper halves of the karsts, giant upthrusts of granite covered almost to their summits by forest creepers. The air grew thicker and warmer and the noises of the forest grew louder. The river began to narrow and the forest began to threaten its very passage. Adam should have felt alone and afraid among strangers in a far country, but he was now beginning to feel like a famous explorer as he scanned the river ahead with his telescope. But he had grown weaker since that terrible Thursday and the warm air overcame him. Bing Wen caught him as he began to doze and slide forward. The brothers laid him in the bottom of the boat using their army packs as pillows.

The boat chugged on for another half kilometer, then turned into a strong current from the right. They had left the Pearl and joined the Si-Kiang. Along its banks the forest spilled into the water.

On went the boat. "Wake up, little one," said Bing Wu. "See what is ahead." Silhouetted against the sun and projecting from the forest was a huge flat rock, and on it was a lone figure clad only in a loincloth. He waved and shouted to unseen figures.

The current almost drove the boat backwards as it rounded the rock. Guang Csai had to reverse the engine. To the left side was another rocky projection. They were entering a small natural harbour with deep water.

Tied to a large landing stage were ten brightly-painted fishing boats with nets drying in their bows. In one of them were two men, who jumped out and clambered onto the jetty as the riverboat drew alongside, passing a ladder down into the boat. One of them grasped Adam's arm as he struggled to climb, but he refused their help and nearly fell; the two men caught him in time. Bing Wen and Bing Wu climbed onto the jetty and the two fishermen bowed reverently.

"Come and help our guest", ordered Bing Wen.

Guang Csai had spent his life on the river and did not depend on the local landowner for his living. He did not subscribe to all this deference.

"These are my sons," he said proudly, "Jun Wei and Jun Wui."

They grinned at Adam and he grinned back. "This is Der Deutsche Junge," said Guang Csai.

Adam's smartly-pressed tropical trousers were covered in oil stains, and the fisherman pointed to similar stains on his father's clothing, as if Adam was one of them.

Adam had had had a long day, and could go no further. He collapsed onto the jetty and his crutches fell with him. He was afraid the others would treat him as an object of pity, but although at first they were amused at the young European's discomfort, they soon began to treat him with every kindness.

"You will walk no further," said Bing Wen and made a sign to the two fishermen. They hauled Adam to his feet. Bing Wu took care of the crutches and Bing Wen the suitcase.

Watching over the jetty was a Pagoda-style gateway which was brightly painted in red lacquer and decorated with carvings of fish and birds. Dominating the archway was a huge yellow dragon. Jun Wei bent down and held Adam in his arms. The brothers bowed as they went through the gate and Guang Csai said his goodbyes with a special word for Adam. He looked at the oil-stained trousers and said, "You'll have something to remember me by!"

A tangle of trees and plants confronted them, but a few yards further on, the paved path became broader. Standing in the centre of the track was a bamboo sedan chair.

"This is yours, Deutsche Junge," said Jun-Wei, lifting him up and placing him in the chair.

The two fishermen took the carrying poles, hoisted the chair on their shoulders and the journey into the forest began.

The air was hot and humid and Bing Wen and his brother were uncomfortably hot in their uniforms. The path was lined by stone pillars joined by ropes which kept the bamboo at bay. Butterflies as big as fans played across the path, their colours changing as they were touched by shafts of sunlight.

The group moved towards a stream which had become a waterfall at the inlet, crossing a bamboo bridge which swayed a little. It led to a large flat smooth rock which shone in the sunlight. Lizards scurried from it into the undergrowth and the rock looked down on a dark deep pool. Bing Wen and Bing Wui smiled at each other as if it were a friendly, familiar place.

They left the rock and entered the forest once again, climbing steadily on steps carved from the rocks. Water dripped down from the trees and Adam flicked unfriendly-looking insects from his legs. They reached the summit of the hill and the path opened up. They recrossed the stream by a bridge made of stout timbers. The trees parted to reveal a large clearing and the rear wall of a house.

The darkness of the walls was relieved by the brightness of the blue sky and the tops of the green and blue karsts. The only sound was the gurgling of a tiny stream which disappeared underneath the wall near some stone steps.

Wooden tubes hung on a heavy wooden door and Bing Wen agitated them. They made a haunting sound. The door was opened by a servant dressed in white cotton. The brothers carried Adam to the centre of a quadrangle, placing the sedan chair onto a cobbled surface.

CHAPTER FIVE

The house had been built on three sides of the quadrangle. The rear wall seemed to have been built as protection from the jungle. The lower part of the roof, covered in red barrel tiles, curved upwards in traditional fashion.

The windows had wooden shutters illuminated by lanterns. The servant began to light them as the daylight failed. The smell of perfumed tallow filled the air and the advancing dusk made shafts of red and yellow light. He finished his task and was acknowledged by both sets of brothers before he scurried off to his quarters near the rear gate.

The surface of the courtyard was made of river pebbles, some of which reflected the light of the lanterns. In the centre was a deep, circular pond surrounded by bamboo poles joined by silken ropes. Lanterns on each side of the main door to the house illuminated bronze statues of lions.

The two fishermen took the sedan chair and quietly left, leaving Adam standing with the aid of his crutches. There was silence except for a large koi which disturbed the surface of the pond, and the distant call of a nightjar in the forest.

Bing Wen approached the large cypress double doors of the house and opened them in ceremonial fashion. Out stepped the hosts. "This is my father Huang Yuxiang and my mother He Quiao Gui," said Bing Wen reverently. They both stood perfectly still, as if they were statues to be venerated.

Yuxiang was of average height. He had long silver-grey hair tied in a pigtail and wore a circular silk cap. His cheongsam was a deep blue decorated with a yellow dragon. His thin face seemed pale and striking in the failing light. The slope of his shoulders suggested he might be sixty or seventy years old.

He crossed his hands in front of him. His fingers were long and slender, bearing one copper ring. His face seemed to be fixed in an amused, tolerant half-smile but his piercing blue eyes projected authority.

"You are welcome, Adam von Saloman," he said.

"Thank you sir," answered Adam.

He Quiao Gu was younger than her husband and seemed to be in her mid-forties. She wore a deep orange yellow quipau. Her face was round and her eyes small and brown. Her teeth protruded a little and her smile was warm. She started forward when Adam's head dropped and held his face in her hands. "You will come inside and rest now," she said anxiously. She was not challenged by any of the men. They knew the authority she possessed inside the house. She kissed her son, saw the stains on Adam's trousers and grimaced.

Pain lanced through Adam's whole body and Bing Wen caught him as he fell. He picked him up and took him into the house, to a room specially prepared for the patient, who had fallen asleep in Bing Wen's arms.

The older brother placed the guest on a low-lying bed with a chicken feather mattress. Quiao Gui removed the oil-stained trousers and socks and deck shoes. She placed the straw hat on the stool at the foot of the bed. Overlooking it was a rosewood cabinet with double doors. Quiao Gu unpacked the suitcase, except for Adam's changes of clothing.

"What are these?" she asked picking up one of the Lancers. Bing Wen placed his hand on his mother's arm. "I will take care of these," he said firmly. He arranged the soldiers on top of the cabinet in a semi-circle so they could look down on their commander in his sleep. "His grandfather made them for him," explained Bing Wu. "He is to be a soldier one day." Quiao Gu placed Adam's bedside clock near the window and the three of them quietly left.

Adam woke up just before ten o'clock the next morning to see sunlight filtering through the shutters. There was silence, except for the birds.

His leg felt a little better, and he had no back pain. He stood up slowly and stretched, looking around for his clothes. He found his empty suitcase and was relieved to see the soldiers on the cabinet. Then he saw the straw hat, the cheongsam and his deck shoes and guessed he should draw the cheongsam over his head. He explored cautiously.

He stepped into a short corridor towards a partly opened door. The shutters had been drawn back and sunlight flooded in. He felt he was being drawn towards the light. He stopped and went back, afraid to go on.

Adam rubbed his eyes and looked at himself in a mirror. He noticed his stomach had grown in size because he had had no exercise for weeks. He felt despondent and wanted to pack the soldiers and go home.

Then he heard voices. He didn't want anyone to think he'd been the last to get out of bed, so he quickly returned to the front of the house. Barefoot, he stepped into the sunlight, onto a patio bound by silk ropes, and looked around in wonder.

Yuxiang's house stood on a hill, perhaps a hundred metres high and faced south. To the left and right was thick forest. The drop in front of him was sheer, and was broken only by stone steps leading to a rocky shelf fifty metres below.

Tall flags, which seemed to grow out of the rocks, waved in the breeze. He retrieved his telescope. He saw monks at prayer and Adam knew he had intruded, so he retracted the telescope.

The valley below was still hidden by the remains of the morning mist. Creeper-covered karsts protruded from the white veil and Adam wanted the mist to roll back. He could see villages at the feet of the karsts and people moving around like insects, the morning sun shining on paddy fields.

There was a slight noise behind him. "Did you sleep well?" asked Quiao Gu, holding a tray with a porcelain tea pot and two cups. "We will take morning tea outside," she said, pointing to a stone seat overlooking the valley. She saw the telescope. "You have introduced yourself to our friends below?" she asked.

His face turned red. To Adam's surprise, Quiao Gu took his head in her hands and kissed him on the forehead. She laughed and poured him some tea. He tried not to look too curious at the few tea leaves floating in almost colorless water. His concentration lapsed as the pain returned, and Quiao Gu understood. She held Adam's hand. "My husband is a good doctor. Soon you will feel better", she said. "You're hungry?"

She brought a bowl and a square-headed spoon which contained rice porridge, and she twirled a toffee like substance into it. He ate ravenously. She reappeared with the main dish in a bamboo container. "This is Qinzen," she said.

He peered into the container at a piece of dried fish. It was a new taste for Adam, but he remembered his manners and pretended to enjoy it. His spirits plummeted when Quiao Gu said, "We eat again in the late evening."

"Would you like me to feed your soldiers?" she asked. Adam enjoyed the joke and laughed.

Bing Wen and his brother arrived to greet their friend and turned to salute the soldiers. They had work to do on the estate, they said, and would see Adam later. "Your treatment will begin very soon," said Quiao Gu. "You must be brave, little one," she added ominously.

Adam was left alone for a short while until Yuxiang appeared. He approached so quietly he seemed to materialize out of thin air. He wore a blue silk shirt with a tight collar with a simple peasant loin cloth and a pair of canvas slippers, and carried a leather bag.

"The gods have decreed that you will live, my little friend," he began. "Therefore there is a good prospect for your recovery. Please lie on the bed and roll up your garment."

Yuxiang rubbed his palms together furiously for nearly two minutes. He breathed in and out noisily several times. "Now Deutsche Junge, we will begin," he said. His features softened. "It will not be comfortable," he warned.

Yuxiang gently rubbed a sweet smelling oil into the injured leg. Adam mistakenly thought that this was the treatment. The Chinese doctor slightly twisted the knee and pressed his thumbs into the livid scars and Adam shouted with pain. Yuxiang took no notice. He pulled at the leg and Adam cried out. Yuxiang rubbed his palms together furiously and kneaded the whole knee. Adam sobbed with the pain, tears streaming down his face. "You must be brave, little one," said Yuxiang.

He reached down inside his leather bag and withdrew several long needles, each with a coiled spring at its end. "This will not hurt you," he said as he pressed each needle into selected spots between Adam's left hip and the side of his foot. "Look at your clock, Adam," said Yuxiang. "Do not move for thirty minutes. I will return soon."

Adam felt as if his whole body was on fire, but it was bearable and he lay still until Yuxiang returned. He retrieved the needles and helped Adam off the bed. "Put your weight gently on the left leg only," he ordered. Adam tried but winced with pain. "That will be enough for today," he said.

The treatment was repeated for three days with little result. Adam began to despair; he even wanted to get rid of his model soldiers, a constant reminder of what he would never be able to do. He wanted to explore but was trapped by his disability and it seemed no one wished him to know anything else about the house. Quiao Gu was the most sympathetic but even she gave the impression that he could do nothing without his Chinese host's permission.

He began to feel homesick, because even Bing Wen and his brother hardly came to see him. The only time they were all together was in the evening, at dinner time. His hosts behaved correctly, but only Quiao Gu showed any warmth.

Adam had been attracted by small statues set in recesses in the walls of the house. One of them, a monkey wearing a crown, seemed to mock him. Bing Wen saw that Adam was interested in the figure, and said mysteriously 'You will be better when you get the monkey off your shoulder like this." Bing Wen's withdrawn palm shot forwards and stopped a centimetre from Adam's chin.

"Show me how you did that," demanded the young German. Bing Wen said firmly, "My father will explain in his own time and you must never ask." Then he left. Adam tried to repeat what he had been shown, with little success, but was determined to discover more. He thought Bing Wen had made a real gesture of friendship and felt much better.

Yuxiang seemed different on the fourth day. The treatment was repeated, but this time with a difference. He helped him from the bed. "Today you will walk," he announced. He held Adam's hands.

"Hold your head high," he commanded. "Walk as slowly as you can, like a sleepwalker. Be fearless. I will guide you."

The leg seemed to burn, but not with pain. Adam put his left heel down cautiously. He looked anxiously at Yuxiang. "Now little one, this is the moment," said Yuxiang. He lifted Adam in a bear-hug and gently lowered him to the floor, taking his hands and drawing him forwards into his first steps. The numbness Adam had felt for months had gone, and he felt alive once more. He extended his arms and pretended to fly. Yuxiang caught him before he fell over, holding him tightly as if he were his own son.

"Now you must rest," he said. "Go to your room and sleep."

Adam felt drowsy, sleeping until mid-afternoon. That night, he held the little prayer book his mother had given him and gave thanks for Yuxiang's family. "At ease," he said to the Lancers and slept soundly. He knew he could live again, and the next day he was able to bear the treatment more easily.

When Yuxiang had finished, he said to Adam," I have something to show you." He led Adam into parts of the house he had not been allowed to see up until then. Adam thought he was in the Chinese equivalent of a church and he gazed at the wall facing the valley.

"This man is the father of my thoughts," said Yuxiang, pointing to a picture of Confucius, the centrepiece of the wall. "He is my conscience, and this gives me peace," he added, laying his hand gently on a statue of the Buddha. "These are our household gods, Adam" he said, pointing to the statues set in recesses in the wall. "My son says you like the monkey. He is no longer on your shoulder, but you must always watch and respect him."

Adam was puzzled. "If you are a good student you will know more in time," added Yuxiang. Adam wondered why he had called him a student.

"Have you ever been without food?" asked Yuxiang. Adam shook his head. "Have the wind and the water ever carried away your house?" asked the doctor. Adam shook his head. "Sleep well, Adam von Saloman. We will talk again tomorrow and you will get to know us better."

They bowed to each other. For the first time in many months, Adam was not troubled and slept soundly.

When he woke up, he hauled himself off of the bed but forgot the weakness in the muscles in his left leg and fell over. He looked for the green cheongsam. It was no longer there. On the bedside stool were a long loin-cloth and a sleeveless cotton shirt. His faithful straw hat and deck shoes were still there. After Quiao Gu brought him morning tea, the brothers appeared, dressed similarly. They led Adam to the head of the stone stairway overlooking the valley.

A thin blanket of mist covered the valley floor and a breeze blew from the high hills north west of Canton. Adam felt his leg stiffen with the cold. Bing Wen offered him a stick to help him down the hundreds of steps, but he refused. As they began to descend a small bird flew down the pathway, startling Adam, and he fell, grazing his weak leg and drawing blood. He carried on grim-faced until they reached the rocky platform. Four Buddhist monks in bright maroon robes faced the valley in prayer and rose as if expecting the small party. They blessed their visitors and showed Adam their brightly coloured flags. One of the monks presented him with a bright orange flag. "Tie it up in the wind," he said, "and your prayers will be answered."

The path ended on a dusty cart track. In the near distance a great karst loomed up in front of them. A river flowed past its base and crashed down over a waterfall on its way to the Si-Kiang. On the near bank of the river was a collection of mud-brick houses. Everywhere there were rice paddy fields, as far as Adam could see. The village was cut off from the outside world and its lifeline lay through the Si-Kiang house.

Two men approached in a bullock cart. They dismounted and took a wooden box from its rear. They were emptying live fish into the water and seemed unaware of the visitors. Adam recognised Jun Wei and his brother and they broke into broad grins. Jun Wei brandished the empty basket and shouted a greeting and Bing Wen chided him for his familiarity. The young peasant showed no fear, only resentment.

Bing Wen led Adam down a narrow earthen track towards a collection of mud-brick houses where a line of women were gathering rice knee deep in water. They turned to greet the visitors as if expecting them. Adam was welcomed because he was with the Huang brothers. All the women turned back to their work except one, who motioned him to join them as if by arrangement. Adam rolled up his loin cloth, to the brothers' surprise, plunged into the water and waited for instructions.

As the visitor discovered, there was more to harvesting rice than he thought. One of the women raised her voice to Adam but he wasn't discouraged. The brothers allowed events to unfold.

A small drama was unfolding in the next dwelling, close to a copse of mulberry trees. There were shouts of frustration as a small stocky woman drove a little black pig out of the house. It burst through a mulberry thicket as Adam was being helped out of the water. As he placed one foot on the trackway the squealing pig crashed into him and both Adam and the pig fell in.

The pig was in trouble and its owner's anger turned to anxiety as Adam's head disappeared under the water as he tried to capture the pig. The two sets of brothers were convulsed with laughter as the young German aristocrat struggled out of the water with the animal. Its owner bowed to the rescuer and invited him into the house.

A child lay asleep in a manger amongst a few simple pieces of pottery. A bamboo seat occupied one side of the hut. The roof was made of rushes gathered from the swamp which divided Yuxiang's estate from the country north of Canton. The woman led Adam to the seat. He noticed her hands were white and creased, from a lifetime working in paddy fields. She brewed tea for all of them.

Some of the neighbours peered through the doorway at the visitors. They tried to get a closer look at this western curio, but Bing Wen noticed Adam grimace. His leg was painful and it was time to return to the house. Adam thanked the lady and said goodbye to the baby. In that short time, he had become a celebrity.

Jun Wei and Jun Wui returned with the bullock cart. Jun Wei grinned broadly and with one sweep picked Adam up and placed him in the cart. A little boy perhaps four years old ran up to the cart and stared at Adam. He said something to Bing Wen and bowed. As the cart bumped and rattled along, Bing Wen said "He asked if he could be your friend, Adam." The young German broke into tears.

There was little mention of the visit to the valley during the evening meal. Yuxiang was animated about an important visit from downriver. Adam was used to being excluded by now, but there was a sudden change of attitude. Yuxiang said "Please join my wife in the kitchen, Adam."

He had seen her tossing ingredients in the air with a cast-iron pan and Adam's reward was to be taught how to cook. Quiao Gu invited Adam to try. He made a mess of the kitchen and was told to clean it. His hosts watched him solemnly, as if the task was part of an apprenticeship. He sensed what was expected of him and didn't complain. The task was part of the day's training, and he had passed the tests with flying colours. His hostess presented Adam with three recipes in the form of scrolls of rice paper tied with red ribbon. The brothers told him he had been granted a great honour.

Until that moment, he had sat on the opposite end of the table to Yuxiang, but the following evening he sat next to him. Adam had always had a keen sense of what was expected of him. Just before he fell asleep, Yuxiang said to him, "Goodnight Adam. You have done well today and you are worthy of this family's friendship." He was living and learning as Yuxiang's family had done.

After dinner one night he was promised a musical evening, and Quiao Gu entertained the family on an ancient Chinese lute. Adam listened politely, but soon his head began to fall.

His concentration was suddenly restored by an incident after Quiao Gu's recital. Bing Wui made a comic remark about his mother's playing as Adam left the room. He turned to see Quiao Gu playfully grabbing her son's long sleeve with her hand shaped as if she were playing the lute. She pulled him down powerfully and he collapsed laughing onto the floor, pretending to beg for mercy.

The effect on Bing Wen and Yuxiang was immediate. They turned on Quiao Gu and reprimanded her. This shocked Adam, because his hostess seemed to be the real ruler of the house. He left the room deeply embarrassed, but couldn't help hearing raised voices, and heard most of what was said. "You must not betray our secrets, mother," said Bing Wen sharply, and Yuxiang agreed. "But what about our standing with the German legation?" Bing Wui reminded the others. Adam understood nothing of this but didn't forget what he had seen.

He made the situation worse the following day by enquiring how Quiao Gu had subdued her son, even playfully. It embarrassed his hosts. For two days there was a wall of silence on the subject and Adam began to want to return to Canton. Then he remembered how Bing Wen had taught him to get rid of the monkey. He thought the incident must be something to do with it. He felt compelled to ask, but decided it was wise not to do so in case he was sent home. He did not know he was being used as a pawn in the politics of the river.

Bing Wen remembered that Adam enjoyed fishing with his grandfather and he arranged for him to join Guang Csai's sons at the wooden jetty. It all seemed innocent enough, but the Chinese family wanted to be sure that their guest had shed the superior attitudes he had shown at first.

The brothers waited on the wooden jetty beside three wooden cages. Inside each of them were two cormorants and the remains of several fish. In the brightly-painted boat lying on the shingle beach next to the jetty were neat piles of hempen rope, each one ending in a small leather collar.

Adam and Jun Wei pushed the boat into deep water and Jun Wui picked up one of the bird cages. When they had rowed out to the deeper water, the collars were attached to the birds. The boat stopped in the centre of the inlet, and the two birds perched on the bow. Other cormorants were waiting patiently on a sandbar. They detected a shoal of fish and began to feed. Jung Wei stood up and frightened them away. His brother released the tame birds and they brought fish after fish to the boat. Adam fished with a rod and line the brothers had made for him; they watched disdainfully. He had no success at all, which his companions found amusing.

The brothers left the inlet and rowed upriver against the powerful current. A family of giant river otters frolicked in the water while the three of them lay low in the boat. The otters were joined by others, who had found a shoal of fish, which they drove towards the boat. The brothers leapt up and threw weighted nets into the water. They harvested the fish and returned to the inlet more than satisfied.

They asked their guest what he thought of their achievements. Adam hadn't caught anything and thought he'd been treated as a spectator. "That was cheating," he said. "My grandfather and I do it properly with a rod and line." He looked enviously at the pile of writhing fish in the bottom of the boat and failed to understand that it wasn't a leisure activity for the brothers.

They were just able to understand what he had said and laughed out loud. "Your grandfather must be a better fisherman than you," said Jun Wui. Adam's face turned red just as Bing Wen and his brother walked through the gateway. Jun Wei pointed at one of the struggling fish, which Adam had seen during his journey upriver. Its head was out of all proportion to its tiny body. Jun Wei pointed to it, then at Adam and christened him, "Little Big Head."

Bing Wen overheard the joke and was furious. He looked as though he might strike one of the fishermen, then thought better of it. "I will speak to my father about this insult to our guest," he said. The fishermen were crestfallen, bowed to Adam and apologised. He did not understand the joke, which was a relief to Bing Wen, who was mindful of the other reason for entertaining their guest.

On the way back to the house Adam asked what had happened.

"They insulted you, my little friend," said Bing Wen. Bing Wu remained silent. "What did they say?" Adam asked him. Bing Wen had tired of Adam's curiosity in the last twenty four hours. "We will say no more of it," he said dismissively.

Adam did not give up so easily and he asked Bing Wu again for an explanation. He grinned. "You are now known as Little Big Head, Adam," he said trying not to laugh.

After the evening meal, the brothers had promised to join Adam by the side of the pool. He waited and waited and there was no sign of them. Instead Yuxiang appeared.

"Last night my family behaved badly in front of you, our guest," he said. Adam couldn't have known how difficult it was for him to say that. Yuxiang had to be sure Adam made a favourable report of his stay on the Si-Kiang to his parents. At the same time he was determined that Adam should change during his stay.

Now he had to alter his plans, because slowly but surely he had become fond of Adam and was making a decision to share some of China's most closely guarded secrets with the young German.

"Tomorrow," he announced, "You will learn some of the secrets of old China. My family has agreed you should know at least a little. But you must make a promise to me. First, no one must know you have seen such things. Few people outside China have seen the things you will be shown. You must swear never to teach the things you are about to see and never to use them except in self-defence."

Adam stared at the koi in the pool and wondered what might happen in the morning. He believed he had watched a game, and wondered at the serious purpose behind it.

At eight o'clock the next morning, Adam rolled off his mattress and rubbed his eyes. His cheongsam and loin cloth and shirt were missing. In their place was a green silk trouser suit. He turned it over, and there was the yellow dragon.

Quiao Gu waited on the stone seat with morning tea. She was dressed in a similar outfit but in a deep bright blue. She seemed different. When Adam had finished his tea, she made a surprising announcement.

"I will be your instructor to begin with," she announced. "Are we going to play the monkey game?" he asked. She laughed and shook her head. "Come Adam," she said. "We are going for a short walk."

She led him down the forest trail. It was in shade at that time of the morning and quite cold. The sun was still rising, but as yet there was no oppressive heat. They stepped carefully, because overnight rain had made the shaded areas slippery. Adam moved his head cautiously round hanging mosses and creepers. The birds chattered and the morning chorus of cicadas had begun.

They crossed the first bridge and came to the rock platform which faced the rising sun. To their right, water cascaded over three tiers of rock into a deep dark pool.

"Face me. Put your hands together like this and bow," she said. Her friendly little grin had disappeared. "Face the sun," she commanded, standing behind him. "Don't think of anything. Empty your mind. Turn whenever you wish to find me."

Adam thought it was like playing games with his grandfather and thought Quiao Gu would be just as slow. But time and again he tried to catch his host, and time and time again he failed, until his frustration made him tired of the game.

"You are not listening," Quiao Gu said. "Forget the noise of the forest. Forget all the noises in your head. Relax downwards. Listen for my footfall."

He tried again and again but always chose wrongly, becoming angry and frustrated because it seemed like an attempt to humiliate him. Quiao Gu had forgotten he was a small boy in a foreign land who was missing his parents.

Then he realised how to find her. He waited until she betrayed herself with some tiny sound. Then he found her and grinned.

"You think it's a game Adam, don't you?" she said "Try again."

This time he heard her move quickly and turned. One inch from his nose was an upturned fist, and he started back fearfully. Close to tears, he asked what he should do, anxious to please his host.

"Stand like this," she said holding her arm across her face and pressing her other palm down at her side. "Turn around and try again." He found her and realised what was expected. He deflected Quiao Gu's fist above his arm, but still believed it was a game.

"It's a good start," she said. "You wanted to know how to play the lute, little one. Stand close in front of me. Try to grab my right arm." Adam tried to do so time and again. His teacher simply moved her body weight onto her rear foot. He became quite frustrated. "Try it once more," she said. He tried again and this time he was off balance. She seized his sleeve and pulled him downwards, catching him before he fell. He laughed as his frustration turned into fascination.

"Chinese soldiers have won many battles using what you have seen today" she said. His face lit up. He thought his military training had begun.

"You have been defeated today, but we are still equals, Adam" she said. "Never forget the humanity of your opponent. We bow to each other like this."

"My grandfather would like you," he said. He seized her shoulders and kissed her on the forehead. Her seriousness melted away and she became a motherly figure once more.

"Practise for half an hour and join me in the kitchen," she said. He had found a new obsession and a new home and didn't reappear for an hour, practising furiously.

"Will I meet Jun Wei and Jun Wui again?" he asked Quiao Gu in the kitchen.

"You won't be allowed to meet anyone again if you don't finish cleaning those vegetables," she joked. "You'll meet them both soon. It is all arranged for tomorrow. My husband will teach you this time. Be at the rock at eight o'clock."

The next morning the sun was hotter and the rock teemed with lizards and insects, but there was so sign of Yuxiang. Adam's mind drifted away and he realised he had no one to play the new game with.

"Good morning Adam," said Yuxiang. He had stolen up unobserved. "I am glad you are thinking." He wore a green silk suit and was barefoot. They bowed to each other. An empty backpack lay on the ground and he attached it to an overhanging branch.

"Stand on your left leg," he commanded. "Sink into the earth."

He stood in front of Adam. "Parry my fist and kick my stomach," he ordered. Adam looked dumbfounded and Yuxiang looked disappointed. "Yesterday did you not learn through obedience?" he asked impatiently. "Why are you afraid? You couldn't hurt me." The little boy was reassured and a determined look crossed his face.

As Adam's right foot arrived, his teacher stepped aside and the foot crashed into the sack. "Kick harder, kick harder Adam!" shouted Yuxiang. "Now parry my fist and kick, never drop your guard, hide the fist. Try to strike upwards with your fist."

Adam's determination increased and his movements quickened. He was feeling a new power, and Yuxiang had lost some of his powers with age. Adam struck him in the midriff and his teacher staggered backwards. Adam rushed to help his teacher, but Yuxiang sprang to his feet and his fist stopped a centimetre from Adam's ribs.

"Hold your place, never drop your guard!" he warned, placing his hand on Adam's shoulder. "Only for defence Adam, only for defence," said Yuxiang. "Sit here by the pool. Now I will teach you something else." He pointed to the rushing water.

"Do you see life in the angry water, Adam?"

The young German knelt down and immersed his hand. He saw no sign of life and shook his head. "Do you see how shallow the angry water is?" Adam picked up a handful of stones from the stream bed and let them drift through his fingers.

"Look at the pool in front of you Adam. What do you see?" Yuxiang asked. Adam stared at the pool at the foot of the waterfall and saw fish rise from the depths to take insects.

"Here the water is deep and the fish find their food. Put your hand in the water again. What do you feel?" asked his teacher and Adam said it was quieter and warmer.

"I am told you can be angry when you don't get your own way," he added and the pupil smiled.

"Did you enjoy your visit to the village?" asked Yuxiang. Adam grinned broadly.

"They like you Adam, and that pleases me," he continued. I will tell you some important things now, because there will always be secrets between friends." They sat down together on a smooth rock. "Those poor people all owe me rent because I am their landlord and some do services for me instead of payment. You saw the servants in the house. As long as I stay here safe they have a future." Adam wondered where Yuxiang was leading him. "I am friendly with General Chiang and my sons do military service in the army." A conspiratorial smile crossed the landowner's face. "It is useful for General Chiang to have my support. But you see Adam, things may change. I need another protector who could be as powerful. Now I have a new friend from a powerful country. Do you think your father might help us? Do you see, little one?"

"I'll ask him to help," promised Adam. The landowner no longer saw the young German as an intrusive foreigner but he had not forgotten that his guest had been a victim of the Communists. Yuxiang was well aware of what would happen if they ever came to power in Canton. The landowner had told him something of the politics of the river, but only so much.

Quiao Gu packed Adam's suitcase and the lancers were carefully wrapped in rice paper. The oil and moss stains had gone from his tropical trousers. When he emerged from his room, Quiao Gu was delighted and clapped her hands, because Adam had chosen to travel home in his cheongsam even if it didn't suit his straw hat.

He walked in the courtyard with the family and had one last look down the valley at the karsts. He had missed his parents and his uncle Jacob, but here he had found another home. One day far in the future, his stay here would renew his life. He walked down the forest path to the landing stage with his new friends. Quiao Gu was in tears and held onto him all the way.

They walked through the pagoda gate to see people running back and forth. Moored to the wooden jetty was a small junk about forty metres long, with bright red ribbed sails. It was painted with red and yellow lacquers and its stern stood high out of the water. The mast at the stern flew two flags, one the Nationalist twelve-pointed star, the other the Stars and Stripes of the United States. Most of the shouting came from a team of twenty men who stood nearly up to their shoulders in water, pushing for all they were worth to stop the craft going aground. Standing on the stern, shouting orders, was a tall stocky figure wearing a long loincloth and, on his head, a bright red bandanna.

The man with the red bandanna, sporting a neatly trimmed grey beard and huge side-burns, yelled in Adam's direction "Just give me a minute young man. I have some business to attend to. Careful with that," he said, as his crew passed a large wooden crate down to the jetty. It all clearly involved Yuxiang, who walked up to the crate watching it anxiously. "You could open the crate. It'll be easier to carry," suggested the junk's captain.

Jun Wei attacked the crate with a crowbar. It fell apart to reveal a cast iron bath and Quiao Gu purred with delight. Four men picked it up and set off towards the Si-Kiang house. Yuxiang gave the captain a small silver ingot for services rendered.

"So this is Der Deutsche Junge," said the captain. "Are you sure he's only seven years old? Come here young man," he commanded in a genial manner. Adam ran up the gangplank and joined him on his vantage point. "I'm Ned Travis and I run most things around here," said the big American, holding out a huge hand. Adam's disappeared inside it. Ned had spoken in German, but Adam answered in English.

"That's enough of that young man. They'll think we're impolite," said Ned. "We gotta go while there's no wind. We don't want to get caught up in a typhoon. It's time to say your goodbyes."

Adam ran back down the gangplank. He embraced each of the family in turn, which amazed Ned. He'd known Huang Yuxiang's family for years and a display like this was unusual.

The two fishermen were very deferential and contrite. "Goodbye sir," they said in turn. Adam whispered to them. "You may call me Little Big Head!"

They tried desperately not to laugh because Bing Wen was watching them carefully. Jun Wei picked Adam up and pretended to throw him in the water. He glared defiantly at Bing Wen.

Adam climbed the gangplank to receive another surprise. Seated in the waist of the ship was Huang Lin Hui, the Warlord of Canton. He sat on a bamboo throne protected from the sun by a Western-style umbrella and waved an arm in Adam's direction. The young man was frightened and looked to Bing Wen for support. Bing Wen rushed up to the gangplank and embraced the young German like a brother.

"Wait Ned," said Adam. He opened his suitcase and took out two of the lancers. He dashed back down the gangplank. "I want you to have these," he said to the brothers. "It is a great honour little one," said Bing Wen. "Your soldiers brought us together."

"Hurry up young man," shouted Ned. Adam raced back to the junk, waving furiously at the family.

There was no wind in the inlet and the junk was towed by six fishing boats each with four oarsmen. Adam looked around at the crew. All of them were armed, some with swords, others with pistols. One evil-looking man leered at Adam. He had grown a moustache and sideburns like Ned and he too wore a red bandanna. Ned treated him with caution.

Adam noticed he carried a pistol. He had seen a similar one carried by the driver at the Consulate. It was a German Luger, and Adam wondered how he had got it.

"Are you going to ask me why you're here and not bumping your way down a dusty track?" asked Ned.

"I don't mind. I couldn't go back with my friends," answered Adam.

"I'm told those guys in Canton were upset they didn't get you, so you're safer here," said Ned grimly, looking down at Adam's injured leg.

When the junk was safely downstream on the Pearl, Ned invited his passenger to join him at the tiller. He said to Adam, quietly pointing towards Lin-hui, "He asked to be here today and there are things you ought to know. Huang is a common name round here Adam. You know that?" Adam nodded. "He's Yuxiang's brother. He wanted to be on the boat with you."

Adam wasn't reassured. Lin Hui was one of the few people he had met he really disliked.

"Stand behind the mast. He won't be able to see you. Use your telescope and look downstream," said Ned. What do you see?"

Adam scanned the river bank and saw the remains of a wooden jetty.

"Lin Hui's son drowned there, Adam. He was your age. Yuxiang never forgave him. He isn't allowed to land at the Si-Kiang. But he took a shine to you as soon as he met you."

The Warlord's bodyguards ordered Adam to stand in the waist of the ship. A bony hand alighted on his shoulder and he remembered the long cracked fingernails and the smell of opium. Adam turned to face Lin Hui as politely as he could. Lin-Hui's yellow eyes seemed devoid of feeling.

Adam shivered when he asked in a high-pitched monotonous voice, "How is the beautiful mother of Der Deutsche Junge?" He felt his blood run cold. "Stay here with me, Deutsche Junge," said Lin Hui. "You are all under my special protection." He returned to his bamboo throne. A relieved Adam returned to his new friend Ned.

"That guy down there has become my friend. You'll find that hard to understand," he said.

"One other thing you need to know. Huang Yuxiang thinks Chiang might not last. That's what China's like. He needs his brother's private army as protection in case the Communists come back," said Ned. "And maybe you know where they get the guns," he added quietly.

Adam would discover the contents of the *Derfligger*'s hold in the near future. Ned thought he had said too much and began to talk about the river instead.

Within two hours, the junk approached Canton and prepared to melt into the melee of small ships and fishing boats. As Adam prepared to leave, Ned casually asked him a question or two. The American had watched dredgers making a deep channel to Canton. The *Derfligger* could now anchor quite close to the town. He asked Adam the date of its next visit and the young man told him. He hadn't developed the caution he was soon to acquire.

Within a few days two carefully-chosen members of the junk's crew had volunteered their services as dock workers and members of Lin Hui's private army had made sure they were accepted.

The junk rounded Shamian Island. "You can help me bring her in," said Ned. He allowed Adam to hold the tiller, helped by a well-armed helmsman. "He looks after me," Ned said quietly to Adam in English. As they approached the wooden jetty Adam saw a familiar face. Guang Csai's boat was setting out upriver in a cloud of blue smoke. He shouted and waved, but the old man looked only briefly towards the young German and seemed anxious to leave as quickly as possible.

Adam looked at Ned for an explanation. "Don't forget the company you're keeping kid," he said. "Lin Hui usually collects a river tax from him, but not today. That heap of dung in the middle of this ship is waiting for the old man to do well before the next bill."

Adam lost concentration and the helmsman said something insulting in dialect as the boy's clumsy efforts led the junk to bang against the side of the jetty. A fuel drum fell from the deck and rolled into a handcart full of fish pushed by an old man with a long beard. The old man fell over, pinned down by his cart.

"Let Lin's people off the ship first," ordered Ned, but Adam rushed down the gangplank to help the old man. The small crowd seemed hostile but Adam wasn't deterred and righted the cart, while others collected the fish. He calmly returned to the ship. The American was impressed, but he was afraid of the Warlord, casting an anxious glance in his direction.

Lin Hui summoned Adam to the waist of the ship and placed his hand on the boy's shoulder. "The old man is known to me," he revealed. "Now all those people down there are your friends, because I have decided it should be so. Tell your father who protected you." Adam bowed. Huang Lin Hui was helped down the gangplank and met by a frightening array of about fifty armed men who melted away into the waterfront.

The old fisherman pointed; half his fish had slipped through some of the planks into the harbour. Ned calmed him down and gave him two dollar bills. The old man beamed.

Then an army lorry arrived and two soldiers jumped down and ran towards Adam. A young woman stood in front of him. "I will look after him," she announced. The old fisherman was her father, but a soldier threatened her with his rifle. The young German stood between them and the soldier lowered his gun.

Ned watched all this in admiration. "Get yourself in that lorry young man and I damn well hope I'll see you again and soon," he said. "Go show off your leg to your parents. These guys don't like Chiang and that means they don't like you. Get going." Adam leapt onto the lorry and waved furiously to Ned Travis. "Bring me some business!" The American shouted.

Käthe, Peter and Jacob Meissner were beginning to think Adam wouldn't return as the afternoon wore on. They heard shouts as Adam shouted goodbyes to his escorts and there was a loud clang as the gates closed.

An unfamiliar figure walked slowly towards them wearing a cheongsam and a battered straw hat and carrying a small brown suitcase. He looked careworn and his mother's heart sank. Adam continued his little charade for a moment and limped towards her, but he could not bear her crestfallen looks any longer. He dropped the case, opened his arms, ran towards her and threw himself into her arms. Käthe gasped in surprise and delight and Peter embraced him with a broad smile.

"We shall always be grateful to you, Jacob," he said, his body shaking with emotion.

"Welcome home Adam," said Jacob, close to tears himself. "May I examine him now?"

"Of course," replied Peter. Peter and Käthe sat holding hands in the apartment.

"Has Huang Yuxiang given you exercises?" asked Jacob. Adam was not forthcoming, but the doctor understood. "Please I must know," he insisted and he showed Jacob some of the things he had been taught. Adam knew even more of south-eastern China's best kept secrets, but he did not share them with either Jacob Meissner or his parents.

Chapter 6

By the time the Von Saloman family had been resident in Canton for nearly three years, Käthe was beginning to think of little else but returning to Germany. The infrequency of letters from home made her feel worse. Her parents wrote regularly, but the theme of the letters was always the same; they wondered when Käthe would return to Hamburg. There were times when she thought the only thing that kept her sane was her relationship with Adam. She was still prepared to use him to gain her own ends.

A letter arrived from Frieda and Gustav. They were almost demanding to see their grandson at Die Schwanen for Christmas. Käthe read the letter to Adam by the fountains. "Look my darling," she began, but then a photograph fell out of the letter. It was a picture of Greta, the housekeeper.

"Do you remember your little games with her in the kitchen?" she asked. "There's another picture here, my darling." She showed Adam a photograph of two dachshunds with very long ears. He laughed. "There's no room underneath them, Mama," he joked. She encouraged the mood. "What are their names?" he asked.

"They're called Hansl and Gretl, my darling. They've bought them for you." Adam too began to think of going home.

Käthe read the letter to Peter together with Adam and persuaded him to plan the trip home. Then came a bitter blow for Käthe. The Foreign Ministry demanded that Weidling and his deputy establish their precedence over the British and French in Nan-king, Chiang Kai-Shek's new capital. It would involve repeated flights by Peter and his aides. He became obsessed with this new mission, constantly boring and irritating Käthe with tales of the resurgence of the new Germany and his part in it. Adam could look forward to seeing his new friends on the river, but Käthe had nothing to divert her.

CHAPTER SIX

She had another means of gaining her freedom. She informed Jacob that Peter had contracted rheumatic fever in 1918 and thought his new responsibilities might endanger his health. Jacob agreed to examine him and discovered he had a weak heart. He felt bound to inform Käthe, even though he knew she might use the information to persuade Peter to go home.

She made an appointment of her own to see Weidling and was shocked by his obedience to the Foreign Ministry's demands. "I am sorry Käthe, but Peter is indispensable to German prestige in the far east. He must stay on for now," said the Consul. Jacob was appalled by Weidling's weakness; all he could do was keep a careful eye on his patient.

Suddenly life improved for Käthe. She was allowed escorted shopping trips into Canton.

One of the expeditions disturbed and puzzled her. Adam had told her about the fish stalls on the waterfront and she insisted on paying them a visit. While they were making their way there, Adam began to regret telling his mother anything about the waterfront. His parents were not supposed to know how he had got back to Canton. He had promised Bing Wen he would never tell.

When they arrived, hostile looks greeted their escort. "They won't do anything, Mama," said Adam confidently. She was uneasy and couldn't understand Adam's complacency.

Lin Hui's soldiers bowed to Käthe, and Adam laughed. The old man behind a fish stall on a two-wheeled cart recognised him. He pretended to shake his fist at the young German because of the incident of the fuel drum. He laughed from a toothless face and gave Käthe two large fish. She looked hard at Adam, who just stared ahead. "We have to pay for the damned fish," said a voice behind them.

A member of Ned's crew called out "Come and say hello to the Boss." They were hauled away behind waterfront houses to Ned's mooring. Adam was terrified his mother would discover the truth.

Ned was standing on the junk's stern. Some of the crew saw Adam and cheered and when they saw Käthe they began to applaud. Ned realised he had better remain anonymous, although he wondered how Adam would explain all this. It was as well he spoke better Chinese than his mother.

That morning Käthe was restless and had risen early. She saw Adam dressed in a green silk trouser suit performing the strangest movements, and wanted an explanation. Her son was her best friend and the day's events had created a distance between them.

The most important ritual of the day to Käthe was to say goodnight to her son. She felt almost afraid of him after his mysterious behaviour. "I thought I knew everything about you Adam but I don't, do I?" she said. "Please tell me what happened to you." He laughed and threw his arms around her neck, and kissed her. "Promise me you won't tell Papa," he said. "It's to heal my bad leg. That's why Uncle Jacob is interested." He thought a game would help. "Hold this pillow at arm's length, Mama," he ordered. He swayed on the thick mattress and balanced himself, then aimed a powerful kick at the pillow. Chicken feathers flew around the room. She pretended to be annoyed, but laughed out loud.

They both cleaned and swept the bedroom. "Your father is coming home tomorrow," said Käthe. "Shall we ask him to go to the waterfront with us, my darling?" she asked mischievously. She wanted Adam to know she knew some of his secrets and had guessed how he had returned to Canton. Adam grinned and said "Only when it's safer, Mama." She was happier; the conspiracy had been restored.

The silver Junkers slowly lost height as it approached Canton. Peter and his new aide felt satisfied with their work. His briefcase contained a big order for German guns. It was agreed the cargos should continue to be landed in Canton now that a channel had been dredged to allow the *Derfligger* to anchor just off the city. The weapons would then be sent north via the new railway to Wuhan and beyond. The whole process was far less conspicuous than the alternative of landing the guns in Shanghai.

For once, Peter didn't subject Käthe to a celebration of his achievements. He seemed tired and it was the first time he had returned to the consulate in darkness. The cook provided a light meal, but Käthe noticed Peter's lack of appetite. She stroked his head and kissed him longingly. He responded and pulled her to her feet and began to waltz round the room. Her arms tightened round him and he pulled the straps of her dress down her arms. She felt his hands and arms suddenly release her.

Then he sank backwards into a chair, breathless and clutching his chest. Käthe ran to the hallway. "Adam, Adam!" she called. He was down in seconds.

"Get Jacob, quickly," she said urgently. She loosened Peter's shirt collar. The doctor burst in, examined him and was sure he had suffered a heart attack.

The three of them watched over Peter during the night. He recovered, but the doctor was in no doubt as to what could happen and saw Karl Weidling in the morning.

The interview was stormy. Jacob concluded the interview by banging on his desk and demanding that Peter be sent home. Weidling relented and gave Peter six months' leave without seeking the Wilhelmstrasse's permission. As the German right wing became more powerful in the Ministry, there were a few who would question Karl's reliability. His decision would come back to haunt him.

The *Derfligger* was not due to arrive for several weeks and Peter was given light duties. Chiang sent a letter of sympathy wishing him a speedy recovery and another letter arrived for Adam from Yuxiang and his family. Peter's illness was supposed to be a closely-guarded secret, but the date on the letter showed the Si-Kiang family had found out before Chiang.

Christmas came and went, but now Frieda and Gustav knew their family would return to Berlin in the spring. Peter and Käthe began to think about Adam's education. Gustav had already laid plans and Adam was to go to school for the first time.

Chapter 7

The journey home was long and uneventful. Now that Käthe was freed from the confines of the consulate, she began to behave as she had before the family's time in China. Peter was thankful for the change and knew the decision to come home was the right one.

Adam left his parents' side to watch as the ship passed through the Suez Canal and Käthe saw an opportunity to raise her husband's spirits. She leaned over the ship's rail and gave him a chance to show off his knowledge.

"My darling, I know I embarrass you sometimes but this is worse than anything so far." He looked puzzled. "Which country is this?" she asked bashfully. He patted her on the arm. "It is Egypt, my love," he answered. "And whose soldiers are those?" she asked.

Peter was amazed. "They are British soldiers and we have to pay them a toll," he said regretfully. "But that's terrible Peter," she said. "That must annoy you."

Käthe was pandering to Peter's expertise and prejudices. She gave in to his every need, determined they would never return to Canton. Peter appeared to have recovered, but she was a realist. At any time he might have another attack, and the next might be fatal. When they were together, she painted pictures of him as the master of Die Schwanen and for the time being he seemed to enjoy it.

As the ship entered the Bay of Biscay, the world seemed to turn grey. Käthe and Peter hid in their cabin from the biting winds and driving rain, but Adam enjoyed the pitch of the ship and the white-topped waves. The Biscay wind died and the ***Derfligger*** ploughed its way through the English Channel towards the Baltic and Hamburg. The weather turned cold once more and the ship set course for the mouth of the river Elbe.

CHAPTER SEVEN

The ship's horn blew and a pilot boat approached. Adam waved at the pilot and shouted, "Take us in please." The mile-wide mouth of the Elbe was lined by derricks and fuel storage tanks. The great transatlantic fleet lay at their berths, including the immobile liners of the Hamburg-Amerika company.

Soon the ***Derfligger*** approached its berth beyond the International Bridge. She and ships like her were keeping Germany's commercial sea-going ambitions alive, and her reception was enthusiastic as pilot boats and other small vessels blew their horns.

Peter's credentials guaranteed quick passage through the arrival halls. There they were met by Käthe's parents, Kurt and Lisa Holman. Kurt was a railway official on the docks. The less generous among their friends had labelled Käthe as a social climber. Adam didn't remember his Hamburg grandparents and he treated strangers politely but distantly.

The family stayed at the Holmans' apartment for two days. Kurt and Lisa begged Käthe never to leave Germany again. Adam said very little. When his grandparents pressed him to ask questions, he promptly asked the wrong ones.

"Who are the men in the red shirts marching in the streets?" he asked.

Käthe's heart sank. She knew her father was active in the Communist party and his answer would incriminate him in Adam's eyes. Kurt answered proudly, "They are the comrades of the Communist party, Adam. They march so that people will have jobs again and their families will have enough food."

"Communists tried to kill Mama and me in Canton, grandfather," Adam remarked. An embarrassing silence descended on the room, as no one in the family had been told about the attack. Kurt was upset, demanding to know the details. His efforts to explain it fell on deaf ears, including Peter's.

Käthe tried to come to her father's rescue. "People here can come and go as they please," she said sharply. "They can march in the streets if they wish," she added, clumsily.

"Perhaps some people shouldn't have that freedom," interrupted Peter. None of this was lost on Adam.

The remainder of the two-day stay couldn't pass quickly enough for Peter and his son. Käthe was close to tears all the way to the airport. She was disgusted at the insensitivity of the other two. They weren't apologetic.

"Look at our aircraft," said Peter as they walked towards a single-engined

Junkers. "It's just like mine," he said proudly to his family. "I do a lot of my work on it," he added and the family basked in their VIP status.

They made a perfect landing at Tempelhof airport in Berlin and were met by a deputation from the Foreign Ministry. Peter was congratulated on his achievements and Käthe was presented with flowers. He was instructed to call briefly at the Foreign Ministry for a debriefing, which lasted one hour. Their chauffeur was then to drive them to Die Schwanen.

Käthe loved springtime in Berlin and wanted to buy from every flower seller she saw. They had planned to drive down the east-west axis of the city, down the Kurfürstendamm, past the victory monument and on to Wilmersdorf.

She suggested a change of plan because she knew Peter was obliged to spoil her. "Could you ask the driver to take us to Julius' shop in Kreuzberg?" she asked.

"Of course my dear, I will instruct our driver" he answered, grinning at Adam. "You and I will have to amuse ourselves for two hours while your mother tries on a lot of clothes."

"We'll go for a walk Papa. Do you think we might get to the zoo in the Tiergarten?" he asked hopefully. Peter thought it a good idea.

The car turned off the Wilhelmstrasse towards the unfashionable area of Kreuzberg. Peter was suprised that Frieda and Käthe had developed such a loyalty to the wizened little Jewish shop owner in such an area. They approached the square and heard shouting and cheering. Dozens of people passed the car as their driver tried to find somewhere to park. A policemen saw the flag of the Republic on the bonnet and offered to help. "You may be able to park over there but it will be difficult for you to exit the square sir," he said.

A speaker's dais had been set up at one side of the square and technicians were testing microphones. The crowd increased and was ringed by men in brown uniforms with swastika armbands. The police made way for a long black Mercedes saloon and four burly men in brown uniforms sprang out of the car. One opened a rear door and threw out his right arm in a Roman salute. A small man with narrow aquiline features limped from the car. He wore a leather coat and a Homburg hat. Each of the men in brown uniforms raised his arm in salute.

"There's Julius, Mama," said Adam as the shopkeeper appeared, looking terrified. He was carrying a large bunch of keys and seemed to be about to close the shop, glancing anxiously around him. Peter's attention was rooted on the speaker.

The policeman approached the car again. "May I suggest an alternative route sir?" he said. "Thank you officer," replied Peter, "But I think I would like to hear the speech. Pray tell me, who is to speak today?"

The policeman replied as politely as he could. "Have you been away from our country, Your Excellency?" he asked. Peter was told that the speaker was the National Socialist district leader for Berlin, Dr Josef Goebbels.

The speaker waited for silence. His first topic was the restoration to Germany of territory lost in the war, and Peter showed interest. He was, after all, an instrument of German expansion. "Listen Adam," said Peter.

Suddenly the crowd swayed towards the car and Dr Goebbels stopped speaking. Men wearing red shirts appeared out of side streets and began to heckle and interrupt. His brown-shirted supporters responded immediately. Several of them drew rubber truncheons and used them on the intruders. Some of the crowd cheered but others were silent.

The police suddenly intervened and some of the red-shirted intruders were bundled into police vans and driven away. Adam applauded from inside the car and the speaker resumed, on a new theme. He blamed Germany's defeat and present mass unemployment on the Jews and he looked menacingly towards Julius' shop. Peter had changed his mind. He now felt nothing but revulsion.

Käthe was dismayed and disgusted by the things she had heard. "What would these people do to Julius?" she asked.

Adam was watching a group of boys dressed like the International Scouting Movement. They too wore swastika armbands. Neither of his parents was aware that Adam was watching the boys, who behaved as if the mention of the Jews was a cue. They walked menacingly towards Julius as he locked up his shop and folded a sign. As the boys stood over him, he held out his hands and tried to reason with them. The biggest boy seized the sign and smashed it to pieces. Another boy produced a can of paint and wrote 'JEW' on the shop window.

Adam watched angrily as a third boy pushed the old man to the ground and spat at him. Then he opened the car door and ran towards Julius and the three boys. He pushed the third boy away from the shopkeeper and placed himself defiantly in front of the old man.

"Please Peter, do something!" Käthe pleaded. Peter opened the car door and tried to push his way through the crowd. He waved furiously at Adam, who stood defiantly with his arms folded.

"Thank you young man, but this is not your battle. Please leave," said the shopkeeper. Adam took no notice. "Pick on someone your own size!" he shouted at the boys. By now, an audience had gathered round. "Fetch the police!" shouted one man.

The three boys sneered at the young aristocrat in front of them in his starched collar and pin-striped suit. "Give the toff a good thrashing, Berndt," said the smallest boy to the biggest. "I'll teach you some manners," said the biggest boy as he advanced on Adam.

"Adam, Adam!" shouted Käthe fruitlessly.

The boy was tall, blond and well-built and there seemed no doubt of the outcome. Some supported Adam, but many watched sullenly. The big boy did not check his quickening stride. His left hand reached out to seize Adam's collar and his right fist began its journey.

The encounter ended in a split second. Adam lifted his arms and parried the blow. He stepped forward with a shout that rang round the square, pushed the boy under the ribs with both hands and lifted him off the ground, throwing him into his two friends. The pot of paint spilled over the cobblestones.

The crowd watched open-mouthed as Adam stood in a martial stance with both hands turned to fists. Peter and Käthe were speechless.

Two Brownshirts arrived. "There were to be no demonstrations like this today. You will be punished for this!" shouted one of them. He hit the smallest boy across the face when he appeared defiant.

Their supporters had lost face, and the other Brownshirt turned on Peter. "Is this your boy?" he asked accusingly. "These boys are the future of Germany. You will have to learn to control your son, or it will be worse for you."

"How dare you threaten me!" replied Peter. "If these boys are the future of Germany, then God help us."

A policeman whispered something to the Brownshirt, pointing to the car with the pennant parked nearby. The Brownshirts bowed to Peter and retired. The crowd slowly dispersed, but several approached Adam. "Well done young man," said one.

"Are you all right, Julius?" asked Käthe anxiously.

"Thanks to your son, I am, madam," he answered. "I must say, it is so good to see you again after so long, and you sir. I cannot open my shop for you, I'm afraid. It will be held against both of us."

"But the crowd has gone," objected Peter.

"The policeman is still watching, and so is that cruel man on the dais," said Julius.

The speaker waited for Peter's car to leave, as if he wished to be sure who it was carrying. He nodded to Peter as the car passed, but Peter ignored him.

"I would like you to sit between us, Adam," said Peter, before they left the square.

Adam was afraid of what Peter would say. His parents looked inscrutable. A few people drifting away from the meeting looked threateningly at the car.

As they turned onto the East-West axis, Peter and Käthe breathed out audibly. Adam glanced at both of them anxiously. To his relief, Peter grasped his hand and shook it warmly. "I am so proud of you, Adam," he said. Käthe was amazed. She had expected Peter to be angry. This was not the first time she had misjudged him.

"What were you thinking, Adam?" asked Peter.

"I thought of Uncle Jacob," he answered.

Peter patted his son's arm and smiled and Adam waved to the animals as they passed the zoo. The planned visit would have to wait.

The car passed the victory monument and crossed the Spree Bridge, turning south down the Avus towards the Berliners' playground, the Grünewald forest. The family had never been so relaxed together and pointed out every landmark to each other. They were coming home.

Just before the Avus Joined the Potsdamer Chaussée, the car slowed down and crossed the railway tracks, turning into the forest on the last of the public trackways. The car slowed for a group of runners and turned into an insignificant-looking track to the left. Here the woods darkened and black squirrels darted impudently from branch to branch. Some stopped to watch the mechanical intruder as it stopped in front of forbidding-looking iron gates. The chauffeur got out of the car and pressed a small button behind the left-hand gate post. The gates swung inwards.

The car crunched its way on a gravel track into even darker wood. Käthe strained her eyes to see the light she knew lay ahead. The travellers emerged from the trees into a sun-drenched park and Käthe squeezed Peter's hand.

One of the gardeners waved. "It's Stephan, Mama," said Adam waving furiously. The old gardener abandoned his spade and wheelbarrow and hurried towards the house. A grove of walnut trees led to an open area in front of the house. Käthe was still as awestruck as she had been when Peter first introduced her to Frieda and Gustav. She cast her eyes once again along the length of the building.

Die Schwanen was a two-storey baroque house with a frontage of about a hundred and twenty metres. The long period windows were French influenced and reminded her a little of the consulate. The house was painted in a deep yellow and seemed to absorb the sunlight. Three marble steps led to a double outer door of oak and divided the two wings of the house. A brass ring with the head of a cherub hung from a leather strap. It had never been replaced as the doorbell.

"Look Adam, Greta's at the tea house," said Peter. He had just seen her formidable figure go back into the kitchens at the back of a wooden platform about three metres high which protruded from the north-east wing of the building. It dated from a time when there was a fashion for all things oriental. Inside its cedar-wood outer ring was a circle of spiraeas, their tiny blooms just beginning to appear.

The red lacquered tea house was a place of privacy. Its main appeal was a view over the Wannsee and the tiny shingle beach at the rear of the house.

A breathless Stephan, clad in a leather apron, opened the front doors. "They're here sir, madam," he said. It was the signal for the welcoming ritual to begin. His parents loved to welcome all their visitors formally, and Gustav was the first to appear.

He had a shock of wavy silver hair and a bushy moustache. His once-burly frame was now racked by arthritis and he steadied himself on a silver-headed walking cane.

Frieda stepped lightly through the front door. She was small and deceptively frail looking. Her face bore an aristocratic hauteur and an unflagging resolve. She wore a deep red dress and two strings of large pearls. Frieda saw herself as the moral conscience of the family and behaved accordingly.

Greta Hoffman, the housekeeper and cook, appeared. She had dedicated her life to her mistress Frieda and was of medium height and a full figure. She had modelled her behaviour on that of her mistress, and looked every bit as formidable.

On her left was her daughter Helga, tall and slim with long blond hair. She was nearly fourteen years old and had never known life away from Die Schwanen. Helga had no intention of remaining in service. She knew how to behave towards her employers, but her subservience was only skin deep. When she looked at Adam, Helga saw a model well-bred young man who might be a passport out of the world of service.

Adam bounded out of the car, clutching a model soldier in each hand. He placed them on the car bonnet, saluted them and ran to Gustav.

"Careful Adam," mouthed Käthe, noting the old man's frailty. Gustav bravely tried to lift him, and he threw his arms round his grandfather. Gustav kissed him on the forehead and his eyes filled with tears.

"How are you my boy?" Gustav asked Peter, furiously shaking his hand and embracing him. "You're safe now." He laughed as he turned to Käthe and kissed her thankfully.

Peter had never seen his mother shed a tear before. She embraced them all in turn and straightened Adam's battered straw hat.

"Where did you get that?" she asked.

"You may take charge of him now Greta," said Frieda. The housekeeper seized him. "My darling boy," she said. Adam began to feel a little bruised and battered.

Helga curtsied with just enough deference and tried to catch the young man's eye. She was patient. She waited for the opportunity she was sure would come.

"You may bring them now, Helga," said Frieda. Helga disappeared indoors and reappeared with a dachshund under each arm. They were intended for Adam and were part of a deeper scheme to persuade Peter never to leave Germany again. Helga put them down and quickly brushed their brown coats. They barked at Adam, then changed their minds and lay down at his feet with their legs in the air.

"Adam!" said Peter, reminding him of his duty. Peter, Käthe and Adam shook hands with all the servants and Adam shook Stephan's hand vigorously. Peter took Gustav's arm. He glanced upwards and saw flaking paint and rotting wood in the eaves of the house. He wondered why it had been allowed to decay. Frieda watched her son and thought Peter should not concern himself with such things on such a wonderful day.

"It's a beautiful spring day. We will gather in the tea house. Greta has prepared everything," she announced.

Greta and Helga waited at the great oak table ready to receive the family. A few bottles of Käthe's favourite hock stood by the sweetmeats and cakes. She wondered how she could avoid revealing what had happened to Adam but two or three glasses of wine soon loosened tongues. Adam knew it should be a secret and said very little. Gustav was disappointed, encouraging him to say more.

Käthe tried to put the best gloss possible on her life in the consulate, but her story disappointed Gustav. "It was a foreign country, you must have had some excitement," he insisted. "I expect you did some expensive shopping my dear," he added with a wink.

"Oh we did, Grandpapa," interrupted an enthusiastic Adam, "When it was safe." Käthe and Peter glared at Adam, and he realised his mistake. His face reddened. "Safe from what or whom?" enquired Frieda. Peter decided they had to tell his parents, but they evaded the seriousness of the injury.

"But you didn't tell us, Peter," said Gustav. "You know it is our tradition to tell everything."

Frieda came to the rescue. "You are all here safe and that's all that matters," she said.

Gustav looked at the floor as he was upset by something else. "What's the matter, Grandpapa?" Adam asked innocently.

"Old Julius has telephoned your grandmama, Adam," he began. He looked at Peter and Käthe. "And you allowed Adam to intervene?" he asked.

Frieda wanted to tell them that Gustav hadn't been himself lately. Adam usually turned to Gustav for warmth and to Frieda for guidance, and she didn't let him down.

"Please raise your glasses to our grandson," she began. "He has defended the weak against the strong." Gustav seemed humiliated, but was soon to demonstrate he could have his way in some matters.

Käthe had told him years before that Peter might have a heart defect. He asked his son to walk with him on the shingle beach. They both sat down on an upturned rowing boat painted a bright yellow, and Gustav tapped it with his stick.

CHAPTER SEVEN

"You remember the hours we spent in this boat before the war, my boy?" he reminded Peter. "I told you everything then, and I will tell you everything now. Things are not going well. You've noticed the condition of the house? Well of course you have. You always wanted to learn how to repair things, but your mother said it was none of our business."

Peter knew where all of this was leading. "My tenants cannot pay their rents in the East. I can no longer afford to invest in the land Peter and I cannot see the way forward," said Gustav.

Frieda had persuaded Gustav to obtain a diplomatic post for their son, but Gustav convinced himself that Peter would not continue long in the job. Now that had backfired, because Peter was the most successful German diplomat in south-eastern China. He wanted to return, but Gustav wanted him to stay and manage the estates. All Peter felt he could do was to promise to examine the estates accounts for his father. The old man was distressed, but there was little he could do.

Käthe and Frieda examined the family photographs in the tea house. One of them showed them taking tea with the Goerings at Horcher's restaurant in Berlin. "The circle is really looking forward to seeing you again," said Frieda. Käthe looked dubious when Frieda mentioned Goering. Georg Holman had told his daughter that he was a leading light in the National Socialists.

"You needn't worry my dear," her mother-in-law assured her. "Goering's new lady Karin has told him to behave himself and the others think it's still acceptable to take tea with them.

"Really?" said Käthe, surprised at Frieda's apparent naivety.

"Yes, and he is now President of the Reichstag," she added. Even Käthe was prepared to forget the events in the square at Kreuzberg for the sake of resuming her social life in Berlin with such an important man.

When Peter and his father returned from their stroll on the shingle beach, Gustav summoned everyone to the tea house. He stood at the head of the oak table and banged his walking stick against the wooden floor to gain attention.

"I have an important announcement to make," he began and he turned to his grandson. "Beginning next Monday, Adam, you are to attend the Martin Luther school for boys in Wilmersdorf." He waited for a reaction from his grandson. Adam was delighted.

"Is there a uniform, Grandpapa?" he asked.

"There is indeed," replied Gustav. "It is waiting for you in your room. You are to try it on immediately and report to us all here. Be quick, my boy," he said, waving his walking cane. Adam scurried off.

The announcement caught Peter and Käthe by surprise because a decision they should have made had been made for them, but Peter was pleased because Adam was to go to his old school under the guidance of his old Principal, Dr Stiebert. Gustav was from a Protestant background and insisted against Frieda's wishes that Peter should attend a Protestant school. He was determined that the same should apply to Adam. Käthe was the newcomer and had no choice but to agree.

Adam returned in a stiff collar and an outfit not unlike his ordinary clothes and wearing a straw boater, much to Käthe's delight. "Look after it, my darling," she said smiling.

Then came a lecture from Gustav. "You must study hard for your Abitur," he said. "It is a necessary qualification for you to enter the military college at Potsdam." Adam saluted his grandfather, who felt his pre-eminence had been restored.

"Can I change and row the boat papa?" asked Adam. Peter nodded and Adam tore off to his room. Käthe looked worried as she slowly finished her last glass of wine and nibbled on a remaining canapé.

"Don't worry my love," Peter tried to reassure her. "When he goes to school, He'll forget all this soldiering." Käthe wasn't so sure.

They all watched as the solitary boy launched the small rowing boat without any help. Adam rowed powerfully along the shore away from the pleasure steamers. "Two Chinese fishermen taught him how to do that, father," said Peter.

Helga interrupted her cleaning duties to watch Adam's performance through the large side window. Adam strained and strained at the oars to try to forget his fear of going to school. He became obsessed with what the other boys would think of his injured leg.

Gustav had made an appointment for Käthe, Peter and Adam to see the school Principal, Dr Stiebert, at eight o'clock on Adam's first morning. They were to review his educational progress and introduce him to his first-year classmates after the first lesson had begun.

CHAPTER SEVEN

Käthe annoyed him by constantly adjusting his straw boater and Frieda supplied a briefcase and a supply of pens and pencils. Gustav insisted Peter drive them to the Martin Luther school in his pride and joy, a 1922 American Buick saloon. The cream-and-maroon car had not seen the light of day for some time and Gustav was now unable to drive because his arthritis was too severe.

The building lay behind a row of legal offices in its own parkland. The car reached it in ten minutes and Peter guided it down the avenue of elm trees leading to the main entrance.

Käthe glanced at Adam. He said very little. He didn't want to get out of the car and stared at the gaunt building, its square lines broken only by two soaring spires at each end.

A senior student directed the car to the visitors' parking area and led the family up granite steps to the huge double doors. On each was the image of a brass eagle clutching a branch of oak leaves. A caretaker who was polishing the eagles bowed and opened the doors for the visitors.

The entrance hall had a high dome and every sound echoed and carried. It was possible to hear a conversation twenty or thirty metres away, and their footsteps rang on the parquet flooring. In the centre of the hall was the statue of an eagle. At the foot was a copper nameplate bearing the names of former pupils lost in the war.

Their guide knocked on an oak door and ushered them in. Dr Dieter Stiebert was seated behind a heavy oak desk. He had just finished briefing his secretary, who bowed and left. He sprang to his feet with a not inconsiderable effort for a man close to retirement. He was tall and distinguished. His rimless spectacles sat on a firm but caring face, which lit up when he saw Peter.

"It is Herr von Saloman, one of our most promising mathematical and engineering students, is it not?" he enquired eagerly. "I am charmed indeed." He shook hands with Käthe. But he was not to be diverted from his purpose and quickly discovered the extent of Adam's knowledge, from a summary which Käthe produced. He announced that he was generally impressed, but there were areas where remedial measures had to be taken. He peered over his spectacles. "No formal physical training I see," he remarked. "Herr Rust will take care of that, I am sure."

"Please don't be concerned" he assured Adam's parents. "I will conduct this young man to his first lesson." They shook hands with the Principal and left, leaving Adam more scared than he had ever been.

"Now, von Saloman," began the principal. It is your first day in a public school, I believe?" They stopped at the eagle and the war memorial. "Why does the bird hold oak leaves, do you think?" he asked.

"It is the old German badge of bravery, Herr Stiebert," Adam answered with a falter in his voice. The Principal paused at the memorial and bowed. "We do this as we pass here," he said. He lifted his hand for silence as they reached a door inscribed with gold letters. It read 'Professor Rohrman - Science and Engineering.' He knocked quietly and listened. A distant sharp voice said "Come in."

Dr Stiebert entered the science laboratory, followed by a quaking Adam. Bunsen burners and flasks occupied three sides of the room and there was a smell of sulphur and ammonia. Every desk was occupied except one. Professor Rohrman stood behind an oak desk. He was tall and slim and wore a threadbare suit, patched at the elbows. He looked severe and impatient as he consulted a list on his desk.

"You must be von Saloman," he said.

"Yes, Herr Professor," answered Adam in a respectful stutter.

"May I leave him with you, Rohrman?" asked the Principal.

"Yes, of course. Please step forward and be introduced," said the science teacher.

The door closed quietly and Adam was on his own. He noticed three boys seated at the back of the class. One of them seemed uncomfortably familiar and fixed a hostile stare on the new pupil. At the front were two wide-eyed little boys who eyed Adam curiously. They looked at Adam as if they wanted him to say something, and he thought they were twins.

Next to the only vacant seat sat a dark-haired, pale-skinned distant-looking boy. As the teacher spoke, he seemed disinterested. As Adam faced the class, red-faced, this boy looked out of the window.

"This is von Saloman," said the teacher, inviting Adam to sit next to the boy, who shifted uneasily. Adam opened his bag and nervously produced pens and pencils.

CHAPTER SEVEN

"Von Saloman, your neighbour is Grabowsky," said Rohrman. The two boys exchanged a nod.

On the teacher's desk was a working model of a steam engine. The smell of methylated spirits was still in the air. "Would you please describe to me the principle of the sun and planet wheel, von Saloman?" asked the teacher.

Adam froze. Jacob had told him, but he had forgotten. He had to say something. "I have oiled a steam engine on the Pearl River in China Herr Rohrman," he answered. "But I don't know the sun and planet wheel."

The three boys at the back sniggered and Adam remembered who they were – his opponents in the square at Kreuzberg. The teacher drew a small cane and rapped the desk and the three boys were temporarily cowed.

"Klaus Gutman," the teacher said to one of the twins. "Would you like to help von Saloman?" Adam's neighbour grimaced. What followed was an encyclopaedic description. "Thank you, Gutman," said Professor Rohrman with a hint of relief. A bell sounded and the teacher gave Adam a text book to study at home.

Adam's neighbour said nothing and hurried away to the next lesson. The twins waited for Adam. "I'm Theo," said one. "I'm Klaus," said the other.

"Are you any good at music?" asked Theo.

"Quite good," said Adam distantly.

"Well look," said Klaus. "If you help us with music, we'll help you with science."

"Yes, I'd like to help," answered Adam, and they shook hands. He towered above them. At the beginning of the music lesson, Theo told the teacher that Adam was good at music, which embarrassed him.

Before they sat down, Adam's pale neighbour told the twins off for embarrassing the new boy. Adam was asked to give a recital. He played a little, and applause thundered round the room. The three boys at the back didn't join in but the mysterious Grabowsky began to show some interest.

It took five minutes to reach the maths lesson. This time Grabowsky waited for Adam and the Gutman twins. He'd enjoyed Adam's recital. "Can you do anything else?" he said to Adam smiling mischievously. Adam smiled in return and quietly chuckled.

Theo and Klaus were not to be left out. "Adam," said Theo. "This is Bruno. He speaks to us when he's in a good mood."

"Not like now, you mean," retorted Bruno. Adam had begun to enjoy himself.

None of them had been watching the three boys who had hung back, and they now quickened their pace. One of them deliberately walked into Klaus and tore his school bag from his shoulder, throwing it on the floor. "Pick it up, Jew," he said threateningly. Klaus tried, but the biggest boy kicked it away.

"C'mon Jew, pick it up," he said. There were no teachers or senior pupils in sight. The attackers had picked their time carefully.

Adam stepped between Klaus and the big boy, never taking his eyes off him, as he had been taught. "I'll pick it up, Klaus," said Adam, and he returned the bag. The big boy's arrogance turned to cautious hostility. "It won't be long before we bring toffs like you down to size," he said, trying to retrieve his loss of face. Adam smiled indulgently at him. "Please lead us to the maths lesson," he said to the three boys. He didn't see Bruno smiling.

Bruno ruled the roost in maths, hotly followed by the twins. It was clear Adam had never been taught much algebra and Bruno helped out on the invitation of the teacher.

On the way to the dining hall, Bruno said, "I see you're stealing my friends. Haven't you any of your own?"

The question hurt Adam. "I've just borrowed them for a while. May I have them a little longer?" he asked.

"You can have them for as long as you want" said Bruno. "They're really hard work. They think there's prehistoric monsters in the Grünewald."

The twins overheard. "No we don't," said Theo, anxious to maintain their standing with Adam.

"I think I've heard them at night," said the new boy, and Bruno enjoyed the joke.

The four boys queued up along a long table where ladies doled out sausage, bread and a generous helping of pork stew. "I'm Frau Gluchs and I expect you to behave yourself" one woman said, smiling. She gave Adam an extra helping. The twins laughed and Bruno expressed mock disgust. "You haven't been here two hours and you're cook's favourite," he said. They sat down together.

"Where was your last school?" asked Theo.

CHAPTER SEVEN

"I've never been to school," said Adam. "My parents and friends taught me."

"Where?" asked Theo. Bruno pretended to be embarrassed, but he wanted to know.

"Canton," answered Adam.

"Where's that?" asked Klaus.

"China, you half-wit," muttered Bruno.

"Who are they?" asked Adam, nodding towards the three boys he had met in the square. The twins allowed Bruno to do the talking. "Watch them," he said. "The big one's Berndt Schuster. He used to be OK. Then he got in with that lot and joined the Hitler youth."

They paused to make serious inroads into the stew. "Slow down, you boys!" shouted Frau Gluchs.

"I'm in the Catholic Youth," said Bruno. "That lot try to bully us." There was another pause as they wiped their plates with huge chunks of black bread. "Are you allowed to do that Adam?" asked Bruno. Adam chuckled again.

"Why was Schuster afraid of you?" asked Klaus. "Is it because you're a toff?"

Bruno looked at Adam as if there was no hope for the twins and all three stared at Adam curious to know the answer.

"I can't tell you," he said.

"Well that's a good start, I must say," remarked Bruno. As they left the dining hall, he asked Adam privately, "Why did you pick that bag up?"

Adam looked at Bruno with the self-assurance his grandmother had taught him. "Because someone had to do it," he answered. Bruno looked impressed, and nodded.

Before the new friends left for home in mid-afternoon, Adam was treated to an inspirational hour neither he nor Bruno would ever forget. Theo and Klaus dragged their feet as they approached the history room. "They're not interested in anything unless it has an engine or it goes off with a bang," explained Bruno.

"Dr Diercks isn't like the others," he said.

"Stupid old fool," said one of Schuster's friends.

The four boys had barely walked through the door when a kindly figure with hands clasped together met them. The old history teacher radiated enthusiasm. "You must be von Saloman," he began. "Please sit down. You have a very interesting surname. I shall research it for you."

The walls were covered with flags and heraldic emblems. Behind the classroom door was a rusting suit of armour. Dr Diercks launched into a lecture about Frederic II, the great Hohenstaufen. Adam and Bruno hung on every word and so too did Berndt Schuster. The twins nearly fell asleep.

"There is to be a competition," announced Dr Diercks. "You will each write an essay about Frederick II. You must do your own research." He opened a drawer. "And this will be the prize," he said, unfurling a two-metre long yellow pennant. On it were sewn the three black lions of the great emperor.

There was another group of boys in the centre of the class who were yet to reveal anything about themselves. A serious looking fair-haired boy sat amongst them.

"I shall expect great things from you, Harro," said the teacher. "And I look forward to your effort too von Saloman," he added.

"Where's your bicycle?" asked Theo just as Peter and Käthe arrived in the Buick. The bustle around the bicycle sheds came to a halt as the car pulled up noiselessly. Berndt Schuster and his friends pretended not to be interested. Theo and Klaus peered into the car windows. "Stop it you two," ordered Bruno and they looked hurt.

Peter got out of the car first and opened the door for Käthe. She looked her usual elegant best. "Please introduce me to your new friends, Adam," said Käthe. Bruno bowed and shook hands. He smiled at Käthe without any shyness. The twins bowed and stared.

"Bruno, Theo and Klaus," said Adam. "My new friends." Adam looked at Bruno hoping for approval, but didn't suspect he was already the dominant partner.

"I'll remember these names easily," said Käthe. "I'm sure we'll see you again."

"It's running tomorrow," Bruno reminded Adam quietly before he got into the car.

Theo opened the car door for Käthe and shyly smiled at her. "Thank you very much," she said graciously.

CHAPTER SEVEN

Käthe asked questions for both of them as Peter concentrated on the road. Adam couldn't wait to tell them about the history competition. "Bruno wants to win too," he said.

"Where does he live?" asked Käthe.

"In an apartment block near grandmother's lawyers," said Adam casually. He wasn't thinking of Bruno's apartment or of anything else except the athletics lesson in the morning. Neither Peter nor Käthe knew how self-conscious he was about the scar on his left leg.

Dinner was a celebration of Adam's first day at school. It was a welcome diversion for Peter as he remembered his enjoyable days at the Martin Luther school. The adults were excited about Adam's first day at school, but drifted into talking about their own experience. None of them noticed Adam slipping away to bed early, except Käthe. She found him sitting up in bed staring at his two remaining soldiers.

"What are they telling you my darling?" she asked. "Are you afraid of tomorrow?" He nodded. Then she guessed. "It's athletics tomorrow, isn't it?" she asked. Again he nodded.

"Are you worried about your leg?" she continued, and he admitted he was. Käthe suddenly remembered how old her son was. "I like your new friends," she began. He was pleased because he wanted his mother's approval of them.

"I watched them as the car drew up," Käthe continued. "They all think you're wonderful, Adam. Did you know that? And why shouldn't they, my handsome son?" Käthe had made it possible for him to face the next day. "And as far that scar is concerned, Adam," Käthe said, "that's nothing compared to the things I saw in the Berlin military hospitals."

She kissed him goodnight and closed the door quietly. He could face his soldiers once more, and saluted them.

The following afternoon, a school bus took Adam's class to an old pier by the side of the Wannsee. There they were to be met by Herr Alfred Rust, their physical training instructor. Senior boys supervised them on the way to the lake and they had trouble keeping Schuster and his friends quiet; they seemed to be planning something. The twins thought they had most to fear and they clung to Adam, their new protector.

The boys went as quiet as the grave as they got off the bus in front of an old shed painted bright blue in the school colours. Waiting by an open door was their instructor, a bald, square–headed man with a carefully trimmed oblong moustache. It was a cold day, but he didn't flinch as he read out the boys' names from a clipboard.

He looked sharply at Adam. "Von Saloman," he asked.

"Yes, Herr Rust," answered Adam.

"This announcement is for your benefit" he said loudly. "Class selections for all events in Sports Day have been made except for the javelin and the three thousand metres. Our training here in the Grünewald will enable these selections to be made. I would like to say that Harro, Schuster and Grabowsky must not take their selection for granted."

Adam's heart sank. His new friend was good at athletics and he hadn't told him. Adam turned and saw Bruno grinning.

"That's enough, Grabowsky," said the teacher. "Showers are available in the usual place. And there is one other announcement. I will remind you," he said severely. "You must all respect the Private Property signs at the end of the lake."

It was Adam's turn to grin and Bruno's to be puzzled. "Report to the start in ten minutes," ordered the teacher. He had seen that Adam was nervous.

Herr Rust broke into a half-smile. "Have you done this sort of thing before?" he asked. Adam shook his head. "You are in good hands, von Saloman. Grabowsky and the twins will look after you."

He turned away to supervise the others. "I told you he was all right," said Bruno and they all clustered around the start. One of Schuster's friends saw the scar. "Would you like a wheelchair, von Saloman?" he asked. "Your little Jewish friends could push you."

Bruno stepped in to defuse the situation. "I'll push you if you like, Adam," he said. His new friend wasn't amused. "OK, Adam, listen," he said. "Just try to follow me. I'll go slower today. Those two can look out for prehistoric monsters."

"We'll look after Adam as well," said Klaus.

"If you insist," said Bruno.

"Schuster and Harro always win," said Theo.

"Run past me, Adam," said Bruno, who didn't run all that slowly, but Adam did as he was told. Bruno caught up. "Run past me again," said Bruno.

Adam was enjoying himself and his leg didn't hurt him. They finished sixty metres behind Harro and Schuster, but they had beaten everyone else. "You're not bad at this," said Bruno.

Herr Rust called them over to stand with Dieter Harro and Berndt Schuster. He continued to display his more kindly side. "Well done, von Saloman," he said. "Selection now will be even more difficult. You have all returned a good time today. Shower as quickly as you can."

Dieter Harro shook Adam's hand. "That was a good performance for your first try," he said.

Adam asked Peter to take himself and Bruno to the Grünewald at least twice a week over the next four weeks and the twins followed them on their bicycles as the willing timekeepers. After one month, Adam finished ahead of Bruno and only ten metres behind Schuster and Harro. Dieter was delighted, but Berndt became even more morose and anti-social.

Bruno noticed a trait in Adam. "That lot really have it in for you," he said. "But you never say anything bad about them." It took years for Bruno to find an explanation.

Chapter 8

Adam chose the time carefully to ask about Bruno's Catholic youth group and forgot about Theo and Klaus. They were upset if they were left out of a conversation and always looked over their shoulders. "Schuster and his friends watch us all the time," explained Bruno.

One stocky little boy seemed to be the eyes and ears of Berndt Schuster's group. "We don't like Müller," said the twins. "He's the one that starts all the trouble." The friends didn't know that Uve Müller kept a notebook. He now had a new subject, the comings and goings of Adam von Saloman. He insisted that his leader Schuster read the reports in detail, and Berndt Schuster read them for fear that he himself was under scrutiny.

Adam had to extract the details of the Catholic youth group from Bruno. He seemed to want Adam to think his life was a collection of closely-guarded secrets, but was always cheerfully surprised when his new friend made enquiries.

"Is it the sort of thing you'd do?" asked Bruno when he had described the barbecues, the singing and the less-than-airtight log cabins. Adam was keen to try it out, particularly when Bruno mentioned a uniform. Peter and Käthe were more enthusiastic at first than Adam, as they knew their parish priest was involved. The weekend away was to be spent at Allgau in the Black Forest in Bavaria.

Peter drove Adam and Bruno to Berlin's central station and Bruno insisted on being picked up at school. The boys took a train to Heidelberg. "Don't get selected to look after the flag," warned Bruno. "The priests never take their eyes off you."

When they had settled down in their compartments, Adam said he would like to meet Bruno's father. The question pained his new friend. "All I know is he was gassed while fighting the French" said Bruno. "He caught tuberculosis and died. His name was Wilfred. That's all I know. Mother doesn't want to talk about him. Let's not talk about it again."

Adam had no idea that Bruno was in awe of his new friend's family and looked for any chance to increase his own prestige. The introduction of Adam to the Catholic youth group was one example. Adam thought it was a game and hatched a scheme to impress Bruno that landed them both in serious trouble.

Berndt Schuster and his friends had become worried at the progress of their rivals. They thought only of selection and victory in the three thousand metres. The training had become a means of cementing a friendship for Adam and Bruno and they began to lose sight of the contest on Sports Day.

For the twins, it was a different matter. A victory for Adam or Bruno might guarantee them some safety, so they badgered them to do better. The two became quite annoyed with the twins, who constantly brandished stop watches. Only four weeks before sports day, Adam thought his moment had come. This was the time to impress Bruno.

During a training run, Adam eased his pace, as if he didn't care whether Harro or Schuster won or not. "I want to beat the pants off Schuster, even if you don't," Bruno reminded Adam. They reached the signpost near the end of the lake marked 'private property' and Adam stopped.

"Let's have a look," said Adam.

"No," answered Bruno, "We'll be thrown out of school if we do."

Adam rode roughshod over Bruno's objections. "We'll have a look," said Adam.

"Why is this so important to you?" asked Bruno and at that point the twins caught up. Klaus developed more courage than usual. "That's stupid," he said.

"It's for Bruno and me," said Adam.

The twins wandered off, thinking they had been permanently excluded. "There was no need for that," Bruno said. "Let's get it over with." If it was important for Adam, he decided, he would have to go through with it.

"We'll have one look and stay in the trees," said Bruno, trying to convince himself he was in charge. He didn't see Adam press the button behind the left hand gate post which activated a warning in the kitchen.

The gates opened silently and the two boys crept down the path. The trees made a dark archway that made Bruno feel safe for a few moments.

"I've had enough," he said, tiring of the dare.

"We'll just go to the end," said Adam. "Hide behind that big tree Bruno." The house came into view. Bruno peered out from behind the tree to see Die Schwanen in the sunshine, just as the front door opened and Greta appeared with Hansl and Gretl. She strode down the path towards the intruders.

"Run!" hissed Bruno.

They sprinted back through the main gates and left them open. Bruno was furious, "The old girl with the dogs saw us. We'll be for it now," he said.

"She didn't see us," replied Adam in the safe and sure knowledge that Greta wasn't wearing her spectacles.

Herr Rust was disgusted with their performance. Even Theo and Klaus beat them. He didn't think to ask why, though he soon regretted he had not done so.

The following morning, Adam and Bruno shuffled into assembly in the great hall. Adam and Bruno sat on the front row. They flushed proudly when Dr Stiebert announced several sporting successes and an entry into Tübingen University. He encouraged the boys to greater efforts because Berlin had been chosen to host the Olympic Games in a few years' time.

Then his expression changed and he bowed his head. He produced a piece of paper and his hands fell. "I am ashamed to say," he began, "that two boys who must be pupils of this school have trespassed on private property and what is more, have done so in school time."

Bruno felt the muscles in his face contract and sweat poured down Adam's forehead. Dr Stiebert continued. "I expect the boys who are responsible to report to Herr Rust after assembly. If they do not do so, the class will be punished collectively."

Bruno was angry, not just because they had done something wrong. He felt hugely let down.

"What do you suggest we do now?" he asked.

"See Herr Rust," mumbled Adam.

"You can do the talking, Adam," said Bruno, "but I'll take the rap as well," he added in a low voice.

"Thanks Bruno," stuttered Adam.

Quaking, they knocked on the staff room door. Alfred Rust was not expecting these two and was almost speechless. Before he could say anything, Adam blurted out, "It was all my fault, Herr Rust. Please don't punish Grabowsky."

"Go back to your class, Grabowsky." I'll deal with you later," said the teacher. Bruno left, knowing he now had to face the twins and Schuster and his friends.

"Why did you risk embarrassing your family, von Saloman?" asked Herr Rust. "Do you realise, were it not for your family's connection to this school, you would face expulsion? This is the course of action you will take. You will write a letter of apology to your family. I am sure your father will know how to deal with you. Furthermore, you and Grabowsky will make a full apology to your fellow pupils in class. You must do that now in the history class. You may go."

"Herr Rust," Adam began weakly, "Grabowsky didn't know it was my family's house." Alfred Rust had to suppress a smile as he guessed what had happened. His attitude softened. "Most of your new classmates look up to you, von Saloman, particularly the Gutman twins and Harro. You bear a great responsibility. Go now and make your speech."

As Adam walked down the echoing corridors, he remembered his grandmother's words. "Always Adam, remember who you are."

He knocked quietly at the door and stole in, to be greeted by a stony silence. Bruno stood by the teacher's desk, red-faced. Uve Müller grinned smugly. He nudged his neighbour, Rolf Schneider. They intended to enjoy the humiliation of their enemies.

"Do you have something to say, von Saloman?" said Dr Diercks.

"I have made the class look very bad in front of the school and I have upset my friends. I am very sorry," Adam said.

"Yes and I'm sorry too," Bruno added in a timely gesture of support.

Uve Müller and Rolf Schneider believed pre-eminence had passed back to their leader, Berndt Schuster, and Dieter Harro was afraid they might be right.

"Leave them alone," he said to Müller.

"Shut up, Harro," said Rolf Schneider, "or it'll be worse for you."

In the next few weeks, the Hitler Youth's assumption proved badly wrong.

The Gutman twins had no choice but to remain loyal and Adam's apology had impressed the class.

Dr Stiebert's letter arrived at Die Schwanen the following morning. Gustav and Frieda were furious, and Peter was ashamed. With the letter was an apology from Adam and Bruno and he thrust it into Käthe's hand. Peter believed that his wife overindulged their son, but was still mildly jealous of the conspiracy between them.

"The other signature," said Käthe. "Isn't this his new friend Bruno?"

"Yes," replied Peter.

"There can be no question of allowing the visit this weekend."

"I think it might be more effective if you told him, Käthe," Peter said, implying that the whole matter was Käthe's responsibility. This made her angry.

"This is no more than a childish prank that has gone wrong" she snapped. "He's never had a friend before. It's just harmless showing off and he's probably suffered enough already."

Peter thought it a lame excuse, but to everyone's surprise, Gustav thought the boys should be forgiven and Frieda agreed. Poor Gustav had been ignored too much lately and she thought the balance should be redressed. They both made Käthe promise to be more firm with Adam in the future. She thought they were interfering, but didn't dare say so.

When Peter met Adam after school, his face was stony. "We will speak later," he said. "But first you must meet your grandfather in his workshop." Peter said nothing else all the way home, but his thoughts turned once again to Käthe's over-indulgence of Adam.

Gustav was seated in his favourite oak chair with his old mountain jacket draped over the back. The smell of lacquer was heavy in the air. There was row upon row of pots of paint to be applied to the latest of Gustav's model soldiers.

His grandfather was upset. "Your mother and father wished to cancel your friend's visit," he said. Adam's spirits sank. "Your friend will be allowed to come, on one condition. You have let him down. Nothing else matters my boy," he said patting Adam on the cheek. Adam threw his arms round Gustav's neck. "Have you apologized to your friend?" he reminded Adam and remembered that he hadn't.

Bruno lived close by in Wilmersdorf and Peter knew the address. The

Grabowsky apartment was in the same building as the one owned by the Foreign Ministry. They rang the doorbell and the concierge telephoned Frau Grabowsky on the first floor. Within two minutes Bruno appeared with his mother. She was determined he would forget nothing. "Please Mutti," Adam heard him say. "I have everything."

Renate Grabowsky was small, slender and as well dressed as her limited income permitted. She had managed to obtain a post as a librarian after Bruno had started to attend the Martin Luther school. Her hair was dark auburn streaked with grey and she peered anxiously over a pair of half-moon spectacles. Her skin showed little sign of her age. Peter thought her in her early forties.

Renate didn't want Bruno to go anywhere without her. He was all she had and Bruno never spoke of aunts or uncles. She wrung her hands anxiously as Bruno attempted to say goodbye.

Adam was very gallant. He sprang from the car and introduced himself. "Thank you for allowing Bruno to visit us," he said.

She looked slightly suspiciously at Adam through her dark eyes, then decided she liked him. "Don't let Bruno stay in bed, Adam," she said.

"Mutti, please," begged an embarrassed Bruno. She squeezed his hand through the open car window.

"Sorry," said Adam as the Buick took them towards the forest.

"Don't mention it," said Bruno as the car joined the Avus in the southern half of the Grünewald. Bruno watched the trams because he was too afraid to speak. He managed to grin at Adam as they approached the end of the forest. Peter had been anxious to build bridges with his son and had agreed to play Adam's game and surprise Bruno. The car turned into the forest. Bruno looked at Adam, who continued to stare ahead.

"I believe you do some of your training here, Bruno," said Peter.

"Yes Herr von Saloman," answered Bruno.

The car stopped in front of the gates and Adam opened them. He climbed back into the car. "Would you like to meet the old girl with the dogs?" he whispered to Bruno, who was in a terrible state as the car drew up outside the house.

Peter had overheard Adam. "The old girl with the dogs is called Greta and she will make a tremendous fuss of you. From now on Adam, will behave himself," said Peter. Adam looked suitably ashamed. Bruno muttered to Adam, "You rat!"

The family and the household filed out of the front door and Bruno was confronted with another world as he stepped cautiously out of the car. He looked upwards at the house and seemed rooted to the spot.

"Do you intend to join us later?" joked Adam.

Bruno was welcomed in turn by the gardener, the handyman, the cook, the housekeeper, Frieda, Gustav and Helga, who pretended not to notice him. When Bruno met Helga, she curtsied and held out her hand. Bruno held onto hers much more than anyone else's. He smiled mischievously and Helga turned bright red.

Frieda announced grandly that all were to go to the tea-house. "Will you take my arm, young man?" she asked Bruno. He walked as if in a dream, with Helga walking close behind. No one sat until Frieda and Bruno had taken their chairs.

He gazed at the spread on the old table. There were several solid silver cake-stands and a Meissen tea service. "Please choose, Bruno," said Frieda. Adam hadn't enjoyed himself so much for a long time.

Bruno dropped a huge chocolate éclair onto his lap and his face turned a deep red. Greta came to the rescue. "Take another," she said. "There are plenty. I didn't know it was you two."

"You should have set the dogs on us, Greta" joked Adam.

Helga held a large cake. "Helga has baked it for you Bruno," said Greta proudly. "Would you like to try some?"

Bruno said he would, not entirely out of politeness. Helga spent as long as she dared cutting him a piece.

Käthe made a fuss of him. She asked him about his chosen career, which was architecture, and hoped against hope Adam would be deflected from his military ambitions. She became fond of Bruno and they became great friends.

Gustav disappeared behind the house in the hope that the visitor would be curious about his shed, and Peter told Adam he could have Bruno all to himself. They staged one of Adam's mock raids on the kitchen. Greta pretended to drive them out with a large ladle, but gave them several biscuits.

"I can't eat any more," said Bruno.

"Then we'll explore," suggested Adam.

Bruno stood at the foot of the main staircase in the entrance hall. He had never seen marble steps in a house before and gazed at the gold paint on the ceiling.

"I didn't know you liked architecture," said Adam.

"What do you want to do?" asked Bruno.

"I shall join the army and become an officer in the infantry. Grandfather and I have planned it for a long time. Look at this Bruno." He was standing by the long side window overlooking the lake. He pointed to a small rowing boat lying on a shingle beach.

"Is the boat yours?" asked Bruno.

"Yes," said Adam. "And the beach."

"What's your grandfather doing?" asked Bruno.

"Making another battlefield, I think," said Adam. "That's his workshop. I'm the only person allowed in there."

Bruno thought Gustav's shed should be the next item on the itinerary. "He might let you in," said Adam. The old man was surprised and delighted when he saw the two boys. "You know you're the only one allowed here," said Gustav.

"I know Grandpapa, but this is my best friend," said Adam.

"Shall we show your best friend the war room, Adam?" asked the old man.

"Yes please Grandpapa," he answered.

Gustav reached underneath a bench for a tin box. He produced two brass keys, and got out of his seat with some difficulty. He refused help and hobbled to the rear of the house. Part of the walls was covered by thick ivy over a few stone steps which led downwards. There was a loud squawk as a jackdaw was disturbed and flew off. The smell of moss and decay was everywhere. Gustav stepped downwards and unlocked a small door at the foot of the ivy and threw a light switch.

"May I join you?" said Peter. Gustav looked at his son with a pained expression. Ever since the end of the war, Peter had refused to go to the war room with his father. Now he felt able to go.

"Of course you may," answered Gustav.

"This is really good now you're here, Papa," said Adam.

He produced the second key, which unlocked a door at the head of six stone steps which climbed to the centre of the house. Gustav opened the door into complete darkness. There was no electric light, only candles placed at the four corners of the room. Gustav lit them in turn.

At the far end was a suit of medieval armour. Behind it on panelled walls were hung swords, spears and shields. Adorning one long wall to the left were portraits of Germany's generals. On the long opposite wall was a life-size military scene in a tent. Nineteenth-century commanders pored over maps and held empty glasses with sherry bottles standing on a trestle table.

Covering three quarters of the floor area was a diorama of a battle. French flags flew from wrecked buildings. Wounded men, cannon and horses lay on their sides.

There were hundreds of models, a lifetime's work, each one beautifully painted. Standing on raised ground facing each other were the unmistakable figures of Napoleon Bonaparte and the Duke of Wellington. Bruno stood in front of the Duke as if he expected to be introduced.

"Look Bruno," said Adam, pointing to the black guards of Prussia galloping into the north-east corner of the battlefield. Bruno pointed to a regiment of lancers kneeling down in front of them, his fingers gently touching their distinctive headgear.

"Those are my soldiers," said Adam proudly.

"What is the battle, young man?" said Gustav to Bruno.

"I think it is Waterloo sir," said Bruno. "I think this is Marshall Blücher coming to the rescue of the English. Dr Diercks told us sir."

"You are a very clever young man," said Gustav. "Do you know what Adam wants to do?" he asked his new friend. Adam stood tall. "He will go straight to the military school at Potsdam when he is old enough and train to fight in the infantry," said Gustav.

Peter remained silent. He'd seen the horrors of the trenches and was already planning a future for his son in the diplomatic corps. Secretly he had not regretted the lack of contact between his son and Gustav in recent years. Käthe too hated the idea of Adam becoming a soldier, and now Gustav was undoing all the good work again.

Peter knew Gustav had never seen front-line service, but he could never tell his father he knew. He chose his moment to remind everyone they should rejoin the others when he thought the boys had had enough of Gustav's brand of militarism.

CHAPTER EIGHT

The evening continued to revolve round the two boys. "Bruno wants to be a famous architect," Adam announced. He had added 'famous' for effect. Frieda was delighted and wished to know Bruno's taste in buildings.

"My mother has promised to take me to Florence one day to see a famous old bridge," said Bruno.

"That's something we should do," said Käthe hopefully. Peter agreed, but Gustav grunted sullenly.

"Have you begun your essay for the competition at the end of term?" Peter asked Bruno, changing the subject.

"Oh yes," said Bruno. "I have a book at home about Frederic II." He said it as a throwaway remark and hadn't mentioned it to Adam who looked nonplussed. Käthe watched and listened carefully and more and more thought that Bruno was a good friend for Adam. The young aristocrat might have all the advantages, but Bruno was determined his new friend would find nothing easy.

Helga served dinner that evening and Käthe noticed the number of unnecessary trips she made to see if everything was all right. Käthe thought it was far more interesting than their Berlin social circle and Bruno became her little project.

Early on Sunday morning, the family and their guest took Holy Communion at the parish church but Bruno was uneasy and had to be guided through the service. Adam had wrongly assumed that his friend had had a Catholic upbringing because of the link with the Catholic youth. He told his mother it was something Bruno didn't want discussed.

The people of Berlin came out to play in the Grünewald on a Sunday afternoon and the noise carried over the wall from the forest into the gardens. Gustav suggested that Peter row the boys along the edge of the lake. Käthe looked horrified and Frieda forbade it on the grounds of Peter's poor health. Gustav had been overruled again.

"Why don't you row Bruno along the lake?" she suggested to Adam.

"Surely the boy isn't strong enough," objected Gustav. "And there is the danger from the pleasure steamers." Adam announced that he had had some training from two Chinese fishermen. Gustav looked at his grandson as if he'd been betrayed.

"It's all right Grandpapa. I can do it," he assured him, sensing the old man had been left out. Käthe saw it also. "I'll keep a careful eye on them both Gustav," she promised. Käthe had spoken, and Gustav was happy.

"Please can we take the dogs?" said Adam as they came out from under the table and nuzzled his legs. It was a wonder they were able to row. The boys had already had a light lunch, but Greta appeared with rolls, sausages, eggs and lemonade. Each of the dogs was provided with a cushion, and Adam and Bruno were resplendent in white trousers and straw boaters.

Soon the adults had dozed off in the tea house in the hot afternoon sun. Adam rolled up his trousers, threw his deck shoes into the boat and stood knee deep in the water, passing the dogs to Bruno. They failed to settle at first, showing a great deal of interest in Greta's picnic.

"Keep to the shore, boys," said the old family retainer. "Look after the dogs."

Adam pushed the boat out and jumped in. His trousers were wet through and he still wore his battered straw hat.

"Have you done this before?" asked Bruno. Adam sniffed contemptuously and produced a display of power rowing. "Be impressed," he said to Bruno.

"I am," retorted Bruno. "You can row for the rest of the afternoon."

The dogs slept and revived briefly to sample some of Greta's sausage. Bruno began to doze as the sun grew hotter, dangling his right arm over the side into the cool water. "You're not allowed to go to sleep on me, Bruno," said Adam.

"Of course not Herr von Saloman," replied Bruno. He pretended to snore and shook his legs. Hansl and Gretl woke up.

"Are we in heaven?" asked Bruno.

"Ask those two down there," answered Adam pointing at the sleeping dogs.

"They'll be really useful if we're ever attacked," said Bruno.

They drifted away from the shore and Adam began to doze. A pleasure steamer bore down on them. "Adam quick, the oars," shouted Bruno as he revived. Adam swiftly rowed with all his might out of danger, but the steamer's wake hit the boat and nearly turned it over. The dogs whimpered and both boys were soaked by the spray.

CHAPTER EIGHT

Adam's old straw hat threatened to float away and he leaned over to seize it, nearly capsizing the boat.

"You young fools. Stay by the shore!" shouted a crew member from the steamer, and worried passengers hung over the rails.

"Would you like to row back?" asked Adam.

"No thank you," replied Bruno. "You've done a great job so far."

The boat grounded on the shingle beach and Bruno jumped into the shallows carrying a dog under each arm.

"Are you really serious about going into the army?" he asked.

"Of course I am," answered Adam. Bruno began to doubt his own choice.

While the boys were on the lake, Gustav once again talked with Peter about his financial situation. He surprised his son by admitting that he had already sold off parts of their eastern estates, but proudly re-affirmed that he would never sell Die Schwanen, Peter's birthright.

"Your mother knows nothing of our situation, Peter," said Gustav, staring over the lake. Peter nodded and was thankful.

Unknown to Gustav, the family solicitors Berger and Schöler had briefed Frieda. She had doubted Gustav's competence for years and had already begun to move what remained of their investments into gold, secure in a Swiss bank. Her little chats with Adam went largely unnoticed. They were nearly all about his future security.

Bruno was euphoric about his weekend and couldn't wait to reveal every detail to his mother. When the door of their apartment had closed behind him, Bruno was obliged to describe his experiences in detail. She wasn't impressed by Gustav's battlefield but enjoyed the story of the boating picnic. Bruno left out the detail of the near-collision with the steamer.

Then he mentioned his attendance at Holy Communion, and his mother's face darkened. "You should have asked my permission to do such a thing," she said angrily, saying very little to him for the rest of the evening. He believed his visit to the church counted against him for the next few weeks.

As usual Gustav and Peter sat together after breakfast in the tea-house. Gustav remarked on the beauty of the lake and the forest in springtime.

"Do you enjoy your life here in Germany, Peter?" asked his father.

Peter knew what was coming. "I have decided my role has nothing to do with enjoyment, father. My duty lies elsewhere," he replied and Gustav became impatient.

"And your duty to your wife and son?" he said quickly.

"I am concerned about Käthe, Father," Peter admitted," but there is no need to worry about Adam. He will prosper anywhere."

Gustav raised his voice and placed his hand on Peter's arm. "But surely Adam must stay in Germany if he is to attend the military academy at Potsdam?" he said anxiously.

Gustav had cornered Peter. "Are you not here because of your poor health? Look, Peter, you could stay here and manage my estates."

Gustav had barely finished his appeal when a courier arrived from the Foreign Ministry with two letters. The first announced that Karl Weidling was to be transferred to Nanking, Chiang's new capital, and Peter was to be promoted to the post of Consul in Canton. The letter contained the personal thanks ofVon Neurath, the Foreign Minister. Peter showed his father the letter. "I didn't know you had served your country so well," he admitted. "You are a credit to all of us," Gustav added with moist eyes.

Peter tried another approach. If it was not possible for him to leave his post, he would send Käthe and Adam back to Germany for regular special holidays.

"My boy," continued the old man, patting him on the arm. "I would also like to see you regularly." The second letter was from Jacob Meissner. He enquired after Peter and Adam's health and missed the family terribly. "So you see Father, the pressures I have to face."

Jacob knew Käthe would dread the return to Canton and made an interesting offer.

Karl Weidling had given the doctor permission to set up a waterfront surgery to improve relations with the local people. Nurse Müller would have to remain at the Consulate and he would need an assistant on the river front. Jacob asked Peter to consider allowing Käthe to help him.

Peter thought the idea was conceived in heaven and enthusiastically broached the idea with Käthe, but she was lukewarm. She and Frieda had just re-established contact with the Goerings at Hörcher's restaurant, and the two women thought the National Socialist leader was the soul of charm. "We didn't think Dr Goebbels was the soul of charm in the square at Kreuzberg, my love," he retorted.

"But we do have to consider Frieda, Peter," she reminded him. Peter thought this part of Käthe's life empty and selfish. Without her approval, he replied to Jacob Meissner and accepted the offer.

Adam and Bruno were forgiven for their trespass and it was wiped from the school records, all at the behest of Alfred Rust. They were now deeply obliged to their new benefactor and threw themselves into their training with great gusto. They trained with the twins during school time and found another supporter at weekends. Helga followed them with a stopwatch on her bicycle.

The four friends planned their approach to the hostile boys over Frau Gluch's stew in the dining hall. The twins listened while Adam and Bruno did all the talking.

"Schuster is not so bad," suggested Adam. "We could get on with him."

The twins stopped eating and looked at each other, dismayed. "Forget it," said Bruno. "He's being watched by Schneider and Müller. Schneider is the worst."

The three Hitler Youth boys walked past carrying fingers of bread, which they were pretending to use as clubs. Uve Müller nudged Theo. Adam saw it and began to get up.

"Rust is watching," said Schneider. He leered evilly at Adam. "You're not in his good books yet," he warned.

Adam thought Schuster worth bothering with because of the character he had displayed in his training. Adam remembered such things and if someone appeared not to like him, then that needed correcting. Bruno was uncompromising. "Keep away from all of them," he advised.

Sports day was a bright sunny day at the Martin Luther school. The forbidding buildings had been restored to give the impression that a new day had dawned under the Republic. Senior pupils waited to greet the visitors at the main door leading to the Principal's office and were conducted to specially-built stands commanding a view of the amphitheatre, a bright green oval, broken by the red gravel running track and the areas reserved for field events.

Gustav was too ill to attend and Frieda stayed behind. Peter and Käthe called for Renate. Käthe got out of the car and demanded that Renate stood still while she was inspected. "You look wonderful, my dear," said Käthe. "Together we shall make a huge impression." Renate laughed nervously.

They were soon at the school. A welcoming committee of senior boys met them and one made a short speech of welcome. The party were greeted by Dr Stiebert and Herr Rust and escorted to a special enclosure close to the finishing line. Behind them dutifully stood Theo and Klaus Gutman, who had volunteered to look after Adam's parents. Käthe recognised them immediately. "They must sit next to us Peter," she insisted.

The two boys were a little tongue-tied at first because Bruno had given them strict instructions not to lecture the guests on science and engineering. Peter had been briefed by Adam and was keen to hear all about their interests. He nearly missed the beginning of the proceedings as the wide-eyed enthusiasts talked about rocket fuels.

"And do you really make your own fuel?" asked Peter. To Käthe's delight, Renate took to them immediately and promised to invite them to tea.

The school orchestra played the national anthem and Dr Stiebert opened the sports from a raised dais in the centre of the field. He stood behind an oak table on which were arranged the silver trophies and the school emblem, an eagle clutching oak leaves. Only one of the trophies bore the symbol, the trophy for the first-year boys' three thousand metres. A ripple of interest had appeared among the senior pupils. They usually only showed a polite interest in the junior boys, but had heard of the rivalry among the competitors in the three thousand metres and knew threats of physical violence were involved.

The rest of the afternoon had passed predictably and the Seniors waited for the race as eagerly as the junior boys. Some were determined that Schuster should win because they were members of the same Hitler Youth group. Others were Catholic youth group members who supported Bruno and Dieter Harro. Adam was an unknown quantity but he now had the secret support of the Gutman twins.

"May I take a photograph of the competitors?" Käthe asked Herr Rust, who was preoccupied with the starter.

"Of course," he replied patiently.

The boys looked embarrassed and impatient as Käthe snapped them, but Dieter Harro looked distant and calm. Berndt Schuster stared down the track stamping his feet. Adam and Bruno looked nervously at each other and the rest of the field jogged impatiently. Herr Rust held up the starting pistol and the crack reverberated around the field. They were off.

Berndt Schuster immediately went into the lead and the rest bunched. He set a furious pace and intended to win from the front. After one thousand metres, the pace began to tell and most of the runners fell far behind the leader, except for the lone figure of Dieter Harro, who began to catch Schuster.

Käthe clutched Peter's arm. "What are Adam and Bruno doing?" she asked anxiously. Her question was answered at fifteen hundred metres. Adam and Bruno broke free of the group and began to catch Dieter Harro. Käthe stood up biting her fingers and Peter glared at her. He took her arm and told her to sit down, but she refused. Berndt Schuster began to slow and Adam and Bruno paced each other as they had practised in the Grünewald. Little by little they caught up with Dieter Harro, who seemed unperturbed as he ran smoothly along. The three of them were content to sit behind Berndt Schuster for the time being.

They closed with him, and the shouting and cheering told him he might lose the race. At five hundred metres he found new strength and maintained a lead of twenty metres over his rivals, but they drew closer and closer.

Suddenly Dieter Harro burst in front of Schuster, who fought back and regained the lead. They tussled until their shoulders began to roll. The noise was deafening. All eyes were on the two leaders.

Käthe abandoned her dignity. She stood up in a vain effort to shout directly at Adam. "He must see me," she thought as he and Bruno seemed to run lazily past her. "You must show a little decorum my dear," whispered Peter in her ear. She took no notice. At two hundred metres, they closed with Dieter and Berndt. Staff and pupils ran to the side of the track and Dr Stiebert began to worry about the image of the school.

With one hundred metres to go, Bruno burst past Dieter and Berndt, hotly followed by Adam. Theo and Klaus were beside themselves.

With twenty metres to go, the four runners were giving everything they had. Adam was the most powerful, and burst past Bruno. He threw his arms out as he breasted the tape. He staggered to a halt, looking down at the scar on his left leg and stood bowed with his hands on his hips. He was completely exhausted, but as soon as he had got his breath back he congratulated his opponents. Dieter and Berndt looked stunned.

Bruno just grinned at Adam. No one could have been more pleased at coming second. It was too much for Peter, and his reserve disappeared. He marched over to the finishing line. "Please, Herr Rust, have those four boys brought to me," he demanded.

The teacher waved them over just as Dieter Harro recognised he was king no longer and congratulated Adam. Renate forgot herself and hugged and kissed Bruno, which the twins enjoyed enormously. "But Mutti," began Bruno. "I haven't won."

"Ah but you have all won today," she said.

Adam, Bruno and Dieter walked over to Peter still gasping for breath, but there was no sign of Berndt Schuster. He's over there with his Hitler Youth Friends," said Bruno.

"Leave him alone Adam," he advised. Adam ran over to him.

"Come with me Schuster," said Adam. "My father wants to congratulate you on your performance."

Adam needn't have bothered. The only security Berndt Schuster had at that moment was his friends, who stared coldly at Adam. Schuster said resentfully to Adam. "Perhaps you would like your parents to recognise me?" he said.

Adam had forgotten the incident in the square and turned on his heels to rejoin the others. "Schuster feels ill," said Adam lamely to his father and Herr Rust. The teacher placed his hand on Peter's arm. "It is better left there, Herr von Saloman," he said.

Peter addressed the remaining three of them grandly. "You are all a credit to your school and your country" he said. He smiled. "And I include your faithful supporters," he added, turning to Theo and Klaus, who beamed with pride.

"We helped them train sir," said Klaus.

"Well done," said Peter.

"This is too much," whispered Bruno. "They're taking all the credit."

Adam received the trophy from Dr Stiebert. He held it aloft and a proud Käthe took a photograph, of which a copy was made. That copy was framed and stayed for many years to come on a rosewood cabinet near the figures of household gods in the Si-kiang house.

When the party returned to Die Schwanen, Gustav rose from his chair to embrace his grandson. "You know what the oak leaves mean Adam," he said. "You have already been decorated for bravery."

A dubious look appeared on Peter's face. Adam retired to his room and carried out an inspection of his two remaining Uhlans, finding them in good order. Before he went to sleep he asked himself if Huang Yuxiang would have approved of his behaviour today. He decided he would, and slept soundly.

Alfred Rust asked to see Bruno and Adam at the door of the staff room the following day. They assumed they had done something wrong, but when the sports teacher appeared he had a kindly look in his face. "You two did very well yesterday. The race will be remembered for a long time to come," he reminded them. "But you can't know why I've sent for you." They looked puzzled. "Berndt was one of the favourites to win the race, but you know that. All your training was based on beating him, wasn't it?" he asked. They nodded.

"You were beaten into second place, Grabowsky but you are able to bear it, I see." Bruno grinned at Adam. "You see, you worked for each other, those other boys did not. Do you see?"

They nodded again, not quite understanding the point. "And your mothers were there and we certainly noticed your mother's support, von Saloman," he said smiling.

"You are their heroes. You can be anything you want to be because they were there. There was no mother or father there for Schuster. He lives with his aunt and his father is away in the army. I'll say no more. You may go," said Alfred Rust. The teacher had thrown a lifeline for Berndt Schuster. "You tried," Bruno said to Adam.

Professor Rohrman announced Adam's return to China to the whole class. To their astonishment he said. "We will miss von Saloman. One day he might be a fine engineer." He presented Adam with a new science textbook.

"Study hard for your Abitur for when you return," he said. There was a ripple of applause and Adam turned to acknowledge it. Berndt Schuster nearly joined in but thought better of it when he sensed he was being watched by Müller and Rolf Schneider, who fixed Adam with a deep hostile stare. There was no going back for him and he looked forward to the day when he would make Adam pay.

As they walked to the last lesson with Dr Diercks, Dieter Harro's friend, the studious Armin Schurmann predicted that Adam would win the essay prize. The entries were all pinned to the rear wall.

"I am delighted with your efforts and have commended the class to Dr Stiebert," began the teacher. "The departure of von Saloman is sad indeed," he continued. "Our best wishes go with him. And now the results," he announced. "The winner is Grabowsky and the runner up is Schuster."

The twins were upset and fearful. Bruno tried not to look too cheerful because he thought he was about to lose his best friend.

Adam began the round of applause. He turned to face Schuster and half-waved to him. Berndt nearly reacted, but changed his mind, and Bruno stepped forward to accept the pennant. "This belongs to both of us," he said quietly to Adam.

Peter waited for Adam at the front steps of the school. The twins and Bruno looked lost, but they shook hands with Adam's father.

"I don't suppose we'll ever see you again," said Bruno.

"Of course we will," said the twins, hopefully. They were aware that they were being watched by Müller and Schneider from a respectable distance.

"You'll write to Bruno and he'll tell us everything," said Theo with tears in his eyes.

Adam solemnly shook hands with them all, fighting back tears. Peter shook hands with Bruno again. "You're important to our family, Bruno," he said. Adam climbed into the Buick and didn't stop looking back as he was driven away.

While Adam and Käthe packed the cases and tin boxes helped by Greta and Helga, Peter was briefed at the Foreign Office in the Wilhelmstrasse. It was a world away from the consulate, where Peter had really been the leading figure. Here in Berlin, it was a very different matter, as he was soon to discover. He knew Principal Secretary Wilke well but not the other man in his office, who wore the uniform of a Colonel of Military Intelligence.

"This is Colonel Rudinger," said Wilke. "He is here to help us with your briefing."

The Colonel dominated the briefing. "Do you believe in a much stronger Germany, von Saloman?" he asked baldly.

Peter replied, "Of course Herr Colonel. We have promoted the Republic at the expense of France and Britain in China." Rudinger looked at Wilke and then at Peter.

"I think we can forgive your son's rash behaviour in the square at Kreuzberg, Herr Consul," said Rudinger pointedly.

Peter looked perplexed and thought it was a good time to listen. He realised his reliability was being questioned.

"It is our belief that very soon, the National Socialists may become the dominant partner in a coalition. Germany's foreign policy may, shall we say, enter a more active phase," said the intelligence officer.

Peter was worried by Colonel Rudinger's admission that the family had been watched. He wondered if that might continue in Canton. He was soon to be given an answer. A younger man in a uniform similar to Rudinger's appeared.

"This, Herr Consul, is Lieutenant Manfred Weiss," said Rudinger. "He is to be your new intelligence assistant and Deputy Consul. His passage had been booked with you on the ***Derfligger***.

Weiss clicked his heels. "I am honoured to meet you, Herr Consul," he said.

He had a pale, unexceptional face and his hair was plastered back on his skull, but his movements were deliberate and deft. "I have taken the liberty of examining a copy of the new diplomatic codes, Herr Consul," he announced. "Also a list of consulate personnel and their function."

Peter soon discovered that Manfred Weiss had committed the contents of his briefcase to memory. Peter was concerned that his new assistant was an intelligence officer.

On Adam's final afternoon in Germany, He was to go fishing for pike with Gustav in the lake margins. Adam pushed the boat into the shallows, put up the rods and waited for his grandfather, who had promised to bring the bait. But Helga, not Gustav, appeared and she wasn't wearing her domestic uniform but a simple white blouse and a full blue skirt and ankle-length socks. It was the uniform of Hitler's League of German Maidens and she knew it made her more attractive. She had decided Adam would not forget the next few hours.

"Herr Adam, your grandfather feels too ill today to go fishing," she announced. "If you would still like to go fishing, I could help."

"But I must see my grandfather," said Adam.

"He says you must go fishing and then tell him everything, Herr Adam," she said. "I have brought a picnic. You see, I'll be all right," she said, wading through the shallows and jumping into the boat. She threw off her shoes and socks and said without a trace of deference, "You may row me to the fishing grounds."

She watched Adam as he pulled on the oars. She didn't take her eyes off him and he turned a deep red. There was no one here to maintain the hierarchy of the house and Adam was trapped with a pretty fourteen-year-old who intended to reap any advantage she could. Helga passed her hand through her blond hair, then smoothed her skirt down over her knees.

"Will you remember us all when you're back in China?" she asked. She decided to risk mocking him a little. "Who will you play soldiers with when you're there?"

"With my Chinese soldier friends," he said defiantly. Adam had every right to reprimand her, but she knew he wouldn't.

"If you want to be a soldier when you come back, You'll have to join the Hitler youth," she said.

"They're all just bullies," he said firmly. "I saw three of them trying to beat up an old man."

Helga laughed. "They're not all like that," she said. "They do the same things as the Catholic youth."

She tried to stir jealousy in Adam. "Bruno told me about all the things you do on your weekends," she said. She was thrusting out her breasts. "Do you know what this uniform is?" she asked, sure that he didn't. Adam shook his head sheepishly.

"This is the uniform of the league of German maidens," Helga stated proudly. "We make picnics for people like you."

Adam didn't laugh, and when the boat grounded in the shallows he jumped out and Helga pretended helplessness. She held out her hand and Adam, still a deep colour of red, helped her from the boat.

She pretended to fall over and he caught her. "Thank you so much Herr Adam," she said and kissed him on the cheek. To her relief, he smiled.

They sat close together and ate some of the food. She pursued her advantage. "Will you write to me?" she said. Adam said he would, but would ask permission first.

"But they will say no," she said gently. "You must do it on your own."

She removed his old straw boater and tried it on herself. She was choosing her moment carefully.

"If you want it back, and I know you do, you must kiss me," she said. He reached forward and took the hat and left Helga stranded, so now she was frightened. Adam leaned forward quickly and kissed her on the lips. She pulled him towards her slightly and stroked his head, then his arm. Her hand fell to her side.

"We'll always remember this," she said. "Now we'll go back to the house."

Helga was holding Adam's hand and Frieda and Käthe saw this from the side window of the house. Frieda was deeply upset.

"Helga's behaviour merits dismissal Käthe, but I cannot do such a thing," she said. "She is the daughter of my greatest friend and supporter. Can I afford to do nothing?"

"Will you leave it to me?" said Käthe. Frieda thanked her. Helga's dismissal would have forced Greta to go also, and that Frieda could not face.

At dinner that evening as Helga leaned over Käthe to replenish her wineglass, Käthe whispered. "You were seen."

If Käthe even half-believed that Helga would be racked with guilt, she was sadly mistaken. Greta's daughter thought she had done a fine afternoon's work. Adam would not forget his fishing trip in a hurry.

And if that enterprise failed, there was always Bruno. He made her laugh and he was nice looking and intelligent, a much better proposition than most of the Hitler youth she had met. But she would never forget her first choice, the future master of the house.

That last dinner was a sad affair and the conversation was stilted. Gustav had seriously thought of disinheriting Peter until he was wounded and decorated. He had compensated by looking to his grandson to preserve family traditions, but as his health began to fail and he grew older he changed his mind. He was devastated by the prospect of Peter's return to China.

That night Adam was restless and he seemed relieved to see Käthe. "Did you enjoy your fishing trip my darling?" she asked. He didn't reply but kissed his mother full on the lips. She stroked his head as he lay back. "My handsome, handsome boy," she said and kissed his forehead. Adam slept soundly and she crept from his room like an illicit lover.

The three travellers dreaded the appearance of Stephan with the Buick that last morning. Gustav was in severe pain and held Adam tightly as if he would never see him again.

"I will look after your grandfather for you," Frieda promised. Greta held

Adam so tightly that he could hardly breathe.

Helga had done her work and stood dutifully in the background until invited to shake hands with Adam. The leather suitcases and the boxes were strapped into the trunk of the car and the three of them climbed in. Peter and Käthe sat together holding hands as Stephan drove the car as slowly as he could towards the gates. They turned round and saw Gustav steadying himself on his walking stick and waving painfully. Frieda comforted him as he broke down and sobbed.

Chapter 9

Lieutenant Weiss met the family at Tempelhof airport in the VIP lounge. He asked if Adam and Käthe might wait in an adjacent room while he briefed Peter, who thought Weiss quite rude. Peter was an expert in communications, yet Weiss showed him a document signed by Wilke giving Weiss complete charge of the radio room at the consulate. Peter was prepared to admit that Weiss knew more of the new codes than he did but, as Consul, he expected that all information pertaining to the Consulate's business should be shared. Peter was assured he would have full control of negotiations with Chiang Kai-shek. He wondered what changes there had been at the Foreign Office.

Manfred Weiss apologised to Käthe and Adam for keeping them waiting. To Peter's surprise, he proved to be a lively companion and offered to help with Adam's education. Any suspicions Peter had were allayed, for the moment.

Captain Fischer personally welcomed the family on board the *Derfligger* and they were assigned the same cabins under the bridge. They were invited to the captain's table that evening and drank more than usual.

This was only the beginning of Käthe's plans for the evening. She closed the cabin door and they both laughed as the lights flickered and threatened to go out. Everything was restored as the ship's generators seemed to be working properly once more.

A large ship passed on the port bow. It rocked the *Derfligger* and caused Käthe to spill her wine. Peter caught the glass before it hit the floor, but the bottle shattered and Peter hurriedly swept up the glass and Käthe's expensive American stockings were ruined.

They stared at the pool of wine on the floor as if it was an achievement. "I will have to remove the remains of my stockings my darling," said Käthe.

"I'll find something to clean this up," said Peter.

He reappeared carrying several towels and a bucket. Käthe was lying naked on cushions on the floor. She put her finger into the pool of wine and smeared a little on her breasts.

Peter dropped the towels. She shifted slightly and rolled over on one side. Her hand stroked his leg. "Kiss the wine away," she said.

Without removing any clothes, he did so and felt her nipples grow erect in his mouth. He stood up and threw off his clothes. Käthe dipped her hand in the wine once more and touched the tip of Peter's erection. She kissed the wine away. "Quickly, my darling. Quickly," she moaned.

She arched her back and Peter entered her joyfully. "As deep as you can, my love," she moaned. He moved slowly, then furiously, until they were exhausted.

Käthe gladly agreed to become Jacob's dockside nurse. She hoped she could pass the time in China in another way, looking after the child she wanted so badly, and it seemed reasonable to raise the issue after their lovemaking.

Peter seemed unenthusiastic. "We must consider the age gap between Adam and any future brother or sister," he said.

When Käthe failed to become pregnant, Peter's attitude was all the more galling. The days passed more slowly as the days grew hotter and hotter and Käthe looked in vain for signs of pregnancy. Peter buried himself in his papers and seemed uninterested in further lovemaking.

On the Si-Kiang and the waterfront of Canton, Adam was a prince awaiting a kingdom and he couldn't wait to take the tiller of Ned's junk once more. Most of all, he had missed the brothers and the tranquillity of the Si-Kiang house.

The ship sailed close to the sandbank where she had run aground in 1923 and Adam watched fascinated as it responded to shouts of 'Hard a-starboard,' and the ringing of the steerage bell just above the family on the bridge.

The *Derfligger* approached the Pearl Delta in the late afternoon and followed the marker buoys setting out the newly-dredged channel up the Pearl to Canton. The ship's horn blew a greeting to Whampoa Island as they passed. The riverboat was getting up steam for the last time in the day and Adam waved furiously at the passengers.

CHAPTER NINE

For a few moments, Peter and Käthe felt apart from their son as he hung over the bow rail and took in every detail. He seemed detached as he stared at the yellow waters of the Pearl and spoke to them almost as if they were strangers.

He told them about the folklore of the river. An egret settled on a sandbank close to the ship and a small long yellow snout appeared nearby. The bird idly flapped its wings and the alligator slid silently towards it. It was all over in a few seconds. The alligator rose out of the water and took the bird, dragging it under water. Käthe was horrified.

"It's all right Mama," said Adam. "The alligator can do anything he wants. He is a god. He made all life in the river. He can take it away."

Käthe wondered what had happened to Adam's Catholic upbringing.

A pilot boat guided the *Derfligger* to its anchorage off Shamian Island. Constant soundings had delayed the ship and it took nearly three hours to cover the twenty-three kilometres from Whampoa.

Jacob Meissner, escorted by armed police, waited for them on the wooden jetty. Close by was a small army of volunteers who had suddenly materialised when they heard that Der Deutsche Junge was returning.

Jacob held out his arms as if he were welcoming a personal lifeline. "Welcome my friends," he said and embraced them all in turn. Then he was distracted by a fight for the honour of carrying the luggage to the consulate. Three men waved furiously at Adam and pointed to Käthe's luggage. He nodded and they seized the tin boxes but the police demanded that the luggage be carried in a waiting army lorry.

"Oh I'm sorry Lieutenant," said Peter. "This is Lieutenant Manfred Weiss who is my new deputy. This is our respected Doctor, Jacob Meissner."

Weiss clicked his heels, but he seemed coldly polite and formal towards Jacob. Peter had forgotten that Weiss had conducted research into some of the Consulate personnel, and Jacob was conscious of Weiss attitude even if the others were not.

Peter lost no time in installing Manfred Weiss in his new quarters. He had not yet assigned a detailed list of duties to him, but Weiss volunteered his services. "Your Excellency," he began awkwardly. I would like to interview the doctor."

He seemed very ill at ease. "I would like to establish that his activities have been pertinent to the business of the consulate while you've been away."

"That will not be necessary," replied a puzzled Peter. "I have absolute confidence in Jacob Meissner. I myself will see if he had anything to report." Weiss seemed relieved and Peter wondered why he had made the offer. The new Deputy withdrew and set up his equipment in the radio room without delay.

Barely a week had passed before Jacob began to express some misgivings about the new man. Peter and the Doctor resumed their old custom of walking in the gardens before dinner. Jacob was worried.

"Peter," he began, "Given that I'm a lowly doctor here and not a member of the diplomatic community, there is probably very little I am allowed to ask."

Peter patted his friend on the arm. "You, Jacob, may ask whatever you wish," he assured him.

"What impression have you gained of your new Deputy?" asked Jacob.

The question didn't surprise Peter. "He was a lively and sophisticated companion during the voyage, Jacob," he said. "Then a few days before we arrived, I began to have my doubts. Weiss made enquiries about our political sympathies, in a jovial kind of way, you understand. I remember feeling worried when Käthe announced she was a reformed communist."

"Why did you ask?" said Peter.

"Why does he feel it necessary to be rude and dismissive towards me?" asked Jacob. "When and if it happens again, Jacob, please tell me."

"I have charted the rise of the National Socialists in Germany, Peter. They are not at all sympathetic to my religion. Might there be a connection?"

Manfred Weiss of all people then joined them and greeted them both cordially. After dinner, Peter said to Jacob. "There my friend, you have nothing to worry about." Jacob was skeptical. He was worried by Peter's apparent naivety.

Manfred Weiss began to make friends with Adam. As the weeks passed and there was, as yet, no sign of Bing Wen and his brother, the friendship became genuine. Weiss was an educated man with a degree in philosophy and was interested in helping with Adam's education when his duties permitted. He was delighted to discover his new pupil's interest in military history.

Peter and Käthe were delighted. They would have been more concerned had they known that Adam had told Weiss far more about his trips to the Si-

Kiang than they themselves knew. Manfred Weiss kept a detailed private notebook, and in went the name of Ned Travis.

As Peter's trips northwards resumed, Weiss promised to maintain separate contacts with Chiang's troops in Canton and he meant those on the waterfront. Peter was a little naïve in such matters and had no idea that Weiss had begun to build a network of paid informants there. His new Deputy had a grasp of administrative detail which Peter lacked, and soon discovered discrepancies between what was landed from the ***Derfligger*** and how much arrived at the Consulate.

Weiss selected information and conveyed it to his real masters in military intelligence, and some of them were distinctly favourable to the rise of the National Socialists. He suggested to Peter that the old office in Canton should be reopened as a front for Germany's real activities.

Peter remembered he had given no thought at all to the ground maintenance staff at the airfield.

"One of them has just reported for treatment to an injured leg, Peter," said Jacob. "And I think he smelt heavily of drink,"

Peter leaned over his desk and asked Elizabeth, his secretary, for the personnel records of the two men involved. He found two photographs dating from the beginning of the war of Willie Novka and Rudolf Schlemm. Peter guessed that they would look somewhat different now. Without telephoning ahead, he informed Manfred Weiss that he was to pay a visit to the airfield.

As Peter's car approached the security barrier at the airfield, it became clear that the guards did not welcome surprises like this. As one of them lifted the barrier, the other waved towards the hangar out of sight of Peter.

"Please park by my aircraft," said Peter to his driver. He got out and saw a small figure clambering across one of the wings. It was a Chinese woman carrying a pot of paint. Then there was a tremendous racket from the rear of the hangar and Peter recognised the sound of a generator. The rest of the noise sounded like a grinder. Working on a machine was a short stocky figure, and by now the Chinese lady had made him aware of Peter's presence. He was confronted by a short but powerfully-built man with distinct bow-legs, wearing an old flying jacket over an oily overall, and a pair of very old flying boots.

He lifted his goggles, staring at Peter and his soldier escort, and Peter's identity dawned on him. "Oh good morning Your Excellency," he said with a broad grin.

"And who might you be?" asked Peter.

"Chief engine artificer Novka, Your Excellency," he replied, straightening with pride.

Peter had already noticed the three wooden structures at the rear of the hangar and it had already occurred to him that he had no address for the two maintenance men.

Two of the wooden buildings were about three metres high and could be described as dwellings. In between them was a small mock-up of a Chinese aristocrat's house. By now, the overalled painting lady stood proudly at its door, inviting Peter in.

"Aren't there two of you?" asked Peter.

"Oh, over here Your Excellency," said Novka, leading Peter to the hut in the far corner.

The door was closed, but heavy snoring indicated that it was occupied. Sound asleep on a straw palliasse was a tall balding figure with a handlebar moustache. His left trouser leg had been cut away and the leg was heavily bandaged. Peter retreated and closed the door, anxious to discover something about the Chinese lady, who by now was bowing every few seconds. He had decided that further enquiries about the sleeping figure could wait.

Novka announced, "This is Madame Ling. She lives here, sir." He pointed to the dwelling in the middle.

"We made it for her, Your Excellency," said Schlemm, emerging from slumber and staggering towards his employer.

"This is assistant engine artificer Schlemm, your honour," said Novka.

"Oh indeed," said Peter, trying hard to disapprove of everything he saw and failing.

Schlemm was anxious to explain the presence of Madame Ling. "She's his really sir," said Schlemm, "But she cooks and cleans for both of us. We give her a little money out of our wages."

Poor Schlemm was clearly in some pain. "How is your leg, Schlemm?" asked Peter.

"Oh much better your honour," he replied. "Dr Meissner is very good."

Peter wanted to know the whereabouts of the new aircraft. "It's here sir, in pieces," said Novka, leading Peter through a small door in the rear of the hangar. There, already partly assembled, was the fuselage. The rest was still crated.

"Can two of you assemble and maintain a tri-motored transport aircraft?" asked Peter.

"Ah sir, we have help. There's a man who helps us," said Novka sheepishly. Schlemm looked hard at his partner.

"And who might that be?" continued Peter.

"He is a clever American sir," said Schlemm thinking that was enough.

"And his name?" persisted Peter.

"He is Mr Ned Travis, and his men help us with heavy work."

"In return for what?" asked Peter, walking over to a ramshackle shed which bore a sign saying 'fuel store'. "Please open this," ordered Peter. Novka found a key while Peter produced a copy of the ***Derfligger***'s manifest pertaining to fuel delivery. Novka and Schlemm looked hard at each other.

"We're a drum short, Your Excellency," explained Novka. "Test flights."

Test flights for an aircraft which not yet been assembled seemed curious to Peter. He was very anxious to meet Ned Travis.

Peter decided to leave well alone except to require Rudolf Schlemm to report to Jacob for help to limit his drinking. Peter's kindness would cost him dearly. He didn't mention any discrepancies in deliveries to Weiss, who already suspected they must exist. There were certain people who would prefer to call Peter's kindness weakness. Peter suspected nothing.

Chapter 10

A letter from Chiang assured Peter that the Communists were no longer a danger. They had been dealt with, he claimed, and were hundreds of miles away in the interior. The general had acquired a suitable building for use as a surgery and Dr Meissner could start as soon as he wished. An army lorry was made available and it met the three of them at the consulate gates.

Jacob wore a white coat and a stethoscope. Adam wore a cheongsam and his old straw hat, much against his mother's wishes. He leapt into the back and helped Käthe up the ladder. She wore a spotless brand new nurse's uniform with a large red cross over her left breast. They bumped and banged their way to the waterfront.

The 'suitable building' was an abandoned customs shed and a plank was missing from one side. Jacob opened the creaking door after fighting with the rusty padlock and recoiled from the stench inside. Käthe had anticipated such a problem and produced a supply of leather gloves and caustic soda. Within twenty minutes, most of the stench had gone.

Jacob was despairing. "Where shall we find hot water?" he asked. Adam disappeared and within five minutes, he had found a brazier and a supply of timber. A quietly curious crowd gathered. Käthe was uneasy because she thought the stares were hostile. Adam told her not to look, as everything was all right.

Then two of Huang Lin Hui's men appeared. They stood either side of the surgery door, their hands resting on the hilts of their broadswords. Several fishermen had been standing on the sterns of their boats for a better view. When they saw Lin Hui's bodyguards, they melted away. The crowd grew bigger. He knew it was a waiting game, but Käthe grew more frightened. They were surrounded.

CHAPTER TEN

"Please Jacob, we must leave," said Käthe. She looked anxiously at Adam, who stood perfectly still with his hands crossed in front of him. There was no sign of the police or the army except for two old soldiers who watched from a distance.

Some of the crowd by the water's edge moved backwards. They had parted for Ned and his two bodyguards but he walked awkwardly. The two men caught him as he stumbled and his face twisted in pain.

Adam recognized the bodyguards and bowed to them. One of them made a mock fist and waved it in front of Adam's nose. A few people in the crowd laughed.

"Do something Jacob, please," whimpered Käthe. Adam became impatient with his mother and glared at her.

"Good morning young man," said Ned. "Are we open for business here?" Adam proudly took Ned's arm and led him towards Käthe. "This is Mr Ned Travis, Mama. He lives on the river and is a great man. And this is the wonderful Dr Meissner, Ned, my friend and teacher."

"I am charmed indeed," said Ned. "But I must point out that I am in some pain and require your assistance." His face twisted again. Lin Hui's men stood aside and Jacob knew this was the test case of his life. He led Ned to a trestle table in the hut. "I will need the assistance of my nurse, Mr Travis," said Jacob. "I'm afraid I will have to ask you to reveal your lower portions. Are you in agreement?"

"Anything you say," answered Ned. "My concern is for the lady – I take it you're Adam's mother?"

Käthe was attracted to Ned because he was so striking, and he radiated the consideration of many Americans she had met at diplomatic receptions. "Anything I see will be a closely guarded secret," answered Käthe.

They disappeared into the shed and the crowd waited as Jacob lifted Ned's hips and cracked the bones on both sides. "Try that, Mr Travis," he said. Ned cautiously rolled off the table and felt no pain. He appeared at the door with Adam and they both punched the air. It was a signal for mayhem, and the crowd surged towards the wooden hut.

Jacob and Käthe worked for nearly six hours. Some came with newly-broken limbs, others with untreated breaks. Most, at least, they could help. The last patient placed a year-old pig on the trestle table. It squealed in pain with a broken leg. Jacob couldn't turn her away and Käthe made a splint for the leg.

Peace descended on the waterfront and the three of them waited for the army lorry. Jacob collapsed and slept in his surgery. Peter had to carry Käthe and Adam to bed.

When he left early in the morning with Manfred Weiss for Nanking, Käthe knocked on Adam's door. She crept in, but he was still asleep. She recalled his utter lack of fear on the waterfront and his greeting from Ned's crew and Lin Hui's bodyguards. She knew he would soon reacquaint himself with the brothers from the Si-Kiang and had to admit to herself that Adam liked the company of soldiers. She began to wonder if all her work on his education was in vain.

The surgery flourished, but ran into unexplained shortages of medical supplies. Jacob asked Käthe to see if Adam could help by using his contacts on the waterfront. Käthe was surprised he'd asked. Jacob persisted until she agreed.

As Jacob and Käthe attended to the patients, Adam slipped away into the crowd.

His short walk was well timed, because a shipment of medical supplies had just been landed on the island, bound for the French embassy. Within a week, two of Ned's crew appeared at the surgery with a sealed box and a note from Ned. It read "I hope this solves your problem. On this occasion, no payment is required."

Jacob opened the box and found syringes with doses of morphine. For once, Ned had been careless in assuming things would go no further. To Jacob this was sheer criminality and he informed Manfred Weiss of the transaction. Weiss expressed his gratitude and his attitude to Jacob softened. He had added to the case against Ned Travis.

Adam waited in vain for the reappearance of the brothers. Manfred Weiss informed him that the Nationalist forces were now heavily engaged against not only the Communists but the Japanese. Bing Wen had been promoted to lieutenant and the two of them were in action in northern China.

Ned brought the invitation to Adam to visit the Si-Kiang house and this time there would be no ride hitched in the old army lorry with soldiers going on leave. Nationalist casualties were rising and all leave was cancelled. Ned offered Adam a ride upriver but said the offer depended on his parent's agreement. Neither of them were enthusiastic, but Peter thought a refusal might upset Yuxiang, an important supporter of the Nationalist cause.

Adam told Weiss he would not be able to attend any lessons for at least a week. The deputy consul had not been informed through the proper channels. Not only did he feel sidelined, he assumed there was an arrangement between Peter and Ned. Nothing could have been further from the truth, but Weiss made a note of his assumption and it shaped much of his thinking.

Adam was escorted to the river-front by armed police. When he reached the foot of the junk's companionway, the escort left. He ran up the companionway to look for Ned. His cabin door opened and an attractive Chinese woman appeared, introducing herself as a friend of Ned's. She bowed deferentially and invited Adam inside. Ned's disarray suggested the encounter with the lady had gone well beyond taking tea. He left Adam to change into his favourite cheongsam while he and his lady walked to the head of the companionway. When Adam emerged from the cabin, the American was deep in conversation with the man on the tiller. They both looked to the south-east, where the yellow-blue haze became a dark grey. Ned decided the junk would sail because of the importance of his passenger, but the wind was not favourable. As the boat cleared the dock, it had to make headway with the engine.

Adam had never seen the crew so concerned. One of them approached him. It was the man he had seen before who kept small figurines in a leather belt, and he had no small influence among the other crew members. He told Adam almost accusingly that the voyage would not be taking place if he was not there. They were all aware of the prevalence of typhoons at that time of year.

The man with the figurines looked into the water and tried to read the signs, hanging on grimly to one of the ropes securing the mainsail.

"Take no notice of him," said Ned as he stood with Adam by the tiller.

"Do you miss your home Ned?" asked Adam. The American looked surprised and avoided the question. "My home is here Adam," he answered and said nothing for at least ten minutes. His relationship with Adam had nothing to do with river politics. He was only doing Yuxiang a favour which was costing him time and money. He liked Adam and thought he deserved some answers.

"I will tell you something which may cause you to see me in a different light, young man," he said. " No one here knows this and no one else must know. Do you understand?" The young German nodded.

"I too was a soldier once," he said. I was a volunteer in the United States army of General Pershing in France in 1918. I had a difference with a young officer which caused me to confuse him with the enemy. This led me to leave the area in a hurry. Unfortunately, the military authorities have not forgiven me and would still like to interview me. The young officer was not too badly hurt," he added with a reassuring smile.

Adam had not believed Ned to be completely harmless but this surprised him as it involved an attack on an officer. Ned was such a dominant, genial character that Adam forgave him instantly. Adam grinned and said nothing. Ned was relieved because he liked Adam and wanted his respect. He had been honest, and it had worked.

The air was heavy and oppressive and the junk made laboured progress. Giant otters and yellow alligators moved to the nearside bank of the river while cranes and egrets disappeared into the juniper scrub on the river banks. Ned fell silent and the crew were edgy and nervous. Adam noticed the splintered remains of what had been a wooden jetty.

Three crew members stood amidships. The man with the figurines ordered the others to sit and they refused to work. We must go back, they said. Their lives were being risked for the sake of 'Der Deutsche Junge'.

Ned looked at the advancing storm and knew there was no time to lose. "Man the tiller, boy," he said to Adam as he stamped towards the waist of the ship with one of his bodyguards. He didn't try to reason with the men. He lifted the man with the figurines off the deck and dropped the frightened individual as if he was a rag doll.

The bodyguard drew a pistol and the three men begged for mercy and scuttled back to work. Ned returned to the tiller. "We've more chance running upriver with the storm," he said to Adam. "Reef the sails!" He ignored his bodyguard's brutal behaviour, as if it was normal.

The sky went black from the south-west and it started to rain. At first it fell vertically in torrents and water washed from the stern to the bow. Adam put on a brave face, the rain streaming down his forehead. The wind started to howl round the upperworks of the junk and blew the bow towards the riverbank. The boat was out of control and the stern began to swivel round. Ned's voice could hardly be heard.

"Get into the waist of the ship," he shouted to Adam, who was hanging on to the upperworks for dear life. The wind howled and whistled. The half-reefed sails were carried away and the main mast crashed into the deck. A crew member lay unconscious, bleeding from a head wound.

The junk threatened to capsize as it was blown towards the shore. The wind lifted the boat out of the water onto a sandbank. "Abandon ship. Get onto the sandbank," ordered Ned. The remainder of the crew obeyed the order and huddled in the shelter of the creaking hull. The injured man was left on the deck and his crewmates looked up helplessly at the upper deck.

As quickly as the storm arrived, it died, but it left a sorry sight, the boat's crew lying stranded in the middle of the river. As the tide ebbed, the water level dipped and three of the crew tried to rescue their comrade, but he was already dead. His body lay spread-eagled across the sandbank and the crew stared at him.

"You can't help him now," said Ned. "Help me save the ship." They were afraid of the bodyguards and obeyed. They climbed on board and salvaged two rowing boats.

The boats made some progress and then the crest of a white wave appeared in front of them. The flash floods of the hills were bearing down on the survivors and they didn't need telling to row for the bank. The man with the figurines stared back at the dead crew member on the sandbank. "Row you idiot!" shouted Ned, but the other boat with one of the bodyguards landed first. "You've done well young man," said Ned.

"What will we do?" asked Adam.

"We either fight our way through the jungle on the banks or we risk the swamp. Guang Csai's sons told me about a path though the swamp to the north," said Ned.

"Couldn't we wait for Guang Csai's boat?" asked Adam.

"He isn't expected for another week. He always waits for the next load of fish and reed baskets," replied Ned. He forced a smile. "So we wait for the morning and then strike north."

The sun turned orange and sank quickly. Its fading light was hidden by more yellow black clouds and the tops of the karsts to the north slowly disappeared under the clouds. Forked lightning danced into the swamps followed by deafening peals of thunder. It turned cold and hailstones battered the survivors. The crew huddled together and looked to Ned for guidance.

"These guys are scared of this place Adam. We've got to keep them moving. Get the machetes from the boats," he said quietly to Adam. "Bring 'em back here to me where I can see 'em." He called one of the bodyguards. "Look for the path to the north, Chen," said Ned. "Adam'll help you." He grinned. "A silver ingot to the man who finds it."

For nearly two hours they hacked in turn at the tall grasses and willow scrub in the fading light, but nothing resembling a path appeared. There was a cry of alarm. Adam and Ned found one of the crew members sinking in quicksand. Adam threw a rope to the trapped man, who was just able to raise his arms and hold it. Adam and Chen pulled him out, and he sat shaking and reeking of the putrefaction of the swamp.

It was now dark and superstition got the better of the crew. Two of them walked towards the boats and Ned barred their way. His hand rested on his revolver. The two men ignored Ned, walked past him and climbed into one of the rowing boats. "We go to Canton," said one of them.

Ned calmly fired several shots into the side of the boat. Then he levelled his gun at the men. He looked for a moment as if he intended to shoot them. Rigid with fear, the two men climbed out of the sinking boat and rejoined the others.

Adam drew the wrong conclusion. He called out, "We'll work again." He grabbed a machete in an attempt to get the crewmen to forget their fear. He hacked at the grasses and willow scrub like a madman. Then he stood in front of the man with the figurines and handed him a machete. "Work with me," he commanded. Adam stood nearly as tall as the man. "Work!" he said and hacked away until he was exhausted. Adam sank into the mud sobbing, a twelve-year-old boy once again.

Ned thought the men would never forgive the young foreigner for his imperious behaviour. It stopped raining and Ned fell asleep, exhausted. Adam's protection had gone for the moment. Even the bodyguards had turned against him.

"HAI HAI!" called a timely voice from the swamp. "Mister Ned!" called a second voice. "Little big head, little big head," called the first voice and lanterns appeared.

"Ned, wake up!" shouted Adam. "Over here, over here," he called. "It's Jun Wei and Jun Wui." Superstition and resentment seemed to vanish. The tall grasses parted and the brothers appeared. Jun Wei threw his machete down and picked Adam up.

It was not an easy passage through the swamp after the torrential rain. After two hours, Adam's leg began to hurt him. His clothes were soaked and heavy and his spirits sank. Ned didn't desert him for a moment, but Adam's head spun with exhaustion and he collapsed.

The brothers looked to the crew for help, but from their sullen looks it was clear that they believed their bad luck was Adam's fault. For all they knew, they no longer had a boat to crew, and Ned had been a lifeline for them.

Jun Wei and Jun Wui carried the young man in turns till they reached the edge of the village paddy fields. He was carried to the house of the woman whose pig he had rescued. The brothers laid him on a straw palliasse by the light of a lantern. Adam slept throughout the night and into the next day.

He woke up and rubbed his eyes. He had no idea of the time and had almost forgotten how he arrived there. He put some weight onto his leg and it felt better and walked out into the morning sun but there was no one to be seen. His only company was a family of black pigs in a small pen, who pushed their snouts through the wooden slats.

Then it struck Adam that the village was at work, and might have been for some hours. He walked down the track outside the house and saw the villagers harvesting rice in the distance. He turned to walk back to the Si-Kiang house, sure that he knew the way. He found the foot of the steps to the house and half way down them was the figure of Jun-Wei signalling Adam to climb the steps. He sprang up the steps and joined him.

"There's no time to lose," said Jun Wei. "Follow me." They sprinted past the house and down the jungle track to the jetty. Yuxiang and He Quiao Gu waited at the end of the wooden platform, and Adam saw the reason for the deserted village. Most of the men were here in the fishing boats and were loading grappling hooks. Adam approached Yuxiang and knew there was something wrong because Ned's crew were all standing with the landowner and Yuxiang was angry. Adam bowed to him but Yuxiang only nodded. Even Quiao Gu seemed distant.

"We will talk later," said the landowner. "You have something to prove to these men. You must show they are equal to you and you are not the bringer of misfortune. Go now with Ned."

"We are going to try to rescue my boat, young man," said the American. "It's the least I can do for them." Then he said quietly in English, "They won't work for me unless I do this thing. Take a position behind an oar in this boat."

The small fleet of fishing boats stood out into the Si-kiang. He glanced back and saw Quiao Gu give the smallest possible wave.

Ned stood in the raised prow of the leading boat; he had never hoped so much for a miracle. He prayed the junk was still intact. Without it his authority was gone.

The landlord of the Si-kiang watched the fleet of fishing boats as it joined the Pearl. He had decided on this course of action to cure the young German of his imperiousness.

Ned swept the Pearl with a telescope, and at first saw nothing in the heat haze. The only sound was the oars striking the water. Then he breathed a sigh of relief when he saw the stricken junk with the broken mast lying across its waist with several cormorants perched in a row on the upperworks. They flew lazily away on the approach of the fishing boats.

Ned had calculated that the rising tide could refloat the ship in one hour, provided it could be righted and repaired. The fishermen planted the grappling hooks on the side lying upward. Every man pulled with all his might using the heavy sand and the keel as a brace.

The ship slid back and back again. Finally after three attempts it was upright, and Ned was the first to board to check for leaks. The hull was intact. He looked upwards and gave thanks, then remembered his other responsibility. Adam lay exhausted at the end of a rope beside the man with the figurines. He let go the rope and sat on the sand. He could do no more and tears streamed down his face. The man with the figurines took out one of his statues and wrapped Adam's hand around it. It was a sign of forgiveness.

"It's all right," shouted the American, and sail-makers and carpenters swarmed all over the junk. Soon everything was ready and the water began to rise. It swirled round the ship. The men remained on the ropes to hold the ship steady until the water reached their shoulders. Then one by one they were hauled on board.

The anchor held, and the craftsmen set to work. The broken mast was thrown over the side and the engine restarted. "We're a little late young man, but we have an appointment to keep," said Ned as he gave instructions to set course once again upriver. The man with the figurines paused while repairing the ship's rail. He turned to Adam. "Well done little big head," he said.

Just before the junk reached the wooden jetty Ned said to Adam. "Be careful who you tell about this."

"I'll wait till I'm in the army before I tell Papa and I'll never tell Mama," he said. Ned laughed.

The junk's return was triumphant and it was loaded with preserved fish and live animals to be sold at the Qing Ping market. Before any return Ned had to reward the villagers for their help. This time he did not charge money or services for the trip downriver.

The locals seemed pleased but not overjoyed. Ned asked Jun Wei what else he might do for them. The big fisherman pointed to the depths of the junk's hold, where Ned kept a quantity of very strong beer. "Break it out," said Ned. "You must make your own way back to the house, young man," he said to Adam. Nothing was heard from the jetty for the next few hours.

There was no sign of Yuxiang when Adam returned. He had entered the forest after bidding a stern goodbye to Adam in search of rare herbs used in his treatments. Quiao Gu knew it was a snub and her husband was avoiding Adam. She tried to explain Yuxiang's attitude, but she didn't say her husband was beginning to regret giving Adam such a privileged status.

She was grateful for Adam's company because she had heard nothing from her sons since their departure for northern China. She made Adam promise to write to her, thinking they might never see each other again, and confided in him that the village was deeply troubled. Two of the men had left their parents to make the dangerous trek to the north-west to join the communists.

"Try to forgive Yuxiang," she said. "His family had suffered at the hands of foreigners. He decided many years ago to live in safety of the Si-kiang, many miles from Canton."

Adam woke the next morning to find her waiting with porridge and morning tea. "He expects you at the rock," she said.

Yuxiang kept Adam waiting for one hour. When he arrived, he looked stern and distant. "Ned and I have talked about your behaviour in the swamp, Adam. What did you learn from your first visit to the village?"

"They have nothing and I have everything," answered Adam.

"What did I show you in the house on your first visit?" he asked. Suddenly Adam realised that his treatment of the crewman with the figurines had another deeper meaning. "We worked together on the ship," said Adam. "I think we are friends."

Yuxiang held the boy's face in his hands. "It is difficult for you to be friends with my people," he began. "The Russians brought Communism from Europe. Look what happened to your people. The Americans forced Japan to trade pottery for guns and now we face them in Manchuria. And your country uses us as guinea pigs to test weapons."

Adam defended himself. "I'm not like that, I'm friends with Bing Wen and Bing Wu. They'll always write to me."

Yuxiang's attitude softened. "I know," he said, "but we may never see them again." Adam now knew the reason for Yuxiang's distress.

Käthe came alive once more as she re-discovered her old vocation. Jacob rediscovered his first love, his interest in tropical medicine, and Nurse Lisa Müller saw more and more patients at the consulate surgery because of the doctor's new commitment.

Jacob Meissner developed an entirely separate interest and was seen taking walks with Heidi Schepke, a secretary and friend of Peter's secretary Elizabeth. Then, for no apparent reason, Heidi stopped meeting Jacob. She cancelled an appointment to see him and insisted on being treated by nurse Lisa or Käthe. Manfred Weiss had been forced, in Peter's absence, to expand his responsibilities and had found he enjoyed it, but this was a new and unwelcome challenge.

Several of the staff at the consulate refused treatment from Jacob. Weiss left the doctor a note suggesting they meet after dinner by the fountains. Jacob had not forgotten Weiss' initial attitude and he dreaded meeting Peter's deputy, particularly in Peter's absence.

Jacob was preoccupied with a possible outbreak of yellow fever in the town when he met Manfred Weiss. He had begun to consider leaving the consulate for friendlier surroundings. Weiss wore civilian clothes, which surprised Jacob. He was correct but slightly more cordial than he had been.

"Good evening Doctor," began Weiss. "I trust the new surgery is doing well."

"Indeed," answered Jacob without offering any details. "I have received a particular request, Doctor, which I must bring to your notice, although I realise you will have drawn your own conclusions."

Jacob waited for the worst. "Fräulein Schepke and two other women have asked to be treated by either Frau von Saloman or Fräulein Müller," he said with some difficulty. "I am sure you are aware of the rising popularity of certain political views. I have informed these ladies that neither Frau von Saloman nor Fräulein Müller are competent to treat most of the medical problems brought to our surgery."

Weiss forced a smile. "They have been told that you are our doctor and that will not change. They have also been informed that regulations require that treatment is compulsory."

He waited for it all to sink in, and then announced that that was all that needed to be said on the matter. It appeared that this was not an attempt to socialize and that Weiss had gone no further than his obligation to enforce regulations.

Just as he turned to go he said "Thank you for your information on the theft of morphine, Doctor. I regret your relationship with Fräulein Schepke could not be continued."

The morning sun rose above the rock shelf, which glistened with overnight rain. Adam had received a command to stand for one hour. His training had crossed a barrier and become a penance. The clouds gathered behind Adam, rolled over him and threatened to envelop the forest. The air crackled and exploded. A nearby tree was shattered by a bolt of lightning. The rain fell in torrents and he stood still, his arms outstretched as commanded. The storm died and Yuxiang appeared. He carried a broadsword and it was heavy and cumbersome. "Hold your hands as if in prayer," said Yuxiang. He placed the sword in Adam's hands. "Hold it there until I return," he said. "Sink into the rock and face the forest."

Yuxiang slipped away, and returned when he knew Adam had reached the limit of his endurance. He took the sword from Adam's hands and stood in front of Adam. They bowed to each other.

"Do you remember how to fall?" asked his teacher.

"Choose your moment. Circle," said Yuxiang, arms hanging limp by his side. Adam closed and pushed into thin air. He was spun round by a blow on the shoulder. He recovered and kicked again into thin air. A hand descended on his outstretched leg and grasped it. He was spun around and discarded like a rag doll. Adam sprang to his feet and waited for the next attack.

Yuxiang's right hand descended on his shoulder. Adam stepped forward and parried it. His right fist moved forwards and upwards. He stopped before contact.

"Why did you stop?" asked his angry opponent. "Because I did not need to hurt you," answered Adam. "You're my friend," he added with tears in his eyes.

He wanted to know why Yuxiang had punished him. His teacher became calm and looked at his teacher's clothes as if they were not appropriate. "I have learned from you today, Adam," he said. "I am no longer worthy to be called your teacher and I am ashamed." Adam held out his arms and grinned and the ageing Chinese landowner held out his arms and they embraced like father and son.

That night Adam slept soundly. Part of him would always belong here.

Before the junk returned to Canton, it had to be rededicated to the river. The ship still bore signs of its ordeal, but the crew believed it possessed a new immunity. A group of alligators appeared and the crew intoned prayers to the gods of the river.

Yuxiang and Quiao Gu led a small procession down to the Si-kiang. Their honoured guest stood between them and Yuxiang's reserve seemed to have gone. Ned was waiting on the jetty. He strolled up to the landowner and his wife and bowed. He was anxious to return to Canton with his new cargo.

The last of the consignment had just been loaded when Yuxiang turned to Adam and spoke so that all could hear. "I was more harsh to you than I ever was to my own sons," he said. Jun Wei and Jun Wui grinned broadly. Neither of them bowed and Yuxiang didn't seem to object.

Quiao Gu felt she had been left out and seized Adam and embraced him. "You must come back," she said. "My sons will always write to you. How will I manage without you here?"

"I know you will be a soldier one day, meine Deutsche Junge. Be just to your men," said Yuxiang.

Adam walked slowly backwards up the companionway and fell into Ned's arms at the ship's rails. The fishermen climbed into their boats and towed the junk into the main channel. Adam waved at them furiously.

As the junk made its way from one safe channel to another on the Pearl, Ned thought carefully about his future. He had been made aware of Lieutenant Weiss' enquiries. He knew of Peter's visit to the airfield and could only assume the worst, and it occurred to him that his acquaintance with Adam had not helped. The river front police had been corruptible until the arrival of Manfred Weiss.

Life for Ned Travis might become very uncomfortable and like Lin Hui he could be forced to hide in the old tenements of Canton. He even began to consider a return to the United States and a possible court martial.

Chapter 11

The list of dockside patients grew to an unimaginable size. Adam was spurred on to greater efforts by the rediscovery of Professor Rohrman's science textbook, and Jacob helped whenever he could. The other new influence on Adam's education was Manfred Weiss. His diffident and quiet manner hid talents which the staff of the consulate learned to respect. He never forgot a name and his mind was a card index of events. They learned to keep on the right side of him as he constantly made inquiries about individual beliefs.

Peter's secretary Elizabeth Bruning was impressed with Weiss in a different way and they began a relationship. With Peter's permission, Weiss offered to provide the staff with a regular news bulletin of events in Germany. He had well-placed contacts and his detailed radio reports were eagerly awaited.

Heidi Schepke and her friends showed great interest in the disorder on the streets of German cities and met regularly with Weiss. One evening a German newspaper report of a big National Socialist rally in Berlin was posted through Jacob Meissner's letterbox. He became steadily more uncomfortable, much preferring to be at the Riverside surgery. As the power and influence of Manfred Weiss increased, Peter was no longer the dominant influence. He was never insulting towards the doctor, always correct. The new Deputy Consul never gave the doctor reason to complain to Peter.

If anyone had any doubts about Manfred Weiss' political sympathies, they were soon dispelled. Over the next few months, his radio bulletins turned into an account of the rise of Hitler's National Socialists, and a number of the staff refused to be treated by Jacob in defiance of Weiss' instructions. Poor Jacob became defeatist and kept Peter in ignorance of the growing problem.

The letters from home were lifelines for all the staff and it was Elizabeth's job to distribute the mail when it arrived. Weiss called her to his office when the signal announcing the *Derfligger*'s arrival came.

"You may inform the rest," said Weiss, handing Elizabeth the message. His hand lingered on hers. She had thought her unexceptional looks would condemn her to spinsterhood until the arrival of her Manfred. She seized the message and ran towards the von Saloman apartment, because she knew Adam would want to go to the dockside with her.

Adam was sitting in the window tapping a pencil on the table when he saw Elizabeth coming, and he asked Jacob if he might be excused from his maths lesson. He ran outside. "The post's here Adam," she called, smiling broadly and waving the radio message. He kissed Elizabeth on the cheek, seized her hand and dragged her towards the gate. Weiss let them out and Adam dragged Elizabeth all the way to the dock.

The ship's pinnace was a hundred metres away from the pier. The officer with the postbag saw Adam and held up the brown postbag. Elizabeth was the unofficial postmistress and took charge of the bag before Adam dragged her all the way back.

The staff waited by the fountains and Elizabeth handed out the mail. She found a letter with a Berlin postmark and showed it to Adam. "Thank you Elizabeth," he said, seizing the letter and running to his bedroom. He had never received a letter from a friend before and tore it open.

"Now you men, listen," he said to the two Uhlan Lancers, propping himself up on the bedhead.

> *"Dear Field Marshall",* it began. *"A catastrophe!! There has been an explosion in a Science Laboratory. Do I write of Professor Rohrman and an experiment gone wrong? No, it happened somewhere in Schöneberg in a wooden shed. The shed caught fire but two scientists escaped without some of their hair. They had to have two days off school, but Theo and Klaus are back. How many times have I heard the story? I leave you to guess. They both say hello to you and want to know when you are coming home. Every time Müller bullies them Theo says they had better watch out because you're coming back. Dieter wants to run against you again.*
>
> *Schuster and his friends are worse than ever, now that Hitler is on the radio. Thanks for that weekend. I've kept all the photos. Please do something bad and come home.*
>
> *Auf wiedersehen*
> *Bruno*
> *(love from Mutti to everyone)*

Elizabeth personally delivered Peter's mail. He was busy with a tourist who had stolen souvenirs from the Qing Ping market..

Peter turned to several letters left by Elizabeth and chose the one with the Berlin postmark, addressed in Frieda's handwriting. He skip-read the letter, fearing the worst. Then he saw the words "Your father passed away on November 20th."

Peter let the letter fall to the desk. Frieda had added detail she knew they would all demand. "A few weeks ago I found him in his workshop holding a paintbrush, he could hardly use. He was sobbing. He ordered the War Room padlocked and no one is allowed in now. The doctor diagnosed a rheumatic heart and told me to expect the worst. We're at a loss what to do. Greta and Frieda send their condolences. We've told Renate and Bruno. We miss you now more than ever. I thought you would want the photograph."

Frieda had enclosed a picture of Gustav taken many years ago with his arm round Peter. Adam was inconsolable and sobbed night after night for nearly a week. He loved his Chinese friends, but wished he'd never given away any of his Uhlan Lancers.

Manfred Weiss rushed from the radio room to Peter's office on the fateful day of January 30th 1933. He was flushed and excited, a rare condition for him. "Your Excellency!" exclaimed Weiss. "The National Socialists have made a coalition with the Nationalists and the centre. Our leader, Adolf Hitler, is Chancellor of the Reich!"

He was followed by Elizabeth Bruning, who was never far away from Weiss these days. She burst past her boyfriend. "Your Excellency, our Führer is Chancellor. Germany is saved from the Communists. May we have a celebration?"

Peter could hardly refuse. A small group, perhaps a third of the staff, gathered on the lawns and Peter was forced to preside over it. After all, the new government were his new bosses. Jacob Meissner stared out of the surgery window, feeling more isolated than ever before. He watched, dismayed, as Käthe was feted for her links with Goering.

Käthe tried hard for Peter's sake, but her lukewarm attitude did not go unnoticed. Over the next few weeks, she formed an alliance with the supporters of the doctor, which would not have been so dangerous had she not been the Consul's wife.

CHAPTER ELEVEN

Once again, Käthe raised the issue of a second child. Once again Peter was dismissive and it made Käthe's defence of Jacob Meissner seem nagging and incessant. She accused Peter of cowardice because he wouldn't discipline Jacob's opponents.

That resulted in a terrible argument and Adam tried to intervene as he had done before. This time he was rebuffed by both of them and they began to behave as if it were their right to argue on a regular basis.

The decline in their relationship became a talking point in the small closed community. Without Peter's permission, Weiss despatched a message to the Foreign Ministry which hinted at a serious decline in morale. It was not long before there was a reply.

"What does this mean, Weiss?" asked Peter with the door of the office firmly closed. The signal began with congratulations to Peter for his work in Nationalist China. It then said that because of the 'increasing complexity' of diplomatic life, it was thought necessary to appoint an additional advisor to Peter. The new advisor, Karl Wendt, was to travel to Canton on the ***Derfligger*** within the next two months.

Then Peter looked ruefully at the second part of the signal. "Dr Jacob Meissner is relieved of his post with immediate effect. His duties will be performed by Nurse Müller. He is allowed only to treat patients at his dockside surgery and will be expected to return to Germany on the ship bringing Karl Wendt to Canton."

The signal was signed by a member of the secretariat of the Reich Chancellery, not by an official of the Foreign Ministry. Peter failed to see its importance. It was a bigger threat to his independence than he realised.

"Well Weiss, I am aware of your political sympathies, but that should not stop you from explaining this new appointment," said Peter. Manfred Weiss liked Peter and his family and relaxed his guard.

"The new man is a political officer, Your Excellency," he answered in an almost apologetic manner.

"You mean we are to be watched, Weiss?" asked Peter.

"The party calls it coordination sir," said Weiss with a half-smile. "If it is any comfort to you, I will be watched and reported on as much as anyone else."

Then Weiss surprised Peter. "May I express my regrets on the dismissal of Dr Meissner?" he said. "I now realise he is greatly respected here."

"Don't you think your change of heart is a little belated?" asked Peter sharply. Weiss was surprised that Peter knew of his offhand treatment of Jacob and was embarrassed.

"Perhaps", answered Manfred. "But we will both come to realise there is little we can do to protect him. We now work for a government which will make life difficult for Jews."

"What do you think prompted this signal?" asked Peter, knowing that, if anyone knew, Weiss would. Manfred Weiss felt very uncomfortable, but he was honest. "I felt it my duty to report on the situation here, Your Excellency," he replied hesitantly. "I cannot but regret the effect it has had on the doctor. Perhaps I have been guilty of naivety, and for that I'm sorry."

"Thank you for your apology Weiss, but that will not help Jacob Meissner," replied Peter angrily.

By now Manfred Weiss was very contrite. "Will this episode affect my commitment to your son's education Your Excellency?" he asked pessimistically.

Peter thought it better to keep his deputy within the orbit of the family. "My son enjoys your company, Weiss. I see no reason to terminate the relationship," he said. The Intelligence Officer was relieved.

By force of habit Weiss gathered information even within his growing friendship with Adam. He taught him maths when Peter was absent and introduced his pupil to military science. His pupil lapped it up at a speed which astonished Weiss. He showed a genuine interest in Adam's life at Die Schwanen. Adam was one of the first to realise that the mask which was Manfred's face could be modified.

Elizabeth Bruning had begun to have an effect. They talked of Adam's life on the river and the Huang family. He cheerfully told Weiss more than he had told his family.

"Look I've still got bruises from a big metal drum that fell on me," said Adam, proudly displaying what seemed to be a distorted finger. Manfred couldn't resist reverting to his natural instincts.

"You wouldn't happen to know what was in the metal drum, would you?" he asked quietly. He regretted asking the question when he saw Adam's smile disappear. Manfred quickly said. "It is of no importance."

CHAPTER ELEVEN

Weiss didn't need additional information from Adam. He had already built a case against Ned Travis and made friends with reliable police on the river front. He couldn't decide whether to give the dossier to Peter or relay the details to Berlin. He chose the latter.

Peter and Käthe saw Jacob together and he seemed breathless and defeated. He believed he had found a comfortable post a long way from the anti-semitism of Europe, but now the tentacles of the National Socialist state had reached out even to South Eastern China.

"What will you do Jacob?" asked Käthe.

He sighed. "I can only return to my family. I suppose I'll be allowed to treat other Jews," he replied sadly.

"Surely it won't be that bad," argued Käthe. "You have a reputation."

"Yes, I know," he said. "But I have written too many papers which will make me a target. Perhaps I can find another profession."

Adam was angry when he was told, remembering Schuster's treatment of old Julius in Kreuzberg. "Uncle Jacob won't have a chance," he said. "We have to help."

Käthe continued to enjoy Jacob's company in spite of growing hostility in the Consulate. Peter suggested things might calm down if she saw less of Jacob. Käthe was furious and accused him of cowardice. Their relationship reached a new low.

A new signal ordered Jacob to leave all his medical equipment at the Consulate. Manfred Weiss knew some of it belonged personally to Jacob and he made an inventory of everything in the surgery and excluded items Jacob wished to keep. Two weeks remained before the next visit of the *Derfligger*.

Four men occupied the foc'sle of the ship, as it approached the Pearl delta. One of them, a young doctor, sat in a deckchair apart from the others and was reading a medical textbook. Hidden in the pages was an article written some years ago which engrossed his attention. Its author was Dr Jacob Meissner.

The other three leaned over the ship's rail and talked over what was to happen in the next few weeks. One of them was tall with a shaven head. He had high cheekbones and an aquiline nose and was immaculately dressed in a tropical suit. In his jacket lapel was a Nazi party membership badge. The other two seemed very deferential. They all seemed ill at ease and uncomfortable in a sub-tropical climate. The doctor overheard a few of the remarks made.

"Don't worry," said the tall man. "It will be only a few hours and you will be able to return with your prisoner."

His companions were members of the newly-formed State Security Police, the Gestapo. One of them said quietly and malevolently. "Soon the Jew Meissner will get his desserts."

Captain Fischer had been instructed to signal Gestapo Headquarters in Berlin as they approached Canton. A further signal was relayed to Peter.

"It is expected that Herr Wendt and his companions will have an official reception," it began. "Before this takes place, Dr Meissner is to be handed over to the State Security Police."

Peter was shocked to hear it was a matter for state security. He told Käthe and they now knew Jacob was in real danger. He had to be told. But when he heard, he seemed resigned. He unlocked a drawer in his desk and showed Peter and Käthe a letter which had arrived on the *Derfligger*'s last visit.

His brother described the beginning of Jewish persecution in Germany. His relatives were preparing to emigrate and his brother wished to go to Israel. Their parents had decided to stay. "I will support them," said Jacob. "This has happened to my people before. We will survive."

He sat down on a large suitcase. "Perhaps it would be unwise if you wrote to me, but I will try to write to you," he said. "That way you will be safe."

"I'm sorry to remind you the ship will be here soon, old friend," said Peter. "We will drive to the river front with an escort despite the demands of these people."

The family sat with Jacob in the surgery. Adam stared at him in disbelief, his mind racing with ideas of how he might help. He threw himself at Jacob and embraced him.

Jacob shed tears. "Be the best you can for your parents," he said.

Adam walked over to Jacob's top drawer and pulled out a stethoscope. "You can't leave this, Uncle Jacob," he said. "All good doctors have one." He draped it round Jacob's neck.

The doctor smiled close to tears and stuffed it into a large coat pocket. A large black trilby hat had perched on a hook for the best part of three years. Jacob removed it and placed it on his head. "How do I look?" he said to Käthe.

She couldn't speak and embraced him. The hat fell to the floor and Adam picked it up and replaced it on Jacob's head.

Jacob looked around him. He had saved lives in this surgery, including Adam's, and believed he would never enjoy such freedom again. He was afraid to go through the surgery door into the courtyard, but he knew he had to lead the way.

As the four of them emerged, they were met by Manfred Weiss and Jacob's supporters. To his surprise, Elizabeth Bruning rushed towards him with a bunch of flowers. Others did not appear to say goodbye, afraid their names might appear in a notebook somewhere. They just stared out of the windows.

A uniformed Manfred Weiss opened the gates when the car had arrived from the airport depot. Jacob insisted on walking because he loved the view over the rooftops of the city and the glistening Pearl in the distance. Käthe walked arm in arm with him. Adam preceded them, trying to look as important as possible. He carried the old naval telescope in the belief it might somehow make a difference. Käthe remembered Adam's defence of Julius in Berlin and had already told Adam to make their friend's departure as easy as possible.

A small crowd waited on the jetty. At the front was a lady with three children who visited the riverfront surgery each week. She pushed the children forward and each presented Jacob with a posy of flowers. He was deeply moved.

Adam watched the ship drop anchor. Davits launched the ship's pinnace and he watched several figures emerge from the waist of the ship and climb into the small boat. The swastika flag of the new Germany fluttered at the stern. Adam thought of Berndt Schuster, Rolf Schneider and then of Theo and Klaus.

The crowd grew bigger and more restive. The sailor with the figurines pushed his way to the edge of the bustle. He stared at Adam and then rushed forward.

"What is happening to our doctor, Little Big Head?" he asked and the crowd looked expectantly at Adam. Käthe put her arm round his shoulders in an attempt to restrain him, but he gave his mother a withering look and pushed her arms away.

He walked up to the edge of the crowd. "What is happening, Deutsche

Junge?" asked the woman with the three children. Adam shouted, "Your doctor is being taken back to Germany by bad men who will hurt him."

The ship's pinnace was still a few minutes from the quayside. Käthe made a feeble appeal to Adam to go back but he ignored her. "Your Excellency, please restrain your son," advised Manfred Weiss. Two of Ned's crew appeared, armed with broadswords. "Can we help?" they said.

"You can save the doctor," said Adam. "Grab these cases," he shouted. A gaggle of volunteers followed him to the car where two policemen stood guard. Ned's crew members stood in from of them, hands on sword belts while the volunteers seized the cases. "This way," shouted Adam. Jacob watched open mouthed as his belongings disappeared into the crowd.

Adam ran up to him. "There's no time to lose, Uncle Jacob," he said urgently. He seized the doctor's arm. Manfred Weiss intervened. "Go doctor," he said. "I have a story prepared."

"Yes go Jacob, go," said Peter and Käthe.

Peter pushed him gently and Adam led him to the water's edge, where the crowd parted. The volunteers with the cases asked for instructions and Jacob looked at Adam bewildered. "To Ned's boat," said Adam, but Jacob hesitated. "I have to help my family in Germany," he said. "I've seen them attacking old men, Uncle Jacob. You won't have a chance."

"He's right," said Weiss. "Run for your life."

Jacob turned incredulously to Weiss, who told him to go. Adam disappeared into the crowd and it closed round the fugitives, preventing any pursuit. Breathless, Jacob stopped at the base of the gangplank. He gazed at the red sails and the collection of piratical-looking characters in front of him.

Ned appeared, hands on hips. "Come aboard young man," he said "and bring your friend." Adam helped the doctor up the gangplank, and the luggage volunteers followed.

"I have to go now Ned," said Adam urgently. "Can you hide Jacob please?" he asked Ned. Lin Hui sat in the waist of the ship and he gestured Adam to go to him. "We will help our doctor I think Mr Travis," said the Warlord. Now go, Deutsche Junge."

Adam tore down the riverfront to rejoin his parents, who were on the point of welcoming the visitors. A guard of honour of six Nationalist soldiers approached, lined up and presented arms. Käthe turned round and straightened

Adam's jacket. She patted him on the cheek. "Now for God's sake, behave yourself," she said.

The political attaché Karl Wendt was the first to ascend the ladder to the jetty. He waited for his companions before any introduction. Peter had expected Wendt to be officious and arrogant, but he seemed genial and engaging. He first shook hands with Peter and gave the Nazi salute. He greeted Peter's reluctance to return it jovially.

"I'm honoured to meet you, Your Excellency. We are all aware of your service to the Reich. The salute will come in time," he joked. He turned to Käthe and gave her a long look of approval.

Käthe had decided to remain icy and reserved, but she soon found that difficult. "We have heard so much about your work on the riverside surgery and I believe you have been a wonderful hostess to our ally General Chiang-Kai Shek," said Wendt. He had a winning, almost mischievous smile for Käthe.

Then he turned to Adam. "This must be Adam," he began. "I have connections with the Martin Luther School and I am led to believe one day you will represent our Fatherland in the Olympic Games." Käthe found herself hanging onto every word of his carefully-prepared compliments.

Wendt treated Manfred Weiss as if he was a subordinate he had already met. Then he took Peter on one side. "Your Excellency, these two gentlemen behind me have some unpleasant business to conclude," he said, trying to disassociate himself from what was to follow.

The two security policemen behind Wendt were two of the most forgettable people Peter had ever seen. "Where is Meissner?" one of them asked rudely. Karl Wendt intervened. "May I ask of the whereabouts of Jacob Meissner, Your Excellency?"

Excuse me Herr Wendt," said Manfred Weiss. "I think I am the best informed of the facts of the case. Dr Jacob Meissner is no longer with us. On receipt of the news of his dismissal, he left the Consulate. My informants tell me he has taken refuge in the French Consulate on Shamian Island."

Manfred didn't know that only a full blown embassy would permit such a thing. Wendt might have known it, but if he did, he concealed his irritation well.

"So my travelling companions are to leave empty handed?" he said. "I should like confirmation that Meissner is indeed in French hands, Your

Excellency," he added to Peter. "I will leave that in yours and Weiss' capable hands."

The fourth member of the landing party had been largely ignored. He was Jacob's replacement and received no more than a few curious glances from Käthe. She nudged Adam, who stepped forward to greet this shy-looking, bespectacled character. Adam cooperated because he felt obliged to, and he did not wish to greet any replacement for his friend and teacher warmly.

The man bowed and introduced himself. "I am Dr Albert Transier," he said. He seemed very ill at ease and had spent many hours worrying how he might replace a popular figure. He wore a white tropical suit and carried a large briefcase. He put it down and produced a large leather wallet containing his travel documents. He seemed to think Adam might want to see them and sweated profusely. Adam forced a smile and managed to say something. "We only have one car, doctor. You and I will have to walk."

Transier had seen the restive crowd on the jetty and was afraid. "The soldiers will escort us, doctor," said Adam coldly.

Wendt spoke with the two security men before they re-embarked. They were angry because their prey had escaped, but Wendt knew what to say.

"Perhaps gentlemen, Dr Meissner is not in such safe hands at all. What, I wonder, will the French do with him when the Führer has defeated their armies?" he suggested. They exchanged salutes and reboarded the pinnace. The car disappeared in a cloud of dust and Adam walked to the Consulate with Dr Transier, in silence.

Peter had preferred to keep the office adjacent to the family apartment. Karl Weidling's office had remained vacant and was assigned to Wendt. Käthe thought it better if she and Adam kept out of the way while Peter showed Wendt his new quarters. The newcomer thanked Peter and produced two packages. He proudly opened both of them. One contained a swastika flag, which he announced was to replace the flag of the Republic outside Peter's office. He became quite emotional when he presented Peter with the contents of the second. It was a portrait of Adolf Hitler, to be hung behind Peter's desk. Peter had learned the art of compromise, but this was nearly too much. Wendt, so far, had been the soul of charm, and was to continue to be so in Käthe's company. In everyone else's he behaved differently.

He lost no time in taking the initiative. He knew Peter was to fly to

Nanking to meet Chiang the following day. He called a meeting of himself, Peter and Weiss to discuss its implications, appointing himself as Chairman.

Peter was appalled at Wendt's high-handed behaviour. The purpose of the meeting turned out to be the drawing up of a list of instructions to Peter, underwritten by the Chairman himself. Peter objected.

"You know yourself, Herr Wendt that I am on good terms with the Nationalist leaders" he said. "I think they, not us, will decide on strategy."

"I think not," said Wendt. He produced a typewritten sheet prepared in Germany for Chiang's adviser, Von Falkenhausen. Manfred Weiss was shocked.

Peter decided to agree, but to simply ignore all the new instructions. He was relieved when Wendt announced he would stay at the Consulate while Peter was in Nanking. He asked Käthe to be as hospitable as she could to Wendt. She reluctantly agreed, but reminded Peter that she had the odious task of helping Albert Transier to settle in. Peter flew off to Nanking with his aide not realising the danger in which he had placed Käthe.

The atmosphere at the waterfront surgery was strained. Transier was at a loss what to do when many of the patients insisted on treatment by Käthe and not by him. She appeared to encourage them. Albert Transier's frustration boiled over. "Frau Von Salomon," he began. "Do you hold me responsible for the removal of Dr Meissner?"

"I cannot help but think so," she retorted, as she secured a dressing on a child's arm. "I applied for this post in complete ignorance of the circumstances and may I remind you of our professional duty to our patients, both here and at the Consulate."

He reached for his briefcase. "This is my favourite paper on tropical medicine," he said. He showed her Jacob's article on the treatment of malaria, produced at the Consulate with Käthe's assistance. She apologised, realising that the new doctor was probably blameless.

She turned to the queue of patients and called out, "Dr Transier is a friend of Dr Meissner. He is a good doctor." A few approached Transier cautiously. Suddenly there was a crowd of volunteers to carry the doctor's equipment back to the Consulate.

Käthe and Albert Transier talked for the first time. And he decided to take a risk. "May I venture to suggest that your friendship with Dr Meissner means you hold liberal views?" he said to Käthe.

"Perhaps," she answered, cautiously.

"I have accepted this post,"Transier began,"because I am tired of the over-regulation of the medical profession in Germany. In my naivety I believed that distance might make a difference, yet now I am in a situation where it appears I am involved in the smearing of a good doctor's character. I have had to pretend to support the views of those brutes who occupied the first-class cabins. I occupied a second-class cabin, I might add."

"I have to pretend to support the Catholic Centre Party for my husband's sake," said Käthe, warming to her new colleague.

"You won't have that privilege any longer, Frau Von Salomon. The Catholic Centre has just disappeared. And please be careful of Wendt," he warned. He paused, removed his hat and wiped the sweat from his forehead. "Have I said too much, Frau von Saloman?" he asked.

"It's Käthe," she answered and he was very relieved.

She felt obliged to invite Albert Transier to dinner in the family apartment. Adam thought his mother was betraying Jacob at first and said very little. He preferred to develop his friendship with Manfred Weiss now that Bing Wen and his brother were in Northern China. Adam invited Weiss to dinner without asking Käthe.

It was the beginning of a social circle of which she was the hub. At first Weiss was lost in such talkative and warm company. Käthe suggested he bring Elizabeth Bruning. She flattered her shy new man friend even during the first dinner date. Manfred had been afraid to speak, but this all changed. Elizabeth announced he had a degree in Philosophy, which embarrassed him. Käthe was very impressed and their guest appeared to change.

"I have heard you are a capable pianist, Frau von Saloman," he said. "Might you perform for us?"

Käthe looked reprovingly at Adam for betraying a secret. He took no notice and insisted his mother display her skills. Piano recitals involving Käthe and Adam began to make their little soirées memorable and were a welcome relief from the dull routine of the Consulate.

But the little gathering had made a serious omission. They had failed to invite the new political adviser, although he seemed to find solace in dinner dates with his secretary Christina Schultz. After a signal from Peter that he expected to be delayed for at least one month, Karl Wendt decided to disrupt

Käthe's social arrangements. He showed particular interest in Manfred Weiss' investigation of the riverfront smugglers and insisted on receiving a duplicate copy of all documents relating to the Warlord, Ned Travis and Huang Yuxiang. He suggested to Manfred that protocol required him to dine alone with Käthe and Adam from time to time. He had no objection, he said, to the continuation of the dinner arrangements at the von Saloman apartment.

Käthe had made enough concessions in the past to know Wendt was right. Elizabeth Bruning told her that he was a charming companion to Christina Schultz, and she had nothing to fear.

Wendt prepared the ground carefully, and asked to see Käthe in his office. He explained that it was, of course, a state requirement that Adam attend school. He understood that was not possible, but he was happy with the existing arrangements. He made a point of meeting Käthe when she returned from the riverfront surgery and listened patiently and politely to her stories of the day's events.

She had dreaded the prospect of dinner with Wendt, but now began to look forward to it. He showed no impatience to fix a date but promised it would take place soon, despite his busy schedule, and each time they met he paid her compliments. It had been a long time since any man had done so regularly.

Wendt gave Käthe twenty-four hours' notice, and she searched her wardrobe anxiously for the appropriate evening dress. She chose one she usually reserved for Peter after one of his long absences. She replaced it and then took it out again.

Käthe prepared Adam as if he was about to attend an interview. He found the whole process embarrassing and annoying, but as always, he would be on his best behaviour for his mother's sake.

Wendt paid attention to detail. First, he decided to establish that his guest would feel honoured to dine with a dignitary of the new German Reich. Then he slowly relaxed her and made her the centre of attention. Candelabra and fresh flowers adorned the table and a waiter stood in attendance all evening.

Käthe had been made to feel anxious about Adam's education, but he quietly announced that he had written to the Minister of Education to assure him that everything was in place. Wendt had sensed that Käthe would be impressed by any display of authority and influential contacts. He allowed her to describe the social circle of which she had become a part in Berlin, and seemed to be impressed by her encounters with Hermann Goering and his wife Emmi. He listened patiently to Adam when he described very reservedly his favourite things at Die Schwanen. He didn't mention Bruno. That was reserved for people he liked.

The dinner dates became more frequent. Wendt's compliments, always well timed, became more fulsome. Adam found himself left out more and more and made a forlorn attempt to get his mother to see sense. "Dr Transier says he was very rude to the ship's crew Mama," he said hopefully.

The reply was predictable. "Perhaps he was treated badly my darling, and besides he is never rude to us," she retorted, hardly pausing her preparations for yet another evening of cajolery and flattery.

"I don't like him, Mama," said Adam.

"Then perhaps you ought to stay with our other friends Adam."

Adam went with Käthe once more, but he had never felt so left out. Wendt and Käthe behaved as if he wasn't there. On the next occasion, they dined alone. Käthe had crossed the line, and tongues began to wag.

The next day, Albert Transier held his morning surgery and there was only one patient. Wendt's secretary, Christina Schultz, strode secretively through the door and sat down apologetically. "How may I help, Fraülein Schultz?" he began.

She began sobbing and could hardly speak. Albert rose from his chair and tried to comfort her. "Please, what's the matter?" he asked.

"I dare not stay long," Christina began, looking furtively out of the window. "I have no one else to turn to," she spluttered. "It is Herr Wendt." She couldn't find the right words. "He won't leave me alone doctor," she said. "He threatened me if I said anything."

Albert Transier felt equally powerless. He believed Christina, but there was no police force to turn to because the Consulate was a self-governing body. He considered telling Manfred Weiss but was convinced he was a creature of Wendt's. Worst of all, Peter, the only person to outrank Wendt, was not expected for some time.

"I'm sorry Christina," said the doctor, "but I'm powerless."

Christina was now safe from Wendt because he had become bored with her. He threw her over to concentrate on the pursuit of Käthe. Her good luck was Käthe's misfortune. She seemed impatient when she dined with Adam and her new friends. She began to bore them with tales of Wendt's supposed prowess and his influence in Berlin. It had all been contrived by Wendt for her benefit. Manfred Weiss was in a position to validate Wendt's claims, but he knew better than to challenge them. Adam was irritated and embarrassed when his mother appeared to continue to fall under Wendt's influence. He reacted in the only way he could. When Käthe pushed open his bedroom door to say goodnight, he turned away and pretended to be asleep.

Wendt had sensed tension between Käthe and Peter, and his experience told him how desperate a woman might be in pursuit of another child.

Käthe had always dressed conservatively away from Peter's company but she abandoned her policy for Karl Wendt. She lay awake at night and pictured herself in her American evening gowns with the immaculately-dressed Wendt. She even imagined herself complimenting him on his athletic figure and receiving similar compliments. Finally after dinner, she imagined Wendt dancing a waltz with her and leading her to his bedroom.

As she prepared to leave for Wendt's apartment, she allowed the fantasy to become a reality. She wore the most flattering evening gown she possessed and her headiest French perfume. As she stared at herself in the mirror Käthe decided she was at her very best. She tripped down the stairs and saw Adam leaving for Manfred Weiss' apartment. "Goodnight my darling," she called. Adam ignored her but watched anxiously as she disappeared through the door of Wendt's apartment.

"You are looking very lovely tonight, Käthe," said Wendt in a practised soft voice.

"Thank you Karl," she answered, allowing him to kiss her on the cheek. There were fresh camellias on the table. The Chinese cook had been instructed to serve small courses but to be ready with a plentiful supply of hock.

"These evenings are very important to me," said Wendt. "I cannot imagine more wonderful company than yours."

Just then she made a fatal mistake; she leaned across the table to touch the flowers. Her fingers shook as Wendt's hand covered hers. She didn't withdraw her hand. The predator now believed she was in his grasp.

Wendt thought it better to allay suspicion. He invited Weiss, Albert Transier and Adam to the next meal and behaved as if nothing had happened. The evening turned out to be entertaining as they discussed the more amusing features of life on the waterfront. Even Adam dropped his guard for a while.

Then he announced in front of the others that he would be unable to dine with Käthe because he had to host receptions for Nationalist Officers from the training college at Whampoa Island. Käthe felt rejected and distraught. She wanted Wendt, but wished it to happen on her own terms.

Manfred Weiss had seen enough of Wendt's behaviour to suspect Käthe might be in terrible danger. He overheard him threatening Christina Schultz with dismissal if she ever revealed details of his behaviour to anyone. Weiss liked Käthe and preferred to lay the blame for what was happening at Wendt's door, but he felt he could do nothing. He was isolated and powerless.

He sat staring at the new enciphering machine and looked for the courage to send a signal to Peter. He looked out of the window and saw Karl Wendt driving through the gates, and his courage failed him.

Then Albert, Christina and Adam burst through the door. "This area is strictly off limits to any but authorised personnel," said Weiss sharply.

"Enough of that Manfred, we demand you send this signal to Nanking at once," said the doctor.

Manfred took the piece of paper from Albert. It read: "FAO the German Consul in Canton. Your presence here is urgently requested."

"My mother can't help herself, Herr Weiss," pleaded Adam. "Please send it."

"Yes please, for all of us," said Albert.

"I cannot," said Manfred. "If nothing happened here, can you imagine our position?"

Adam was disgusted and ran to his father's office. There he found Elizabeth Bruning. "Please come," he said and explained what was happening. She needed no prompting.

She found Manfred staring at the new teleprinter, his hands on the table.

"Please send it, Manfred," she said.

"God help us all," he said as he put on the headphones and tapped out the message.

Albert watched Käthe making simple mistakes at the waterfront surgery, such as dropping a syringe. He had already decided that such a compassionate character as Käthe did not belong with the likes of Karl Wendt. She suddenly appeared to be very busy as a way to make amends for her carelessness in the surgery.

"Käthe is there anything you would like to discuss?" Albert asked quietly, seeing her turmoil. But Käthe had been drawn too far into Wendt's web to escape.

"Of course not Albert, of course not," she insisted.

"Would your son agree there was nothing to discuss?" he retorted.

She looked guilty and called in the next patient. All Käthe could think of was Karl Wendt.

Manfred and Elizabeth called on her before the dinner date that evening. "You can cancel Käthe. We'll take the message," she said.

"Of course not," Käthe answered. "I am well able to handle myself and it would not be right and proper to behave like that. "

That night Käthe wore her most expensive and eye-catching evening gown. Manfred began to wonder if she really was a victim. "Come Elizabeth, we can still get to the Opera House in time," he said, pulling her away. He looked up and saw Adam's face in the first floor window. How he must be looking forward to seeing Peter, he thought.

Wendt waited for Käthe at the door. Other faces watched from apartment windows. Some of them did not feel Käthe was a victim. One of them, Heidi Schepke, hoped that a scandal would lead to her departure.

Wendt greeted Käthe with a kiss on the cheek, then drew her inside and kissed her on the mouth. "There – I have done it Käthe," he exclaimed, continuing to hold her. "You may call for help if you wish, or share a special meal cooked by a French chef."

She preferred to believe it was a light-hearted kiss. "I forgive you Karl, but I may consider telling your wife," she joked. She took his arm and was led to the table. Wendt withdrew her chair for her. He snapped his fingers and the electric lights were switched off. Only the candlelight remained.

He spoke softly to her and plied her with hock. He asked her to stand up in the candlelight and announced he had never seen such a beautiful woman. She ought to be paid far more attention, he said. Käthe had always left at eleven o'clock, but now she lingered. She was enjoying an adventure in the otherwise dull world of the Consulate, believing she was safe in the company of the waiter and the chef. The two men were sent home. She could have made an excuse and left, but now she wanted Wendt to make love to her.

The air was hot and oppressive. Wendt turned on the electric fan and invited Käthe to stand under it. The gentle breath of cool air made her close her eyes and her auburn curls danced on her peach-like skin.

Wendt wound up a phonograph and played a waltz which he knew she loved. He drew her towards him and kissed her neck. Her hands stroked his neck playfully and she drew his hand downwards. His hands reached behind her and unbuttoned her gown. He slid one strap off her shoulder. His hand caressed her behind. Suddenly alarm bells rang.

"Please Karl, not now. I would like it to be on my terms. I'm sorry to embarrass you. I really must go now."

He hid his disappointment and pretended to be courteous, covering her shoulders with her mink stole. Käthe fled through the brightly-lit courtyard to her apartment. Eyes still watched, some with relief, others with disappointment.

The Führer's political advisor in Canton burned with a gnawing desire to have Käthe, and his ego had been seriously bruised. He resented his rejection and was afraid his image among Heide Schepke and her friends had been damaged. He had been cheated of his prey this time, but he was certain Käthe would not refuse him again. She had had the security of the staff of the Consulate at close call. He would make sure that was not the case next time.

Käthe couldn't sleep. She found herself trying to choose between Peter and Wendt and naively believed she was in control of the situation. She decided not to choose until Wendt had made love to her. Only then did she think she could she make a proper comparison. It would, of course, be on her terms. But Peter would be back soon. And then she realised she would have to give in to Wendt at the next dinner date.

The bright silver Junkers aircraft descended from Wuhan towards the airstrip at Canton. Peter drummed a pencil on a piece of paper as he wondered why such a cryptic signal had been sent.

Käthe and Albert returned from the waterfront surgery almost exhausted.

He volunteered to return the unused medical stores. "You're exhausted Albert," she said. "I'll take care of that. You go to your apartment and take a nap."

He was grateful for the offer and left Käthe in the surgery. He looked around the courtyard, wondering why it was so quiet, and then remembered that Wendt had given the staff permission to go on a shopping spree at the Qing Ping market.

Manfred had reluctantly left his post to accompany Elizabeth and her friends. Normally meticulous, he had missed a brief signal which protruded from the teleprinter. It read "Acknowledged, von Saloman."

Weiss felt guilty as he wandered round the market. The Consulate was almost deserted. He should be at his post, he believed. He walked quickly back and directed his steps towards the radio room. He waved to Käthe, whose face briefly appeared in the window of the surgery.

He saw the signal from Peter and picked up the telephone for the gatehouse. "Ludwig, take the car down to the airport now," he ordered. He sat down and waited, wondering if he had overreacted.

Käthe took far too long to replace the supplies. She lingered deliberately and cursed herself for not allowing Wendt to seduce her. She looked into the courtyard. There were always one or two people near the fountains, but it was deserted. Perhaps she ought to change and go to his apartment. She decided that was too blatant. She would wait for another dinner invitation.

"Hello Käthe," said Karl Wendt, appearing in the doorway of the surgery. He was dressed in a white tropical suit and cravat. She looked him up and down and apologised for her own appearance.

"It doesn't matter how you are dressed," he replied, taking her arm and checking the blinds were drawn. "We'll forget the end of our last meeting Käthe. I forgive you. You can make it up to me now."

She thought his condescending tone was a form of playfulness, but she was sadly mistaken. He was there to perform a ritual to establish his superiority over her and avenge his humiliation. He drew her towards him and kissed her hotly and roughly. She felt his hand move above her knees. She moaned and allowed her hand to fall and stroke his legs.

"You have tortured and tortured me," said Wendt as he manoeuvred her towards the treatment couch. She tore off her headdress and allowed her hair to tumble over her shoulders. Her hands stroked his legs urgently. He picked her up and laid her on the couch. She had avoided looking at him until now.

She assumed he had a streak of decency, but she was about to be disillusioned. She looked into his eyes, hoping for softness.

"Please say you love me Karl, before we make love," she said weakly. Tenderness had no part in Wendt's plans. His hands fell on the softness between her legs and he rose above her in triumph.

"Don't be ridiculous Käthe," he said. "We are like two beasts in the jungle who must feast themselves on one another."

Käthe went cold, suddenly realising she was in the power of a monster. Wendt put his hand over her mouth and knelt between her legs. She broke away and rolled off the couch, striking her head on the floor. He seized her and threw her on the couch. She felt weak and her struggles began to subside. She sobbed uncontrollably. He raised himself over her once more.

Just then the door crashed open. Peter, with Weiss at his shoulder, stood there horrified. Wendt mouthed an excuse and began to re-arrange himself. Käthe lay there sobbing, her forehead bleeding.

"Your wife has taunted me and led me on, von Saloman. These things will happen you know," said Wendt weakly. Peter did not think for one moment that his wife was complicit and he advanced on Wendt, striking him across the face in the old Imperial gesture that usually led to a duel.

"You filthy Nazi swine!" exclaimed Peter, hitting the now ridiculous half naked figure of Wendt time and again. "You're as bad as all these filthy lower-class upstarts who form our Government today."

Manfred Weiss took hold of Peter's shoulders from behind, trying to stop him. Wendt cowered in a corner, trying hastily to dress himself. Peter knelt down and put his arm round his distressed wife, but she hardly dared to look her husband in the face.

"Manfred, send for Transier," said Peter. "If you see Adam, send him back to the apartment."

He had made the mistake of ignoring Wendt, who had now composed himself. He had not lost his presence of mind and understood his Führer's belief that morals were trite and only the decisive and fit should survive.

"Come with me Weiss," he ordered sharply.

"I must get the doctor," countered Manfred.

"You must come with me Weiss," shouted Wendt, "now!"

Albert Transier had been wakened by the noise and he marched through the door, and ordered everyone out.

"Follow me Weiss," said Wendt as he marched towards the communications room. They were there in a few seconds. Wendt seized a notepad and began to draft a signal. Manfred Weiss stood watching incredulously.

"Compose yourself Weiss," said Wendt. "You look as if you've seen a ghost." He finished the draft, read it through and nodded with satisfaction. "You will send this at once," he ordered. Manfred read it.

> *"It is my duty to report disloyal behaviour on the part of Herr and Frau von Saloman. Both have shown disrespectful attitudes to the Führer and other Party Leaders including Reich Minister Goering. His Excellency Herr von Saloman is reluctant to display the flag of the New Reich.*
>
> *I am sorry to have to report this inappropriate behaviour in one who has done so much for Germany.*
>
> *Obediently, Wendt (Political Advisor).*

Manfred looked at the draft in dismay. "You cannot send this, Herr Wendt. These people do not deserve it," he said.

"You know where your duty lies, Weiss. You are directly responsible to me. Send it."

"I refuse," retorted Manfred. "I am a witness to the worst behaviour I have ever seen."

"You don't understand, Weiss," sneered Wendt. "You are associating yourself with their behaviour." Yet Manfred stood firm.

The staff were beginning to return from Canton. Wendt wanted to remove what he now believed to be a minor obstacle, and he knew how to do it.

"You will remember Weiss, no doubt, your story of the departure of Dr Meissner?" Manfred said nothing, wondering what was going on in the mind of this monster. "You informed the landing party that Dr Meissner fled to the French Consulate on receipt of the news of his dismissal, I believe?" continued Wendt.

Manfred's blood ran cold. He had made one mistake since his arrival and was about to pay for it.

"I have interviewed Fräulein Schepke and her friends. They insist the doctor did not go until the day, indeed the moment of my arrival," said Wendt. "It also appears that His Excellency's son is as much to blame as you are. I am not sure all this can be overlooked."

Manfred Weiss was speechless. Wendt handed him the draft of the signal and smiled triumphantly. "Send it, Weiss," he ordered.

"To the Foreign Ministry?" asked the defeated Manfred.

"Oh no", added Wendt, "to Gestapo Headquarters, No. 8 Prinz-Albrechtstrasse, for the attention of Kriminalrat Kloster."

Manfred shuddered. He encoded the signal and despatched it. As he did so, Elizabeth Bruning appeared at the door for an afternoon briefing.

"Good day," said Wendt calmly. He turned to Weiss as if a routine matter had been concluded. "All in complete confidence of course, Weiss," he said. "Yes, Fräulein Bruning, please come in."

Early the next day, Peter drafted his own signal to the Foreign Ministry in Berlin recommending the instant recall of Karl Wendt. He stated Wendt had assaulted Käthe. He handed the signal to Manfred in his Deputy's Office. Manfred showed it to Wendt, who destroyed it as soon as Peter had left. "I'm so glad you have seen sense, my dear Weiss," said Wendt.

Both Wendt and Peter waited anxiously for a reply. Both were confident the outcome would be favourable. But Wendt had been doubly clever. Not only had he been able to blackmail Manfred Weiss, he had made the problems of the Consulate a security matter. He understood his new masters in Berlin well.

Later that day, Käthe was approached by Karl Wendt as she sat by the fountains. She shuddered as he came close but noted the bruises on his face with some satisfaction.

She turned her head away as a sign she wished to have nothing to do with him. But Wendt hadn't finished with her. "Don't you think he deserves to find out Käthe?" he asked evilly. He didn't expect an answer. He swept off officiously towards a waiting car.

The internal telephone rang in Peter's office. It was Albert Transier, requesting an urgent interview. "Please meet me in the surgery, Your Excellency," insisted Albert.

When Peter arrived, the blinds were drawn. "Your excellency, I do not wish to be seen in your office for any length of time. I wish to divulge a confidential piece of information which I know to be unprofessional, but I think the needs of the moment demand it."

"Go on," said Peter.

"Christina Schultz has also suffered from Wendt's unwanted attentions. She may not reveal this to anyone else, but if you were in need of support in the near future, you now know of a potential witness."

Wendt had powerful friends. Peter welcomed the thought of extra support for Käthe.

Käthe was now terrified of Wendt, who took every opportunity to remind her of her near unfaithfulness. One morning Heidi Schepke appeared at the surgery, bringing a note from Wendt for Käthe. "No reply is required," she said with a look of utter contempt on her face.

Käthe read it. "I will choose the time and place, Käthe. Perhaps some time in the near future would be the best. A decent man like that ought to know." He signed himself "Yours Karl."

Käthe began to neglect her appearance and lose weight. She found sleep difficult, and moved from Peter's bed. He was devastated, but Albert Transier told him to expect such things for some time. She found solace in the waterfront surgery. There in the guise of a nurse she could be her old self once more. When she returned to the Consulate, she dreaded seeing Wendt or any of his supporters.

Then one day, while walking back down the tree-lined avenue from the waterfront surgery, she heard footsteps behind her. The steps quickened.

"May I speak with you, Frau von Saloman?" asked Christina Schultz. She was aware she had not been allowed to approach the Consul's wife except in formal circumstances.

"May I speak frankly?" she asked. "This is very difficult and I may seem part of a conspiracy of tongue-waggers," she said hesitantly. "Elizabeth Bruning is my friend." She let that take effect. Käthe now knew that details of the assault had spread. Christina had decided to take a chance because she was desperate for a powerful ally. "May I be yours?" she asked.

She revealed Wendt's harassment of her. It was fortunate for her that Käthe needed someone to talk to.

"The man is a monster," said Käthe. "You have done the best thing possible."

Christina was delighted, and stood wringing her hands. Käthe embraced her and felt a little relieved.

"We must meet regularly," she said.

"Perhaps under his window where he can see us," said Christina impishly. They made the mistake of thinking they had gained the upper hand.

Peter now paid more attention to Adam, and couldn't resist asking him to describe every detail of Käthe's behaviour. Adam revealed that dinner parties involving Wendt had taken place. He never mentioned that Käthe had dined alone with him.

Night after night Käthe lay awake staring at the moonlight. Some two weeks later, a terrible storm hit the Consulate. Wind and rain battered the windows and water flowed from the roofs of the apartments and offices and tumbled down the courtyard. Käthe drew the bedclothes over her face. Her body shook and she sobbed. She hardly heard the bedroom door open above the noise of the wind.

"Are you all right Mama?" asked Adam. She couldn't speak and he was almost afraid to approach her. She whimpered to him, "Will you hold me my darling?"

Adam lay on the bed with her as he had always done. Her arms circled his neck tightly. She kissed his forehead, and he stroked her hair and returned her kisses. When he read Bruno's letters, he thought of Helga. But now he didn't need her. He had been restored to his mama.

"Are you ready to tell me things about your friends on the river?" she asked. He told her about Ned and Ned's women. "Do you think that makes him a bad man?" she asked pointedly. Adam grinned mischievously. "Oh no Mother, of course not," he replied.

"I'm very tired now my darling," she said and Adam rolled off the bed. She held out her hands and grasped his. "Is it to be me or your soldiers?" she asked.

"Always my Mama," he said. He blew her a kiss on the way out.

A young boy in a conical peasant hat and reed sandals ran up the tree-lined avenue to the Consulate and handed a message to the guards for Der Deutsche Junge, then stood with his hands out waiting for a tip. One of the guards threatened to kick him, and he fled. The guard took the message to

Peter's apartment. The cook took the message to Adam, who was enjoying a biology lesson with Dr Transier. Adam excused himself and ran to Käthe, who was chatting with Christina Schultz by the fountain.

"Ned wants to see us right away on the waterfront, Mama," exclaimed Adam.

"It looks as if you'd better go Käthe," advised Christina.

"We've forgotten the keys to the surgery" said Käthe.

"We're not going to the surgery, Mama," Adam said. "We're going to Ned's junk."

"Please, I can't," she said. "Those men are so frightening."

Adam continued to drag her towards the riverfront until they reached the foot of the gangplank to the junk. The Warlord's bodyguards were there and they leered at Käthe.

She shuddered. One of the men, who had a huge broadsword and a pigtail hanging down to his waist, offered her his hand. He led her up the gangplank to be confronted by Lin Hui, whom she recognised instantly.

"Go and talk to him, Mama," said Adam. The Warlord said mysteriously, "I cannot offer you protection inside the Consulate." Käthe felt sick to the stomach that news of the scandal had spread to the Waterfront.

Then Ned appeared. He looked Käthe up and down. "You seem worried Ma'am," he remarked, "I think you need a tonic."

Ned's latest mistress appeared and bowed to Käthe. She held out her hand and led her to Ned's cabin. She peered into the half-light and saw the smiling face of Jacob Meissner. They embraced.

"What are you wearing, Jacob?" she asked. He now wore the uniform of a regimental Chief Medical Officer of the Nationalist forces.

"I take up my post depending on the rains in the next few days," he said. "Chiang has secured a seat for me on a flight to Nanking on the Consulate's aircraft, I believe. Ironic, don't you think? Herr Wendt is of course in complete ignorance of the arrangement."

His final words were for Adam. "I have a future because of you, and I shall never forget you. Look after your mother."

Käthe and Adam walked along the riverfront, deeply saddened. Then Käthe said, "Look, how many of these people know us, Adam? Doesn't it make you feel proud?" They walked slowly past the wooden surgery, now securely locked,, and wondered if it would ever open again.

Manfred brought the reply from Berlin to Peter in defiance of Karl Wendt's instructions. "I am sorry, Your Excellency," he said. Peter could hardly believe the message. The signal curtly recalled Peter, not Wendt. He was instructed to return at the beginning of April and on that day, Wendt was to become Consul.

Peter let his hands fall to the desk. He looked hard at Manfred.

"I too sent a signal, Weiss. Is there no reply?" he asked anxiously.

"I was directly responsible for Herr Wendt, Your Excellency. I'm deeply sorry," replied Manfred.

"So my signal was not sent?" Manfred shook his head.

"You had better take this to your master. Otherwise I feel your stay here will not be very comfortable," said Peter.

He knew he must tell Käthe immediately. He rose from his chair and felt dizzy and his breathing became laboured. He quickly found Dr Transier at the surgery and Albert insisted on a full examination.

The driver Ludwig met Käthe and Adam at the Consulate gates. "Will you please go to the surgery immediately, Madam?" he asked. They passed Wendt seated by the fountains, dictating a letter to Christina. He smiled at Käthe with an amused tolerance. She turned her head away, but Adam stared fearlessly at him. Käthe knew Peter must be in difficulties. They found Albert Transier in the adjoining pharmacy preparing treatment for Peter and he invited them to go through.

Peter lay on the treatment couch breathing heavily. Käthe kissed him and held his hand and he tried to hoist himself up.

"Please do not exert yourself, Your Excellency," ordered Albert. He turned to Käthe. "I have discussed your husband's condition with him. It is my opinion that His Excellency should be relieved of his duties forthwith," he continued.

Peter took the doctor's arm. "I must speak with my family now, Transier," he said.

"Sir, I must insist, no more than five minutes," said Albert.

Peter told Käthe and Adam the bad news. Only then did she realise the extent of Wendt's callous and vengeful nature.

"What about your friends in the Foreign Ministry?" asked Käthe. Peter told them that Manfred Weiss had destroyed his signal on Wendt's orders.

"What does it mean, Papa?" asked a puzzled Adam. "It means we have to go home Adam and begin again. You will soon see Bruno and Theo and Klaus again and we will have a proper home. You will see your grandmother again and Greta and Helga," he added.

Käthe forced a smile for Adam's sake. She had begun to believe that wherever she went, Wendt's threats might turn into reality.

The prospect of returning to Germany was no longer the same for Adam. He hadn't heard from Bruno for some time. He worried about him because he knew his new friend had derived much of his courage from the new friendship.

He remembered Schuster's words, "Wait until we are in power", and wondered if Bruno would be safe. Adam thought of Uve Müller and especially of Rolf Schneider and their threats against Theo and Klaus.

"I shall fight my case at the Foreign Ministry," said Peter. "You know I have friends there Käthe. You too have your influential contacts, I believe," added Peter, thinking of her contacts with Goering.

"Of course we will be all right," she replied." If the worst comes to the worst, you can retire and run the estates. I can return to nursing, and Adam is very popular at school."

"We will be returning in the spring my love," she said stroking his hand. "You can rest and recuperate in the tea house and we will all make a fuss of you." She turned to Adam. "You and I will write a long letter home. Just think, your grandmother need not worry any longer. Bruno will be happy and you can row Helga on the lake," she added mischievously. Adam coloured. They left the surgery and began preparations to leave.

Adam retrieved his battered brown suitcase for the long journey home and lovingly packed his green silk martial clothes, Quiao Gu's recipes and the little book of Confucian thoughts Yuxiang gave him. He wrote a letter to the Si-Kiang family in Chinese characters, with the help of the cook. The letter was short and he wondered if the family would think him discourteous. Adam included his German address and enclosed a photo of himself and Peter and Käthe. "Bing Wen and Bing Wui will be all right," he wrote. He ended the letter on a sorrowful note. "I will never see you all again and I am very sorry, Adam."

Peter was forced to see Wendt to finalise matters. The new Consul leaned back in his chair, crossed his hands and spoke in an indulgent manner. "You have achieved great things here, von Saloman," he began. "I feel therefore you need not use the proper form of address to me."

Peter was infuriated, but bit his lip because of the need to finalise diplomatic matters. "How will you deal with our Chinese friends, Herr Wendt?" he asked.

"I have not concerned myself greatly with that issue," Wendt answered. "I'm sure it will be a simple matter. I don't think they care which German official sells them guns, do you?" Peter feared his good work would quickly unravel under Wendt's direction, but he said nothing.

Wendt called in Christina. "I think Herr von Saloman will wish to write a formal letter of resignation, which we will do together now," he said, enjoying the moment because he knew he was also hurting Christina, who was fond of Peter. Then Wendt asked her to wait in her office.

"Do you think you might apologise to me?" he said. "Oh, but I think that unlikely. You will please me if you clear your desk immediately. Please bring relevant documents here and give them to my secretary. I'll find something for you to do here."

Christina had already decided on another course of action. She followed Peter to his office. The flag had already been removed and placed outside Wendt's office. When the two of them had finished emptying the filing cabinets, she had a surprise for him.

"Excuse me, Your Excellency," she began.

"Yes Christina?" Peter answered.

"I have decided to resign and will return to Germany on the *Derfligger* with you sir, and I would like to remain in your service in whatever capacity you think fit." She hesitated and added, "My inside knowledge might be of use to you in the future. Perhaps you will need help when you return to Germany."

"I am grateful for all your help, Fräulein and I'm touched by your loyalty. I will do everything in my power for you," he said.

As the *Derfligger* approached Canton, the National Socialists were burning books in Germany. Wendt would have preferred to see the family leave quietly, but there was a conspiracy on the waterfront to see that it would not be so. Everyone who had used the surgery joined the quiet throng of people by the landing jetty, except for some who thought it better to keep out of sight, concealed amongst the wooden tenements.

Wendt announced that the official car would not be available to take either the family or their belongings to the riverfront. Peter, Adam and Albert Transier stacked the boxes and cases onto trolleys. Even the servants had been forbidden to help. The three of them stood on the step overlooking the quadrangle. The only people they could see were Heidi Schepke and her friends seated round the fountains.

Adam ran back up the stairs to his room to take a last look at where his soldiers had stood. Käthe had no such feelings about the Consulate surgery. "Adam, quickly" she called, "We must go."

When they reached the apartment entrance the family saw a moving sight. One by one the doors of the offices opened and the staff gathered outside Manfred Weiss' office. He appeared in uniform and led them towards the piles of luggage. He assigned cases to each of them and approached Peter and saluted.

"If necessary Your Excellency, we will carry your belongings to the waterfront," said Manfred. Adam grinned and returned the salute. Then Wendt appeared and strode up to the volunteers. "This is not in order," he said weakly.

"There is work to be done." Elizabeth replied. "We are doing the decent thing, Herr Wendt, would you care to join us?" He was silent and joined his supporters by the fountains.

The volunteers pushed the trolleys, helped by Adam, to the gates. The family's Chinese cook insisted on carrying Peter's biggest case by hand, but he collapsed sweating at the gates. Wendt had not finished. He appeared holding the keys and announced that anyone except the family who went through the gates would be locked out.

Peter, Adam, Manfred and Albert Transier carried the boxes and cases through the gates. "I presume we will be an exception to your order, Herr Wendt," said Manfred. Wendt nodded. There was no sign of Christina Schultz. She appeared at the gates with her belongings, and Wendt was taken by surprise.

"My resignation is on your desk Herr Wendt," she said defiantly.

He was taken aback. "You are leaving the service, Fräulein Schultz?" he asked sounding genuinely disappointed.

Christina enjoyed the slight she had administered and had another surprise. She had made a call to the airfield without Wendt's permission and the news of the family's departure had spread. A strange cavalcade approached the gates from Canton, heralded by the roar of two motorcycle engines. They were ridden by Willi Novka and Rudolf Schlemm and were followed by a limousine flying the flag of a yellow snake on the bonnet, driven by one of Lin Hui's bodyguards. Novka and Schlemm jumped down from their motorcycles. They both wore their uniforms from the Western Front.

"Good afternoon Your Excellency," said Novka. "One sober luggage detail reporting for duty." Peter was overcome and thanked them.

Each of the motorcycles was tethered to a two-wheeled cart. Peter helped the two mechanics pile the array of cases onto the transport. Meanwhile Lin Hui's bodyguard stood silently holding a rear passenger door open in the limousine, and Adam clasped hands with him. Peter was amazed. He had had no idea of the extent of his son's involvement with the people of the Pearl River.

"My master awaits you all on the waterfront," said the bodyguard. He invited Christina to sit by him in the front seat.

Some of the crowd had run from the waterfront to watch the family's progress. The car was driven as if it were a royal procession. People peered into the windows so that Käthe might recognise them.

The crowd at the jetty parted to allow the car through and it stopped inches from the drop to the water. At the front of the surging mass was the lady with three children, who tried to touch Käthe as if she had magical powers.

Suddenly the crowd went fearful and quiet. It parted to allow Huang Lin Hui and two bodyguards through. He acknowledged Peter and Käthe and waved his long, gnarled fingers in Adam's direction. Adam bowed and Lin Hui presented him to the people.

"I give you Der Deutsche Junge," he said. He unstrapped his broadsword and presented it to Adam. Then he melted away into the crowd with his bodyguards and Adam stood open-mouthed.

That was a great honour young man," said Ned as he appeared out of the crowd with his crew. "Well maybe this is the end of the line."

His handshake with Adam was like a trial of strength. "How do you expect me to carry on without seeing your mother again?" Ned asked, turning his attention to Käthe.

"Oh my Ned, we will see you again, I am sure," she said kissing him on the cheek.

"I should hope so madam," he replied. "I have a sore back just now." He smiled broadly. Then he too looked grave.

"Are the rumours true about that man and you?" he whispered. Käthe hardly dare reply because she had felt so degraded.

"I have some friends who can fix him" said Ned. Peter watched, completely bemused.

"Father," said Adam. "Meet Mr Ned Travis."

"Sir, it is a real pleasure," said Ned, "but I feel I may have been a thorn in your flesh for some time."

They shook hands. "You have been a worthy opponent, Mr Travis," replied Peter.

"I would prefer that we part on the best terms possible," said Ned. He produced a leather wallet stuffed with American dollars. It was done openly as a gesture of repentance. "You have my permission to buy something expensive with it for your beautiful wife and maybe restore the rest to the German Treasury when you return, sir," suggested the American. He gave it to Käthe, who placed it in her handbag.

"I have business to conclude," said Ned. "It's been a real pleasure."

He disappeared in the direction of the junk's mooring and Adam was deeply saddened at the departure of yet another friend. Ned turned, grinned at Adam and punched the sky with his fist.

The men concealed in the tenements watched Ned's donation through a pair of binoculars from the waterfront tenement. The information was passed not to Manfred Weiss, but to Karl Wendt, who immediately saw it had potential.

Captain Fischer stood on the bow of the *Derfligger*'s pinnace as it approached the jetty. Peter stared at the swastika flag on the stern and wondered how the captain and Wendt could serve under the same emblem.

Captain Fischer requested Peter to board as soon as possible. Lighters from the wharf were already on their way to the ship to unload its latest cargo. The light would soon fail and he wanted the option to stand out to sea before darkness fell. The captain helped them all onto the pinnace personally, except for Adam, who leaped from half way down the ladder.

The captain paid special attention to the ladies, but especially to Christina

Schultz. "Cast off," he called and the boat turned towards the ship half a kilometre away. Adam stood in the stern waving at the crowd, tears rolling down his face. Käthe joined him.

Captain Fischer decided not to risk the narrow passage in the river until the morning. Adam refused to leave the ship's rail and watched the river as the light faded and the sun dipped below the horizon. He watched the lights of the city and the flashes of lightning in the hills. The cormorants and the cranes on the sandbanks dipped their heads and settled down for the night.

Then Adam heard the noise of a motor boat in the distance. It was the steady chug of an old marine engine. In the failing light he could just see the outline of the bow and a column of blue smoke and knew it was Guang Csai's old ferryboat. It was Illuminated by lanterns in the stern, and Guang Csai cut the engine.

The old man had not come alone. Standing in the waist were Yuxiang and Quiao-Gu, dressed in elegant blue cheongsams. The orange surface of the river was tinged by the light from the lanterns of ten fishing boats. Guang Csai had towed them all.

Each carried a member of a family from the Si-Kiang village. The occupants of the boats waited silently for the family von Saloman to gather at the port rail. Peter and Käthe stood behind Adam. Yuxiang and his followers had no intention of meeting for further goodbyes; it would be enough to stand off at a distance and acknowledge each other.

Adam drew his parents to the rails and Käthe and Peter waved and bowed. Huang and Quiao-Gu smiled. The missing pieces of the story had been provided.

Guang Csai started his engine and the boat turned away into the gathering darkness. Adam waved and waved until the boats and their passengers had vanished, as if it had been a dream. He choked back tears. "That was for all of us," he said.

Peter stroked his chin. "I had no idea how much the people of the river meant to you Adam, until now. I will do everything in my power to return," he promised.

He would never be able to fulfil that promise, but the people of Canton and the Si-Kiang had given Adam a priceless gift, which would one day save his life.

Chapter 12

The Return

As the *Derfligger* left the China Sea, Peter thought of his new responsibilities in Berlin. He had not been able to dismiss the image of his father staring helplessly at Die Schwanen as it slowly decayed. He knew Gustav had possessed no financial acumen and Frieda only a little. Peter suspected that they had handed the job of collecting rents and maintaining tenant farms to others. He had seen the sometimes offhand and often violent practice of corruption in China, and was deeply worried.

Peter had walked away from the problem under the cloak of responsibility to his mission in the East. Now that was gone and his father was dead.

As the ship ploughed through the Mediterranean towards the storms of the Bay of Biscay, Peter wondered about his wife's future. Käthe had become quiet and withdrawn. Peter had never questioned his Catholic faith and he prayed nightly for his wife's recovery.

Peter didn't understand what had happened to Käthe and believed the effects of the attack were temporary. He felt no resentment towards her, as she showed little sign of recovery. He believed, naively, he had the solution. He was the man of the house and he would alter the march of events, but there were moments when he was desperate for the advice of Jacob Meissner.

Now Peter had to get used to the sight of the back of Käthe's head in bed. Her eyes were riveted open and her thoughts were fixed on the most terrible man she had met.

She felt Peter tap her on the shoulder and turned towards him.

"I think you were right Käthe. It would be good for Adam to have a brother or a sister" said Peter. He imagined that his apparent change of heart would be enough. He was shocked and upset to see the fearful, puzzled look on Käthe's face. She said nothing and turned away.

"Käthe, please tell me what is the matter. Look – I know I should have said that a long time ago," he said. She remained silent and stared at the cabin wall. Peter sighed heavily and turned away himself. A few minutes later Käthe got out of bed, threw a few cushions on the cabin floor and went to sleep there. It was another cry for help.

The ship began to pitch and yaw and Käthe was thrown against the side of the cabin. The blow reopened her old head wound. Peter got out of bed, wrapped a blanket round his wife and held her as she sobbed.

The storms grew worse as dawn approached and Käthe panicked and rushed out of the cabin, still wearing a nightdress. "Adam, my darling!" she called into the howling wind. "Where are you?" Peter followed her and threw a blanket round her shoulders. They could just see Adam clinging onto the starboard rail. "It isn't as bad as the storm in the Pearl," he said. They dragged him into their cabin. They were all cold and dripping wet.

"What storm was that Adam?" Peter asked. Adam coloured and told them about the typhoon. At that moment Peter thanked Gustav even less for his influence on Adam.

At last the storms died and the ship entered the English Channel. Christina joined the family leaning on the starboard rail, watching the French shore. "Why don't you write your nursing memoirs?" suggested Christina. "Look how interested Dr Meissner was in your early work."

That was when Käthe discovered new life. She obtained pens and paper from the ship's purser and set to work. To Peter's relief, she welcomed his help on the project. Adam wrote down his thoughts on the riverfront surgery, with several omissions of details he thought would worry his parents.

Käthe began to improve and gained weight, but the ship's doctor watched Peter carefully. His old symptoms were returning, but he put on a brave face and refused to accept treatment.

Brisk winds drove the clouds across the mouth of the Elbe, and the sun shone.

Then the wind died completely, and the *Derfligger*'s progress seemed effortless. The four passengers lined the rails, surveying the grey German coast. The steward appeared with hot coffee for the last time, and on his silver tray was a note addressed to Christina. She thanked him and read the note. "Is there a reply, Madam?" he asked. "No written reply," she answered. "Just tell him yes." The steward smiled and left. Peter and Käthe though it was none of their business, but Käthe couldn't resist a mild enquiry. "Not just for the voyage Christina?" she asked quietly. Adam strained his ears for the reply. "Oh no," she replied.

The International Bridge loomed, and just beyond was the quayside of the Hamburg-East Asia Line. A pilot boat appeared and the *Derfligger* blew its foghorn. The chains were paid out of the bow and stern and the ship came to rest. The family were home.

The quayside swarmed with police and brown-shirted troopers, some of them armed. The passengers' luggage was piled high on the quayside and the inspections began. Dockside workers wheeled a covered companionway up to the side of the ship and Captain Fischer paid his respects to his passengers. Christina lingered for a while. The captain removed his peaked cap and kissed her on the cheek.

Customs officers in new uniforms waited at the foot of the companionway. "Your papers please," said one of them curtly to Peter. He relaxed when he saw the official stamps. "Welcome back to Germany, Herr von Saloman," he said. His attention turned to Adam, who was the last to step onto the quayside carrying his suitcase and the Warlord's sword. The Customs Officer apologised to Peter. "I am sorry Your Excellency. We have orders to search all small items of luggage. Please open your case young man."

Adam opened the case and out fell the two Uhlan Lancers, the recipes and the green silk trouser suit. A small drawstring purse fell out and revealed a silver ingot, the main currency of the Pearl River.

"You will understand this is classed as bullion," said the officer. Peter thought this was bureaucracy gone mad, but explained politely, "These things are all gifts from one of our most important allies in China."

The officer apologised and Adam's belongings were restored to his suitcase. The other customs officer didn't give up so easily. "This is irregular," he said, picking up the sword. "Why are you carrying this, young man?"

Adam drew himself up to his full height, watched by a proud Käthe who nudged Peter. "It was given to me by the Warlord of Canton," said Adam officiously. "It will help me to become an officer in our infantry." The Customs Officer became deferential. "Well done young man," he said.

"Weren't you proud of him?" Käthe whispered to Peter, who admitted he was.

Peter attempted to lift a small case onto a luggage trolley and Käthe saw him struggling for breath. "I have it," said Adam. They left the customs hall and looked for Kurt and Lisa Holman. They were standing by a bicycle rail in front of the taxi ranks. Käthe clung to them both in floods of tears. She didn't want to let go. Kurt noticed her desperation and wondered at the reason. Lisa looked at Peter half expecting an explanation. He shook his head as if it was a forbidden topic.

Käthe's parents turned to Adam. They remembered his distant behaviour which was the biggest source of worry for them at the reunion. "Are you really our thirteen year old grandson?" asked Lisa. Adam couldn't think of life without a grandfather. He had decided to change. He broke into a grin and embraced his grandparents. "I want to know about Michael the street clown," he said to them. Their faces darkened and they rapidly changed the subject. "More later," said Kurt. He waved towards a taxi rank and a taxi pulled into a small layby. Peter tried to lift the cases. "Grandpapa and I will do that," said Adam.

Kurt paid the driver and set off with Lisa to their apartment in the old town on their bicycles. The ship had berthed during the lunch hour and the old city, the Altona, was busy. Kurt and Lisa arrived at their apartment before the taxi. The driver volunteered to help carry the luggage up three flights of stairs. "You sir, will stand and watch," he said to Peter.

He was interrupted by the sound of jackbooted feet as two Brownshirts stood on the steps leading to the entrance. Another demanded to see the newcomer's papers. Peter glanced upwards. swastika banners protruded from window after window and he wondered why they had been stopped. The man handed Peter's and his family's papers back, muttering "Not a healthy place to be staying Herr von Saloman." The three men left.

"What does he mean?" asked Peter. Kurt shook his head.

As soon as they walked through the heavy oak door of the Holman apartment, Kurt became deferential to Lisa. He was a docks railway supervisor, Lisa a faithful Hausfrau.

Käthe produced their gift from China, a set of paintings of the Pearl River Käthe had bought at the Qing Ping market. The couple were delighted that this aristocratic couple had remembered them at all. Lisa nudged Kurt and cleared his throat. "Will you stay with us for a few days?" he asked anxiously.

Peter was preoccupied by the need to fight his case, but he put Käthe's needs first. "Of course we will Herr Holman," answered Peter. For the rest of the stay the von Salomans were allowed to do nothing for themselves.

Hardly had Lisa time to serve coffee and homemade cakes when there was a knock at the door. It was Lotte and Hans Meurer from next door and they had heard about the aristocratic relatives. "Is everything all right Lisa?" asked Lotte, peering over Lisa's shoulder. They were joined by other neighbours, who were invited in. "Should I bring biscuits?" asked Lotte.

Peter and Käthe were besieged. A little grey-haired lady noted for her strong opinions said to Käthe, "You've done well for yourself." Adam thought all this hilarious and introduced himself to everyone.

"Where's Uncle Michael?" asked Käthe. "He was a street juggler, Adam. Remember I told you to ask."

When the buzz of conversation died, Lotte and Hans were the first to make an excuse to leave. The others followed. "What's the matter, Mutti?" asked Käthe. Kurt sighed. "Michael Wolfram was not just a street juggler. He was also very active in the local Communist Party," he explained. Adam's ears pricked up. "They came for him three weeks ago. We haven't heard anything since," said Kurt.

"Can't you make enquiries, Papa?" asked Käthe naively.

"That is too dangerous, my love," answered Kurt. To enquire would be to associate with him. "Your father was a member of the Social Democrats, Käthe," added Lisa. "The National Socialists think they're as bad as the Communists."

"Look how even the mention of Michael's name broke up our meeting," said Kurt. "We have become a nation of cowards and informers, I am ashamed to say."

Adam was quite happy to sleep on the leather sofa and he noticed that all the doors seemed to close by eight o'clock. A silence fell over the apartment block and in the streets outside, but it didn't worry him. He was used to the claustrophobic world of the Consulate.

He couldn't sleep, wondering what waited for him in Berlin. He had never forgotten Bruno. He drew the curtains and gazed into the half lit streets below him. A solitary car was approaching slowly with no lights. Adam strained to look downwards as it stopped outside the apartment block. Three men got out, their faces obscured by the poor streetlights and the wide brims of their hats. They closed the car doors as quietly as they could. One of them looked upwards and saw Adam, who stared back. The three men disappeared as they entered the building.

Kurt came into the room. "Come away from the window," he said quietly and urgently. He pulled Adam's arm and they stood in the centre of the room. He saw beads of sweat on Kurt's forehead as the footsteps came nearer and Adam felt Kurt's hands tighten on his arm.

The three men passed the apartment and ascended to the next floor. Kurt breathed a sigh of relief. There was a loud, aggressive knock on a door, followed by threats and shouting. It sounded as if someone was being dragged down the stairs.

Adam darted to the window and pressed himself against the wall as one of the men looked upwards again. Adam could just see the glint of metal on the fist of one of the police as it crashed down on the prisoner's neck. The half-conscious man was bundled into the back of the car and driven off.

Before breakfast, Adam ran to the bakery for fresh rolls. While he was away Kurt attempted an explanation of the night's events to Peter and Käthe. "They are new people probably on the run," he guessed.

"They did seem a strange couple," said Lisa.

Both behaved as if the new couple were devoid of rights simply because they were strangers, almost making excuses for the police. Käthe wanted to challenge her parents. She knew her father was intelligent but had failed to rise above his present post because he was too compliant. She blamed her mother's supervision of his every move. A discouraging look from Peter stopped her. Käthe clenched her fists and looked away. On his return, Adam sat by the window pretending not to listen as a gesture to his grandparents.

There was a long silence and Peter decided to invite Adam to describe his experiences on the Pearl River. The atmosphere brightened as Adam described the Si-Kiang house and its people. Instinctively he spent some time describing the poor of Si-Kiang, and Lisa was touched. They agreed to talk about the riverside surgery the following evening. Safety lay in the avoidance of politics.

When the family left for Berlin, there was no official car or internal flight this time. Peter made light of it, but Käthe was worried. She began to look for other signs suggesting Peter was out of favour. She didn't have to wait long.

They had used an apartment belonging to the Foreign Ministry in the same building as the apartment belonging to Renate Grabowsky, and this was to be the von Salomans' last visit to it. Käthe had stored clothes, jewellery and a valuable tea service there. The taxi driver agreed to wait for them without extra charge. When Käthe and Peter greeted the concierge, he seemed anxious. Peter's key didn't fit the lock and the concierge was very apologetic. "Herr von Saloman," he began. "I must tell you the locks have been changed. It seems the apartment may be sold off in these hard times. I have your property in my office, if you would follow me."

Everything had been carefully packaged, and the planned sale of the apartment seemed plausible. Peter was not affected in the least, but Käthe's recent state of mind made her a little paranoid. She had noticed Peter's symptoms returning.

The taxi emerged from Wilmersdorf onto the Avus, which joined the Grünewald forest further south. It was the beginning of the weekend and already Berliners were heading into the forest. The von Salomans loved the clear air and the green wall of trees which concealed their family home.

They became silent before the car turned off the Avus, knowing there would be one less in the welcoming committee. The house shone in the sunlight but there were further signs of decay. Trees had lost their shape and flowerbeds encroached on lawns. Poor old Stephan could not cope. He hobbled up to the car to open the doors and help unload.

Käthe, Peter and Adam now faced the Matriarch of Die Schwanen. Frieda was magnificent in a steel blue dress with her usual two strings of pearls. There was the suggestion of a smile on her face as she stood with her hands crossed. She may have just lost her devoted husband, but she intended that everyone around her should derive strength from this survivor of the Imperial era.

Even the two dachshunds were made to sit still until Frieda gave permission for displays of affection. She broke protocol and advanced down the steps and her eyes misted as she embraced Peter. She turned to Käthe, the saviour of her son in a Berlin military hospital, but sensed something was wrong as they embraced.

Then it was Adam's turn. They eyed each other, nearly identical in profile, as if they were heads of state. Their self-possession dissolved and they embraced. Old Stephan scuttled back to his domain in the gardens while Frieda began the ritual welcome in the tea house.

The mistress of the house sensed that Käthe and Peter's early return meant there was something wrong. She didn't press them and allowed them to tell her about all the more innocuous details. All the time, they moved closer and closer to the truth. Frieda knew this was not the same Käthe she had introduced to her Berlin friends.

Adam heard his father mention 'differences' with a colleague in China and saw lines appear on his mother's face. He didn't want to hear any more and excused himself.

He walked on the shingle beach and inspected the rotting rowing boat. When he looked up at the side window of the house, he saw Helga watching him. She smiled and he gave her a little wave. Seconds later, she appeared.

"Have you heard from Bruno?" he asked.

"Oh yes," replied Helga. "Madam invited Bruno and Frau Grabowsky to the house, after you left. They have been here three times." She paused to watch the effect on Adam. "Madam gave Bruno permission to take me out in the rowing boat and we had a good time," she said, meaning every word to strike home. It didn't have the required effect on Adam, who was far from consumed with jealousy. He resumed his life in Germany as if the first encounter on the shingle beach had never taken place.

"Bruno hasn't been for a long time," she said coyly, looking at the boat.

"We will have to repair it," said Adam.

"Are you still in the League of German Maidens?"

"Certainly," answered Helga. "Why? Don't you approve?"

The servant girl thought she had her boss on the defensive. "I don't like those people," said Adam. Helga had been put in her place, but she never gave up hope.

"Helga," called out Greta from the house. The awkward conversation was at an end. He moved on to what he saw as greater things, but Helga never lost her passion for him.

Peter and Käthe chose the moment carefully to explain their early return from China. Peter told his mother the story, or as much as he knew of it. Käthe wrung her hands. Frieda walked over to her daughter-in-law and embraced her warmly. "You must not feel diminished in the least by this monster," she advised. "This house and its people will always be your refuge." She kissed Käthe and her daughter–in-law sobbed in sheer gratitude. She would never have to tell either Peter or Frieda the real story unless Wendt carried out his threats.

"Shall we stay away from the Berlin scene for the moment?" asked Frieda.

"I think so," replied Käthe. Peter muttered approval and Käthe said she would like to return to nursing.

The weight of guilt on her shoulders was growing heavier and heavier, and she lived in daily fear of discovery. All she could to relieve the feeling was devote herself to her husband's happiness.

The next day a letter fell through the letterbox suggesting strongly that Adam return to school as soon as possible. It was signed not by Dr Stiebert but Dr Rolf Schaub, who, it appeared, had replaced him. It invited Peter and Käthe to accompany Adam on his first day and was couched in terms Dr Stiebert would have considered rude. The letter almost suggested that Adam was a truant. Peter was deeply offended, but had calmed down by the following Monday when Adam was to return to school.

Peter revived the Buick, with Stephan's help, and the family arrived at school at eight o'clock. Everything seemed normal until they reached the Entrance Hall. They were confronted with a huge poster which shouted at the students. They must redouble their efforts at athletics because Germany had been selected to host the Olympic Games, it said. A young pupil strode purposefully across the hall and nearly bumped into Käthe. He apologised profusely, but then several other pupils nearly did the same. It seemed the pace of life in the school was more frantic.

Their guide knocked at the Principal's door. Dr Schaub abruptly opened it and invited the trio to take a seat. He was in his early forties, tall and fair haired, and he radiated energy and enthusiasm. Käthe had misgivings when she saw the Nazi party badge on his lapel. Dominating the room was a large portrait of Adolf Hitler on the wall behind the desk. In front of Schaub was Adam's school record.

Peter handed the Principal the offending letter, for which he apologised, explaining that there was a national drive to get all young people of school age to attend. "We hope for great things from you von Saloman," he said to Adam. "Herr Rust speaks very highly of you."

He noticed the textbooks on Adam's knee and asked to see them. He quickly scanned the titles without opening them. "Professor Rohrman and Dr Diercks gave me the books to study at home," said Adam helpfully.

"Ah," continued Schaub. "Dr Diercks has been retired and I am sorry to say that Rohrman was guilty of disloyalty and has been dismissed."

Adam remembered that the science teacher had commended the efforts of the Gutman twins to the rest of the class. Perhaps that was classed as 'disloyalty.'

"This science textbook is no longer permitted," continued Schaub. "It is too sympathetic towards the so-called achievements of Jewish science." Before Käthe and Peter had said anything further, Schaub said. "It was nice to meet you both. The guide will conduct you back to your car." He pressed a bell on his desk and the interview was over. The Principal looked at his watch. "Follow me von Saloman. It is nearly eight thirty and I must conduct the daily briefing," he announced.

Peter and Käthe were abandoned in the office. The secretary took pity on them and directed them to the car park. Adam was marched to the Assembly Hall and told to stand at the rear with senior boys. Schaub mounted the stage and surveyed the perfectly-ordered ranks. He concluded his brief order of the day.

"You must all be successful," he demanded, "Because you are Germans."

Adam's class had left the Assembly Hall and were already standing behind their seats in the Science Laboratory when Adam arrived. The new science teacher, Professor Kreisler, demanded silence as he reintroduced Adam. "Be seated," he ordered. There was a rattle of chairs and desks. Adam felt very exposed and he looked around quickly for Bruno.

CHAPTER TWELVE

Staring at him malevolently were Berndt Schuster and his friends, all in Hitler Youth uniform. Uve Müller looked at two empty seats and then at Adam. They had been occupied by Klaus and Theo Gutman. Behind their old seats was a poster proclaiming "Jewish Science has poisoned the German people."

Just before he sat down Adam caught sight of Bruno in the far right-hand corner close to Schuster's group. He was staring out of the window. Adam thought he saw bruises on Bruno's face. He gave no hint of recognition of Adam, who drew the obvious conclusion that their friendship was at an end. He felt excluded, and the only solution seemed to be to immerse himself in the lesson. Within half an hour, during which time Adam hardly lifted his head, a bell rang and the class spilled out into the corridor. Adam waited hopefully, but Bruno dawdled at the rear.

Berndt Schuster backtracked and jostled Adam. His friends joined him.

"Leave him alone," said Armin Schurmann.

"Mind your own business," said another Hitler Youth Adam didn't know. This boy, Ulrich Semmering, was to prove a thorn in Adam's flesh. "Von Saloman is ours now," he smirked. Adam was aware of Rolf Schneider's malevolent gaze.

The Principal called for the boys to move on and make their way quietly to the next lesson. "We'll see you in the Dining Hall," threatened Semmering.

Armin Schurmann sat with Adam in the Dining Hall. He felt much better until Semmering and Schneider told Armin to go away, which he did sheepishly. The two boys sat down on either side of Adam. He was finding it hard to obey Yuxiang's instructions.

Then Semmering knocked Adam's soup onto the floor and Schneider called to the supervisor. "Von Saloman wishes to clear up a mess. Please bring a mop and bucket," he said. But the two boys made it impossible for Adam to clear up. "More water please," shouted Semmering as he kicked over the mop bucket. The two boys basked in the new power they enjoyed.

"Von Saloman will not clear up the mess. You will Semmering, and Schneider," said a voice sharply and clearly. The athletics teacher, Alfred Rust, and several other boys had appeared to help, among them Armin Schurmann and Dieter Harro. Dieter glared at Semmering and Schneider. He shook Adam's hand. "It's good to see you again," he said. "We shall have a good contest again this year." Dieter was too well respected to be a target.

Alfred Rust appeared with bread and soup. "Get this down you, von Saloman. Then you can start thinking about getting in shape for this year's race," he said cheerfully.

Semmering and Schneider slunk off bearing buckets and mops and Rolf Schneider gave Adam a withering look as he left. The rest crowded round Adam to watch him finish his lunch. "You've put weight on," said Dieter. The rest laughed.

The wolves had gathered. This time they had been thwarted, but they were patient and believed their time would come. Noticeably absent from the dining room were Berndt Schuster and Bruno. Dieter Harro wore the uniform of the Hitler Youth.

The new History teacher welcomed Adam and presented him with a copy of Hitler's biography as if it were a school prize. He had a kindly face but tried to adopt a military bearing. He began the lesson in the worst way possible for Adam. "What can you tell us of the Führer's life in the German Army from 1914 to 1918?" he asked the new boy, who admitted he knew nothing. Schuster and his friends laughed mercilessly. "Silence," ordered the teacher.

Bruno shot a disapproving glance their way and they replied with threatening glances. He continued to stare out of the window. The teacher asked to see Adam after the lesson. "You will have noticed changes in the school, von Saloman," he began. But Adam interrupted. "Where are my friends Theo and Klaus Gutman?" he asked.

"Let me explain," began Herr Leitgen in an indulgent, fatherly manner. "You have returned to witness the rebirth of the Fatherland. Germany has been given back to us and we must fight to keep it. Theo and Klaus cannot help who they are, but it is better for our folk community that they be educated with other Jews. I'm sure they are all right," he explained. He smiled like a kindly old man. "I know this must be hard for you, but you must learn to face the future."

He struck a chord with Adam. "I have seen your record von Saloman and you bear a great responsibility. You are from a distinguished family and the Führer looks to young men like you for leadership." He allowed his words to sink in. "What is your chosen career?" asked Herr Leitgen.

"To follow my father and grandfather into the infantry and serve in an elite unit," answered Adam proudly.

"Well done von Saloman, well done," said Herr Leitgen enthusiastically. "But there is something you must know. Membership of the Hitler Youth is now required for career soldiers." He smiled. "They're not all like Schuster and his friends you know." He paused once more thoughtfully. "You need a good friend I think. I suggest you talk with Grabowsky. He's very intelligent."

Adam thanked the teacher and thought what an ironic suggestion that was because for the moment, friendship was the issue, not Adam's career. He was beginning to think he should make friends with Dieter Harro and Armin Schurmann and treat Bruno as a lost cause. He consoled himself by thinking that Bruno wasn't worthy of his friendship, because he hadn't shown any courage, and his wearing of that uniform was unforgiveable.

Peter waited for Adam, which was fortunate. Schuster and his friends also waited, and they were no longer afraid of what Adam might do. Although he was the biggest and most prominent of the hostile group, Schuster always seemed to hang back. The burden of hatred seemed to fall on Uve Müller, Rolf Schneider and Ulrich Semmering.

Peter sensed the threat. "Who are these boys?" he asked.

"Not friends of mine," mumbled Adam in reply, determined his father would fight none of his battles.

"Where's Bruno? Has he left school?" asked Peter.

"I suppose he's with them," answered Adam.

"And Theo and Klaus?"

"They've been sent away. Just like Uncle Jacob Papa," said Adam almost tearfully.

They drove home in silence. Adam's former triumphs in school now seemed as nothing.

The next two days were bearable for Adam with the support of Dieter and Armin, and Alfred Rust appeared whenever trouble threatened. Still Bruno said nothing and Adam had had enough. He would tell his father that the friendship was officially at an end. He waited for the inevitable clash with Schuster and his friends. Dieter Harro and Armin escorted Adam to the Buick and Peter was pleased to meet Armin and see Dieter again. The wolves watched them.

As Peter drove onto the Kurfürstendamm it was clear that there was a delay ahead. Several policemen slowed the traffic as a detachment of Brownshirts crossed the road. They were followed by a large squad of Hitler Youth carrying black ebony flags, and Adam wound down the windows to get a better look.

"Those two boys would make good friends," suggested Peter. Adam didn't answer as he stared at the military precision of the marchers. The procession passed and Peter impatiently tapped the hub of the steering wheel, casting several glances into the rear view mirror. One of the policemen waved Peter on. He looked again in the rear view mirror as the car moved off.

About two hundred metres behind the car was a youthful figure wearing Hitler Youth uniform, furiously pedalling a bicycle. The car drew away from the cyclist, who redoubled his efforts. The car slowed down once more for traffic signals. The cyclist nearly caught up. Peter looked hard into the mirror and smiled to himself. It was Bruno. Peter pretended to be worried.

"Don't look back Adam, we're being followed," said Peter. "He's wearing a party uniform." Peter kept a straight face as he turned the car into the Avus. He drove as slowly as he could, to the annoyance of other motorists. Peter turned into the forest and then into the access road to Die Schwanen. He stopped at the iron gates. At the same time, Bruno lost control of his bicycle and crashed into the bushes. Adam grinned and leapt out of the car. Bruno hauled himself out of the hedge, limping.

"How's your leg?" asked Adam. "Not as bad as yours was," said Bruno. They stood staring at each other.

"Are we still friends?" asked Bruno. He drew himself up to his full height. He was now nearly as tall as Adam. He didn't stand as erect and square as Adam and his shoulders were narrower and slightly stooping, but the old look was still there, gentle permanent mockery. He tried to look contrite, which made Adam point at him and laugh. "Not with that ridiculous look on your face we're not!" answered Adam. They shook hands furiously.

"You look terrible," said Bruno. "Have you had a bad time at school?"

"Dreadful," answered Adam. "Would you like a tow?" He looked at the battered cycle. Peter improvised a repair by battering the front wheel with a large stone, then shook hands with Bruno. "I'll walk the rest of the way," answered Bruno. They both walked, preceded by Peter driving very slowly and tooting the horn to alert the house.

Helga was the first to appear. She looked behind her to make sure no one else was there and ran up to the two boys. First, she curtsied to Adam not taking her eyes off his. Then she turned, and before anyone else came out of the house, she ran up to Bruno and kissed him on both cheeks. Greta behaved as if Helga had done this before, but asked Helga to apologise to Adam for such a public display. Adam wondered how he might ask Bruno how and when he had made such progress.

Käthe appeared, wearing a wide-brimmed straw hat, an apron and a pair of gardening gloves. Stephan was right behind her carrying a choice of garden tools, stacked up in a wheelbarrow. When Käthe saw Bruno, she was overjoyed and ran up to him, kissing him on both cheeks. Adam noticed he wasn't in the least embarrassed. Frieda's sunhat was just visible over the rails of the tea-house.

Käthe grasped Bruno's hands. "If you ever fall out again, you will telephone me with an explanation. If you don't," she warned, "I'll set these dogs on you." By now they were making a fuss of Bruno and pretending to bark. "We'll see you both in half an hour," said Käthe.

The two friends walked along the shingle beach and Bruno patted the old rowing boat. He became serious. "I didn't write because I thought you'd never come back." he explained. Adam understood but then said, "How did you get this?" pointing to the bruise on his face, "and that?" pointing to the uniform.

"We've no choice but to join. If you want a career you have to do it," he said grimly. "You'd love it," he said, forcing a smile. "We're always playing soldiers, but there are some things I can't stand." He pointed to the bruise. "I got it from Schuster in a boxing match at camp."

Adam asked tentatively, "Can we still be friends if I don't join?"

"I suppose so," said a disappointed Bruno.

They walked for a few minutes in silence. Bruno knew what was coming. "Do you think Theo and Klaus are all right?" asked Adam.

"I just don't know," answered Bruno, "I haven't heard from them for a long time. It's too dangerous to ask. You don't know how bad Schneider is."

Herr Leitgen and Bruno had planted a seed, and that evening Peter asked Adam what he thought of the Hitler Youth. He had noticed the respected Dieter Harro in uniform and believed Adam should consider joining. To Peter's surprise Adam trotted out details of Hitler's early life. He had been doing some homework.

To Peter's dismay, Käthe left his bed once more and spent more and more time in the garden, as if she were retired. Frieda tried to persuade her to revisit the Berlin social haunts once more, but Käthe said she was not quite ready. She ached for the day Adam would hold her and kiss her again, and Peter wondered if his wife was capable of resuming a nursing career.

He found a new diversion from scrutinising the estates accounts. He and Stephan tinkered with the Buick. Frieda was annoyed by the constant engine revving at the rear of the house and decided to intervene. She stepped through the front door with Greta in hot pursuit, but her mission was interrupted.

"Madam," called out Greta holding the internal telephone. "There is someone at the gates called Gunther Graf who demands to be allowed in."

"Tell him to make an appointment, Greta," retorted Frieda. "I have an important matter to deal with here. This house and its grounds are beginning to sound like a racing track."

Greta caught up with Frieda as she approached the grimy couple at the car. "Madam," said Greta. "He says he's here by the authority of the National Socialist Party."

Frieda forgot her mission. "Peter," she called above the noise. "You are required at the front of the house. We have a visitor."

Before Greta reached the phone, they heard the sound of drums. A detachment of Hitler Youth emerged from the trees in perfect order, headed by an overweight man in his early forties. "Halt," he ordered, as the formation reached the front steps.

Adam had been watching from an upstairs window. He dashed down the steps carrying his copy of Hitler's biography.

The boys were in two columns. The boy at the head of each carried a black flag bearing the name of his unit in gold lettering. A boy at the rear carried a black eagle holding a golden scroll. Adam was flushed with admiration.

"At ease," ordered the group leader and the drums ceased. He strode officiously up the steps and threw out his arm in the National Socialist salute. "Do I have the pleasure of addressing Herr von Saloman?" he asked. Peter nodded.

"I am District Leader Graf," he said, "and I am on an important mission." His lips tightened and his face reddened as he projected his self-importance.

He produced a letter and read it as if making a public proclamation. "I have here a letter signed by Principal Dr Rolf Schaub of the Martin Luther School listing the achievements of your son. It is a matter of his deep regret and mine that your son is not yet a member of our formation," he continued. "Therefore," he continued, "by the authority vested in me by the Führer and Reich Youth leader Von Schirach, I am here to insist that your son enrols as a member forthwith."

Peter stood open-mouthed and speechless, while Frieda carefully surveyed the boys. She knew Bruno, who tried not to grin at her. He had clearly been the guide. Her attention moved to one boy near the rear of one of the columns. All the rest had been trained not to look at anyone but to be passive and unapproachable. The exception was a dark-haired boy who cast a glance at her so malevolent she thought he was the personification of evil. She had made eye contact with Rolf Schneider. Frieda shuddered.

Bruno stood near the rear of one of the columns, carrying a small parcel. Dieter Harro was there with Armin Schurmann. Schuster stood at the head of one of the columns, his friends lined up behind him. Now that Adam saw all his new friends in uniform, he ignored Schuster and his followers. He looked towards Bruno and then down at the parcel.

Frieda whispered to Peter, "How dare he make such an insolent demand? Who does he think he is?" Peter had lately become a student of realities. "I'm afraid he is more influential than either of us could imagine," he whispered back.

Graf began to drum his feet impatiently. "I will allow my son to decide for himself," said Peter, anxious to delay matters and prick Graf's bubble of self-importance.

Peter turned to Adam. "I would like to join, Papa" he said. Armin, Dieter and Bruno nearly broke ranks. "Forward Grabowsky," barked Graf, and Bruno marched to the front bearing the parcel.

"Here is von Saloman's uniform," said the leader.

"It's the biggest we've got," said Bruno.

"Silence!" barked Graf. "You will be expected to attend the home for induction next Wednesday at the Wilmersdorf Church Hall, von Saloman, that's all." Graf bowed to the family, the drums resumed and the Wilmersdorf and Charlottenburg Hitler Youth marched away. Gunther Graf had achieved his aim by recruiting the talented son of a local aristocrat. His superiors were bound to be impressed.

Adam rushed upstairs to try on his uniform. He emerged from his room and nearly knocked Käthe over. "You should have joined us at the front of the house Mama," he said. "All my friends were there."

"Yes I know darling," she answered looking him up and down as if she felt sorry for him. It was hardly the moment to tell him about the dying and broken men she had tended during the last war, and she could never tell him.

"Don't you like it Mama?" asked Adam. "You look very smart," Käthe replied flatly.

Adam's euphoria didn't prevent him from asking Bruno the following day about Theo and Klaus Gutman.

"They stopped coming to school at the end of February," began Bruno. "I thought they were ill and then that poster about Jewish science appeared. I telephoned them, but they don't live in Schöneburg any more. The man who answered said, 'Only good Aryans live here now.' Theo telephoned me a week later. He knew I would be worried. He said his family were all right but his father had lost his lecturer's job. They've just started another school. He said, "Don't try to contact us, it's too dangerous. The police and the Brownshirts watch us.'

"I miss those two," said Bruno sadly. "They say "Hello" to you."

Neither of the two friends said much for the rest of the lunch hour. When he reached home, Adam fingered the pages of the leather-bound volume of Confucius given to him by Yuxiang. His Chinese experience now seemed far removed, and perhaps irrelevant. He found a passage he had studied with Yuxiang. Confucius had written that people must go with the flow of events as a natural solution. Adam was happy, because that was exactly what he had done.

Adam believed that the incident in the square at Kreuzberg was long forgotten. He was now a member of the group he had once hated and compromise, he believed, would surely follow. The Hitler Youth group in school, Adam believed, was a more attractive proposition now that it included Dieter Harro and Armin Schurmann.

Bruno was far more of a realist. He didn't take his eyes off Schneider and Semmering for one moment, and even less so when Schuster's group began to be side-lined. Rolf Schneider and Ulrich Semmering constantly hinted to Berndt Schuster that something must be done.

Schuster welcomed Adam and Armin to the Hitler Youth 'home' in Wilmersdorf without any hint of unpleasantness. Adam began a campaign to rehabilitate Berndt Schuster among his own group, telling them he had a talent for organisation. It became a joke between Bruno and Adam that Adam must have another agenda because of his promotion of Berndt Schuster. Bruno didn't see that his friend had a serious purpose.

The new group began to be pre-eminent, but they underestimated Rolf Schneider and Ulrich Semmering, who were always at Schuster's elbow. These two boys watched Adam's group carefully, certain their intended victim would make a fatal slip. One boy asked Armin Schurmann if he knew anything about the fate of the Gutman twins. Armin told him about the telephone conversation between them and Bruno. The boy was a creature of Rolf Schneider, who could not believe his luck, and he passed the information on to Berndt Schuster. Schneider said he was sure that Adam was the instigator of the telephone call, knowing it to be a lie. He fed Berndt Schuster's shame at being toppled as a running champion by Adam. Ulrich and Rolf didn't think they had quite enough against Adam to spur Berndt into action, but Adam handed them the opportunity they had been waiting for.

Dr Kreisler had chosen not to parrot National Socialist propaganda in his next science lesson. Instead he chose to talk to the class about the internal combustion engine. Adam had joined Peter and Stephan in tinkering with the Buick and was very interested. Then the teacher unveiled a motorcycle engine. Adam's group wanted to crowd round, but Herr Kreisler asked them to return to their seats, to the delight of Schuster and company, who made their enjoyment of Adam's groups' embarrassment obvious. Several of the classes in the school had to endure the rowdyism of Hitler Youth elements.

As the teacher resumed the lesson, Semmering and Schneider began to chat loudly to each other over the teacher's voice. Bruno gave them black looks, but Adam went further. Out came his streak of rectitude. He stood up and turned to face Schuster's group and got the silence he waited for.

"Will you please be quiet and let the teacher speak," said Adam. Even Dr Kreisler froze for a moment, knowing the influence of the Hitler Youth in schools. Bruno shuddered and wondered what Adam was doing. He tapped him on the shoulder and motioned him to sit down.

"That's enough Adam," whispered Armin Schurmann.

Adam had handed Schneider and Semmering a gift by belittling the 'home' leader in front of the class. Even Schuster looked hard at Adam, who didn't budge. When he thought he had made his point, he sat down.

"I'm sorry Herr Kreisler," he said, thinking that was the end of the matter. Bruno was fearful of the consequences. The course of his life was about to change.

Dr Leitgen met them both in a corridor, adjusted his spectacles and suggested they visit the Senior Library. In his position as History teacher he had been informed of a new intake of military literature and he gave special permission for Bruno and Adam to visit the Library. It was in the senior half of the school on the first floor. They climbed a spiral staircase and entered a different world. A carpeted floor led them down an oak-panelled corridor and a modest sign told them they had reached their destination.

There were no slogans here. Adam and Bruno stopped outside a large oak door engraved with the Eagle and oak leaves. A helpful character emerged from the library and said "Knock and go in. Don't be frightened of the librarian. She isn't a bad old bird."

They were greeted by an officious middle-aged lady who treated them like trespassers. This was her domain and these two interlopers had better have a good reason for being here. Bruno presented her with Dr Leitgen's permission and her attitude changed. It seemed they were now entitled to humanitarian treatment, and she was pleasantly indulgent.

"So you are interested in books on military technology," she began. "I must tell you, your time has come," she said, leading them to a new section. Adam chose a book by the Army Chief of the Fuhrer's bodyguard, and Bruno went along with Adam and chose a book by an Englishman on tank warfare, expecting to be bored by it. They thanked the Librarian, who watched them disappear down the corridor clutching their trophies. In her left hand was a letter containing her dismissal for 'uncooperative behaviour.' She had paid the price for her membership of the Social Democratic Party,

As for Bruno, he became fascinated by armoured warfare. When he reached home, he took pencil and paper and copied a picture of an armoured car.

CHAPTER TWELVE

As Adam, Bruno and Peter sat in Peter's study poring over the military literature, other members of the Hitler Youth were making plans. They met in the small park outside the 'home.'

"This will be perfect," said Ulrich Semmering. Rolf Schneider agreed and suggested they take action before the planned weekend in the Black Forest.

"I'm not so sure," said Berndt Schuster.

"You can't back down now Schuster," said Semmering. "You know it is our duty to discipline if necessary."

He squared up to Berndt. He seemed overweight and short, but powerfully built. Schneider joined in with an impeccable sense of timing. "You have been humiliated again. You cannot show weakness. If action is not taken, von Saloman, not you, will command the 'home.' He paused and added "If you don't act now, everyone will know you did nothing to punish a friend of the Jews."

This was an outright threat. Schuster knew it, but was helpless. He believed Adam was challenging for the position of 'home' leader and he was no longer the "cock of the walk" in athletics.

"What do you intend to do?" he asked weakly.

"We'll take care of him," said Semmering. "All he'll get is a gentle beating. We won't touch Grabowsky."

Berndt Schuster had been backed into a corner and had allowed control of events to pass into the hands of these two boys. He accepted their promises at face value. He couldn't have known these two brutal young men had an agenda of their own.

Chapter 13

Käthe began to accept Adam's commitment to the Hitler Youth and his decision to spend less time with her. Frieda constantly reminded her companion that the reunion with Bruno meant Adam's life had taken on a new purpose and direction.

Frieda noticed a distinct improvement in Käthe during their early morning lakeside walks. "Would you like to see our old friends in Berlin again?" she asked tentatively. Käthe was not enthusiastic but said she would for Frieda's sake, and Frieda had already booked a table at Hörcher's. She had spoken with some of her old friends, who said how buoyant the mood was now in the capital. Frieda asked Stephan to drive them to town in the Buick.

Their favourite waiter was still there and wanted to see Käthe again. He usually flirted with her and this occasion was no exception. They were a little short of goose liver pâté, he said, but he had reserved some especially for her. Käthe knew he had no control over the supplies of goose liver pâté, but she was amused and flattered by the attention.

"Oh look, there are Gerhard and Inge Back," said Käthe suddenly, warming to the occasion. "They know Peter from the Foreign Office," she explained. She caught the man's eye and lifted her hand. She repeated the gesture, but the couple turned away. The waiter intervened sympathetically. "It has been some time, Madam," he reminded her. "Would you like a formal introduction?"

"Thank you. As usual you wish to promote our interests, but on this occasion I don't think it's wise," said Frieda.

"As you wish Madam," he said, and he bowed and disappeared into the kitchens.

"Today we will enjoy each other's company," said Frieda.

"We will finish our meal as soon as possible," retorted Käthe. The changing of the locks and this apparent snub had made her very uncomfortable and concerned for Peter. That night, she returned to his bed. They made love in sheer relief.

Peter examined the estate accounts and noticed a big decline in the rental income. The new Minister of Agriculture had ordered the lowering of rents, but it didn't explain the huge shortfall. He told Frieda about it.

"I am ashamed to say I think I may be able to explain the discrepancy," she said. She searched her bureau and found a copy of a letter written by Gustav to an agent who collected rent for the family, allowing him an agreed percentage. But even the deduction of the percentage didn't explain the discrepancy. Peter knew it might be a matter for the Criminal Police. Before he approached them, he remembered what might appear to be a serious omission in China. He had paid a small portion of the receipts from arms sales into his own account in the Deutsche Bank. That sum, though trivial, would have to be transferred to the Foreign Office account.

The police could not possibly be interested, he believed, but everything would have to be made right before he could approach them on the other matter. Peter didn't know that someone else had already made their own enquiries into his financial dealings.

Peter drove Adam and Bruno to the Old Church Hall well before the beginning of the weekly meeting. Peter and Frieda had discussed the less savoury-looking characters in the group and advised Adam and Bruno not to show off their new-found knowledge.

Even Bruno ignored the advice. They discussed it, laughed complacently and strode eagerly up the steps of the church with a cheerful greeting to the caretaker. They had decided to tell Berndt Schuster about their library books, convinced he wasn't as bad as his friends.

The meeting went like clockwork. Every boy knew his exact role for the coming weekend and was made aware of the punishments for failure. Berndt Schuster read them from a list drawn up by Group Leader Graf. Bruno was given special responsibility for guarding the flags. Dieter and Armin were to extinguish all camp fires. Adam's name was not mentioned, but neither were those of Ulrich Semmering or Rolf Schneider. They seemed unconcerned and were pre-occupied with two new boys.

At the end of the meeting, Adam and Bruno chatted to the caretaker while they waited for Berndt Schuster, but the hall was empty. They were the only people there.

"You young gentlemen have half an hour to wait, I believe," said the caretaker rattling his keys.

"If we're lucky," answered Bruno. "Herr von Saloman sometimes has an evening nap."

"It's started to rain," said the caretaker. "I don't mind waiting a little longer. Stay inside for a while and keep dry."

"Thank you," said Adam. "He'll be here soon. We don't mind waiting."

"As you wish," replied the caretaker. "Goodnight boys." He disappeared into the steady drizzle on his bicycle and Adam and Bruno walked towards the Park Gate. They were used to walking slowly through the park, whiling away a few minutes waiting for Peter and the Buick.

Most of the park lights had been switched off, but enough remained to reveal the central walkway lined with the occasional wooden seat. Dull yellow lighting illuminated the steep landscaped sides of the pathway with tree roots rambling wildly down the slopes. The trees and the upper half of the slopes were in darkness.

"We're glad you could come," said a voice from the upper half of the left hand slope. The subdued light hid the upper half of his body, but Adam and Bruno recognised the voice of Berndt Schuster. Bruno looked ahead. Their way was blocked by the two boys who were new to the meeting. Adam glanced behind. Walking stealthily towards them were Rolf Schneider and Ulrich Semmering. They stopped and Berndt Schuster spoke hesitantly.

"You are charged with bringing shame on the Home, von Saloman" he said. "You have associated with Jews and protected them from due punishment. You have insulted me, your hut leader, openly in school for which no apology has been received. Due punishment will now take place." Then he added, "Keep out of it Grabowsky. This is none of your business."

Bruno didn't move. The rain became heavier and plastered their hair to their heads. He prayed for Peter's arrival.

"Stand aside Bruno. This is my fight," said Adam.

"Don't be stupid Adam. You don't stand a chance," replied Bruno.

"Stand aside Bruno," said Adam firmly. Bruno took a few hesitant steps.

"Keep out of this, Grabowsky," said Rolf Schneider. The four boys advanced and stopped at a signal from Ulrich Semmering, reaching into their shorts pockets. Each drew a small rubber truncheon. Berndt Schuster realised he had been hoodwinked.

Semmering fixed his eye on the scar on Adam's left leg. He intended that Adam should never win another race. The four of them circled Adam, who stood perfectly still and watched.

Bruno looked to Schuster to intervene. "This isn't what you intended, is it Schuster?" he said, hoping for a last minute stay of execution but Schuster said nothing.

One of the two strangers leapt at Adam who tried to dodge the first blow. It missed his head but caught his shoulder a stinging blow. He winced with pain and almost simultaneously the other stranger raised his right arm. Adam's left arm parried the blow. He leaned towards the boy, throwing him off balance. Adam threw his right leg into the boys' chest. He cried out with pain, dropped his truncheon and fell backwards onto a tree stump, where he lay writhing helplessly. Before the other new boy could move again, Bruno grasped him round the neck from behind. They rolled over and over on the muddy bank. Schneider and Semmering had waited. This was to be their moment, but they would pay for their hesitancy. As the stranger collapsed onto the tree stump, Schneider ran forward and lifted his right arm, sure that Adam had been distracted. The truncheon began to descend on his head.

In a split second, Adam turned and parried the blow with his left arm. As Rolf Schneider's body weight fell on him, Adam drove his fist into Schneider's chest. He collapsed gasping.

Bruno hung on grimly and Ulrich Semmering stopped in his tracks. Berndt Schuster quietly said, "Enough." Bruno and his adversary stood up slowly, their uniforms coated with mud. Bruno was flushed and triumphant, the other boy half frustrated, half ashamed.

The initiative had passed forever from Berndt Schuster. Adam was now to seize it in a way that astounded his friend.

"On your feet," shouted Adam. "Face the Hut Leader!" His face burned with anger and contempt. He coldly hauled the stranger off the tree stump and the boy sobbed with pain. "Face your Hut Leader," commanded Adam. "Pick Schneider up, Semmering." Ulrich Semmering saw the blood issuing from Rolf Schneider's mouth and hesitated.

"Out of the way," said Adam as he hauled Rolf Schneider to his feet. Even Bruno was concerned for the fate of this boy who had plotted a brutal nemesis for Adam.

"Get in line," ordered Adam striding up and down in front of them and treating Bruno as if he was one of them. "Raise your arms," ordered Adam, still burning with fury. "Salute the Hut Leader." Berndt Schuster still hadn't moved.

To Bruno's dismay, Adam lifted Rolf Schneider's arm. It fell backwards as he cried out in pain, but the rest saluted.

"What are your orders, Hut Leader?" asked Adam sharply.

"Dismiss," said Schuster weakly, walking down from the top of the bank.

"Schneider'll need help Berndt," Bruno said quietly. Schuster nodded. "Thanks Bruno," he replied and joined the assailants who staggered out of the park. He briefly turned to Adam, a look of pleading on his face. By now Adam had regained his self-possession. "None of us will ever speak of this again," he said. Schuster lifted his hand in acknowledgement.

There was no sign of Peter. Adam sat down on the tree stump and reaction set in. He began to shake and sob. Bruno was relieved at this after a display of pitiless naked ambition he would never want to see again.

"I've hurt Schneider badly," Adam said, staring at Bruno as if he was seeking forgiveness.

"Don't feel sorry for him," replied Bruno sharply. "Schneider and Semmering wanted to put you in hospital."

"You don't understand Bruno. I promised never to use it." insisted Adam.

"If you hadn't, we'd both be a pile of bones by now, you clown," said Bruno.

Adam forced a half-smile. They saw headlights in the distance. "Pull yourself together Field Marshal. Your father's here. Don't you have anything to say?" Bruno reminded him.

"Oh thanks for helping, Bruno," said Adam. "Don't ever tell anyone what you saw tonight."

They heard the car come to a halt. "Where did you learn that?" asked Bruno.

"An old man and his wife in China," replied Adam. Bruno shrugged his shoulders.

"Hurry up you two," called Peter. "You're wet through. I'll get you both home quickly." Peter stared at Bruno's mud-bespattered uniform. "War games I suppose?"

"Not really," answered Bruno mischievously. Adam prayed Bruno would honor his promise to say nothing.

"We planned for the weekend away," said Bruno, enjoying his friend's discomfort and grinning at him.

That night a young man in Hitler Youth uniform was stretchered into the local hospital. With him was a policeman in uniform. The young man was operated on immediately and the policeman waited anxiously outside the operating theatre. The policeman was Sergeant Schneider and he waited to see if his son would survive.

After three hours, the surgeon appeared, looking exhausted. He removed his gloves. "Only time will tell Sergeant," he said. "You should find out who was responsible for this."

Rolf Schneider's father was not entirely blameless and conducted no enquiries. He bitterly regretted a decision he had made earlier. His son Rolf had asked him to ignore anything that seemed unusual in the park at a certain time because an important disciplinary measure was to take place by order of the District Leader. Sergeant Schneider had agreed to look the other way.

"Herr Peter, it's the Foreign Ministry for you," said Greta at the foot of the stairs as Peter descended at the usual time of eight-thirty in the morning.

"Thank you Greta," said Peter, picking up the phone. "Von Saloman speaking."

"Good morning Herr von Saloman," said a curt voice." "This is Herr Neumann of the Secretariat. We must see you urgently. You are expected here at nine o'clock on the coming Monday morning. The car will be sent for you at eight-thirty. I trust that is in order?"

Peter replaced the telephone and felt uncomfortable. He was usually addressed as 'Your Excellency,' and he expected to be called by Herr Wilke, not Herr Neumann, of whom he knew nothing. He returned to his study and retrieved every document he possessed relating to the behavior of Karl Wendt. He found Christina Schultz's telephone number and began to believe he might need her as a witness after all.

Greta appeared on the stairs carrying the remains of Peter's and Käthe's morning coffee. She was especially cheerful today because she had served the couple's coffee in the same room. She squeezed Peter's arm and retreated to the kitchen.

The following Monday, Peter waited in the entrance hall for the Ministry car. He had decided he would not demean himself by waiting on the steps. His visitors would have to ring the doorbell.

"My darling, will you please leave the contents of your briefcase alone?" asked Käthe. Peter sighed heavily and tried to compose himself. "They'll give you a new assignment somewhere in Europe, you'll see. See if you can get Paris," she joked.

At nine o'clock a black saloon bearing a swastika pennant came slowly down the drive. It stopped and the chauffeur opened a rear passenger door. He stood and waited without making any attempt to climb the steps. He bowed as Peter stepped into the car.

The traffic was not too heavy and the car drew up to the Foreign Ministry in the Wilhelmstrasse a little over thirty minutes later. Peter had rehearsed his case against Wendt over and over again. Surely, he believed, his old colleagues would rally round him.

He mounted the steps and glanced upwards at the unsettling sight of the swastika banner flying high into the entrance hall, and gazed in admiration at the stone reliefs on the walls depicting Germany's past triumphs. He began to feel confident as he walked to the Secretariat. An usher opened the door to an ante-room and he was invited to sit down and wait.

It was fully half an hour before anything happened. Peter had passed the time nervously fingering his papers. An older female secretary came in and unlocked a cabinet. "Good morning Your Excellency, it's good to see you again," she said warmly. He felt much better now.

He brushed his jacket lapels and straightened his bow tie for at least the tenth time. The door opened noiselessly and the usher invited Peter through. Two men sat behind a large oak desk on which stood a silver eagle and swastika. They stood up abruptly and gave the National Socialist salute. Peter thought it safer to salute as enthusiastically as the two men.

One of them, a thin bespectacled man in the dress of a senior administrative official, perhaps in his mid-forties, invited Peter to be seated in a red leather upholstered chair in front of the desk.

Staring down on the scene were portraits of Bismarck and Hitler on the panelled wall behind the desk. The only sound in the room was the almost imperceptible ticking of an ornate gold clock on a wooden stand.

The other man wore a plain grey suit. He was in his mid-forties and was already completely bald. His head seem square, his jaw weak and his skin white. He sat perfectly still, surveying Peter through rimless spectacles. His only distinguishing feature was his small piercing blue eyes.

"Good morning Herr von Saloman," began the official. "I am Principal Secretary Neumann." He paused for effect before he introduced his colleague. "This is Kriminalrat Kloster of the Geheime Staats Polizei," he said. Peter's blood ran cold. It was to be the first of several unpleasant surprises.

"The Foreign Ministry would like to thank you for your efforts on behalf of the Fatherland," said Neumann, in such a manner as if it were of no consequence and an obstacle in the way of the main agenda. Neumann stared at Peter and the tone of his voice changed. He placed a sheet of paper in front of him and checked a detail. "You were a loyal and reliable servant of the Reich until I believe – November of last year."

He spoke as if he were reviewing a set of accounts. The policeman continued to stare at Peter. "I do not understand, Herr Principal Secretary," he replied puzzled.

"Well let me enlighten you, Herr von Saloman," replied Neumann. "I have here a detailed report on your conduct during recent months," he continued, "and it makes disturbing reading."

He shuffled his documents and produced one. "It has come to our notice that considerable parts of consignments meant for the Nationalist forces of General Chiang Kai-shek have gone missing. Were you aware of this, Herr von Saloman?" asked Neumann.

Kloster had started to roll a pencil over and over in his fingers. He stopped and prepared to make notes.

"Of course," answered Peter. "Some small arms and ammunition were diverted to local warlords who supported Chiang Kai-shek."

"And how were you paid by these warlords?" asked Neumann.

"The traditional currency of the area is small silver ingots," answered Peter.

"And how was it transferred to Germany?" persisted Neumann. "Under lock and key on the *Derfligger*, of course," answered Peter, beginning to wonder where this interview was going.

"All of it?" asked Neumann sharply.

"No, of course not," answered Peter. "I always kept a certain amount in reserve for future negotiations."

"A certain amount you say," said Neumann. "I must say that only a negligible amount has reached us."

It now began to sound like an accusation. Neumann moved on. "And who is Ned Travis, Herr von Saloman?" asked Neumann, suddenly leaning towards Peter.

"He is a well-known dockside smuggler and provider. He is also my son's friend and protector," answered Peter. He suddenly regretted saying this, but it was too late. He remembered with horror Manfred Weiss' spying activities on the waterfront. His dossier on the subject must have been passed to Karl Wendt, who would instantly have seen its possibilities.

Neumann produced a photograph and handed it to Peter. It showed Ned handing Peter the wallet full of US dollars. "How do you explain this?" asked Neumann.

"This payment was in recompense for all the trouble he had caused," answered Peter. "It was a negligible amount."

"And where is the money?" asked Neumann. Kloster was furiously making notes. "It is a personal matter Herr Neumann," said Peter.

"We are not inclined to agree, Herr von Saloman," retorted Neumann.

"Are you accusing me of dishonesty Herr Neumann?" asked Peter sharply.

Neumann answered equally sharply. "We will ask the questions," he said. "I suggest you pay the money into the Foreign Ministry's account in the Deutsche bank as soon as possible. Now," he continued, "Kriminalrat Kloster has some questions." He turned to Kloster, who suddenly seemed animated. His voice was high-pitched and the thick lenses of his spectacles magnified his stare. He carefully selected a document and pretended to peruse it for effect, though he already knew its contents.

"It seems you have displayed hostility to the Reich Government, Herr von Saloman," he said in a monotone.

"Please explain," said Peter cautiously.

"This emerged through the unacceptable treatment of a party member, His Excellency Karl Wendt."

"Are you aware of the reason for my treatment of Wendt, Herr Kloster?" asked Peter, hardly giving him time to complete his statement.

"Continue," said the Gestapo man.

"I caught Wendt assaulting my wife. You would already know the details of Wendt's behaviour, had he not intercepted and destroyed my signal. That in itself was serious insubordination, Herr Kriminalrat," said Peter, with a hint of condescension.

Kloster was not to be deflected. "But we have only your word for that, Herr Von Salomon," retorted Kloster.

"Nonsense," said Peter sharply. "Have you bothered to talk to Lieutenant Weiss of the Abwehr?"

Kloster kept his even tone. "We have indeed spoken with Weiss," he answered. He paused and almost smiled. "He does not support your story."

Peter wondered what pressure had been brought to bear on Weiss, or where Manfred Weiss' real loyalties lay.

"I would ask you to moderate your tone of voice Herr von Saloman," snapped Neumann. Peter said nothing and glared at him.

Then he discovered why Kloster was present. "It is a matter of interpretation, Herr Von Salomon," said Kloster. "You see, we have the evidence of several witnesses who are sure your wife's behaviour towards Wendt was, to say the least, dubious."

He paused to see the effect on Peter, whose face grew redder and redder. "Frau Von Salomon's opinions of some leading National Socialists are quite insulting, to say the least," Kloster went on, his high-pitched voice retaining its monotone. "They are so insulting, Herr von Saloman, that they are of great interest to a man in my position."

The threat was clear, but Peter did not realise how serious it was. He wasn't aware of the opinion his wife had expressed during her dalliance with Wendt, and Kloster knew it. He was merciless. "You will not be aware of your wife's encouragement of Herr Wendt's attentions I suppose," said Kloster with a new a note of menace.

This was too much for Peter. He stood up and banged on the table with his fist. "Apologise at once for what you have just said!" he shouted. He turned to Neumann. "You have sat there and behaved in a manner which would have disgraced a once honourable profession, Herr Neumann!"

Equally red faced, Neumann stood up. "You are in no position to demand an apology, von Saloman. You are hereby dishonourably dismissed from Foreign Ministry service."

Peter sat down deflated, but Kloster wasn't finished. "There is also your complicity in the disappearance of Dr Jacob Meissner to consider," he said, staring hard at Peter.

"You may go," said Neumann unceremoniously, leaving Peter to worry about Kloster's last threat.

Peter stepped out onto the street. He felt like a freemason who had been expelled from his lodge. For the first time for years, there was no waiting car, no chauffeur. Berlin was enjoying a warm spring, but Peter hardly noticed as he tried to hail one taxi after another. Even the taxi drivers appeared to be part of the conspiracy to reject him. One eventually stopped. All the way home, Peter went over what had been said. He had the disturbing conviction that it had all been rehearsed.

He wondered why Kloster had emphasised the things Käthe had said. As far as he knew, no policeman had ever asked to interview her. Peter was afraid of what he might discover in the course of time.

He chided himself for thinking such things. He became tight chested and breathless when he thought how his son's future career might be affected. After all, Ned Travis was Adam's friend. Using Weiss' intelligence network, Kloster must have made a point of knowing it. Peter was beginning to understand this faceless, seamless creature whose malice had begun it's work.

He felt even worse as the taxi travelled down the Avus. It stopped at traffic lights and the driver turned round. "Are you all right sir?" he asked.

Peter felt thankful for his concern, but wondered how he was to explain himself to Frieda and Käthe. He considered the shame of dismissal and the effect it would have on his mother.

"Well done Neumann," said Kloster to the First Secretary. "The plan is proceeding perfectly. I will notify Party Secretary Bormann's office immediately. I am sure they will know how to reward you."

Neumann assumed he had become Kloster's confidant. "And the next stage Herr Kriminalrat?" he asked.

The Gestapo man resumed his coldness. "That is not for you to know, Herr Neumann and now I must leave," he said, impatiently taking his coat from the usher.

Frieda, Käthe and Greta waited anxiously all morning. Fearing the worst, they were all afraid to go outside to greet Peter as the taxi drew up. They saw him get out anxiously searching his pockets. The driver was sympathetic when his passenger asked him to wait. Peter said nothing as he brushed past the three women looking pale and distraught. He reappeared and paid the driver, who bowed and drove away.

Peter asked the women to join him in the tea house. He did not even remove his coat before he began, but undid the buttons and sprawled helplessly in one of the wickerwork chairs. His hands shook as he spoke but his account of what had happened was very selective. He noticed Käthe's hands shaking.

"We'll never understand those people," he began. "They don't respect decent behaviour. They had no intention of listening." Peter spoke as if he were talking to himself. He raised his head to see the effects of his words on his mother.

Frieda listened, looking every inch the aristocratic matriarch. In the past her strength had lain in her impassive, judicious look, but now she was angry. She spoke as if making a public address.

"These people are not worthy of you Peter," she began. "They are lower-class upstarts who enjoy making the lives of their betters uncomfortable. You have conducted yourself well. It is their loss."

Käthe saw Peter was in difficulties and placed her hand on Frieda's, but she was waved away. Frieda had more to say and would not be deflected.

"I have consulted our lawyers and made the following decision," she announced. "You are not to wait for my death to inherit. The deeds of the house have been altered and witnessed. Die Schwanen now belongs to you and Käthe."

This was news to Käthe, but she now believed her husband faced a more pleasant future. His diplomatic career had gone, to be replaced by another as the owner and manager of the family estate. She prayed for a positive response from Peter.

"I have already begun," he announced. "I must tell you that I am already conducting an investigation into the shortfall of rents and intend to visit our tenancies in the east as soon as possible."

Their relief was almost tangible. In one day Peter had altered the whole direction of his life, convinced now that he was in sole charge of his destiny as a landowner. As if to complement what had happened, Käthe's application to nurse at the local convent hospital was accepted; she was to care for the long term disabled of the last war. None of them had yet realised that the National Socialist state didn't believe in people having sole charge of their lives.

That night as they lay in bed, Käthe wanted to know if Peter approved of her return to nursing. She need not have worried. "I am alive because of what you did for me in 1918," said Peter. "And I know these poor old soldiers will have better lives because of you my love." He was not aware of Käthe's plans for the rest of the evening.

"Do you remember when I fed you my darling?" she said mischievously. He smiled and stared at the ceiling. "I enjoyed it so much," he said.

"In that case I will do it again," Käthe said reaching over him and picking up his half-empty coffee cup.

"Open up," she said, spoon feeding him. "Will that be all Lieutenant?" she asked in a schoolgirl voice. Käthe sat up and drew her nightdress over her head. Her hands crept under the bedclothes, stimulating him. She stroked his nose and straddled him, stroking his erection and guiding him inside her. They made love slowly and deliberately, feeling they had rediscovered their lives.

Peter fell asleep before Käthe. She was sure now that her greatest fears would never be realised. After their lovemaking Peter could never believe she could prefer any other man to her husband. The monstrosity of Wendt and his threats began to dwindle; Käthe was at peace.

Chapter 14

Adam was worried about his reception at the Church Hall, which irritated Bruno.

"If this lot inside knew what had happened there'd be a celebration," he said.

"You make it sound as if nothing much happened," objected Adam. "Have you forgotten Schneider?" That served to irritate him even more. "It was his fault and he probably won't be here," retorted Bruno. "Are you going to stand there all night or are we going in?"

They had said all this within earshot of two policemen who regularly patrolled the area. One of them seemed uninterested, but the other stared hard at Adam as if he intended to remember his face. Constable Schneider was sure he now knew the identity of the boy responsible for his son's injuries.

Bruno had underestimated Adam. When he was sure Rolf Schneider would not put in an appearance, the young aristocrat did everything he could to bolster Berndt Schuster's authority without being obsequious. Slowly but surely Adam made himself and Bruno indispensable. During the course of the evening Adam casually suggested to Bruno, "When Berndt's finished with the arrangements for next weekend, why not tell him about our reading?"

Bruno's mouth opened in amazement. "I'll tell him, Field Marshal," he answered. Adam had read Berndt Schuster well and understood he was permanently beholden to him. The 'Home' Leader suggested that Adam and Bruno tell the whole group about their library books. The two readily agreed and the group listened to Adam and Bruno explaining how Germany would win the next war.

Adam slowly became the sun around which the planets revolved. Berndt was now trapped by his recent behaviour, but was grateful to Adam and Bruno, who were true to their word and revealed nothing of the events in the park. Berndt had no idea that his family background had been described to his rivals or that they were sympathetic.

Ulrich Semmering made no apparent effort to make amends, probably because he didn't know how to. Uve Muller had not been invited to join the punishment detail and boiled with resentment in isolation. He was now powerless and friendless.

Ulrich gravitated towards Adam and Bruno, but was allowed near them only as a subservient being – or at least that's how Bruno would have preferred it.

Rolf Schneider's name was not even mentioned as he was airbrushed out of the life of the 'home'. Bruno asked a special favour of Berndt – to be informed of Schneider's progress, but not to mention it to Adam.

The Berlin groups took trains to Heidelberg and disappeared into the forest to play soldiers. Lorries carried them into the darkness and secrecy of secret clearings. Here, believed their leaders, they would be in touch with their Teutonic ancestors.

Hundreds of them formed two giant circles to renew their oath to Chancellor Hitler. A figure who was unknown to most of them stood on a wooden dais behind a bank of microphones and required the boys to solemnly promise to risk their lives for the Führer whenever required to do so.

They walked and ran through the forest, climbed crags and fell into mountain streams. Failure to help each other was rewarded by instant punishment. Just a few had doubts about one Hitler youth obsession – boxing.

One of the few was a studious-looking bespectacled son of a university lecturer, Benno Roepke. "Stick with us Roepke, you'll be all right," Bruno assured him. The instructors picked on the bigger boys for the purpose of the demonstrations and Bruno prayed they didn't use Adam.

The instructor's finger passed up and down the line. Bruno and Berndt exchanged glances, both realising the risk of choosing Adam. The finger stopped. The burly instructor put his hands on his hips grinning. He pointed to Adam.

"What will he do?" Berndt asked Bruno.

"He'll let him hit him," answered Bruno.

"Quiet," said the instructor to Bruno.

"Strip to the waist," ordered the instructor, who was wearing an athlete's top which clung to his muscles. Adam obeyed at lightning speed.

"Hold up your fists boy. Like this," said the man. He demonstrated how to defend and touched Adam gently on the chin.

"Now defend yourself," said the instructor. Adam moved around in expert fashion as if he intended to evade the blow, but it caught him on the chin and he reeled backwards. Adam threw out his arm in salute, which was returned. Berndt Schuster grinned at Bruno. Ulrich watched open mouthed and Berndt and Bruno enjoyed his confusion.

Partners were chosen for each boy and Bruno was partnered with Semmering. Both looked embarrassed. Semmering was fearful of the consequences of hitting Adam's friend. Poor Benno Roepke was confronted by a boy of similar height but stocky and rough looking. The boy rubbed his gloves with glee when he saw Benno.

"Wait a moment, Semmering," said Bruno. He leaned over and said to Benno's opponent, "Watch my friend before you fight Roepke." Another big and rough-looking boy had been chosen to fight Adam. He threw punch after punch, all of which found fresh air as the instructor watched. Adam knew he had to hit the boy. He struck him once under the ribs and the boy collapsed gasping for breath.

Bruno said to Benno's opponent, "That's what'll happen to you if you hurt Roepke."

Benno threw punch after punch, which missed, until he collapsed exhausted. His opponent did not have to hit him.

"Let's fight Grabowsky," said Semmering , who saw an opportunity to re-establish himself. The 'home' watched fascinated as Bruno made a bad mistake. He took it seriously and threw a violent punch at Ulrich, which missed by several inches. Bruno received a stinging blow on his left ear and fell sideways. Semmering was almost apologetic.

"Well done, Semmering," said Adam. "That'll teach him a lesson." Berndt Schuster was stunned into disbelief and Bruno berated his friend. "You rat!" he said, sounding deeply hurt.

"Sorry Bruno," said Adam loftily, "but we need Semmering on our side." It was a long time before Bruno understood.

Peter inspected the remainder of the family estates in Eastern Germany.

He met Nicholas Seebring, who rented the biggest farm. Nicholas showed Peter the neglect on several farms and made it clear that the agent had cheated both parties. Peter promised to invest in the revival of the estates and returned to Berlin sure he was about to revive the family fortunes. He decided to contact the criminal police, unaware that Kloster had already done so.

Die Schwanen and its grounds were bathed in dappled sunshine as the sun stole upwards above the trees. The waters of the Wannsee glistened in the stillness and the cranes and egrets cruised lazily over the surface, looking for an early meal. Silver aircraft rose into the sky from Gatow airfield, but the distant noise failed to intrude on the piece of the house and the promise of a new summer season.

Peter was surveying a small crack in the bathroom shaving mirror when Greta respectfully knocked at the door. "Herr Peter, there are some men at the gate demanding to be let in. What shall I say?"

"I am afraid you must let them in Greta," replied Peter. He knew who they probably were, and that this would herald a new dark period in his life.

A black Mercedes saloon crunched its way down the gravel path. Two men in dark raincoats and Homburg hats got out of the back seat. They sprang up the steps and banged loudly on the door. Peter decided he would not hurry in the face of such impertinence. The rest of the family appeared at the top of the stairs. "Who is it?" asked Käthe anxiously.

"I fear they are the minions of the policeman Kloster my love," answered Peter and she rushed downstairs followed by Adam.

"Can I help Papa?" he asked.

"I'm afraid not," answered Peter. "The longer they are made to wait the worse it will be for us I think," he added.

There were two more loud bangs on the door. Greta opened it and the two Gestapo men rudely brushed past her. One of them said, "You must come with us Herr von Saloman," but Peter demanded to see their identification. They were surprised and irritated. "We are the Gestapo. That's all you need to know," said one of them. "You will come now."

Frieda stepped forward to lecture the unwanted visitors, but Käthe restrained her. "May he take some things?" asked Käthe.

"No Madam, he may not," was the reply of one of the faceless intruders.

CHAPTER FOURTEEN

Peter was hustled to the car, and Adam followed. "Go back to the house," threatened one of the policemen, "or it will be worse for you."

"Do as they say," said Peter. Adam stood still and watched helplessly. Before Peter climbed into the back of the car, one of the men produced handcuffs. "Is this really necessary?" Peter asked. One of them leered and replied condescendingly. "It is regulations." The two men were enjoying humiliating a member of the aristocracy in front of his family.

Käthe tried to kiss Peter, but she was pushed away rudely. Adam ran towards the car and confronted the men. One of them thought it better to smooth events. "Your father will be back soon," he said. "Attend to your mother." The car doors were slammed. The family watched as Peter was driven away.

The traffic appeared to melt away in front of the car, which took little more than half an hour to reach Gestapo headquarters. None of the three men had spoken to Peter. He was dragged out of the car and made to run up the steps between two motionless guards in black steel helmets and blue uniforms. A giant swastika banner waved gently over the main door. Peter was pushed into a dull cavernous entrance hall and made to sit down in front of a glass fronted reception desk, manned by a faceless individual in a grey uniform. He heard Kloster's name mentioned before the two men who had arrested him signed a form and left, after handcuffing their prisoner to a chair. He was abandoned for nearly two hours.

At length a door opened in a partition at the end of the hall and two men in grey uniforms and peaked caps walked towards Peter. They unlocked the handcuffs and lifted him roughly to his feet, saying nothing. Peter remembered the strong smell of body odour on them. They frogmarched him through the partition and turned right down an inner corridor. On the inner side were small barred windows set high in the wall. On the other side were a series of offices bearing the names of Gestapo officers.

The guards stopped and restrained Peter. A man in his sixties, barely able to stand, faced two guards. His legs were chained. Peter's guards waited impassively as the man was struck several times in the face by his guards, who pushed him into a chair and handcuffed him. Peter's presence there was not accidental.

The corridor appeared to follow an inner courtyard. After another fifty metres, Peter was pushed into a chair and handcuffed to it, then abandoned for another hour. The guards reappeared and the door opened. Peter was almost lifted through it and pushed down into a chair in front of a large desk.

He could not see the man behind the desk as a light shone directly into his eyes, but he recognised the high-pitched voice of Kloster. The two guards stood either side of Peter's chair.

"Are you in good health, Herr von Saloman?" asked Kloster. Peter replied that he was.

"Has your family resettled well in Germany?" Peter nodded.

"I am pleased to report that the State Bank has received all outstanding amounts of silver bullion and cash, a good addition to the Reich coffers I may say," said Kloster in a flat voice.

Kloster paused, then reached over and turned the light away. He leaned over the desk and stared at Peter. In an instant the atmosphere changed.

"We are concerned at your wife's attitude to our Reich leaders, Herr von Saloman. How do you explain this?" asked Kloster sharply.

Peter was aware only of Käthe's reaction to the attempted rape. "I assume you refer to the assault on my wife by Herr Wendt?" asked Peter.

"Go on," said Kloster.

"My wife said things in the heat of the moment which she has since sincerely regretted," answered Peter.

"But events have a way of making people reveal their true feelings, have they not?" countered Kloster. He waited to see the effect of what he had said on Peter, well aware that he possessed information which Peter did not. "She made remarks hostile to the Reich whilst not under pressure, Herr von Saloman," said Kloster triumphantly.

He thumbed the pages of a dossier and read out a list of the remarks supposedly made by Käthe about Hermann Goering. Wendt had lied profusely, thought Peter, and this was one more example.

"You have only the word of that man Wendt for all this," said Peter.

"Her opinions would not be surprising I think, because they agreed with yours, Herr von Saloman," retorted Kloster.

That was too much for Peter.

"That moral bankrupt tried to rape my wife!" he shouted. "How would you expect me to behave?" Peter rose up from his seat. Kloster stood up and the guards laid heavy hands on Peter shoulders.

"Sit down, von Saloman!" he barked. "We have treated you leniently so far, but that may change."

Peter didn't give up. "Do you know of Fräulein Christina Schultz?" he asked. Peter thought it a good time to introduce a favourable witness. "Don't be naïve" said Kloster. "Of course I do."

It suddenly dawned on Peter that the Gestapo were interested only in rooting out disloyalty in any circumstances. He suddenly felt very afraid.

"Perhaps you have realized, Herr von Saloman, that you do not enjoy a privileged position any longer. It is possible that you and your wife may suffer for your complacency," said Kloster." Perhaps your son will suffer despite his prospects." He turned away from Peter. "Take him to his cell," he snapped.

Kloster believed his deeper purpose would soon be realised. He had not mentioned Käthe's liaison with Wendt and never intended to do so. His superiors would have been pleased. Käthe's indiscretion could be used in the future.

Peter was handcuffed once again and taken to a cell a short distance away, deeper into the building. The door was opened and he was told to take off his coat. The two men pushed him into the cell, and instantly he began to shiver. His hand brushed one of the walls. They ran with damp.

The cell contained a wooden bunk, a straw palliasse and a bucket. There were no blankets. The guards took Peter's watch and pushed him towards the far wall. The door was slammed shut and locked.

A bright light shone permanently in the inner courtyard and Peter could only guess when daylight had faded. He lay down on the bunk and tried to sleep, curling himself up into a ball. He managed to sleep for two or three hours. He began to shiver once more and his head ached. He had no idea of the time when he woke and heard a movement in the next cell followed by a cry of pain.

He lay awake thinking of a strategy for the next interrogation, which he believed must come soon. Peter believed he might be contrite. Perhaps that would satisfy Kloster. But then he thought about the threats against his family.

There was an eerie silence for some time and Peter guessed it might be morning.

Suddenly, there were commands from the courtyard, followed by a single pistol shot. He heard the sound of a hose washing down a wall. Then his guards arrived.

Bruno waited in the Charlottenbrunnestrasse for his lift to school. The Buick appeared on time, not being driven by Peter. Bruno nodded to Stephan and climbed in, noticing that Adam wasn't in Hitler Youth uniform. The morning's conversation nearly always began with a derogatory remark by Bruno answered in kind by Adam, but today his friend only nodded and stared ahead.

"What's the matter?" asked Bruno. He had seen Stephan's worried look through the rear view mirror.

"The police have taken Papa away," said Adam to a stunned Bruno.

"Why?" said Bruno. "What's he supposed to have done?"

"Something to do with China, I think," answered Adam. "I don't know anything else."

"Can you ask?" suggested Bruno, not very hopefully.

"I don't think so," replied Adam. "You should have seen the men who came". I'll damn well ask if no one else does," said Bruno defiantly.

"Thanks," replied Adam. "But don't. They're like Schneider." It was the first time Adam had mentioned Schneider's name since the attack.

"What will you do?" asked Bruno, feeling sure that Adam must have a plan.

"I don't know," answered his friend. "I'll think of something." Then he said earnestly, "don't tell anyone Bruno."

"But they'll all ask why you're not in uniform, you know that," Bruno reminded him. "I'll deal with it." He made a fist and tapped his friend's arm. "It's nothing to be ashamed of," he added.

Bruno was true to his word. He saw Berndt as soon as the car reached school. In no time, they all huddled round Adam. Ulrich Semmering approached Adam cautiously.

"I'm sorry von Saloman," he said. "He'll be all right." Bruno's eyebrows raised as he exchanged a glance with Berndt. Semmering's rehabilitation was going well. Only Uve Muller remained detached and isolated.

Peter was hauled to his feet and frogmarched down the corridor once more. This time Kloster did not enquire after his health. He produced a document and slid it across the table.

"Do you recognise this signal, von Saloman?" he asked abruptly. The Gestapo man lit a cigarette while Peter re-read it. He had dreaded this moment, because he knew it involved Adam.

"The signal ordered you to dismiss Jacob Meissner and surrender him to the authorities," said Kloster stating the obvious and therefore repeating the charge against Peter. He stubbed out the half-smoked cigarette and leaned over the table. "But it is worse than it looks, I believe," continued his interrogator. "You informed Herr Wendt that Meissner had escaped without your knowledge before the arrival of the new Deputy." Peter said nothing.

"I think perhaps, your son might be able to tell us the whole truth. Perhaps you can picture him sat in your chair, von Saloman," threatened Kloster.

Peter was tired and exhausted but the threat to Adam and his contempt for Kloster refreshed his spirit. By now he had decided that Manfred Weiss belonged with Kloster and his like.

Peter quietly said, "Dr Meissner was helped by another official at the Consulate." Kloster got up and banged the desk. "You were responsible, von Saloman, not Weiss!" he barked, knowing very well who Peter was about to accuse. Kloster sat down. "He was merely your deputy."

Peter realised now where much of Kloster's information had originated. It appeared that Weiss' courage, displayed on the waterfront, had finally failed him. Now worse was to follow. Kloster quietly went on "There is the incident involving your son in the square at Kreuzberg. I must tell you that Reichsleiter Goebbels was not impressed." He paused, knowing that Peter was finally trapped, and then tried to sound considerate.

"It is possible we might forget that as he appears to have put some of his old loyalties behind him" he said. Peter knew the threat remained, and Kloster knew his plan was nearly complete.

Peter began to shiver uncontrollably and his chest pains reappeared. Kloster saw his prisoner's discomfort but pity was not part of his agenda. "You will return to your cell to ponder your misdemeanours," he snapped. "In the meantime, we will decide what is to be done with you." He turned to the guards. "Take him away!"

All the family felt they could do was to resume some kind of routine while they waited for news. Käthe and Frieda resumed their morning walk by the lakeside. They watched early day trippers on the lake steamers enjoying a freedom which the family had just lost. The two women walked in silence for some time.

"Do you know of anything which might help Peter?" asked Frieda. Käthe cast a guilty sidelong glance at her companion, but decided the inquiry was entirely innocent. They walked on slowly.

"My only son is in the hands of these upstarts," said Frieda grimly. "What is to be done, Käthe?" They stopped as a patrol boat passed close to the shore and its wake washed the shore. Käthe 's expression changed. "Time is short. But there is much to be done Frieda," she said resolutely. She spun on her heels and marched back to the house, leaving a puzzled Frieda. When she was within a hundred metres of the house, she saw Stephan holding the car door open for Adam. She shouted furiously, "Wait Adam, wait!"

She ran up to the car, almost out of breath. "Adam, you will not go to school today. Go upstairs and put on your uniform and wait for me here." She turned to the old family retainer, "Stephan, you will be driving today, but not to school."

"Hurry my darling," she called to Adam as he ran up the steps. He turned and asked. "What are we doing today Mama?"

Käthe placed her hands on her hips and said imperiously, "We're going to get your father out of that hell hole."

Adam grinned from ear to ear. "Well done Mama," he said and ran to his room.

Frieda caught up and Käthe described her plan. Frieda was horrified.

"You cannot involve Adam," she said. "It's too dangerous."

"I can't do this on my own, Frieda," replied Käthe. "I depend on my son and he would never forgive me if I left him out of this."

"I have lost my husband and I may now lose my son, and you wish to place my grandson in danger," retorted Frieda angrily.

"Oh Frieda! When Adam and I are together, no one can resist, can they my darling?" she asked Adam as he appeared in his Hitler Youth uniform. He kissed Frieda. "We'll be all right, Grandmama," he assured her.

"Where to Madam?" asked Stephan.

"Gestapo Headquarters in Berlin, Stephan," said Käthe. The poor man's face fell. Frieda felt for her old retainer but knew Käthe was right. "Do this for all of us Stephan," she said. He drove as slowly as he could, hoping his passengers would change their minds as they approached Prinz Albrechtstrasse.

"Are you sure this is where they took Herr Peter?" He asked nervously, and Adam held his mother's hand; she had started to shake.

The car drew up to the front of the steps in front of the building. Käthe glanced upwards at the blue uniformed guards and the swastika flag flying lazily over the entrance. Her courage began to fail.

"Mama, this is the most important thing you've ever done," Adam told her. He gripped her arm and kissed her. "After this, everything will be all right," he added with a half-smile. She wondered how much he knew as they climbed out of the car.

"Madam, you cannot park here," said a traffic policeman.

"We are on official business, we won't be long officer," said Käthe, feeding on her regained courage. The policeman would always remember the impressive Hitler Youth with one of the best-dressed women he had ever seen. He bowed. "I will remain here with your driver until you return," he said.

"I'll go first," said Adam. "Hold yourself straight Mama. Look at them like Grandmama. Walk quickly." Käthe found it hard to breathe properly as they marched through the entrance. The guards didn't move.

"Now you take over Mama," said Adam as they approached an expressionless receptionist seated behind bulletproof glass. Käthe breathed in and tried to look at the man as if he was a servant.

"What is your business here, madam?" asked the receptionist coldly.

"I wish to see Kriminalrat Kloster," said Käthe.

The face behind the glass was unmoved. "You may only see officials of the Gestapo by appointment Madam," he said. "We make the appointments."

Käthe stood her ground, deriving strength from the man's offensive attitude. "My name is Frau von Saloman and I will stay here until I see Kloster," she said. Adam nodded behind her, but the receptionist was unaffected. Käthe and Adam stood there for fully three minutes as the man appeared to ignore them and continue with other work. Then suddenly he picked up the telephone and looked at Käthe and Adam as he spoke. He replaced the telephone, turned and thumbed a sheaf of documents. "Please, sit over there," he said sharply.

Peter was hauled in front of Kloster at seven o'clock in the morning. He was now plainly ill. To Peter's surprise, Kloster pushed a cup of coffee in his direction. Peter didn't move, as if the gesture was a prelude to some form of punishment.

"Take it," said Kloster. The liquid was hot, dark and sweet and Peter felt revived. He was still convinced that an onslaught of fresh charges and abuse would follow. He didn't know that Kloster had nearly concluded his work.

"Your family, I believe, have experienced some financial difficulties of late," began Kloster. Peter managed to open his eyes a little wider, but was no longer surprised at the breadth of the Gestapo man's information.

"We have uncovered the disloyalty of you and your family to the Reich," he reminded Peter. "Do you see any way to resolve these problems, Herr von Saloman?"

Peter remained silent, knowing any such solution lay in the interrogators' hands. The Gestapo man paused and produced a small sheaf of documents. "May I suggest a solution to your problems?" he said. Peter said nothing.

"It has come to my notice that you have prematurely inherited your family's property in the Grünewald." Kloster continued. Peter wondered how the Gestapo man could possibly have known that. Berger and Schöler, the family lawyers, would never betray such details, he thought. But then, they employed clerks, and Peter now knew how far the tentacles of the secret police force could extend. He waited for Kloster to continue.

"The sale of your property would provide a solution perhaps," he said. Peter thought the suggestion impertinent, but was in no position to say so. "Here is an estimate of its market value Herr von Saloman," said Kloster pushing a document towards Peter. On it was printed an estimate of the value of Die Schwanen which far exceeded any Peter would have made.

"May I ask who is the interested party?" enquired Peter.

"The Reich Government, of course Herr von Saloman," answered Kloster and in that instant Peter knew that he was being blackmailed into surrendering his family house. Kloster continued as if he were an estate agent.

"It is proposed that your family occupy a permanent lease at No. 1 Charlottenbrunnestrasse, which I think you know was a Foreign Ministry property," continued Kloster. "In return for this generous gesture, the Reich Government is prepared to forgive any misdemeanours of which your family is guilty."Then he added menacingly. "We do not of course destroy our records – regulations, you understand."

Peter sat shivering in an open-necked shirt. His priority at that moment was to sleep for as long as he was able, and he knew he had no choice but to agree.

Kloster found himself in a position he would rather have avoided. His superiors expected the arrangements to be concluded as quickly as possible, but the Gestapo man would have preferred to draw out the process to show he was not so dependent on the result and to intensify any remaining hold he had over the family. He stared at Peter and arranged and re-arranged the documents in front of him to give the impression he might change his mind. Then he pushed a copy of the new deeds across the table.

"It must all be concluded now, Herr von Saloman," he announced blandly, pushing a pen across the desk. The telephone rang. Kloster picked up the receiver, said, "there's no hurry," and replaced it.

Peter picked up the pen, took off the cap and signed away his rights to Die Schwanen.

Kloster lit another cigarette and offered one to Peter, who declined. The interrogator began to treat Peter almost as an equal. It irritated him to see his jailer ignore his medical condition and spend the next thirty minutes chatting about the international situation. Then a telephone call announced the arrival of Käthe and Adam. The Gestapo was not at the beck and call of any visitors, who would be made to wait.

Kloster gathered up the documents and placed them in a briefcase. Without another word he left his office and made a signal to the two guards, who conducted Peter to his cell. He found a blanket on the straw palliasse and fell asleep.

Kloster did not go to the reception area for some time. He first made a telephone call to Martin Borman's office at Hitler's chancellery.

Two hours later, Kloster appeared in the entrance are hall flanked by two guards.

Käthe tried to gain an impression of the bland-looking man who confronted her. She remembered him as of average build. His face seemed square, his skin pale and his mouth small. His rimless spectacles seemed to fit flush with his features and his trousers billowed out before reaching his shiny knee length boots. He walked with a measured even tread and revelled in his power over the formerly influential and important.

"Why do you wish to see me, madam?" he said impatiently. Adam sprang to his feet to give the National Socialist salute. Kloster returned it, knowing it was the only obligation he had at that moment.

Nevertheless, Adam's enthusiasm surprised him, placing him a little on the defensive. "My father should not be here, Herr Kriminalrat," said Adam stridently. "He is a good man and has done a lot for Germany."

Kloster merely nodded and turned to Käthe. "My husband has been wrongly arrested and should not be here," she began.

Kloster decided to regain the advantage. "He is here because he expressed disloyalty to certain members of our government, as I believe you did also," he answered sharply. He paused and stared straight into her face. "We have proof of this," he added.

Adam turned to give courage to his mother, and her anger grew. "Do you mean proof from Karl Wendt, a moral bankrupt? Have you spoken to Fräulein Schultz, Herr Kriminalrat?"

"Of course we have, Madam," lied Kloster. "I see no point in continuing this conversation." With that he turned and disappeared behind the partition.

"Herr Kriminalrat!" she called after him.

"Sit down, madam," said the receptionist sharply and Adam led his mother to the uncomfortable seats. Käthe was tearful and despairing. Her carefully-contrived charade, it appeared, had failed, but Adam's attitude was different.

"Mama, they haven't ordered us to leave. We might see Papa after all."

She grasped his hand and kissed him hesitantly. Such a gesture did not seem to belong in this building.

The receptionist and everyone who entered and left the building ignored them. Käthe kept glancing at her watch. At least an hour must have passed, she thought.

Peter woke, not knowing how long he had slept. Shadows passed across his eyes as he struggled to focus and raise himself from the bunk. The cell door was wide open and there were no guards. He stood up and fell back against the damp wall, but found the strength to walk to the doorway. He peered both ways down the corridor; it was deserted and silent.

Peter had difficulty in remembering the way out of the building. He turned right, expecting at any moment to he seized roughly and thrown back into his cell. He took one uncertain step after another until he reached the grey partition, which was open.

He could just see two figures seated by the entrance. His eyes began to clear; he knew who they were. He stepped through the door and began to shake and sob. Käthe ran towards him and he fell into her arms. Peter turned to Adam and embraced him.

"I should have known you would come" he said. Adam led him to the nearest chair.

"It was Mama's idea, Papa," said Adam, and Käthe looked at her son gratefully. The receptionist emerged with a buff-coloured envelope with the eagle and swastika printed in one corner and gave it to Käthe. They helped Peter half way down the steps and Stephan rushed forward to help. The policeman walked away, thinking it safer not to associate with a victim of the Gestapo.

"We must get Herr von Saloman home as soon as possible, Stephan" said Käthe. She placed the envelope in her handbag and, for the moment, forgot about it.

Greta, Helga and Frieda were horrified when they saw Peter. Stephan and Adam helped him upstairs and within thirty minutes Doctor Shraeger had arrived.

"What have these monsters done?" he exclaimed when he saw Peter. He asked to be left alone with the patient and emerged after ten minutes. "Herr von Saloman must be hospitalised as soon as possible," he announced and took Käthe to one side. "His pulse rate and blood pressure are dangerously low. The signs are that he has had a heart attack, and I fear it wasn't the first. I will arrange for Peter to be taken into the convent hospital."

Käthe moved into the hospital to watch over Peter for the next three days. The first forty-eight hours were an anxious time, but then Peter seemed to recover. As his awareness increased, so too did the burden of guilt relating to the loss of the house. He chose, for the moment, to say nothing to Käthe.

On her return to Die Schwanen, she remembered the letter she had been given. The receptionist's attitude had been so offhand that Käthe was in no hurry to open it. She described the Gestapo headquarters to Frieda, who confessed that she had been afraid that Käthe might not return. "You mentioned they gave you a letter," Frieda reminded her. Käthe found it at the bottom of her handbag and handed it to Frieda. She read it and allowed it to fall to the floor.

"What's happening to us?" she asked despairingly.

Käthe picked it up, read it and looked mystified. The brief letter contained a cheque for 40,000 Reichmarks. Käthe didn't recognise the signature and handed it to Frieda. She had recovered by now and smiled when she recognised it.

"Do you remember Peter was about to begin police proceedings against Herr Mecklendorf, our agent for rent collection?" she asked.

Käthe red the covering letter aloud. ***"Herr Mecklendorf is well known to the criminal police,"*** it began. ***"The cheque should redress the balance I think. Therefore our business is concluded. Kloster."***

"What can this mean Frieda?" asked Käthe.

"Whatever it means, I don't like it," Frieda replied.

Peter was home within a week. Dr Schraeger was not optimistic and confided his concerns to Käthe. He admitted that the convent hospital had not managed to restore Peter's blood pressure and advised he should not attempt anything strenuous. Greta and Helga were both told how serious Peter's condition was. He had asked that Adam should not be told. Käthe and Frieda had decided not to press him for an explanation of the cheque.

Peter did not know about Frieda's investments in the Swiss bank. She was confident that the family could stay at Die Schwanen. The two women agreed they should raise the matter of the letter from Kloster with Peter in the gentlest way possible.

At nine o'clock that evening, Greta brought a glass of warm milk on a silver tray for Peter. Käthe sat with him until ten o'clock and then retired to a separate room, to reduce any stress on her husband.

"We have a little extra money now my darling," she said cautiously to Peter before she left.

"What do you mean?" He replied with a hopeful smile and reached out from voluminous pillows to hold her hand.

Käthe reached inside a drawer in the bedside cabinet and produced the envelope. "We thought it might be important and didn't want to worry you," she explained as Peter saw the envelope had been opened.

"Please give it to me," he said sharply. He quickly surveyed the contents and dropped the envelope onto the bedclothes. "Please bring mother," he said.

She quickly went down the main staircase her and found Frieda and Greta together. Helga was dusting the main staircase but turned to listen.

"Peter wants to see us both together Frieda – now. I don't know why. He has seen the letter and seems agitated," said Käthe.

Peter had used the two or three minutes to work out how he might deliver the terrible news. He was very distressed and found it difficult to speak.

"I have betrayed you all," he began and explained how Kloster had threatened action against Käthe and Adam unless he signed away his rights to the house. Frieda was stunned into silence.

"I know I could have resisted," continued Peter. He began to gasp for air, holding on to Käthe's arm.

"We must call Dr Schraeger," said Frieda.

"No," said Peter. "I feel a little better. You must listen carefully," he continued urgently. "Adam must not be told any of this. He must never know he was under threat. He is still not safe. This is what you must do. You must encourage him in his Hitler Youth career. He must achieve everything he can. Father's ambition for him must be realised, if that is what Adam wants. He must show support and sympathy for this monstrous regime. Only then will he be safe. Do you both understand?"

He grasped Frieda and Käthe's hands. "Promise me this. Please!" he said urgently.

They both reluctantly agreed. Peter lay back on his pillows and looked at Frieda hoping for forgiveness. Her reply gladdened him.

"The house is not as important as the wonderful people in it," she began. "You have both escaped the clutches of those terrible people. I have a wonderful son and a wonderful daughter-in-law." She kissed them both. "I cannot pretend this is not hard for me," she continued. "But only because it is difficult for someone of my age to change their habits."

She looked Peter in the eye and smiled. "You may have done us all a favour. Our sort are a thing of the past and we must learn to live as other people. We will rebuild our lives in the Charlottenbrunnestrasse and if what you have been promised is true Peter, we have six months in which to make our plans."

Käthe was thoroughly relieved, but Peter was not pacified. "My son has been cheated out of his birthright," he answered.

Frieda retorted, "This young man – cheated? I think not. He will carve out his own future. I think we all know that."

Despite everything she had said, Frieda left nothing to chance. She usually received no visitors during the latter half of the day, but over the following months she made an exception. Regular visitors might have aroused suspicion, so the car that stopped in front of the house did so only twice over a period of three months. Her callers were Karl Berger and Edmund Schöler, the family solicitors, and they carried documents which would have guaranteed them a long prison sentence if they had been discovered.

Crowds began to flock to the Wannsee, secure in the belief that a new age had dawned. Families sat on the shingle beaches with picnic hampers. They were hardly disturbed by the wash from pleasure steamers as the passengers waved to the picnickers. Cranes and egrets watched in the sunshine from rocky promontories. The old conventions were relaxed as ladies hitched up their skirts to bathe.

Adam and Bruno took turns at rowing Peter up and down the shoreline at weekends. He couldn't remember going so long without wearing a diplomatic shirt. He began to build a new relationship with the two boys.

He found in new ally in Bruno. "What do you do at your meetings?" he asked the boys, as if addressing two sons. Adam was reticent, but not Bruno. "We play at soldiers, box each other and march up and down," he said. "Adam's the best at everything."

"No I'm not," retorted Adam, "I'm not very good at singing."

"Everybody's better than you at singing," agreed Bruno.

Peter enjoyed the banter, knowing he would never be told the truth. They enjoyed being with him and he was grateful. Bruno saw Peter as a substitute father.

They nibbled Greta's huge sandwiches before they rowed back. The boat grounded and the friends helped Peter onto the shore. He didn't want to go back to the house because he was enjoying himself too much, but Greta was firm with him. For as long as he could remember, he had never felt so relaxed.

"We'll do this again soon, boys" he said.

"We will, Herr von Saloman," called out Bruno as Peter was led back to the house. Bruno looked worried. "He's not well, is he Adam?" he remarked.

"I think I shouldn't go away on the army exercise. Mother needs me here," said Adam.

"We all need you at the home and you can't change anything here," answered Bruno. Adam nodded in agreement.

CHAPTER FOURTEEN

Helga appeared from the direction of Gustav's old workshop, having taken delivery of a large wooden crate addressed to Adam. The post office official drove back down the drive. "Herr Peter has a gift for you, Herr Adam," said Helga, grinning broadly at Bruno. They stood side by side as if they were part of a conspiracy. The sound of creaking and breaking timber came from the direction of the old workshop and Stephan appeared brandishing a crowbar.

"It's done," he said. He pushed the workshop door open and wheeled out a gleaming black and silver bicycle. Stephan produced an oil can and applied it to the moving parts. Adam gave the bicycle a puzzled stare.

"It's a present from Herr Peter," said Stephan. "I shan't need to drive you to school again."

Stephan replaced the tools and set off to prune trees with a large saw, but not before he had exchanged a mischievous glance with Helga, as if they knew an embarrassing secret was about to be revealed.

Bruno wheeled the cycle up to Adam. "Now Field Marshall, I expect a demonstration," he said. Helga was shaking her head behind Adam. "I must go now Herr Adam," she said. "My mother needs help."

Bruno began to entertain a small suspicion, as Adam seemed reluctant to mount the bike. "You're not going anywhere, Helga," said Bruno, who suspected Adam had never ridden one. "Those medical skills you've learned with your lot might come in handy, Helga," he added.

"Perhaps we might have the cycle lessons on the path by the shore," suggested Helga.

"I agree," said Bruno. "We only want two witnesses to this."

Both of them had ignored Adam, who was squirming with embarrassment. Bruno was enjoying himself immensely. He had never seen Adam looking sheepish before and was looking forward to enjoying his friend's discomfort for just a few minutes.

After they reached the path by the lake, serious lessons began and Bruno stood twenty metres in front of Adam. "See if you can reach me without falling off," he said.

Helga tried not to laugh but then became more sympathetic. Adam was so serious Bruno couldn't resist a joke. "The army'll discover bikes one day," he said.

The cycle wobbled. "Don't look at the ground, Herr Adam," said Helga, standing by Adam's side. "You can do it," said Bruno. The front wheel slipped down the steep tarmac edge and the cycle began its progress downhill towards the lake, with Adam hanging on grimly. Ten centimetres of water covered the front wheel, and then it hit a rock, throwing Adam into deep water. Helga ran after him anxiously.

"Help him Bruno," she said, annoyed with his behaviour.

Adam emerged from the lake dripping wet. He stood still at the edge of the water and began to laugh. Bruno knew why. He could forget the blow from Ulrich Semmering now.

Bruno retrieved the bicycle and saw it was undamaged. He wasn't surprised when Adam seized it and made off for the Grünewald. "I'll do this thing on my own," he said and proceeded to teach himself how to ride a bicycle some distance away.

Helga made no move towards the house. As she and Bruno saw Adam's rear wheel disappear into the woods, they laughed and embraced. Bruno pulled her towards the lake shore and the cover of some rocks. "Not yet, Bruno," she said after a few minutes. He had to be content with a lingering kiss.

They emerged from the cover of the rocks to see a triumphant Adam riding towards them with only one hand on the handlebars, but even as they watched he fell off again. Helga rushed to help him. Adam had no idea what had just happened behind the rocks. He could ride a bicycle, and Helga was still interested in him.

Doctor Schaub watched the athletics training with interest; he expected an inspection soon and was well aware of the authorities' interest in athletics success.

"Why is Schuster training alone?" he asked Alfred Rust impatiently. "Surely he would achieve his best if he trained with von Saloman and his friends?" Alfred explained he had done his best to bring the boys together. "Come Rust," replied Schaub. "Please make further efforts."

Alfred Rust bowed and talked to Adam and Bruno, who said they would try again.

"Are you going to ask him to join us, or shall I?" asked Bruno.

"I'll ask him," said Dieter Harro.

"Thanks Dieter, but this is between Adam and me. We'll tell you about it some day," answered Bruno, who then wandered over to Berndt Schuster.

"Dieter and I want you to join us, Berndt," said Bruno cheerfully. "We need someone to cut von Saloman down to size. Are you with us?"

Berndt was relieved to be asked. Even Ulrich Semmering joined them, and the training began. Berndt Schuster trained with a ferocity which surprised them all. He felt the other boys had given him permission to become champion again. Schaub watched with deep satisfaction. He could face the inspectors with confidence.

Peter was too ill to attend the next sports day at the Martin Luther School. Frieda insisted that Käthe go with Renate, but for the second time, the family matriarch would miss her grandson's achievement.

Before the three thousand metre race for the Third Year Boys began, a soldier and his female companion sat down just behind the front row of the visitors' stand. Doctor Schaub spotted the uniform and walked over to introduce himself.

"May I ask who is your son, Sergeant? he asked.

"I am Sergeant Schuster and this is my Sister Hanna, who looks after Berndt," replied the soldier. Schaub may have been an enthusiastic supporter of Germany's Government but he did not neglect his social responsibilities. He asked Alfred Rust, who was priming his starting gun, to join him.

Alfred was delighted to meet Sergeant Schuster and insisted the visitors sit in the special enclosure with Käthe and Renate. Alfred bowed to the women. "These are the parents of Berndt's friends," he announced.

Sergeant Schuster and his sister sat down very near the starting line and prepared to watch the race. When Alfred Rust told Berndt his family were watching. He couldn't wait for the start and jumped the gun, so he was severely reprimanded by Rust. However, he stormed home in first place, with Adam and Dieter joint second and Bruno third. The prizewinners were saluted with five hundred pairs of outstretched arms, and the Hitler Youth boys of the Third Year were finally united.

Käthe was her usual gracious self. When the Sergeant heard the family name, he said he recalled a Lieutenant von Saloman who had served in a Saxon Regiment during the final push in France in 1918. The afternoon's heady proceedings ended with an invitation to Sergeant Ernst Schuster, his sister Hanna and Berndt to visit Die Schwanen as soon as possible. By now everyone had conveniently forgotten Klaus and Theo Gutman.

The terms of the lease for the Charlottenbrunnestrasse apartment arrived at Die Schwanen. It was to begin just before Christmas, and the family agreed they would enjoy their last summer at the house to the full.

Frieda ordered that nothing be spared in the effort to welcome the Schuster family to Die Schwanen. Even Peter was able to help. His spirits had revived a little because of the grant of a small pension for his services to the Foreign Service. He began to think that Kloster was behaving apologetically, but he could not possibly have guessed that the Gestapo man was tidying up loose ends.

Stephan conveyed the guests to Die Schwanen in the Buick. Berndt and Bruno cycled, to make room in the car for their parents. Adam was in charge of receiving the guests, but he had asked Berndt and Bruno to arrive early. They had been asked not to wear Hitler Youth uniform, which meant Hanna had to shop for clothes for Berndt, which they could ill afford.

Adam lay in wait behind a large sweet chestnut tree with a box camera. This opportunity would be too good to miss. Helga had not given up and she suddenly appeared at Adam's elbow. She was pleased because he didn't seem embarrassed. Adam ran out from behind the tree and snapped the two boys pedalling sedately down the drive in their suits.

"Herr Adam," said Helga anxiously, "the car's here, everyone's coming down the steps."

They leaned the cycles behind a large bush and Bruno and Berndt joined their parents as Stephan opened the car doors for them. Bruno had threatened to expose Adam's lakeside performance on the bicycle if he ever showed the photos to anyone else in the 'Home'. Sergeant Ernst Schuster wore dress uniform and Adam was impressed.

Frieda, Käthe and Peter welcomed them formally and aperitifs were taken in the entrance hall. This was to be a celebration of German youth, amongst other things, and Helga had received a formal invitation as a representative of the League of German Girls.

Renate and Bruno settled quickly, but the Schusters were ill at ease. Peter relaxed Ernst Schuster by swapping experiences of the last war in France. Käthe and Frieda soon settled Hanna, but poor Berndt didn't know what to do with himself. He was at the mercy of Adam and Bruno and he graduated towards them, hoping for the best. Bruno was determined that Helga wouldn't be left out and thought it a good idea to introduce Berndt. He bowed awkwardly. He had never seen anyone as attractive as Helga as she smiled and came to his rescue.

"You're the Home leader, aren't you?" she began. "I've heard all about you. I know you're good at organising everyone." Don't overdo it, thought Bruno.

"I am not supposed to do this tonight, but for you I will make an exception," she said to Berndt, pouring him a glass of champagne. He drank it quickly and his face was soon flushed. Adam and Bruno drank theirs quickly too so that he would not be embarrassed, and they all retired to the tea house, where dinner was served.

Another genteel drinking session began at the end of the meal. It was awkward for the boys, because Frieda had insisted grandly they had should tell her all about their Hitler Youth experiences. Berndt was relieved when she moved on to the other guests.

The conversation began to die and the evening became cooler. No one noticed a side sash window open in the house at a signal from Frieda. Greta placed a phonograph on the table near the open window. Just as the guests were running out of words and had been reduced to smiling warmly at each, other the strains of a Viennese waltz filled the air. Stephan and Greta began to clear the tables, helped by Sergeant Schuster and the boys.

Adam knew his father could only watch, so he asked his mother to dance. Berndt stared open-mouthed at the display of expertise, but Bruno was not to be outdone. He got up and floated round the patio with Helga. Ernst Schuster now felt it his duty to do the same with Hanna, and Poor Berndt was left high and dry, but not for long as Bruno whispered something in Helga's ear. The phonograph was rewound and Helga asked Berndt to dance. He was in a terrible state and muttered that he didn't know how to. Bruno whispered in his ear, "We'll tell the rest you turned down an offer from one of the best-looking girls in Berlin. Go on, it's easy, she'll show you."

Helga patiently taught Berndt the waltz steps and his efforts were applauded by everyone. Berndt had arrived, to the delight of Ernst and Hanna, and they thanked Adam and Bruno for befriending him.

Ernst Schuster vowed never to neglect his son again, and before he left he delivered a pleasant surprise for the boys. "I may see you during the forthcoming exercise," he said. The three boys glanced anxiously at each other. Berndt had had no idea his father would be part of the army contingent. When everyone had left, Bruno said to Adam, "We've got to make him look good." Adam agreed.

For a few hours the von Salomans had tried to resurrect a bygone era, but only Frieda believed there was a chance of saving the gallantry of the old empire. Käthe and Peter knew the attempt was illusory. Both of them had suffered at the hands of the worst of the new order, Peter at the hands of the grey functionary Kloster and Käthe because of Wendt's treatment of her.

Käthe was very fond of Bruno and watched him being drawn into her son's circle. Peter believed he had become the controlling influence in his friendship with Adam, but Käthe believed otherwise. She now realised that Gustav's ambition lived beyond the grave, and Adam saw himself as already training for the life of a soldier.

Bruno had done most of the talking and made nearly all the jokes, but Käthe knew that Bruno basked in the reflected glory of friendship with the young aristocrat and that he had abandoned his ambition to be an architect. Here at Die Schwanen Adam was king. He had expected Bruno to make the evening a success, and his lieutenant had not let him down.

Renate had sat in a corner of the tea house and hardly moved at all. She watched the blossoming relationship between Helga and Bruno with unease. They met more often, and Bruno invited Helga to tea, only informing his mother on the same day that she was expected. There was a cool atmosphere throughout the tea party.

Bruno was upset and begged his mother for an explanation after Helga had gone. "None is needed," was Renate's reply. "This girl does not suit you and it will not last."

"I like her and she does suit me," he retorted.

"Please don't speak to me like that Bruno!" she said sharply. He didn't want to upset his mother who, he realised, was very lonely, and apologised.

Bruno had no intention of giving up Helga and he planned their meetings carefully.

Renate worked part-time in the local library and on Helga's day off, Bruno skipped school to meet her in Charlottenbrunnestrasse. Renate returned home early and surprised them together in the flat. They hadn't gone very far, but it was too much for Renate, who icily ordered Helga out of the flat, threatening to report her to Frieda.

Bruno was angry and rounded on his mother, demanding an explanation of her attitude. He failed to understand when she replied, "You must have nothing to do with such people. Please promise to have anything more to do with her." Bruno glumly made the promise but continued to see Helga whenever he could. He mistakenly believed that Renate didn't like Helga because she was a serving girl.

Chapter 15

"We'll check everything, Berndt," called Adam. "If your dad wants you home early, you'd better go." Berndt Schuster grinned thankfully.

"Can I help?" offered Ulrich Semmering, who by now was a creature of Adam's.

"Of course," answered Adam, who now had no reason now to doubt his loyalty.

Bruno didn't like him, but he kept quiet for his friend's sake and in no time at all everything was ready for the joint exercise with the army in the Black Forest.

"Do you think it'll be like the books?" enquired Bruno, picking up one of the old carbines and turning it around in his hands.

"It's bound to be," answered Adam hopefully.

"OK if I go?" asked Ulrich. Adam nodded.

The caretaker appeared with his keys and the boys collected their bicycles from his office and set off. Bruno paused to take an oil can from the leather pouch behind his saddle. Then he glanced down the street in the direction of the lawyers' offices. "Isn't that your car?" he asked, straining his eyes to identify a vehicle parked in the darkest part of the street away from the lights.

"My family only go out in the daylight now," said Adam, anxious to get home to see his father. Bruno continued to stare, unconvinced, but let the matter go and they cycled away.

Bruno was right. It was the Buick, on a dangerous errand. Stephan looked both ways for police patrols. "I think it is safe now, Madam," he said.

A light appeared in the doorway of the offices of Berger and Schöler. The shadowy figure in the doorway signalled Frieda to go in.

"It's cold, Stephan. Why don't you come in and wait for me?" suggested Frieda.

"It's all right madam. I'll stay here and look after the car," he answered.

Frieda stole across the street and Karl Berger closed the door behind her.

"You have the documents?" he asked.

They entered his office and Frieda placed a small black portmanteau on the table, extracting a sheaf of papers. Berger scanned them and nodded.

"You have all signed?" said the lawyer. Frieda nodded and Berger smiled. "You are a very resourceful woman," he said.

He was looking at a set of deeds pertaining to Die Schwanen. They were not however, the new deeds drawn up by the Party Secretariat and now locked away in Martin Borman's Office in the Reich Chancellery. These were new, witnessed by Peter and Käthe and secretly drawn up by Karl Berger and Edmund Schöler.

"Now Schöler," began Karl Berger. "You are steadier on your legs than I. Can ask you to secure these deeds?"

Edmund Schöler placed his hand on a baroque fireplace in a corner of the room and it swung open to reveal a safe. Schöler unlocked it and lovingly placed the new deeds inside.

"Just in case the new Reich doesn't last for a thousand years, we will both swear that the sale of your house was carried out under duress and the rightful owners are Peter and Käthe von Saloman," Berger assured Frieda.

Only one dim light was left on as Frieda left the building. She looked for police patrols, and saw none. She signalled to Stephan to emerge from the unlit area of the street and the car slid forward. Stephan's heart thumped as he drove the car back to the house as slowly as he dared, but they saw no policemen.

Käthe waited with Greta in the entrance hall of Die Schwanen and breathed a sigh of relief when the Buick returned. Frieda mounted the steps and Käthe opened the front door. They embraced. "It's done," whispered Frieda.

Three hundred Hitler Youth assembled on the Berlin Central Station concourse late on the following Friday. Each company assembled under its flag and every boy was issued with a twenty kilogram pack, an old carbine and a few provisions. Adam and Bruno tried to hide those provided by their mothers, but they were not spotted by any of the Wilmersdorf group.

"This is an infantry exercise, Bruno," said Adam. "No ride in an armoured car for you this time!" The Charlottenburg, Spandau and Wilmersdorf Hitler

Youth boarded a special train for Stuttgart. A convoy of army lorries took them from there to Freudenstadt, where they spent the night in youth hostels. At six o'clock the next morning, the lorries took them to a large turning in the Black Forest cordoned off by military and civil police. Adam, Bruno and Berndt jumped down from their seats and looked around. There were no tanks or armoured cars, only a few soldiers issuing instructions, and Adam's jaw dropped in disappointment.

Company Leader Graf appeared. "Line up in your companies," he ordered. "There'll be a kit inspection in ten minutes." Then came the next surprise. There was to be a forced march with rifles and packs to the next rendezvous.

By the time they reached their destination, most of the boys were exhausted, but they were practised in not showing it, except for one small boy in the in the Spandau Company. He sat down on a tree stump and was treated with contempt by Gunther Graf. "You have let your comrades down!" he barked. "Take no further part in the proceedings." He stalked off.

Bruno knew the boy. "That's Benno Roepke," he said. "He's a great boxer, Adam." His friend grinned when he remembered. "He wants to be a doctor," added Bruno.

"He looks terrible," said Adam. Graf reappeared. "Attend to your duties," he reminded them, and Benno was abandoned.

Each hut leader was given a sheet of instructions and Berndt read them out. Concealed in the forest, they said, were regular army soldiers wearing dark blue ribbons on their wrists. The boys were issued with light blue ribbons. Whoever you surprised had to hand over his ribbon and became your prisoner.

The paths in the forest were pointed out by marshals. "The army is waiting for you up there," explained one. "Their headquarters are about six kilometres away."

Benno Roepke sat disconsolate on his tree stump. He had brought his medical kit and he faced redundancy.

Berndt thought he had an advantage because two of his company had read books on the subject. They crowded round him as planning began. He showed the maps and the instructions to Adam and Bruno, who looked carefully at them and then at each other.

"Did you see that other path into the forest behind us as we came in?" said Bruno.

"Yes," replied Adam.

"We can strike north and by-pass the army position," said Bruno. Berndt listened apprehensively. "We've been ordered to use these other paths," he reminded them.

"We'll get the chop if we try anything else," said Uve Müller.

"I'll take the rap if they don't like it," promised Adam.

"No, interrupted Berndt. "I will. We'll do it. Get yourselves ready. Graf's waving a starting flag. Strap your rifles across the back of your packs."

A small voice said, "Can I be your Medical Officer?" It was a hopeful Benno Roepke.

"Why us?" asked Bruno.

"I like you three," he replied. "I want to help you to win."

"We won't stop for anyone, Roepke," warned Adam.

"I'll look after him," said Semmering. Bruno shuddered.

Graf dropped his flag, and three hundred boys entered the forest. In the confusion the Wilmersdorf group slipped back down the main track to the old forestry path. Adam was the leader in all but name, and felt as if he had forged a fighting unit. Like the great commanders, he would disobey orders, if necessary. He felt uplifted.

The Wilmersdorf 'home' advanced down the forestry path at a furious rate and the going was easy for half a kilometre. The path came to an end at a pile of newly-felled trees and ahead was dense, dark forest. Most of the boys looked downcast.

"Follow north on the compass Bruno," said Adam. Hardly any light penetrated the trees and rifles snagged up on low branches. "Keep going," shouted Berndt. "Carry your rifles."

Some were frightened of the forest and began to slow down. Adam ran up and down the line, urging them on. This time he would not lose control as he had after the typhoon on the Pearl River. Even Bruno began to think they were on a fool's errand, but said nothing.

There was a crash ahead as one boy fell down a small ravine and reappeared with cuts and bruises. Benno assured him there was nothing seriously wrong.

Two boys said they had seen a bear. Another disturbed a deer, which leapt away startled. "Keep going!" shouted little Benno.

They found a clearing and on the edge was a wooden hut. A woodcutter was swinging a large axe. One panic-stricken boy pointed his carbine at the unfortunate man and shouted "hands up." Berndt pushed the gun aside and apologised to the woodcutter. On they went.

A stream, set in a deep culvert, lay across their path and a fallen tree straddled it. They all got across except Armin Schurmann. He plunged into the icy water below at the foot of a small waterfall.

The expedition had given Benno Roepke strength he didn't know he had. He plunged down the bank and Ulrich Semmering followed him. They hauled Armin out of the stream and sat him down on a flat rock. Benno bandaged his damaged foot. "He can walk," shouted Benno. "Help him up."

A chain of arms hauled Armin, clutching at boot and sock, back to the trail. Benno supervised as the boot was put back on. "Try it," he said. Armin managed to walk. "I can carry on," he assured Berndt.

"I'll scout ahead," said Bruno, who disappeared for half an hour. By this time Adam thought the whole exercise would soon be over. Bruno reappeared with bleeding hands and arms, having fallen into dense brambles. "False alarm," he said. "We're not there yet."

By now the boys were cold and miserable, their uniforms dirty and tattered. They ploughed on until Bruno reappeared, after another scouting expedition. "Get down and keep quiet," he whispered urgently. "They're over there." He was pointing to a gap in the trees. He led Berndt and Adam to the edge of the clearing. They lay down in the long grass and surveyed the scene.

"Look," said Bruno. "There's District Leader Graf." He seemed embarrassed as he assessed his boys' efforts so far. At least two hundred wretched-looking boys had already been taken prisoner. "What a bunch of amateurs," whispered Bruno.

Graf ticked off names on a clipboard while talking to an army Major. By the Major's side was Sergeant Ernst Schuster and Adam grinned from ear to ear. Berndt seemed worried. "It'll be all right," Adam assured him.

"Who are they?" asked Bruno, pointing to two men sitting at a trestle table underneath an oak tree at the far edge of the clearing.

"Forget them," replied Adam. "This is what we must do."

"Listen all of you," said Berndt quietly, turning to the others.

"Berndt, take half to the other side of the clearing, through the trees," said Adam. "I'll wave to you when we're ready. We'll deal with the Major. Ignore those two under the tree."

Off went Berndt and Armin Schurmann, who had taken off his boots and strung them round his neck. Adam gave the signal and twenty dishevelled fourteen-year-old boys rushed into the clearing. Berndt and Adam stepped forward grandly and Adam did the talking.

"We demand your surrender, Major," he said. "Please hand over your ribbons." There was a buzz of excitement among the boys who had been taken prisoner and they watched to see what had would happen next. The Wilmersdorf 'home' had failed to notice that none of the officers in the clearing were wearing any ribbons. The horrified looks which turned to anger on the faces of Gunter Graf and the Major told Berndt Schuster and his followers they had made a ghastly mistake.

The boys remained kneeling, pointing their carbines at the Major and Sergeant Schuster. The Sergeant's main concern was his son's behaviour. At first he didn't know where to look, but he quickly regained his presence of mind.

"On your feet and stand to attention!" he shouted to the boys. They stood at ease, looking sheepish. The Major made a gesture and a copy of the order of the day was handed to him. He walked up and down in front of the boys.

"Have you seen a copy of this?" he snapped.

"Yes sir," was a subdued collective reply.

"Who is your group leader?" he asked. Berndt stepped forward and threw out his arm in salute.

"Are you responsible for what happened here?" asked the Major.

"Yes Herr Major," Berndt answered.

Suddenly Adam and Bruno stepped forward and saluted. "Permission to speak Major," said Adam confidently and the officer nodded. "We share the responsibility Herr Major," said Adam.

Gunther Graf interrupted, knowing he would bear the ultimate responsibility. "Please allow me to deal with this, Herr Major," he said. He tore the insignia from Berndt's shoulders. "You are hereby stripped of your rank, Schuster. Your group will lose all privileges until further notice and you will not join the campfire celebrations. Get yourselves cleaned up and dismiss." His face was as red as a turnip.

"Wait!" said a voice sharply from the edge of the clearing. The two men at the trestle table stood up and walked towards the boys. All the troops snapped to attention.

"At ease," said the smaller man of the two. He was of average height and dapper and his movements were brisk and deliberate. He stood in front of the boys with his arms behind his back. He wore the insignia of the Führer's army bodyguard.

Adam was trained to look over the shoulders of superior officers, but his glance was drawn towards the uniform of the other man. He wore black with silver braid. The boys had heard of the new SS Soldiers and here was one who, Adam believed, wore the uniform of the Uhlan Lancers.

His pulse raced and he felt the blood rush to his head. The regular army officer, a Colonel, walked up and down the lines of the bedraggled members of the Wilmersdorf group. He passed in front of Benno Roepke and saw the medical kit.

"Was there much work for you today?" asked the officer.

"Yes sir, a little," stammered Benno.

He stopped in front of Adam, Bruno and Berndt. "I see you have lost your rank young man," he began. "Do you know why?"

"Because we disobeyed orders Herr Colonel," answered Berndt humbly. Sergeant Schuster had decided his son had done his best and suspected his son's new friends might bear most of the responsibility.

"Whose idea was this?" asked the Colonel. Berndt half turned towards Bruno and Adam. Bruno had decided his friend should do the talking this time, and Adam did not disappoint.

"It appears it was yours," said the officer to Adam. "Why did you not submit your plans to your superiors?"

Adam's answer scandalised the listeners. "They would not have understood, Herr Colonel," answered Adam, without a trace of repentance. The SS Officer's eyebrows went up. "I see," said the Colonel. "Why did you use this manoeuvre?"

Adam half-turned to Bruno, anxious his friend should share any credit. Bruno would rather have been left out of it. "Permission to speak Herr Colonel," he said. The SS Officer began to stamp impatiently. "Because it was unexpected Herr Colonel," said Bruno.

The officer looked interested. "And what did you hope to achieve?" he asked Adam.

"Complete surprise, Herr Colonel," answered Adam.

"Do you know why you succeeded?"

"Yes Herr Colonel, the enemy's attention was diverted by the main frontal attack. We have a good unit and pressed ahead despite difficulties. I knew we would win." answered Adam, sensing he was about to turn the tables.

"Were the ideas your own?" continued the officer.

"We read two good books in school Herr Colonel," answered Adam.

Sergeant Schuster realised his son would not be disgraced and felt relieved. The Colonel recognised something of himself in the arrogant youngster who did not realise the book he had read was written by the officer in front of him. He turned to the SS Officer, who had been making notes.

"Well Sulzbach, do you see anything to interest you?" he asked.

"What are your names and units?" asked the SS Officer. As he wrote Adam's name, he scribbled something after it and the Colonel read it. "So your people will give him a hard time, Sulzbach," he said quietly.

"What is your ambition?" the SS Officer asked Adam.

"To be an officer in the infantry, Herr Captain," he answered, successfully guessing the officer's rank.

"Why?" asked Sulzbach.

"Because they do all the fighting sir," replied a completely revived Adam.

"Perhaps we will meet again, young man," said the Colonel as he turned to leave. He paused in front of Gunther Graf. "You have a talented bunch here Graf. Look after them for me."

There were no punishments. Graf recovered from his embarrassment and saw the episode as an opportunity to raise his profile and that of the West Berlin Hitler Youth. The campfire celebrations centred on Adam, Bruno and Berndt, who was reinstated as Hut Leader. Graf asked a deputy to return Berndt's insignia away from the glare of the celebrations. The army exercise was to be the highlight of the Hitler Youth magazine and Graf insisted on posing with the three boys for the photographs.

The euphoria continued on the train from Freudenstadt to Berlin and Graf honoured the three boys with a visit to their carriage. He caught Berndt and Bruno in an embarrassing moment as he was reminding Berndt of his dance steps. Adam's head was buried in his book.

"Stay seated," said Graf, continuing his campaign to enhance his reputation.

He wanted to imply that he moved in high military circles. "Do you know who those two men were?" he asked Adam, who confessed he had no idea. "The Colonel wrote the book you have there, von Saloman," said Graf. "Captain Sulzbach belongs to the first SS division. They are the new guardsmen, the Führer's personal soldiers." With that he swept out of the carriage, hoping he had left the boys suitably impressed.

Just as the three let out sighs of relief, Benno Roepke approached them shyly, his medical kit still strapped around his waist. "Can I sit with you three?" he asked.

"Why not?" answered Bruno. "We owe a lot to you."

Adam grinned. He allowed him to scan the book and the would-be medical officer was at peace.

"I'll be all right, Helga," said Peter irritably as he walked towards the rowing boat on the shingle beach. She wondered if she ought to tell her mother or Frieda.

"Please Herr Peter, you are not fit enough to do this," insisted Helga.

"I'm much better now," he said impatiently. "Please help me to launch the boat. I promise I'll be back in half an hour."

He was desperate to prove he could do something unaided and Peter knew his only chance lay in Käthe's absence at the convent hospital. Reluctantly she helped him to push the boat out, dropping the two dogs into it. They stood on the bow spar as Peter gently rowed away from the shore.

"I'll wait her for you Herr Peter. Remember, only half an hour," she called after him.

As Peter disappeared from view behind the house, Helga began to regret allowing him near the boat. She kept checking her watch and looked towards the rear doors of the house, fearful of Greta's untimely arrival.

Peter slowly came into view rowing slowly and the dogs began to bark when they saw Helga. He seemed all right as the boat grounded in the shallows. Hansl and Gretl jumped into the water and nearly disappeared. Peter climbed out with a reassuring smile and helped Helga to pull the boat onto the shore, the dogs splashing gleefully through the water's edge.

But as he turned to thank Helga, he collapsed on to the ground. "Stephan, Mother!" Helga cried at the top of her voice. Stephan was polishing the car at the rear of the house and was the first to arrive. Greta had seen what was happening from the side window on the first floor and rushed out of the house carrying blankets. The two women made Peter as comfortable as they could while Greta telephoned Dr Schraeger.

Frieda now appeared. "We cannot leave him here," she said, as she saw how the colour had drained from Peter's face. "We must carry him inside and Madame Käthe must be told," said Stephan. They were not able to move him further than the entrance hall, where they laid him on the chaise longue. Then they leaned against the wall, exhausted.

Dr Schraeger arrived within ten minutes. Stephan had recovered enough to help carry Peter upstairs to bed. "Please leave us," said the doctor and they waited downstairs.

Frieda clung to the banister at the foot of the stairs. She peered towards Peter's bedroom door and began to sob silently. The doctor came slowly downstairs, looking grave. Just then Käthe burst through the front door. Dr Schraeger stopped her. "Please Käthe, before you go to see him," he began. He pursed his lips. "I have done everything I can for Peter. I'm afraid it's only a matter of time. I can't promise more than a few hours at best."

"That can't be!" Käthe replied. She dashed up the stairs to find Peter unconscious. His mouth was half open and he breathed in short gasps. His face was colourless. The others quietly climbed the stairs and joined her.

"I will stay with you as long as you wish," promised Dr Schraeger.

Stephan knocked on the bedroom door and came quietly in. "Shall I meet Herr Adam and Bruno?" he asked.

"Why yes, of course Stephan," answered Käthe. "Please be as quick as you can, and say nothing." He understood and left to drive to Berlin Central.

Peter's eyes half opened and he reached out slowly in a desperate attempt to touch someone. Käthe took his hand. "We're all here, my darling" she said. He seemed aware of everyone in the room. Käthe and Frieda sat either side of the bed and Käthe stroked his head. He opened his eyes a little more and attempted a smile. He managed to gently squeeze Käthe's hand. "Where's Adam?" he asked.

On and on went the self-congratulation on the Berlin–Freudenstadt train. "Come with us Berndt, we'll give you a lift," said Adam as the train pulled into the station and the three hundred boys began to dump their kit on the platform.

The three friends walked to the station concourse and threw their rifles and packs onto a wooden seat, and the Buick drew up in front of them. As Stephan got out, Bruno knew something was wrong. "Can we give Berndt a lift to Charlottenburg?" asked Adam. Then he saw Stephan's grave expression.

"Herr Peter is very sick," he began. "We must go to the house immediately."

"We'll be all right," said Berndt. "We'll find our own way."

Bruno followed Adam to the car. "Phone me as soon as you know anything," he said. Bruno knew this might be the end, and he dreaded his next visit to Die Schwanen. The pleasures and achievements of the last few heady days drained away as he watched the Buick leave the station.

Stephan said nothing else until they reached the gates. "They are all waiting for you Herr Adam. I'll take care of your kit," he promised.

Adam jumped out of the car and raced up the steps. Greta met him. "They're all in your father's room," she said tearfully. Käthe put her finger to her lips as Adam burst through the door, desperate to talk to his father.

Peter tried to say something. "Ssh!" whispered Käthe. "Save your strength, my darling." She had seen him like this before, in a Berlin hospital bed in 1918. He had recovered then and Käthe hoped against hope that he would recover now.

Frieda, Käthe and Adam took turns at keeping vigil through the night. Greta came in early in the morning and drew the curtains slightly. Peter seemed to respond, and Helga brought a light breakfast for him. "He might need it, madam," she said half apologetically to Frieda. She couldn't forget she had allowed Peter to go rowing.

Peter had gone still and silent, and Adam took his cold hand and copied Yuxiang by rubbing it, but there was no response. Käthe looked for life signs. There were none. Peter had gone. Adam fled to his room threw himself on the bed and sobbed.

Dr Schraeger arrived shortly afterwards and promised to take care of everything. Within an hour, an ambulance had arrived for Peter. The family and their servants watched it drive slowly back towards the darkness of the Grünewald. Stephan removed his cap as Peter left Die Schwanen for the last time.

CHAPTER FIFTEEN

That night Adam stayed with his mother until she had sobbed herself to sleep. He left the house to walk the grounds and noticed a flickering candlelight in the tea house. He mounted the wooden stairs to find his grandmother staring at the moonlit waters of the lake. She had gone there for solitude, but was grateful to see Adam. She placed her hand on his.

"The torch has passed to you, Adam," she said. "I wonder what you will do with it." He couldn't give an answer, and Frieda expected done. "It's time to sleep," she said and they went into the house.

Over the next few days Adam rarely left his mother's side, but she insisted he return to school before the authorities sent their bloodhounds to Die Schwanen. Bruno had paved the way. He telephoned Dr Schaub, who prepared the class and enlisted Dieter Harro to make things easier. Bruno tried to treat Adam's return as a normal school day until he saw him dissolve into tears. The first to offer sympathy was Ulrich Semmering.

Frieda and Käthe lovingly organised the many photographs of the China experience. "I have asked Adam to say a few words at the funeral, Käthe. Do you approve?" asked Frieda. "The photographs will help him," she added. But their thoughts were elsewhere and Frieda slammed the photographs down.

"I cannot tolerate the thought that my son has died in disgrace Käthe. This is what we will do. You will inform the newspapers and I will telephone the Foreign Ministry." She let her fist descend gently to the arm of her chair. "These people will speak to me. They will be told."

They were surprised by the reaction. Frieda phoned the Secretariat but was made to wait. Herr Neumann himself answered the telephone and apologised profusely for the delay. He promised that he himself would send a signal to the China station announcing Peter's death. Frieda and Käthe would never know that Wendt had been dismissed in disgrace for his philandering, but most of all for his inept handling of Chiang Kai-shek and his friends. The new Consul returned the signal, promising to inform the family's old contacts.

It was as if Peter had never been investigated. Locked away in Neumann's safe was a memo from Kloster ordering that normality be resumed as soon as possible. He added that Peter von Saloman was to be remembered as a true servant of the Reich.

Neumann telephoned Käthe to inform her that the Chinese Ambassador was to attend the funeral. She thought it all diplomatic hypocrisy, until she saw the Ambassador carrying two large wreaths. The first to be placed by the graveside was attended by a letter from Chiang Kai-shek. It read ,"To my friend Peter, who will be missed by us all. Greetings to my favourite German family."

The Ambassador presented the second wreath to Adam. The dedication, like the first, had been specially telegraphed. "Please accept the flowers of the Si-Kiang," it read. "Our thoughts are with you and your family. The family of Huang Yuxiang."

Bruno supported his friend as his turn came to speak to the congregation, standing side by side with him. Adam thanked the congregation. He managed the words "Best friend and supporter," before he broke down, and Bruno helped him back to his seat. Peter was laid to rest beside Gustav, and Käthe was left to wonder why Renate had not attended the funeral. As they left the church, Bruno explained that his mother was not feeling too well. Bruno had brought a wreath, but Käthe thought it was not enough. She was surprised and offended by Renate's absence, although she knew better than to press Bruno to explain.

As usual Helga visited the local bakery before eight o'clock that morning. She was not aware that she had been followed. As she emerged from the bakery with her basket full of bread, a stranger introduced himself as a colleague of Renate's from the local library. He pressed a sealed envelope into Helga's hands and rode off on a bicycle. Intrigued, Helga placed the bread in her bicycle pannier and opened the letter. It was an invitation to take tea at Renate's flat and it said emphatically that Bruno would not be there. The meeting was to take place in mid-afternoon.

Helga stood her cycle on concrete supports outside the apartment in the Charlottenbrunnestrasse. It was raining heavily and she hurried inside after shaking the rain from her headscarf. She was not looking forward to the meeting.

There was silence in the building but Helga, like all newcomers, was being watched. She had lived a privileged existence at Die Schwanen. What she had to say was governed only by the conventions of politeness. She was entering the arena of a new set of rules, set by the whisperers, who were suspicious of all strangers.

CHAPTER FIFTEEN

As she mounted the stairs, chinks of light escaped from the doors as pairs of eyes watched her carefully. The chief whisperer left her door slightly ajar permanently in the daylight hours so to miss nothing. Just inside her door was a small table and on it a notebook and pencil. She was pale, tight-lipped and alert. Even indoors she wore a black hat with a silver hatpin. Her dark coat lay draped over a chair, one of its sleeves displaying a swastika armband, which afforded an unmarried lady like this some protection in National Socialist Germany. She was at the centre of a web and the other whisperers were her creatures, anxious to prove their own conformity by reporting the apparently deviant behaviour of others. This lady was Fräulein Ilse Diels.

She was sure that the fair-haired visitor had knocked at the door of the quiet little librarian who lived further along the corridor, and waited patiently until the visitor emerged after a short time, her face flushed and tear-streaked.

Ilse picked up her pencil, and the others strained their ears. "It's for the best if you don't see him again," said the quiet librarian.

"How could he not tell me?" asked the visitor, as if she had been betrayed.

Her hostess took her arm. "Because he doesn't know," she replied.

The young visitor was angry and resentful. She stared at the hostess in disbelief through her tears, convinced that what she had been told was no more than a clever ploy to break up her relationship. The blonde girl ran down the stairs and the door down the corridor closed. Ilse Diels scribbled furiously. There were people she knew who would be interested.

Twenty Nationalist Chinese soldiers, exhausted and bedraggled, stopped when they heard the sound of rushing water. They were on the northern side of an westward-flowing river in northern China close to the Manchurian border, and they were on the wrong bank.

Scouts had reported that the Japanese had thrown bridges over the river to the east and west of the small pockets of survivors. Most of them were young recruits from the south who had long ago lost interest in fighting a resourceful and well supplied enemy. They had not been paid for months and longed to return to their families in the Pearl Delta.

To become a prisoner in this war was a fearful prospect. They had heard too many stories of the maltreatment of Chinese prisoners by the Japanese. Their officers were dead or had deserted and they turned for leadership to their doctor. Dr Jacob Meissner had become an expert at begging, borrowing or stealing medical supplies and was their only hope as they settled down in what they are all hoped was a safe bivouac for the night.

The fire burned low and the noise of insects grew louder. Suddenly, there were shots and cries. A squad of Japanese soldiers burst into the camp, pushing one of the perimeter guards in front of them. The frightened young soldiers neglected to bow to the Japanese officer and one of them was struck on the head by a rifle butt. The doctor rushed forward to help, but stopped when a rifle barrel was thrust in his face.

The barrel was pushed aside by the officer, curious to know why the Chinese unit had a European medic. The prisoners were roped together and began a long march to a Manchurian prisoner-of-war camp. Few of them would survive.

Dr Meissner was not roped together with the others. The officer examined his passport and remembered that Germany was now a friend of Japan, so he was given food, which he insisted on sharing with his men. Then his captors discovered he was Jewish.

Autumn and early winter passed quickly at Die Schwanen. The family prepared to spend the last Christmas at the house, but Frieda didn't abandon her usual practice. A huge Christmas tree and nativity scene stood on the lawn near the foot of the steps. She held open house and friends visited them over the festive period. Christmas Day was cold, and nearly half a metre of snow fell. The ceremonial opening of Christmas gifts took place under the tree with Greta and Helga's wild boar roast.

The family had dreaded Christmas without Peter, but there were some compensations. For the first time Kurt and Lisa Holman agreed to spend Christmas at Die Schwanen.

Käthe received a telephone call from Christina Schultz, who announced that she was to marry Captain Fischer of the *Derfligger*. The ship was shortly to be taken out of commission and Captain Fischer had brought a special package from Canton. It was addressed to Adam, who opened it alongside the Christmas gifts, which included an overweight-looking doll sent by Bruno that was meant to look like District Leader Graf.

The package from China contained a wooden model of the Si-Kiang

House, and wedged in the courtyard was a small scroll. Adam had not handled Lin Hui's broadsword since his return from China. The scroll contained instructions on how to train with it.

Adam drifted into another world and didn't hear his mother call, "Adam, Bruno's here." He remembered one sentence more than any other: "Rotate the sword round the body like a shield. Then strike like the wind."

Käthe looked over his shoulder, "You'd like to go back, wouldn't you?" she said. Adam didn't know what to say as he looked at her and then at Bruno. He remembered the doll and started to chuckle. He picked it up and pretended to feed it with a large piece of crackling. "He can take more than that," quipped Bruno.

Adam said 'Auf Wiedersehen' to his friend at midnight. Käthe put her arm around her son and said, "I would never get permission to leave Germany now, let alone go to China."

Chapter 16

Christmas had hardly passed when Karl Berger rang to make arrangements to sign the house away. Stephan drove Frieda to the lawyers' office on a bitterly cold January day. The old family retainer had thought of nothing else but his own future in the last few weeks. Frieda had tried to think of a way she might employ him, but he looked as though he would have to be made redundant. She didn't know how to tell him.

Frieda stared at the frost-covered trees and metal railings as Stephan drove the Buick carefully on the road's frozen surface. She was terrified at the thought of who might be present at the signing ceremony. Most of all, she would find the humiliation of it all hard to bear.

As the car slowed down, she saw a long black saloon flying a swastika pennant parked outside the offices. It reminded her of the imprisonment and torture of Peter, and she clenched her fists against the cold.

Stephan helped his mistress climb the icy steps and rang the doorbell. Despite the cold, Frieda held herself erect, determined not to suggest that she had been complicit in a property fraud. She contented herself by repeating to herself over and over again that the authorities had committed criminal acts against her family.

Edmund Schöler answered the door and directed Stephan to a small waiting room. Then Schöler opened the door to the main office. Behind a long table sat an array of lawyers and party officials. They stood up and bowed as Frieda came in, never relaxing their displays of excessive politeness.

Frieda was invited to sit in a red leather chair and offered coffee, which she declined. The relevant documents waited for her signature. She peered individually at everyone in the room, as if they were there by special invitation. Her reputation had gone before her, and her indulgent stare made some of them nervous.

"Shall we proceed?" said one of them. Karl Berger offered Frieda a pen, which she imperiously waved away, to the discomfort of several of the officials from Borman's office.

"There is one other matter," said Frieda grandly. "I note that I am to rent the apartment in Charlottenbrunnestrasse." She put a distasteful emphasis on the word 'rent.'

"Do I take it you would prefer the option to buy, Frau von Saloman?" asked the man from the Party Secretariat. Frieda nodded and the man said a few words to a colleague. "Before we proceed, may I make a telephone call?" he asked, and returned within ten minutes.

To Frieda's surprise, she was allowed to buy the apartment, and the offer price for Die Schwanen was revised upwards. She signed the documents and left, declining to shake any hands. She cast a worried look at Berger and Schöler and then at the fireplace.

Stephan and Frieda returned in silence after the old retainer had expressed sympathy. She climbed the front steps and stared at the ice-encrusted wooden crates which would soon contain her most precious possessions.

Greta already knew she would stay on as housekeeper and general help, and Helga had acquired a position as housekeeper in Charlottenburg. Stephan stared at the crates, hoping to prove his indispensability by helping to load them.

He relieved Frieda of the responsibility of dismissing him the next day. He finished a piece of his beloved topiary, put the tools in their place and said goodbye to Frieda as if he were having his day off. He pushed his cycle down the snow-covered drive without leaving a forwarding address.

Frieda made arrangements of her own, not mentioned in the new house deeds. No one could fail to hear the banging and sawing and the noise of collapsing timber in the vicinity of Gustav's War Room. Adam knew it would remain padlocked for the time being, but was sure that one day it would be opened once again, though he knew that could not happen until after his grandmother's death. He gazed at the huge brass padlock on the door.

Then one day he came home from school and the padlock had gone. So had the door. Adam saw only an expanse of seamless oak panelling smelling of fresh varnish, applied so that no part of it would be conspicuous. He walked to the rear of the house, to the steps that led to the secret door over which was an ivy-covered window. The window had been bricked in and the entrance was masked by a pile of fuel meant for the boilers in the cellars. Frieda was determined that the shrine to her husband would never be defiled by the new owners.

The carpenters responsible disappeared as quickly as they had arrived into the maze of walkways in the Grünewald. Frieda asked if she might say goodnight to Adam in his room. She kissed him as he lay dozing and he opened his eyes wide. She lifted her fingers to her lips and whispered. "You will live through these terrible times and one day I know you will open the War Room. There are others who know of this sacred trust who have promised to see you inherit. Goodnight Adam." She stole out of the room as if she had been part of a dream.

The family had to endure one more slight before they left, when a small convoy of trucks trundled down the drive. Tradesmen got out, wearing aprons and carrying carpenters' tools. A pompous little man marched them into the house, hardly bothering to introduce himself and treating the family as if they were trespassers. He lifted his clipboard and barked out instructions. The older carpenters gazed in awe at the wooden panelling and the sweep of the old staircase. Their spirits sank at the thought of the vandalism they were about to commit. The Party Official told them to stop gazing at the walls and ceilings and to get on with the work in hand. He was proud of his planned alterations for the Entrance Hall, and incapable of realising that one of the trademarks of the Government he was working for was extreme bad taste. The entrance hall was to become a bar, and the only things he carefully removed were the paintings, which became part of Hermann Goering's private collection.

The bedrooms would soon lose the stamp of ownership as they became overnight stopping places for the Party privileged and their guests. A few graced the bedrooms with their wives, others with playthings they had met in Berlin nightclubs.

"Where do you want this?" or "Where do you want that Madam?" echoed round the rooms of No. 1 Charlottenbrunnestrasse when the removal men disappeared. Frieda and Greta looked bewildered as they moved slowly from room to room, and Greta broke down. "What will we do, madam?" she asked.

CHAPTER SIXTEEN

Before Frieda could revitalise her old housekeeper and friend, there was a knock at the door and in walked a deferential but cheerful figure, cap in hand. "Good morning ladies – Albert Hartman, concierge, at your service," he announced jovially. "May I say I know everything about this place, and you look the sort of people who deserve to know about it!"

Käthe introduced everyone. Frieda had an immediate effect on Albert, who decided that from then on he would try to be chief handyman and her head butler. He muttered to Greta, fingering his cap, "I'll always ask you first." He announced he would have to tell them everything at once, because a police registration team would be here shortly. "I do know you're friendly with the Grabowskys on the first floor. Very nice," he said. "And may I ask a favour? Frau Reymann wants an introduction. She's a fine lady from a good family. I shouldn't say such things," he said, "but I would be careful of Fräulein Diels on the first floor." He hesitated and whispered. "She watches and listens and writes things down."

With that Albert set to and helped the ladies settle in, clashing gently with Greta after making a suggestion as to how to stack cooking pots.

There was another knock at the door and a well-groomed lady with a hesitant smile walked in. Martha Reymann welcomed everyone, insisting they join her for coffee after they had settled in. She had a habit of clasping her hands to make everything she said sound interesting. None of them need have worried about Adam's reaction to the apartment. He was in the same building as his best friend.

Now a new institution took shape in Wilmersdorf: the Charlottenbrunnestrasse Ladies' Circle. Word quickly passed round that a minor member of the aristocracy had moved into the building. Already Martha Reymann had introduced herself and offered Frieda, Käthe and Greta coffee. The gesture was returned. Renate Grabowsky joined them as a matter of course and during the meeting Martha Reymann mentioned that she had a shy friend called Hanni Dirksen. Would Frieda mind if she joined them, assuming of course, another meeting took place?

Greta had now taken charge, anxious to justify the continuation of her employment by Frieda. The kitchen became a hive of activity prior to the meetings and Greta's cakes and biscuits became one of the main attractions of the circle.

Martha introduced her friend Hanni from an apartment block across the street. She was thin, shy and pale but sat erect with bright eyes and was good at making the other women seem interesting. She only took a cake after circling it warily with her hand and then nibbling it apologetically.

There was a problem in the form of Ilse Diels. She was not invited by anyone because they didn't like her, but one of her creatures was a member and reported back to the 'Chief Whisperer'. The Ladies' Circle seemed to be in dire danger, but Martha knew where to turn. "Shall we ask Adam and Bruno for advice?" she suggested. "Ilse seems to like them."

The boys had a sure touch in such matters. The Hitler Youth had prepared them for almost anything, and a message had just appeared from Ilse saying she expected to be invited.

"Ladies," advised Adam, "wouldn't you rather have Frau Diels where you can see her?" The ladies nodded and Frieda glowed with pride in her grandson. "And you, Bruno?" asked Frieda. He put his hand to his mouth and said thoughtfully, "You have to pretend you like her. You should also spend at least five minutes in turn talking to her." Käthe laughed, but knew it was sound advice.

So Ilse Diels was invited. She was never seen without her black hat and silver hatpin. Her chin was always withdrawn, military fashion, and she was ill at ease. She was regularly abandoned in a corner, but not for long, and soon assumed that chair was her own.

Adam and Bruno paid a price for their advice. Ilse thought they were wonderful and after that she regularly intercepted them by Albert Hartmann's office. They sometimes had to give her more than five minutes.

Albert Hartman tapped on the door early one evening and seemed concerned. "Frau von Saloman," he began anxiously. "Two policemen are here and wish to see you."

"Please invite them in, Herr Hartman," replied Frieda confidently.

Constable Schneider and his assistant walked in, refusing offers of refreshment and even of a seat. "Who is in charge here?" asked Schneider, sharply.

"Well I'm the owner of the flat, officer," answered Frieda.

"What is the purpose of your meetings, madam?" he enquired officiously.

"Well, we discuss wallpaper, and sometimes the price of fish."

Schneider became annoyed. "Are you aware that meetings of this size require police permission?" he asked.

Just then Adam appeared from his room, not realising who had called and hoping to give support. Schneider gave him a withering look and he went back to his room.

"Madam," continued Schneider. "You are to report to the local Police Post to apply for permission to hold your meetings. That's all I have to say."

Schneider's partner called the next day to say that permission was not necessary. It appeared that the sale of Die Schwanen continued to give Frieda some influence.

The Ladies' Circle grew in size and flourished, to the point where eager applicants had to be turned away. Once again Frieda had become a social focus and she hadn't enjoyed herself so much in years. But as Adam became the real centre of his Hitler Youth 'home,' his confidence became arrogance.

The new way of life in Charlottenbrunnestrasse was blighted by quarrels between Adam, Frieda and Käthe. Hitler's latest gamble had paid off. Austria was now part of Germany, and Adam became insufferable in his support of the regime.

Frieda chose to lecture him on the criminality of Germany's leaders and Adam was openly rude to her, to Käthe's disgust and amazement. It was not Greta's place to take sides, but she let Adam know her feelings by giving him a succession of black looks.

Soon the boys would have to do labour service. Käthe and Frieda privately agreed that Adam should leave home and do his as soon as possible. The three women were glad to see Adam go, at least for a short time. He helped to build the Hanover-Berlin Autobahn, and Bruno worked on a farm in Bavaria.

Adam managed to return home from time to time and during these periods he developed a new taste. He knew he had upset his mother and grandmother and decided to repair the damage. Käthe suggested they might go to the cinema together, and Adam agreed. She didn't know he had another idol besides the Führer. He jumped at the chance of seeing a film starring the Reich's heartthrob, Christina Sodenstern. Not even Bruno knew his friend had begun a scrapbook of her photographs.

Adam was determined that Bruno should share his new enthusiasm and couldn't wait for the end of his friend's labour service. Käthe had only moderately enjoyed the film and warned Bruno it might be a trial. "If he likes it, I probably will," promised Bruno.

For the first time in years the two friends wore casual civilian dress for the expedition to Central Berlin. Bruno watched Adam as he stared at the naïve-looking blonde on the screen. He watched his friend grip the top of the seat in front as Christina's body floated down a river surrounded by garlands. Bruno thought Adam had taken leave of his senses.

On the way home, they did not say much until they got off the train a short walk from Charlottenbrunnestrasse.

"Well, what did you think of her?" asked Adam hopefully. Bruno stopped and placed his hand on his friend's shoulder. "My old friend," he began. "I think she's a disaster."

Adam was crestfallen.

"She's not a real woman," Bruno went on. "She doesn't do anything useful. On top of that, she doesn't look very bright, which shouldn't suit you."

"But she looks right," retorted Adam. "She's a real German woman."

"She's not real, she looks soft and silly, not my dear idea of a real woman at all," countered Bruno. The atmosphere became heated and a policeman stared at the two boys arguing at the corner of the street and passing ladies looked embarrassed.

"Well, what's your idea of a real woman Bruno?" asked Adam, resuming his condescending attitude. Bruno realised that apart from his relationship with Käthe, fantasy was all his friend possessed.

"Well, take Helga for instance," he continued. "She's got a great face, a great figure and the grip like a vice on a ten-mark note. That's my idea of a good woman. And she looks as if she knows things."

Adam lapsed into a sullen silence and then suddenly remembered something. "Bruno!" he exclaimed. "We have to get back. Aunt Martha's niece is visiting and I promised Mama we'd be back in time to be introduced."

They sprinted the last few hundred metres to the apartment. "Hello Herr Hartmann," shouted Adam to the concierge, hardly noticing the taxi waiting outside with an irate driver tapping his fingers on the bonnet and looking at his watch.

"If Frau Diels has trapped her I'll go to the rescue," promised Bruno as they arrived breathless at the apartment door. The door was slightly ajar and the Circle meeting was breaking up, to the sounds of Greta collecting crockery. The two friends peered through to see what was going on.

There was an animated conversation at the far side of the room and the friends could see Frieda and Käthe, but not the face of the young girl talking with them. She wore a brown belted woollen coat and a small woollen hat perched on the side of voluminous blonde curls.

Adam and Bruno burst through the door and apologised, just as the young guest turned round to place an empty cup and saucer on a table. "Adam, Bruno," said Käthe. "Come and meet Gabrielle."

Bruno shook hands and bowed first, followed by Adam. He couldn't release his hand, and she didn't want him to. Gabrielle was nearly as tall as Bruno, but a few inches shorter than Adam. She had a full figure with a narrow waist and smiled as if she had been pleasantly surprised. She had a small, well-formed mouth and a round face. Her blue-grey eyes danced mischievously as she surveyed the young aristocrat.

Still neither of them released their hands, and everyone stopped talking. Bruno stood close to Käthe and she whispered to him, "I've lost him, haven't I?" Bruno couldn't answer as he stared in disbelief.

Those who were about to leave stopped in the doorway, including Martha Reymann, who was anxious for her niece to catch the train to Münich. Adam released Gabrielle's hand.

"Gabrielle is going to Münich to train to be a teacher," said Käthe, trying to kick-start a conversation between them.

"What subjects will you teach?" asked Adam nervously.

"I will teach mathematics as a main subject and my second subject will be architecture," she answered.

"That's very interesting," said Adam. So far, so good, thought Bruno.

Renate and Käthe thought they had better relieve the tension by striking up a conversation, but left one ear open in case of developments elsewhere. "I believe you two are famous Hitler Youth Leaders," said Gabrielle brightly, casting a quick glance at Bruno and then continuing to stare at Adam.

Bruno behaved loyally. "He's the big leader," he said encouragingly.

"You have my permission to describe your achievements," continued

Gabrielle. Martha waved to her and the taxi driver stood behind her. "But it will have to be another time," she said. "But it was lovely to meet you."

"Please come and see us again," said Adam awkwardly.

"Yes, I would like that," she said. "You could tell me about your ambition to be an officer in the army," she added as she walked towards the door.

Bruno could see his friend was running out of initiatives. He knew he would have to prompt Adam as Gabrielle disappeared into the entrance hall. Frieda remained seated, a mysterious smile on her face. Bruno grabbed Adam's arm. "Get after her!" he said urgently. "Say you're interested. Get her phone number."

By the time Adam moved, Gabrielle had climbed into the taxi and the driver was preparing to move off. Bruno dropped his hands in despair. His friend might have to settle for Christina Sodenstern after all. Adam had never felt so deflated, and Martha took his arm as the taxi moved off. Gabrielle turned and waved through the rear window, and Adam waved back.

"I think she was only flirting with you," Martha assured Adam. "She is to be engaged to a young man who is doing well in the Ministry of Education. I'm so sorry Adam." She kissed him on the cheek.

Bruno and Käthe knew Gabrielle was not flirting, and Adam didn't give up. He persuaded Aunt Martha to give him Gabrielle's address in Münich. He wrote three times and she answered the third letter. It was short and to the point. "Dear Adam," she began. "I am flattered by your attention but I must tell you I am soon to be engaged. We must not see each other again. Yours, Gabrielle." Her fiancé had stood over her as she wrote.

Adam reacted by immersing himself in his future career. He asked Gunther Graf to research training programmes, especially those connected to the SS. Then he found to his dismay that the Waffen SS did not encourage applications. Bruno had done all he could, but one evening Adam discovered that it was his friend that needed help. He came home one evening to discover a terrible atmosphere. Käthe and Frieda seemed reluctant to speak to him. Even Greta didn't emerge from the kitchen.

"Sit down Adam, please," ordered Frieda. She looked at Käthe as if they had rehearsed what was to be said and she was wringing her hands.

"Do you remember what you were doing last Wednesday?" she asked anxiously.

"Of course Mama," he replied. "I was with District Leader Graf until quite late discussing an army career."

"You gave us to understand Bruno was with you," interrupted Frieda. Adam broke into a sweat when he realised his campaign of lying for Bruno had been exposed. Käthe was mortified at her son's behaviour and became officious.

"You know that Renate has a part-time job in the evenings at the library. She came home early and found Bruno and Helga on the sofa." Käthe left the rest to Adam's imagination. He tried hard not to find it amusing.

Käthe crossed her hands in front of her. She had more to say. "Renate has just paid us a visit, Adam. She has just lectured Greta in front of us and blames the failure to control Helga on her. None of us are very pleased with you at the moment, Adam."

Frieda fixed Adam with her most penetrating stare, and he withered. "My main concern is the health and happiness of my most faithful servant and friend. Please repair the damage now and apologise," she said. The matriarch had spoken, and Adam dutifully went to the kitchen.

Greta had heard every word and was pretending to work furiously. She dropped a plate and Adam picked it up.

"I am ashamed I covered for Bruno," he admitted, "but I really don't know what can be done."

Greta wiped her hands on the tea towel and smiled. " Bruno should be grateful to have friends like you, and I do like him, "she whispered. Greta kissed Adam on the forehead and the formidable housekeeper was pacified.

" Why is Renate behaving like this, do you think?" Greta asked Adam, but he had no idea. The rift with Greta was healed, but Renate began to treat Adam in the most formal manner.

Adam continued to cover for Bruno, but in so doing he discovered another side of his friend's character. Three weeks after the rift Bruno asked Adam to lie for him again. He had just returned from the butcher's shop at two o'clock in the afternoon when Adam assumed Bruno and Helga were together. He waved to Greta, who was on the telephone. He was about to store the beef joints for her when he overheard a little of the telephone conversation. She was talking with Helga. Then Adam remembered that on at least two occasions when the Wilmersdorf Hitler Youth had met the local League of German Maidens, one of the girls couldn't stay away from Bruno. Adam discreetly enquired who the girl was and found out she was called Karin Haller. He didn't let Bruno know that he knew, but refused to cover for him again. Adam had another loyalty, and that was to Helga.

Adam was obsessed by the prospect of joining the Waffen SS. Gunther Graf told him he would have to apply to the Lichterfelde Barracks in Berlin. Bruno and Adam applied for admission to training, and the reply was immediate; they could only be invited to apply. One month later came another letter from the Lichterfelde Barracks. Adam and Bruno were told to attend a medical at the SS school at Braunschweig. Their parents had to go with them and bring a family tree, authorised by a lawyer.

Berger and Schöler produced a glittering family tree for Adam based on documents stored by Frieda. It showed clearly that the family was not tainted by Jewish ancestry back to the year 1750, as required. But Bruno's family tree did not have such clarity. There was a grandfather who had disappeared and then reappeared in the United States in the 1890s. There was a problem with Bruno's father because there were no baptismal records available for him. He had died on the Western Front in 1914 and a photograph of his grave in the German Military Cemetery at Langemarck in Belgium accompanied the family tree. A footnote from the lawyers stated there was little doubt that the family was solidly Aryan.

There was no flexibility in the appointment with the SS, even though the applicants lived in Berlin, so it should have been no problem for them to attend at ten o'clock in the morning. They joined the train at Charlottenburg, but even this suburban station was alive with police, checking identities.

Bruno and Adam stared at small groups of soldiers who appeared from different directions to board trains heading eastwards. "Is there an emergency, officer?" asked Käthe, forgetting the inadvisability of making almost any enquiry of a policeman. "That is not for you or me to ask," he replied. The huge oil-filled engines pulled flat cars and tarpaulins covered the unmistakable shapes of armoured vehicles.

The train to Braunschweig was delayed by twenty minutes. Travelling away from Berlin, it would normally have been empty, but the open compartment was full of SS military personnel.

CHAPTER SIXTEEN

The two women felt uncomfortable, even though they had dressed as unpretentiously as they could. "My mother looks like Ilse Diels today," Adam whispered to Bruno. Within earshot of the soldiers Käthe and Renate began to fuss over the two young men's appearance, to the amusement of the onlookers. They looked Adam and Bruno up and down. One of them whispered to Adam, "Are you going to training school?" Adam nodded.

"Keep your mouth shut and do as you're told. You'll be all right."

"Thanks," said Adam.

A businessman was reading the early edition of a newspaper and Bruno pretended to look over him at the view through the window. The man seemed annoyed and folded the paper inwards, but not before Bruno had read the headline: "Gleiwitz Radio Station attacked by Poles." In smaller print, just underneath, Bruno just managed to read "Führer says since 4.40 this morning we have begun shooting back."

Bruno rushed back to join the others. "Mutti," he said. "I think another war's starting." Renate grasped his hand.

"So the madness starts again," Kathe said.

"Keep your voice down, Mama," warned Adam, who had noticed an unhealthy interest from one of the soldiers.

The train stopped at Braunschweig station and Renate made every excuse she could to turn back. It began to rain and she and Bruno stood under the umbrella on the small town station while she berated her son for blindly following Adam.

Bruno had been long-suffering on his mother's behalf because of her circumstances, but now he felt she had gone too far. He hailed a taxi.

"I intend to go Mutti," he began, "with or without you. If you don't come you can tell yourself you stopped me doing the thing I wanted most."

She stared at him tight-lipped and climbed into the taxi as if she was stepping off a cliff. It carried them north of Braunschweig into a forested area. The small country road gave way to a gravel track, which seemed to be swallowed by the darkness of the forest. The trees grew further apart until the taxi reached a large open clearing. Käthe was dismayed by the view in front of them, and the driver behaved as if he wanted to go no further and return as soon as possible.

A grey stockade with a timber guardhouse blocked their path and it was still raining from leaden low clouds. The only colour visible was in the swastika banner flying high on the flagpole. Two uniformed guards stood motionless, apparently unaware of the visitors. Just then a group of runners appeared out of the forest, wearing white vests with an SS flash.

Renate paid the driver. Käthe wanted to walk arm in arm with Adam. "Not here Mama," he said sharply. "Walk faster. Show them we're not frightened." They were all very conscious of the noise made by their feet on the gravel path as they approached the guardhouse.

A grey uniformed man appeared with a clipboard. "Von Saloman and Grabowsky?" He enquired. He demanded to see the women's papers, which he examined and returned dismissively. "Come this way," he ordered.

They stopped at a wooden building on the far side of a quadrangle. Adam and Bruno had already seen the dimly-lit barracks on the opposite side. The guard knocked at the door and a middle-aged female assistant answered. She was uniformed, with a bright SS flash on her left collar. There were no preliminaries. "The doctor is ready to see you now," she said curtly. They were led past two other women working typewriters who seemed to be trained to ignore visitors.

"Please wait here. I require your certification now," she said. Käthe and Renate handed over their family trees. The two women were tempted to check the appearance of their sons. Adam and Bruno glared at them. They waited for ten minutes.

A door opened and a white-coated official with SS flashes on his sleeve told Adam to go in. His family tree was handed back to Käthe with a firm nod from the woman who had examined it. She didn't hand over Bruno's family tree. The assistant consulted another official in a separate office, who looked dubiously at Bruno's papers.

Adam was made to stand in front of a large desk on which was a collection of medical equipment. Watching in the corner was a stocky sergeant with a bony face and bushy eyebrows. Adam thought he ought to react to him, but the man motioned him to stand at ease. That would the last sign of generosity Adam experienced from Sergeant Julius Kolb for some time to come.

"Strip to the waist," said the doctor. He listened to Adam's heartbeat, then checked his hearing and his eyesight. His teeth were checked one by one. The Sergeant was silent because this young applicant was yet to enter his Empire.

"Get dressed," ordered the doctor, "and wait outside." It was Bruno's turn.

Renate waited anxiously for the woman to reappear with the family tree. It was half an hour before she did so. Renate was close to tears and sat wringing her hands.

"Everything is in order," said the assistant. "He may go in."

The Sergeant appeared. "You have both been accepted." he said. "From this moment you belong to us and must now act accordingly." He glared at the two friends.

The presence of their mothers was now irrelevant and the young men snapped to attention. Sergeant Kolb ignored the parents as he marched the two off to another office while Käthe and Renate had to make their own way to the guard house. The sentry phoned for a taxi.

"What have they done wrong?" asked Käthe as they climbed in and waited for their sons. Renate was equally fearful. "Perhaps they'll be treated like that all the time," she said gloomily.

Sergeant Kolb lined Adam and Bruno up in front of a Lieutenant, who barely acknowledged them as he reached inside a metal retractable file and withdrew some documents. He chose one, turned it round and pushed it towards Adam. "Read it," the Lieutenant ordered.

It was Captain Sulzbach's report. Adam glanced quickly and disdainfully through it, then glanced at Kolb, who had already read the report with some misgivings. It included the words 'Headstrong', 'Opinionated' and 'Self-centred.'

"You are lucky to be here von Saloman," Kolb remarked. "Do you understand?"

The Lieutenant surveyed the young men in front of him. Adam was tall, muscular and erect. The officer noted the arrogant potential in his face, even though the young recruit stared past him.

"You will both report for training in one week's time," he said. He handed each of them a list. "Do not exceed this list of allowable personal belongings or you'll be punished. You belong to the Führer and the Leibstandarte now. Heil Hitler," he said and gave the half salute, which the two young men hesitantly copied. Kolb had seen it all before and didn't react. "You may rejoin your parents," he said and gave Adam a long hard stare as he left.

It had stopped raining and the two women waited outside the taxi. Adam and Bruno were ignored by the guards.

"What did they mean when they said we would belong to them?" enquired Bruno.

"Do you still want to find out?" asked Adam.

"I'll hide behind you," joked Bruno. "Let's look as if we're pleased." They both realised this was not the Hitler Youth or the Labour Service and they had been confronted with a hint of the brutal reality to come.

"We really enjoyed that," said Bruno to Käthe. She wasn't amused and pushed them both into the taxi.

Back at the apartment, Käthe examined Adam's list. "You'll get everything in your rucksack Adam," she said. "Will you take your crucifix?"

"Of course I will Mama," Adam replied.

The Ladies' Circle gathered to say goodbye to Adam and Bruno. The friends wanted to leave as quickly as possible but the ladies made that difficult. Käthe clung to him and sobbed, then dried her tears and delivered a surprising piece of advice. "Do as you're told," she said, "and please write every week." She let him go so that Frieda could embrace him. She too had dissolved into tears. "Forget the house," she said. "Come back safely and don't take too many risks." She knew that would fall on deaf ears.

Renate had all but repaired the rift with Bruno. She hugged and kissed him. He was embarrassed as she stroked his face.

"Who will make us laugh?" she asked him. "I'll invite Helga to tea. I promise," she added.

Ilse Diels shook hands with both of them, because an embrace was difficult. "You are the Führer's soldiers at last" she exclaimed grandly, pulling her chin in. "I know you'll make us proud." Finally, to show she was true to her word, Renate called into the entrance hall and Helga emerged from Albert Hartmann's Office.

Renate took her arm and led her to Bruno. Helga gave him her photograph and they kissed passionately. Then she turned to Adam and kissed him on the lips, which scandalised the older women. She felt safe now because she was no longer employed by Frieda. "You can go now," she said to them both.

Greta grasped them both and couldn't let go. "Look after each other," she whispered hoarsely. The gathering waved furiously as the taxi turned the corner.

"Do you still want to do this thing Bruno?" asked his friend, well aware of his responsibility for changing the direction of Bruno's life. "Yes," replied Bruno, "but that little shit of a sergeant scares the hell out of me."

Chapter 17

They walked the four kilometres from the station at Braunschweig to the camp because neither of them wanted to be seen arriving in a taxi. Bruno hesitated in front of the guardhouse, as if he was looking for a lead from his friend.

"Helga likes men in uniform. She told me," said Adam. "Follow me and we'll say hello to the army."

A corporal emerged from the guardhouse. "Outside Hut One," was all he had to say, and the two friends joined a collection of slightly lost-looking characters fidgeting nervously with small suitcases and rucksacks. Two of them stood apart and seemed to know each other.

"We'll try them," said Bruno. He shuffled up to them, trying show he knew what he was doing. "I'm Grabowski, this is von Saloman," said Bruno hopefully.

The bigger of the two wore a brown leather jacket which had seen better days. His jaw was square and his nose flattened and he behaved as if the attempted introduction was an intrusion. He looked Adam up and down and noticed his expensive clothes. That was too much for him. He grunted and turned away.

His companion seemed embarrassed by the big man's behavior. He was of average height with a lean face, sunburned skin and a slightly hooked nose. His eyes were bright and he seemed prepared to make friends.

"I'm Stamm and this big oaf is Thaelmann," he said. Bruno thought he had found a friend and shook hands. The big man declined to shake hands with either Adam or Bruno and seemed to resent Stamm's attitude.

"Watch out," warned Bruno. A short stocky figure appeared out of the building on the far side of the clay-covered quadrangle and made straight for the recruits with a quick purposeful step. He stopped in front of the group and surveyed them, hands on hips, as if they were verminous intruders. "Attention!" he snapped.

They shuffled into line. He walked up and down the assembled recruits, then turned and barked. I'm Sergeant Kolb. Identify yourselves." He waited as they called out their names. He walked up and down the line making his first assessment, stopping briefly in front of each man. He paused for a few extra seconds in front of the proud young aristocrat, as if making an effort to remember Captain Sulzbach's written caution.

"Go into the hut in an orderly manner," he barked. "Stand in front of your bunks and face inwards."

Kolb gave them no time to think about the placement of their belongings. All except Adam laid their belongings on the floor. His lay on the bed, and the verbal assault began.

"Never on the beds!" shouted Kolb. "Open your rucksack." Kolb tipped the contents onto the floor. "Replace them!" he barked. Adam did so. Kolb opened a window and threw the rucksack outside. "Replace it!" ordered Kolb. "Bring back only those articles permitted."

"Yes Sergeant," said Adam in a vain attempt to appease his persecutor. Adam retrieved his belongings and separated out an empty photo frame. Kolb stared deliberately at the crucifix and his disapproval was cold and unrelenting. Adam was made to march at the double ten times round the quadrangle. The punishment was light for someone of Adam's strength, but humiliation was intended.

When Adam had finished, Kolb announced that the delay caused by the new recruit might cost him dear in the near future. He was already on probation, the sergeant announced, and even Adams' eyes shifted towards his persecutor when he announced emphatically, "You have let your comrades down."

Two of the new recruits, Hans Thaelmann and Martin Schröder, had enjoyed Adam's humiliation. Bruno guessed that the reason for the Sergeant's attitude lay with Captain Sulzbach, but the more he studied Kolb's non-Germanic appearance in contrast to Adam's, the more he wondered if the Sergeant's verbal assaults were more personal.

The sergeant pointed to a building at the north end of the complex. "Form a line outside the quartermaster's store," he ordered. "At the double."

They were issued with a rifle, helmet, two shirts, two pairs of trousers, socks, boots and a pack and told to stow their civilian clothes in the metal cabinets. If any part of that clothing saw the light of day, Kolb threatened, a fatigue would be automatic. "There'll be an inspection in thirty minutes," he warned. Then he stalked off to the sergeants' mess, giving them just enough time to get into their uniforms. Kolb stopped in front of Bruno. There was tarnish on his belt. That evening he had to clean the toilets.

Kolb allowed them to take a light lunch of bread and sausage in the mess hall. Franz Stamm chatted to the two friends while Adam behaved as if he was a mildly interested party and kept a distance. Stamm was not in the least intimidated and spoke loud enough for Adam to hear.

"Do I need your permission to speak to him?" Stamm asked Bruno. This produced one of Adam's indulgent smiles as he pretended to look into the distance. "Wait till he's eaten a sausage," answered Bruno. He's a different man."

Another surly character, Martin Schroeder, joined Thaelmann. Together they decided that Adam didn't belong there. All of them suffered a little from shyness and made mistakes at first.

Kolb burst through the mess hall door. "Assemble in fifteen minutes outside your hut with full kit," he ordered. A fifteen-kilometre route march followed. Kolb left them all behind.

Halfway, they met Sergeant Heinz with the recruits of Hut Two. Kolb exchanged a joke with him on the move about the inadequacy of the recruits. They were meant to hear and they tried harder. When they'd finished, Kolb made them stand to attention for nearly ten minutes. Kolb stopped in front of Kurt Janke, who was pale and exhausted. The Sergeant noted that there might be a future problem.

Bruno could hardly feel his legs, and his boots were the wrong size. He decided to choose another time to say so. "Lights out at ten," announced Kolb. " Assemble in PE kit at 06:30." He strode off to the sergeant's mess as if he'd abandoned them.

The beds were made of grey metal. The cabinets were grey and the walls and ceilings were grey. Even a single heating pipe next to the floor was grey. There was only one picture on the walls, a portrait of Adolf Hitler, and it had been chosen carefully. The Führer's expression seemed benign, as if he intended some hope for his future soldiers. All other pictures were forbidden. Even family photographs could not be displayed openly. All the recruits were able to do was look at each other and the Führer. When Kolb threw Adam's belongings out of the window, he spared one article, Rommel's book. Adam lay on his bunk absorbed by it and read bits of it to Bruno.

Half the hut had fallen asleep by nine o'clock, but Thaelmann, Stamm, Schröder and Seebring were still wide awake. Seebring told the other three he was concerned about Janke, whom he had befriended, but only Stamm shared his concerns. The other two were interested only in making mischief at Adam's expense.

Adam and Bruno had taken a break from Rommel and were going through the contents of their wallets. Bruno held up a photo of Helga, kissed it and made a loud noise, writhing on the bed as he did so. "He'll make you do another fifteen kilometres for that," said Adam.

Neither of them saw Stamm point his thumb in their direction. Thaelmann strode up to the end bunk, towering over Adam and Bruno, and Stamm stood behind him. In a quick movement Thaelmann grabbed Bruno's wallet and tossed it half the length of the hut to Martin Schröder.

"Examine his papers, Schröder," ordered the big man, staring malevolently at the two friends.

Bruno looked worried. Schröder looked at the photos of Renate and Helga. He tossed Renate's photo aside contemptuously and drooled over the photo of Helga. "Not your sister then?" he asked and threw the wallet back at Stamm, who returned it to Bruno.

"And yours, von Saloman," said Thaelmann. Adam smiled indulgently, to Thaelmann's intense annoyance. The young aristocrat was the main target and several of the others were awakened by the noise. "Shut up, you noisy bastards," said Kroll.

Thaelmann told Adam to hand over his wallet. Adam did so, staring his adversary full in the face and lying back unconcerned on his bunk. The wallet was handed to Stamm. He withdrew a photo of Frieda which looked as though it belonged in a society magazine and gave it to Thaelmann. "She doesn't look like you," he remarked.

The atmosphere was now tense, but Adam refused to react and Stamm threw the wallet to Schröder, who imagined he'd become friends with Stamm and Thaelmann.

Seebring had been watching with disgust. He knew Adam was his father's landlord's son, but had told no one. "Give it back," he said to Schröder. "Show some respect."

Schröder grabbed Seebring's braces and threatened him. That was too much for Adam. He leapt from his bunk and strode over to Schröder. He flicked his fingers and opened his hand, demanding the return of the wallet. Schröder looked to Stamm and Thaelmann for support, but there was none. He had believed his left-wing background would have been enough to impress the other two.

"You handled that well, Schröder," remarked Stamm, and Bruno chuckled. Martin Schröder handed over the wallet. "Well done," said Adam. "You have done the right thing."

"I'm going for a piss," announced Stamm.

"So am I," said Bruno. "Would you like us to clean the urinals for you, gentlemen?" asked Stamm.

As they were about to button themselves up Stamm said, "I have your boy ahead on points so far."

Morning PE was followed by a route march in appalling weather. High winds drove heavy rain, and a military cape was the recruits' only protection. Kolb pushed them harder and harder, once again looking for an opportunity to humiliate Adam.

The first victim was Kurt Janke, who collapsed exhausted in the driving rain ten kilometres into the march. This time the recruits had to carry full packs and rifles. It was too much for Janke. He was the son of a Protestant Pastor and had come late to the Hitler Youth. He was not prepared for the brutal reality of the Waffen SS.

"Help me pick him up, Thaelmann," Adam said. They got Janke to his feet. "Can you carry on?" asked Adam. Thaelmann stood aside and wanted no more to do with it. It made no difference to Kolb.

"Leave that man there," he ordered harshly. "He must learn to fend for himself."

He confronted Adam. "Thaelmann, over here," he ordered. The rain dripped down through the necks of their capes as Kolb berated the two. "Next time, ask permission. You will both do fatigues tonight. Toilet cleaning in both huts." Hans Thaelmann thought Adam would always attract trouble.

The march continued. "That was shit," remarked Bruno.

"Enemy ahead!" shouted Kolb. They had been told to throw themselves sideways flat on the ground and the Sergeant had chosen his time carefully. Adam threw himself into a tangle of bramble bushes and emerged scratched and bleeding with a torn cape. Again, he was berated.

Thaelmann threw himself into a pile of horse manure. Both of them took all evening to clean their kit and the heating was inadequate. "I'll fix it," said Seebring. To everyone's admiration he found the courage to approach the stores to obtain a set of spanners and fix the heating.

"I think you might know his family," said Bruno as they prepared to fall asleep. Adam leapt off his bunk and apologised to Seebring. "We've got to stay together," said Seebring.

Kurt Janke was still awake. "Can we come down and talk to you two?" he asked.

Bruno was writing a letter home. "What can we tell 'em Stamm?" he called out loudly. Franz Stamm had suddenly become interested in anything to do with Adam and Bruno. "Tell 'em von Saloman's had his arse kicked again, but you're all right," suggested Stamm.

"Tell 'em nothing," said another voice.

Bruno was at a loss what to write, but twenty minutes later, amidst loud snoring, he had finished. The letter to Renate included such phrases as 'good friends', 'tough training' and 'food not bad.' Adam heard Janke's story. It was another tale of frustrated ambition and he looked across to Bruno. Adam wondered if Bruno felt any regrets at having to abandon his.

Hans Thaelmann didn't like the new association between Adam and Seebring and his campaign to isolate Adam seemed to be failing. Stamm was concerned for his friend. They had been brought up together in Hamburg. He was afraid Hans, not Adam, was becoming isolated and he had seen Thaelmann's temper get him into trouble with the Hamburg police.

At six o'clock, Kolb walked up and down the hut, banging two mess tins together. Twenty minutes later, the trainees faced gruelling physical training. Kolb outlasted them all. A light breakfast of bread and sausage was followed by a punishing assault course – in high winds and driving rain. A swollen, violent stream faced the group in the centre of the forest ten kilometres from the camp.

"Permission to speak, Sergeant," said Adam. Kolb nodded. "What is your solution, trooper?" asked Kolb.

"Throw a line and pulley, Sergeant," answered Adam, "I'll secure it to a tree."

Kolb had other ideas because he intended to make the crossing a supreme physical test. He knew there were some who didn't fit in.

The men waded into the icy water carrying ammunition boxes above their heads. The current was very strong and the water reached to chest level. Kolb paired Norbert Abs and Kurt Janke, but it seemed the pair would be swept away. They dropped the boxes and Abs grabbed a submerged tree root, pulling Janke to safety. Janke collapsed exhausted on the far bank.

That evening Julius Kolb sat in a Braunschweig bar with Sergeant Heinz and told him about his concern for Janke. "Keep going," advised Heinz. "The rest'll pull him through." But Kolb wasn't so sure. He began to punish Adam and Hans Thaelmann together. He'd seen the rift and intended to heal it his way. It backfired. Parade ground drill was regular and harsh and Kolb caught Adam and Hans slightly out of step as they stumbled on the rough ground. The rest continued the mindless drilling while Adam and Hans elbowed their way over the ground holding their rifles a few inches clear. They cleaned themselves up and washed the bruises and abrasions.

A kit inspection followed. Adam's and Han's uniforms were still soiled and both missed the next sports session. This pattern went on for weeks, until Thaelmann had had enough. He confronted Adam in the hut before lights out.

"On your feet von Saloman," he said. Schröder and Maschman watched with interest, sensing victory for their side. Adam this time sprang off his bunk and faced Thaelmann. "You have something to say?" he asked.

"You attract trouble," Thaelmann began. "A few of us think things won't get better until you leave."

"I've said so from the start," chimed in Martin Schröder.

"Your sort don't belong here, von Saloman," added Thaelmann.

"You can take Stamm's toilet friend with you," said Schröder.

Bruno leapt off his bunk and jumped from one bed to another to get at Schröder. He seized him by the braces and hit him in the face. Blood spurted from his nose onto his pillow. Franz Stamm pulled Bruno away. "What the hell are you doing?" he asked. Bruno started to calm down. Schroder cowered on his bed but Hans didn't give up. "Well?" he continued, still confident of support.

Adam stood four-square in front of his adversary. He half-smiled and announced. "You have my permission to leave, Hans. For my part, I have no intention of leaving until I've made a soldier out of Kolb."

The ripple of laughter relieved the tension and Franz Stamm stared at his friend Hans. "Shake his hand, you big oaf!" he demanded. Hans Thaelmann extended his hand to Adam for the first time.

"Hey," shouted Maschmann after chatting with Bruno one Saturday evening when boredom threatened. "Von Saloman was in China."

"Fuckin' good," said another voice.

"What a bedtime story," said Franz Stamm.

"Spill the beans," said Thaelmann, and they crowded round Adam's bunk. Adam told them about the river and its people, and they were spellbound. Ned Travis was their new hero, but Adam didn't mention Jacob Meissner.

"I think Kolb's from fuckin' China," said Schröder. Stamm joined in. "His dad's that bastard with the bad teeth and the sword," he suggested.

When the rest fell asleep, Hans quizzed Adam. "You've been to Hamburg?" he asked.

"My grandfather lives in the old town near the docks," answered Adam. "He works on the railways."

Stamm breathed a sigh of relief. At a stroke the tension was relieved. "I like the big ships too," said Adam.

There were three farmers in the hut, Kroll, Seebring and Abs. They all had their stories and Seebring wanted to tell his. "I like horses," he said. He told them his father had nine horses but they were all sent to the front in the last war and none came back.

"We got two more," he said. "They had two foals. I helped to deliver one. They want you to talk to them," he assured everyone. There were nods of agreement from the other two farmers. Only Schröder said nothing. Privately Adam found out his background was similar to Berndt Schuster's but promised Schröder he would tell no one.

Kolb regulated their sleep and permitted them to eat. He insulted them in turn and imposed a kind of equality. His justice was rough and certain and the punishment negative and humiliating. Hut One waited for the tread of his boots as he left the earthen quadrangle for the concrete square outside the hut. They sprang to attention and waited for the axe to fall. He always left them alone for the last two hours of each day. They could gaze at the portrait of their Führer as if he were a distant last resort. The belief grew that he alone was blameless and would shoulder all their troubles.

Every morning the trainees did rigorous PE before breakfast and Janke appeared to grow stronger. His friendship with Norbert Abs and Klaus Seebring appeared to sustain him.

On one particular morning, there was no banging of mess tins, no call to PE, no parade-ground drill. Sergeant Kolb did not appear until eight o'clock, just as a line of military trucks turned off for the autobahn towards the camp. They stopped in front of the assembled ranks of trainees, all in battledress with rifles. Every officer wore a helmet. There was, as yet, no explanation.

Kolb stood in front of Hut One, Sergeant Heinz in front of Hut 2. They had been ordered to say nothing and for once, it wasn't raining. The lorries bumped through several kilometres of dark forest until they reached open scrubland.

"Form two lines!" shouted the sergeants. Other units joined them and soon the two grey lines extended for nearly half a kilometre. The trainees were ordered to strap their rifles to their backs. Then the sergeants told the men what was happening. They were to experience live shellfire.

"You will advance when the signal is given," said Kolb. "Artillery will lay down a curtain of fire in front of you. You must keep going at a steady pace. The next salvo will fall behind you."

A signal flare arched up into the sky and the sergeants waved the men forward. They saw the flashes from the guns on slightly higher ground and heard the whine of the shells.

The ground erupted fifty metres in front of them. "Keep going," yelled Kolb. Some of the shells overshot and showered the men of Hut One with earth and stones. None of them knew the aiming point of the next salvo and relied on the men either side of them. Janke turned and ran before the second salvo. No one saw him as the shells whined overhead and burst behind them.

CHAPTER SEVENTEEN

The first sign something was wrong was the appearance of a squat military ambulance. The trainees were marched quickly back to their transport, as the broken body of Kurt Janke was removed. The officers assessed the exercise and pronounced it, overall, a success. This time, the casualty rate had been low.

Kolb was ordered to assemble the men of the Hut One on the parade ground on arrival. Very little was said on the return journey when they realised Janke had not reappeared. "I'm sure he'll be all right Seebring," said Adam. The others joined in with weak reassurances. They each drew their own conclusions.

The Sergeant was not his usual aggressive self as he ordered them to assemble on the parade ground. They shuffled nervously as a Lieutenant announced Janke's death.

"I have to announce the loss of Trooper Janke," he said. The rest of the speech staggered the men. "Obedience to orders and support for your comrades are our main requirements here at Braunschweig. Janke failed on both counts. Therefore his family must mourn his loss, not you. You must all look to the future." He spun on his heels and left in a staff car.

Very little was said in Hut One after the evening mess. Seebring and Abs were stricken with grief and anger at the callousness of the speech they had heard. Klaus Seebring got off his bunk and put on his tunic. "Where are you going, Seebring?" asked Stamm as Klaus reached the door.

"Something must be done," he said angrily. "I'm going to see Kolb." Adam realised he meant it and would probably be punished. "Wait!" he called. "You are right." He stood at the end of the hut and invited every man to join him in a memorial. "We must remember our comrade," said Adam. "What would you like to say, Seebring?" he asked.

Seebring said he'd lost a good friend and a decent man and Norbert Abs agreed with him. Bruno said a few words, but the rest were tongue tied. The demonstration was in defiance of orders. Kolb watched through a small window in the door and approved.

Julius Kolb and Gerhard Heinz sat on two high stools in a local bar. "Do you still have a problem with von Saloman?" asked Heinz.

"Sulzbach was right. He's too big for his boots," replied Kolb.

Heinz downed the rest of his beer and started to pull on his greatcoat. "But is he a good soldier, Julius?" asked Heinz.

"Damn good," answered his colleague and friend.

"Then live and let live for the sake of the others," advised Heinz.

Kolb nodded but was not deflected from the campaign to drive the condescending look from Adam's face. He was sure he knew how to do it.

There'd been a hard frost during the night and the pipes burst early in the morning after breakfast. A fountain of water landed on Thaelmann's bunk and it took Seebring nearly ten minutes to stop it. Kolb arrived and they snapped to attention. Thaelmann's kit was wet through and his bed stood in a large pool of water. Seebring stood erect, spanner in hand. Hans waited for the inevitable fatigue, but it didn't come. He could be fair and he had their surprise for the men.

"Today we move ammunition boxes over the assault course and there will be a time limit. If the schedule is not met, the hut will miss the next sports session," he began. Some thought they saw a half-smile appear on the sergeant's face.

"I will supervise. Von Saloman will take charge of the movement of supplies. We assemble in ten minutes," he concluded, leaving Hans Thaelmann to contemplate the thought of the assault course in a wet uniform.

Kolb swept out of the hut. "What the fuck's he up to?" asked Schroeder.

Bruno thought he knew and was sure the exercise would end up in humiliation for his friend. After the loss of Janke, it would not be good for the men in Hut One. But Bruno, like the rest, believed Kolb incapable of subtlety. They were soon to be proved wrong.

"This is all wrong" said Franz Stamm. "it's personal for Kolb. von Saloman's better than any of us. He's the best shot, the best runner, the best at fuckin' everything. What's going on?"

Even Schröder expressed some sympathy for Adam. "He doesn't look worried," he remarked as Adam returned from the breakfast hatch.

"Aren't you worried Bruno?" asked Stamm. "Before he sits down, listen," warned Bruno. " We'd better all be worried, because Adam will knock the shit out of us."

Stamm was puzzled. They fell into a numbed silence as Adam sat down and split them up into squads.

CHAPTER SEVENTEEN

It was a bitterly cold morning as Kolb marched Hut One up to the assault course. He had allowed three hours to complete the course and a forced march. It was to be carried out in full battledress with supplies of ammunition. The sergeant organised them into three squads led by Bruno, Thaelmann and Stamm. They waited by a starting tape for Kolb's signal to begin. Up till then Adam had been strangely silent. Bruno thought his friend was afraid.

They plunged into the icy water. Giant icicles hung from tree roots protruding from the stream, making it difficult to use them as hand holds. Abs was nearly swept downstream and Adam hauled him out of the water.

"Well done Abs," said Adam. "Rejoin your squad."

Stamm perched on top of the net, hauling his people up. Seebring was not a small man, but Stamm caught him by the seat of his pants and threw him over. On they went, urged on by Adam. Thaelmann hauled his great bulk up the rock face. A field dressing from a dropped ammunition box covered his forehead. He hauled his men up, but Schröder faltered. Adam helped him up and waited for the rest to catch up.

Kolb stood by a table with meagre rations spread on it, but said nothing. The men gathered round and looked pleadingly at Adam. They were cold and wet through and they expected the sergeant to intervene. He had decided that if Adam wished to command, this was his opportunity and he said nothing. Adam decided they were behind schedule and drove them on without rest and refreshment.

The last to arrive at the start point for the exercise were Thomas Lehman, the new man, along with Harold Maschman, struggling with an ammunition box. Lehman wasn't as fit as the others and seemed on the verge of collapse. He was as white as a sheet and Kolb ordered a medic to attend to him.

The buildings were still white with frost as they marched to the gatehouse. Adam was not popular at that moment. Even Bruno was surprised at the display of naked ambition from him. Thaelmann told him later he was thinking of murder.

"Form up by the duck pond," ordered Kolb. "At ease," he said sensing the resentment amongst the men.

"Von Saloman, take five steps forward," he ordered. "Your report."

"The men have done well Sergeant. We are here ahead of time," said Adam confidently. Bruno thought he was trying to behave like an officer and expected Kolb's wrath to descend on him.

"Lie down on your stomach, von Saloman," ordered Kolb. Adam hid his look of surprise and obeyed the order. "I require four volunteers to show appreciation of von Saloman's performance," said Kolb.

The weary men began to show signs of life, while Adam expected another fatigue as he threw himself on the frozen ground. He didn't see the sergeant gesture towards the duck pond and the half smile that appeared. They all wanted to volunteer except Seebring and Abs. Bruno beat them all to it, followed by Hans Thaelmann, Franz Stamm and Martin Schröder. They stood to attention in front of Kolb. Adam lay quietly on the frozen ground. "Continue," Kolb said quietly.

Each of them took hold of an arm or a leg and hurled Adam into the pond. His heavy body crashed through the ice and the four volunteers re-joined the ranks expressionless.

Adam staggered out of the pond and tried to snap to attention in front of Kolb. He looked ridiculous with strands of pondweed hanging from his hair and uniform. His helmet was still perched on the ice. "Retrieve it," ordered Kolb quietly. "The rest of you dismiss." The hapless Adam waited for the next phase of the Sergeant's treatment.

"Report to quartermaster's stores and ask for Sergeant Kolb's special uniform," he ordered.

A euphoric reaction had set in by the time Adam reached hut1 bearing a brown paper parcel. They were falling over each other in the scalding hot showers cursing and swearing. Adam followed them.

Martin Schroeder had regained a little courage after a recent toilet fatigue. "Don't leave any of your pondweed in my nice clean shower, von Saloman," he said.

Adam remembered the time on the Pearl when he had treated the junk's sailors badly, and he felt ashamed. "Sorry Schroeder," he said. He had used his comrades for his own selfish, ambitious ends and they left the shower when he used it. He emerged quietly and sat down on his bed and began to open Kolb's parcel. The rest pretended not to look.

Adam held up a drab grey uniform and looked in vain for the SS flashes. He held up the tunic in front of a grinning Bruno who suddenly changed his expression. Painted in bright yellow letters across the breast pocket were the words 'Cleansing Department Braunschweig.'

They were all stunned into disbelief. "The bastard's gone too far this time," remarked Hans Thaelmann.

"Be careful what you aim for on the rifle range Adam," said Franz Stamm. Even Schröder was sympathetic. "Hard luck von Saloman," he said. "This is shit."

Klaus Seebring patted Adam on the shoulder and found something light hearted to say. "You can't sit around like that. You'll have to put that damn thing on," he advised. Adam had never felt so dejected and humiliated, but he put the uniform on and shook hands with every man and apologised. He sat down on his bunk and recovered his confidence. "Kolb's clever," he said. "We'll kick the hell out of anyone now." They agreed, but Kolb wasn't finished.

It was Saturday evening and talk turned to what they had done before they joined up. "You wouldn't do that with her tonight, Schröder," remarked Stamm. "It's too fuckin' cold." The heating had failed again, but Seebring came to the rescue before anyone's belongings were soaked.

It was so cold that some of the water which had showered the window turned instantly to ice. Bruno scraped some of it away and peered into the floodlit quadrangle. The wind howled and giant snowflakes were beginning to fall; they contemplated a weekend of card games and recovery from training.

"I'll set fire to the fuckin' place," said Franz Stamm.

Bruno continued to look through the window. "Shut up Franz. Come and look at this, all of you," said Bruno. They crowded round the windows. A procession of orderlies wearing capes, pushing loaded trolleys, approached Hut One from the direction of the Mess Hall. Sergeant Kolb was leading them. Heinz was helping him steady a trolley full of crates. The trainees were just able to see them through a snowstorm driven by a gale-force wind.

The double doors swung open to shouts and the clanging of metal and a snow flurry swept down the hut. Two orderlies wedged the door and in came the sergeants. "At ease," shouted Kolb as he and Heinz removed their capes and shook them outside.

Steam rose from giant food containers perched on top of the trolleys and two more men appeared, carrying collapsible wooden tables. As the men of Hut One sat and watched bemused, two long tablecloths were thrown the length of the flimsy wooden structures. The orderlies laid a place for each man in the hut with huge knives and forks from the mess hall. Kolb and Heinz watched expressionless, their hands behind their backs.

The cutlery was followed by soup plates. The lids came off the hot containers and the smell of cooking drifted down the hut. "Close that door," shouted Heinz, but not before Kolb had disappeared into the vestibule and reappeared pushing a trolley full of crates of beer.

He personally placed a litre mug at each place. "You may move your chairs up to the tables," he said. The two sergeants lifted down the crates of beer and filled each glass to the brim. Kolb poured one for Heinz and one for himself.

Norbert Abs was completely nonplussed. "Lift your glass, Abs. Don't be afraid," Kolb assured him and he lifted his own. "To our Führer, Adolf Hitler," he said gravely. "To the Führer," muttered the rest.

The civilian orderlies served dumpling soup, a piping hot pork knuckle and a small pile of sauerkraut to each man. "We will leave you now," said Heinz. "You may celebrate whatever you wish and I'll be disappointed to see any bottles remaining."

Then Kolb announced. "This is a gift from your sergeant. It will not happen again." He pointed to mops and buckets the orderlies had left near the door. "Clean the place up when you've finished. Goodnight gentlemen," he said.

The men of Hut One waited for the outer door to close and heard a key turn in the lock. They stared at the feast, hardly daring to make a move. Klaus Seebring picked up a ladle and poked a container full of gravy and pork knuckles. "This is really the best," he said.

"Why are we just staring at it?" said Stamm, picking up a large spoon and wading into his soup.

There was a respectful silence, broken only by the banging of cutlery on plates and litres of beer being downed noisily. "Is Kolb a shithead or isn't he?" asked Schröder. Bruno answered, "He is, but he's our shithead!"

They ate as if it was the last meal of the condemned. Kolb had provided exactly the same amount of food for each man, and almost as if he had intended it, they finished at roughly the same time so the serious drinking could begin.

Franz Stamm picked up a crate and placed it on the table. He made a mock bow to Adam. "Permission to begin, von Saloman," he said. There were loud guffaws. Even Seebring saw the joke. "I expect you'll just want to supervise," Thaelmann said to Adam.

"No, he fuckin' won't," remarked Bruno, who had watched Adam's main weakness develop over the last few years.

The orderlies had been watching anxiously, hoping for a chance to clear the crockery. One of them opened the inner door. Hans Thaelmann glared at him and he retreated with the others to the Mess Hall. Thaelmann didn't believe Bruno. He looked Adam full in the eye and downed a bottle in one draught. Adam followed him and banged the empty bottle down. Hans drank another; so did Adam.

Martin Schröder decided he was the referee. He said he had never officiated over anything in his life before. "Whoever falls over or falls asleep first cleans the shit up in the morning," he announced. He downed a bottle himself before declaring the contest started.

Before the end of the meal they drank two litres of the strongest beer they'd ever seen. Klaus Seebring was the first to show its effects. "Just because von Saloman is wearing a shit inspector's uniform," he spluttered, "doesn't mean he's got to clean up." He had just drunk his third litre and staggered over to the referee. "You're the biggest shit Schröder. You should do it." He fell sideways onto Abs' bunk.

Hans was distracted from the contest with Adam. "Wait, von Saloman," he said, "I'll be back shortly." He staggered over to Norbert Abs and placed his hand on his shoulder, then patted his cheek. "Hello Abs," he slurred. "Listen all of you," he went on. "Abs thinks he's a nobody. It's not fuckin' fair." Abs threatened to collapse and Hans gently stopped him falling and held him in a bear hug. "He's my friend now," said Hans, slurring every word. Norbert Abs began to cough and splutter.

"Let him go you big oaf," said Franz Stamm. Hans did so and grabbed Stamm by his braces. "One day," he said "one day," and threw a mock punch which missed. Hans fell over and crashed over the table.

"You've lost!" shouted Schröder. "You're cleaning the shit up!"

Hans staggered to his feet to be faced by Adam, who banged another empty bottle on the table. Hans tapped Abs on the cheek. "I'm sorry my old friend," he said with a loud hiccup. "Are you there Abs? No, no this is serious," he said swaying badly.

"How would you deal with Kolb?" asked Thaelmann. "Tell us all, Abs."

Poor Norbert passed out. Stamm shouted, "I'd turn von Saloman's granny on him."

Adam's head fell forward and knocked his glass over. The unconscious Abs was now the centre of attention.

"Piss off Stamm," said Hans. "I'm asking Abs." Norbert Abs suddenly jerked his head upwards. He crawled onto his bed and hauled himself up, steadying himself on a metal cabinet. He patted it affectionately and waved his hand for silence. He refused to begin until they were all silent.

"I'll tell you what I'd do," he began, beginning to slide back down to the floor. "I'd ask my granny to get a pitchfork. And do you know what she'd do? She'd stick it up his arse."

It was time for Adam to say something. "Well done, Abs' Granny," he said, sinking into a chair. He dragged himself up. "Three cheers for Abs' Granny," he said and fell back again. He stared ahead and his head moved as if he were a puppet. He tried to smile indulgently at everyone. "I'm thirsty," he said.

"Open wide," said Bruno. Adam leaned backwards while more beer was poured down his throat. Then he suddenly sprang to his feet, and began to pick bits of flesh from pork knuckles. "These are the best bits," he said, tapping Bruno on the head with a huge bone.

"I'll tell your Granny you're a fuckin' vulture," promised Stamm.

Suddenly Adam looked at his watch. "Inspection at 22:30 in two minutes," he announced. He staggered from man to man and lifted them to their feet. He tried to lift Hans and fell forward. Hans struggled to his feet and lifted Adam, who decided to make some room. He lifted one of the tables and threw it on top of the other, smashing all the crockery.

They lined up, leaning on each other and threatening to fall sideways like a row of dominoes. "You're wearing the wrong uniform Grabowsky," began Adam. "You're the worst. You've always been a damn disgrace. You're past help. Do a fatigue."

"Which one?" asked Bruno.

"Any one you want," answered Adam. "Listen," he said trying to sound earnest. He tapped the badge on his breast pocket. "This is the right uniform. I'm a shit inspector. Schröder, you're a shit inspector. You're all shit inspectors. Let's drink a toast to shit inspectors." Everyone still standing solemnly raised a glass. "To all shit inspectors!" they mumbled.

CHAPTER SEVENTEEN

One by one they staggered to their bunks, except for Adam, who slept on one of the tables. The last noise to be heard was Harold Maschman trying to remember what time to turn up for PE in the morning. "Fuck PE," said Stamm.

Silence reigned and two of the orderlies arrived to clean up. They gave up when they saw Adam snoring heavily on one of the tables. One of them left a brand new uniform on his bunk.

There was no PE at dawn. Sergeant Kolb appeared at eight o'clock to inform the men of Hut One that they were expected on a rifle range at nine thirty. Adam sat in a corner, too ill to speak to anyone, while the rest dismantled and cleaned their rifles. Bruno cleaned Adam's and wasn't punished.

Stamm and Thaelmann walked either side of Bruno to the rifle range as Adam dawdled behind. "Why is he your friend Bruno?" asked Thaelmann. Bruno grinned broadly and slapped Hans on the shoulder. "Because he showed me how to like other people, including you, you big shit!" he answered. Hans made a fist and gently touched Bruno's chin.

Each morning Klara Bettinger's husband drove her to the SS School at Braunschweig. Her post as a civilian assistant to the Colonel brought in a much-needed income. She began to see herself as a real part of the school, proud to be associated with the Führer's elite soldiers. Every day she carefully brushed her tunic, but two evenings a week Klara assumed another identity. She was the Principal of the local school of dancing.

She kissed her husband outside the gatehouse and walked smartly to her office to be was met by the Colonel, who seemed ill at ease.

"Frau Bettinger," he began awkwardly. "Please come to my office." He invited her to sit down and nervously fingered some papers. "You have been chosen to make a contribution to the future of the Fatherland," he continued. "I am unable to reveal much detail."

At the same moment, the doors of Hut One burst in and Kolb appeared. "At ease," he said. "Von Saloman, follow me. We are expected at the Colonel's office." Adam threw on his tunic and followed him across the parade ground.

Klara Bettinger was no stranger to the secrecy surrounding the SS. She listened patiently, prepared as ever to carry out instructions.

"Frau Bettinger, I would like you to teach two of the trainees to dance," said the Colonel.

"Of course Colonel," she answered, prepared to waive her usual fee if it was in the national interest. Over Klara's shoulder The Colonel could see Kolb and Adam marching smartly in their direction. "It will be done here over the next three weeks in my office, Frau Bettinger. You will be very well paid. What do you say?"

There was no reason for her to refuse. "Of course I will, Herr Colonel," Klara said enthusiastically. "When will I meet the young men involved?"

Bang on time, there was a rap at the door. "You will meet one of them now," the Colonel replied. "Yes Sergeant, come in."

Adam stood stiffly to attention after saluting. "At ease, von Saloman," said the Colonel. "You may leave us, Kolb."

The Colonel cleared his throat. "Von Saloman, you have been called upon to perform a great service for the Führer and for Germany." He cleared his throat once more. "For that reason Frau Bettinger will teach you how to dance. Frau Kranzmuller will assist." He flicked his fingers and Klara's assistant Bettina appeared with a phonograph and several records. She quickly wound it up and stood in attendance. "There will be three one-hour weekly sessions and you will begin now," the Colonel announced. "You will also put in extra time at the rifle range, von Saloman. Is that clear?"

"Yes, Herr Colonel," answered Adam.

"You will begin now," said the officer, retiring quickly from his office. "Please close all the shutters, Fraulein Kranzmuller," he added on his way out. Bettina switched on the lights and left the two together.

Adam had been through the most rigorous training he could have imagined. He had been humiliated to an unacceptable degree and one of his new comrades had died in an exercise with live ammunition. Germany was at war, and he was to be taught to dance.

Klara was as mystified as he was. "Please do not ask why," she said. "I have no idea. Have you danced before?"

Adam realised that Klara was in a difficult position and remembered his manners. "Of course," he answered. "But you must never question the plans of the SS. I am to be taught to dance. Therefore I could not possibly have known how to. Shall we begin?"

CHAPTER SEVENTEEN

The strains of a Viennese waltz filled the room. Without hesitation Adam swept Klara round the office. "What shall I say in my report?" she asked. "Say enough to guarantee we will meet for more practice," he advised.

"I have been instructed to teach you how to dance intimately," said Klara as if it was an afterthought. "This is what you must do," she said dropping her hands and drawing him closer. She had noticed Adam several times through the office window and had been given no such instruction. She wanted to feel his reaction to her closeness. His face coloured, but he looked her in the eye and they chatted the time away easily. After exactly one hour, Bettina came in to retrieve the phonograph.

The door opened as soon as Bettina had opened the shutters and the Colonel stepped in hesitantly. Klara delivered her report, stating that an initial awkwardness had yet to be overcome. Adam had to repress a smile. "Until next week, trooper," Klara said. Adam bowed and left to join his comrades on the rifle range.

It was another bitterly cold day. The men lay prostrate in their greatcoats, fingers protruding from the end of mittens.

"Where the hell have you been?" asked Bruno.

"You won't believe it," answered Adam. He refused to say anything, even after the evening meal when tongues wagged as at no other time. "This lot have just accepted you. You've got to say something," Bruno reminded Adam.

Bruno and Stamm organised the audience at precisely nine o'clock and they gathered round Adam's bunk. He had been dozing and was suddenly aware of them.

"Spill the beans," said Hans Thaelmann. Adam glanced at his expectant comrades, trying to gauge the possible reaction of each one. "I've had a dancing lesson," he said quietly and looked at them in turn.

"While we were freezing to death on the fuckin' rifle range, you were having a dancing lesson?" remarked an unbelieving Schröder.

"With the Colonel?" said an even more incredulous Franz Stamm.

Bruno chuckled. "With Frau Bettinger," Adam said.

"That's the one with the big tits that Abs fancies," Schröder informed the gathering. Poor Norbert tried not to look interested.

"Ask von Saloman to put a good word in for you Abs," continued the insensitive Schröder. They all had the same look on their faces. "I've no idea why," admitted Adam.

"Maybe von Saloman's better at dodging bullets now," suggested Harold Maschman.

"Show us," said Hans Thaelmann.

"He's a good dancer Hans," said Bruno.

"Show us the steps," insisted Thaelmann.

"Partner him Bruno," said Stamm. "Fuck off Franz," answered Bruno.

They allowed Adam to go to sleep. Bruno and Franz chatted after lights out. "I don't like it," said Franz. "It isn't right and I think Adam doesn't like it either."

"Let's all forget it and leave him alone," advised Bruno.

"You're right," agreed Stamm. "We'll be shat on if we ask too many questions."

Chapter 18

Adam's Christmas leave in 1940 was one to remember, for all the wrong reasons. He and Bruno knew the deception practised in their letters would have to continue. So much the women said seemed trivial to Adam. He missed his father and imagined that he would have understood the experience of the training camp much better. He made one excuse after another to be with Bruno, which hurt Frieda, Käthe and also Greta. But Bruno spent as much time as he could in Charlottenburg, where Helga was close to her live-in job as a housekeeper. Käthe felt the strained atmosphere could be something to do with Adam's failure to re-establish contact with Gabrielle.

Adam's worst experience was an encounter with Renate Grabowsky in the local bakery. Renate had not attended a single meeting of the Ladies' Circle since Adam had come home, and now he politely enquired why not.

"I trust you are well Frau Grabowsky," began Adam. She seemed cold, hostile.

"I have hardly seen Bruno," she answered sharply.

"He misses Helga, Frau Grabowsky," he reminded her.

"He's all I have Adam," she said. "And you have led him away from a respectable career as an architect."

Adam couldn't resist trying to correct her, which made things worse. "You should be proud of him," he began and told her how respected Bruno was in Hut One. "We will soon be risking our lives in the defence of Germany. If he wishes to spend time with Helga, then he must," Adam said tactlessly. Renate lost no time informing Frieda and Käthe of Adam's attitude. Unfortunately for Renate, she did so in Ilse Diel's company. Frieda and Käthe demanded that Adam apologise, which he did for their sakes. He assumed Bruno knew the reason for Renate's attitude, but when Adam broached the subject, Bruno was as mystified as he was.

When the two friends left for Braunschweig, the bad feeling seemed to have been forgotten. The women behaved as if they would never see the two men again. As they were throwing their rucksacks over their shoulders after they had said goodbye, Albert Hartman called through his outside window, "I'll look after them for you."

As winter gave way to spring, the men of Hut One basked in one German victory after another. France had been defeated and British troops had fled across the Channel. These young Germans believed this was all that was necessary, because the humiliation of 1918 had been reversed.

Bruno discovered his calling on a cold and wet afternoon on the North German plain. The men of Hut One lay in a series of shallow slit trenches. It had stopped raining and the sun appeared almost apologetically.

"Our trench is wetter than yours," Schröder called over to Adam and Bruno. "Abs has pissed himself."

The chuckles were silenced by Sergeant Kolb, who gave Martin Schröder a latrine fatigue. Kolb stood hands on hips and faced the men of Hut One. "When you hear the engines behind you, get your arses out of the trenches and follow," he ordered.

Diesel engines roared behind them and Bruno looked behind to see a brand new eight-wheeled armoured car. A lieutenant wearing headphones stood in the turret. Adam, Thomas Lehmann and Harald Maschman leapt out of their trenches. Bruno hesitated for one moment, distracted by the armoured car. "Move Grabowsky," ordered Kolb. Just before Grabowsky ran off to join the others, he shouted to the officer. "I like your machine, lieutenant," and at that precise moment, it broke down.

"Grabowsky!" shouted Kolb. Bruno ran back. "Lieutenant, he's good in the engine shops. Do you want him?"

Bruno was amazed and delighted. "I'll leave him with you," said Kolb. "Please give him a hard time."

Bruno fixed the engine. "What am I supposed to do with you?" asked the Lieutenant.

"I can read maps. I could hitch a ride Lieutenant," answered Bruno.

"Hang on to the grenade shields," ordered the officer. The armoured car bumped its way over the heath with Bruno hanging on grimly. He spent the afternoon in the engine shops. One of the mechanics took a black forage cap and put it on Bruno's head. "It suits you son," he said.

Bruno appeared at camp at eight o'clock that evening having walked fifteen kilometers. He wisely reported to Kolb, who simply said. "Get yourself cleaned up. You'll have your chance one day."

Kolb crashed through the double doors after breakfast. "Von Saloman, you are required in the Colonel's office now," he said, and Adam was marched briskly across the parade ground. Kolb knocked respectfully and ushered Adam inside. He snapped to attention and saluted.

The Colonel sat down. On either side of his chair, stood two black uniformed men from the Ordinary SS.

"Sergeant," began the Colonel, "has this trooper been guilty of serious misdemeanours within the last six months?" The sergeant assured the Colonel Adam had no such stains on his recent record and was dismissed.

"Frau Bettinger," he called, and Klara appeared with a large package which she laid on the table. "Open it," he said to Adam. Inside was an SS dress uniform. Adam had never seen one before, and his eyes were drawn to the silver braid and the dagger.

"Try it on," ordered the Colonel. "You may use Frau Bettinger's office." Klara remembered the separate package containing black leather shoes. She pushed her office door open and handed it to Adam. He reappeared in a few minutes and the uniform was a perfect fit. The two SS men nodded in approval.

"You may leave us, Frau Bettinger," said the Colonel. "You and your unit have been honoured, von Saloman. You have been selected to perform a great service for our Führer and the Fatherland." He glanced at some notes in front of him. "This service will help to guarantee the future of our new order in Europe." Adam thought he was to join one of the new commando units. "If you divulge even the smallest detail of anything that has happened here or what takes place at the weekend, you will suffer the severest punishment," the Colonel went on. "It will be looked upon as treason and punishable by death. Do you understand?"

"Of course Herr Colonel," answered Adam.

"A staff car will collect you and Trooper Seeler here at six o'clock on Saturday morning. You will be provided for. Take only your trainee and dress uniform and other essentials. You are dismissed."

Adam gave the Waffen SS half salute, and the two SS men threw out their arms. "Remember," the Colonel reminded Adam. "Not a word to your comrades."

The Colonel watched him walking towards Hut One. The officer was an old army man who had transferred to the Waffen SS. He thought of the so-called mission and reflected that it was no way to treat a promising recruit.

Adam knew he would have to face a barrage of questions from his comrades, but Kolb had already warned them not to be inquisitive. Bruno was only the one who said anything. "I think you've been chosen to try out a new punishment," he said. "Shut up Bruno," said Franz Stamm. Adam managed a half smile.

Adam and Johannes Seeler waited underneath the guardhouse lights. At precisely six o'clock the staff car arrived, driven by an SS chauffeur who opened the rear passenger doors for the two troopers. They were driven quickly down the Hanover-Berlin Autobahn, reminding Adam of his Labour Service days. Seeler too, had worked on the road but neither mentioned the mission.

Within an hour they reached Berlin Central Station, at the beginning of the rush hour. Early-morning travellers found their way blocked by police and were made to wait while the entire station concourse was cordoned off.

Other staff cars arrived. Each one contained one or two passengers and were quickly directed to an area beyond the ticket barriers. A special train of two carriages waited. A huge oil-fired locomotive lay idly building up steam. Adam, Seeler and the others were surrounded by SS security men. An SS Major addressed them. He warned them not to make themselves known to each other or arrange to meet again.

Railway staff waited impatiently for the privileged party to leave the station while an SS officer led the twenty young men towards the train for Munich. Before they settled into first class reserved seats, they looked quickly at each other; they were not all in military uniform. Some wore the tunics of the Ordensburgen, the National Socialist Universities. Just two wore civilian clothes, each wearing a party badge. They had one thing in common. All were blond or sandy-haired and were of similar height and build.

CHAPTER EIGHTEEN

The young men settled into an uneasy silence in one carriage. The other was used by servants and party officials. Two SS security men watched them all the way and white-coated attendants with an SS flash on their collars attended to the passengers' every need.

The young men stared out of the windows at some of the finest scenery in Germany. It seemed a safer thing to do than speak to the person next to you. The waiters served a light lunch, which Adam noticed came with expensive bottles of French wine. One of the passengers in Ordensburgen uniform misunderstood his privileged position and attempted to drink a second glass. One of the security men smiled at him and took the bottle away.

The great oil-fired engine was given priority and didn't stop until it reached Münich. They waited nearly two hours there, surrounded by police and yet treated with excessive courtesy.

The travelling public were ejected from the station restaurant so that the special party could wait in comfort for their special coach. It carried them in the direction of the Austrian border.

Johannes Seeler felt guilty because he hadn't spoken at length to his Waffen SS comrade. "I think the Führer comes here before he makes his decisions," he said hopefully. Adam just nodded. They drove for half an hour before the coach slowed in front of a sign, its directions hidden by a sheet. Several guards with dogs patrolled the turning. A junior officer directed the driver towards a broad forest track and the coach laboured up the rough road for a further twenty minutes. The track was so narrow and the trees so tall and densely planted that the driver switched on his headlights.

As the coach climbed, it became colder. The forest opened up and it stopped at a security barrier where there were more guards with dogs. An SS officer checked the drivers' papers and counted the young men. The coach was driven slowly towards what appeared to be an Alpine hotel. Its name had been obscured.

The coach stopped at the foot of the steps. SS orderlies carried any heavy luggage and placed it at the foot of a winding wooden stairway in the entrance hall. None of Adam's party had noticed that another coach had followed them at a discreet distance. It stopped at the security barrier until the passengers of the first coach had entered the hotel. An orderly checked the young men's papers and escorted them up the stairs.

Adam glanced through a door to the right of the reception area and thought he saw a formally-dressed man go in with a violin case. The orderly invited Adam into his room but kept the key and told him he had one hour to refresh himself. The orderly bowed and left and Adam inspected his surroundings.

Adam's feet sank into a thick piled white carpet. The table in the centre of the room had two expensively-upholstered chairs and a bottle of champagne in an ice bucket graced the centre. An open log fire bathed the room with a red glow. A fire screen kept some of the heat from two armchairs. Glass doors opened up onto a balcony with views of the Bavarian mountains. Adam walked onto the balcony, convinced that he and his new colleagues would soon go to war in a new and secret phase. He looked sideways and waved to Johannes who was admiring the view.

There was a knock at the door and an orderly brought the uniform Adam had tried on and laid it on the bed. Adam called out his thanks and looked out again over the mountains as the other coach arrived. He counted twenty young women getting off the coach, supervised by several women in nurses' uniforms. He looked at Seeler, who was equally puzzled.

The girls wore woollen coats, but some had left them unbuttoned, even on this cold December afternoon. They were all wearing the uniform of the League of German Maidens. Adam stepped back, afraid he was being too curious.

He took a brief look at the bedroom before he took a shower. Another log fire burned there, and the carpet pile seemed even thicker. The centrepiece of the room was a large four-poster bed, and on it lay a large bunch of roses.

He showered, changed into the dress uniform and sat and waited as instructed. On the hour the telephone rang and a curt voice said he was expected in the entrance hall. Stricken now with doubt, he descended the stairs as slowly as he dared, looking around for clues as to what might happen next. He met Seeler, who was just as uncomfortable.

They were ordered into a room with rows of seats, a film projector and a screen. A very senior SS officer stood waiting on a stage with several SS nurses and doctors. He announced that a film would be shown. It lasted half an hour and showed a selection of people from the cities and the countryside, who all seemed to be poor. The next part of the film dealt with the educationally challenged, and was not at all sympathetic. Adam glanced sideways at the man next to him. He was leaning forward with his hand on his chin nodding in agreement. Adam felt nothing but revulsion, and thought he didn't belong here. His doubts increased when he saw that many of the audience were not soldiers.

When the lights came on, one of the doctors stood in front of the lectern and shuffled documents. If these young men had no idea why they were here, they were soon to find out.

"We have shown you here," he began, "one of the Reich's greatest problems. Within the ranks of the Aryan peoples of the Fatherland lurk the racially unsuitable. Most of those will die a natural death. For others, intervention may be necessary."

Adam remembered Theo and Klaus, but he knew this was not the time and the place to stand up and object. The doctor continued, "You represent the finest that Germany can offer. You stand today as the breeding stock of a people which will one day rule the Reich, and tonight you will make your first contribution."

He sat down and the senior officer delivered instructions. "Shortly you will join other guests in the hotel. These twenty young women are the best Germany has to offer. You will leave here in single file and occupy the vacant seats in the hall. It is important that you conduct yourselves in a manner worthy of your calling. At this point selections will be made. You will accompany your partner into dinner and make appropriate conversation."

Adam glanced sideways. His neighbour now seemed to be harbouring doubts and was fidgeting nervously.

The officer continued to issue instructions as if they were fire regulations. "There will be a short programme of dancing, after which you will conduct your partner to your room," he continued. Then he paused and cleared his throat. "I must tell you, there will be no cause for concern. These young women have been highly trained in the art of conception."

He concluded by warning them that any attempt to extract details of the girls' identities would result in the severest punishment. "You will vacate the rooms at 07:30 hours," he informed them.

As the young men were led out in single file, most betrayed little sign of anxiety. Seated down one side of the entrance hall were the twenty young women, all staring straight ahead of them. Adam looked away, desperately needing something to absolve him from all responsibility, and thought Frieda would never forgive him. He was the last to be seated and had never before felt self-conscious in formal dress. He longed to be somewhere else.

The girl seated opposite was very attractive and wore traditional Bavarian dress. She looked hopefully at Adam and he stared coldly back. She dropped her eyes and turned a bright red. Adam felt sorry for the embarrassment he had caused her and wanted to get up and apologise. He placed his hands on his lap and tried to compose himself and his dress uniform gloves fell on the floor.

Five SS nurses marched up and down behind the girls, surveying the men. The girl opposite Adam continued to make hopeful glances in his direction. Suddenly one of the nurses marched over and took the hand of one of the men and marched him over to her. It was Johannes, and Adam was relieved. He allowed his eyes to stray down the line of girls to the far end and became aware of another pair of eyes watching him. The girl leaned forward and continued to look in Adam's direction, but he stared ahead. She leaned forward again and this time she seemed familiar. Then he saw the billowing blonde curls and she smiled mischievously. It was Gabrielle, and his pulse began to race.

One of the nurses walked behind the remaining young men and spoke to a doctor out of Adam's sight. He heard the sharp rap of footsteps on the wooden floor behind him, and a hand fell on his shoulder. "Please come with me," said the nurse. She led him to Gabrielle. "This is your partner for the evening," she said.

Now began the pretence that they had never met. "Good evening," said Gabrielle brightly and Adam bowed. They shook hands. It had taken this long, and these circumstances, for it to happen. He stood there helplessly as his partner pretended to look past him.

An SS waiter approached the pair and bowed to them. "You will occupy table nineteen," he informed them. Gabrielle took Adam's arm and they walked towards the restaurant. She had been instructed to smile warmly at her partner, but Adam was afraid to look at her.

"Relax, for God's sake," Gabrielle said. "We can fool these people. You can start by smiling." She squeezed his arm. "You're an expert charmer, you know," she whispered. Adam didn't feel his feet touch the wooden floor on the way to their table.

Another waiter appeared, who withdrew a chair for Gabrielle. He did the same for Adam and now he could look at her. Her curls were tied back with a large dark blue bow and her shoulders were covered with a lace top. She wore a full-skirted blue dress.

"Now what would Bruno do?" she asked. He lifted his eyebrows and smiled, and Gabrielle was relieved. He stared at her transfixed, forgetting the revulsion he had felt while watching the film. Bruno's advice rang in his ears. This time she would not escape, he thought.

The realities of the situation escaped him for the moment. "Careful," mouthed Gabrielle as a wine waiter approached the table. He poured them half a glass each and told them there would be no more. Then began a stilted conversation which nearly made both of them laugh.

"It's a wonderful hotel don't you think?" said Adam.

"Indeed it is," Gabrielle replied, "and what a wonderful location." The waiters seemed to listen carefully to every word.

"Did you know the Führer stays not far from here?" asked Adam, too loudly.

"Indeed I do," Gabrielle replied. The waiters withdrew after the couple had placed their order, and they began to breathe normally.

"Well Field Marshal, here we are," she said. He was flattered; she had used his nickname. Then he asked himself how on earth she knew it. His hands shook as he nervously fingered the cutlery. "May I call you Gaby?" he asked.

"Don't be crazy," she whispered. "Wait till we get out of here."

The waiter reappeared and resumed his robotic vigilance. "The mountains are beautiful at this time of year," said Gabrielle. Adam wanted to stop the trite conversation.

The twenty couples made almost no noise as the dinner proceeded, and the only sound was the rattle of cutlery. A bell rang and a small light orchestra filed onto a stage at the far end. Whether the couples had finished or not, the waiters cleared the tables and moved them to the sides of the room. The conductor lifted his baton and the orchestra began to play a waltz.

The young men were jolted into reality as they held their partners for the first time. Some moved competently, others awkwardly. Adam and Gabrielle glided round the floor, to the consternation of some of the couples and the delight of the SS officers. The SS Major on the stage noticed the lack of jollity on the dance floor. He had been assured by the chief nurse that the mission could be jeopardised if the right atmosphere was not achieved.

The last dance was a Viennese waltz. After the first few bars, Adam and Gabrielle relaxed their hold and moved closer together. She squeezed his hand and his mouth went dry. He pulled her towards him.

"Not here," she said.

"To hell with these people!" said Adam. In a gesture of revolt he swept her towards the stage before the gaze of the SS officers. One looked at the pair suspiciously. Gabrielle couldn't stop him and decided to enjoy the adventure, but just then the music stopped. "Retire to your allotted rooms," said an SS Major. They were the first out of the restaurant.

"Why didn't you write back to me?" Adam asked plaintively.

"I did, if you remember," Gabrielle replied. "Karl stood over me. No more questions like that please. Let's enjoy our time together."

The nurse who had paired them, Fraülein Agnes Felsen, followed them up the stairs holding a stool and they fell silent again. She opened the door of Adam's room and ushered them in. The door closed and they heard a key turn in the lock. Gabrielle leaned backwards on the door and used it as a springboard to launch herself into Adam's arms. He paused to look at her before kissing her longingly and she pressed the whole length of her body against his, until they nearly fell over.

Then she felt his body stiffen. "What's the matter?" she asked.

"This isn't right," said Adam.

"Of course it's not right," answered an annoyed Gabrielle. "What else can we do?"

The tone of Adam's voice changed. "Why are you doing this for these people?" he asked. His warmth had gone and his rectitude had returned. Gabrielle was dismayed.

"Adam, has it ever occurred to you I might have a good reason for doing this?" she asked. "Do you seriously believe I am interested in improving the racial stock of Germany?" She threw her handbag on to a chair in utter frustration. "You were born with a silver spoon in your mouth, Adam. My parents lost everything in the depression, but I think your family did rather well."

This stung Adam, but before he could reply, Gabrielle continued the lecture. "The pension I will be paid will help to pay off my father's debts, and

I'll have you know, my fiancé's a good man. We have been together for two years and you and I for two hours. You don't own me."

"So this is just an adventure for you?" he suggested. This spurred Gabrielle on. "And what about your motives Adam?"

"What do you mean?" he asked defensively.

"I'm sure you couldn't avoid joining the Hitler Youth, just as I couldn't avoid joining the League of German Maidens, but why the Waffen SS? This government has stolen your family home and wrongly imprisoned your father, and you have joined the most politically extreme soldiers. Why?" She paused and said quietly, "Perhaps you do not like the Jews."

He could have forgiven all her remarks except this. "How dare you suggest that?" he shouted. "I have defended them. Apologise immediately." Gabrielle was stunned by his reaction.

The door burst open and Fraülein Felsen stared at them incredulously. They were her pet project, and they had betrayed her. She had also heard things which placed them in her power, and they suddenly realized it.

"You must come with me now," she said to Gabrielle. "And you trooper, will be reported to your superiors."

She grabbed Gabrielle's arm and led her outside, slamming the door, Gabrielle burst into tears. "For God's sake, I'm only human," she said. "You knew we wanted each other from the start." She paused and took the nurse's arm. "Look, we've met before. It really is only a lovers' quarrel." Fraülein Felsen's granite expression softened. "Please!" begged Gabrielle. "You will have your child tonight." She led the nurse to her stool looking around, saw no one was watching, and kissed her on the forehead.

Gabrielle strolled back into the room, where Adam was slumped in a chair, emptily staring into the fire. She was afraid his feelings for her had disappeared. She knelt down on the thick pile rug in front of him.

"I'm so, so sorry," she said. "I know about Theo and Klaus and Julius, my darling. Your wonderful mother told me. I can be such a bad tempered cow." She kissed his hands. "That taxi driver had to wait until we had met," she added. She stroked his face and drew him forward.

"I'm sorry too," he said. "I was afraid of what my grandmother would think."

She laughed. "Don't you blame it on her," she said with a chuckle.

They lay on the rug kissing. "Take that damn uniform off," she ordered, standing up and shedding her clothes. They knelt down together and she drew his hands to her breasts. He kissed them, then looked at her and smiled.

"They said I shouldn't make you wait too long," said Gabrielle, guiding his hand between her legs. "You must stimulate me like this, my darling," she whispered. His fingers found her opening and she moaned. Her hand reached down and stroked his erection. "Please now," she said. He entered her easily and joyfully but she begged him to move more slowly. She lifted her legs to allow him to penetrate more deeply. She grasped his hips and smiled lovingly. He gasped and ejaculated. They continued to move until Gabrielle had reached her climax.

The log fire began to die and the room grew cooler. Adam stood up and surveyed the woman of his dreams. He wanted her again. "Let's go to bed and get warm," he suggested.

"I'm very tired," she said playfully. "You'll have to carry me."

Gabrielle was not small, but she was amazed at the ease with which Adam knelt down and picked her up. He carried her into the bedroom, where the fire still gave off some heat. She wriggled under the bedclothes and he followed her. "You're a very good pupil, my love," she said. "My nurse said you might have no idea what to do."

"Living in the same hut as Bruno and Franz Stamm is a great help," admitted Adam.

"I've been told you owe Bruno a lot," she said. "Your mother told me he's quite a ladies' man." She paused and stroked Adam's chest. "But he isn't here and you are."

Adam attempted to describe his comrades in Hut One. Gabrielle pretended to listen and allowed her hands to fall. She turned over laughing and knelt over him, guiding him in once again. They both moaned loudly, to the relief of the nurse whose ear was glued to the door. She wondered if any of her colleagues had heard her charges quarrelling. She could argue that they were worth the trouble because they were so gifted racially.

Gabrielle slid out of the bed to go to the bathroom. When she returned Adam was in a deep sleep with a half-smile on his face. He made a little noise and the smile broadened, but he didn't wake up. She tiptoed to her handbag and drew out a black leather purse given to her by her Aunt Martha. She threw a robe over her shoulders and stood by the window, where there was enough moonlight to see the photographs. She picked one of herself in uniform. She tiptoed to Adam's side of the bed and took his leather wallet from his tunic, nearly changing her mind. It was a selfish thing she was about to do and must place Adam in terrible danger. She returned to the window and opened the wallet. She saw photographs of Käthe and Frieda and decided that Adam would have wanted her to do this. Gabrielle placed her photograph underneath Frieda's.

She could not bear to leave the hotel without any hope of seeing Adam again and was convinced he felt the same. At the same time she was determined not to coerce him in any way because of the danger. She returned the wallet to his tunic and slid back into bed.

Adam rubbed his eyes to confirm he was still in bed with the woman of his dreams. He wanted her again and kissed the back of her neck. She turned over, smiled and kissed him. There was a loud bang at the door. "You have ten minutes!" someone shouted. They leapt out of bed and threw on their clothes.

The couples gathered on the ground floor. One of the men gave his partner a polite kiss on the cheek and two couples shook hands. It appeared their mission had not been accomplished. Adam and Gabrielle stayed inside their doorway for as long as they dared, clinging to each other. "I'll find you one day after the war," he promised. "Of course you will," she answered. She knew it was too dangerous because both of them might be under surveillance.

"Trooper von Saloman," called the officer who had disturbed their bedroom bliss. Just before Adam tore himself away, Gabrielle slid her hand inside his tunic and tapped the wallet. She turned round twice while descending the stairs.

Gabrielle was the last to climb into the coach and she knew Adam would be on the balcony. She surreptitiously blew a kiss, but an SS nurse impatiently pushed her onto the coach. Only one of the other men, Johannes Seeler, appeared on his balcony. The two young men felt so liberated they were no longer afraid. As the coach moved into the blackness of the forest, Gabrielle and Johannes' partner waved furiously out of the rear window of the coach. It turned sideways on before disappearing. Adam and Johannes continued to wave and all the other girls waved back.

The girls who had become pregnant were taken to a secret site somewhere in Germany, where SS nurses waited for the births of the new super-Aryans and SS doctors supervised. They had orders to report the births to the office of Reichsführer Heinrich Himmler, the Chief of the SS. There were a few disappointments, including miscarriages and some stillborn children. But to the men in the white coats, they were no more than statistics. They ordered Gabrielle's nurse and her friend to dispose of the dead foetuses. Because supervision of the order proved an embarrassment to the doctors, the two women were entrusted to carry out the task as they saw fit, but they did not obey the spirit of the order. They buried the dead children between two of the nissen huts where the girls had given birth and gave each child a small wooden cross.

Gabrielle had planned her life carefully. She was soon to qualify as a teacher and would shortly marry a high flyer in the Ministry of Education. She was as determined to become a School Principal as was Adam to become a Senior Officer in the Infantry. Her old attraction to him had surfaced in the Black Forest, but she believed that was now ended and she could look forward to a privileged life. The threat of severe punishment would deter her from ever considering seeing Adam again.

She was now almost sorry to have left her photograph. That, Gabrielle was convinced, had been merely an impulse. As she lay waiting to give birth, she longed for Adam to be there. Fraülein Felsen understood her anguish.

Suitable foster parents in a childless marriage had been selected, and they looked forward to the adoption of their new child. Their identity was intended to be a closely guarded secret, but one of the nurses penetrated the security screen and waited. The foster parents were delighted with their child at first, but then found that she didn't respond to them. They suspected she might be educationally backward, but assistance for such children could be double-edged in National Socialist Germany. Many such children mysteriously disappeared. This child's foster parents used their party influence to gain whatever help they could. They were allowed to advertise for a specialist nurse. One appeared who pleased the couple; they did not know she was the nurse who had had supervised their foster-child's birth. Fraülein Felsen was able to continue her project, although she regretted the absence of the natural father.

All the young super-Aryan men were scrutinised by security men as they boarded the coach, and hands fell on selected shoulders. Pockets were turned out, but only one felt any fear, the one who had taken details of his partner's identity.

This time Johannes escaped. He and Adam exchanged a few words, but Adam would have preferred silence. He indulged Seeler because it seemed safer at the rear of the coach when it appeared the security men had lost interest.

"Was your girl nice, von Saloman?" Johannes whispered. The security men were talking with the driver. It seemed safe. "She was wonderful Seeler," said Adam mechanically. "And yours?" "Wonderful," said Johannes. "She was the girl sitting opposite you," he said proudly. Adam smiled back; the girl he had embarrassed was very attractive.

A few minutes passed as the coach was driven quickly down the autobahn. "Would you like to see your child?" asked Johannes.

Adam became interested. "Of course I would," he answered, his voice charged with emotion.

"I also would like to see mine. I would like to see my partner again," said Johannes. They both realised they had said enough.

Chapter 19

"What the fuck's the matter with you von Saloman?" enquired Martin Schröder. "It's bad enough round here without you turning miserable. If you keep this up you'll get yourself blown up like Janke."

"Piss off Schröder, you big shit," said Franz Stamm.

Seebring glared at his tactless neighbour, but they were all unnerved by Adam's attitude since his return. "They're right, my old friend," said Bruno quietly. "What the hell is the matter with you?"

"We can't talk about it Bruno," answered Adam.

Bruno wouldn't be diverted. "Have you killed someone?" he asked. Hans heard the question, which stimulated his dark sense of humour. He leaned towards the two friends. Adam continued to sulk in the corner, playing with his wallet and gazing at Gabrielle's photo. He threw the wallet off the bed and Hans Thaelmann got up and seized it as he had done nearly two years before. Adam looked as though he might kill him. Thaelmann sat on the end of Adam's bed, holding the wallet open. The photographs fell out and Bruno and Hans saw there were three.

"Who the hell's this?" asked a bemused Hans Thaelmann, staring at the photo of Gabrielle. He showed Bruno. "Who is it, laughing boy?" Bruno stared at it open-mouthed, then snapped "Put it back Hans, now!"

"Sorry Adam," said the big man. Hans had aged several years since the beginning of his training.

Klaus Seebring joined them. "Leave him alone, all of you," he said and they trudged back to their beds and prepared for lights out.

"Do you want to talk?" Bruno asked Adam.

"I didn't know the photo was there," answered Adam.

"You've seen her again, haven't you? What the hell's going on?"

"Don't ask," said Adam. He turned over and tried to sleep.

CHAPTER NINETEEN

The doors were flung open at five-thirty. The men of Hut One sat up in bed rubbing their eyes. Seebring was slow to get out of bed and received a toilet fatigue.

"Lieutenant Gröner will be here in fifteen minutes with some gifts for you," said Kolb. "Prepare yourselves."

They knew that whatever Gröner was about to tell them it would involve extreme discomfort, because they lived with it from one minute to the next. It was usually accompanied by Bruno's dry remarks and Schröder's rudeness and callousness. Two men held the door open for Lieutenant Gröner. He was followed by one of the trainees from Hut Two, pushing a trolley laden with packages. He grinned at the men of Hut One as if they were heading for a hard time.

"At ease," he began and waved an official document at them. "I have here a request from Reichminister Von Ribbentrop from the Foreign Office. The Leibstandarte has been granted the privilege of providing an honour guard for certain foreign embassies. I must remind you that perfect discipline is essential. Sergeant Kolb will give you the details."

The men from the quartermaster's store broke open the packages. Each contained a black uniform, and one was hung behind six of the bunks. With each uniform was a shining black helmet with a swastika flash and almost knee-high shiny black leather boots. The men from the stores were dismissed and Kolb allowed the men of Hut One to gaze at the uniforms. The six men with the uniforms wondered why they had been selected.

"Thaelmann and Seebring will guard the Hungarian Legation, Abs and Schröder the Yugoslav Embassy," Kolb began, striding up and down, his hands behind his back. He stopped in front of Adam. "You, von Saloman, and your friend Grabowsky have a special treat. You two will guard the Chinese Legation. And remember, you're there to show them who's boss in this town, especially the Chinks." Adam cringed. "The Colonel's impressed with you lot," Kolb continued with a half-smile.

He looked carefully at those not chosen to go. "Why not you, Maschman and you Kroll? Well, Sergeant Heinz, the Colonel and myself thought these six enjoyed lousy weather." Kolb warned them there would be an inspection on the hour of the two-hour stint and retribution would follow if anyone so much as moved.

None of the chosen six slept very well. Occasionally the hut was filled with Martin Schröder's violent snoring. "It's like Seebring's fuckin' farmyard," commented Harold Maschman. Things got worse. The snoring suddenly stopped and Schröder dashed to the toilet, where he retched violently. Peace reigned at roughly two o'clock.

Kolb crashed through the doors at five-thirty and ordered the six into their uniforms. "Be ready for inspection in thirty minutes. A big noise from the Foreign Office wants to make sure you can scare hell out of anyone," he said.

Reichsrat Braun from the Foreign Office scrutinised the six men. He was small, round, bespectacled and self-important. "You must not forget you are playing a part in the Führer's policy towards other countries," he began. "You are to impress these people with the firm intent of the Fatherland." What he really meant was they were to be symbols of bullying and contempt.

The rain hammered on the tarpaulin cover of their transport as they sped down the Hanover-Berlin autobahn. The noise of the speeding vehicles gave way to city traffic.

"Must be in Spandau," said Bruno.

"Heavy traffic on the Spee Bridge," said Adam.

"Thanks for the tour guide," said Hans Thaelmann, pretending to yawn.

The lorry came to a stop amid heavy rush-hour traffic and a chorus of shouts and orders. They heard Kolb lecturing a traffic policeman and threatening him with SS retribution. The lorry moved off towards the diplomatic quarter and each pair got out, until only Adam and Bruno were left. The lorry trundled on for another five minutes.

"Out you two," ordered Kolb. "You're allowed your greatcoats." They soon found out why. It had started to snow.

They were in the least fashionable area of the diplomatic quarter, although the design of some of the buildings harked back to Frederic the Great's Berlin. The narrow street was quiet except for the passage of one or two cyclists. The buildings reared up five storeys high, darkening the streets between them. Only one looked as though it might belong in the diplomatic quarter and a large metal grille, heavily padlocked, guarded the way into it. Adam glanced upwards and was moved by the sight of the twelve-pointed star of Nationalist China.

Kolb stationed the two friends outside the wrought-iron metal gate, which reached upwards for nearly four metres. Behind it was a large wooden double door studded with metal, which seemed to groan under the weight of the thick stone walls above.

Kolb rang the bell in the outside gate and an Embassy official appeared. He looked surprised when he saw the SS uniforms. Sergeant Kolb explained rudely that the SS decided who would provide the honour guard. Adam cringed again, but if this was meant to upset the official it failed. He bowed and retired. It was the first time Adam had seen the bright-blue uniform for many years.

"Expect Sergeant Heinz and myself at any time," said Kolb to the two friends. "Your tour of duty will last two hours." A small staff car arrived to carry the sergeant's from one post to another.

After half-an-hour the cold began to bite their hands even through the white gloves. Adam began to wonder why the German government believed the Chinese would feel slighted by two guards who said and did nothing.

The wind howled, the clouds fell and it began to snow. Small drifts began to form in this wind tunnel of a street. The two men stared ahead and thought of life two hours ahead.

After a few minutes, a black saloon car turned down the narrow street and slowly approached the legation. The wooden doors and the metal grille opened noiselessly and the car turned into the entrance and stopped. Adam and Bruno presented arms as the car stopped just before it entered the legation. A figure in the uniform of a senior officer peered through the rear side window in Adam's direction. The car moved to the inner courtyard and the gates closed.

Twenty minutes passed and there was no sign of the two sergeants. The wind dropped and it began to snow more heavily. The inner wooden doors behind them opened quietly and there were gentle footfalls in the snow. They opened and in a few seconds closed again and Bruno was sure they had just been inspected. He glanced to one side, expecting Kolb's staff car to appear, and then glanced downwards.

"Look to your left," he said quietly.

"Shut up, Bruno," said Adam.

"No look now," his friend insisted, as large flakes of snow began to stick to their helmets. Adam sneaked a look and standing between them was a toy soldier. It was about twenty centimetres high and even though the paint had flaked, Adam knew it was an Uhlan cavalryman. He forgot the cold and Kolb's threats. He knew that one of only two people could have placed it there. Whoever had done so had gone and would probably never return. Adam recalled the last time he had seen the brothers on the Si-Kiang and remembered that neither would have been intimidated by their SS guards.

After a few more minutes, the gates opened once more and the Uhlan disappeared.

The men of Hut One crowded round the six guards before lights out. They expected a lively break after a monotonous few days, but the wrong person spoke first.

"That must be the most fuckin' boring experience in my life," said Martin Schröder. "I felt like fuckin' shooting at something."

Schröder's sufferings were usually greeted with either disdain or merriment. "Did you crap yourself, Martin?" asked Harold Maschman, which forced a smile from Bruno and Stamm. "Piss off, Maschman," said Martin. That was the best response he could think of.

"Did you scare the shit out of the Chinese?" called Sepp Kroll down the length of the hut to Adam and Bruno.

"It was too fuckin' cold to scare anyone," answered Bruno.

"Did you see any of your old friends, Adam?" asked Klaus Seebring.

"All we saw was a toy soldier," answered Bruno, who thought that was one of his weaker jokes. There were no more questions. The lights went out and for once Martin Schröder didn't snore.

Bruno began to worry that Schroeder was becoming isolated and believed that Kolb wouldn't approve. A few days later he saw Adam talking with Schroeder on the rifle range. Adam listened patiently and Schroeder seemed deferential. When the conversation was over Adam clapped Schroeder on the shoulder and the normally obtuse trooper almost bowed as he withdrew. Sergeant Kolb's influence was more pervasive than the men of Hut One realised.

Sergeant Heinz and the men of Hut Two appeared in full uniform in the quadrangle on a bright, cold sunny day after morning PE as their comrades of

Hut One sat in the sunshine cleaning and oiling their rifles. Kolb strode up and down with his usual look of permanent disapproval, looking for candidates for fatigues. He didn't allow Adam to settle. "You're wanted in the Colonel's office now," he announced.

As Adam strode off to the other side of the quadrangle, there were mutterings from Kroll and Maschmann. They lapsed into sullen silence as they saw Kolb approach. Bruno felt uneasy as he saw Adam disappear through the office door.

Klara Bettinger produced the uniform of a qualified storm trooper. "You've ten minutes to put this on, von Saloman," said the Colonel. "You've been selected to welcome a guest of the Leibstandarte today. You will be allowed thirty minutes only with our guest. I must tell you his country is not in favour with the Führer at the moment and this is a special concession to an anti-Communist military attaché." With that, the Colonel and Klara left.

Adam wasted little time changing, although he looked at the tunic collar thinking how it might be improved with three or four pips. As he marched over the parade ground, the men of Hut Two, led by Sergeant Heinz, began to form up into two lines in front of the Colonel's office. A long black saloon glided into the barracks. Adam knocked, went in and snapped to attention; the Colonel and Julius Kolb were waiting. Heinz shouted "Attention," outside and two minutes passed, followed by "Dismiss."

The office door opened and the visitor came in. He was smart, of medium build with a small black moustache and wore the bright-blue uniform of a Chinese Nationalist soldier. Adam saw he was a Lieutenant Colonel, but stared past him.

"May I present the Chief Military Attaché to Germany of the Republic of China, Lieutenant Colonel Huang Bing Wen," said the Colonel. "This, Excellency, is Adam von Saloman. I trust it is the man you remember," he said to the visitor. "At ease, von Saloman. If our visitor is in agreement, protocol may be relaxed at this point." Bing Wen nodded and the Colonel and Kolb left. "You have thirty minutes only," added the sergeant.

The door closed and Bing Wen and Adam shook hands furiously and embraced. "Please Adam, your news first. How are Käthe and Frieda?" asked Bing Wen, beaming from ear to ear.

"You know about Father of course," Adam began gravely.

"Yes, of course," replied Bing Wen. "I'm so sorry. I know you idolised him. Generalissimo Chang still speaks of him."

"My mother is still wonderful and beautiful and Frieda is well," said Adam. My grandmother is the rock of the family. We have lost our house and live where we can afford. And what is your news, old friend?"

Bing Wen became solemn and his head fell. "My brother is missing and is believed captured," he began. "There are terrible stories of ill-treatment of prisoners by the Japanese." He paused. "I must also tell you that Dr Meissner has also fallen into their hands."

Adam was crestfallen. "We must be strong in these terrible days," said Bing Wen. "I do have good news. My mother and father are well and send their greetings. Guang Csai and Jun Wei are well, although they do not speak of Jun Wui any longer. He has joined the Communists." Bing Wen smiled broadly." They still talk of 'Little Big Head' in the village. And I have a surprise. You will not know of the American volunteers who help us in the South West against the Communists. One of our helpers sends his greetings, Captain Ned Travis."

Adam laughed out loud. "You have proof of this, old friend?" he asked.

"Only that it is so unlikely, it has to be true," answered Bing Wen. "He enlisted with his whole crew!"

Bing Wen glanced towards the door. "We have very little time left, Adam. What I am about to tell you comes from the highest levels and must not go beyond these walls." He paused as if unsure whether or not to go on. "Your Führer will attack Russia in June. There were even signs on the exercises I have just seen. The Waffen SS are to be the shock troops of this invasion. Your life will change, Little Big Head. You must be careful." His face saddened. "It will be a war of hatred and conquest."

He took Adam by the shoulders. "Don't let yourself be corrupted, my old friend."

Adam stared at his old friend in disbelief. "I cannot believe our Führer could be so foolish," he replied impatiently. "The world will not stand by and watch us do such a thing."

Bing Wen shook his head. "You always took your life into your own hands even as a young boy. I'm sure you'll survive," he said. Adam wondered what he meant.

Bing Wen gave him a penetrating look. "You must try to seek safety in seniority, Adam," he added. He glanced at his watch; the thirty minutes had passed. "I must go. My friend in the High Command can't protect me any longer." He grasped Adam's hand. "I know we'll meet again."

The door opened and Bing Wen was ushered out. Adam watched the embassy car drive away and thought it was for the best. Such men as Huang Bing Wen did not belong in this forbidding, gaunt fortress.

The next day Kroll's friend from Hut Two met Adam on the parade ground.

"The Gestapo came for Seeler last night," began the newcomer." It happened so quickly. Sergeant Heinz tried to shake hands with Johannes, but one of the bastards drew a gun. I thought you ought to know."

"Thanks, Selzner," said Adam. "Don't be seen talking to me." Selzner scurried off. Adam thought he should destroy Gabrielle's photograph, but in a minor gesture of defiance, decided not to.

Bruno was reading the latest letter from Renate before lights out. He began to chuckle. "Spill it," said Thaelmann.

"I have to announce," began Bruno, "that the Ladies' Circle of Wilmersdorf has decided to have a pet's protection society until the war's over." The ripple of laughter was cut short by the appearance of Kolb, who was nearly apologetic. "Von Saloman, you're wanted in the office now." They marched briskly over the dimly lit parade ground past a black car with the swastika pennant. "I don't like it, von Saloman. Be careful what you say," warned the sergeant.

The Colonel was not himself and for once didn't seem to be in command of the situation. "Please go into Frau Bettinger's office, Trooper," he said. He looked worried. Klara had gone home hours before and seated in her chair was the unmistakable figure of Kriminalrat Kloster. He motioned Adam to sit down, giving no indication that they had met before.

"I am told you are a promising trainee, von Saloman," he began in his customary attempt to disarm potential victims. Adam nodded, trying to forget he regarded this man as verminous.

"The interests of our Fatherland require we have this informal chat," he continued. Adam remained silent and watchful. "You were recently reunited with your old friend Huang Bing Wen, I believe," said Kloster in his high-pitched voice. Adam nodded. "Please summarise your exchanges," he said. Adam now knew why Kloster was here. He began to wish his old friend had not divulged the secret of the invasion of Russia.

Adam was offhand. It was the best attitude he could summon for this contemptible little man. "It was an exchange of trivia between friends," said Adam flatly.

Kloster's attitude changed. "Trivia to you, von Saloman, but not to me," he answered sharply. He produced a file. "You are lucky to be here," he continued. "You have a track record of choosing bad friends, beginning with your school friends I believe." Adam remained silent, feeling oddly safe in the barracks even though Seeler had been arrested.

"I am informed you have performed a valuable service for the Fatherland," he went on. Adam went cold. Gabrielle's picture was in his breast pocket. If Kloster insisted on a personal search, his career and possibly his life might be ended. The Gestapo man could only have mentioned the hotel episode because he believed Adam was a security risk.

"We will conclude, for now," said Kloster. "You are not as talkative as you used to be. You may go." They exchanged salutes.

Kolb conducted Kloster to his car. The sergeant was a gruff, simple man and was not averse to showing his likes and dislikes. "You're uncomfortable in the presence of the Gestapo, Sergeant," observed Kloster.

"We do have one thing in common," said Kolb as he held the car door open for the policeman. "It is unlikely that either of us will see service at the front."

Kloster stared at the sergeant and quickly slammed the door.

Adam stalked into the hut in the semi-darkness. "What's up?" asked Bruno. Adam behaved as if his friend was the only one there. He slammed his fist into his cabinet. "What's going on in this damn country?" He asked.

Adam, Bruno, Hans and Klaus climbed into the back of a lorry, followed by Sergeant Kolb. This time they would miss Sports Day. Kolb had told them they were to be considered for officer training and that this day there would be an important test.

The sergeant seemed ill at ease. It was a fine day, but the tarpaulin cover on the rear of the lorry was hauled over them. They had no equipment and their sergeant didn't tell them where they were going. He preferred to sit in the cab because he didn't approve of the trial to be undergone by these four young men, and he didn't wish to display his lack of enthusiasm.

The lorry careered down forest tracks and a small convoy of staff cars built up behind. One of the vehicles was a field ambulance. The driver stopped to check his position. After a few minutes, the tarpaulin was drawn back and the lorry continued through the forest until it reached a clearing. Kolb ordered the four men out and a Lieutenant appeared, checking the four men's names against a list.

The clearing echoed with the noise of revving engines and clouds of blue smoke issued from the edge of the forest. "Wait here," ordered Kolb. He went off to report to an officer sitting at a trestle table on the edge of the clearing. The sergeant stumbled over deep marks left by caterpillar tracks.

Kolb ordered his four men towards a wooden rack containing spades and pickaxes. Parked just behind the rack underneath the trees was a black saloon with a driver and two passengers. One of them, an SS major, got out of the car and approached the four men, who sprang to attention.

"You should be proud of your selection for today's exercise," he said. "Good luck."

Adam glanced sideways across the clearing towards the sound of the engines. Four tanks emerged from the scrub at the far side fifty metres away and underneath the gun on the sloping armour was painted a red star.

"Today you must prove your worthiness as candidates for officer training," the officer began. "Each of you have twenty minutes to dig a trench for yourselves. You'll lie in it and the tanks will pass over you."

The looks on the faces of the four men betrayed nothing. Adam thought training with live ammunition was one thing, but this was quite another. Two men painted oblong white shapes on the ground where the trainees were to lie. Klaus Seebring stole a plaintive glance at Adam, who thought he heard Bruno say "shit" under his breath.

Adam looked at the hard stony ground and then at Klaus Seebring. He had to do something, even if it meant jeopardising his career. "Permission to speak, Herr Major," he said assertively. The officer seemed startled and Sergeant Kolb's ears pricked up.

"Any reluctance to comply will result in instant transfer to the Regular Army," he said coldly. "Well, trooper?"

"Permission to speak with the men before the exercise?" said Adam.

"Granted," said the officer with some reluctance. Kolb breathed a sigh of relief.

The man in the car, whose uniform was covered in silver braid and oak leaves, looked impatiently at his watch as Adam turned to his comrades. "You've dug slit trenches before," he began. "Don't look at the tanks. Keep to one rhythm. We can do this, men. See you all in twenty minutes," he added cheerfully, trying to hide his own fear. The officer gave the signal and the four began to dig. Adam looked up and saw Hans and Klaus watching the tanks. "Don't look at the tanks. Keep going," shouted Adam. Their engines revved and they slowly moved forward.

Klaus Seebring seemed transfixed and did nothing. Bruno shouted at him, "Klaus. Do as you're fuckin' well told or I'll tear your bollocks off!" Julius Kolb tried to hide his anxiety and looked as impassive as he could.

Klaus carried on frantically. Sweat poured down their faces as they hacked at the ground, but Hans fell behind. "Thaelmann – don't spoil this or you're for it!" said Adam, and Hans speeded up. Pieces of earth and chips of rock flew. A piece hit Adam in the face, leaving a large cut. On and on they went. The tanks' engines revved once more and the steel monsters moved even closer to the four men. Thaelmann had not dug a trench deep enough to take his bulk and his tank was ten metres away. Adam looked at him, horrified. "Lie down, now men," he called, and they obeyed.

Seebring lay quivering and sobbing in his trench. Bruno and Adam gritted their teeth, their fingers clawing the strong ground. Thaelmann shouted, "Fuck you," and hurled his spade at the tank. He threw himself into his inadequate trench, clawing the ground and shouting defiantly.

As the tank passed over him, he screamed with pain. His cries were the only sound in the clearing as the tank engines were switched off. The others were unscathed. Adam jumped up and ran towards Hans Thaelmann. He was lying face downwards and his uniform had been ripped from his back. He had suffered terrible abrasions and lay motionless in the dirt.

Adam saw the Major taking notes, and his fury got the better of him when he saw no movement from the medics' table. Julius Kolb intervened; his anger too had spilled over. These were his men, and he never tolerated hesitancy. "Medics!" he called, but they still hesitated, waiting for orders from the officers.

He ran to one of the medics and shouted in his face. Finally the man ran to helped Hans.

Bruno went to Klaus Seebring, who sat in his trench weeping because he had soiled himself. "It's OK," said Bruno. "We've all been there." He helped Klaus to the lorry that was to take them home. The medic tended Hans and gave him penicillin shots and temporary dressings. He was just able to stand, but he pushed the medic away and leaned on Adam. They both staggered to the lorry.

Kolb snapped to attention in front of the Major, expecting punishment.

"Not the disciplined display I was led to expect," said the officer. "Dismiss." Kolb did his best to hide his fury.

Bruno hauled Hans up the lorry's tailgate, but the injured trooper couldn't suppress moans of pain. Adam pushed himself under Hans' hindquarters and helped by his Sergeant, finally got the injured man on board.

Adam was about to climb into the lorry when he received a surprise. "You did well today, von Saloman," said the Sergeant.

"Thank you Sergeant," said Adam politely, without a trace of condescension. Their confrontation seemed to be over.

They queued to see Hans in the barracks hospital and the doctor assured the men of Hut One that he would be fit in three weeks. After the announcement, the friendly abuse began. "You spoilt the whole fuckin' performance Thaelmann," said Bruno. "I'm going to give you a thrashing when I get out of here Grabowsky," promised Hans.

He just managed to raise his fist to shoulder level and Bruno lowered his face so that the big man from Hamburg could reach. "The doctor says you can hand out the thrashing in about two weeks, Hans," said Adam.

Thaelmann had stretched out his arm as far as he could to shake Adam's hand. He knew he probably owed his life to the young aristocrat and developed an interesting habit. He began to ask Bruno if it was all right to speak to Adam. Bruno kept that little titbit to himself.

Nearly all of them qualified as fully-fledged stormtroopers; they had expected no more. Hans Thaelmann and Franz Stamm were to train as NCOs and both agreed their role model was Julius Kolb. Adam and Bruno were to train as officers at Bad Tolz in Bavaria, while Klaus Seebring was quietly drafted back into the regular army.

A familiar, slightly bow-legged figure strode across the parade ground towards the men of Hut One. Sergeant Kolb walked up and down the line of twenty men and shook hands with each of them. "You'll be all right Schröder," he said. "You'll find someone like me to kick your backside. Don't go too hard on recruits," he said to Stamm and Thaelmann, and then he reached Adam and Bruno. "Perhaps you'll be happy as Lieutenant?" he said to Bruno, who thought he was probably right.

He stared Adam full in the face. "Perhaps your way is the best, von Saloman," he said and marched briskly back to the NCOs' mess, disappearing through the door without turning round.

Sepp Kroll and Martin Schroeder seemed lost and were the last to move from the parade ground to the hut. They both sat on their bunks in silence and wondered what to do next. They slowly began to pack their belongings, realising Sergeant Kolb would no longer do their thinking for them.

The two friends caught a train to Charlottenburg. Adam was about to open a wedding invitation he had just received. Bruno grinned because he liked to catch his friend off balance. It was an invitation to Bruno's wedding to Helga in two weeks' time. Bruno looked out of the window, waiting for his friend to say something.

Adam tossed the envelope onto the seat to see what Bruno would do. "What was that for?" he asked.

"This invitation seems like an afterthought to me," said Adam. He stared at Bruno reprovingly.

"Would you be my chief witness?" asked Bruno.

"I suppose so," answered his friend. "I have nothing else planned on that day. And where will it take place, may I ask?"

"Oh, it's to be a civil ceremony at Herr Berger's Office in Wilmersdorf," answered Bruno.

"And of course, you wish to be married before we get to Bad Tolz?" enquired Adam.

"Helga's pregnant," said Bruno.

"Congratulations, my old friend," said Adam shaking Bruno's hand. "The SS would approve."

"As the Chief Witness, I am entitled to be familiar with the guest list," said Adam.

"I've asked half the Wilmersdorf home to come," said Bruno cheerfully. "Do you think your family would come?"

"You haven't asked them?" enquired an amazed Adam. He wondered what the next feature of the shambles would be. "Your mother's coming of course?" asked Adam.

"Only because it's a civil ceremony," answered Bruno.

"At least the SS would approve of a civil wedding, Bruno," said Adam. "And my family will be there."

In spite of the venue, the wedding was a grand affair. Frieda and Käthe insisted that the reception be held at the von Saloman apartment. Bruno was resplendent in SS dress uniform and Helga was dressed in bright blue with a coronet of flowers in her hair. Karl Berger conducted the ceremony in the presence of the guests of honour, the von Saloman family. Helga's employer turned up in a Brownshirt uniform and congratulated Helga on her choice of husband. He found the couple an apartment in Charlottenburg at a lower rent.

The Ladies' Circle waited for the guests to arrive in Charlottenbrunnestrasse and threw armfuls of flowers over the couple as they arrived. The wedding car was the Buick, and Adam doubled as driver and chief witness. The ladies thought the wedding the social event of the year. Hanni Dirksen had brought her equally shy civil servant husband along, and he spent much of his time bowing to everyone. Ilse Diels sat on a high-backed chair in a corner glaring at everyone. She resented not being invited to the wedding and let everyone know it. It was a National Socialist wedding, she said, and the Blockleiter should have been invited. She didn't remove her hat during the entire reception.

Bruno expected his mother to welcome all the guests, but she was slow to do so and spent most of the time in the kitchen with Greta, who would have preferred someone else's company. She was rescued by Bruno, who insisted that Renate show some enthusiasm. Ilse Diels heard the conversation from just inside the living room and committed as much as she had heard to her notebook. She craved the chance to lecture someone on the subject of conformity and marched into the kitchen, dismissing Greta, who was afraid of her.

"Why are you behaving in this manner, Frau Grabowsky?" Ilse demanded.

"To what manner do you refer?" retorted Renate.

"This is a National Socialist wedding and I don't think you are aware of it," said Ilse, thrusting out her chin.

"Don't you know a wedding of convenience when you see one?" asked Renate defiantly.

Ilse's faced turned a dangerous red. "This will be seen as an act of disloyalty, Frau Grabowsky," said Ilse pompously.

"You will mind your own business, Frau Diels," said an angry Renate, pushing her way past her. She joined Bruno and Helga and assumed a bogus air of cheerfulness.

"It's time for the presents," said Käthe, unaware of the confrontation. There was a round of applause as the proceedings began. "Stand by me Adam," Käthe said, gently holding something square and heavily wrapped. "You open it Helga," said Käthe. Helga let the wrapping drop and showed the framed photograph to Bruno. It was Bruno with his damaged bicycle standing on the steps of Die Schwanen on the day of the friends' reunion. He let out a joyous laugh and clutched it to his chest, turning to shake Adam's hand. It was almost like a reaffirmation between blood brothers.

Martha was usually the life and soul of the Ladies' Circle, but not on this occasion, and Frieda was trying to comfort her. Adam had been reluctant to approach Martha, but now he had no choice because Frieda asked him to join them.

"How are you, Aunt Martha?" asked Adam.

"You remember Gabrielle, Adam?"

"Of course. I hope she's well."

"I can't answer that," said Martha. "I rang my sister yesterday and asked how Gabrielle was." Martha became tearful and grasped Adam's hands. "She has lost touch with her. Can you imagine how terrible that must be?"

Adam's heart skipped a beat. "I rang the college in Münich Adam, and do you know what they said?" Martha continued. Adam shook his head. "They told me I was to make no further enquiries, but I insisted. They said she had to attend a health spa somewhere on the Baltic Coast, as part of her course. I asked what was wrong with her and they told me to ring off because Gabrielle was on party business."

"That's terrible," said Adam, trying to sound as genuine as possible.

"It's much worse," said Frieda. "Tell him, my dear."

Martha managed to compose herself. "The police have been to my flat. They said if I make any more enquiries, I will be evicted."

"Then there is nothing you can do, Aunt Martha, but wait," advised Adam, desperate for information about the love of his life. "Gabrielle will tell you what has happened," he advised, wondering what on earth these wonderful women would say if they knew the truth. He realised Gabrielle was pregnant and longed to be with her.

"I would like to help but as you know we have had a brush with the police before Papa died. I'm afraid we all have to become cowards now," Adam warned regretfully.

Martha reached inside her bag and withdrew a letter. "This is for you, Adam," she said. She wanted him to open it there and then in case it gave some information about her favourite niece. She looked at Adam pleadingly, and he opened it, praying the contents would be short and circumspect, and knowing he would have to read it to Martha.

The letter was short. "Give my best wishes to Bruno and Helga," Gabrielle had written, signing it, "love Gabrielle." Adam saw it as a form of shorthand. She had said enough. He now knew why she had gone to the so-called spa. He felt fraudulent, but most of all he longed to tell Käthe what was happening.

Bruno and Helga had been watching and she prodded her new husband into asking the cause of the distress. Bruno cornered Adam in the kitchen. He didn't show his friend the letter at first. "I saw Martha give you a letter, Adam. If you can't be honest with me, who can you be honest with?" he said.

Adam showed him the letter. "You know damn well why she's gone, but I won't press you for an answer," said Bruno.

"I've seen Kloster again and he's scared the hell out of me," Adam warned. "Aunt Martha's had a visit from them. If I reveal anything to you, we're all for the chop."

"What's the matter with you?" objected Bruno. "You're afraid of your own shadow. This isn't like you at all."

Adam looked sullenly at his friend. Bruno slapped him gently on the shoulder. "You know where I am if you need me," he reassured him.

Albert Hartman appeared in the doorway, waving his arms. The gathering went quiet. "Turn on the radio quick!" he said urgently.

The announcer said that the German army had responded to repeated provocations on the Soviet border and the armed forces had begun to shoot back. The room was deadly silent, except for an outburst of patriotism from Ilse Diels. The rest glared at her.

"Why couldn't the Führer tell us himself?" said Albert. Ilse seemed to think his question was worth recording. The next day she went to the police station, and the duty officer braced himself as she strode up to the counter.

"This woman should be watched carefully," Ilse said, opening her notebook at the relevant page and banging it down. The duty officer thought he had seen Renate's name before. "Günsche, make a copy of this," he ordered, passing the notebook over his shoulder. Like everyone else he did not dare to appear inactive.

Six months later, Manfred was born to Bruno and Helga.

Chapter 20

In February 1943, the training school at Bad Tolz received a message that the German Army needed new divisions to make victory certain. Within a few hours the Reich Military post had delivered the shoulder flashes and armbands of the new divisions.

"Ah well, it's nice to see the High Command is honouring tradition," the Colonel said to himself as he examined the names of the two new units.

"Please sit down, gentlemen," Colonel Leuter said to Adam and Bruno, pouring each of them a small glass of schnapps. "The Führer has agreed to the formation of two new SS Panzer Divisions. You two are to serve in one of them." He smiled and paused. "You have both prematurely passed out as lieutenants. Please remove your training insignia and have these sewn on," he ordered.

Adam smiled broadly at Bruno when he saw the name 'Hohenstaufen.' The Colonel handed them sealed orders which included the location of the new division and a list of the men in their platoons. He warned them that a lot of those men were not trained SS but had transferred from the Army.

"You may open your sealed orders on the train to Berlin" he concluded. "Good luck gentlemen."

Most small boys dismiss their childhood fantasies, but grandfather Gustav's prediction had been a thread holding Adam's life together. Now he had truly joined the officer ranks of Germany's elite soldiers. Bruno decided he was enjoying himself and conveniently forgot his mother's promise to take him to Florence one day.

The orders told them to proceed to Brussels and from there to the Gare du Nord in Paris. There they would be met by a staff car and taken to a secret destination. Bruno had never been outside Germany and knew next to nothing about France and the French. He had heard interesting rumours that French women were obliging, and checked this stimulating piece of knowledge with his friend. Adam had had enough of Bruno's meanderings and told him so.

Their destination was an area outside Rheims. As they drove along, they examined the names of the men in their platoons.

"What does yours look like?" asked Bruno.

"I have Hitler Youth draftees with no training, a few volunteers from the Army and two sergeants with no battle experience," said Adam.

"My lot don't look too bad," said Bruno. "They can drive armoured cars, it says, and read maps, and most of them are not bad gunners."

"Then it looks like you'll have an easy time my old friend," joked Adam.

Five kilometres outside Rheims, the car approached a barrier manned by SS military police. One of them told Adam that his two sergeants could not take up their posts and two other trainees from Lauenberg had been sent down. "Here are their names, Lieutenant," said the policeman. Adam concealed his reaction. The SS had made a glaring mistake, which he felt they would have to rectify. They had sent him Staff Sergeant Hans Thaelmann and Sergeant Franz Stamm.

Adam showed the slips of paper to Bruno. "They're friends," he said. "I must report the mistake."

"Say nothing Adam," advised Bruno. "Those two guys really looked up to you. You'll handle it and they'll help you. They'll have your platoon organised before you arrive."

They forgot the problem of Thaelmann and Stamm when they saw the array of military might in front of them. As far as they could see stretched lines of brand new half-tracks, armoured cars and tanks with mechanics crawling all over them. Some of the vehicles still displayed factory grey, while others were already painted in camouflage colours. The air was filled with the smell of exhaust fumes as soldiers rolled newly-delivered drums of fuel to hidden dumps in the trees. The roar of the engines drowned the issue of dozens of orders as sergeants drilled new recruits.

Between the vehicles, stood lines and lines of hastily-erected tents. Motorcycle messengers churned up the ground delivering messages from Divisional Headquarters to companies. An army cooperation plane landed in the churned up ground, its stilt-like undercarriage threatening to turn it over.

CHAPTER TWENTY

"This is where we part company," said Adam, spotting his company flag.

"See you on leave," replied Bruno.

"We'll watch Christina Sodenstern floating down the river together," quipped Bruno. "Then we'll finish off a bottle of schnapps. I'll need it."

They shook hands solemnly and Adam watched his friend march off to the site of the Reconnaissance Battalion. He marched towards the company flag in time to see Hans Thaelmann berating a new recruit

"Attention!" he barked and Adam's new company stood rigidly to attention. Franz Stamm introduced Wachtel and Gensche, two veterans from the Russian front.

"Soon we will talk," said Adam to the two men, realizing how much he could learn from them. He was pleased the two sergeants had trained the other men. Already a new recruit was performing latrine duty.

Later Adam sat in his tent with the two sergeants. "Do you have any problem with the situation?" he asked. Thaelmann said he hadn't. "We should report this. We could be in serious trouble," Adam reminded them.

"I don't give a shit, Lieutenant," he said. "You were the boss in the barracks. Even Kolb thought you were. You're the boss here, that's good enough for us." Stamm nodded in agreement. "We won't mention it again, Lieutenant," he said with some authority.

Adam always carried a bottle of schnapps and they downed a glass each to cement the arrangement. It was easier for Thaelmann and Stamm as they had never considered Adam a close friend. Their friend was Bruno.

The dull routine was interrupted in an unexpected way. The soldiers of the Ninth had become used to the vapour trails high in the sky made by American bombers flying east. Adam was trying to make conversation with a thin-faced young private who had impressed on the rifle range. He spent much of his time by himself, cleaning and oiling his rifle.

They glanced up at the now-familiar vapour trails. "What does it mean, Lieutenant?" asked Private Michael Kaspar.

"It means the Americans don't like us, Kaspar," answered Adam, thinking the simple approach would work. Then one of the bombers fell out of the sky. It had lost most of one wing and half its fuselage as it spiralled into the ground. The remainder of its fuel exploded and a black pall of smoke rose. Two parachutes appeared three hundred metres above the camp and drifted into a small copse close to where Adam and Kaspar were standing. One of the airmen had survived and was quickly surrounded by military police and taken into captivity. The other man was already dead. He hung in a tree, his head slumped forward, his arms hanging limply.

He was buried in a local churchyard with full military honours and Adam was ordered to attend. He took Michael Kaspar with him. After the brief service Kaspar was persistent in trying to extract Adam's views on the Americans. "It is the Führer's business Kaspar. We are his firemen. We will deal with anything." He seemed happy with the reply.

Kaspar was a loner and treated the new recruits with scant respect. He took an instant liking to his lieutenant and let Adam know he could be relied on. He would only ever ask Adam for advice.

The survivors of the First Army fell back on the town of Tarnopol in Byelorussia. They received yet another order, from the Führer, to hold fast. The tired, demoralised men were squeezed into a pocket several kilometres long between the small towns of Kamenetz and Podolsk. Hitler relented, for once, on his customary policy of ordering the fight to the death and assured the survivors that help was on its way. The Hohenstaufen Division was to make its debut on the Eastern Front and to try to retrieve something from yet another defeat.

One April morning in 1943 the entire camp at Rheims sprang to life. Hans Thaelmann interrupted Adam as he was shaving, and he cut himself. "We are expected at the local railway station in two hours," he announced. Adam decided he wouldn't bother to change his blood-stained vest and threw on his tunic.

The local rail network around Rheims became out of bounds to all but military police and the eighteen thousand men of the Hohenstaufen. The Ninth had to be entrained in time to rescue their comrades in the East and avoid yet another attack from the air on the railway yards. The roofs of the carriages had been hastily painted in camouflage colours and bristled with anti-aircraft guns. The mechanics made last-minute checks. Tanks were driven on to flat cars in clouds of smoke, accompanied by the clank of chains securing them.

"You'll get nowhere without us," shouted Helmut Wachtel at a familiar tank crewman, as the infantry marched into the yards. "Shut your mouth, Wachtel," ordered Franz Stamm. The tank crewman waved and grinned.

CHAPTER TWENTY

Adam's platoon marched past a line of armoured cars. The Lieutenant in the hatch of one of them, an eight-wheeled Puma, shouted into the interior, "Stop moaning about your girlfriend Wem, or I'll have you transferred to these loafers marching past."

"Unusual fighting crew you have there, Lieutenant Grabowsky," called out Adam. Bruno glanced towards the fuel tankers and stubbed out his cigarette. "Getting better by the minute," he replied, returning Stamm and Thaelmann's salutes.

"Get your platoon on the train as soon as possible," ordered a military policeman. Adam refused to be hurried. His sergeants cast an eye over every man's equipment, backpack, field rations, field dressings, steel helmet and rifle. The machine-gunners came last and stowed their equipment amid cursing in the entrance to each carriage. Every man had to be on standby, ready to de-train and fight at a moment's notice, with enough ammunition to last nearly a week.

The locomotive's wheels gained a grip on the rails and there was a judder as it stopped and then finally started. Anti-aircraft gunners in the railway yards waved to the departing troops and then resumed their anxious watch on the sky.

The train picked up speed. It slowed as it passed prisoners of war wearing khaki uniforms filling in bomb craters. Adam wondered if they had been captured in France or in Greece, and then turned to the care of his men. He showed his orders to Thaelmann and Stamm. They outlined the plan to rescue the remnants of the First Army. They both nodded, but their half-smiles showed that they understood that the Ninth could be drawn into the same trap.

Franz Stamm suggested that Wachtel and Gensche could tell them how to do it. Adam grinned. "Perhaps you're right, Stamm," he replied. They were acutely aware of their lack of experience.

The soldiers saw little sign of the war until the trains reached Berlin. The Central Station had received direct hits. Gangs of labourers, some of them prisoners of war, toiled to remove rubble and repair railway lines. Adam couldn't help but think of his family.

The train crossed East Prussia through the type of farmland once owned by the von Salomans before turning south-east and crossing the Polish border. The train slowed and stopped again. "Outside!" shouted the sergeants. Partisans had blown the line.

The delay lasted an hour and the journey continued, but not before Adam had a puzzling experience. The officers ordered the men at ease now that there appeared to be no danger. All the time, they had been watched by Polish labourers in the fields. Trooper Walter Breitman of Adam's platoon was slow to return to the train. He tried to speak to one of the labourers, a silver-moustached old man.

The farmer dropped his gaze to Breitman's sleeve and saw the silver bird of the Waffen SS. He fell on his knees and begged for mercy. Breitman backed away embarrassed and returned to the train.

Adam had watched the whole thing – so too had Wachtel and Gensche. He looked for answers from them. "You'll see what we've done ahead," said Gensche. "Then you'll understand." A more unsympathetic voice spoke so that only his comrades could hear. "Serve the old bastard right," he said.

The further east the Ninth travelled, the colder it became, and Adam was transfixed by the scene. The train slowed frequently at small halts used for decades by small towns or villages as links to the outside world. Some of those small communities were now barely visible, victims of total war. Village after village was wrecked.

The Ninth was nowhere near the front, but this was a war zone. The train slowed down once again, to the disgust of the officers, and Adam used the delay to compose a letter home. He wrote to Martha Reymann and asked her to pass the letter on to Gabrielle. Then he remembered the fate of Johannes Seeler, and destroyed it.

After a few hours into the journey, Adam was convinced that these young men would give a good account of themselves. He noticed Trooper Kaspar socialised for a short time but then wandered off to enjoy his own company. One of the young recruits said to him "What's wrong with us, Kaspar?"

"Mind your own business," replied the young isolate.

"He wants to be at home with his mother," remarked another trooper. Kaspar grasped his tunic collar and pushed him over, all within sight and sound of Adam and Franz Stamm.

"Order!" barked Stamm. The quarrel broke up and the two guilty men snapped to attention. Stamm handed out extra latrine duty to both of them, to be performed on arrival at camp. "I'll see them both, Sergeant," said Adam, ordering them to join him at the end of the compartment. "We shall soon be at grips with the enemy and you are comrades. This will not be forgotten." They both apologised and shook hands. The recruit seemed penitent, but not Kaspar.

"Wait," ordered Adam, who had noticed the badge of a sharpshooter on Kaspar's sleeve as he walked away. Adam hoped that if the young trooper couldn't identify with his comrades, he might with the nearest junior officer. Kaspar turned and once again snapped to attention.

"At ease Kaspar," said Adam. "You will be very useful to us all." He pointed to the cross-guns. "Is it something you did in peacetime?" he asked.

The young troopers' bland expression disappeared. "I am a good shot, Lieutenant," he said. "My trainer says I could represent Germany in the Olympics."

"You practise hard?" enquired Adam.

"Yes Lieutenant, we hunt in the local woods. I shot fifty pigeons in one afternoon." Adam felt a chill, but had to show enthusiasm. "Well done Kaspar," he said. Adam suspected Kaspar's comrades knew something he didn't.

The train went on at a steady pace as the light began to fail. It slowed down to the squeal of brakes and turned off the main track to park in a siding for the night. Adam thought they must be near Krakow. He toured the carriages with Thaelmann and Stamm. Some of the men were still playing cards, a few writing letters, while Eric Graffe and his friends were asleep.

"We'll keep them on their toes with a kit inspection in the morning," said Adam.

"You rest," said Thaelmann. "We'll watch out for fights breaking out," he added with a grin.

Adam settled down in his seat, but couldn't sleep. He looked at his watch and remembered he had gone to bed with Gabrielle at exactly this time. He wandered past his sleeping platoon and stepped off the train, pulling his greatcoat over his shoulders.

The sky was clear and the marshalling yards bathed in silver moonlight. There was a light covering of snow. As Adam stepped down, the frozen snow crackled.

"Good evening, Lieutenant," said a military policeman. "Please keep close to the train. There are partisans here."

"May I join you, Lieutenant?" said Kaspar.

"Of course," replied Adam. "Couldn't you sleep either?"

They walked up and down for five minutes, hazarding guesses as to their destination. Then Kaspar peered into an area shrouded by a line of trees. "Is that another train parked over there?" he asked.

"I believe it is," answered Adam.

Kaspar's keen eyes saw grey-uniformed guards walking up and down a collection of what seemed to be freight cars. Curiosity got the better of Adam and he decided to make a brief enquiry. He approached a guard, who saluted him. He wore the death's head cap badge of the SS.

"Are you on your way to the front?" asked Adam. The guard seemed reluctant to answer and was soon distracted. Each of the wagons had one small barred window. A small hand, perhaps a child's, protruded through the bars. The fingers extended as if their owner was drowning. In an instant, the guard unhitched his rifle. He grasped the barrel like a club and struck the hand with the stock. There was a sharp cry of pain from inside the wagon.

Kaspar started forward, but Adam restrained him. "Who is inside these wagons?" he asked the guard sharply. A Lieutenant ran up to the scene. "What are you doing here?" he asked Adam curtly.

"You do not outrank me and I demand courtesy at least Lieutenant. We are in transit for the front. May I ask you what you and your men are doing?" Adam replied equally sharply.

"You may not," was the reply. "I advise you to join your train immediately."

Adam stood his ground until they were interrupted by the military policeman who had advised caution. "Lieutenant, I have just received orders that you must rejoin the train immediately" he said. Adam turned to see an officer watching them from one of the carriages.

They wandered back. "What's going on here Lieutenant?" asked Kaspar quietly. Adam felt ashamed not to be able to give him an adequate answer. "I have no idea," he replied. "We have learned to look the other way in Germany today. I think we should concentrate on fighting the Ivans."

They returned to their seats in deep disquiet and neither shared their experience. In the future, what had passed that day would serve to reinforce the bond between the two men, although Adam had begun to entertain doubts about Trooper Michael Kaspar.

The train moved on at first light and Adam gazed at the flat featureless countryside, still partially covered by snow. The train passed village after village which had been reduced to charred timbers with little sign of life. There were no signs to indicate where they were, as if there had been a deliberate campaign to reduce these old communities to anonymity. A few wrecked tractors, the first mechanization seen by Russian farmers, lay overturned in ditches. One had been equipped with improvised armour plate.

The few Russians they saw were resentful, gazing at the occupiers in the fatally-mistaken belief they had come as liberators from Stalin's rule.

"Have we come here to fight for this dump, Lieutenant?" asked Sergeant Stamm.

"I'm told it has hidden benefits," replied Adam.

"For all I care, they can keep them," said Stamm, trying to keep warm.

A few hours before dark the train slowed and the soldiers of the Hohenstaufen prepared to tread on Russian soil for the first time. They had stopped at a small village because, once again, the rails had been torn up. Every building was wrecked save one, restored as some sort of reception for the German rescue force. The young soldiers of Adam's platoon stared uncomprehendingly at the scene. They moved slowly, until Stamm and Thaelmann barked at them.

Previous trains had brought the armoured vehicles first. The soldiers had been used to seeing them parked in imposing rows, but here they were dispersed because the Russians controlled the skies.

Then came a deadly time. The ammunition train arrived, bristling with anti-aircraft guns. Adam behaved with the complacency of inexperience, watched anxiously by Wachtel and Gensche. Three German aircraft put in a token appearance, to be greeted by cheers and waves from the younger troopers, but the two veterans knew this was no cause for comfort.

One extra train arrived, pulling wagons with double sliding doors. Troopers placed ramps at the doors and Germany's main field transport appeared - horses. Corporal Eberhardt took charge of them without waiting for orders.

"Friends of yours?" said Adam.

"They're better than people," replied Eberhardt.

Spring had not arrived here and biting east winds still swept the landscape. A few centimetres of partially-melted snow still covered the ground and the soldiers shivered in their greatcoats. There was no time to be lost, as camp had to be set up close to Tarnopol before dark. The luckier ones rode on half-tracks slewing around on the unmade roads. The Panzer Grenadiers of the Ninth realised why forced marches had become second nature to them. This was just another, and it was like the north German plain in winter.

Adam felt the freezing metal of his machine-pistol through fingerless mittens. Breitman, Graffe and their group raised spirits. In the Waffen SS, permission to speak to a junior officer was not required. "We're OK, Lieutenant," shouted Graffe. "There go the field kitchens."

The men of the Ninth crawled their way over the Steppes to Tarnopol. The soldiers could see a kilometre or so ahead on the trackless waste. Helmut Wachtel and Hubert Gensche's eyes searched the skies to the east, but their appeals to the young soldiers to do the same fell on deaf ears.

The two veterans were the first to see the approaching dots in the sky. "Fighter bombers!" they shouted, without reference to Adam.

"Throw yourselves flat!" shouted Thaelmann and Stamm. The dots grew larger and approached faster. "Leave it to the flak," shouted Gensche. One of the half-tracks began to describe a circle on the ice and snow. Wachtel jumped onto it and pushed the driver out of the way, taking control as the first bombs fell. The first aircraft flew into a hail of fire and exploded. The second flew straight at Adam, Kaspar and Graffe, and the ground erupted round them. Wachtel's half-track was thrown on its side by the blast.

When the surviving aircraft had receded into the clear eastern sky, Adam and Kaspar ran to the damaged vehicle with Gensche following them. It was half on its side with Wachtel's body hanging out of it. "Help me," shouted Hubert Gensche as he struggled to remove his friend's body. "He's dead, Gensche," said Adam quietly. "We will remove his body together and give him a decent burial." Adam had seen his first battle casualty.

Kaspar retrieved Wachtel's helmet and rifle from the wreck as Graffe and Breitmann stared at the corpse. Kaspar helped Gensche and Adam to remove it. "Hurry," said the Company Commander. He didn't wish to seem insensitive. "Was he your comrade?" he asked Gensche.

Helmut Wachtel was buried at Gensche's request by the side of the smouldering half-track, his helmet and rifle resting on an improvised cross. As the platoon marched away with the rest of the division, the fuel in the half-track exploded. There was no more singing on the march for the rest of that day.

The sky in the east turned grey as the light began to fail and it rained steadily. A horse-drawn convoy approached from the east and kept a distance. In the gathering gloom the men could just see a large red cross on the side of the wagons. The vehicles were field ambulances packed with German wounded. The soldiers were forced to march in a narrow column, as the land either side of the track was boggy and they were thankful for the gathering darkness. There would be no hostile aircraft in the sky until the next day. The alien shapes of the spires of Tarnopol were visible through gaps in the forests.

A roadblock lay ahead, the first sign that they were close to the front line. The guards informed them that the division would be dispersed over two kilometres. Adam's platoon was lucky, as they were close to their bivouac. He surveyed what passed for a defence line and knew what Kolb would have said. Groups of bedraggled and unshaven soldiers sheltered in foxholes, with makeshift roofs of waterproof capes.

Gensche shook hands with one of the survivors of the First Army. "Welcome to Stalin's holiday camp," he said grimly. Gensche told him to report to Adam. "Our boys are stuck between Kamenetz and Podolsk. Tarnopol's here in the middle. There's thousands of them," he said grimly. "The Ivans are patrolling in front of us, Lieutenant."

Adam swept the horizon with his binoculars in the rapidly failing light. He could just see shadowy figures moving in the distance. "They want us to see them, Lieutenant, to scare the shit out of us," he added.

"Thank you Private," answered Adam.

"Careful when you come back," the private in the foxhole called out. "There's big drainage ditches out there."

The tents were up in no time, covered in camouflage netting. There were flashes to the east and shells whined over the trees. It lasted a few intense minutes. The Russians had now informed their enemy that they knew they were there, and it didn't stop raining. Gensche informed everyone that Russian rain was different and sooner or later their privates would drop off.

Eberhardt and Gensche were to guard the company's area for the first half of the night. Kaspar and Johannes Krebs, a Hitler Youth recruit, were to take the second half at two o'clock. They were then to join the advance at five thirty.

It began to snow at the beginning of the second watch and Krebs stamped on the ground, wishing Kaspar was there to talk to. Even the reticent Kaspar was better than no one. By three o'clock he could hardly feel his feet.

"Try this Krebs," said a familiar voice. Adam handed him a small portion of schnapps. The young trooper remembered that for the rest of his life and Adam snatched another two hours of sleep.

They were to attack in two columns. Each was to make one side of a corridor through which the survivors of the First Army would pass and it was to be carried out at the utmost speed.

As five thirty approached, the Reconnaissance Battalion said the way ahead was clear. Thank God, Adam thought, Bruno must be safe. "Stick together," he told his platoon. "Watch me and your sergeants."

Just before five thirty, clouds of blue smoke issued from the exhausts of the tanks and half-tracks. There was still no reaction from the Russians. Adam's unit was ordered to probe the way ahead. "That's a great honour, isn't it Gensche?" said Breitmann. "If you insist," answered the more experienced soldier. Heavier units were to follow, protected on their flanks by artillery. Gensche knew that the smaller guns were useless against Russian tanks.

There was no enemy response to the German advance and Gensche stuck like glue to Adam. "I don't like this Lieutenant," he said, as the metal giants made steady progress through scrubland followed by the bulk of the infantry. Adam hung on every word of advice from the experienced man. They marched almost casually towards the spires of Tarnopol. It seemed they had surprised their enemy.

They had advanced nearly two kilometres towards Tarnopol when the enemy opened fire on the infantry after the tanks had passed. Adam and his platoon jumped off the half-tracks to deal with the Russian machine-gunners and snipers hidden in the scrub who had been waiting there all night for the German attack. The recklessness of the Russian infantry dismayed the men of the Ninth. They shot dozens of them down, to find them replaced immediately by more. Finally the firing died down and the Russians melted away.

Adam crawled over to Graffe and his friends. "We're all OK, Lieutenant," he said hoarsely, out of breath. Two dead enemy soldiers lay almost in Graffe's position. Adam retired to his shallow foxhole, falling over one of the two Russian soldiers he had just shot down. The dead man's face was turned away from the young officer, as if he was aware of Adam's feelings even in death. Adam knew this was no time for pity.

Ten metres away was a wounded man who lifted a hand for help, but the

Ninth had been told to take no wounded prisoners. The interpretation of that order was left to individual units and tragic consequences followed. The Russian soldier was left to an unknown fate.

"Your whole life is behind you, Lieutenant," said Gensche. "Welcome to the twilight zone." Adam nodded grimly as he remounted his half-track.

The advance continued towards the town, past charred farm buildings. They looked like good defensive positions, but there was no further enemy response. "Shit," cursed Gensche. "The fuckin' tanks have gone." Adam had made his first mistake and lost touch with the main body. He didn't panic and continued the advance. Only Gensche was aware of the mistake, and he kept it to himself. The orders were to make contact with First Army soldiers and that Adam intended to do. He sent Breitmann and Kaspar to scout in front of them. They reported back that there was no movement in the nearest buildings.

The platoon pressed on into the town, hugging every wall. A church was the only building which seemed untouched. They listened for telltale signs. Adam took cover behind rubble, scrutinising every building. "Train your binoculars up there Lieutenant. They'll be holed up in the top floors," warned Gensche. The platoon moved cautiously forward. "Stop yapping Schaefer," said Graffe to his more nervous friend. "You're giving me the willies."

The soldiers reached an open square. The battered timbers from market stalls were still there. The wind increased and blew old wicker baskets across the open space. The platoon advanced down one side, using the market stalls as cover. A collection of shawls, all the same colour, still hung from one of them. Schaefer reached for one as a souvenir. Then a shot rang out and the young trooper fell dead.

Mayhem broke out as machine gun bullets made patterns on the ground. Discipline held and fire was returned. Adam saw the telltale smoke from a sniper's rifle and signalled Kaspar to move forward, pointing to the roof of the building from where the shot had come.

Michael Kaspar rolled over, fitted a telescopic sight to his rifle and crawled out of sight. Twenty minutes passed. A shot rang out and the Russian slumped forward over a parapet.

"I think he's the only one Lieutenant," reported Kaspar. "Useful lad," whispered Gensche to Adam.

The cautious advance continued, and Schaeffer was abandoned. Adam trained his binoculars on groups of soldiers running from house to house, wearing German helmets. "Give them cover," Adam ordered. "Bring the half-tracks up." The retreating soldiers thought they were in a trap and bullets bounced off the walls behind Adam. "We're SS, you stupid bastards!" shouted Franz Stamm.

Walter Graffe dashed from safety towards the retreating soldiers, bullets ricocheting off walls behind him. He threw himself down behind a heap of rubble and peered at the haunted-looking dishevelled soldier by his side. "Stop firing at my fuckin' mates," he said breathlessly.

They were joined by another First Army soldier, a red-faced bearded corporal with sharp eyes. He surveyed the young trooper wearing camouflage and carrying the latest submachine gun. "That's a dangerous toy you've got there sonny," he said. "But thanks all the same."

Graffe led nearly one hundred men to the safety of Adam's position. The red-faced corporal introduced himself as Fritz Eberling from a tank-hunting regiment. "I'd get these vehicles out of here as fast as you can, Lieutenant," he advised. Adam looked at his watch. He had left only four hours to regain contact with the bulk of the division.

As many men as possible piled on to the three half-tracks, while the rest retreated out of the square. Two mortar bombs landed among the last to leave. Five of the First Army survivors lay on the ground, at least one of them badly wounded.

Overconfidence had gripped the Soviet soldiers, who tried to gain the cover of the old market stalls and were driven back with heavy casualties. The survivors were taken prisoner. One hundred and sixty Germans left the town fighting repeated rearguard actions. Their pursuers broke off and Adam did not understand why. The vital minutes enabled the Germans to regain their corridor of retreat.

Adam held up his hand in the lead half-track and scanned the horizon to the west. There was no sign of the rest of the division. All he could do was to resume the retreat. The next five kilometres were to seem like a hundred. There were no friendly troops in sight and no apparent cover.

"Look Lieutenant," said Stamm, scanning the horizon to the North. A force of some strength seemed to be about to march across their line of retreat. At the same time dots appeared in the sky behind them and to the north.

Adam knew they couldn't be German aircraft. After the fighter-bombers had gone, Adam counted the casualties. There were three dead First Army men and two wounded from Adam's platoon. Three of the badly wounded were from Eberling's section.

Eberling looked hopefully at Adam, but was not surprised at the answer. "We must leave them," said the young lieutenant. Gensche stared at Eberling, who realised the men must be left.

The three men were left clutching field dressings and Eberling left them cigarettes. One of his comrades joined him and sat down with the wounded men. "Move," ordered Hans Thaelmann, but the First Army soldier refused. Thaelmann levelled his machine-pistol at him. "We need you," he said grimly, "but the enemy can have you dead." The man glumly rejoined the rest, jumping onto the last half-track. "SS bastard," the man muttered to himself.

The only feature on the landscape was a copse of trees several hundred metres to the left. More Soviet soldiers appeared from the north and Adam trained his binoculars on them. Leading them was a tank. "Make for the trees," ordered Adam. The pace quickened as heavy mortars fell in front of the leading half-track. Shrapnel tore pieces from the front of the vehicle and the anti-tank gun it was towing slewed round. A Russian armoured car accelerated from behind the tank in a reckless display of bravery. Eberling and trooper Renecke unhitched the anti-tank gun and set the armoured car on fire. The Russians replied with mortar fire. Eberling and Renecke jumped on to Adam's half-track and abandoned the anti-tank gun, which suffered a near miss, throwing it on its side.

The German soldiers fled into the trees as shells rained down on them, and there were more casualties. "Krebs, Kaspar, position yourselves in the centre with the prisoners," Adam ordered. "Shoot anyone who crosses the perimeter."

He crawled over to Eberling. "How are your men?" he asked. Eberling spat the remains of a cigarette onto the ground, looking round at the demoralised collection of soldiers. "As well as can be expected," he replied forcing a smile. Adam looked at his watch and the sky. "The light is failing. There'll be some safety in darkness."

"Perhaps they'll fight," Eberling said.

"Look at this," said Stamm. Three Russian soldiers were walking slowly towards the German position. One was an officer, another carried a white flag. "Who speaks the language, Eberling?" called out Adam.

Renecke stepped forward. "Are you ready for this, Renecke?" asked Adam. The hard-bitten trooper seemed to think it a pointless question. Adam and the First Army soldier walked slowly towards the Russians, watched carefully by Michael Kaspar, who carefully adjusted his telescopic sight. Adam looked at the Russian officer as if he had no business to be there, and they saluted each other.

"Your position is hopeless," said the Russian. "We offer you an honourable surrender." Adam thanked him for his offer and retired a few metres to talk with Renecke, as though he was taking advice. Adam's main thought was that this was his platoon's first action, the first fight of the new division. He felt he could not surrender, even taking into consideration the state of the first army survivors.

Adam thanked the Russian for his offer but turned it down. The officer half-smiled and returned to the safety of his own unit, shaking his head. Adam walked briskly back and ordered the defenders to make ready.

Nothing happened for ten minutes and then the Russian tank began the attack seven hundred metres away. Three hundred Russian infantry moved forward, some concealing themselves on the uneven ground while others followed the tank. Enemy machine-gunners gave intense covering fire and bullets splintered the bark of the trees around the defenders. Some of Eberling's men had begun to regret meeting this particular SS platoon. When they told him of their doubts, he told them to shut up and fight for their lives. "Hold your fire," ordered Adam.

"You didn't expect him to surrender did you?" asked Thaelmann.

"He didn't surrender to Kolb," answered Stamm. "Why now?"

The tank's engine noise became louder and Adam crawled from man to man. "We're OK," said Graffe. Adam looked at these eighteen and nineteen-year-old faces and understood now the consequences of his own ambition. And they had no defence against the tank.

"Lieutenant!" called out Eberling. Adam crawled over to the First Army man, who pointed at the anti-tank gun which had broken free of the half-track and then at the badge on his sleeve. Adam understood. "Do you feel lucky, Eberling?" he asked. Eberling thought it was another pointless question. "What else do we do?" he asked.

"It will take three of us to right that gun," Eberling reminded him. Adam scanned the ground near the weapon. The caisson of shells was intact.

"Renecke," called out Eberling. His comrade joined them. When he heard the proposal, he just nodded. "We'll crawl for thirty metres," said Adam. "Stamm – lay covering fire when we get up," he ordered. "Then we run like hell. You lay the gun Eberling. Renecke and I will load and fire." The three shook hands and crawled out.

They crawled unseen until they were fifty metres from the overturned gun. They had only one or two minutes to right it and shelter behind its armour plating.

The Russian tank disappeared into a gully and reappeared, its gun pointing to the sky. At that moment the three men rose and sprinted for the gun, surprising the Russians. They reacted quickly and despatched a hail of bullets, but the three men reached the gun unharmed.

A deadly time began as they tried to right the weapon. Twice, the gun fell back on its side. Bullets ricocheted off the metal and whined into the distance. One last superhuman effort righted it. But before Renecke could shelter behind the armour he fell dead from a sniper's bullet.

"Shit," growled Eberling. Adam rolled over on his side away from the gun to retrieve one shell. They had time for only one shot. Eberling struggled to aim the weapon on the uneven ground. He had to fire over open sights and a direct hit was a forlorn hope. Adam opened the breech and rammed in the shell. The tank crew saw them and its gun swivelled round. A shell screamed past the two men and plunged into the copse.

"Wait, wait Lieutenant," said Eberling. "Now!" Adam pulled the cord and the shell hit the tank at the base of the turret, detaching it from the hull. Eberling grinned at Adam. "Let's get the fuck out of here," he said.

A bullet ricocheted from the barrel and left a red streak on Adam's face. Blood poured down his tunic as they waited to time their run to safety.

"Now," said Adam and the pair tore through the scrub. Thirty metres from safety a bullet hit Eberling in the thigh and he fell, face down onto the stony ground. Adam threw himself down beside his wounded comrade. "You go Lieutenant," said Eberling, clutching his leg. Adam got up amidst the hail of bullets and threw Eberling over his shoulder.

One bullet tore an epaulette from his uniform. He ran, then staggered as a bullet removed the heel from his left boot. He was not sure where he was, and blood was pouring down over his eyes. He collapsed just inside his own perimeter, gasping for breath. Graffe dragged the injured corporal to safety. "Look after Eberling," Adam whispered hoarsely.

The light failed and the Russians stopped firing. Adam and his two sergeants took stock of the situation as a medic bandaged his face. "Organise a patrol, Thaelmann," he ordered and three volunteers crawled out beyond the perimeter. Hans Thaelmann was back in thirty minutes, the lower half of his body covered in black slime.

"There's a drainage ditch to the west," he reported. " I couldn't see any Ivans."

"See if we can get across," ordered Adam, and the sergeant disappeared into the darkness once again, followed by Stamm with a machine-pistol.

Adam went from man to man to assess morale. Everywhere there were murmurs of congratulation. When he found Michael Kaspar hidden in the scrub on the perimeter, the trooper patted the barrel of his rifle. Adam realised Kaspar might have saved his life with a good shot or two. Adam peered into the gloom. "Careful, Kaspar," he warned. "The patrol's coming in."

Enemy infantry lay concealed only two hundred metres away and they were calling out to their intended victims in bad German. "Surrender before dawn or you will die," said one. "Enjoy our countryside while you can," said another, accompanied by raucous laughter.

Hans Thaelmann and Franz Stamm returned after thirty minutes, Thaelmann wet to his armpits with stagnant water. "We can cross the ditch," he announced. "I don't know what's beyond. I didn't see anyone. I don't know how far away our lines are."

It was their only hope, and the word was passed round that they were to leave. The Russian prisoners were terrified. One of them, a private soldier, knelt before Adam to beg for his life. Another, a junior officer, turned away in disgust. Adam waved him over to him. "These two will be released," he said, "but you must come with us."

Adam knelt down beside Eberling, "We will carry you over a ditch. Whatever it takes we'll get you back," he promised. Eberling tried to smile but grimaced with pain. "Always the optimist," he replied, "and Renecke?"

Adam shook his head. "Why did that man beg for his life?" he asked.

"Why do you want to know Lieutenant?" replied Eberling. "You've learnt enough to last you a lifetime." The wounded man was open and honest. "Every time we occupied a town Communist officials were hung in public. Sometimes the Jews were shot on the spot. Some of our men volunteered." Adam remembered Bing Wen's warnings.

Kaspar and the other marksmen manned the perimeter as the rest crawled towards the ditch. A Russian soldier called out in the darkness, "You will have no sleep tonight." He was answered by a burst of automatic fire. "Who the hell was that?" demanded Adam.

Hans Thaelmann and volunteers stood in the stinking water and passed the wounded over their heads in silence. Gensche stumbled on an obstacle. It was the decaying corpse of a horse, and he stifled a curse. Last to leave were the snipers and Adam.

Kaspar slipped into the cold stagnant water. He was the last man before Adam. "I don't like this," whispered Kaspar. He stopped and listened. Adam held his machine-pistol above his head and peered into the darkness. All he could see was the back of Michael Kaspar's steel helmet; he heard nothing. They moved forward again.

A burst of machine gun fire made fountains in the water and Adam felt a dull thud in his left shoulder. Everything became indistinct and he began to slip under the water, into unconsciousness.

Hans Thaelmann had left the others in Stamm's charge and stood in the cold stagnant water waiting for Adam. He saw him slip forward and Kaspar helped his sergeant to keep his head above water. Graffe joined and together they hauled the young officer to safety. They laid him on the damp ground and a medic stanched Adam's bleeding.

"Take his arms Kaspar, I'll take the legs," said the sergeant. The rest continued to crawl forward, through deep ruts in an old path, expecting at any moment to be discovered.

Then Franz Stamm stopped the men and probed forward. He heard twigs crack and thought - this is it.

"Halt," called a nervous guard. "Spring awakening," answered Stamm in a subdued voice.

Two men appeared on either side of him covering him with machine-pistols. They saw the badges on Stamm's sleeve and lowered their weapons. "We have wounded," said Stamm.

Within a few minutes, stretchers and medical teams arrived. Eberling was conscious. "How's the Lieutenant?" he asked. "He'll be all right," said a medic evasively. Adam was bleeding slowly from the mouth. "Punctured lung," said one medic to another. "We'll look after him," said the medics to Stamm and Thaelmann. "Get yourselves cleaned up or you'll catch swamp fever."

Adam briefly regained consciousness in a field hospital as a nurse was cutting away at his uniform to reach the wound. The doctor examined it and shrugged his shoulders. "Clean flesh wound," he said flatly and went to treat more urgent cases. Adam blacked out once more.

His next memory was the sound of feet marching smartly up and down a wooden floor and the noise echoing against a high ceiling. His eyes cleared enough to allow him to recognise ancient painted windows with gothic arches. The bottom third of the medieval stained-glass windows was obscured by screens forming cubicles. This church was now a military hospital.

The pain became unbearable, but Adam uttered hardly a sound. Two nurses stripped off the field dressing to find a serious infection. He was given morphine and penicillin and fell asleep.

A pretty young nurse appeared. "Is there anything you need, Lieutenant?" she asked. She passed his rucksack to him and he thumbed through his Confucius. The contents now seemed alien and irrelevant.

Would I understand any of that?" the nurse asked politely.

"Don't be offended," Adam answered, "but you probably wouldn't. I'm not sure I understand it now." She stayed with him and told him about her boyfriend in Germany. Adam feigned tiredness after deciding she wasn't in a good relationship and politely dismissed her. He began to ache for Gabrielle.

Sister Klederman burst into the ward, followed by a small army of cleaning staff. The morning's peace and tranquillity was at an end. The patients were washed and changed and the floor scrubbed as if it were a penance. Doctors paced up and down, supervising every detail. Then suddenly the cleaning staff melted away and the clatter of mop buckets receded down the corridor. The doctors and nurses waited, hands behind their backs, eyes riveted on the entrance to the ward.

A roar of motorcycle engines outside was followed by the sound of military boots in the corridors. Two SS military police held open the swinging doors and in strode Adam's Battalion Commander with an aide carrying a number of small containers and one parcel. He spoke to every soldier who was conscious. The officer stopped by the bed at the far end. Adam strained his eyes but couldn't hear what was said. He presented an iron cross to the soldier, who was so badly wounded he could hardly speak.

Then the doctors and nurses gathered round Adam's bed and the pretty nurse stood next to him as if taking sole responsibility for his recovery. The officer reached Adam, saluted briskly and broke into a broad smile. "It is von Saloman, is it not?" he asked. "Bad Tolz spoke highly of you. I have a pleasant duty to perform."

His aide handed him a small box. "I present you with this in recognition of exemplary leadership, not only of your own men, but of First Army soldiers," he said and pinned the Iron Cross First Class on the pocket of Adam's battered tunic, which was draped over the chair.

"This is not all, von Saloman," continued the Battalion Commander. The aide handed him a parcel which contained a captain's tunic. The officer held it up as if he was expecting Sister Klederman to arrange it on Adam's bed. "You will join your company shortly, Captain. Congratulations," the Brigadier concluded.

He marched off smartly and was gone with more roaring of motorcycle engines. The young nurse stayed behind and said how proud she was of her patient. Adam's admirer kissed him on the cheek and fled to another patient at the end of the ward.

The man in the next bed came to life. "Better than a shot of penicillin eh?" he said. He grinned, made a half-salute and fell asleep.

Chapter 21

The bombers made their first visit, in strength, to Berlin on the nineteenth of November in 1943. The Ladies' Circle felt safe in the suburbs as they watched fires burning in the Lichterfelde District. The drone of the bombers increased as they turned for home over the south of the city. Then the noise receded, and that seemed the end of the danger.

Constable Schneider made repeated appeals to the ladies to use the newly-completed shelter under the municipal buildings, a few blocks away. They turned to Frieda, not to Schneider, for advice. She and Martha Reymann stridently agreed that the enemy were attacking the government in the city centre and the suburbs would be untouched. Martha's cheerfulness and Frieda's resolve won the day and the ladies slid into complacency.

On the night of the twenty-second, searchlights probed the sky on a particularly cloudy night and some reflected off the cloud base in an eerie display. There were multiple flashes high in the sky, some orange and some silver. Red and green lights drifted downwards. A burning aircraft fell, twisting its way through the night sky. The ladies watched from the garden outside the rear window, well wrapped up against the autumn chill. The doorbell rang and Albert Hartman announced that Constable Schneider wished to check that none of the ladies were breaking the curfew.

The local sirens sounded and the policeman advised the ladies to go to the shelter at once. Martha repeated her belief that Wilmersdorf would not be attacked, but Liselotte Wenniger decided that the policeman deserved support. "I'll go if someone will go with me," she said defiantly. "We really ought to go, you know," she said staring at Martha for support.

"I shall go with you," said Martha. "I can't stand the thought of you on your own down there and I think the Ladies' Circle should be represented."

Greta made sandwiches for the two women and Käthe found blankets for them. She volunteered to tell their Civil Defence Worker husbands. Hitler Youth and Civil Defence Workers handled the large queue well and Martha remarked that the sky seemed empty now. The eerie half-light from the searchlights had gone and the moon was barely visible. It was a relief to escape from the darkness and enjoy the wall lighting in the shelter.

In a short time nearly five hundred people had been herded in. Some lay on mattresses on the concrete floor, while others were lucky enough to find space on the metal seats attached to the wall. There was still a strong acrid smell of cement dust. Martha and Liselotte said a prayer for their friends as they settled down for the night.

The ladies drank coffee sleeplessly in Frieda's apartment. Käthe parted the blackout curtains over the French windows at the rear. For the first time, there were fires in nearby Spandau and Charlottenburg. The dogs whined and paced about nervously.

At midnight the building was shaken by a huge explosion and window panes fell on the road outside. It began to rain heavily and Ilse Diels remarked that the explosion must have been close by. They heard shouts in the streets and Käthe ran to the entrance hall to find Albert Hartman. She gazed into the street and saw the buildings opposite lit by the glow of a huge fire.

Albert ran in. "Madam," he said breathlessly, "I think there's been a terrible tragedy. I'll find out. Young man," he said to a Hitler Youth volunteer running past.

"I can't stop," he replied. "We think it's the shelter." He ran back." Where are the water mains, madam?" he asked Käthe. She didn't know and he ran off.

"Get inside," shouted a fireman. "There is nothing you can do."

Käthe's first thought was her friends in the shelter and her second was professional. She quickly ran inside to retrieve her nurse's cape. "I'm coming with you," said Renate.

A throng of volunteers and the inevitable sightseers headed towards the ominous glow. Käthe and Renate pushed their way through to be stopped by police clearing the way for ambulances and medical teams.

A huge cordon had been thrown round the remains of the Municipal Buildings. A policeman wouldn't allow Käthe through, even though she wore a nurse's uniform. She could see already the charred remains of victims laid out in rows and begged him to change his mind. "Madam," he said sorrowfully.

"I believe it is only a matter of counting the dead."

Käthe and Renate gazed at the glowing crater where the shelter had been. They held each other and sobbed for their lost friends. "Who will tell Gabrielle?" asked Käthe.

They returned to the apartment in silence. It was as if their friends already knew. They could no longer bear to stay together and drifted back to their own apartments.

Adam's latest letter lay on the rosewood table. Käthe picked it up and reread it. She knew its blandness hid realities and that almost any letter home from a soldier was likely to be read by a censor. From now on, she no longer believed in her son's invincibility and she prayed for Adam and Bruno as never before. She desperately tried to remember things Martha and Liselotte had said before they went to the shelter so that she could tell the two young men.

The following morning, events took a bizarre turn. The apartment dwellers were assembled by their Block Leaders and for once, Ilse Diels showed no enthusiasm for the task. Armed police arrived and announced that the zoo in the Tiergarten had been hit and wild animals roaming the streets should be reported immediately.

The remaining ladies gathered in silence for the next meeting. Frieda solemnly asked them if it was their wish to continue?. There was no response at first. Ilse Diels said "If we didn't meet again, it would be an admission of defeat." For once, they agreed with her and the meetings continued. The tragic circumstances allowed the admission of new members.

As Berlin's agony continued, the old house in the Grünewald seemed to stand aloof. Privileged party members attended conferences there which were no more than organised junketings. The Führer decided that such behaviour could have a bad effect on morale and thought his minions should practice some self-denial.

Die Schwanen was boarded up and padlocked. It quickly became home to jackdaws and pigeons which gained entry through the broken windows. Any peace it had enjoyed was shattered in January 1944, when the forest and its maze of tracks and retreats were torn by high explosive and incendiaries. The trees close to the garden wall were scorched or uprooted. The wall itself was breached and burning embers were carried from the forest to settle on the roof and on Gustav's workshop. They were fanned by the wind and the roof began to burn, but a sudden downpour extinguished the fire. The rain soaked into the holes and onto Gustav's workbench.

Over time, damp rot collapsed part of the roof. The workshop was gone but Gustav's chief memorial remained because the secret room remained intact. Barbed wire surrounded the house along the perimeter and signs read, "Entry Forbidden." The building's survival lay in the hands of benevolent ghosts stalking its corridors.

The park in Wilmersdorf was no longer a pleasant retreat. Some of the iron railings were twisted and uprooted and all that remained of most of the trees was splintered stumps. At the risk of severe punishment, some residents had turned them into fuel.

The grassy banks where Adam had defended himself were now burnt bare. The benches remained intact but unused. When the wind blew, small clouds of ash eddied upwards.

The newspapers were still delivered. Some small shops remained open and one even advertised a sale. Each day Herr Poganowska delivered the milk. Greta kept a few lumps of sugar when she could for Hans and Ilse, the two horses that pulled the milk cart. The trains still ran but few used them, except to visit relatives and friends. There was little point in visiting the centre of Berlin, and police didn't encourage travel.

And so dullness entered the lives of the Ladies' Circle and their neighbours in Wilmersdorf, a dullness which was interrupted by an incident which, in the opinion of a few, changed Frieda von Saloman's behaviour. Rumours reached the apartment block that an English bomber had crashed nearby and there might have been survivors. An Air Force police lorry reached a pile of rubble on a road which he hoped would take him out of Berlin and to the south. The driver found himself driving slowly down Charlottenbrunnestrasse. He was annoyed and looked for directions and approached Käthe as she returned from an unsuccessful visit to the butcher's shop. He said he needed to exit the city urgently and Käthe wondered why. She glanced towards the back of the open lorry and seated there were two steel-helmeted guards. Between them was a pale, frightened-looking young man with a bandaged head. He wore a flying jacket and the uniform of the enemy air force.

A crowd began to gather. Most of the onlookers were merely curious, but there was an element who were far less generous. One of them, a man in his forties, wore a Brownshirts' uniform. He shielded whatever he said behind his hand to the lady next to him, who nodded in approval. She turned and said a few words to other onlookers.

The mood began to turn ugly. Ilse Diels had been watching from one of the upper floors and she intervened. She joined the more hostile people and began to shake her fist at the English prisoner. She shouted, "Do you know what the Führer says we should do with people like you?"

The young flyer looked puzzled and some of the crowd led by the Brownshirt began to advance menacingly on the lorry. Then Frieda appeared with Albert Hartman. Some of the crowd shouted at the two guards, who seemed impassive, and their officer remained in the cab.

Frieda braced herself and marched towards the lorry's tailgate. She seemed too small to push her way through, but push through she did. She folded her arms and tried to look as dignified as possible in her imperial style dress and two strings of pearls.

"Do you have something to say, madam?" asked the Brownshirt.

"Mind your own business," shouted one woman. "You don't live in that big house now." She pushed Frieda.

Ilse Diels didn't know what to do. She was wearing her coat with the swastika armband and had apparently already taken sides. "Leave her alone," shouted Käthe trying to push through the crowd to rescue Frieda.

The hostile element closed in and reached the tailgate, standing menacingly in front of the guards. Their officer climbed out of the cab and fired his pistol in the air and there was silence. "I will shoot anyone who tries to take our prisoner," he announced. "Disperse and go to your homes." The Brownshirt muttered something about reporting the air force officer, but decided to retreat with the rest of the crowd. Albert Hartman told the driver how to exit the city.

"Ask them to wait a few minutes," shouted Greta from the front entrance. She appeared with five packs of sandwiches and gave them personally to each occupant of the lorry. She thrust the English flyer's food into his lap and shook her head. "If only your mother knew what you had been doing," she said. The guards grinned at each other and the lorry picked its way carefully out of the suburbs towards the Avus and disappeared.

CHAPTER TWENTY ONE

The ladies gathered in the street and pronounced judgement on Ilse Diels. "I don't care who she is," said Hanni Dirksen angrily. "She shouldn't be allowed at our meetings." There were murmurs of assent. Ilse stood in the road with a penitent look.

Frieda surprised them. "Frau Diels is a lonely lady. She doesn't think before she does things. She may change," she advised. And so Ilse was allowed to attend the meetings. She was careful now never to be too assertive. The police still monitored the Ladies' Circle, but they had decided long ago that they were not the focus of a resistance movement. Constable Schneider and his partner still visited the circle because they were offered refreshment.

A Civil Defence Worker called one afternoon in the early spring of 1944. He begged Frieda not to hold the Circle meetings at night, but his advice was ignored and complacency triumphed once more.

Ilse was delighted with Adam's promotion, to such an extent that she cycled down to the Martin Luther School and personally informed Dr Schaub. Käthe, Frieda and the rest of the circle were more worried about Adam's wounds. As the spring approached, a telegram arrived announcing leave for him and Bruno. The two women's lives were now dominated by preparation for the return of the two young men.

Their euphoria was blighted a little. Käthe had never forgotten Gabrielle's effect on Adam. She wondered how Adam would take the death of Martha Reymann, his friend and only link to Gabrielle.

The Ladies' Circle barely heard the warning sirens on the night of the twenty-fourth of March. The noise waxed and waned in a spring gale and Käthe parted the blackout curtains on the french windows. It seemed that the city centre was once again the target. The Ladies agreed it was likely to be an isolated raid, because there had been no attacks for several weeks. A temporary shelter had been built, but superstition bred fear and the ladies preferred to stay in the apartment. Ilse Diels thought the English had lost the battle for Berlin, and everyone agreed with her.

Hanni turned on the radio. Two or three of the ladies listened to enthusiastic reports of success on the Russian front. The rest saw the reports as thinly-disguised news of defeats.

Käthe had left the hospital early to be at the meeting. She had a small surprise, a small amount of sausage she had begged from the hospital kitchens. Ilse Diels saw it before Käthe passed it on to Greta in the kitchen. Her old repentance disappeared and she accused Käthe of depriving patients at the hospital.

Hanni Dirksen was only half Ilse's size, but she confronted her. "You will apologise now," said Hanni, in a shaky tone which didn't disguise her real fear of Ilse Diels. Käthe joined him. "I will inform Captain von Saloman of your attitude, Frau Diels," said Käthe.

Ilse began to dither, seemed to shrink to Hanni's size, and apologised to Käthe. She was slowly becoming a figure of fun. Then the ladies discovered from Constable Schneider that Ilse had been told not to badger the police so frequently.

The gale was blowing much harder at twenty thousand feet, and the bombers were blown off course. They had planned to wreak further devastation in the city centre but the wind carried them to the south, before those who survived turned for home. The sirens continued to sound but the ladies heard nothing. Käthe was standing at the front of the great cooking range wondering what she might do with sauerkraut and sausage. "Please be patient," she called out.

In years to come Frieda would always remember the appeal from the kitchen and the small, pale, alert figure of Hanni Dirksen, sat cross-legged in front of the French windows. Everyone froze when they heard the whistling of a stick of bombs.

Albert Hartman threw open the door of the apartment when he heard the terrified screams. Frieda lay on the floor whimpering and moving her arms aimlessly. Ilse Diels knelt on the floor, her hand in her mouth, but there was no sign of Käthe.

Albert looked towards the kitchen area to the left of the remains of the French windows. Pieces of the roof had collapsed into the doorway. Then he saw Hanni's contorted body, thrown by the blast against the far wall.

Albert led the survivors to the safety of his office and they sobbed ceaselessly. Only Ilse Diels retained the presence of mind to ask Albert where Käthe was, and he returned to the flat followed by Ilse.

"She was in the kitchen, Herr Hartman," said Ilse sobbing. Albert stared at the blocked doorway and heard the distinct crackling of fire. Smoke began to pour from the collapsed timbers in the doorway. Albert brushed past Ilse and ran to the rear of the building just as firemen and Civil Defence workers arrived. The upper floors had collapsed at the rear and incendiary bombs had penetrated the mass of timbers and started a huge fire which seemed to envelope the kitchen.

"Clear the building at once!" ordered a fireman. "All of you to the church hall immediately!" shouted a Civil Defence worker, but Greta refused to go. "My mistress is trapped in there," she said tearfully, pointing at the remains of the kitchen.

Firemen hacked at the wreckage but were met by a wall of flame. "It's one of those damned incendiaries, Captain," said one of the firemen.

"Clear the area," shouted the officer.

"It's hopeless sir," said a Hitler Youth helper as a small explosion in the kitchen showered them all with sparks.

"Find the water main, Weiskopf," said the captain to his deputy. "It's been smashed by the bomb sir," he answered. All they could do was to allow the fire to burn itself out.

"If she's in there Weiskopf, that's a funeral pyre," said the captain.

Ilse Diels clung to the fireman's sleeve. "Please dear lady," he said. "We have done everything possible." Ilse left the scene, her hands hanging limply by her sides. Frieda remembered that moment because Ilse was hatless for the only time she could remember.

A new member of the Circle, Lizzy Kranzmuller, who had not been subjected to the edge of Renate's tongue, remembered Bruno's mother had not been accounted for and told Frieda and the captain of firemen. He asked for the location of her apartment and took two men through the front of the building. The rear portion of the four floors had collapsed and burned, but Renate lived on the street side of the building. When the captain carefully made his way through the piles of rubble and smouldering timbers which now reached beyond the door of Frieda's apartment, he found the bottom half of the stairs in a state of collapse, burning timbers obstructing the entrance to the top of the stairs.

"Frau Grabowsky!" called the fireman. Ilse Diels had followed and ignored orders to go back from Deputy Weiskopf. A tiny voice answered from the first floor. "She's there," shouted the captain and a frightened Renate opened her door slightly.

The fireman and his colleague climbed the stairs and removed the burning timbers. The captain was on the verge of collapse because of smoke inhalation and a Hitler Youth volunteer climbed the remains of the stairs. He led Renate carefully down and Ilse embraced her, their old animosity forgotten. Ilse lost her interest in her role as Guardian of the National Socialist State in the apartment block because her loneliness had been relieved through membership of the Circle.

The loss of Käthe drew her closer to Frieda, who had shamed her over the incident involving the English flyer. She conveniently forgot the damage she had already done, assuming her old contacts with the police would have no consequences.

The Police President himself arrived to inspect the damage and gave Frieda and Greta permission to salvage whatever they could from the ruins. Lizzy Kranzmuller helped Frieda and Greta rummage through the remains of their belongings.

A minor miracle had happened. Although the glass frames were broken all the photographs from the far wall were intact. Frieda picked up Käthe's, taken at the Waterfront Surgery in Canton, and placed it reverently in the ruins of the kitchen.

Fires had started in the bedrooms on the street side and little remained. Adam's room, kept so immaculate for his leave, was reduced to a blackened shell. Greta searched it for any memento of the young soldier. She tried to reach the tall cupboard in the corner but the debris shifted dangerously and she abandoned her search.

Frieda and Lizzy joined Ilse and the rest in the Church Hall. Nearly fifty people had crowded onto the small floor space. Frieda and Greta stared at the scene in disbelief. A short while before, they had been the guiding hands of a country house in the Grünewald. They had improvised and lived tolerably well in the apartment and Frieda had become the social hub of the area through the Ladies' Circle. It couldn't meet for the foreseeable future now that Käthe was gone. And now the two women were reduced to this.

In two days' time, Adam would begin his leave and would be in mid-journey by now. No telegram could reach him and Frieda knew he was about to face the greatest trial of his life. There were two small crumbs of comfort. "Are these yours Madam?" asked a Hitler Youth helper who couldn't have been more than fourteen years old. He carried a dachshund under each arm.

CHAPTER TWENTY ONE

Hansl and Gretl whimpered when they saw Frieda and Greta. "They were on the other side of the street, madam," said the young man. "They were staring at the old park. It was hard to get them to come with me." They thanked the young man but knew it would be difficult to find food for the dogs in the future.

Renate returned to her apartment with Albert Hartman's help. He repaired the stairs and Renate offered her flat as their new home. Ilse's flat was intact, but she had always been reluctant to invite anyone in. Speculation as to what might be there had grown more and more bizarre.

When the bombers came, Käthe had been standing in front of the great iron cooking range. The first and the nearest bomb collapsed the rear apartments and burning timber and rubble cut off her only avenue of escape, the internal door to the main living space. Furniture from the apartments above crashed through splintered floors. The kitchen roof began to creak and flames licked through the timbers. A heavy chest of drawers burst through the roof, followed by a lifeless figure. The body lay like a rag doll on the floor and pieces of burning timber began to cover it.

Käthe screamed, but her cries were lost in the wind and the fire. Rubble and burning timber began to fill her survival space. She climbed on top of the cooking range and sheltered under its stone archway. The flames became intense and slowly consumed the remainder of the oxygen. She stared fearfully at the drum of paraffin, still untouched in the far corner by burning timbers, and passed out.

The shifting wreckage allowed some air into the living space. Käthe revived, tried to escape and fell from the cooking range, her head striking the stone paving. She passed out once more. Again, she revived and began a panic-stricken crawl across the now hot paving stones. Käthe clawed at the wreckage and sobbed each time it shifted. A piece of smouldering timber fell on her left leg. She started with the pain but continued to claw at the wreckage. Her fingers bled and her nails splintered. Her clothes began to smoulder. She coughed and spluttered, unaware of where she was or who she was. Her knees began to bleed as she dragged herself along the stone floor in total darkness. She reached the far end of the kitchen, where it joined the neighbouring apartment. The rubble collapsed inwards and Käthe felt a draft of cool air. She strained her tired eyes and saw the smallest of gaps. With a superhuman effort she scaled the rubble and found herself staring at the stars.

She fell, twisting her left leg. Her hands slipped into a bomb crater.. She dragged herself to her feet. There, staring at her obediently, were Hansl and Gretl, whining gently for a show of recognition. Käthe ignored them and began to walk, dragging her left leg. She limped past the ruined apartment and stopped at the edge of the pavement. The dogs followed and stopped. They watched as Käthe drifted away aimlessly, her tattered dress billowing in a gale.

When she reached the apartment block on the other side of the street, she turned automatically towards the park, watched by the dogs. A voice drifted on the wind. "Hansl, Gretl!" called Greta. Neither of them moved. Behind Käthe the kitchen walls moved once again and her escape route was hidden. To all intents and purposes, the kitchen was a tomb.

Käthe wandered on and on in a south-westerly direction. Her legs buckled and she sobbed, like a lost child. She wasn't aware of the gaunt building in front of her in the total darkness, or its white-painted gates. She collapsed against them, her eyes darting wildly around and her mouth quivering. She didn't hear the soft footfalls inside the gates or the quietly spoken voice. "You're safe now, my dear," it said. "Please help me lift her, Sister Matthew."

Adam waited for six hours in Krakow, his shoulder still painful. An army lorry drew up beside him and one of the drivers jumped out. "Herr Hauptstürmführer," he said to Adam. "One aircraft is available to fly twenty men to Tempelhof in Berlin. Would you like to choose the lucky ones? We've no officer here."

Adam chose the first twenty men who lived anywhere near or in Berlin and the rest seemed resigned to a long wait. He realised the lucky ones had adopted him. He hauled himself into the back of the lorry. One three-engined transport aircraft waited on the airfield, its propellers already spinning. Adam wondered how it had come to this that Germany could afford only one aircraft to ferry the wounded home. There was silence during almost the whole journey.

Adam waited for some time at Tempelhof airfield while stretcher teams moved the badly wounded. Another aircraft bearing a red cross taxied behind Adam's aircraft and Bruno was helped down the steps. He spotted Adam and waved a crutch.

They swapped stories. Bruno's armoured car had been hit by an anti-tank shell which had removed the rear wheels. "Everyone got out?" asked Adam.

CHAPTER TWENTY ONE

"We joined the damned infantry," said Bruno. "It's a damned site more dangerous, as you can see." He tapped his injured leg.

"How's Wem?" asked Adam.

"His girlfriend's chucked him. We can all breathe now. I'll tell him you asked."

A collection of requisitioned vehicles took the passengers from Tempelhof Airfield to Berlin Central Station. Adam and Bruno were shocked at what they saw. Row upon row of apartments were shattered. Gangs of workers moved rubble from the shattered buildings and filled bomb craters. One half of an enemy bomber lay across a heap of broken stone and smashed timbers, its Perspex nose pointing to the sky. Many of the workers were prisoners-of-war, some in the unmistakable khaki tunics of the English army. Bruno remembered Gustav's battle diorama. "Wellington's soldiers have reached Berlin," he said. Adam smiled grimly.

Much of the Central Station had been wrecked, although the trams still ran. The two friends walked to the tram terminus, to be told there were very few running.

After a two-hour wait, one finally appeared. People pushed and shoved to get on and many of them cast resentful glances at the uniforms of the two friends. Bruno lost his crutch, which was retrieved by a policeman. He took the soldiers to the front of the queue with the muted approval of those left behind.

The tram swayed along, making slow progress. At one point it lurched suddenly but continued. Bruno looked out of the window and saw that they had almost fallen into a bomb crater. They stared in silence at the scenes of devastation on either side of the Kurfürstendamm. Adam craned his neck to look at the Tiergarten and saw a sign announcing that it was closed until further notice following the escape of the animals. "You liked going there," Bruno said. Then he fell silent.

"What's the matter old friend?" asked Adam.

"Mutti and I don't get on too well. I'm as worried as hell," answered Bruno.

"She didn't stop writing to you did she?" asked Adam.

"No," answered Bruno. "I'm frightened she'll give me hell if I go home to Helga first," he added. The tram lurched again. "And your magnificent duo?"

Adam shook his head. "I fell out with both of them," he answered. Bruno laughed. "They worship you. Everyone in the district will know you've been promoted and decorated," he said, trying to reassure his friend. "You know your big fault? You love both of them too much."

"I know, I know," said Adam impatiently. "But I wish Grandmama smiled more."

"I wish you did!" said Bruno. "You're too damn serious. You're just like her," he added.

Adam helped Bruno off the train at Charlottenburg. He stood at the top of the metal steps as the train moved off and watched Bruno wave a taxi down with one of his crutches. He smiled to himself and prepared to face the light of his life, his mother.

The tram didn't get as far as the Brandenburgerstrasse before it was forced to stop while gangs worked to repair the lines. Adam felt strong enough to walk. He had hardly got off the train when a small open staff car braked to a halt. An SS Major in the car had seen Adam's left sleeve flapping idly. "Can I give you a lift, Captain?" he said. Adam received a lift to the end of Charlottenbrunnestrasse.

He was saddened when he stared through the gates at the spot where he had faced his Hitler Youth enemies. The benches were blackened, but the elderly were still using them. He recognised the lady in her fifties sitting on the nearest bench.

"Good afternoon, Frau Kranzmuller," he called out. Lizzy recognised him immediately, but she said nothing. She waved weakly and turned to her newspaper. It was not her place to tell him what had happened.

Two Hitler Youth ran up to him when they saw his badges of rank and his Iron Cross, and asked for his autograph. He thought the request ridiculous, but obliged them.

When he reached the apartment block, he opened the front door and stopped. Beyond the foot of the stairs was a mountain of rubble, some of it still hot. Adam stared at the shattered stairway and the rubble beyond it. There was a chill in the air from the gaping holes at the rear of the building.

He knocked as usual on Albert Hartmann's window. The concierge was reading a newspaper. He put it down and came to meet the young officer. His thinning wavy hair had turned silver and the cheerful attitude Adam remembered had vanished. Albert hadn't intended to tell Adam his mother was dead as it was not his business to do so, but he grasped Adam's arm in sympathy. "I'm so very sorry," said the faithful concierge. "Please wait here for one minute."

CHAPTER TWENTY ONE

As Albert climbed the stairs to announce Adam's arrival, Adam pushed open the door of the apartment. When he saw the blackened walls and the pile of wreckage that had once been the kitchen, he knew he had to prepare for bad news.

Albert called him up the stairs. He retreated past Adam to his office, not daring to look the young soldier in the face. "They are in Frau Grabowsky's flat," he said. "Careful on the stairs Adam." Adam climbed cautiously, kicking pieces of burnt timber out of his way. Renate's door was slightly open.

Frieda and Greta got up from their chairs and clasped their hands in front of them. "Where is Mama?" demanded Adam. Frieda propped herself up on a table trying to compose herself. "Frau Käthe has gone, Adam," said Greta.

Adam carefully placed his suitcase on the floor and removed his cap and tunic as if the words had not been said. "How?" he asked.

"She is believed to have died in a terrible fire in the kitchen," said Frieda, hardly able to speak. Neither of them moved towards him, afraid of his reaction.

He cloaked his grief in anger. "Why wasn't I told?" he demanded, raising his voice. Frieda lost her composure and threw her arms around her grandson. He grasped her tightly, moving her from side to side in his grief and they clung to each other. He sobbed and sobbed, then sat down, Frieda hanging on to his hands. Renate knelt in front of Adam and threw her arms around him.

"Helga doesn't know," Greta whispered in Frieda's ear. "Shall I telephone?" As an afterthought she asked if she ought to invite Bruno. She knew he too would be very upset and Adam might need his support. Frieda whispered back. "Ask them to come tomorrow."

Greta picked her way down the stairs to the only working telephone in the building, which was in Albert's office. He had placed a pewter mug, already full of marks, by the phone.

"I'll find Mama," announced Adam, springing up from his chair. He raced down the stairs to Albert's office, oblivious of the pain in his shoulder and ignoring the two dogs following him.

"Albert, we have work to do," he announced. We need all your heavy tools to find Mama. You'll help of course," he said. Albert meekly brought picks and shovels and followed Adam to the garden at the rear.

"There is nothing you can do," said Albert quietly. "The Civil Defence workers are coming today to clear the wreckage. It has become quite dangerous."

"Do you wish to help or not?" Adam asked sharply as he began to pick away at the rubble. Some timbers four or five metres above his head moved and came crashing down. The dogs kept whining gently.

"What the hell do you think you're doing?" said a voice behind Adam. A steel-helmeted Civil Defence worker with a policeman and a group of Hitler Youth volunteers had arrived.

"Will you help or not?" asked Adam impatiently. Constable Schneider behaved sympathetically towards Adam for the first and last time. "We believe Frau von Saloman was cremated in there," he began. "We are sorry, we all liked her."

The Civil Defence officer became impatient. "You have no authority here, Captain." he said. "My men wish to begin work. If we find anything I will speak to you personally," he promised.

Adam stood and watched, refusing to go away, as the site was cleared until only the shell of the kitchen remained. He stared at it until long after the workers had gone, and still the dogs stayed with him. He knelt down and stroked them, then lifted them up in turn and kissed each of them on the nose. Then one of them seized his trouser leg and pulled him towards the site of the kitchen. Hansl was still whining continually. He stroked them once more and rejoined Frieda and Greta.

Renate's attitude to Adam had now changed." You're welcome to share my apartment with the others," she offered. Adam knew the offer was impractical, but a timely one came from Albert Hartman, who quickly made up a spare bunk in his office.

Renate picked her way down the blackened stairs holding two envelopes, one addressed to Adam the other to Bruno. Both bore the crest of the Martin Luther School. A letter from anyone at that moment was an irrelevance, but he read it.

"You are cordially invited to preside over a special school assembly which will celebrate your promotion and decoration," it read. The letter informed Adam that Bruno had also been invited. Adam turned the letter over in his hands, trying to guess who had informed the school that the two of them were on leave. He showed the letter to Frieda and Greta, who told him Ilse Diels was responsible.

"I'm obliged to turn down the invitation, Grandmama," he said. "This is not a good time."

"Perhaps not," replied Frieda, forcing a smile. "But I must let you know the lengths to which Frau Diels has gone. She has already contacted the Leibstandarte Division at Lichterfelde and arranged for a staff car to take you to school.

"Then that must be cancelled," replied Adam without hesitation.

Bruno arrived with Helga and Manfred, who became the centre of attention and provided a much-needed diversion from the terrible sadness hanging over the family. Bruno had to resist the temptation to stand by Adam all the time he was there. He remembered Stamm and Thaelmann were on his mailing list and thought they should know.

"You have read your letter?" asked Bruno.

"Of course," answered Adam, "and we must decline at this time."

There was a knock at the door and in walked Ilse Diels, hat and all, in a celebratory mood. "May I welcome home our heroes from the Russian front?" she said grandly. She shook hands solemnly. "May I have the honour of delivering your letter of acceptance to Dr Schaub at the Martin Luther School?" she said. Ilse was puffed up with pride and Bruno looked at Adam as if he had no choice to accept.

"Of course, Frau Diels," Adam answered. Frieda produced a pen and writing paper while Ilse waited impatiently for Adam to write the letter. As soon as he had sealed it, she set off for the bicycle store.

Adam and Bruno would never forget the sight of Ilse dressed all in black with hat and hatpin setting off down Charlottenbrunnestrasse, wobbling uncertainly on her bicycle. Bruno embraced his friend. He himself had always been a little in love with Käthe and would miss her terribly.

When Bruno and Helga left, Bruno made a mysterious parting remark to Adam. "This school visit is more important than you could possibly know," he said, escaping without explanation. As Bruno walked away holding Manfred, he smiled to himself as he remembered the letter he received from Martha Reymann before she died in the shelter disaster.

The next day, Adam and Frieda walked in the remains of the park. It was a bright, sunny, windless day and people had gathered there in the hope that this would be the last spring of the war. There were green shoots on the shrubs and new growth had appeared at the foot of the blackened and splintered trees. The birds sang louder than ever.

"I want you to tell me everything Mama said in the last days," Adam said. Frieda was relieved, as she had been waiting for the opportunity to do so. "She was worse than Ilse Diels at telling everyone about your achievements," she said. "She worried about you all the time, but she was so proud of you." Then Frieda added mischievously. "Your mother said Gabrielle would be proud also."

He stopped and made her face him. "Grandmama, that is a little invention. You should be ashamed of yourself," he said.

"No Adam, it's true. She really liked Gabrielle."

Adam began to feel the blood flowing in his veins again. "Has anyone seen her?" he asked hopefully.

"I'm afraid not Adam. Now that poor Martha's gone we'll never see her favourite niece again," she said. "Will you be all right at the school?" she asked, wanting to change the subject.

"Of course I will Grandmama. I will have the best friend anyone could have with me," he replied.

"Bruno was very insistent you go, Adam," said Frieda. "Perhaps he is looking forward to you both meeting Herr Rust again."

"I'm sure you're right Grandmama," Adam replied.

Renate was reminded that Adam was her closest link to her son. Both tried to imagine Ilse Diels' effect on Dr Schaub and agreed that he would never be the same again.

"Do you think she'll make him volunteer for the Waffen SS?" asked Renate.

"Perhaps, but he'll be a little out of breath," said Adam. Renate giggled.

They overheard Frieda and Greta talking on the stairs, and Renate held her finger to her lips. They could just hear Greta saying she felt haunted by the apartment building and Frieda's reply wondering where on earth they could go. They were soon to discover it had been decided for them.

Forty-five minutes before the special assembly was to begin, an SS staff car arrived. Bruno wasn't allowed to call for Adam. The driver was under strict instructions to do everything. He rapped sharply on Albert's window and the concierge ran smartly up the stairs to inform Adam of the arrival of his transport. Ilse was allowed to have her moment as the two officers were driven off. As Frieda, Greta, Renate and Albert waved, she stretched out her arm in the National Socialist salute. Tears streamed down her face as she said to the other women "Aren't you proud of them?"

"Indeed Ilse," they felt obliged to say.

Dr Schaub met his guests on the school front steps with a welcoming committee headed by the new Deputy Principal, Alfred Rust. He swelled with pride when he saw his former pupils in dress uniform. Another car pulled up at a respectful distance behind Adam and Bruno's car. It carried two press men who were to report on the assembly and conduct interviews later in the staff room. The government was not going to miss an opportunity like this to propagandise the youth of Wilmersdorf and District.

The staff and school waited in respectful silence for the two young men, and Dr Schaub led the procession onto the stage. The school stood in ordered lines. "Heil Hitler," called Schaub and the stage party exchanged salutes with pupils and staff.

The Principal welcomed his guests and invited Adam to speak. He felt a dreadful sense of emptiness as he delivered the expected homily to the students. He must have done it well, because there were smiles all round. He revived when invited to present the prize to the winner of the junior three thousand metres. As Adam shook hands with the winner, he looked for Bruno's reaction. He wasn't paying attention but looking round anxiously.

One member of the audience amongst the staff at the rear of the hall wasn't smiling. Her heart pounded as she wondered how she was going to get through the next few hours.

The school was given the afternoon off and the celebration of the two young officers' achievements was to continue in the staff room. Two photographers waited there and asked the three to pose.

The double doors were open and there was a buzz of conversation inside. Adam and Bruno exchanged glances. They had never faced their teachers on an equal footing before and the two young officers were not at all comfortable. Dr Schaub read their feelings.

"I must tell you both that most of your teachers are no longer with us," he said. "I am ashamed to say that some have been brought out of retirement to fill vacancies." He was referring to the politically unreliable. "Everyone under forty has been drafted into the forces. I'm afraid we're already drawing up a list of the dead and wounded."

This was not the ebullient Dr Schaub they had met before, and he added a detail of which he seemed ashamed. "Please don't be surprised by the latest additions to our staff. Shortages have compelled us to employ two young women. I hope this doesn't make you feel uncomfortable," he added quietly.

They posed for one more photograph. Alfred Rust announced their arrival and Dr Schaub held the doors open. The two officers joined the gathering, to a round of applause. Alfred said quietly to Adam, before the staff descended on them, "Please be sure to see me before you leave. I have an interesting offer to make which concerns your family."

The conversation was polite and predictable, until they reached a fifty-year-old bespectacled zealot who offered the National Socialist salute. His outstretched arm sent a glass of wine flying. He recovered quickly, insisting on a report from the Russian front implying he had important contacts.

"I believe we are to make a temporary peace with Stalin," he began. "This should mean we keep millions of hectares of land for our farmers in the east."

Adam and Bruno had never heard such fantasizing, but were tactful. The teacher persisted. "Our troops are resisting impossible odds," he continued. "You are to be congratulated. Pray tell me where, in your opinion, the summer offensive will strike?"

The two friends had had enough and Adam knew how to scare him off. "In Germany today, we have had to resist speculation," he said. "Such talk may be seen as dangerous." He leaned towards the teacher, who scurried off. Bruno laughed. "You've learnt something from that bastard Kloster," he quipped.

The two women teachers were deeply engaged in conversation in a far corner of the room. One was standing, the other sitting, obscured by one of the photographers leaning towards her. Alfred called over the one who was standing.

"May I introduce Fräulein Eva Knopke?" he said. He winked at Adam. "Eva teaches chemistry in the old tradition," he said. Alfred left them after reminding Adam he had something important to tell him.

Eva was tall, slim and a little angular, but she had large brown eyes and radiated an amused awareness. She was also Karin Haller's friend, and Adam knew Bruno had not forgotten Karin.

Adam turned and looked accusingly at Bruno. So this was the reason for his friend's enthusiasm for today's events. He wanted to re-establish contact with Karin through Eva. If it hadn't have been for his promise to see Alfred, he would have made an excuse and gone home.

Dr Schaub interrupted. "Eva mustn't monopolise the guests," he said.

Bruno gave Eva a knowing look. "Oh, before you move on," she began." You must meet my friend and colleague. Excuse me," she said to the photographer, who stood away from the lady he was talking to. "My apologies gentlemen," he said.

"Gabrielle, may I introduce Captain von Saloman and Lieutenant Grabowsky," said Eva, almost wickedly. Gabrielle turned to face the guests, and the cup and saucer in her hands began to shake. "Thank you Eva, we've met before," said Bruno.

Adam and Gabrielle stared at each other, hardly knowing what to say. She flushed deeply. "I'm so sorry to hear about your mother," she said.

"Thank you," began Adam, "and Martha too, was a terrible loss," he said, feeling himself go light-headed.

Bruno made frantic signals to Eva that the couple should be left alone and they strode off into a corner. Alfred appeared inconveniently at Adam's elbow. "I see you're getting on well," he began. "Why don't you show our guest your new mathematics laboratory, Gabrielle?" he suggested. "It's very impressive."

The pair said nothing for fear of discovery as they marched down the hundred metres of corridor without even exchanging a glance. Gabrielle quickly looked behind them when they heard footsteps. Bruno and Eva had stepped outside the staffroom to give the couple a cheerful little wave.

Adam wondered who else knew, but then he had a good feeling. His friend had risked all to unite them. They reached the maths laboratory and Gabrielle looked anxiously up and down the corridor as she unlocked her room. She was not so sure of Adam's feelings. She pulled him through the door and leaned backwards on it as it closed, her speech of rejection ready. As her hands left the door handle, Adam pulled her towards him. She threw her arms round his neck and pulled his face down to kiss hers. They kissed wantonly, nearly falling over.

Tears streamed down Gabrielle's face as her pent-up feelings were released. Adam kissed her face, her neck and her shoulders. She was wearing the same lace top she had worn at the mountain hotel. It fell to the floor. They stopped to breathe and take each other in, no longer afraid of Kloster and his ugly apparatus. Gabrielle remembered she had to say the important things first, and thought a flippant remark would make Adam think twice. She touched the scar on his face and then his Iron Cross.

"You didn't cut yourself shaving did you?" she asked playfully. His reaction was not flippant, his left hand stroking her cheek, his right resting on her left breast. They began kissing once more and Gabrielle stroked his left leg with her right. He lifted her as if to pull her towards the desk. They ached to make love. One of her shoes fell off and she kicked it away.

There were steps in the corridor. "Oh, my God no," she breathed.

Adam had already unzipped her dress and it was falling off her shoulders. The footsteps stopped and there was the quietest of knocks at the door. Bruno poked his head round. "Is this the officers' mess?" he said. Gabrielle giggled. "Our host has sent me to retrieve you two. Would you please compose yourselves and follow me?"

They said little as they walked as slowly as they could back to the staff room, holding hands. They released each other just in time. The photographer who had been so attentive to Gabrielle burst through the staff room door and photographed the three of them. Just as they went in Bruno whispered to Adam, "I'm damn proud of you. Oh, and by the way you've forgotten your cap."

"Let us offer a final toast to our guests," said Dr Schaub. As glasses rose, the cameras flashed. The photographer wanted one more picture of the Principal with Adam and Bruno, who thoughtfully removed his cap.

The staff began to drift away in twos and threes. Alfred Rust took Adam by the arm. "I know you have to go but please, convey this offer to your grandmother and her housekeeper" he said. He thrust a letter into Adam's hand. "It contains an offer to share my house in Schöneberg," he said.

Adam realised how generous an offer this was. He shook Alfred's hand warmly with an anxious Bruno looking on, but there was no sign of Gabrielle. Eva came back through the staff room door and said something to Bruno.

"If you would like to retrieve your cap Captain, Gabrielle wants to present it to you in the maths room," said Bruno. "You've got half an hour before the caretaker locks up. And for God's sake be careful, we're all in this now."

Gabrielle was sitting at her desk writing furiously, with Adam's cap beside her. He gathered her up once again and kissed her lovingly, but there was no time to make love, and both realised this was hardly the place.

"What happened?" asked Adam. "Do we have a child?"

"We have a wonderful little girl," she answered and then issued a warning, which deflated him. "You can do nothing until this terrible government goes. I am watched regularly and have to report to the police station."

The warning went over Adam's head. "Please tell me where she is," begged Adam.

"You can't see her," answered Gabrielle. "Her adoptive parents love her. She is watched like a hawk by her SS nurse."

"I'll track her down," he retorted.

"No," she said firmly. "We have to be patient. You'll put both of us in danger if you do."

"And what of you?" he asked.

"I'll be all right," Gabrielle answered. "I'm married to a party high-up and there's no escape. Remember, Bruno's involved. Please read this letter, my love." She handed him an envelope. "I'll tell you a little of what's in it." She stroked his face. "It asks you to be my lover," she said softly.

He looked at her searchingly, but knew it all had to be on her terms. Then she said something curious. "The SS nurse is the one who brought us together, my darling."

Adam knew at that moment that Gabrielle intended he should meet his daughter one day.

There was a sharp rap on the classroom door. The caretaker appeared with a large bunch of keys and the encounter was over. Adam walked out of the classroom, forgetting his cap. Gabrielle was tempted to place it on his head, but she decided the caretaker's life was probably complicated enough already and placed it in her lover's hand.

Adam returned to Frieda and Greta with Alfred Rust's exciting new offer, which included a suggestion that the Ladies' Circle should meet at his house.

On his way home, Adam felt sudden guilt at his behaviour during the day. His grandmother's words "Remember who you are," rang in his head. Perhaps he had behaved with indecent haste and dishonoured his mother's memory. Then he realised that such a thought was ridiculous. Käthe was disappointed her son had apparently lost Gabrielle and now Frieda had changed. It seemed the move to the streets had done her a great deal of good.

Adam tapped his tunic pocket. His most treasured possession now was

Gabrielle's address, but he knew he must not be reckless, even though he was desperate to see his daughter. He dealt first with the most pressing matter, presenting Alfred's offer to the two ladies, who gratefully accepted. Adam now knew he had a child, but who was the link that made all that possible? Adam would not discover the answer until far in the future.

Franz Ackerman went from strength to strength at the Ministry of Education. They were impressed by his choice of a wife, but expressed a small reservation. He was slapped on the back at receptions and reminded that the Führer needed a child from the rising star's marriage, and his wife assured him there would be children. Gabrielle's ambition was as strong as her SS lover's, but she could never tell her husband the truth. Tests showed she could have no more children, and this was the death knell of the marriage. Ackerman said he had been betrayed, and they parted.

Gabrielle now belonged to a disadvantaged group of Germans, single woman without children. But she had a protector. Despite strong suggestions from above, Dr Schaub refused to consider her dismissal.

Chapter 22

The memorial service for Käthe took place on a sunny, warm spring day. Adam, the two women and Father Albert Wendel waited patiently for the few people who had been invited. They would have been grateful for the attendance of just these few because of the near collapse of Berlin's transport system.

The time at which the service was due to start, ten o'clock, approached. The survivors of the Ladies Circle arrived at precisely ten and the priest prepared to begin. Then the rest arrived. Karl Berger, Edmund Schöler and their entire staff came late with apologies. A nurse pushing a man in a wheelchair came into view from Charlottenbrunnestrasse. The old man in the wheelchair waved to Adam as if they had met. As the breeze stirred his remaining wisps of hair, he introduced himself as Michael Renneker, a former comrade of Peter's during the last war and a favourite patient of Käthe's. "For a Saint," he said handing a wreath to Adam.

Over the next ten minutes nearly all the tenants from neighbouring apartments arrived, all anxious to make themselves known to the chief mourners. Someone laid a bicycle on the side wall just out of sight and it clattered to the ground; it was Frieda's faithful retainer and driver Stephan. He placed his wreath in the ruins and bowed to Frieda and Adam in turn. Frieda shook his hand warmly and asked him to remain behind after the ceremony.

There was, as yet, no sign of Bruno and his mother. Father Wendel had just announced he was to begin when they appeared. Adam remembered her reluctance to attend Catholic ceremonies, and was pleased she had changed her mind on this special day.

Bruno carried two wreaths. The first was inscribed with his and Renate's names. He turned the inscription on the second towards Adam, and he saw Gabrielle's name. He fought back tears when he realised she wished to share his grief. Adam remembered that Bruno was the messenger.

The service was brief, but not without uncomfortable moments; Ilse Diels was joined by an unknown stranger in civilian clothes. At the end of the service, he whispered a question into Ilse's ear and she pointed to Bruno and Renate. Adam saw it all and wondered if Gabrielle's wreath might cost the freedom of at least one of the mourners.

Constable Schneider too was in uniform. Adam wondered if the attention he had paid to the family had another motive.

Not so far away, an attractive woman in her early forties stared out of a long window. Her burns were bandaged and she was still in some pain. She had dragged herself from her mental torpor, climbed out of bed and reached the window with the assistance of a crutch.

She stared at the remains of a children's playground with a curious look on her face. She half-smiled at the twisted and splintered trees. The longer she looked, the more she felt unsafe and afraid; tears ran down her face. The door opened quietly and a nun took her arm. "Come my dear," said Sister Matthew. "You must rest."

The sister stayed with her patient until she had fallen asleep and then left the room to discuss the mysterious guest's future with the Mother Superior. "We must tell the police," said Sister Matthew. "Only they will be able to identify her."

"That is correct, Sister Matthew," said the Mother Superior. "But might that be dangerous in the times in which we live?"

Sister Matthew possessed no political instincts and asked for guidance. "She shows signs of mental disturbance," began the Mother Superior. "If we hand her over to the police she may never see the light of day again. I think it would be better for her to stay with us until things improve outside."

The woman recovered from her burns and regained the full use of her left leg. Sister Matthew noticed how comfortable she was during church devotions. She was obliged to follow the Mother Superior's advice and over time, their guest became the lay helper. She was baptised and given the name Michaela.

One day a small boy in Hitler Youth uniform was brought into the orphanage with a deep cut on his left arm. The neighbour who had brought him said the boy had lost his parents in a raid. Sister Matthew had nursing experience, so the boy was brought to her. She was about the apply lint and disinfectant after the wound had been cleaned when an otherwise passive Michaela intervened. "The wound must be stitched," she said and added, "Of course you may help, Sister Matthew."

Sister Matthew ran to the Mother Superior for further guidance; the Mother Superior counselled tolerance and offered support.

They looked on fascinated as a lay helper expertly stitched the wound and announced, "Our patient must stay with us for observation. There may be a danger of infection." The watchers realised the helper had treated wounds before and thought she had found her calling. The army had long ago commandeered the services of the orphanage doctor.

Michaela filled the void and soon expressed the wish to become a novice. The need to teach her a little humility was clear, but she responded well. On completion of her novitiate, she was named Sister Michael.

Adam walked the dogs for the last time before he returned to Poland. It had been Käthe's job every evening before curfew, and he wondered if he would see his four-footed friends again. He carried them, one under each arm, down the rickety staircase, attached their leads and walked into the street. They pulled on their leads towards the garden at the rear, and Adam didn't resist. He wanted to pay his respects to Käthe for the last time and the flowers would soon be withered and gone.

Hansl and Gretl began to dig at the base of the small mountain of flowers. He pulled them away and dragged them towards the street. They stopped on the edge of the pavement, whining softly and staring towards the park.

"Good evening Captain," said Constable Schneider's colleague. "I was sorry to hear of your loss. Frau von Saloman often took the dogs in that direction."

The journey to Krakow took nearly seven hours. Time and again, the train pulled into sidings to allow what appeared to be freight trains pulling cattle trucks to pass through. Adam told Bruno about the incident in the siding on the way to Tarnopol, but his friend could offer no explanation.

Adam thought Bruno seemed callous. "To hell with freight trains," he said. "Let's survive this war and keep our women happy." He paused and grinned broadly. "Which reminds me, how is it with you and Gabrielle?"

"Nothing else has happened," replied Adam grimly. "Oh and thanks for the wreath."

"Well, at least you're consistent," remarked Bruno. "May I offer some advice? Go to that husband of hers, give him a good hiding and show him who's boss. Failing that, which might be difficult for you, meet her regularly at a nice comfortable venue. The rest I'll leave to you!"

"Thank you Lieutenant," replied Adam. "I knew I could depend on you."

An hour before they reached Krakow Bruno sprang a surprise. "It's your birthday soon, isn't it?" he asked. Adam was puzzled, because Bruno didn't usually bother to remember it. He had announced blandly that he didn't intend to try because he couldn't compete with any of the women at present-giving.

"It's the Führer's birthday soon," replied Adam, "and I don't suppose you'll be sending him a card either." Bruno became serious and reached inside his haversack, unfurling the three Lions of Frederic II he had won at school. "I want you to have this and before you refuse, listen," he continued. "You're more likely to survive this war than me."

Bruno surprised and shocked Adam. "I can't accept it," he said.

"No," insisted Bruno "Take it."

Adam could see it meant a lot to Bruno and replied, "On one condition, that I return it to you after the war, even though you'll look a damn fool." Bruno muttered agreement and the train pulled into the remains of the Polish station.

Adam watched Bruno striding out towards a line of brand new armoured cars and recognised the not very military-looking figure of Herbert Wem, driver and mechanic supreme. Bruno was entering the small world where he was king.

"Good journey Lieutenant?" asked Wem. "How's the family?"

"Fine," answered Bruno, his mind a long way away. He reached inside an inner pocket to caress a perfumed envelope from Karin Haller, but it wasn't there. He had left it in his civilian suit hanging in the wardrobe in the flat in Charlottenburg. He cursed himself for his carelessness.

"He'll be here soon," said Sergeant Hans Thaelmann after a bad-tempered kit inspection. Franz Stamm marched over after an equally bad-tempered one. "Get hold of yourself Hans, and read this," he said handing him the latest letter from Bruno announcing that Käthe was dead. It concluded, "watch his back and don't be afraid to stand up to him."

"So his mothers' dead," said Hans. "God help us all."

By 14:00 hours when the new company assembled, Hans Thaelmann's warnings had travelled like wildfire. Each new recruit had been told to feel privileged to be half dead from the extra training they would receive. A Kubelwagen staff car roared over the uneven ground and came to a halt in front of the assembled company. Every man went rigid as Adam approached them.

"Krastner, take care of the captain's luggage," barked Stamm.

A fresh-faced young recruit ran up to Adam, saluted and seized his luggage, then disappeared into a tent. The new captain inspected the unfamiliar platoon first and met Lieutenants Brugman and Dorsch. He had already read a copy of their records.

Adam approached the last of the four corporals and Stamm and Thaelmann watched carefully. Every man in the company knew of the destruction of the Russian tank. The Company already had its own mythology.

The corporal gave the reluctant smile of a hardened veteran. It was Eberling, the newest volunteer to the Hohenstaufen division. Adam was both delighted and relieved; delighted to see Eberling again as a comrade on a permanent basis and relieved to see that he too had been awarded the Iron Cross First Class.

They shook hands warmly and Adam remembered the debt he owed to this veteran of the First Army who had seen Adam as a promising apprentice and risked all to save the survivors of Adam's platoon. The debt was mutual, because this young officer's behaviour had given him a new future. Eberling had staked everything on the Hohenstaufen division and he was to repay the debt with absolute commitment.

Adam received permission to fly the three lions of Frederic II outside his tent. Hans Thaelmann and Franz Stamm made sure that the whole company knew of the competition at the Martin Luther School. It was rumoured that the Ninth would soon be in action again on the Russian front. The division was to practise anti-paratrooper tactics, because there was a threat of landings in rear areas by Soviet partisans. Fatefully, that training was to be used a long way from the Russian front and would involve a crucial turning point in Adam's life.

Chapter 23

A three-year-old child danced along the edge of the lake by the Grünewald, holding her leather sandals. She waded further and further out to make her nurse feel more anxious. The child stopped as the nurse took off her shoes and splashed into the water. The little girl laughed and pointed to a lake steamer. She refused to move until her nurse joined her in furiously waving to the passengers.

"Come quickly," said the nurse. "Your Aunt Gabrielle will be here soon."

The child waded back to the shore and lifted her foot painfully as she stepped on a sharp stone. Her nurse helped her to replace her sandals just as a figure emerged from the trees looking anxiously behind her.

The newcomer pretended to admire a clump of primroses as a police patrol car passed by. The child ran to the visitor who picked her up and kissed her. The little girl lifted her hands, demanding to know what gift her Aunt Gabrielle had brought. Then the girl ran behind her visitor to see the present she was hiding behind her back. It was a small grey cloth elephant with huge ears. The little girl seized it and ran off into the forest laughing.

The nurse was always worried by these meetings in case shows of affection revealed the real relationship between the little girl and the visitor to a hostile watcher. She hid behind a tree. Gabrielle chased her and picked her up again.

The little girl dropped the elephant and pointed to a large deserted house behind a ruined wall, a short distance away. "Who lives there, Aunt Gabrielle?" she asked.

"Oh, no one we know," she answered, and turned to the child's nurse. "Are we safe?" she asked anxiously.

"I can never be sure," was the answer.

Both were afraid the little girl might tell her adoptive parents of the meetings, but the nurse was clever. "This is our little secret," she told her charge over and over again.

CHAPTER TWENTY THREE

In June 1944, North-West Europe was affected by bleak, stormy weather. As the sixth day dawned, the German defenders of the Atlantic Wall on the coast of Normandy mechanically scanned the horizon as the wind howled around them. The sky was turning a yellowish grey.

An officer picked up his binoculars and apathetically scanned the horizon. It was time for an early breakfast. He let his binoculars fall and turned towards the entrance of the concrete gun emplacement, then something made him decide to take one more look.

He almost dropped the binoculars in shock. The horizon was black with ships and he could see flashes among them. Seconds later high-explosive shells began to fall on the coast. By the time the Führer was out of bed, thousands of Allied soldiers had gained a foothold on the beaches of Normandy.

A field telephone rang in Adam's tent as he was shaving. He normally cut himself when an emergency arose, and this was no exception. He mumbled something to himself about his clumsiness and picked up the telephone. His expression changed and he threw on his tunic.

Already, outside Adam's billet, the whole leaguer of the Hohenstaufen division was a hive of activity. Within a few hours, the eighteen thousand men of the Ninth had begun to make their way 400 miles across Europe to the Normandy coast. The Ninth would have to steal its way to its destination under the cover of darkness, because the Allies now controlled the skies. Even so their faith in final victory under the leadership of their Führer was complete. Outside Adam's tent flew the three lions of Frederic II. The men of his company believed that no other officer would have been allowed such a privilege.

It was days before the Hohenstaufen reached its destination behind the Normandy battle front. During the day tanks gouged their way through hedgerows towards the protection of woodland. At dusk, the machines belched smoke and resumed the advance down the straight roads of France. When the soldiers reached their destination behind the battlefront, they were exhausted, sleeping underneath camouflage netting on their first day. They pitched hundreds of tents and farmers had to share their houses and barns with officers.

Klaus Eberling found what he considered to be a substitute for a mattress on a barn floor. When he woke up his fellow corporal, the ex-farmer Corporal Eberhardt, brewed him some imitation coffee and gave him a length of sausage. Eberhardt shared the feast and said little, smiling to himself.

"What the hell's the matter with you?" asked the gruff Eberling.

"Oh, it's that mattress of yours Klaus," was the answer. "It's the finest vintage pig shit I've ever seen."

Eberling shrugged his shoulders. He had survived the night on it. He threw a groundsheet over the solid excrement and threatened everyone in the barn with retribution if they stole his spot.

Adam watched the young replacements. "What do you think of them, Stamm?" he asked his old comrade.

"They're OK, Captain," he answered. "They all want to die for the Führer." Adam smiled grimly.

One of them, Trooper Bastian Wolters, seemed different. He was not afraid of officers or sergeants. He wasn't afraid of approaching Kaspar, who could be forbidding.

"Do you give free lessons?" he asked Kaspar, who was in the midst of his favourite activity, cleaning his rifle.

"Piss off sonny," Kaspar answered.

"You're the most miserable bastard in this company," rejoined Wolters.

Kaspar's expression changed suddenly. His bluff had been called. "Get your rifle," he said. "You can have a free lesson. And keep your mouth shut while I'm talking."

Wolters grinned and called out to his friend Heinrich Henne so that Kaspar could hear. "You're right. He's a miserable bastard but he's speaking to us!"

At five o'clock the next morning, the ground shook with the noise of engines and camouflage netting was dragged from guns and tanks. Quartermasters quickly went from platoon to platoon handing out field rations for the next three days.

Kit inspections were rigorous but no fatigues were handed out because of the trials these untried recruits would soon have to face. Hans Thaelmann watched Wolters with interest. The young lad checked kit for all his friends. He gave his friend Henne a mock punch in the shoulder and told him he deserved a fatigue.

Adam had found an old table in a wrecked barn. He spread a map out on it and briefed his lieutenants and the four sergeants. Franz Stamm peered at the maze of country lanes. "Don't worry, Stamm," said Adam, "we're here." He pointed to a spot near a road junction. "And this is where we're going," he continued cheerfully, pointing to a tiny hamlet called Rauray. "We hold that and the boys behind go through us to the coast. Is that clear?"

"Yes," answered Thaelmann, trying to be cheerful. "We get the shit, they get the glory."

"That's correct," answered Adam.

He carried out a final inspection of the company. Every man wore camouflage uniform and was armed to the teeth with machine pistols and bandoliers of ammunition. But the effect seemed blunted by the small branches each man had threaded through the netting on his steel helmet.

Adam spread the veterans amongst the raw recruits. Wolters had stopped grinning. "Are you all right trooper?" asked Adam. The young man nodded. Adam clapped him on the shoulder. "Stick to your sergeant," he ordered and said a silent prayer for all of them.

Two armoured cars from the Reconnaissance Battalion returned and reported that there was no enemy activity ahead. The veterans constantly watched the sky, but there were no enemy aircraft. The low cloud rolled back and the sky cleared ominously.

The hour of advance approached. Helmets were tightened and hand grenades issued. Machine-gunners threw their weapons over their shoulders. There was to be no artillery bombardment which might warn the enemy. Each unit was ordered to cling to the hedgerows. It had just stopped raining and water dripped onto their uniforms, and there were a few curses. There was to be absolute silence.

Adam's company was one of the first to advance and Stamm ordered a section to sprint over the cross roads and begin their advance. It seemed the war had not reached these leafy lanes. The sound of gunfire seemed some distance away and it appeared the Hohenstaufen had achieved surprise. The soldiers marched on, the young ones desperate to say something to a comrade. A track led off to the right. Lieutenant Brugman spotted ruined farm buildings hidden in the trees.

Adam waved Thaelmann forwards. Covered by Michael Kaspar's rifle he crawled up to a roll of rusting barbed wire. Trooper Winter crawled along the ground to join Thaelmann, and the young man raised his head. Thaelmann grabbed him by the neck and made him lie flat. Hans looked cautiously into the first building. Three hens perched on rafters flew down and startled the two men. Ernst Winter grabbed one of them, exposing himself. Thaelmann grabbed him again. There was silence. The old farm seemed deserted and Thaelmann signalled the company forward.

Winter tried to seize the chicken again. "Keep your dirty hands off it," ordered Corporal Eberhardt. Trooper Rolf Kastner went looking for eggs in the barn and reappeared triumphantly with a handful. He walked towards his friends holding his hands open, displaying his windfall. Just then a shot rang out and Kastner fell dead, the broken eggs staining the ground beside his outstretched fingers.

Wolters thought he saw a movement by some rusting farm machinery and raised himself sufficiently to throw a grenade. It tore the rusting metal apart and Lieutenant Dorsch led a charge, but the enemy sniper had melted away. Adam ordered medics to stretcher Kastner's body to the rear.

He reformed his company and the advance continued. He looked at the faces of the young soldiers staring at the ground and knew they had just learned a terrible lesson. Adam knew the enemy too had made an even bigger mistake. They had revealed their presence and a friendly tank caught up with them, its hull shrouded in branches.

Adam needed an observation position in this deadly game of cat and mouse and the tank commander invited him to climb up behind the turret and scan the area.

"He's taking a hell of a risk," Eberling said to Stamm. "After what's happened to those kids."

"You ought to know better, Eberling," breathed Stamm. "Different set of rules for him."

The company had to scout ahead to find a safe passage for the tanks. The best eyes on the battlefield were those in the air and the German Air Force was completely absent. The company waited until relieving troops caught up with them. Adam was embarrassed to hand over a position that seemed to be of no importance. They resumed their advance, walking cautiously down a winding lane. The only sound was running water made by a small stream which crossed the road winding away to the left. Adam consulted his map, which showed they were nowhere near Rauray.

CHAPTER TWENTY THREE

Adam waved Wolters forward. He was half-way over the stream when there was the sound of a tank engine and a long gun protruded round the corner at the top of the hill. Eberling made a signal for everyone to lie in the hedgerow and moved forward with an anti-tank rocket.

Adam was sure the tank commander must see them as he rounded the corner. They froze in the hedgerows amongst the sharp spines of hawthorn and blackthorn. The tank stopped level with Eberling, then slowly lumbered towards the others. Thaelmann thought the enemy tank commander must have seen them as it changed direction towards him. He tried unsuccessfully to wriggle through the bottom of the hedge.

Eberling waited until the tank had passed him and nearly detached the turret from the hull with an anti-tank rocket. The mutilated body of the English tank commander collapsed down the side of the tank. Hans Thaelmann spat the earth out of his mouth.

The tank driver had survived. He opened his hatch and climbed out slowly, white-faced. Adam waited for the gunner to emerge, but there was no movement and Adam signalled the driver to walk to the rear. He shook his head in refusal, not wanting to turn his back on his captors.

"Leave him Captain," advised Stamm. The hedgerow to their left was torn by machine-gun fire as supporting enemy infantry spotted Adam and Stamm talking. They threw themselves to the ground.

Lieutenant Dorsch led a squad round the flank of the enemy soldiers, but a battery of mortars found the range of Adam's company. It was a new and terrible experience for the young recruits. Trooper Henne lay behind an empty concrete water trough. A mortar bomb landed inside it and cracked the casing. He lay there clawing the earth and shaking, turning for re-assurance to Lieutenant Dorsch. A mortar bomb landed where the officer was lying. For a few minutes, he uttered a few pitiful sounds. Then the mortaring stopped.

Adam believed the men should be taken as far away as possible from the remains of the Lieutenant, but the needs of the moment meant there was little he could do.

"Get that man to the rear," he ordered pointing to the prisoner, who refused to move. Kaspar gave him a cigarette and the company went on. Adam found a vantage point and saw a tank half a kilometre away moving slowly towards them. He handed his binoculars to Eberling.

A long aerial protruded from the turret and the commander was speaking into a transmitter. Adam asked Eberling's advice. He turned to one of the other veterans. He asked to see the tank and knew what was happening. "Get the lads out of here Captain," he said urgently. "The bastard's directing aircraft onto us, I saw it in the desert."

He pointed to three dots in the sky, barely three hundred metres in the air. Those who dared looked up to see the white streaks under the wings. The aiming point was a half-track a short way ahead, which burst into flames. The whole area erupted and in a few seconds it was all over. A young trooper tended his wounded friend as Adam assessed the damage.

"Where's our fuckin' Air Force, Captain?" he asked nearly in tears. Corporal Eberhardt stared into a field at the bloated and rotting corpses of horses, their remains once again disturbed by high explosive. He turned to Adam and shook his head.

One soldier hung lifeless on a fence. Adam cursed himself as he could not identify him. He was from the new platoon and they had suffered most. There was no sign of Lieutenant Martin Brugman.

The mortaring began once more and this time English infantry attacked in force, supported by tanks. Klaus Eberling and his gun crew destroyed four tanks but noted that for every one knocked out, two more appeared. After two days the Hohenstaufen attack petered out before they had ever seen the sea or even the village of Rauray.

Adam had lost nearly one quarter of his company, nearly all from the platoon he didn't know.

A new challenge faced the exhausted soldiers when they returned to their billets. They were forced to stare at the empty wooden seats and bales of straw where missing comrades had sat. The young recruits turned to Bastian Wolters, but he was sensible enough to allow Kaspar to dispense advice.

"Sergeant Stamm's alive, so's Thaelmann. The Captain's still here and so am I. Stick with us, you'll be all right," advised the veteran.

Wolters looked sceptical. He needed more. "Before the next attack, touch that yellow flag outside the captain's tent. He won't mind," said Kaspar. "You'll be one of us then. You'll be all right," he added.

"We touch the flag and the enemy air force fucks off," suggested Wolters. Kaspar grabbed hold of his tunic. "Don't try to be smart with me sonny," he warned. Wolters was shocked into conformity and apologised.

CHAPTER TWENTY THREE

The Hohenstaufen rested for three days. Then the Battalion Commander arrived to address everyone down to Lieutenant. He looked grim. "This is the message from General Harzer," he began. He draped a map over a large board. "The Canadians hold this hill. They must be driven off it gentlemen. They look down on us from Hill 112 and they're close to our rear area. The Hohenstaufen is once again privileged to be selected to save the German front. The Führer has faith in you and watches us closely." With that he left and Adam wondered how he might motivate his survivors. He needn't have worried. Thaelmann, Stamm, Eberling and Wolters had done it for him, with a little help from Kaspar the grey eminence.

"It's time, Captain," called Franz Stamm through Adam's tent flap at three o'clock in the morning. His company had marched nearly ten miles the previous day to the jumping-off point. They had the advantage of a surprise attack by night and it was not wasted. Even in the moonlight, the hill was an impressive feature. One road, an old track, wound its way short of the summit. It was overlooked by small limestone cliffs, perfect vantage points for an enemy. If the Ninth could fight its way past the cliffs to the system of clearings beyond and hold a line, it could be counted a success.

"Touch the flag or I'll kick your ass," Kaspar warned Wolters.

"Bollocks," said Heinrich Henne, out of earshot of the loner.

Michael Kaspar surveyed his new friends as they marched either side of the track, making an unacceptable amount of noise. "Shut your mouths!" he hissed. A young deer leapt out of a thicket and fled down the trackway and Henne pretended to shoot it. Kaspar shook his head in dismay.

The company advanced past the cliffs. That meant the Canadians must be entrenched on the summit. They reached a group of wrecked farmhouses. There was a movement behind one of them and the company threw itself flat. Adam and Stamm crawled forwards.

Like ghosts in the fading darkness three individuals appeared. One of them was pushing a handcart down a path towards the SS soldiers. The man was a local farmer, the other two his wife and daughter. Adam looked into the cart. It contained a mirror, two or three chairs and two piglets nestling in straw. The man seemed resigned and pointed to his treasured belongings. Adam waved him on to the track going eastwards.

The company reached more houses, part perhaps of the same hamlet they had just left. Stamm whistled out of the side of his mouth to some of the young recruits who had fallen behind. As they reached him, bullets hit the trees around them and mortaring began. A tank came up in support. It crashed through woodland and scrub and advanced on the farmhouses, the defenders' bullets bouncing harmlessly off the hull. "Now," shouted Adam running behind the tank and firing into the ruins. Wolters followed with a light machine gun. The Canadian survivors emerged, their hands in the air. Stamm waved them to the rear.

Beyond the house was a partially-ploughed field, an abandoned plough in its centre. An enemy tank appeared out of the woodland and seemed unaware of the German tank. Adam heard the shriek of the German shell and saw it strike the turret of the opponent. It failed to explode and passed clean through, missing the commander. Adam saw his hands fall away from his binoculars and he staggered out of the tank, collapsing on the ground.

Fifty metres away, Kaspar levelled his rifle. Adam's hand rested on the barrel. "Leave him Kaspar. He will never fight again." Kaspar seemed disappointed. The tank reversed and left the commander kneeling on the ground weeping. The German tank prepared to follow, and its commander fell into a trap. As he exposed part of one flank, there was a shriek of another tank shell from the left of the clearing. It hit the Tiger in the tracks and disabled it. The crew scrambled out and joined Adam's men. One was slow and a sniper shot him in the shoulder. He collapsed in the bushes.

Canadian soldiers charged across the clearing in a display of reckless bravery that belonged to another age. They were met by a hail of automatic fire and driven back. They tried again, to the dismay of Adam's men with the same result until the clearing was strewn with their dead and wounded.

There was silence. Then a white flag was cautiously waved from the bushes on the far side of the clearing. "Hold your fire," called one officer after another and a Canadian captain walked slowly into the clearing as a group of jackdaws settled on one of his dead comrades. "Fuck off you bastards," said a voice in the Canadian position. His voice echoed round the clearing in the eerie silence. The birds flew off as if they had been found out.

Michael Kaspar signalled Adam to walk out after he had patted his rifle on the barrel. When he was sure the Canadian was unarmed, Adam left his machine pistol in Kaspar's care.

CHAPTER TWENTY THREE

The Canadian officer waited in the centre of the ploughed field. Adam walked slowly towards the man.

"May we remove our wounded captain?" he asked.

"You may do so," replied Adam in perfect English. "The truce will last for thirty minutes."

Adam looked at the maple leaf on the Canadian's sleeve and wanted to ask him why any of this was his country's business, but he thought better of it. The truce overran because some of the wounded had to be treated on the spot, but both sides behaved well. There was clearly no advantage to be gained from breaking the truce, because both sides were well established. The Canadians knew the truce was over when they heard the sound of tank engines revving from the German side, and they retreated to prepared positions further up the hill.

When Adam's company rushed to the other side of the ploughed field, they found their opponents had gone. They moved forward cautiously and the mortaring began again. Adam ordered a multiple mortar forward, which silenced the Canadian mortar battery, the forest erupting in flames as its shells landed. The ground levelled off once more onto another plateau. Another farmhouse with an adjoining wooden store lay in the centre of a clearing.

The Canadians were well hidden and had learned the virtue of patience. Silence descended once more. "I don't like this, Captain," said Hans Thaelmann. Adam felt the same way, but they had been ordered to take the top of the hill.

"Covering fire," Adam ordered. He signalled two half-tracks to the edge of the clearing and assigned two battle squads to the assault. Adam's arm fell and a storm of artillery fire descended on the far side of the clearing. He raised his arm and the rush to the farmhouse began.

They ran into a minefield. Two men were killed instantly. No one else could move until the armoured vehicles had made a safe path through the danger. Adam had begun with ten men. He was now down to five. Wolters and Henne lay gasping on the farmhouse floor.

Adam had made a mistake. The building was a perfect target and shells came through the walls and windows at close range. A shell splinter hit Heinrich Henne in his left arm. "Get into the outbuilding behind the house," ordered Adam, and Wolters helped Henne.

Stamm led the way in, after forcing a rusty bolt with a piece of farm machinery. It appeared safe. "Get the hell out of here, it's a fuel store!"" he suddenly shouted. He had noticed the smell of paraffin.

Wolters and Henne were the last out as the rest rushed for the trees. Adam looked back to see Henne trying to make his own way out of the shed, waving Bastian Wolters to go on alone. A shell hit the store and Heinrich Henne was covered in paraffin, which quickly caught fire and ignited the ammunition in a bandolier round his neck. Wolters stared at him, stupefied.

The Canadians ceased fire and Henne lay barely moving. He reached upwards and then his hand fell limply. Adam ordered Wolters to leave him to the medics. The Canadians were driven off the top of the hill, but dug in on the reverse slopes. The Ninth was relieved and returned to their billets to count the cost.

Adam threw his machine pistol onto the old trestle table, tearing the map. It seemed a comment on all the effort and frustrated aims. He walked as purposefully as he could to find the remains of his company. It was a bright sunny day and they were lying everywhere it was possible. Some were propped up against straw bales, some against the walls of the old farmhouse. Others lay on the grass with open tunics, smoking. The veterans seemed relaxed, but some of the young recruits shook. They made a pretence of getting up and snapping to attention. Adam waved them back.

One of the survivors was missing. "Where's Wolters?" demanded Adam. Eberling appeared from the direction of the medics tents. He too had been looking for Wolters. "He's over there," said Eberling pointing to a figure emerging from the tents.

"I know they were all told to keep out of the medic's way," said a tired Eberling, who then wandered off to his special mattress in the barn and fell asleep, barely acknowledging Adam.

Wolters approached Adam. "Have you seen Henne?" he asked, expecting the worst. Wolters just nodded. The young trooper, schooled in the heartless obedience of National Socialist Germany, expected some punishment.

"How is he?" asked Adam. Wolters shook his head and was close to tears. "Did you know him well?" continued the young captain.

"My best friend, Captain," he replied and volunteered information which surprised Adam. "He was a toff," said Wolters. "He lived in a big house in Dahlem in Berlin. His family made a fuss of me." Adam thought of Bruno and feared for his safety.

Before he slept that night, Adam pored over his photographs. He had believed that the feeling that he could do anything had come from Gustav, but his mother's death made the young aristocrat see the reality. He missed her terribly and felt his strength drain away as he handled the photograph.

Instinctively he reached for Gabrielle's photograph. He hadn't heard from her for several weeks and the worst fears plagued him. Adam knew the police were likely to discover their reunion and he shuddered when he remembered how reckless they had been at the school.

He began to construct an imaginary world for himself, Gabrielle and their little daughter. His daydreams fired his determination to find her. Meanwhile his responsibility lay with his men. Sergeant Schultz of the new company was dead, his fellow sergeant badly wounded. It fell to Thaelmann and Stamm to pick up the pieces. Nearly a quarter of the company was dead, missing or wounded and no replacements arrived. There was an endless supply of weapons and ammunition without troops to use it.

Adam's company had suffered a level of casualties which might have drained morale in some units. He promoted Klaus Eberling to Sergeant and asked him what he needed. He immediately asked for Bastian Wolters to join the new platoon as a Corporal.

Some Canadian and Polish prisoners were brought through the encampment with an assortment of surrendered weapons piled high in the back of a captured radio truck. Adam, Thaelmann and Stamm examined them. There was hardly an automatic weapon there and the three men wondered how the enemy commanders could send their soldiers against a much better-armed opponent.

The three men of the Hohenstaufen grasped at straws. Surely they must win in the end because they were better equipped, and even Adam subscribed to this fatal belief. Only Klaus Eberling saw the reality and kept it to himself. Too many men had died and for the first time, there were no replacements.

New orders were not long in coming; a motorcyclist arrived from their Battalion. The division was to march behind the German lines to the south in broad daylight to counter a new threat, and was to leave immediately. Adam slapped the order down on his table in front of the messenger. There wasn't a trace of defeatism and he knew the men would fight. But to ask them to move without air support was nothing short of callous. He looked again at the order. It was certain, it said, that the English were about to break into the German rear areas and only the SS could stop them. At least there was a concession. There would be tank support. He looked at the sky as he strapped his machine pistol to his shoulder. The clouds were grey and low. At least enemy observation planes wouldn't see them.

Mechanics had somehow stolen or begged enough parts to get two half-tracks in running order. Eberling's little pets, two heavy anti-tank guns, were hitched to the vehicles and he patted them affectionately. There were no other vehicles to pull the rest of the stores, the caissons of shells for the guns and the fuel supply. A team of two horses under the supervision of Karl Eberhardt, the gentle farmer, was to do the job.

Eberhardt gave the others hope. Alone among the older troops he seemed to remain the same, rejecting the temptation to become cynical. He looked after the two horses as if he was at home on the farm. Without trooper Friedrich's knowledge, Eberhardt removed the bale of hay the young soldier used as a seat in the old barn. Friedrichs complained to Bastian Wolters, "He's fed my seat to the horses."

The Ninth's luck held, for the moment. It made a perfect target confined to such a narrow track, but the clouds were lower and it drizzled persistently. After an hour it stopped raining, but the heat and humidity made the men uncomfortable in their battle kit. Wolters looked up to a patch of blue sky above them, which was getting bigger and bigger. "Shit," he said to himself. Adam, riding on a half-track, examined his map. In half an hour they would be safe from aircraft, having perhaps joined battle.

One small aircraft flew slowly above them. The soldiers watched the puffs of explosions of anti-aircraft shells which failed to bring it down and it flew away to the west. Any banter there had been amongst the soldiers stopped as they anxiously scanned the sky. Adam looked for cover on both sides of the road; by now the sky was almost cloudless.

Three aircraft fell out of the base of a great white cloud, one after another. The soldiers of the Ninth scattered into the ditches by one side of the road or into heather and woodland on the other and buried their faces in the earth.

CHAPTER TWENTY THREE

The first salvo of rockets hit the ammunition store. The fireball destroyed vehicles and incinerated their passengers. The second salvo missed Adam's half-track, giving him a chance to seek cover in a small copse. From there he watched helplessly. The others watched Eberhardt as he struggled with his horses. The terrified animals reared up and refused to go anywhere as more rockets hit the column behind them. Eberhardt struggled to stop the horses overturning the cart carrying the supply of fuel.

"Leave them Eberhardt, leave them. Over here!" shouted Stamm.

"He won't leave them," shouted Wolters, running to help. The first aircraft had turned to attack again and cannon shells exploded all around Wolters, who was thrown to the ground holding his leg. A driverless half-track, burning furiously crashed into the cart, several soldiers hanging over the side lifeless. Burning fragments fell on to the fuel drums. "Run for it!" shouted Wolters, but still Eberhardt refused to leave.

Adam threw his machine pistol down and ran towards Eberhardt and the horses, just as the cart caught fire. "God help him," said Stamm, bracing himself. He ran and dragged Wolters to safety. The young trooper wanted to go back but Stamm restrained him. "You'll be in the way," he warned.

"Cut them free from the cart, Captain," shouted Eberhardt. Adam drew his dagger and began to saw at the leather straps, feeling his arms and neck begin to burn. Eberhardt led both horses away, while Adam ran as fast as he could towards the ditch with parts of his tunic smouldering.

One of the horses reared and Eberhardt fell. Adam turned back to help and was relieved to see Wolters lift Eberhardt's arms. Between them they carried the farmer to safety. The cart exploded as they collapsed into the ditch and Stamm pushed Adam into stagnant water to douse his smouldering uniform. He spluttered, coughed and asked after Eberhardt. The ex-farmer had only been stunned. As he was helped to his feet, the two horses stood and watched.

Wrecked and burning tanks blocked the road and there were no bulldozers to remove them. Ten had been destroyed and thirteen damaged. Ammunition and fuel supplies for the company were gone.

Eberling showed a concern for the ex-farmer which surprised him. He poured water from a stagnant ditch over Eberhardt. "Thank God you're all right, you great fuckin' useless yokel. Help me get this half-track out of the ditch," he growled. They used Adam's half-track to pull it out while Adam's burns were attended to. Thaelmann examined the vehicle with Stamm. "Waste of fuckin' time," he said. "It's knackered."

A military policeman arrived on a motorcycle and handed a message to two officers who were assessing the damage. "You can go back to base, Captain," one of them said to Adam "The English attack has been stopped."

Adam sat on a tree stump and surveyed the scene, bandages covering his forehead and the back of his neck. Wrecked vehicles littered the country lane as far as he could see. His company had suffered more casualties, some with serious wounds and another young soldier, August Kohl, was dead. For the first time he felt a sense of helpless anger. Kaspar sat down by him sensing his captain's mood. "Where was our fuckin' Air Force, Captain?" he asked.

Stamm, Thaelmann and Eberling thought Adam might have to be relieved. Any such thoughts were forgotten when they decided the company couldn't fight without him. He interrupted their conference to assure them he was all right and told them to do a morale assessment. They were ashamed of themselves.

"Friedrichs is in pain, Captain. We have no morphine," one of the medics said. The young trooper lay on an improvised bed a metre above ground. His features were twisted with pain and he couldn't acknowledge Adam. Yet another young recruit was wounded, another victim of a frivolous order.

Adam marched to a field telephone and demanded to speak to the Battalion Commander to ask if morphine could be spared. The answer was negative and Adam replaced the telephone. He thought of little else but young Trooper Ernst Friedrichs. He was Wolters' latest friend and must not be allowed to die. Bastian Wolters stood by his new friend holding his hand. He lost consciousness. "Don't you die on me as well," said the young Corporal.

The company hid under camouflage netting waiting for the inevitable order to join battle and again there were no replacements. Friedrich's cries unnerved the younger soldiers.

Klaus Eberling drew Adam's attention to the insignia on the uniforms of a column of prisoners. He'd recognised the Polish eagle immediately. "I thought we'd beaten that lot," said Eberling ruefully. "The Ivans were supposed to bump off the ones we missed." Adam shuddered.

CHAPTER TWENTY THREE

Another column of prisoners arrived from the south. A panic-stricken cook appeared in Adams billet, afraid he'd have to feed them, and Adam put his mind at rest. These were Americans and carried themselves confidently. The young captain looked ruefully to the south and wondered what this meant.

A long way from Normandy, two teachers sat in a corner of their staff room, separate from their colleagues. Gabrielle had just asked a friend, Eva, to take a risk. She had agreed and her friend passed her a letter. Eva was to post it as soon as possible away from the prying eyes of Gabrielle's husband. Franz Ackermann had intercepted nearly every letter she had posted or received from her lover, determined that a man of his standing would not be belittled and that his wife should not enjoy a relationship outside their crumbling marriage.

Eva knew her friend and possibly she herself were under police surveillance, but accepted that Gabrielle could not tell her why. The rest was up to the Reich Military Post, and this letter was very special.

They watched the Americans trudging off into the distance. "Maybe a few less for us to deal with," said Hans ruefully. As he spoke the post arrived and the company came to life. Adam hoped it was good news for all of them. He had just heard from Frieda and was delighted with the move to Alfred Rust's house. He wasn't expecting more mail but a motorcyclist roared up and presented him with an envelope. "I'll leave you to enjoy it Captain," said Thaelmann, and Adam retired to his tent mystified, having already accepted that it was now too dangerous for Gabrielle to continue their correspondence.

The light was fading and he placed the letter on the old table, removed the map and lit the paraffin lamp. The letter felt bulky and he recognised Gabrielle's handwriting immediately. He used his dagger as a letter opener and inside found another smaller envelope.

> "*My darling,*" began Gabrielle, "*we can talk to one another once more thanks to Eva. Please don't reprove me for asking her to take a terrible risk. She thinks she's in this with us. I have decided at least that you really are part of my family and that you should know a little of its newest member. I won't say any more. The contents of the little envelope will say it all for me. All my love to you my darling, Gaby.*"

Adam carefully opened the small envelope. Inside was a photograph of Gabrielle sitting on a tree stump. On her knee was a little blonde girl with billowing curls who looked just like her mother. The little girl was holding a cloth elephant, which she clearly intended to be the star of the photograph.

The background was a shingle beach with a small rowing boat. The tea house was just visible through the breach in the perimeter wall. Gabrielle had written on the back of the photograph. "I'm Aunt Gabby and this is Katerina with Effy." Adam buried his head in his hands and sobbed himself to sleep.

He never failed to rise at six o'clock to conduct an inspection of the remnants of his company. Some wore helmets, others only forage caps. A few carried machine-pistols, most the standard issue rifle. Michael Kaspar now carried an English rifle with a pillaged store of ammunition. He said it was better for sniping than the German equivalent.

There were two serviceable half-tracks with an insufficient fuel supply. Bastian Wolters had just finished painting a Canadian radio truck with black crosses. His new friend Friedrichs stopped to say goodbye before being repatriated to recover.

The more experienced didn't refer to the youngest recruits as kids any more. They were all veterans who had prematurely aged. They were tired and red-eyed, some with an empty stare. None of them had lost the will to fight and they found it hard to imagine a life away from the battlefield. There seemed to be a self-evident truth. The Hohenstaufen was there to fight until it no longer existed.

The Division had been in Normandy for nearly a month when the last call to battle came in mid-July. Adam's company was to march north-east and was given a map reference centred on a small town called Falaise. Once again, Canadians threatened to pierce the German rear, he was told. The front had to be 'consolidated,' said a voice devoid of enthusiasm at the other end of the field telephone.

Eberling, Thaelmann and Stamm lined up the company under the security of a copse and Adam issued instructions. Gabrielle's letter had infused him with a new energy. He had lost his fatalism and had decided he would not knowingly squander the lives of the men under his command. He even disobeyed an order, refusing to move until they were joined by a column of new Tiger and Panther tanks.

CHAPTER TWENTY THREE

A few brand new tanks arrived and Wolters and Eberling started the half-track engines. Above the noise, Adam announced, "The Canadians haven't learnt their lesson. We march to turn them back again." The few that were left climbed aboard the half-tracks. A motorcyclist roared up to Adam in the leading half-track. "You are to advance round the northern end of the enemy lines," he said.

Adam glanced backwards at his makeshift company. He believed whoever had issued that order must be mad. He looked at the men crammed into the second half track driven by Eberling, who half grinned to show he was ready. Wolters brandished his machine-pistol and pointed to the tattered pennant. Stamm, Thaelmann, Wolters and Kaspar had all touched it. Eberling thought they'd lost their wits.

Another motorcyclist appeared to announce they were to make haste. Adam remembered the books he and Bruno had read as he listened to the noise of the battle behind them growing louder. There, he believed, was the source of the danger. He thought they must soon face American troops.

The Hofenstaufen joined the Frundsberg Division and together they made what speed they could. The two divisions had been led to believe they were threatening the northern flank of the enemy line. In fact they ran into it.

They raced down a country lane which joined a main road running west to east. What remained of the German army in Normandy was trying to escape down it. Adam trained his binoculars on the sorry sight. Thousands of bedraggled and defeated men approached the two Waffen SS Divisions. Dozens of horses pulled what remained of the army supplies. Some even dragged anti-tank guns. The beaten soldiers had even lost the habit of scanning the sky, which was now a clear blue. The retreating soldiers made a perfect target.

Eberling had not lost the habit and when he saw the dots peel out of the sky he jumped onto the captured radio truck and helped Trooper Matthias to man the anti-aircraft gun. When the aircraft had gone, dozens of horses lay dead or dying and bodies were strewn over the road. Bedraggled men appeared from behind Adam's company from the security of the trees and a lieutenant informed Adam that the Americans would soon be here. Adam demanded that he help to form a line of defence.

"Against which line of advance, Captain?" he asked in despair. "The

English, the Poles or the Americans?" He trudged past Adam and ordered his men to join the retreating column. Adam nearly allowed Kaspar to shoot him.

There appeared to be no enemy column on the main road and Adam looked at his map, but his attention was drawn to movements on a ridge twenty metres above them to their right. Then came another order on the radio, which Adam believed was a cruel joke. "Hold the front! Stop the retreat," a voice said. "There are no enemy forces to your right."

Adam trained his binoculars on vehicles moving on the ridge, where he saw weapons carriers and tanks. Straining his eyes, he saw the Polish eagle on their sides. "Make a roadblock, Eberling," he called out. "Get the guns on that road in any way you can."

The way was blocked by a stream with a narrow bridge, just wide enough for the guns to cross and be hauled up the slope. Adam watched the advancing Poles again. They hadn't seen the German soldiers, perhaps because the sun was in their eyes.

Then the shelling began from the west. The first shells tore into trees on the other side of the road. The next salvos fell on the retreating column. Eberhardt stared helplessly at the carnage. "Move across the bridge, Eberhardt," ordered Adam.

The ex-farmer did the best he could. His horses were terrified and he dismounted and tried to lead them across. The shells began to fall nearer and nearer. Eberhardt managed to lead his team across the bridge. Most of the regular troops watched sullenly, as if they believed further resistance was nonsensical. Some resumed their retreat while others halted, afraid of what the SS might do, blocking the way with a team of horses. The Corporal in charge whipped the animals, intent on making his escape.

A shell fell on the road and the horses shied and reared up in terror, crashing into the caisson of shells Adam and Wolters were attempting to get over the bridge. The driver began to whip the terrified horses. Eberhardt ran back over the bridge and told the driver to stop. He took no notice and the ex-farmer levelled his machine-pistol at the man, who pointed to the Corporal's insignia on his sleeve. Eberhardt fired a warning burst into the road and levelled his weapon at the driver once more.

The horses seemed to calm down when their persecutor left his seat. Eberhardt climbed up and tried to calm the horses, but they saw the other animals and tried to follow them to the other side of the stream and Eberhardt couldn't stop them. A shell burst on the bridge at its far side and fractured the trelliswork. The structure cracked and began to collapse.

One of the horses broke its reins and fell into the water. Eberhardt was pulled in but freed himself and began to swim for the bank while the Company watched anxiously. The second horse followed the first as the bridge collapsed sideways. The animal fell on Eberhardt, who disappeared under the water.

Wolters threw his gun on to the bank and threw off his boots. He dived into the water and disappeared into the deep pool under the bridge. The second horse reappeared, thrashing in the water. Wolters' head appeared. He took a deep breath and dived again, but it was too late for Karl Eberhardt. Wolters reappeared with his body, laying it on limestone blocks in the shallows and staring at it helplessly. Eberling rushed down the slope into the stream and began to pump Eberhardt's chest. He looked up helplessly at Adam and held out his hands.

"We must stop the Poles, Eberling," Adam reminded him. Klaus Eberling's soul surfaced for a moment as he knelt protectively over Eberhardt's body and he looked hard at Adam. The young officer placed his hand on his shoulder. "We will retrieve our comrade after we have dealt with the enemy," he said quietly. Wolters lifted Eberhardt's body onto the bank reverently.

Eberling's anti-tank gun reduced some of the Polish vehicles to twisted wreckage and the rest withdrew for the moment. He set up a roadblock on the ridge waiting for the inevitable counter-attack. Kaspar led the surviving horse out of the water and hitched it to an empty wagon. Without waiting for orders, Trooper Kastner helped Kaspar to lift Eberhardt's body into the cart. "He goes back with us," said Adam. "Who can handle the horse?" he asked hopefully. Michael Kaspar took the reins. "Stay here," ordered Adam.

He joined Eberling behind the gun and Eberling patted its barrel. "Knackered, Captain," he said.

"Stay on the road for now," ordered Adam, anxious to show his men had not joined the general retreat.

Polish reinforcements then arrived, and the position had to be abandoned. Adam received another order, a reminder not to retreat. He laughed at a command which he knew had been issued in complete isolation from the battlefield, with the Field Commander already on his way home.

Enemy aircraft attacked the retreating column again. "Jabos, Jabos!" was the cry and the beaten soldiers threw themselves into the ditches. Matthias Eckhardt stayed behind his anti-aircraft gun on the back of the captured radio truck. It disintegrated, hit by a rocket. No one tried to retrieve the remains of the young trooper.

Eberhardt's body lay in the cart by the bank of the stream as the remnants of the Hohenstaufen division fought on. There was no more ammunition for Eberling's anti-tank gun and his crew spiked it in a pointless gesture.

Temporary rescue was at hand. The Tenth, the Frundsberg Division, marched across the rear of the Hohenstaufen. A heavy tank clattered up the road and its commander asked who was in charge. "Get the hell out of here, Captain. They think you've had enough back there," he said. Adam radioed Battalion Headquarters, but there was no answer and the tank commander was the only authority.

He looked at the remnants of his company and the cart bearing Eberhardt's body. "Eberhardt is going home men, and so are we," he said

. "I'll stay and fight the bastards, "offered Eberling.

"You've done enough Sergeant," said Adam.

The jaws of the Allied pincer were closing. The Americans arrived, but too thinly, and the men of Canada hesitated. For the second time in his career, Adam commanded regular army soldiers. He turned to face the west, but the enemy did not come. They had failed to close the jaws of the trap.

The remnants of the Ninth and Tenth had escaped and the battlefield became silent.

Eberhardt was laid to rest and his comrades said a few words. As they walked away from the small copse where they had buried him, Bastian Wolters remarked on the loneliness of the grave. "Some day he will rejoin his comrades of the three lions," Adam assured him, marking the location on the map.

Men from the north and south joined them and Adam found himself commanding nearly five hundred soldiers. They trudged on over the old battlefields of the First World War towards Cambrai, and Adam wondered if his father had fought here.

They were startled out of their limbo when Hans Thaelmann ordered his half-track to stop and scanned the horizon. Enemy tanks crashed through the hedges and Adam joined Klaus Eberling amongst trees, concealing the guns. They waited for what they believed was the inevitable destruction of their small force. The enemy tanks came on unsuspecting. "Well, Captain," said Eberling, "this is just like the old days in Russia. This time we don't have to run for the guns."

There was a roar of aero engines from the east and the soldiers clawed the ground. Wolters glanced upwards. He jumped out of his fox hole shouting, "They're ours, they're ours!"

"You beauties!" shouted Kastner. The aircraft destroyed several tanks and flew away. The daylight failed and Adam ordered his force to slip away to the east. It seemed their agony had ended.

The remaining half-track from Adam's company still flew the yellow pennant, now blackened and torn. During the night the exhausted survivors limped away in the direction of the defences of the west wall. Only thirty men had survived of the hundred and forty from Adam's company.

By the end of July, the Hohenstaufen division was sunning itself behind the west wall. There was no leadership, no direction. They just sat and waited on the banks of the river Rhine. Thaelmann, Stamm and Wolters sat on a bench overlooking the river, staring at the half-timbered buildings on the far shore and half-completed gun emplacements. A single-span metal bridge was just visible to the north.

"Is that the next thing we'll defend, Sergeant?" Wolters asked Stamm.

They wandered back to their new billets to be greeted by some excitement. Civilians had just arrived and a man in a trilby hat had discarded his jacket to enable him to climb a lamppost and secure a loudspeaker. Adam informed his men that they had been ordered to listen to a special radio broadcast, but no one seemed in the least interested. The radio crackled. "Berlin calling," said the announcer, who informed his listeners The Führer himself was to address them.

"That's nice," said Eberling. "We haven't heard from him for a while." The civilian visitors were State Police, who made sure the defeated soldiers were listening. The sharpness had gone from Hitler's voice and he sounded like an old man, but as always he commanded attention. He announced that high-ranking officers in the army had tried to assassinate him. He told his listeners he had been spared by providence to continue his life's work.

Kaspar believed it. "The bastards," he said. "It's like the First War. Someone at home stabs us in the back. I hope they tear their bollocks off," he added bitterly.

Bastian Wolters was in tears and Adam consoled him. "We fight on, Wolters. You can be certain of that," he assured the young soldier.

Magically, the news of the attempt on Hitler's life made Adam's company doubly determined to continue the struggle, if necessary to the death. In the daytime, Adam's professional commitment overrode every other thought. But the late evening was devoted to thoughts of his new family. He never forgot who had made all this possible and did everything he could to discover what had happened to Bruno. Franz Stamm volunteered to find out. Against orders, he wandered into neighbouring leaguers to make enquiries, while military police looked the other way. No one knew anything of the Reconnaissance Battalion except one man. "Radio contact was lost with them," he said. "When we had tanks we needed those boys. They just disappeared."

Stamm was as unwilling as Adam to accept that Bruno was probably dead. He just reported to Adam that no one knew and the police discouraged further enquiries.

Of the eighteen thousand men who had reached the battlefield in early June, six thousand remained. No longer referred to as a division, they were to be called the Hohenstaufen Regiment. This time, they moved in daylight to a secret destination.

The train stopped only once, at Duisburg to take on equipment and a few replacements. It continued north-west over the Dutch border.

"I know where we are," said Hans Thaelmann as the train crossed the Waal into Nijmegen. Franz Stamm was almost asleep, but his interest in the conversation revived as the train rattled over the Waal Bridge. "Thaelmann had a girlfriend here," he mumbled. "He still writes to her."

The Battalion Commander appeared as they were crossing a big bridge over the Rhine. "Welcome to your rest area gentlemen," he said. "This is the town of Arnhem and your only challenge will be the lousy weather."

The survivors of each company piled out of the train on to the deserted platform. The engine reversed out of the station, leaving them high and dry. It was burning hot and the men sat on their kit and laid weapons on the platform. A few Dutch passengers appeared on other platforms to catch what few trains now ran. Every possible vehicle, military or civilian was commandeered to get them to their new leaguers. They were driven through Arnhem watched by civilians behind closed shutters, thankful that the occupiers' army was on the run.

Adam watched the caterpillar tracks of the vehicle in front leaving permanent ruts in the road. It was a small thing but yet another peaceful town was to be a victim of war. He looked upwards to both sides of the streets, remembering the dispossessed farmers in France. He saw nothing but resentment on the faces of the few people who showed themselves in Arnhem.

The Company drove north-west out of the town into featureless country. The monotony of the countryside was broken by a succession of copses in the near distance. Sheltering near them under camouflage netting were tanks and heavy artillery. He guessed that this must be their destination. For once the sky was empty.

The area swarmed with military police. Each company was assigned an area and enough tents had already been erected. Waiting outside them, looking lost and mystified, was the latest batch of replacements. They were intruders, in a sense. These young men, some of them only seventeen years old, were to join veterans.

"What do you want?" asked Hans Thaelmann, standing in front of them hands on hips. One young man with a shock of red hair stepped forward, unabashed, and announced that they were here to join the Hohenstaufen Regiment. Wolters grinned at him and thought he saw a kindred spirit. Thaelmann gave the new soldiers a billet and announced that there would be weapons drill and equipment checks in the morning at six.

It was the beginning of the way back. Bastian Wolters sought out the red-haired recruit, who was sitting round the campfire with three others. They jumped up as if Wolters was an officer. He laughed.

"What's your name?" he asked the red haired recruit.

"Hans Maier," was the reply.

"Are you a miserable bastard, Maier?" asked Wolters. The young newcomer was taken aback and replied defiantly "All the time. What of it?"

Wolters laughed. "I've lost my best friend in Normandy, I need a replacement."

"Why me?" asked the new recruit.

"Because any bugger who'll talk to me must be crazy," Wolters answered. Maier laughed, shook hands and introduced his friends.

They wanted answers. "Listen to Thaelmann, Stamm and Eberling. They're as tough as old boots," advised Wolters. "Our captain is von Saloman. He's the very best. I think he saved us. Do you get it?" he asked.

They thought they did and Wolters slipped off, refreshed and able to face another disheartening talk with Kaspar. He hadn't mentioned the pennant and chided himself for thinking he belonged to an exclusive club.

Adam treasured the letters from home. He loved Frieda's assessment of everyone around her. She now regarded Ilse Diels not as a danger but an eccentric spinster who needed support.

He constantly asked for news of Bruno. Helga had heard nothing since the beginning of July, but Frieda was certain there would be news soon. She chose not to tell Adam about the conversation she had had with Greta when Frieda had enquired after Bruno. Greta told Frieda that Helga had said that it might be better for everyone if Bruno didn't come back.

Chapter 24

Wolters wandered off through the trees with his new friend towards the main road to Apeldoorn, looking southwards towards a dust cloud. Already military police lined the road and one of them was getting ready to direct traffic. Wolters asked a policeman what was going on.

"Reconnaissance Battalion Hohenstaufen is coming in," he replied.

"Follow me Maier," shouted Wolters. The two ran as fast as they could to Adam's tent. "The captain's busy," barked Stamm. Adam was holding a field telephone and looking perplexed and motioned Wolters to wait.

"What do you want?" asked the Sergeant.

"Reconnaissance is coming in, Sergeant," said Wolters breathlessly.

Adam replaced the phone and all four of them ran to the road in time to see the remnants of Bruno's battalion. The roadside was crammed with spectators from several companies peering anxiously at the survivors. First came the motorcycle combinations with machine-guns protruding from sidecars. Not one man wore a steel helmet. A few of the infantry rode in captured staff cars, some standing on the running boards. They stared ahead of them, only one or two acknowledging the spectators. One wore the khaki tunic of an English soldier with the mottled camouflaged trousers of the Waffen SS.

Adam counted not more than eighty men before the rear guard came into view, two dented and scarred armoured cars. Franz Stamm stared through binoculars at the commander of the second one. "He's OK, Captain," said Franz Stamm as he spotted Bruno. Adam trained his binoculars on his old friend, but this was not the Bruno of old.

He was haggard and unshaven. He threw his headphones into the recesses of the armoured car as if he thought they were no longer necessary and he too stared ahead. Adam and Franz looked at him, hoping he would react to them. Bruno seemed to pretend not to see them.

"Brakes, Wem," he ordered. The Puma came to a halt and Herbert Wem's head appeared at the driving hatch. Bruno and Robert Klopp, the gunner, jumped down to greet Adam and his comrades. Some colour appeared in Bruno's face. "Where the hell are we?" he asked. He couldn't have cared about seniority at first, but then he remembered his friend's rank. He saluted as smartly as he could for the benefit of the others. They shook hands warmly.

Klopp reached into the car and waved several bottles acquired in Normandy. "One of those is mine," called another voice from inside the car.

"We kept those in case you were alive." said Bruno.

"Move off lieutenant," said Adam. "We'll celebrate our good luck tonight."

"Flex your drinking muscles, Stamm," said Bruno. He jumped back into the Puma and rejoined the survivors.

"What do you think, gentlemen?" asked Adam.

"He's knackered, Captain. His hands shook all the time," said Hans Thaelmann.

"I agree," said Stamm. We've work to do turning children into men," he reminded his Sergeants. Hans Thaelmann made a telling remark. "Have you forgotten how old we are, Captain, maybe six years or so older than them?"

"How old do you feel?" Adam asked grimly.

Bruno marched past Adam's perimeter guards carrying a bottle in each hand. It didn't seem appropriate to trooper Bergman to acknowledge the visiting Lieutenant, who was clearly intent on a drinking bout, but he did so. "Tell anyone under the rank of Major we are not to be disturbed," said Bruno.

At precisely nine o'clock, as arranged, Adam's friend pulled back the tent flap, strode in and made a dilatory salute, throwing his cap on the table.

"You look terrible Bruno," began Adam.

"You don't," replied Bruno, "but given time you might. I have a considerable amount of drink here." He banged two bottles of Calvados on to Adam's trestle table. "Touché" said Adam, producing a bottle of schnapps.

Bruno hadn't forgotten their other comrades. "Are those two busy?" he asked. "And who's this hard case Eberling?"

"Standing by," rejoined Adam, who produced another bottle, this time of vintage cider.

Within two minutes, Adam appeared with the three men. The visitors shook hands with Bruno and mess tins had to substitute for glasses. "To us and our survival," said Bruno.

Klaus Eberling looked uncomfortable. Bruno took pity on him. "Whose idea was this attempt at suicide?" he asked, pointing to the Iron Crosses. Eberling was still uncomfortable. These after all were officers. "This is different Klaus. You'll soon get the hang of it," said Stamm, filling Eberling's mess tin with more Calvados.

"In this gathering Eberling, everybody talks or there's big trouble," Thaelmann said.

Sergeant Eberling seemed more comfortable when he reminded himself these men were all as hardened as he was. "I believe it was Eberling's idea," said Adam, making his new sergeant the centre of attention.

"But the captain had to carry me back," said Eberling. "I've had to live that down ever since."

"You can be grateful you didn't have to carry the captain," said Bruno.

"Or Thaelmann," added Stamm.

Adam suggested a 'polite' toast. "To the Führer and final victory," he said. The Sergeants left to continue their own celebrations. It was Hans Thaelmann's birthday.

The mood became a little more sombre as the two friends talked of home. Adam said Frieda and Greta had settled well in Alfred Rust's home and Bruno showed Adam a photograph of Helga and Manfred.

The conversation quickly turned to Gabrielle. "You're not going to leave her with that smug party bastard are you?" asked Bruno. "You've got to chase her down."

"I intend to when the High Command gives me an opportunity," said Adam. Bruno's eyebrows rose. He brandished the photo of Manfred, implying there was something missing from Adam's relationship.

"Perhaps not," replied his friend, reaching into his tunic pocket and producing the leather wallet Bruno knew so well. Adam became quite serious. "I had decided before you arrived there was something you ought to know." He showed Bruno the latest photo of Gabrielle and Katerina. Bruno's face lit up. "Yours?" he asked. Adam nodded.

"So there's life below your waist after all!" said Bruno. "I'm truly proud of you."

Adam then told his friend of the risks involved, but not about the Hotel in Bavaria. "I might never see you again, so I don't give a damn for the police," retorted Bruno.

They drank just enough to be able to understand each other. "Well Captain," said Bruno. "Here we are in Holland in a totally uninteresting place. I know you have the ear of the generals. Why do you think we're here?"

"I think the bosses want us to have a quiet month or so before sending us off to plug another gap," answered Adam.

"Show me a map of the area," said Bruno. Adam spread it and knocked over a tin of schnapps.

"Clumsy bugger," slurred Bruno. He took a long hard look at the map and scratched his unshaven chin. "Here we are in Arnhem," he continued swaying gently on his chair. "Which we must agree is a fuckin' awful place even in summer," he added.

Adam attempted to speak, swaying on his chair. "No," said Bruno holding up his hand. "Listen – because I know what's going on. If the bosses had wanted us to have a good time, they'd have sent us to Baden Baden with a few bottles of beer."

Michael Kaspar opened the tent flap to report a change of the guard. "Give me your rifle, soldier," ordered Bruno. Kaspar looked forlorn, but handed over his closest friend.

Bruno nearly fell over backwards in an attempt to place his hand on his friend's shoulder, placing Kaspar's rifle across the map.

"There's a feature of some interest in this area," said Bruno, "and do you know what it is? He stood up uncertainly. "I'll tell you. It's the road bridge over the Rhine." He waited and Adam nodded.

"That clever bastard Montgomery is only sixty miles away," continued Bruno. "The quickest way to our backyard in Berlin is over that bridge," he added, laying the stock of Kaspar's rifle on Arnhem and pointing the barrel at Berlin.

"You can have it back soldier," said Bruno, returning the weapon to its owner. Kaspar tried to hide an almost homicidal look.

"Now," Bruno resumed. "That English bastard kicked our arses in Normandy. He's thinking of doing it again." Adam fell off his chair, then gave his opinion kneeling. "Not him. It'll be Patton, the American."

"No it won't," said Bruno. "He's pissing about down south in a fuckin' forest."

Adam slowly passed out and Bruno watched him. He patted Adam's face and broke into tears. "Bye old friend," he said, kissed him on the forehead and staggered back to his platoon.

Bruno was ordered to return to Germany. He was to help in the assessment of a new model of armoured car at the tank testing site in Thuringia. It wasn't leave, but he was granted three extra days to spend with his family. Two thoughts occupied his mind on the train journey to Charlottenburg. Helga would be delighted to hear about Katerina, but what could he tell her about the circumstances of her birth? Adam had told him nothing beyond the fact of the birth. Helga would demand to know more and Bruno knew she had always been a little in love with his friend. Bruno decided that rather than tell his wife the bald fact of the birth and nothing else, he would remain true to his promise to Adam, extracted before the serious drinking began, to tell no one at all of Katerina's existence. One day it would be safe to talk.

Another thought preoccupied Bruno the nearer the train got to Berlin. Before the Normandy battles began, he had decided to give up Karin Haller. His decision might prove to be irrelevant, he knew, if Helga had found the letter from Karin. He believed that such a meticulously tidy person as his wife was bound to have done so.

Helga was waiting at the station with Manfred. To Bruno's relief, she kissed him and clung to him. He lifted Manfred and kissed him. The little boy stood between them, grasped their hands and pulled them towards the waiting taxi. Bruno couldn't help but notice that every other building seemed to have suffered bomb damage.

Their flat was intact and Helga couldn't wait to show Bruno all the changes she had made, but he showed little interest. He was edgy, bad-tempered and spent much of the time sleeping, except at night when he paced up and down outside the bedroom.

Helga had promised to take Bruno and Manfred to a Ladies' Circle meeting at Alfred Rust's house. The numbers had swelled to such an extent that the couple had to fight their way through to reach Frieda and Greta. Frieda looked a little frail and smiled her greeting. Greta seized Bruno. "You look awful, my dear boy," she said. "Whatever is the matter?" She led him to

Frieda and Bruno kissed her on the cheek. He studied her look of reserve and reflected on how he had learnt how to break down Adam's similar look. He decided this was not the time and place to do it.

Helga's National Socialist beliefs were as strong as ever and she led her husband to the centre of the room with Manfred. She informed the gathering that Bruno had taken part in the heaviest fighting in France. She took Manfred's hand and promised the ladies that victory would mean a better future for them all.

Bruno was embarrassed. "Go on, Hette," said Frieda to a small shy lady who was one of Alfred's neighbours. "You wanted to ask Lieutenant Grabowsky something. Please tell us about Captain von Saloman, Lieutenant."

Most of the time Bruno had spent recently with Adam had been in a drinking bout, which Bruno didn't mention. He told Hette Meisl that the captain was in good health and was admired by his company. Helga cast a few black looks in Bruno's direction because it seemed that was all her husband intended to say.

Another member of the group showed little enthusiasm for Bruno's contribution to the meeting. Ilse Diels turned her head away repeatedly and refused to look him in the eye. Bruno wasn't intimidated and sat next to her when refreshments were served meagre though they were.

"You don't seem to approve of the sacrifices made by the Waffen SS at the front, Frau Diels," said Bruno quietly.

"I approve of the sacrifices made by all good Aryans for the Fatherland, Lieutenant," she replied. Bruno was mystified by her answer but took it as a hint to end the conversation.

When they returned home, Helga couldn't wait to ask Bruno what had passed between him and Ilse Diels. When he told her, her face darkened and she didn't pursue the matter.

"You didn't say very much Bruno," Helga remarked. "They were all specially invited."

Bruno chose this moment to reveal the scale of the defeat in Normandy, or as much as he knew of it. "Two thirds of my platoon and Adam's Company are dead or wounded," he said, believing that this detail would be enough. She stared at him sceptically. He advised Helga to prepare for the arrival of the British and Americans within a few months. She had been attracted to Bruno partly because of his prominence in the Hitler Youth and the reflected glory he enjoyed as a friend of Adam. Now she was frightened and repelled by his fatalism.

"I have begun to be ashamed of your behaviour," she said abruptly. "Do you know people have been shot for saying the things you have said?"

Bruno was annoyed by her condescension. "What do you people know of war?" he remarked. "You know nothing of the deliberate sacrifice of our troops."

"What sort of an example is this for Manfred?" Helga said angrily.

He stared her in the face. "Perhaps I can teach him how to survive," he retorted. She stalked out of the room to attend to Manfred.

In the time remaining, an embarrassing distance grew between them and Bruno was upset when Helga used his behaviour as an excuse to keep Manfred away from him. He found it difficult to relate to his son in the last hours of their time together.

His family saw him off at Berlin Central. He regretted the things he had said but couldn't bring himself to apologise. It hardly seemed worth it because of the differences between them. Just before he climbed into the railway carriage, Helga's eyes filled with tears. She turned her head away as he attempted to kiss her on the lips. Bruno lifted Manfred and kissed him on the forehead.

Two days later, Helga was tidying up an old wardrobe whilst looking for old photograph albums. The only clothing there was an old suit of Bruno's. She tossed it on the bed and sat at the dressing table enjoying the photographs. Then she remembered the suit and Bruno's untidy habits. There were bound to be unwanted pieces of paper stuffed in the pockets. She laughed as she found a handkerchief and threw it in the waste-paper basket.

She reached for the inside pocket of the jacket and withdrew a blue envelope. It was addressed to Lieutenant Bruno Grabowsky, Reconnaissance Battalion. She didn't recognise the handwriting. She withdrew the letter and read it. Before she finished reading, Helga knew who had written it. It was signed. "Your other wife and lover, Karin."

Helga clenched her fist. She had assumed the relationship had ended long ago. She tore the letter to pieces. "Enough is enough," she said to herself angrily.

Chapter 25

Adam's company was ordered to prepare to receive the new Corps Commander, General Bittrich, in less than one hour. On time, the long black Mercedes saloon flying the General's pennant turned off the road into the clearing.

Hans Thaelmann barked and the Company stood rigidly to attention. The General signalled them to stand at ease. The Company had been told to expect a routine award of medals. Adam conducted the General up and down the lines. Michael Kaspar received an Iron Cross Second Class, as did Bastian Wolters, Hans Thaelmann and Franz Stamm.

"Your captain thinks highly of you two," said the General to the two Sergeants.

They had compiled their own report. "Face your men, Captain," ordered the General. Adam received a Knight's Cross amid loud cheering. "You're popular," said the General.

The Normandy fighting had dented Adam's ambition. He hadn't been prepared for the loss of so many men, many of them needlessly. He knew he had to wear the medal as an example to his men.

Adam and Bruno walked in the direction of Arnhem. The two friends had just emerged from the cover of the trees when they heard an aero engine to the west. A lone silver-coloured aircraft dived out of a solitary low cloud and rapidly lost height. It turned sharply towards the road and flew down it northwards, very fast and low. Adam and Bruno threw themselves flat, but there was no cannon or rocket fire. The engine noise receded as the aircraft turned off towards the west. The two friends hauled themselves to their feet. The aircraft reappeared and made another pass over the area, again without firing. It was so low that they could see the pilot.

Adam stared hard at the leading edges of the wings. "It isn't carrying armament, it must have cameras," he remarked.

"A tourist, I expect, unless what I said a couple of nights ago is true," suggested Bruno.

"Can you remember what you said?" asked Adam.

"Better than you could," retorted Bruno. "You were like a tailor's dummy."

"They surely wouldn't attempt the bridge in daylight," said Adam.

"Not now," rejoined his friend. He scratched his beard thoughtfully. "Perhaps they know how knackered we are, in which case we're in trouble."

On Sunday September 14th, on a Suffolk aerodrome, the engines of line upon line of grey-painted American transport aircraft roared into life and hundreds of parachute troops filed towards the aircraft. A Catholic padre, Father Frank McDade, joined members of his flock in one of the aircraft. Most of the men were pleased he was there because he had solemnly promised to keep away from the front line, but Private Gerald Reilly seated next to him knew the padre would find that difficult.

The aircraft shook gently with the roar of the engines. After a while, Reilly peered through a porthole and announced that they had crossed the Dutch coast. The aircraft was shaken a little by exploding anti-aircraft shells as they approached their drop zone. An airman opened the side hatchway and they heard the howl of the aircraft's slipstream. One by one they jumped onto the Hohenstaufen Division's rest area.

The Rhine flowed gently past the quiet Dutch town and there was little movement early on this Sunday morning. The river traffic had almost ceased except for the ferry at Diel, and few vehicles, other than German ones, used the road bridge. Restrictions on travel for the townspeople were more irksome since the arrival of the Waffen SS on the road to Apeldoorn. They hoped liberation would soon come. They looked skywards as they heard the roar of aircraft engines to the west.

Within seconds, the sky was filled with parachutes to the west of the town.

Stamm was checking the sights of a machine-gun mounted on a half-track, watched eagerly by Trooper Maier and some of the new recruits. The low hum to the west became a roar as hundreds of aircraft filled the sky.

Adam stood in the middle of the Apeldoorn road watching the planes disgorge hundreds of parachute troops. Most of his company ran down the road towards him, expecting orders, but none came from Headquarters and the soldiers of the Ninth watched as if it was a display staged for their entertainment. "A lot of those guys wouldn't hit the ground alive if we were there, Kaspar," said Eberling to the sharpshooter grimly.

Adam turned to his men, hands on hips. "Get ready!" he shouted. Why hadn't they dropped them nearer the town? The bridge could have been in their hands by now. He stamped the ground impatiently, waiting for orders, knowing he couldn't advance in company strength. He jumped into the half-track and waited with Kaspar. Wolters manned the machine-gun while his new section piled into the seats. Motorcycles tore out of the cover of the trees further up the road, leading a familiar armoured car up to Adam.

Bruno jumped down and joined him in the half-track. He placed a map across their knees. "Drive through the town towards Oosterbeek," he said. "Set up a line to the west of the town. You're in the northern half. Frundsberg are in the south. If you can get to the Hartenstein Hotel before the enemy, that's your forward headquarters," he added urgently.

"Good luck old friend, and go like hell. It wasn't a tourist after all."

"And you?" asked Adam.

"Some genius thinks the Americans have landed at Nijmegen. We have to stop them crossing the Waal."

Bruno gave Adam a copy of the order and was gone. His armoured car sped towards the road bridge. Kaspar leaned over and touched the battle-scarred pennant. "You do it too," he said to the mystified young recruits. He started the engine in a cloud of blue smoke.

Adam's company led the way in the dash to Arnhem. Kaspar slowed cautiously as they reached the town. "Full speed," ordered Adam, and shutters closed as they clattered through. He consulted his map and found the Hartenstein Hotel outside the Oosterbeek suburbs and directed Kaspar down the narrowing roads. The hotel and the neighbouring mental home, set in woodland, came into view, but there was no sign of the enemy. "All sections stay in contact. Wait for orders. Wolters, Bergman, have a look at the hotel and no shooting. Report back in twenty minutes," Adam ordered.

The two troopers ran from bush to bush, then crawled to a perimeter fence and waited for a few minutes. Soldiers with red berets began to appear down an access road to the hotel. "English paratroopers," breathed Wolters. They crawled back for a short distance and ran, unobserved, the rest of the way. It had felt like the longest Adam had ever waited.

"They're occupying the hotel, Captain," reported Wolters.

"Any artillery, Bergman?"

"No Captain," was the reply. Adam thought the enemy must be mad. "Form a line through the front line of houses," he ordered. An elderly lady stood watching the soldiers as if she thought it all a war game. "Get the civilians out Thaelmann," he ordered. "Keep in touch with the other companies. No shooting until the enemy runs into us."

The lady continued to stand and stare. Adam looked at the young recruits and gave them a reassuring nod, hoping this time the odds were more even.

The Oosterbeek suburbs became a fortress, with the Rhine on its left flank. A middle-aged lady watched as Bastian Wolters and three others entered her living room. Bergman smashed the front window and set up a machine-gun. She cowered in the corner, terrified, and Wolters ordered her to leave. She refused and picked up part of a tea service on the table in front of the window. She huddled in a corner with her arms round the crockery.

Franz Stamm appeared with a box of grenades, ignoring the house owner. "Are you OK men?" he asked. He lifted the lady to her feet, led her to the rear of the house and quickly returned. "You all right Maier?" he asked.

"What are their parachutists, like Sergeant?" asked the frightened young man. Stamm thought it a ridiculous question, but gave an answer. "Crazy, like ours, Maier," he said.

Small groups of soldiers from both sides ran into one another. Orchards, vegetable plots and houses became battlegrounds. A tank demolished a house. Adam ran through the dust cloud it made with Kaspar and Trooper Ernst Unger. A section of English paratroopers rose from behind the remains of the front wall. They shouted and screamed as they charged with fixed bayonets. Adam and Kaspar shot them down at point-blank range. Ernst Unger ran away. One of the enemy soldiers reached for a discarded gun and began to point it at Adam. Kaspar fired and the soldier's body jerked and was still.

Adam hadn't seen two enemy soldiers creep into the rear of the remains and mount what remained of the stairs. Kaspar heard the metallic clunk of the grenade on the metal banisters and threw Adam flat. It exploded a few metres away. He felt a sharp pain and his right trouser leg was soaked in blood.

Kaspar spotted Thaelmann and Eberling signalling from a neighbouring house. They offered cover. "Can you run, Captain?" asked Kaspar. "Of course," replied Adam and they scurried towards the two sergeants. Bullets ricocheted off the walls close to their heads.

Trooper Unger cowered in a corner with Wolters. Unger had soiled himself. "I'll take care of him, Captain," said Wolters. "Get him out of here," ordered Adam. Wolters dragged Unger behind a wall, carrying two machine-pistols. He hit Unger across the face and levelled a gun at him. "Will you fight for your comrades, Unger?" asked Wolters threateningly. Unger stared back and Wolters hit him again. He gently placed a machine-pistol in Unger's hand. The frightened young soldier nodded.

Oosterbeek was now the scene of a recipe for tragedy as the élite forces of two armies clashed. Each house in the outer suburbs of the town changed hands several times. Some were reduced to ruins by artillery fire and casualties had to be dug out after the battle. Only in one area of the front line were the ninth able to eject their enemy, forcing them into the grounds and buildings of the Hartenstein Hotel.

Each house and potential defensive position had to be cleared. Grenades were thrown into the remains of rooms where only the wounded lay. Adam lost touch with his sergeants and fought side by side with Bastian Wolters. His friend Bergman was killed by a collapsing building. Firing continued on the left of the line leading to the river, where the English soldiers refused to surrender because they could expect to be supplied across the Rhine.

Adam and Wolters collapsed exhausted in the front room of a house, not caring whether there were enemy troops there or not. Both men's breath came in sharp gasps. Wolters began to unbuckle his helmet. "Leave it Wolters," ordered Adam. They sprawled in a dark corner for at least twenty minutes. The noise of battle steadily receded. "There's someone in that back room, Captain," whispered Wolters.

Adam dragged himself to his feet. He managed one last effort and walked into the rear of the house. There were two men in a dark corner. One of them held up his hand as if it were an appeal. The man removed his helmet and loosened his tunic to reveal a padre's collar. He held rosary beads. Adam lowered his gun and removed his own helmet. "Please continue," he began. "I too am Catholic."

Father Frank McDade gave the soldier the last rites, even though he was already dead. "I am sorry Father," said Adam "but you must consider yourself my prisoner. It would be unsafe for you to think of doing anything else." The Irishman was surprised to hear such a cultured reply in English from a soldier who, he believed, was a representative of the Antichrist. "Who do I have the honor of addressing?" said the Irishman hopefully as he rearranged the dead man's tunic. Adam gave his name and rank and directed the padre to what he believed was the rear. For once the Irishman did something meekly, because he felt no fear of this young German officer.

Michael Kaspar appeared at the remains of the rear door. "Sergeant Thaelmann says we've been ordered to pull out, Captain," he announced. It began to rain heavily and Frank McDade had noticed Adam's bloodstained trouser leg. "You need treatment for that," he said. Adam was more concerned about the whereabouts of the remains of his company. He returned through several adjacent wrecked houses where he believed his men to be. He met Thaelmann and Stamm, but there was no sign of Klaus Eberling. They said it was possible half the company was lost.

"The Tommies at the hotel have surrendered," said Franz Stamm, hoping to lighten the atmosphere. Adam barely heard him but held up a hand in acknowledgement. His attention was drawn to the body of a Hohenstaufen trooper lying face downwards, spread-eagled over a pile of rubble. Frank McDade sensed it was important to Adam and turned the body over. The face was ashen; the young soldier had died from a single shot to the chest. As the padre moved him, a pair of rimless spectacles tumbled down the rubble. "He looks like a university professor," began the padre. "Except for that damn uniform," he added.

Adam reached for the dead soldier's identification, praying his suspicions would not be confirmed. It was Benno Roepke, and Adam felt sick.

"You knew him, Captain?" asked McDade.

"Oh yes," said Adam quietly. "He should never have been a soldier. He wanted to be a doctor. Like many of us, I believe he has been cheated."

The stunned survivors of Adam's Company gathered on the main road to Arnhem. There was still a great deal of firing near the north end of the bridge, but these men showed little concern. They shuffled towards the stationary ambulance as medics waited for a stretcher case.

"Hurry!" shouted one of them to a stretcher party which had just emerged from the north of Oosterbeek. Adam saw the Hohenstaufen emblem on the man's sleeve and stared at the weather-beaten bearded face. It was Klaus Eberling and he asked one of the medics for his opinion. "He has a stomach wound, but that's only one of his troubles Captain" he said.

A few days later Klaus Eberling contracted septicaemia and died. With him died an inspiration for Adam and the entire company. Half the Russian legend was gone.

SS Military Police guided the Hohenstaufen survivors through Arnhem. Some of the townspeople dared to peer through their shutters and had the satisfaction of seeing their German occupiers even more depleted than before. A damaged half-track broke down in the town centre and a Dutch policeman berated the driver, who stared at him incredulously. The Dutchman thought better of it and relented.

A lone figure on the road to Apeldoorn watched the approach of the survivors. He stood by an ancient pickup truck, half loaded with turnips. Piet Kuyt out was one of the few locals permitted to carry on a normal life by the occupiers. His son was a volunteer in the SS Netherlands Division, which had fought side by side with the Hohenstaufen. He looked hopefully at the young SS Captain, whom he had seen on several occasions. He assumed that any German officer would have news of his son. "I will let you know if I hear anything," said Adam.

Bruno and his platoon sped across the road bridge towards Nijmegen. They hadn't gone more than five kilometres when a message crackled in his headphones. "Keep this damn thing on the level, Wem," Bruno shouted to his driver. "Please repeat," said Bruno, ducking as an enemy aircraft flew low overhead. He threw off the headphones, raising his hand to the armoured cars behind him, which ground to a halt.

Bruno jumped down and issued the latest orders. The Tommies had seized houses at the north end of the bridge. They were to return to Arnhem to assist in dislodging them. "Forget your day out in the country, Klopp," he said to his gunner. "Turn this thing round Wem," he ordered.

Within twenty minutes they had reached the south end of the bridge. Bruno scanned the road and the metal supports. All he could see was the bodies of several German soldiers lying near the blockhouses. The leading motorcyclist asked for orders. "Half way over the bridge," said Bruno.

The two men cautiously rode to the centre of the bridge, but there was no enemy response. They swung their motorcycle and sidecar round and returned to Bruno.

Sergeant Sempel jumped down from the second armoured car. "There's a traffic jam behind us Lieutenant," he said. If Bruno moved forward his car would take the heaviest enemy fire, if indeed they were there at all. Sempel stood waiting for orders, but no one senior to Bruno appeared.

Bruno's brain worked furiously. "If we stay here Sempel, the English or the Americans will come down that road from Nijmegen and kick our arses. We move forward." He felt better when several tanks joined his column. Herbert Wem slipped into forward gear and stared at the three-storey houses overlooking the bridge. He was ready at a moment's notice to jump into the rear hatch and throw the car into reverse.

They crawled three quarters of the length of the bridge, hugging one side and keeping the roadway white line on the left. Wem saw two anti-tank rifles protruding from a window. He began to mouth a warning when two anti-tank rockets hit them.

The first sheared off a small portion of the rear mudguard and did no damage. The second hit the base of the turret and Bruno slumped backwards over the rear of his hatchway. All hell broke loose; machine-gun and rifle fire ricocheting off the metal girders. Wem jumped out of the forward hatch as the other vehicles on the bridge began to reverse.

"Look after the boss," he shouted to Robert Klopp. Wem managed to climb in the rear hatchway and reversed out of trouble behind the shelter of one of the block houses. "Give me a hand, Wem," shouted Klopp. Herbert Wem climbed out and between them they handed Bruno down to two waiting medics. He was bleeding profusely from a head wound and his uniform was wet with blood on his left shoulder. He had already lost consciousness. Herbert

Wem looked stunned as he stared at Bruno. Klopp took him by the arm. "We have to get back to the car before tanks come up," he said.

"We'll take care of him Trooper," said one of the medics.

Wem snapped back into reality. He and Klopp ran back to their armoured car and reversed it away from the bridge to wait for a new commander.

There was a brief truce as the English were offered an honourable surrender. The offer was rejected, but the wounded of both sides were taken to the camp on the Apeldoorn road. The English at the bridge fought on until all hope of relief had gone and their temporary fortress around them was demolished.

The remnants of Adam's Company collapsed on to a grassy bank underneath the trees by their campsite. He talked with each man and thanked him for his efforts. He had a special word for Bastian Wolters. "You could do no more than you did today Wolters," he said. "You are an inspiration to the men." Wolters looked sceptical.

Adam tried to revive them. "It will go down in the history books. You all helped to save the Fatherland today." As Adam wandered back to his tent, he knew everything he had just said was instinctive and it was the least he could have done.

He called Stamm and Thaelmann and poured them each a mess tin mug of schnapps. "We might see each other, after all, after the war," suggested Franz Stamm. The other two remained silent and sipped their drink.

One of the medics turned Adam's tent flap back. "Meisel, is it not?" said Adam, recognising the man who had so often brought them a mixture of good and bad news.

"May I see you privately, Captain?" asked the medic quietly. The two sergeants left quickly. "I have bad news," began the orderly. "I believe you are friendly with Lieutenant Grabowsky of the Reconnaissance battalion." Meisel had become hardened to delivering bad news, but he made a special effort. "The Lieutenant is badly wounded, Captain," he said lowering his voice. "I fear he may not survive the night."

"Take me to him at once, Meisel," ordered Adam. "Stamm, Thaelmann, come with me," he called out. "It's Bruno. It's bad."

Meisel led the three men towards the severe cases. "What the hell are you doing, Meisel?" asked a doctor. "Only one man at a time is allowed. You know that." The orderly looked at the three anxious men and asked the two sergeants to wait outside.

All the doctors were exhausted and they saw Adam's presence as a nuisance. One curtly told him, "You have three minutes". He led Adam to where Bruno lay in a corner, still on the stretcher, now raised a metre from the wet ground. He was pale and unshaven with a bloody swathe of bandage covering half his head. A large dressing covered his left shoulder. He breathed in short gasps and was unaware of anyone round him. Adam placed his hand on Bruno's as if trying to transfer some life into his best friend's failing body.

"Please stand aside," said a doctor to Adam. He gave the wounded man a shot of morphine. "We have failed to restore any real blood pressure, Captain. I feel there is nothing more we can do," he said quietly. He threw the used needle into a fuel tank doubling as a waste receptacle. "I'm sorry Captain, we must attend to those we expect to survive. Your friend will not see the morning. You must make your peace with him. You may remain with him if you wish." The doctor turned away.

Adam became impatient. "Lieutenant Grabowsky's still breathing. You don't understand the power of this man's spirit. I demand you operate immediately," he said. The doctor steadied himself on the blood-soaked planks which covered the floor. "You have no authority in this land of the dead and dying Captain. I must ask you to leave," he said curtly.

For a moment Adams' anger led him to place his hand on his pistol holster. The doctor looked half amused and turned away. Meisel found a chair for Adam while he tended to Bruno. The young captain stared at his friend, sure he would recover sufficiently to say something.

Meisel left to attend others and returned in half-an-hour. He took Bruno's wrist and felt for a pulse. "There is no pulse, Captain," said Meisel. "Your friend has gone. I am so sorry. You may stay for a few minutes, but then I must act on my orders. We are to return the deceased to Germany. You may be assured we will inform next of kin," he added.

"You will leave Lieutenant Grabowsky here Meisel, until I make arrangements to bury him here in Holland," Adam said sharply. Meisel raised his eyebrows. He knew that permission for a private burial would be difficult to obtain.

"Who is the Lieutenant's next of kin, Captain?" asked the orderly.

"I will take care of all that," replied Adam. "Please do as I ask."

Adam left the field hospital to find Bruno's platoon and his own company waiting in the rain outside. Stamm looked at Adam hopefully. Adam shook his head. "Go in if you wish," said Adam, "and then join me as soon as possible."

A few minutes later Hans Thaelmann and Franz Stamm sat with their Company Leader. "Our friend has gone," Adam began. "And we'll take care of him. Please bring me that Dutch farmer as soon as possible. And when you've found him, do everything you can to find that Catholic padre we captured and bring him to me." Adam closed the tent flap behind him. The two sergeants ordered Wolters to allow no one near him for some time while they went in search of Kuyt.

They thought that Piet Kuyt was unlikely to have stayed on the road to Apeldoorn, but began their search there, walking hopefully in steady rain to where they had seen the Dutchman. Kuyt was there, pacing round his broken down pickup truck, mistakenly believing that help had arrived. Stamm and Thaelmann marched him back to the camp. The military police on the barrier seemed uninterested and allowed Kuyt through.

The three men stood dripping wet in front of Adam, Kuyt expecting news of his son. He was disappointed.

"Do you know of a crematorium in this area?" asked Adam. The farmer said he did, but it hadn't worked for some time. "The people there have no pastor," he said. "He was deported for showing sympathy to Jews. Why do you ask, Captain?"

Adam remembered Bruno's wish to be cremated and felt he would move Heaven and Earth to see it was done. The Dutchman scratched his chin. "His assistant is still in town. I could find him for you. Do you wish to see him here?"

Adam said he did and sent Stamm to find Herbert Wem to repair Kuyt's pickup truck. The driver-mechanic appeared with a box of tools within ten minutes and it stopped raining. He asked to see Adam privately.

"Was the boss in pain, Captain?" Wem asked.

"I think he was unconscious until he died, Wem," Adam assured Bruno's faithful follower. Wem felt he could open up in Adam's presence. "He kept us all going, Captain," said Wem.

"And me also Wem," Adam added grimly.

The mechanic joined Thaelmann and Stamm and trudged down the dark open road to the vehicle half in and half out of the ditch. Within thirty minutes Wem had repaired the pickup truck and the three of them backed it out of the ditch amid cursing and swearing. "Why do we bother?" asked Wem. "It's knackered."

The two sergeants scoured the prisoner-of-war compound for any sign of Father McDade. He was sound asleep on a straw palliasse and was not pleased to be wakened by the prod of the guard's boot. "Our captain wants to see you, Padre," announced Hans Thaelmann. The Irishman rubbed his eyes and reached if his tunic pocket for his spectacles. He peered at his visitors in the lantern lit gloom. "Will it not wait till morning?" he asked. "A waste of time asking I think," he added before there was any reply.

A puzzled Frank McDade was led into Adam's tent. The two sergeants stood behind him. "A guard is unnecessary, Captain," the priest said. "Where would I run?"

Adam waved the remark away impatiently. "These two men are here in the capacity of my friends, not my subordinates," he informed his visitor.

"I can't claim the same status, Captain. So why am I here?" asked the padre, mystified.

"I would like you to conduct a Catholic burial service at a Lutheran crematorium, Father," Adam informed him.

Frank McDade chuckled to himself. "Oh, is that all?" he said. "And may I ask, who is the man concerned?"

"He was my dearest friend," Adam said.

"You will be aware this places me in a difficult position, for as you may be aware, Holy Mother Church does not encourage cremation," replied the Priest.

"You are indeed in a difficult position," said Adam with some condescension. "I will do anything to carry out his wish to be cremated," he added, leaning over the table, but Frank McDade didn't enjoy being threatened. "I will try to pretend you are a loyal parishioner and not a Captain in the Waffen SS with the power of life and death over me," he said. Adam drew his pistol and laid the butt towards the priest.

"I'm impressed by your dramatic gesture, Captain. Pray continue," said Father McDade.

"My friend would not receive a decent burial at home. It is likely it would be a secular affair glorifying our efforts at the front," Adam said as a final appeal.

The Irishman carefully picked up the pistol and handed it to Adam. "When does this unlikely event take place?" he asked. "I'm informed I'm to be sent to Germany in the not too distant future."

Piet Kuyt made arrangements for the crematorium to be used after the departure of the other prisoners. By then Adam had seen the casualty lists at the field hospital; Sergeant Kuyt's name was not there. He sent Wolters to tell Piet Kuyt.

The battalion commander gave permission for the service to take place in the strictest secrecy and only Adam, Hans Thaelmann, Franz Stamm and Bruno's crew would be allowed to attend. "I own an isolated plot of land north of Oosterbeek," said Kuyt. You may inter your comrade's remains there."

At seven o'clock on the morning of the seventh day of the Battle of Arnhem, Bruno's body was laid in a makeshift shroud in the centre of one of the few remaining half-tracks in the regiment. Stamm, Thaelmann, Wem and Klopp sat on either side of Bruno. Adam drove with Father McDade by his side. Piet Kuyt was to guide the party to the crematorium. As the engine started, Bastian Wolters ran up to the half-track, carrying a small branch from an oak tree. "The lads sent this, Captain. It's not much but it means a lot to us. Please lay it on the Lieutenants body." Adam thanked Wolters and set the half-track in motion.

Kuyt guided them away from the town and the noise of battle, along narrow straight roads to their destination north of Oosterbeek. A single-storey building of bright white stone fronted by a cross stood alone in the open landscape. Bruno was to leave another memorial as the caterpillar tracks dug into the soft tarmac of the tree-lined drive.

The Pastor's assistant greeted them at the door and seemed impatient and disinterested. "You can have a coffin if you wish," he said. "I don't like to say Captain, but I'll need paying for the fuel," he added anxiously. Adam gave him occupation marks to cover his expenses.

The chapel was unheated and the service short. There was no music and Adam realised he knew nothing of Bruno's musical tastes.

Father McDade invited funeral speeches. There was one only, and all the mourners knew Adam must deliver it.

"Like the Führer, Lieutenant Bruno Grabowsky would one day have designed great buildings, but we who are gathered here will not remember that so much. I have lost my dearest friend and greatest inspiration. I know I speak for my two sergeants, Thaelmann and Stamm. He leaves a wife, Helga, and a son, Manfred. His greatest monument was to make us all laugh."

There were murmurs of assent from the others. Poor Herbert Wem made his own demonstration as Bruno entered the flames. He held up Bruno's damaged helmet for everyone to see. Tears streamed down the mechanic's face.

Piet Kuyt promised to bury the ashes after Adam, Franz and Hans had said their last goodbyes to Bruno in the way they knew best. The bronze urn containing the ashes was placed in a corner of Adam's tent while he broke open his one remaining bottle of schnapps to toast their departed friend.

The peace of the afternoon was disturbed by the noise of a car engine and shouts of, "Heil Hitler", A black saloon flying the swastika pennant drove through the security barrier. One of the guards waved the car towards the safety of the trees and three men got out. The tallest of them asked the guard something and he pointed towards Adam's tent.

Michael Kaspar conducted the party to the tent. "Excuse me Captain, you have visitors," he announced, holding open the tent flap. Stamm and Thaelmann were just thinking of leaving.

Two of the men stepped into the tent. The third, the youngest, waited outside. All wore civilian clothes. One of them was tall, thin and menacing and vaguely familiar to Adam. His assistant was pale-faced, expressionless and carried a briefcase. "Heil Hitler," the thin man barked. The three soldiers answered the salute with their own military half-salute.

Thaelmann and Stamm had got up to leave but Adam had a bad feeling and asked them to stay. His blood ran cold when he realised who the thin man was.

"Good afternoon Captain," he began. "May we introduce ourselves. I am Kriminalrat Schneider of the Geheime Staatspolizei and this is my assistant, Sergeant Rademacher." He didn't mention the young man waiting outside. Schneider looked Adam full in the face as he placed his identification on the trestle table, enjoying the confrontation. It was indeed his old enemy. It was clear that Schneider did not wish anyone to know they had met before and the longer the encounter lasted, the more triumphantly Schneider behaved.

He spoke as if he was entertaining his assistant and took the briefcase from Rademacher. Schneider coughed and glared at Adam as he covered his mouth with a handkerchief, to remind the young captain of the injury Adam had inflicted on him.

"We have documents here which I'm sure we'll be of interest to you, Captain," he continued. There was no mistaking his malevolent tone. Thaelmann thought the man's presence a threat to Adam and glared at the intruder.

"We will begin with this one," said Schneider, handing Adam a single sheet of paper headed with the Eagle and swastika. It was done slowly and deliberately. "Please read it Captain. It proves beyond any doubt," continued the Gestapo man with his arms folded, "that Frau Renate Grabowsky, your dead colleague's mother, is Jewish and that therefore the Waffen SS had a Jewish Lieutenant."

"That's a damn lie," said Hans Thaelmann angrily. "He was a brave comrade and a good German."

Schneider enjoyed the reaction and became condescending. "On the contrary, Sergeant," he continued, handing Thaelmann a second document. "Our sources show Grabowsky's father renounced Judaism but his mother refused to do so."

At that moment, Adam remembered Renate's reluctance to go to church with the family and her disapproval of Bruno's relationship with Helga. The revelations didn't make the slightest difference to Adam's memory of his friend and he was soon to discover that this also applied to his two sergeants. The three remained grimly silent as Schneider continued his mission. He had naively expected the two Sergeants to display shock and horror at least to protect themselves from any charge of disloyalty to the state. There was no such display and the two men stood even closer to Adam.

A machine-pistol lay on the table, a matter of some concern to Schneider. Hans Thaelmann stood closest to it and Schneider's assistant allowed his hand to drift inside his coat. "You are, of course, obliged to co-operate with us," continued Rolf Schneider. "I therefore ask two things on behalf of my superiors at Prinz Albrechtstrasse. I believe, Captain, you have been entrusted with Grabowsky's achievement awards, including the Iron Cross Second Class. This must, of course, be returned to the authorities. There is also the matter of a school award which I believe hangs outside your tent," he continued.

Schneider had looked forward to exacting revenge for his old injury and it would be more complete if the young captain now reacted unwisely.

When he saw that Adam was containing his anger, he said quietly. "But we will overlook the matter of the school award." He moved on to the second demand and pre-fixed it with a calculated insult. "You will understand, of course," he continued, "that it is necessary for the morale of our great German people to accept that Grabowsky died conducting a retreat."

Adam stood up and banged the table with his fist. "He died fighting the English at Arnhem and led an honourable life, which I think to you is an alien conception, Herr Kriminalrat," replied Adam.

"Be careful Captain," retorted Schneider, well aware of the power he possessed. He moved on to the second demand. "Grabowsky's death has saved us all a great deal of trouble," he said. "However, I am a great believer in tidying up loose ends. I am told you have conducted an unofficial service of cremation for Grabowsky. That may be a matter of some concern for your superiors as well as mine." He paused and looked at his assistant to signal the climax of the drama which would finally humiliate his old Hitler Youth enemy. "You have his ashes in your possession, Captain. You are to hand them over to me at once for the authorities to arrange a suitable disposal."

Adam slumped back into his chair, amazed at the depths to which the Gestapo man had sunk. Hans Thaelmann's hands moved towards the machine pistol on the table. Stamm restrained him.

Schneider had already seen the bronze urn and held out his hand. Adam mustered all the contempt he could in one look and handed over the ashes to Schneider, to the disgust of Stamm and Thaelmann.

"That concludes our business," said Schneider. "I will make my report from Police Headquarters in Arnhem and from there return to Osnabruck and then to the Reich Capital. I will, of course detail the extent of your co-operation in this matter, Captain. The badges and the Iron Cross if you please."

Adam handed them over and Schneider half-smiled, knowing his victory was complete. "Heil Hitler," the Gestapo man, said throwing out his arm. The three soldiers reluctantly returned the salute and Schneider strode off to the car. "Come, Kammler," he said to the young onlooker they had left outside the tent.

But the car refused to start. "Tell Kaspar to find someone to get it going," ordered Adam, "but not Wem."

His face burned with anger as he faced his sergeants. "Those wolves killed my father and robbed my family. Now they will do this to my friend," he said, trying unsuccessfully to stifle his fury. He banged his fist down on the table, scattering maps and half-empty glasses. "We owe it to our friend to inter his ashes decently." Adam seemed to look past his two comrades. "Those wolverines stand in our way. Will no one rid me of them?"

The two men waited for clarification, but Adam just stared at them as if he expected some sort of initiative. Adam's words were sufficient inducement to Thaelmann. Franz Stamm thought he knew his old friend from Hamburg, but he was about to receive a rude shock. Thaelmann looked at Stamm, who thought he had read his friend's mind.

"Captain," began Thaelmann. "When these people have finished their business, they will have to drive down the road to Apeldoorn. We know the Dutch resistance has been active here." Adam nodded, though he knew that was not the case.

"The road from Arnhem to Apeldoorn is not lit," continued Thaelmann. "The Herr Kriminalrat and his companions will need an escort to Apeldoorn. May I make the offer, Captain?"

"Schneider would be less likely to kick our arses in his report," suggested Stamm, not realising what was in Thaelmann's mind. Adam remained silent, considering the implications of the offer. He glanced at the corner where Bruno's ashes had stood. It seemed to him that, like their captain, the two sergeants did not intend to survive the war.

"Tell Wolters to make the offer, Thaelmann," ordered Adam. Wolters returned within minutes. "Kriminalrat Schneider has accepted our offer, Captain, and extends his thanks.

"Who will accompany you during your escort duties, gentlemen? Wolters and Kaspar I suggest?" said Adam. The young aristocrat had said all that was needed to make the arrangement sound like a legitimate military operation.

"Stamm and I will do it alone," said Hans Thaelmann.

Adam nodded and dismissed them. They had had the last word, and that was not supposed to happen.

The car and the three policemen drove off towards Arnhem with Rademacher at the wheel. Schneider made a suggestion.

CHAPTER TWENTY FIVE

"I think Thaelmann's behaviour is deserving of some comment in our report. What you think, Rademacher?" he asked. The driver agreed, laughing grimly. Jurgen Kammler, who occupied the rear seat, said nothing for a while but then decided to ask politely what had taken place in the tent when he was left outside, as he had felt surplus to requirements. Rademacher smiled grimly at Schneider, who said evasively that he would be informed in due course.

It was beginning go dark when the two sergeants left in a half-track. Schneider had said he would be returning to Germany that same evening, but the two sergeants did not travel to Police Headquarters in Arnhem to meet them. They chose a spot on the road to Apeldoorn where the way narrowed and the trees were more numerous.

"You know what we must do, Franz," said Thaelmann. Stamm nodded grimly and primed a lantern just outside their vehicle. "We can't let these bastards do this to us," answered his friend, sure of Thaelmann's intentions.

When Schneider reported to Police Headquarters in Arnhem he sent a coded message to Gestapo Headquarters. As yet it was only eight-thirty, which pleased Schneider as they could be in Osnabruck by midnight. "We should stay overnight, Herr Kriminalrat," advised Rademacher, who'd seen an offer of hospitality about to made.

"Have a couple of beers with us Schneider," said the local Gestapo man. "Bugger Berlin." Schneider accepted the offer and a crate of beer appeared. "Here's a chance for you to show you can hold your beer, Kammler," said Rademacher.

They talked about Kammler's attachment to the mission and how politically sensitive it could be for all the police forces. "Careful what you tell your father," said Schneider, well aware that the young man's father was a senior policeman with political connections. The beers slipped down.

"What do you think of our friends in the Waffen SS, Kammler?" asked Schneider. Every enquiry by such a man amounted to an interrogation and Kammler answered carefully. "They have received a terrible shock, Herr Kriminalrat," answered the young man. Rademacher had drunk two bottles of beer and was more frank. "To hell with them," he said. "They've had a well-deserved kick up the arse."

"Indeed they have," agreed Schneider, who suddenly remembered the promise of an escort and a further opportunity to humiliate Hans Thaelmann.

He looked at his watch. "We have to go," he said. "We'll stay in Osnabruck. Kammler, see if our escort's arrived," he ordered.

The young man disappeared into the rain outside. The street was deserted and he reported back. "They're not here sir," he said.

"Shit," said Schneider under his breath. "They've got to meet us somewhere or they'll be answerable to their Captain," he joked. They pulled up their coat collars and ran to the car through the heavy drizzle. Rademacher took the wheel and Schneider sat in the front passenger seat, holding Bruno's ashes. Kammler huddled in the back seat.

"What will you do with those?" asked the driver.

"It's beneath us even to touch them," answered Schneider. "We shall dispose of them at the first public refuse area we can find, a fit end for a Jewish swine, don't you think Kammler?"

The young man tried to impress by suggesting that the SS Economic Office might want the bronze urn. Schneider snapped back, "You are here to observe, Kammler, not make suggestions." Rademacher was a little worse for wear because of his drinking and began to regret that they had not stayed in Arnhem for the night. A few dull lights in the town revealed the kerbs, but Rademacher had to peer through the windscreen carefully to see the road at all as they left the town.

They crawled down the Apeldoorn road. After ten minutes Rademacher saw lights and a barrier and announced that they had reached the Hohenstaufen camp. The guards waved them down and saluted stiffly when they saw the swastika pennant on the hood. They waved the car on.

"There's no sign of them," said Schneider. "The swine will pay for this." They continued down the road.

A kilometre further on, they saw what appeared to be a storm lantern being swung in the rain. Rademacher switched on to full headlights. Two figures stood in the middle of the road. Just visible behind them was the outline of a military half-track parked across the road. Both men were armed with machine-pistols.

"Perhaps this is our escort," suggested Kammler.

"This far from camp?" muttered Schneider. "I think not. I don't like this. Be on your guard," he warned.

CHAPTER TWENTY FIVE

Rademacher slowed to a dead stop and Schneider got out of the car. He immediately recognised Stamm and Thaelmann and stood confidently in front of the two sergeants, hands on hips, the rain dripping from his Homburg.

"What is your business with us?" he asked sharply.

"You have something which belongs to us, Herr Kriminalrat," said Franz Stamm in a flat voice.

Schneider replied arrogantly in the belief he was untouchable. "You refer, of course, to the ashes of the Jew Grabowsky," said the Gestapo man as if he was dealing with two recalcitrant schoolboys.

Thaelmann cut him short. "You will hand over the ashes of our comrade immediately," he demanded, leveling his machine-pistol at Schneider.

The Gestapo man still seemed unruffled. "You will suffer the severest penalty for this, Sergeant," he warned, "as will your captain, who, no doubt, put you up to this." He sneered. "Do not think for one moment your uniform will protect you!"

Rolf Schneider still did not understand the danger he faced and spoke calmly to Rademacher. "Give the Sergeant the ashes, Rademacher," he ordered, believing they would soon be on their way to Osnabruck with one more case to deal with. Rademacher misunderstood his chief's instructions. He walked round the front of the car and slowly opened the passenger door, opening the glove compartment. As he reached for the urn with his left hand, his right hand slipped inside his coat lapel. Stamm saw the pistol and fired a short burst. Rademacher staggered backwards, his blood spattering the car door. The pistol clattered over the mudguard and fell into a muddy pool. Rademacher lay lifeless, his left hand still clutching the urn.

Stamm ordered Kammler out of the car in order to disarm him while Thaelmann trained his gun on Rolf Schneider. For the first time the Gestapo man feared for his life.

"Bring the urn to me," Stamm ordered Kammler. The young policeman prized it from the dead man's grasp and cautiously set it at Stamm's feet.

Schneider started to bluster, hoping further threats would save his life. He correctly judged that Franz Stamm might be reluctant to go further and stared him in the face.

"You have killed a state policeman. You will probably die by beheading," he warned. Hans Thaelmann looked at his friend and nodded. Schneider was doomed.

"Has it not occurred to you, Herr Kriminalrat, that we do not intend to leave any witnesses? Over there," he ordered the Gestapo man as Franz Stamm took a spade from the half-tracks tool kit. Schneider walked slowly to the trees and Thaelmann threw him the spade. "Dig, you swine," he ordered.

"Go to hell, you bastard," answered Schneider. "You'll soon be turned into ashes like the Jewish swine Grabowsky."

He expected the bullets to come from Thaelmann's weapon. But it was Franz Stamm, Bruno's other close friend, who shot Rolf Schneider. Thaelmann dug the policeman's grave himself, watched by Stamm and the terrified Kammler, who sensed it was his turn next. The big Sergeant dug a grave for three people in twenty minutes. "Over here," he said to Kammler.

Franz Stamm desperately tried to think of a reason to allow the young policeman to live. It was one thing to kill Schneider and Rademacher, but this was quite different.

"We can't do this, Hans," he said. Kammler looked at them pleadingly.

"If we let him live, you'll be dead in days Stamm," warned his friend.

"I will have none of it," replied Stamm. "This isn't the battlefield, it's cold-blooded murder."

"Which we have just committed on these two," Hans Thaelmann reminded his comrade.

Thaelmann made Kammler carry Rademacher's body to the narrow trench, taking him out of sight of Stamm. There was a short burst of automatic fire and in a few minutes Thaelmann walked out of the thicket. Stamm knew there had been no choice, but in future he would see his friend's mock threats in a different light.

They returned to the abandoned police car. The urn was perched on the bonnet and they both looked at it, as if Bruno was still there as their Father Confessor. Thaelmann placed it on the front seat of the half-track.

They were left with the problem of the disposal of the car. Stamm said he knew of a line of burnt-out vehicles from a recent enemy attack. They took the spare petrol tin from the half-track and drove the police car to the line of blackened vehicles, leaving it in the centre of the wrecked convoy and setting it on fire.

The two sergeants returned to the camp. The police guard shone a torch over the half-track as a routine gesture. "No trouble from partisans, Sergeant?" asked one of the guards. Franz Stamm shook his head.

CHAPTER TWENTY FIVE

A kilometre away, the police car burned brightly without any investigation from local police. That far away, it was none of their business. Little remained of the car's interior, and nothing of the blood soaked upholstery. Only one item did not burn entirely, the swastika pennant on the bonnet, a sure sign that the car did not belong there.

The two sergeants found Adam waiting for them sat at his trestle table. He looked grim and the bottle of schnapps on the table was half empty. Hans Thaelmann placed the ashes in front of him, expecting some expression of remorse or at least thanks. There was no such expression and Adam spoke flatly and grimly. "Find Herr Kuyt in the morning. I have obtained permission to leave camp to bury our friend. I alone will accompany Herr Kuyt."

Adam made no enquiry about the three policemen. He had decided how to end his war and expected the two Sergeants to join him. He didn't reveal the details just yet and to their dismay he curtly dismissed them.

Adam reached for his old rucksack in an effort to find comfort, reluctant to face whatever Stamm and Thaelmann had done. He fingered his rosary beads and cast them to one side. They were of little use to him now. He felt incapable of prayer, an old solution that he believed no longer applied to him. He reached for Yuxiang's collection of Confucian sayings and re-read the texts he had been told to learn.

He had certainly gone with the flow of events. Then he read the passage about justice and tore the small book in two. "That's not the world I live in," he said to himself. He stared at the remains of the book and never remembered the reason for picking up the pieces and throwing them back in the rucksack.

Bruno's ashes were laid to rest the following morning. Stamm and Thaelmann repeated their daily routine as if nothing unusual had happened. When they reported back to Adam they looked for signs that he had changed. They encountered only his seamless normality.

Chapter 26

Helga's employer insisted on chatting to Helga on many occasions when she wanted to pick up Manfred from a helpful neighbour in her apartment block. She hurried the few streets towards her flat and was not pleased to see the dreadful gossip Frau Mildred Frank waiting, clutching her cat.

"Hello Frau Grabowsky," she began, her eyes sparkling because she had news which she thought was of great significance. "I have news of that strange woman on the third floor."

Poor Helga had just begun to pretend interest in Mildred's news when a motorcyclist from the Reich Military Post interrupted them. He handed Helga one letter. She recognised Adam's handwriting and ignored Mildred.

This couldn't be good news she thought. Helga excused herself, opened it and her face fell. "*Bruno has died bravely fighting the English in Arnhem,*" Adam wrote. *"Herbert Wem told me Bruno kept them going. His crew miss him greatly. I wish you could meet them, I can't say any more. I miss him so much. Don't believe anything you're told by the police."* Adam finished the letter by saying he did not expect to survive the war and she must destroy the letter as soon as she had read it.

Just then a black car rounded the corner and stopped in front of the apartment block with a screech of brakes. Mildred had stopped at the entrance, hoping to share the news in Helga's letter, but when she saw the car, she scurried back inside the building followed by her cat.

Three men climbed quickly out of the car and confronted Helga. "You are Frau Helga Grabowsky?" one of them asked rudely.

"I am," answered Helga, holding Manfred close to her.

"Inside, madam," he ordered, anxious the proceedings were not observed from the street. "You've had a piece of bad luck," he continued, standing very close to her and thrusting his face in hers. "You've married a Jewish swine and had his brat. That's not good for you or for anyone else," he said with a sneer. Helga stared at him defiantly. He struck her in the face with the back of his hand.

Her mouth started to bleed as she staggered backwards. Adam's letter fluttered to the floor as Helga hung on tightly to Manfred. A face appeared over the metal banisters two floors further up. "Mind your own business," shouted one of the men and the face disappeared.

The policeman who had hit Helga calmly announced that he and his colleagues were Gestapo men and her blood ran cold. "And so you see madam, we can do whatever we like," he added.

She was afraid to get up. The man's face was as broad as it was long and he prepared to hit Helga again. As if it were rehearsed, one of the others gently restrained him and helped her up in a gesture of mock sympathy. "You will leave this building within the hour," he began. "Accommodation for people such as you has been prepared in Kreuzberg. You may take one change of clothing. Everything else will be left and given to the deserving. I'll pause and let you take that in, because you can't be very bright," he continued as if he were entertaining the others. "No transport will be provided and you are not allowed to use the S-Bahn. Any money you have will be surrendered to the state. When you arrive, hopefully some time today," he added expecting laughter from the others, "you will report to the officer on duty outside the apartment. You'll give him a list of any visitors you are likely to receive, complete with names and addresses. They are to ask for official permission from their local police station to visit you."

Tears streamed down Manfred's face and Helga looked at him, fearing for his safety. "You will, of course, receive no military pension or state assistance for your child."

"Can't you control that brat?" asked one of the others.

Then came the final insult hinted at in Adam's letter. "I must tell you Frau Grabowsky that any tales you may have heard of an honourable death for your husband are lies." The others nodded in pious agreement. "He was executed for Black Marketing in Holland. But then," he added. "What else could we expect?"

As she was helped up, Helga picked up the letter, out of sight of her brutal visitors, and stuffed it into a back pocket of her skirt. The Gestapo men waited thirty minutes for her. She was searched for an excess of allowances, but the

Gestapo men failed to find the letter. Helga watched them descend the stairs through her half open door and then destroyed it. She closed the door for her last few minutes of freedom.

"I want you to collect all your favourite things my darling, as fast as you can," she said to Manfred.

It was a warm September day, but Helga put on her winter coat. She stuffed its large pockets with everything she could, including her writing paper and envelopes to notify Greta and Frieda.

She opened her wardrobe. In Bruno's half was all his civilian clothing. Helga stroked the lapel of his favourite shirt and forgave him. She took a few items from her own side, and cried as she was forced to leave the dirndl Bruno had brought for her. He had joked that she put all those Austrian milkmaids to shame when she wore it. Hidden at the rear was her BDM uniform. Helga threw it into the middle of the floor.

She looked at her watch. There was time. She went to the kitchen and found a box of matches and a few candles. She lit one of the matches and set fire to her old uniform. It smouldered harmlessly, but she had made a point.

"Come, my darling," she said to Manfred.

"Is it far, Mutti?" he asked, clutching a teddy bear. "Where's Daddy?"

"He'll come and see us soon," she promised. The three Gestapo men watched her walk past two tram stops and then disappeared, satisfied with their day's work.

For the first two kilometres, Manfred pulled his mother along as if it were some kind of game. Helga felt tired after her day's work and she found it difficult to go on. She passed by seats in the first few tram stops, fearful of Gestapo surveillance, but when they reached the city centre, exhaustion overcame fear and they sat down.

Most of the buildings in street after street had suffered bomb damage, but still people came in and out of them as if everything was normal. Once, Helga would have asked the police or a Hitler Youth for directions. Now she dare not and had to settle for a middle-aged lady wearing a headscarf and towing a basket. "Why do you want to go there?" she asked in hostile surprise, but relented and gave directions. The light began to fail.

Poor Manfred desperately wanted to sleep. The streets narrowed and Helga reached a four-storey apartment block close to the main Berlin tram depot. It looked like the building the lady had described. The streets were deserted except for a solitary beat policeman who stood on guard at the entrance. She approached him fearfully, looking around her, checking her pockets and withdrawing the required list and her identity papers. "Frau Grabowsky," the policeman said flatly. Helga nodded and handed over the required documents.

He took out a notebook and made a copy of the names and addresses. His expression changed as he handed her the key to her apartment. He seemed apologetic. "I can't help you dear lady. I'm sure you'll understand," he said.

Helga climbed two long flights of stairs dragging Manfred with her. The policeman stepped inside and watched. He looked outside and ran up the stairs, seized Helga's suitcase and set it down outside her new home. He said nothing as he ran past her to his post outside the building and he was gone before she could thank him.

Helga looked around her for any sign of life. It was eerily quiet and she noticed that all the doors were slightly ajar. Everything was painted a dull brown and much of the paint was flaking. There was a strong smell of detergent. Usually in a block of flats, a conversation or two could be heard echoing from ceiling to floor, but here there was a cold, dull silence.

When Helga reached her suitcase on the first floor, she was utterly spent and Manfred collapsed against the case and slept. She staggered to her door with a barely readable number 18 painted on it. Half the paint was missing from the door.

She let herself in with Manfred leaning heavily on her and surveyed her surroundings. He begged her for a drink of water. "Soon my darling," she promised. Just like the outside, everything was brown. There were no carpets and no lampshades.

A tiny hallway led to the main living space. The only natural light it enjoyed came from a small kitchen window beyond. There was one single bed in a tiny bedroom with no pillows or sheets, only a mattress that was torn and smelt of age. Helga threw a switch in the hall but there was no light bulb. She desperately needed the toilet and was relieved to find it worked.

She cautiously opened the door to the living space. There was a small collapsible table and two upright wooden chairs. The fireplace was as clean as if it had never seen any fuel and a few decorated tiles surrounded it. Helga inspected the tiny kitchen and found the cupboards were empty and bare. The gas stove smelt rancid with grease. Manfred wanted to look out of the kitchen window. Helga picked him up and they peered out. All they could see were wrecked buildings. She held Manfred tightly and sobbed.

There was a gentle knock at the door. Helga dried her eyes and opened the door cautiously. The visitor was a small dark-haired, middle aged woman with large friendly eyes and a small snub nose. She nervously introduced herself.

"Please forgive the intrusion," she began. "My name is Irma Happich. I heard the baby crying and I know you will have little or no food. They don't allow you much you know."

"I have very little food," replied Helga, hoping her visitor could tell her how to get some.

"Come with me and we'll play one of their little games," said Irma. "Oh, and remember two things. Leave your door open, they don't like closed doors. And when you leave your flat, take your food with you. There are some in this building who are easily tempted."

Helga was reluctant to move. She could hardly believe that someone would offer the hand of friendship like this.

"Come, don't be shy my dear," said Irma. Manfred didn't wish to go anywhere and tried to pull Helga back. He let go and sat on the floor crying. Irma knelt in front of him and smiled. She took his hand and led him into her flat next door.

"Look Mutti," he said, smiling and pointing to the picture of a small house woven into the doormat. Irma hid it after the two newcomers entered her flat.

There was very little furniture and no pictures on the wall. "I love pictures, but they don't," explained Irma. There was one rug in the middle of the living space. Like the curtains, it was frayed at the edges and suited the requirements of the Gestapo persecutors.

There were a few fittings and Irma thought she had won a battle. One other feature finally made it a home. In the corner, by the fireplace, on a wooden ledge, stood a birdcage. A small yellow canary hopped from one perch to another and sang its heart out. "They've let me keep it. God knows why," said Irma. "Let me show you something." She led Helga and Manfred into her tiny kitchen. Manfred wasn't interested. He returned to the corner of the living room and peered at the canary.

CHAPTER TWENTY SIX

Irma showed Helga the empty cupboards. "That's how they like it," she said. "They want us to die of starvation." She showed Helga a cupboard containing a small bag of potatoes and a few vegetables. "But I don't intend to do so," Irma said defiantly. "And I know where to get food for your little boy." She knelt in front of Manfred and offered her hand, but he shied away.

Irma heated up a little vegetable soup and produced some coarse black bread, watched intensely by Helga and Manfred. "They try to wear you down. They never let you settle. When they come, always bow to them." Helga was clearly worried and Irma read her thoughts. "You're an attractive girl just like their Aryan ideal, but don't worry. If they try anything with us, they'll be severely punished because you see we're supposed to be infected somehow." She put down her serving spoon and took Helga's hand. "They want us to fade away, but we won't, will we?" She kissed her. They shared the soup and Manfred wanted more. "That's a luxury we can't afford," she said, carefully storing the remainder.

"Now I shall cheer you up," said Irma. "You'll have loved ones who will be worried about you. We have a friendly postman and a friendly policeman. They're both good at pretending to be horrible. By the way, what's a nice-looking Aryan girl like you doing in a place like this?"

Helga pointed to Manfred. "His hair will be very dark I think," explained Helga. Irma nodded and understood. "Mine died at Stalingrad fighting the Russians and some weasels in a Research Office found out his grandfather was Jewish," she explained.

Helga was amazed by the spirit of this little woman who had been a virtual prisoner here in Kreuzberg for more than twelve months. But her main concern was Manfred, and she struggled now to imagine a future for him.

Every other day, Helga had left Manfred with a neighbour and cycled to see Frieda and Greta at Alfred Rust's house. She had only to miss once to galvanise the two women into action. Enough of the tram system had survived the bombing to enable the two to reach the area near the Spree bridge where Helga lived.

They had already met several of the flat owners in Helga's apartment building when Helga and Bruno had moved in and remembered the warm welcome they received. The two visitors were either ignored or greeted with a wall of silence. Greta's knock on the door of Helga's flat was answered by a complete stranger who denied any knowledge of Helga and Bruno. The woman closed the door in their faces and Greta was beside herself with worry. They remembered Mildred Frank and knew she lived somewhere on the ground floor. Frieda spotted the picture of a cat on one of the doors and they knocked cautiously. Frau Frank half opened her door. The cat attempted to greet the visitors by rubbing against Greta's leg.

Mildred gathered it up and said she didn't wish to be seen talking to strangers, but Greta's announcement of who she was softened her attitude. She admitted she had seen the police eject Helga but had no idea where she had gone.

"That's all I can say," said Mildred as she closed the door on the visitors. They heard the key turn in the lock. "We'll ask the police," announced Frieda and they marched off to the nearest police post. Greta trembled.

People were not encouraged to enter police stations unless, like Ilse Diels, they wished to denounce or inform on someone. It was difficult to get any attention and the two women were ignored for some time. The duty sergeant came from behind a glass screen and demanded to know their business. "Lots of young women go missing," he said. "We have our hands full and cannot help."

Frieda stood her ground and said she wouldn't leave until she had information. She stood until her old legs began to buckle, with a look of utter disdain on her face. The duty sergeant had had enough.

"Has it occurred to you that we might forcibly remove you Madam?" he threatened. Frieda smiled condescendingly. "The lady concerned is married to a successful young officer in the Waffen SS," she said. It worked. "And who might she be?" he asked in a bored tone. The sergeant consulted a file and his attitude suddenly changed. "It is a Gestapo matter and you must leave, Madam," he warned.

Greta intervened. "All we require is an address. Then we will leave," she promised.

"Kastner," the Sergeant called out. A constable produced a piece of paper with a Kreuzberg address.

The Sergeant covered himself. "Papers please," he said and his attitude changed once more now he knew he was dealing with minor aristocracy. Frieda sank into her chair and Greta knew her mistress could go no further that day. "We don't wish to see you again Madam," he said as politely has he could. Then he added ominously, "Frau Grabowsky is now a non-person. She will merely take longer to die than others who have disappeared." He retreated behind his glass partition.

On the way home they made a mental list of everything they could cram into two small suitcases. The next day they called a taxi. They travelled along the Kurfürstendamm, sadly surveying the ruins. The driver was inquisitive as to their destination. It wasn't every day his passengers were ladies of quality. Frieda and Greta remained tight-lipped and asked to be dropped off at any point in the southern city centre. He promised to meet them at a time of their choosing.

They showed the address to a beat policeman, who warned them that they had better have a good reason for going there. He walked some of the way with them but was as rude as his colleagues, as if it was expected when dealing with the flat dwellers.

He pointed to a building which was guarded, and they approached cautiously. They were confronted by two Gestapo men. They were rude and methodically searched the two small suitcases. They seemed uninterested in the bed linen, which they casually tossed on the ground.

One of them found the antique figurines Frieda had brought as a special gift. He leered cynically at his companion and slowly and carefully smashed them to pieces on the pavement.

Frieda turned on him. "Do you make a habit of destroying the products of the great German factory of Meissen?" she asked with a half indulgent smile. The man looked embarrassed. Frieda continued "What kind of men are you?" she asked. "Why are you not at the front fighting Germany's enemies?" The answer was well rehearsed.

"Because this apartment block is full of Germany's enemies," one of them said.

Greta restrained Frieda and asked them for Helga's apartment number. "Is that the new woman with the Jewish brat?" one of them asked, trying to needle the ladies into saying something they would regret. Neither were drawn. "Try the third floor," one of them said, in a gesture of mock helpfulness.

They set off slowly up the long flights of stairs, Greta carrying both suitcases. As they reached the second floor Greta glanced upwards and saw a round-faced, dark-haired lady looking down at them over the metal railings on the third floor.

"Have you come to see Helga and Manfred?" asked Irma Happich. She quickly came down the stairs and, even though malnourishment had affected her, took both suitcases and placed them with a triumphant thud outside Helga's flat. Irma tapped at the slightly open door and stood to one side to watch the reunion. Helga threw herself into her mother's arms and sobbed. Greta kissed her face over and over again.

Poor Manfred tugged at Greta's coat for attention. She picked him up and kissed him. He leaned over and touched Frieda's face. She put her silver-headed walking stick to one side and put her arms round Helga and Manfred.

Irma kept watch on the entrance hall, because the police were only too likely to hear displays of emotion and behave as callously as they could. Irma advised everyone to be quiet and to empty the suitcases as quickly as possible. They emptied them, but not quickly enough. Frieda withdrew her hand from the hidden pocket in the lining of her coat. "Stand still," whispered Irma. "Always bow to them." The men who had been on watch when Frieda and Greta arrived burst through the door and demanded to see the visitors' papers.

One of them seemed to approve of the scattering of things all over the floor. "Everything is in order," he joked to his colleague. He spotted a teddy bear that Frieda had brought for Manfred. The little boy had hidden it in the darkest corner, and now he picked it up and hugged it. The Gestapo man took it from Manfred's hands and tore it to pieces. "A valuable antique perhaps?" he said sarcastically to Frieda. She didn't respond, but stared at the man as though he were sub-human.

They had come to punish someone, and Irma was the target. "What are you doing here?" she was asked. She explained she had shown the visitors the way to Helga's flat and advised them how to behave. They took her canary away and reminded the rest to keep the noise down, descending the stairs as slowly as they could. Irma had trained herself not to weep. Such behaviour was a gesture of surrender here, but the removal of the canary was too much for her. She wiped her cheek with her sleeve.

Helga enquired after Renate. She had missed two meetings of the Ladies' Circle, and Frieda said the ladies were very worried. "I've been back to the flats. Albert told me the Gestapo had taken her away," said Greta.

"I never thought I would say this," began Frieda, "but all we can do is to think of ourselves and our families now."

CHAPTER TWENTY SIX

Helga was puzzled by the amount of furniture in Irma's room, until she explained that the policeman on the front door had allowed her and a few others to salvage items from the bomb sites, even though he might be accused of helping looters. He seemed to allow Irma more freedom than the others. The four women worked hard to make Helga's flat habitable, but after only an hour, guards ejected them.

The friendly policeman, whose name was Hubert Gürtner, had become very good at abusing Irma and the others in front of the Gestapo and adopting a quite different attitude when they had gone. For the time being it seemed he had deceived them. Helga was sure why Hubert Gürtner helped Irma when she heard the sounds of lovemaking in Irma's flat. Helga didn't trust Hubert and thought he would betray them. But for now, she needed all the help she could get and decided to give him the benefit of the doubt.

The police never found the considerable sum of money brought by Frieda, nor did they find Helga's favourite photograph of Bruno. In her loss, she had forgiven his philandering and Manfred was taught to believe his father was a war hero.

Soon winter would come and with it the inevitable police restrictions on the use of fuel. The two new friends survived by sharing flats whenever Hubert was on duty. Helga's attitude to Hubert softened even more when he appeared with armfuls of timber from bomb sites. Manfred continued to hang onto the hope that his father was alive and that he would rescue them.

Chapter 27

Adam stared into space, unable to sleep. The generators had been turned off and he found the silence oppressive. He sat motionless in the darkness, plagued by mounting guilt. He had carried out his obligation to his best friend, but at a terrible cost to himself and his closest comrades. He even began to feel regret at the fate of Rolf Schneider, because he knew that Franz Stamm and Hans Thaelmann must have killed the Gestapo man and his companions in cold blood. Most of all, he thought of the young policeman, Kammler, who had died merely because he was in the wrong place at the wrong time. Adam's face flushed hot when he realized what he had made his oldest comrades do. It had been in his power to let the policemen live, but a mere suggestion had taken advantage of the friendship and loyalty of his two best men. And for that, they would probably have to pay the ultimate price.

Adam believed he had betrayed his obligations as an officer and Frieda's words, "Remember who you are," rang in his ears.

Another terrible thought plagued him. He had managed to carry out his obligations, without fault, but only while his best friend was alive.

The young captain decided that he had acted like a common criminal. Before he finally fell asleep he had decided that the only way to atone for what he had done was to die on the battlefield.

Meanwhile Father McDade was returned to his own lines and resolved never to forget the young Waffen SS captain who had given him so much hope. He prepared to try to reach the south bank of the Rhine with the Oosterbeek survivors.

"I know his sort, death or glory," said Hans Thaelmann, drawing on yet another cigarette. Stamm began to cough. "We're not going down with him, Hans," he replied.

They looked at each other guiltily. "What are we saying?" asked Stamm. "We're behaving like schoolgirls. We'd be nobody without the boss. We stick together."

His friend nodded agreement. "Shit, I miss Bruno," said Franz Stamm. "He made me piss myself laughing. He'd know what to do."

On the ninth day of the battle, Adam's battalion commander told him the regiment had won a great victory. The claim went completely over Adam's head when he thought of the sacrifices of the last few months.

"Enemy forces remain in Oosterbeek I believe, Herr Brigadier," he replied. "An offensive patrol down the bank of the river towards the old ferry is necessary to prevent the escape of the enemy over the Rhine."

The Brigadier looked sceptical. "Are your men capable of such a risky enterprise at the moment?" he asked.

Adam displayed his professional optimism. "Of course," he replied. "It would be a volunteer force and morale is still high among the recent recruits."

The Brigadier reluctantly gave his permission. Without delay Adam asked his two sergeants to look for twenty volunteers. They thought the scheme was ludicrous and guessed how Adam had sold the idea.

"Well Franz, our people tell us there's nearly a thousand men left in Oosterbeek. How do you rate the chances of twenty against them trudging in single file?" remarked Thaelmann. "Maybe we're not supposed to have a chance. What do you think, Franz?"

"I'll wait till he briefs us," replied Stamm.

Adam had no difficulty finding twenty volunteers and announced the patrol would take place that same night. He sent Franz Stamm to the blockhouses on the road bridge to arrange for a guide to direct them to the old fisherman's path. He ordered Hans Thaelmann to stay at the leaguer to "look after things there." The young captain guessed that Thaelmann was on the verge of challenging him for the first time since their training, and ordered Franz Stamm to bring up the rear of the patrol. At least he had tried to ensure the survival of his two old comrades. Neither of them failed to notice that these privileges didn't extend to the rest of the patrol.

"He thinks we can really pull it off," Stamm remarked. Hans solemnly shook hands with his old friend. "Just in case you don't," he said.

The patrol set off from the road bridge at 1900 hours. Battle Group von Saloman rumbled up to it in the two remaining half-tracks. It was now firmly in German hands and the debris of war had been cleared.

Adam's half-track slowed as he reached the bridge. He got out and walked to the spot where Bruno had been fatally wounded and stood in silence for a few moments. Stamm joined him.

"Is this the spot, Captain?" he asked.

"Everything all right, Captain?" asked a sergeant from the nearest blockhouse. Clouds scurried in from the southwest. It began to rain and the patrol donned their waterproof capes.

"The path's down here. Erlich show them the way," shouted the sergeant above the wind. A trooper emerged from the blockhouse, pulling on a waterproof cape. "Madness,," he said to himself as he returned to the shelter of the blockhouse.

Trooper Erlich showed Adam where the old fishermen's path began. He looked at some of the faces of the young SS soldiers. He was old enough to be their father and was concerned at the look of utter devotion on their faces. One of them was different and shepherded the others. "Someone's got to do it Erlich," he said with a breezy familiarity.

"Who do I have the pleasure of addressing?" asked Erlich with a tiny amount of interest.

"Bastian Wolters," the young man answered. "The next time you see us, we'll be poking a few hundred prisoners in front of us. Believe it Erlich."

Erlich grinned and waved him on. He went back thankfully to the shelter of his blockhouse.

Moss-covered stone steps led down to the path. Erlich shouted down the river banks, "Be careful. Some of the handrails are missing." As he spoke one of them broke under the grip of Trooper Eric Wunsche. Wolters grabbed his cape and hauled him back.

Franz Stamm looked back as the rain clouds parted and moonlight appeared. The steel span of the road bridge looked stark and foreboding in the dull light. He slipped on the muddy path and cursed, hiding his embarrassment by ordering Wolters to be careful with the machine-gun. He could just see his company commander two hundred metres ahead as he negotiated a long bend in the path.

CHAPTER TWENTY SEVEN

Adam remembered Erlich's advice: "When you see the old jetty at Driel, you'll be close to the enemy." He had sold the idea to the Brigadier because it was just plausible. Now he seriously began to believe in the mission, and finally admitted to himself that he enjoyed the excitement.

Wolters had the keenest eyesight. He joined Adam and Lieutenant Lemp. They all crouched down. "What do you see Wolters?" asked Adam. The young trooper could just see the shadowy outline of the wrecked ferry at Driel. The old ferryboat, now partly submerged, was still tethered to the wooden supports.

"Might we find an enemy roadblock on the road along the bank?" Adam suggested. Lemp thought so and disappeared up the slippery bank with Wolters. Lemp peered around. "What do you see? Wolters," he asked. The young trooper shook his head. There was no sign of life, except for a Dutch couple who had risked a return to their home. They saw the two men and put out the dim light in their room.

The wind eased and the moonlight became more revealing as the scouting party returned to Adam. "I think you're right Captain," said Lemp. "It's too quiet. The Tommies are thinking of getting out."

The patrol inched its way along the path until Wolters spotted three shadowy figures climbing into a narrow boat. Adam signalled the patrol to lie low. The English soldiers seemed to be laying a stretcher case in the bottom of the boat. One of the men held on to an old tree stump on the bank because the river was swollen with rain and currents threatened to turn the boat round. On an old wooden fishing jetty close to the boat, a queue of soldiers began to form. "You can just hear them, Captain," whispered Wolters.

"Go easy with Bamford," said Corporal Harrison as they manoeuvred a wounded comrade into the bottom of the boat. It rocked alarmingly. "Get in, the rest of you," said the corporal. Private Edgerley climbed over the wounded man and trained his Bren gun on the river bank, straining his eyes for any sign of movement. Private Gerald Reilly climbed carefully into the boat, followed by Father McDade. Harrison climbed in last and pushed off with one of two oars, handing one each to Reilly and McDade. The padre was less expert than Reilly and splashed noisily.

Edgerley fingered the trigger of the Bren. "Corporal, there's someone up there on the riverbank," he whispered.

"Shut up Edgerley," said Harrison. "The Jerries think we're still up there."

Edgerley saw the glint of moonlight on a gun barrel and didn't wait for orders. He opened fire on the file of men on the river bank, who returned fire and the water around the boat became alive with bullets.

Edgerley could just see a figure directing the returning fire. He took careful aim, pressed the trigger and saw him spin, clutching his shoulder. Edgerley fired another short burst and the man fell down the river bank.

"Row, row!" ordered Harrison. The wounded man slipped into a deep eddy and was thrown out into the main stream.

Bullets ripped open the fibre of the upper rim of the boat. "Keep rowing," said Harrison as he tried to steer the boat. The firing was directed elsewhere and there were sighs of relief.

No one spoke and the only sound was the slap of the oars in the water. Frank McDade stopped rowing. "Wait," he called. The body of a German soldier appeared a few metres away, swept downriver towards the boat. "Row Father," said Edgerley. "The bastard's finished."

Frank McDade stopped rowing and stared at the others. "I have decided to exercise my rank," he announced as the soldier's body bumped against the boat. "This man is alive. Give me a hand Reilly," he said urgently.

The wounded man showed little sign of life and gently moved from side to side. Frank looked beyond the steel helmet to the three pips on the German collar and the knight's cross around his neck. "I know this man," he said gravely. "Take his legs Edgerley," the padre shouted above the wind.

"Fuckin' madness," said Edgerley. "Reilly, lean against us when I tell you," he added.

McDade's arms disappeared under the wounded German's shoulders and the boat nearly capsized. Reilly lifted the man's legs and immediately his own uniform was heavily bloodstained. "Jesus, he's in a bad way," said Reilly.

On the count of three, they hauled the man into the boat. "Now row for your lives," ordered Corporal Harrison as the boat began to ship water. Frank handed a knife to Reilly. "Cut this," he said, handing him a length of bandage. "Make a tourniquet below his left knee." Edgerley produced a tin mug and began to bale furiously. "One last effort," ordered Harrison casting black looks at the padre.

A light appeared on the bank a few metres away and a rope sailed through the air, splashing in the water just within reach. Two men slithered down the riverbank into the water up to their waists and lifted the bow of the boat to safety. Harrison, Reilly and Edgerley climbed the bank. "Any medics?" they shouted.

Two were waiting. "Have you wounded?" one asked.

"Two," said Gerald Reilly. "And one of them's an officer," he added forcing a grin.

Edgerley threw the Bren on to the soft earth. "The bastard nearly sank us," he said.

Private Walter Bamford regained consciousness, but the German officer showed no signs of life. "Names," said one of the medics.

"Private Bamford," answered Reilly. "South Staffs. The other's German."

Reilly looked at the pale, bloodless looking captain and thought it intrusive to look for identification. "There's no need," said Father McDade, staring anxiously at the wounded man. "He is Captain von Saloman of the Hohenstaufen Regiment. He is twenty-four years old and has just lost his best friend."

Reilly stared at the padre as the medics began to work to save Adam's life under lantern light. In a soft Irish lilt, Gerald Reilly said to Frank McDade, "Didn't you think a man of that size might sink the boat?"

"Possibly," answered the padre. "But I prayed. We were therefore certain to reach safety."

Reilly shook his head. "Would you like to tell me the rest of the story, Padre?" he asked. "I think not Reilly," answered Frank. "You would not believe it."

Dozens more escaped across the Rhine that night and queues of vehicles waited to take them to safety. Frank McDade stayed with the wounded German.

"Will he live?" asked the padre. The medic was doubtful. Within the hour, a doctor found McDade. "He'll live, but I've had to amputate his left leg below the knee."

Frank thanked the doctor and rejoined the boat crew. Just as Edgerley climbed on to a Bren gun carrier, he asked the padre, grinning. "Whose side are you on?"

"The man's a good Catholic you know," answered Frank. "He always wanted to be a soldier. He told me his grandfather encouraged him."

Edgerley slammed the metal door. "Silly old bastard," he muttered.

Doctors fought to save Adam's life. He slipped in and out of consciousness, unaware of his journey from the Allied beachheads of Normandy to the port of Aberdeen in Scotland. He had the faintest recollection of the drumming of the train wheels that took him and other wounded Germans to Thurso and then to the Dunbar hospital.

When he regained consciousness, his first impression was the smell of disinfectant; his second was the grey and brown surroundings. He could see a doctor and two nurses at a central table and heard the doctor tell one of the nurses that Adam was conscious. They both approached his bed. Before they arrived he saw the cage over his left leg and drew his own conclusions.

The doctor and the nurse assumed Adam knew no English. He pointed to himself. "Doctor McFaul," and then to the nurse. "Sister McCracken. Do you understand?" The young doctor pointed to Adam's left leg. "Your shoulder is better now and we are waiting for a prosthetic limb for you," he added, moving on to his next patient.

Sister Jennifer McCracken had bright red hair and a pale complexion. She began to talk to her colleague in subdued tones and Adam closed his eyes, straining his ears.

"Nurse McGregor," she began. "I know we have an obligation to treat our patients equally, but I'm tempted to make an exception of this man."

The nurse raised her eyebrows in surprise. "When you think of the suffering the SS have caused, I would rather treat more deserving patients," she added.

Even in his darkest moments Adam was able to summon up his reserve of condescension. "It may interest you to know, dear lady," he began in perfect English. "I feel the deepest regret at the deaths of both German and English people. It is likely I have lost my entire family in the bombing of Berlin."

Adam stared at her, enjoying her discomfort, and Nurse McGregor tried to suppress a smile. "Please take his blood pressure, nurse," said Sister McCracken, beating a hasty retreat. Julia McGregor leaned over Adam and tied a rubber girdle round his left arm.

"You're brave, staying to face the consequences of the Sister's words," said Adam.

"You remind me so much of my mother." Her face fell a little. "And everyone thought she was very attractive," he added, realising he had been tactless.

This was the last time for many days he tried to speak to anyone, as he plunged into an orgy of self-pity and regret. He cursed himself for the selfish act of risking new recruits' lives in a flawed expedition with little or no hope of success. Each time the nurses tended to him, he thought of Käthe, whose death was the first cruel blow. Gabrielle had helped him to bear his grief, but he had heard little from her recently.

Little Katerina was in the care of someone else. He imagined her smiling at them and looking perplexed when she was introduced to her real father, and he couldn't bear the thought of being treated as a stranger. The final blow was the death of Bruno and the murders of the three policemen. Even if he survived, Adam resolved there and then never to reveal himself to Katerina. And he said little to Julia McGregor, which irritated her. He reminded her of several patients who had died of self-pity.

He isolated himself from the other prisoner patients and his neighbour helped to reinforce his attitude of splendid isolation. Lieutenant Reudinger had served in the U-boat arm and believed the SS officer next to him was as bigoted as he was. He constantly referred to the Fuhrer's next master plan and was certain of German victory. Adam found him tiresome but managed to exchange remarks for a few days. Reudinger suggested he and Adam should keep a watch on the political reliability of the other patients. This was too much for Adam, who retreated into the safe haven of his superior officer status and spoke to Reudinger only when he had to. The word quickly passed from patient to patient that the newcomer was an SS officer, possibly of the worst kind, and not one of them approached him. For the moment that suited Adam.

This went on for two weeks, until the day Adam's new lower leg arrived and he treated its arrival as if it were an intrusion, which angered Julia. She asked the doctor for a few minutes with Adam and drew up a chair. "If you don't exercise, you'll die," she said baldly. He returned her determined stare as if he pitied her. She became angry.

"There are people here far worse off than you," she continued, trying to keep her voice down. "Do you realise you and the Lieutenant are the only officers amongst these twenty men? They look for leadership from you and this is how you behave. You may be in pain, Captain, but I know a selfish, self-centred person when I see one."

Adam gave her a piercing look and she began to go red in the face. Julia sensed she had one more chance. "Who do you think you are?" she asked standing over him. His expression changed. He turned on his side and took her hand. He said quietly, "Only my grandmother can say that to me." Then he threw the bedclothes back. "Help me out of bed nurse, at once, and we will fit this leg of mine. What are you waiting for?"

She broke into a broad smile. "At once, Captain."

As he hauled himself to his feet, blood rushed to his lower body and he gasped with the pain. "Would you like to sit for a while?" asked Julia. "Please fit the leg," he said, ignoring the question. "Good," he said when it was done. "I shall now carry out a tour of inspection. My tunic please."

Supported by Julia, Adam met and talked to every man and enquired into his background. He winced with pain during the whole hour and a half. Finally Julia ordered him back to bed.

One of the prisoner patients, Karl Heinz Ludecke, had at first refused to acknowledge Adam. He had been taken prisoner at El Alamein and had been in Scotland for nearly three years. In that time he had become a 'Trusty' and worked for a local farmer. Then he was taken ill and forced to join the other prisoners in the Dunbar Hospital. He had begun to change his mind about the Waffen SS officer.

Reudinger became officious as Ludecke sheepishly approached Adam, whose head was buried in a Scottish religious magazine. "You need permission to speak to this officer," said Reudinger, desperate to adopt an important role. "That will not be necessary," said Adam.

The two sat together round the central table. The man was afraid to speak and Adam said the matter would be confidential. "I can't hide it sir," he said. "I'm to be married to a Scottish girl."

Adam shook his hand. "Well done Ludecke, and how may I help you?"

A relieved Karl Heinz Ludecke asked Adam to be the best man at his wedding and Adam accepted. He asked Ludecke if he intended to stay in Scotland and the young trusty said he would like to do so. He was afraid Adam would think him disloyal, but he was told it would be a good way to spread German culture.

Ludecke thanked Adam and gave the traditional army salute. He returned, elated, to his friends.

"He's a toff," he said to Maier and the others. "But he's all right, not like some of those other SS bastards."

Ludecke's words, "What is there to go back to?" had struck a chord with Adam. He sat on the side of his bed and took out his old wallet, now discoloured by river water. The photographs were frayed at the edges. When he looked again at the photograph of Gabrielle and Katerina, he knew he would go back to Germany. The photograph of Frieda was in worse condition, but she seemed to stare at him, supervising his every move. His decision not to reveal himself to his daughter was final, but he would do everything within his power to give her a good life.

Lieutenant Reudinger remained aloof from the Christmas activities in the ward. Adam was not aware of the fear the U-boat officer engendered among some of the patients, especially Eric Maier. They had lived for too long under the threat of the Gestapo and the fear of retribution did not die easily, even in captivity. Adam became an unconscious ally of the U-boat man because he saw it as his duty as an officer not to abandon hope for Germany entirely. Unknown to Adam, Eric Maier became the frequent target of Reudinger's threats and he was afraid to approach the SS officer.

While she was on night duty, Jennifer McCracken noticed Eric Maier couldn't sleep. Only the nursing sister knew that he was suffering from severe battle fatigue and she sat with him for a while. He suddenly announced that he wished to go to the toilet and disappeared for nearly twenty minutes. The guard on the ward entrance thought it too long and together with Jennifer went to look for him. One toilet door was locked and knocking produced no result. The guard broke it open with his shoulder. Eric lay unconscious in a pool of blood from a razor cut to his wrist. Jennifer applied a tourniquet and Eric was carried back to the ward by two volunteers. He survived but Reudinger showed no concern. Adam guessed why.

"Have you approached Maier on a disciplinary matter?" he asked the U-boat officer. Reudinger admitted he had. "If you wish to approach the men in future on matters of discipline, you will first consult me," Adam ordered. He knew Reudinger had kept a record of the prisoners' behaviour and Adam demanded he hand it over. "It will be safe with me Reudinger," he assured him. The U-boat officer sullenly complied.

Adam demanded Reudinger's transfer. His last empty threat was directed at Adam as guards led him away. There was a collective sigh of relief from the prisoners. None of them now harboured any doubts about Adam. He gathered them together, reminding them of their origins and their duty as German soldiers. He knew they expected that of him and it was said in full view of the nursing staff. Peace descended on the ward and Adam had a new Company. He had found temporary respite from the nagging consequences of the murders in Holland.

The pleasant unreality of Adam's new situation continued into the Christmas party. He organised a choir, which sang *Silent Night* in German and played a piano duet with the ward sister. Ludecke's farmer employer produced two turkeys and two bottles of whisky. Eric Maier kept some for Adam.

Karl Heinz Ludecke's wedding was a memorable affair. Half the guest list was made up of farming families from Caithness, the other half of German prisoners of war. They packed into the tiniest church Adam had ever seen. It possessed one single large bell set into a triangle of stone above the church door.

Adam thought it sensible to appear in a borrowed civilian suit. When the Pastor discovered Adam's background he nearly called off the wedding, because he believed he was in the presence of the Antichrist. He confronted Adam and demanded that someone else be best man. Ludecke announced that there would be no wedding without Adam and the Pastor was forced to relent. Adam told the Pastor he had been brought up as a Roman Catholic. The priest thought that was nearly as bad as an SS background.

Sister McCracken arranged a treat for the prisoner patients, a visit to the local cinema to see a special matinee performance of *Gone with the Wind*. The excitement in the ward spread to the staff and the guards. But Jennifer's timing was disastrous. The films were always preceded by Pathé news items. It was the beginning of April 1945 and Allied soldiers had advanced deep into Germany. The nursing sister could not have guessed that the prisoners were about to face the worst problem in their lives, or that Adam would be stunned into a new reality.

Adam and Jennifer carried out a brief inspection, mainly for the locals' peace of mind, and sat down together. The lights dimmed and the projector lamp flickered. "Is your leg comfortable?" she asked. Adam nodded, and the show began. The shafts of light from the rear showed advertisements for products which had become rarities.

"Do you have those in Germany?" asked Jennifer.

"No," he answered, teasing her. "But we do have Bach and Beethoven." The reply was pompous, but Jennifer and the staff had become used to that. The cockerel crowed to announce the Pathé news, and the prisoners prepared themselves for coverage of the Allied armies advance into Germany. That much would have been bearable, as they already knew of it from the radio. They made themselves comfortable and shifted expectantly in their seats.

The banner headline read, "BRITISH TROOPS LIBERATE BELSEN." The cameras showed lines of emaciated figures looking like stylised sculptures. Some moved like ghosts, while others sat, no longer capable of movement, staring through barbed wire. There were close-ups of British troops setting fire to long wooden huts, while bulldozers buried the dead in quicklime pits. The camera closed up on the empty face of Josef Kramer, the Camp Commandant and a few of the guards. The SS runes were clearly visible on their collars.

The German audience emerged into the frosty air in a numbed silence. Corporal Rahm approached Adam. "They've done this deliberately to shame us," he said. Adam said he didn't think so. A tearful Eric Maier had similar thoughts. "Do you think it's true Captain?" he asked, well used to film of atrocities, real or imagined, in National Socialist Germany.

"I think I've seen the trains that took them to these places, Maier. That's all I can say," Adam answered. All the while Jennifer clung onto him. Watching the film was bad enough, but to admit the truth of it was to admit a degree of complicity. Karl Heinz Ludecke said quietly to his new wife, "If you wish it, I shall return to Germany." She gazed at him in utter surprise and announced. "You'll stay right where you are." Her decision had a little to do with her being a few months pregnant.

Adam spent much of the rest of the afternoon with his head in his hands. Jennifer McCracken stroked his wrists, trying to comfort him. He whispered to her, "Have I fought for this?"

"I don't believe for one minute that you or any of these men could have done such things," she said, in a hopeless bid to reassure him.

Eric Maier joined them, sure that the young SS Captain would have some plausible explanation. "It might be Allied propaganda," he said weakly.

"I'm afraid not, Maier," answered Adam, casting an embarrassed glance at his SS tunic draped over the bedside chair. Eric Maier returned to his bed and wished no one had found him in the toilet.

A month went by and Adam plunged into periods of moroseness. He could never share the story of the murders and the shame it had brought on him. At least his responsibilities to the soldier patients gave him some respite. Most of the men had recovered and could expect to be transferred to a prisoner-of-war camp. Adam's fate was different.

The news of Hitler's suicide was greeted with indifference, although Adam felt a degree of sorrow he couldn't explain.

One morning one of the guards handed a letter to the doctor in charge. Adam was to return to Germany, to be handed over to the new occupying American authorities. The letter contained no further details. Adam was to leave in two days' time.

Jennifer McCracken packed his borrowed clothes and his tunic and two soldiers and a plain-clothes policeman came to collect him. Every one of the prisoner-patients said a formal goodbye. It was hard for Eric Maier because Adam had given him a reason to carry on. He had told them all about the great house he had lost. Maier couldn't accept it and begged Adam to give him a job after the war.

Corporal Rahm was even more unrealistic. "If there's an army after the war Captain, please don't forget me," he asked.

"Please tell your family you met someone who looked after you," said Jennifer. She kissed Adam on the cheek, followed by Julia McGregor. "We must leave," said the policeman sharply, handcuffing Adam in front of the nursing staff and the men. Eric Maier hobbled up to the policeman. "You're not allowed to do that" he said in broken English. Julia led him back to his bed.

Adam was led down the corridor to a waiting car, which took them to the railway station. He knew it was against the Geneva Convention to handcuff a prisoner of war and chose to remind the policeman of the fact. "I demand you remove these handcuffs," he said sharply. "I'm not a common criminal." The policeman didn't enjoy being lectured and gave his prisoner an ominous answer. "That has yet to be decided," he said. "And I'm only following orders." The universal excuse, Adam said to himself.

Piet Kuyt had obtained permission from the occupying British troops to forage for firewood in the late spring of 1945. Rotting branches crackled under his feet in the neglected woods near the old Hohenstaufen encampment. He forced his way to a clearing and a fallen tree near an area of ground, disturbed by badgers and rabbits, and began to saw furiously before others found the fuel supply.

Then he saw something white protruding from the earth; a human hand.

Once again the Dutch police investigation was watched by an occupying power as British troops watched the exhumations. The Dutch inspector correctly guessed that this was not the work of the resistance, since there were no active military groups in the area. This was a war crime of a different sort. No identification had been left on the bodies. A full-scale search of the area was made without finding any more remains. A British bulldozer cleared the road to Apeldoorn of the wreckage of war.

The vigilant driver found the charred remains of Jurgen Kammler in what was thought to be a staff car. Hans Thaelmann and Franz Stamm had not removed Kammler's identification tag. The Dutch police inspector was ecstatic. This must have been the missing deputation from the Gestapo. Schneider's body was riddled with German nine-millimetre ammunition.

The British authorities had no interest in the case, but were informed that a new German police force was to be set up in Berlin. They wanted to be rid of the case and informed the occupying Americans of the details.

Chapter 28

The tormentors of the Kreuzberg flat dwellers ordered everyone into the street. With a show of mock hostility, Irma's policeman Hubert Gürtner directed them towards a small fountain surrounded by railings. It had been thought good for morale to keep it working. Two Gestapo men stood waiting for them arms folded.

"Irma, listen," said Helga. They heard gunfire to the east. "Silence!" shouted one of the policemen. Before the tormentors could speak, a file of wounded men from the broken army of the Vistula streamed past the apartments.

"Ignore them," the Gestapo man shouted. "There has been a defeatist rumour that you are to be moved to the west of our great capital city. This is rubbish," he continued. "Schöneberg and Spandau are too good for you. You are to stay here."

He told them that powerful reinforcements would pass this way shortly and the flat dwellers' presence in the streets would be a hindrance. He smiled grimly and announced. "After the Führer has driven the Russians back, we will deal with you as you deserve."

Irma looked grimly at Helga and the Gestapo man pounced, standing in front of her hands on hips. "You have something to say?" he said.

"No sir," mumbled Irma, looking downwards. On this occasion she was lucky; he didn't strike her because he saw Constable Gürtner talking to one of the other women. The policeman reprimanded him instead. After the flat dwellers had been driven back to their apartments by a chorus of shouting and cursing, he had a quiet word with the constable. "Don't give me any reason to doubt your commitment, Gürtner," he began. "It is our duty to be hard and unrelenting with these Jewish bitches. I would remind you I have the power to deal summarily with all traitors and defeatists now." Hubert Gürtner bowed.

CHAPTER TWENTY EIGHT

The Russian shelling began and Kreuzberg became part of the battlefield. The air raids had usually lasted for less than an hour, but the shelling seemed endless and wildly indiscriminate. A projectile crashed through the roof and exploded on the top floor and screams reverberated throughout the building. Civil defence workers were allowed into the apartment house and carried two bodies down the stairwell. The guards ordered them to leave them in the middle of the street.

Helga tried to stop Manfred seeing any of this. She wasn't always successful and was worried by the amount of time her son spent clinging to her. When the Gestapo left them alone, one or two of the flat dwellers ventured out into the street, desperate for news, watching streams of exhausted, defeated soldiers streaming in to East Berlin.

Reinforcements began to arrive from the city centre, many of them old men without steel helmets. When there was a pause in the shelling, a young officer gave them words of hope and encouragement, only to be met by blank stares and utter silence. The officer directed the ageing soldiers to an overturned tram, half of it in a bomb crater. They were ordered to fill it with rubble as an anti-tank obstacle. Well-armed SS men looked for any sign of defeatism.

Twenty Hitler Youth helped, most of them barely fourteen years old. One of the old soldiers recognised one of them and told him to go home, just as Hubert Gürtner turned up to begin a tour of duty. The boy told one of the SS men and the old soldier was shot in front of the others. He was left dead in the street and the SS men moved on.

Hubert looked out for the Gestapo men, but there was no sign of them and he guessed that they were afraid to fall into the hands of Russian soldiers. He announced to Irma that they would leave the area that same night.

"It's all over," he said. "I will change into civilian clothes and come back tonight. I have some food stored." He drew her to one side, kissing her on the forehead.

Helga had tried not to listen, but Hubert had made plans for Helga and Manfred. "Frau Grabowsky," he began earnestly. "You must come with us." He knelt down to Manfred. "And you, of course young man. I want you to look after your mutti. Stay away from the doors and windows. Russian snipers won't know who you are."

Hubert finished his tour of duty and Irma and Helga thought they would never see him again.

The noise of battle grew louder and the shelling more intense. Huge explosions started fires on the lower floors. The door lintel collapsed and there seemed no way out. A few retreating Germans tried to turn the apartment block into a fortress. More shells fell and the defenders' remains lay on the ground near the foot of the stairwell.

Helga and Manfred joined Irma in her flat and the three of them huddled in the middle of the floor. Irma joined hands with Helga and her son. "Better this way than the Gestapo," she said. Manfred hugged them both in turn, crying incessantly. "Hubert will never get through now," she added, clutching the wilted remains of his last bunch of flowers.

All water and power supplies were gone. At night the darkness was total, adding to the overall terror. The only light was provided by the flickering of fires from burning buildings.

Helga picked herself up. "We'll not stay here like wounded animals," she announced. "I'm sorry Irma. We can't wait for Hubert. Find your most precious things at once if you're coming with us. We're leaving!"

There was a quiet knock at the door. It was Hubert dressed in a leather jacket and a cloth cap, carrying bags of provisions. "Get your things together – now," he ordered urgently. "Take only one small bag or suitcase."

Helga couldn't decide what to take, a pair of shoes, a hat, personal documents, Frieda's large warm coat, Bruno's photograph? She was afraid to take her identity papers, which had become a death sentence.

"Hurry," shouted Hubert. "We must go now. The Gestapo may return. If they don't, you'll have to contend with Russian soldiers."

He told the two women briefly of his plan. "I have worked out a route which will take us to a friend's house in Spandau. We'll hide in the ruins by day and move only at night."

He looked at his pitiful followers, seeing two underweight women in headscarves and large coats and a tired little boy, who he knew was bound to attract attention. "Are you sure you wish to do this?" he asked. The two women nodded.

The noise of battle seemed to die down as darkness fell. Hubert watched the remains of the entrance at the foot of the stairs and there seemed to be no one there. He decided the use of the front entrance would be too dangerous and had an afterthought. "Bring two bed sheets. The Gestapo have taken down the bottom level of the fire escape at the rear. We'll have to lower Manfred down."

The little party left Irma's flat as quietly as they could. Hubert held up his hand. A light appeared, accompanied by laughter at the foot of the stairs. They crouched down, Helga placing her hand over Manfred's mouth. "Quiet for Mutti," she whispered.

Hubert peered through the metal balustrades. One of the men looked upwards and began to climb the stairs, pointing a rifle upwards. His friend stopped, lit a cigarette and offered it to his companion. Hubert was just able to see the red star, illuminated on his helmet by the match. He hadn't told Helga and Irma what had already happened to other German women in Berlin at the hands of Soviet soldiers.

They found the fire escape. The entrance was boarded up but war damage had loosened the long pieces of wood. Hubert carefully took them down and cast nervous glances down the stairwell.

One by one the rotting pieces of wood came away. The escapers waited until they were sure they had not been heard. The twisted metal of the fire escape made fearful sounds as they descended in the pitch blackness and the cold. Many of the metal stays had been removed from the walls and stopped in mid-air, three metres from the ground. Helga tied one of the sheets round Manfred's waist and Hubert jumped down to receive him. The noise reverberated in the narrow streets and he crouched down until he was sure there was no one there.

Manfred was lowered down gently. Helga peered into the blackness and could just see Hubert encouraging her to jump. She launched herself and he caught her expertly. But Irma was scared and wouldn't jump. She began to sob as her courage deserted her. Then Manfred called out, "Come on Aunt Irma, jump!" She launched herself and Hubert caught her.

They had to sneak through Russian forward positions as well as avoid German defenders. Miraculously, they saw no one as Hubert led them out of Kreuzberg towards the Lützowstrasse. He intended to take them towards the Tiergarten over the Landwehr Canal, but he changed his mind when he realised the area round the Reich Chancellery would be heavily defended by the SS, so they clung to the south, on the roads running parallel to the Kurfürstendamm. They moved at Manfred's speed from one pile of rubble to another and ran into a German patrol, which revealed their presence when a shot ricocheted off the wall, close to Hubert's head.

"Reveal yourselves!" said a voice sharply. Hubert rose from behind a pile of rubble, his hands in the air, convinced the game was up. "The rest of you, come out, hands in the air," said the Regular Army sergeant in charge of the patrol. He examined their papers. "We've more important things to do than to make the rest of your lives hell," he said. "Be on your way and be thankful."

A light aircraft landed on the Kurfürstendamm and Hubert's small party were no longer of any interest to the soldiers.

They hid themselves all day, dependant on the charity of the inhabitants of the ruins. Hubert carried a few provisions to buy the silence of their hosts. The further away from the Chancellery they were, the weaker the grip of the police.

When they reached Hubert's friend's house in Spandau, they found it a deserted ruin. Hubert made the other three hide behind the ruins of a large bus shelter. A tattered picture of the Führer hung from one of the doors. They watched what was probably the last of Germany's manpower marching east over the Spree bridge. The men at the rear stopped, turned and marched west towards the Americans.

For two days and nights, the little party crept from cellar to cellar. Helga and Irma could go no further and little Manfred moved like a sleepwalker. He was so weak Helga could cajole him no longer. She remembered Alfred Rust's house in nearby Charlottenburg. "It can't be far away – they might shelter us," she suggested.

It was a flawed plan because she feared the police would watch premises belonging to any other member of her family. Helga also realised that Frieda must have grown increasingly frail and it would be unfair to give Alfred added responsibility. She dismissed the possibility of her return to Charlottenbrunnestrasse. The police had already come for Renate, and there was also the watchful Ilse Diels.

They awoke from a short sleep in an abandoned building with half a roof. Helga recognised where they were when Irma called them through to the next room. Shelves lined the walls and a till rested on a pile of rubble. It was the old shop so often visited by Adam and Bruno. Hubert suggested they rummage through the ruins, even at the risk of being discovered and charged with looting, but they were too desperate to care. He found a small bag of potatoes, most of them damp and mildewed. "And what will we do with those?" asked Helga bitterly.

Irma sprang to Hubert's defence. "Hubert is trying hard for us," she began. "They're better than nothing."

"Please stop this," said Hubert. "If we quarrel, it will destroy us." Helga apologised.

Irma had imagined a future with Hubert, but his concern for Helga and Manfred seemed to be threatening that prospect. Irma got hold of herself, forgot her selfishness and regained her cheerfulness.

Helga had become skilled in the art of survival. She gazed at her unwashed and starving friends, but especially at Manfred. She gritted her teeth and said to herself, "Bruno will live through my son."

The receptionist came into the staff room with a letter for Gabrielle. She felt sick to the stomach and Eva grasped her arm. "Don't open it now," she advised. "Wait till we return home."

"I can't wait," replied Gabrielle. She fled from the staff room to her own room and locked the door. Her fingers trembled as she opened the letter.

"We write to inform you," it began, *"of the sad loss of Captain Adam Von Salomon of the Hohenstaufen Regiment. We know words are not enough at a time like this. If it is any consolation, he died bravely fighting the English at Arnhem. Please believe us when we say he never stopped thinking of you. We must also tell you that our friend Bruno was also lost at Arnhem. We thought it best to bury him there. We know it is likely you have not been told of this. Yours, Hans Thaelmann (Senior Sergeant), Franz Stamm (Sergeant)."*

Worse was to come in the evening. There was a knock at the door of the ground floor flat Gabrielle shared with Eva. Gabrielle hardly reacted when Eva thought it was yet another police check. The messenger had gone and left a package. Eva picked up the bulky parcel addressed to Gabrielle. "Can you face this?" Eva asked.

Gabrielle opened the parcel cautiously; inside was Adam's rucksack. The dull SS medallion was still attached to one of the buckles. "I'll see if the damn water's on," said Eva, giving Gabrielle some space. She placed each article reverently on the table in front of her, wondering how long ago Adam had opened the torn collection of Confucian sayings. As she touched the rosary beads, her hand began to shake because they were such a powerful symbol of his family. In a separate canvas package was a tattered yellow pennant. She held it up and sobbed for Adam and Bruno, clutching it to her chest.

Then she searched the inner pockets of the rucksack. "His wallet isn't here Eva. There's no identification, no photographs," said Gabrielle.

"Perhaps he was posted missing," suggested Eva. "They wouldn't have recovered his wallet."

"Look at Thaelmann and Stamm's letter," said Gabrielle. "There's no mention of him missing. That's the military mind," she added hopefully. She was beginning to sound excited, but Eva thought her friend mustn't delude herself.

For the time being Gabrielle had to be satisfied with the secret meetings with Katerina and her nurse. The more frequently they met, the worse Gabrielle's anguish became. She dreaded the police checks and was afraid one day she might be followed into the Grünewald.

As dawn broke over the ruin of the old shop, Hubert's little party huddled in the remains of the stock room at the rear. "We must find a secure hiding place" he said urgently. Helga and Irma looked at him hopelessly. Helga put her arm round Manfred. His face was white and he was shivering. He couldn't survive much more of this.

There was one faint hope. "I know of an old house in the Grünewald," said Helga. "It belonged to the party, but they'll have no use for it now." Irma thought Helga was living in the realms of fantasy when she told them where it was. "The house will be padlocked, but I know a way to get in," Helga assured her. Hubert and Irma looked hopeful and Helga smiled. "I was the housekeeper. Do you feel like trusting me?" she asked.

It was too dangerous to walk openly down the Avus, but Helga assured the others she could find her way down the shoreline of the Wannsee, using some of the old public footpaths. If they started their journey at the sports stadium, they could spend much of the time under cover.

Hubert insisted it must be done in one night and Helga knew it was the last throw of the dice. Manfred had stopped complaining, and that worried her. She was frightened by the sores on his face and the growing emptiness in his eyes.

They hid for the rest of the day, and after the last police patrol had passed, they set off for the sports complex at the northern end of the forest. Hubert carried Manfred, but it was still an exhausting trudge for the two women. They said little as they the struggled to the stadium.

The grey, dark walls showed little signs of recent use. The old slogans such as "Strength through joy," were a distant memory. Irma sat down on a tree stump near a signpost barely illuminated by moonlight directing holidaymakers to a steam boat pier. She was silent.

"What is the matter dear Irma?" asked Hubert.

"None of you are Jews," she said hopelessly. "Thank you for everything Hubert, but I'm making it impossible for the rest of you. Just look at yourself, Helga. With a good wash you'll pass as an Aryan. I'm going to give myself up," she announced.

"Irma, you'll get on your feet and carry on," said Hubert. He cleared his throat. "If you don't, how will you become my wife?"

She got off the tree stump, ashamed of her defeatism. She reached up and kissed Hubert on the lips and sobbed. Helga hugged them both. "It's all been decided then?" "Of course," answered Hubert." But for now we'll follow the magnificent Helga and Manfred."

They set off in pitch darkness to try to find Die Schwanen. It was more frightening because the leaves on the trees restricted the moonlight. Hubert carried a lamp and a small supply of batteries and the two women were frightened when he left them to scout ahead. Helga said quietly to Irma well out of earshot of Hubert. "I'm proud of you. You've worked damn hard for this." Irma was astounded and a little offended. She turned to Helga, who stared her in the face with a half-smile. She heeded Hubert's warning and said nothing. Besides, Helga had a talent for survival.

Helga knew the attempt to reach Die Schwanen was a desperate venture. She had privately decided that if she and her child were to die, it would be in the place she had loved most. As they picked their way through the forest, she was more desperate than ever to be reunited with Greta and Frieda. As the hours passed she began to believe in the restoration of the good old days.

Every building they passed was gaunt and derelict. Helga remembered them painted green and white, but they were now forbidding and colourless in the darkness. Hubert tried to force the lock on an abandoned boathouse, but he lacked the tools. He regained the path just in time to stop the others from walking into a bomb crater, barely visible in the few shafts of moonlight.

Irma was so frightened that they walked along the shingle beach of the lake until a rocky promontory barred their way, forcing a retreat back into the woods. Manfred fell asleep on Hubert's shoulders.

The sound of marine engines pierced the silence and searchlights swept the shore. Hubert told everyone to lie behind a fallen tree until the patrol boat had passed. "How far?" asked Irma, near the end of her resources. The sound of more engines from across the lake gave Helga the answer. "It's Gatow airfield," she said. "Not far now."

The roar of aero engines grew louder. "We're nearly there," said Helga. She led them past the rocky promontory and saw the rotting remains of the old rowing boat. The house was in complete darkness.

There was a gaping hole in the perimeter wall made by a near miss from an enemy bomb. A sign written in red said, "Entry Forbidden." Helga pushed it and it fell over in a shower of rotting splinters.

"Wait here," she ordered. Manfred held on to her, terrified of abandonment.

Helga had little time to lose. Daylight would come soon and they had to be out of sight as quickly as possible. A light pierced the gloom from near the main gate. There were voices and the clanging of gates. A motorcycle roared down the overgrown gravel drive, reached the steps and stopped. The steel-helmeted rider ran up the steps and checked the padlocks on the front door. He looked around, remounted the motorcycle and left.

Helga waited until the noise of the engine had died and stepped through the breach to survey the house. A quarter of the roof was shattered and pieces of charred branches still lay across the tiles. All the windows were boarded up. The once regularly-tended lawns had turned into meadows. The weeping willows were rampant, one growing sideways into the grove of walnut trees. Weeds protruded through the gravel and some had advanced up the steps to the front door. Fallen trees and undergrowth covered much of the tea house. Helga's spirits sank.

She crept round to the lake side of the house. A startled jackdaw flew out of a broken kitchen window. The rear door had been left ajar and was jammed solid with weeds and small shrubs.

Helga returned to her friends and assured them that the house was deserted. Manfred clung to her. "Is Papa here?" he asked. Hubert and Irma held each other close as Helga burst into tears. "I'm sorry she spluttered. "Follow me and keep quiet."

The smell of damp and decay was overpowering. They stopped by the splintered, charred remains of Gustav's old workshop. Hubert pushed the door open and shone his torch. The vice was still attached to the bench and the paints and brushes were still in ordered lines.

"Shine the torch here," said Helga pointing to a small paving stone near a tangle of ivy. Helga reached down and tried to dislodge it, breaking a fingernail in the effort. "We'll need one of Gustav's tools," she said.

Hubert disappeared into the shed and emerged with a heavily-rusted wrench. Helga's heart was in her mouth as Hubert levered up the piece of flagging. There, shining in the moonlight, was Gustav's key. Helga had never felt so relieved.

"Over here Hubert," she said, directing the policeman to shine the torch on a tangle of blackberry and ivy. Helga lifted it aside and revealed two large stone steps leading downwards to a small door. She slid the key into the lock and prayed. To her surprise, it opened easily on to a short paved passageway, which led to a flight of four large steps leading to another door.

"Get everyone inside and close the outer door," ordered Helga. When the door closed behind them, they were in total darkness.

Manfred was the first to see the dim light, grasping his mother's sleeve. Hubert climbed the steps to the inner door. He pushed it open gently and the others followed him into Gustav's war room. Standing terrified in front of them, in candlelight, were Frieda, Greta and Alfred Rust.

Chapter 29

Helga threw herself into her mother's arms and they clung to each other desperately. Manfred looked on until it was his turn. Greta picked him up and kissed him. Helga nearly curtsied to Frieda. Her mother's friend and employer held her as if she were her own daughter.

Then Frieda knelt down, taking Manfred's hands and kissing him on the forehead. She faltered as she bent down. "And who are our new friends?" she asked.

"Herr Hubert is a policeman and we're all right now," said Manfred proudly.

"May I present Herr Gürtner and Frau Happich, madam," said Helga. We owe our lives to them. And this is Frau von Saloman, the owner of this house," she announced proudly.

Alfred did his best to be hospitable, but he could not help seeing the visitors as more mouths to feed. He had foraged successfully for food for some months now, but his main supply in the school boathouse by the lake was about to run out.

Hubert and Irma did his thinking for him. The ex-policeman surveyed the pitiful scene and decided he and Irma should leave. Helga demanded they should stay, but Hubert was adamant. He was sure he could very quickly find the American lines. Irma was not so certain, but she had attached her star to his.

They wasted no time, wishing to take advantage of the remaining darkness. Helga walked some way down the lakeside track with them, but she had a dreadful feeling they would never meet again. They disappeared into the trees without turning round and Helga wondered if Irma had the will to survive any longer.

This episode in Helga's life had the opposite effect on her. She returned to the house with one burning thought in her head. Her life was to be dedicated to Manfred, and she would find another protector for him.

CHAPTER TWENTY NINE

Nearly six months before Alfred and the two women had emerged from a bomb shelter to find his house wrecked by a direct hit. "We salvaged as much as we could carry," said Greta.

"Greta insisted we come here to my home," added Frieda.

"We caught one of the last trams to go down the Avus," said Greta proudly. "Alfred salvaged his bicycle and followed us. He's very clever. You'd never find it."

Manfred tugged his mother's sleeve. "It's underneath the rowing boat," he whispered. Alfred climbed through broken kitchen windows and salvaged mattresses and bedding from parts of the house which they didn't dare use. There was always the chance of a surprise visit from a Brownshirt or SS unit.

The noise of Russian artillery fire to the east of the city was constant. It seemed too far away to be of any concern to the little group in the house and they began to relax. Alfred had even begun to go on watch beyond the main gate.

The Avus and the buildings beyond seemed deserted. The eighteenth-century statues stared down at overturned and deserted trams. The sun shone and Frieda and Greta tended some of the flowerbeds. Both had been too inactive, and time had taken its toll on them. Helga watched them anxiously.

Alfred maintained his watch on the main roads while the women became more complacent. He heard gunfire to the south of the city. Shells burst in the middle of the main road and the explosions grew closer and closer. Pieces of tarmac showered the shrubs near the main gate, but Alfred stayed on duty. When military Jeeps approached from the direction of Potsdam, he retreated to the cover of shrubs behind the main gates and ran in breathlessly. "Pick your things up," he said pointing to the garden tools. "Leave no sign we've been here."

The noise of the guns grew louder, continuing for several days. The house shook as shells landed close by and the air was full of the noise of low-flying aircraft. The war-room dwellers huddled in the centre of the floor, praying for it to stop. Manfred cried constantly and clung to Helga. The usually stolid Greta broke down, crying incessantly. Frieda tried to comfort her, but she too was at the end of her tether.

The noise ceased for one day and then another. "We can't stay here like this," said Alfred. "I'll see what's happening. If the Russians are here, we must surrender to them. They can't be worse than our own police. Wait here, all of you."

He unlocked the outer door and let in the sunshine of the late spring morning. It was a windless day and the lake was still. The decaying rowing boat was just visible and so were the handlebars of Alfred's bicycle. He smiled to himself and walked behind the remains of the tea house. Then he heard a motorcycle engine.

Alfred wasn't afraid for himself. He could pass himself off as a harmless civilian, but Helga could be in terrible danger. Soviet soldiers had taken their revenge on the Germans, and it was often at the expense of women.

He reached the laurel bush at the front corner of the house and looked round. A messenger jumped from a motorcycle sidecar and saluted an officer. The motorcycle roared off, spitting pieces of gravel.

A captured Volkswagen staff car was parked at the foot of the steps. The black crosses and swastika had been overpainted with red stars. Alfred began to feel ridiculous. "What could he achieve behaving like this?" he asked himself. He must give himself up and throw himself on the mercy of the new authority.

"Hände hoch!" said a voice behind him. Alfred felt the muzzle of a rifle in the small of his back. He lifted his hands and froze. The Russian soldier pushed him forward with the muzzle, towards the foot of the house steps. "Halt," said the soldier as they met an officer carrying a briefcase. "Krasnov," called the officer towards the house entrance. A Lieutenant ran down the steps and saluted.

"I may need you Krasnov," he began. "Ask him who he is."

The Colonel was a busy man. He resented the intrusion and wished to be rid of the newcomer as soon as possible. The Lieutenant spoke perfect German.

Alfred bowed and replied humbly, "My name is Alfred Rust. I am a games master and sports teacher at the local school."

The Colonel looked Alfred up and down and half-grinned. He could see that Alfred was young enough to be a member of the city's home guard. Some of his men had died even at the hands of these older men. "No you're not," he retorted. "You're another Hitlerite spy and I should have you shot immediately."

He was a big man with bushy eyebrows, small dark eyes and a square jaw. "Why should you live Rust?" he continued. Several rifles were levelled at the schoolteacher. The soldiers had played this game frequently. They thought the Germans deserved it.

CHAPTER TWENTY NINE

Alfred reached for his wallet inside his jacket and the Russian soldiers raised their guns like a firing squad. The Soviet officer held out his hand and Alfred produced what he believed was his trump card, a frayed membership card for the old German Social Democratic Party. "I would have been sent to one of our camps for carrying this," he said hopefully.

The Colonel laughed. "You would have been sent to one of our camps for carrying it," he replied. As far as he was concerned, the interview was at an end. "Take him away to the holding area down the road. Come, Krasnov, we have much work to do." He waved his hand.

"Please wait Colonel," begged Alfred. He felt the gun muzzle in his back once more. "My companions are in the house," he said.

The Russian threw up his hands. "Why should Colonel Malek of the Third Guards Tank Army be bothered with you and your friends? Kryalov, Koba, round them all up. Look out for weapons and watch out for kids. They'll shoot as soon as look at you. Send them all down to the holding area," he said impatiently.

"One is a great lady and she owns this house," Alfred called after him as he mounted the steps. Colonel Malek stopped and Lieutenant Krasnov whispered something to him.

"Kryalov, Koba, bring them up here and line them up outside my office," he said. "So you think there'll be trouble for us if we just send them down the road. You're usually right Krasnov," the Colonel said to his assistant.

Malek was seated at his desk in Frieda's main reception room, flanked by two armed men. "Get rid of this Hitlerite rubbish," he said to Krasnov, pointing to the Nazi emblems that had been torn from the walls. "Set fire to the lot," he ordered. He shuffled a few papers and waited.

Malek stared open-mouthed at the frail but determined-looking lady wearing two strings of pearls over threadbare clothing. Frieda supported herself on her silver-headed walking cane and looked at Malek as if he were a tradesman who had called without an appointment. Greta stood behind her like a bodyguard. Helga stood by Frieda with her hands on Manfred's shoulders. Manfred ran up to the front of the desk and saluted. The Colonel waved him away.

"Who the hell are you lot?" Malek asked, signaling Krasnov to translate.

"I am Frieda von Saloman and I am the rightful owner of this house. May I ask who you are?" she said imperiously. Alfred Rust cringed.

"I am Colonel Antonin Malek of the Third Guards Tank Army, madam. You are now in Soviet power and you must understand that from now on, I will ask all the questions." Frieda fell slightly forwards and Greta caught her. "Bring Frau von Saloman a chair, Yoba," he said to the soldier on his right.

Officially, the Colonel was supposed to dislike and distrust anyone from the aristocracy, but he found this little group interesting and not at all threatening. "And like Herr Rust here I suppose you too were all good socialists?" he asked mischievously, watching them closely, intending they should suffer a little.

Alfred was suddenly aware that Helga and Frieda were staring at him, and it looked like disapproval. Malek watched them all with ill-concealed amusement. "If the answer is no, then I take it that Frau Von Salomon and Frau Grabowsky were Hitlerites," he said. Frieda banged her cane on the floor. "Do not associate me with that deranged thief and murderer!" she retorted. Helga's old loyalty had not completely gone and she cast a sidelong glare at Frieda.

Malek thought he had caused enough mischief. "This house has been requisitioned by the Soviet forces and we have no obligation to shelter or feed you. I shall consult with my Lieutenant as to what should be done. Please wait outside," he said.

"Well Krasnov, what do you think? Enemies of the people? Counter revolutionaries?"

The young Lieutenant was afraid to give an opinion.

"Come Krasnov," said Malek. "We have fought together over the last two thousand kilometers. Your opinion will go no further."

Like most of Stalin's subjects, Krasnov was afraid to make a mistake. He reached for a sheaf of documents. If I may sir, I believe the Politburo has recommended we treat the Berliners well and leave the rooting out of criminals to the secret police," he said.

Malek scratched his chin. "Perhaps I should leave the welfare of the blonde to you Krasnov," he suggested with a half-smile on his face. The lieutenant turned bright red. Malek had made enough people feel uncomfortable. "Of course I agree with you Krasnov, I have decided, call them back in."

CHAPTER TWENTY NINE

Frieda returned as if she was leading a delegation. "Frau von Saloman," began Malek. "We will allow you to occupy the quarters you live in for an indefinite period." He turned to Krasnov. "Lieutenant Krasnov will take charge of feeding Frau Grabowsky and her child. You may from time to time occupy other areas of the house, so long as they are not required by the Soviet forces," he stated bluntly, and then his attitude softened. "You will receive the same food as my troops. On one condition, that your cook prepares a meal for myself and my officers on a regular basis."

Frieda accepted the offer. They were much safer under the wing of the invading Russians than they would have been under the German authorities.

Colonel Malek asked to see their refuge. The stench appalled even a serving soldier. He would never forget the lice-ridden mattresses or the combined smell of human sweat and candle tallow. Then he saw the diorama of the battle and sent for Lieutenant Krasnov.

"Look at this lot," he remarked, turning to Frieda for an explanation. "There isn't a Russian uniform here, Krasnov. Why not?" he asked with mock hostility.

Frieda joined the game of gentle mischief. "Germany and England used to fight on the same side," she explained.

Malek laughed. "Comrade Stalin's right. We can't trust any of them, Krasnov."

He sent for Alfred. "Tomorrow, you will return to your school. Our orders are that everything will be normal. Do whatever you can. You will have an armed escort," he promised.

The Colonel did not dare to abandon the role of interrogator. There were weekly visits from MVD Military Police, who were bound to show an unhealthy interest in Frieda's group. Krasnov advised that they might not be impressed by the feeding arrangements with Frieda, and ordered her group to be kept carefully out of sight in the war room during the police visits.

Malek was obliged to ask Frieda the whereabouts of the men in her family. It pained her to admit that she had not heard from her grandson for many months. Then she said she feared that he had died at the battle of Arnhem.

Gabrielle cycled to Frieda's flat in Charlottenbrunnestrasse to show her the contents of Stamm's and Thaelmann's letter. She had met Frieda there for the first time and it was the obvious place to try.

Albert Hartman met her and showed her the now uninhabitable ruin. Frieda had left a forwarding address, he said, and directed Gabrielle to Alfred's house in Charlottenburg. She found another blackened ruin. Two women approached her to offer directions.

"I'm not lost," said Gabrielle. "I'm trying to find the people who lived here. Did you know them?" she asked.

One said she had seen three people at the tram stop on the other side of the road. "It looked like them," she said. "The two women carried small suitcases and the man was weighed down by containers of all sorts."

"Are you're sure of this?" asked Gabrielle. "Well I think so," was the answer. "But they were at least two hundred metres away."

The story seemed nonsense to Gabrielle. Why would they go south towards the military college? It never occurred to her that Frieda might try to reclaim what was hers, and she turned to the local police. The names did not appear on their casualty lists. Gabrielle had seen the charred remains of victims of air raids who were simply described as unidentifiable. Perhaps that had been the fate of Frieda and her companions.

Gabrielle and Eva waited in their basement flat for Berlin's agony to end. She had not seen her daughter for weeks and although she had cycled several times to the Grünewald, there was no sign of the nurse and Katerina. Perhaps the school had been contacted. There might be a letter waiting there. Gabrielle thought she ought to go.

Eva thought her flatmate was mad and refused to give up the key to the outside door. Gabrielle used all her powers of persuasion. "We have no fuel, food or water. We can't stay here forever, Eva. One of us must try to find help. If you won't try I will," she said.

Eva sat huddled next to the fireplace with a shawl wrapped round her, unable to move. She looked pleadingly at Gabrielle. "Where will you go?" she asked.

"I shall resume a normal life and return to school," Gabrielle announced. "I can be there in thirty minutes or less."

"Will you go by train or taxi?" Eva asked cynically.

"You could go by horse if you could find one that hadn't been eaten," she remarked. "I'll be back as soon as I can," Gabrielle promised. "Keep the door locked."

CHAPTER TWENTY NINE

Eva handed over the key and Gabrielle turned it slowly in the lock. Her head was still below street level and she could see nothing. She reached the pavement. As far as the eye could see, the buildings had been completely shattered.

She began to walk to school in the direction of the Brandenburgischestrasse. She rounded the first corner and walked straight into the arms of a Russian patrol. One of them fired a submachine gun into a pile of rubble and a half-starved cat ran away. Then they spotted Gabrielle. Some seemed hostile, others amused. One seemed to make a lewd remark to his comrade. They laughed loudly, but Gabrielle stood her ground.

A sergeant appeared from the ruins. "Who are you?" He asked in halting German. "Papers," he added holding out his hand.

"I am a teacher and I'm going to school," she replied. There was more laughter and lewd remarks and Gabrielle was afraid for her life.

The sergeant seemed amused, and ordered two soldiers to approach her. One of the others started to unbutton his greatcoat and the sergeant barked at him. He turned to Gabrielle and bowed, much to her surprise.

"These two men will take you to school Fräulein, although they cannot stay there with you," he announced. The two men bowed to her and they set off.

Gabrielle thought the sergeant could have nothing to gain from his kindness and wondered why he had behaved so well. Perhaps it was because she was a teacher.

They walked in silence to the school, passing other soldiers who cast envious glances at their comrades. She smiled at her escorts, who seemed embarrassed. She couldn't imagine what it must be like to be hundreds, if not thousands of kilometres away from home.

Within thirty minutes Gabrielle had reached the gates. The sun shone behind the buildings and she could see very little. The trees lining the approach had been cut down long ago, to be used as fuel. They had helped to soften the image of the school but now it looked forbidding. Many of the windows were broken and she feared for the interior of the school. The two Russians seemed reluctant to leave her, but they obeyed orders. It started to rain and Gabrielle pulled up her coat collar.

The front door had been padlocked, but the lock was broken. Then she noticed that the great oak door had been polished. She stood back and looked on either side. None of the windows were broken and the door was open. She pushed it gently and walked into the entrance hall towards the war memorial. There was no sign of life. Anxiously she looked back towards the main door. Parked just inside the entrance hall was a bicycle.

Her steps echoed in the dome of the entrance hall and there was a strong smell of disinfectant. Doctor Schaub's office door was open. She walked in. There was a smell of polish and everything on the desk was in order. Weeks before she had asked Herr Tietzen, the caretaker, to repair an oak panel behind Schaub's desk under Hitler's portrait. It had been done.

She left the office and walked to her classroom. The door was open and the chairs and desks were in neat, tidy rows. Pieces of chalk lay at the foot of the blackboard, ready for use.

There was a gentle knock at the door. "Good morning, Fräulein Hintzel," said Herr Tietzen, the caretaker, wearing the tattered remains of a home guard uniform. "I apologise for the state of the building, but there is no water supply. I have tried my best, but can do no more."

His presence gave a special edge to what had happened and he found it hard to fight back tears. "May I have your permission to leave, Fräulein?" he enquired. "My morning shift is nearly finished."

"Of course Herr Tietzen, the school is grateful for all your efforts. I trust your family is well?" she enquired. He said they were, bowed and left.

Gabrielle set down at her desk, put her head in her hands and wept. It seemed her only company was Hitler's portrait on the rear wall. She picked up her bag in the belief that nothing could be normal again and prepared to leave.

There was another knock at the classroom door. She dried her eyes and opened it cautiously. Standing there were four, pale, underfed boys in frayed Hitler Youth uniforms. One of them was Bobi Richter, a constant truant, and his steel helmet still hung from his belt.

"Good morning miss," he said brightly. "We thought we'd come to school. What's the matter Miss?"

"It's nothing, Bobi," she answered.

"What are we going to do today Miss?" asked little Gerhardt Magder.

Gabrielle regained her composure, put her hands together and announced, "We'll do what we always do in this room, boys. We'll do a maths lesson. Please sit down."

They all sat on the front row and she looked at the sad collection of teenagers. Their hands seemed bloodless and were covered with sores. Their tired eyes looked at her hopefully. Little Johann Kropp had one eye half-closed. His head began to fall and he was soon asleep.

Gabrielle recalled the distant look in the faces of Adam and Bruno, looks that had divided them from their elders. That look had now gone from the faces of these boys, who looked up to the adult they most respected to tell them what to do.

"Waken up, Kropp," said Bobi, giving him a gentle shove. Even Bobi, the hardened truant, was anxious to please their maths teacher. "Let him sleep Bobi," said Gabrielle.

The rest looked at Bobi expectantly, as he was the spokesman for another important matter. She was in the process of writing some of the simplest equations on the blackboard.

"Excuse me Miss," began Bobi. "May we have something to eat?"

Gabrielle fought back tears, slamming her piece of chalk down on the blackboard shelf, breaking it into pieces. "Come with me, all of you. We will find someone," she promised. First she removed the portrait of Hitler from the wall and threw it in the wastepaper bin. Bobi gave her a dubious look.

Followed by the boys, Gabrielle marched to Schaub's office, more in hope than expectation. She stood behind the desk and picked up the telephone. The line was still live and she dialled the direct number of a certain official in the Ministry of Education. Though they were separated, he might help.

Gabrielle believed that old habits would make someone answer and they did. An unfamiliar voice with a strong accent answered and asked her what she wanted. She told him. "Very well," said the voice. "Wait there."

One of Rolf Schaub's academic gowns still hung on one of the oak-panelled walls. Bobi took it down and suggested Gabrielle put it on. She thought of the implications for her long-term career and smiled at Bobi. She also believed it might impress the visitor, whoever he was.

Gabrielle sat in Schaub's chair and waited. "I'll keep a lookout, Miss," said Johann, disappearing towards the entrance. He reappeared in half an hour. "Quick Miss," he began breathlessly. "Come and look." Gabrielle joined him on the steps outside.

An armoured personnel carrier, packed with Russian soldiers, was grinding its way up the drive. In the front seats were Alfred Rust and her friend Eva.

Gabrielle went back to Schaub's seat and composed herself. "Sit still everyone," she advised. A major in cavalry boots burst through the office door, followed by five soldiers who stood behind him and presented arms. He drew a pistol and gesticulated with it wildly, terrifying the boys. Alfred and Eva came in and stood near the window overlooking the sports field. "They picked us up off the street near the school," explained Eva. "I had to follow you," she added.

The major glared at her, expecting silence, and slammed his pistol down on the desk. He pointed to Bobi's helmet. "You won't be needing that any more sonny," he said in passable German. The helmet clattered to the floor.

"You two, step forward," he said to Alfred and Eva. Although he seemed to have no social graces, the Russian had a pleasant face. He told Alfred to stand close to him. "Is this woman a capable teacher?" he asked gruffly pointing to Gabrielle.

"She is an excellent teacher and organiser Herr Major," answered Alfred. He turned to Eva.

"Do you think that chair suits her?" he asked. Eva grinned at Gabrielle. "Oh yes, it does indeed, Herr Major," she answered. The officer straightened up and asked Gabrielle for her papers. He scrutinised them and seemed satisfied. Then he drew himself up to his full height. "Fräulein Gabrielle Hintzel, by the authority vested in me by the Soviet Government of Berlin, I appoint you Principle of the Martin Luther School," he announced grandly.

Bobi Richter began the applause and the others joined in. The Major waved to them to stop. "That's settled," the Russian officer said. "We will return tomorrow with more students and we'll bring food." He turned to Alfred. "You're more experienced than she is," he said pointing to Eva. "You'll be Fräulein Hintzel's deputy."

Every day the Russians combed the ruins for absentees who they brought to the school, sometimes at gunpoint. Each day, a Soviet army lorry brought crates of tinned food to the school. Some of it disappeared into the local ruins for the benefit of starving families.

Gabrielle was delighted and saddened when she discovered Alfred living in Adam's grandmother's house. Immediately she gave him Thaelmann and Stamm's letter and admitted she and Adam were lovers.

Alfred didn't mention for a while that the love of Adam's life was a colleague of his as he thought it inappropriate. When he told Frieda and Greta, they were overjoyed. The two women tried to think of any way they could to invite Gabrielle to Die Schwanen. Colonel Malek would have none of it, as it would lead to unwelcome attention from the military police.

One spring morning in 1946, the Russians did not appear. Gabrielle rang the old ministry building, but there was no answer and food supplies for the students were in short supply. Gabrielle felt they were without protection.

Little Johann had nearly fallen asleep on watch when he was disturbed by the noise of an engine. A military Jeep with a giant white star painted on the side turned off the boulevard into the school driveway. It was driven slowly and cautiously towards the school entrance. A captain and two military policemen jumped out and approached Johann, who barred their way. "You in charge here?" asked the captain, but Johann shook his head. He ran inside to the school assembly, waving at Gabrielle on the stage. She brought the proceedings to an abrupt end and sent the boys to their classrooms. She met the Americans in the entrance hall.

"Captain Liam Davidson, Third United States Army," said the young officer. "And you are, ma'am?" Gabrielle hesitated to announce she was the school principal. She had been appointed by the Soviet occupiers, and it looked as if these men were her new masters. "This may be a temporary arrangement ma'am, subject to my superior's decisions," he stated. He then announced that Rolf Schaub and his wife had hanged themselves. Gabrielle was upset because she owed Schaub so much. When she expressed regret, Davidson became quite cold, assuming that Gabrielle was a committed Nazi.

The American soldiers and administrators were not friendly. Gabrielle and the staff had to sit through rigorous interviews as part of the 'denazification' process. After months of this, they were awarded a certificate of political cleanliness which the Germans soon christened the 'Persilschein.'

The Americans wished to educate Germans in the proper use of a new free library to be set up in Wilmersdorf. Davidson said that Gabrielle must help to build up a new inventory of books for it. She found lists in Schaub's old files of books which had been banned, and set to work.

Chapter 30

As Adam's aircraft waited for permission to land at Gatow, he surveyed the scene below through a tiny window. The aircraft circled south-western Berlin twice before beginning to lose height. It flew over Die Schwanen before landing, giving Adam time to recall the happy times he had spent there. That was all in the past, and he wondered if the house now had a future.

The aircraft shuddered to a halt after a final rev of one of the engines had enabled it to turn to its resting place facing the control tower. One of Adam's guards opened the hatch and invited their prisoner to step down onto a ladder provided by a French soldier. He smiled at the French private, musing that the old enemy had triumphed again. He stared in the direction of Die Schwanen, refusing to let go of the fantasy that one day, it could be restored to his family.

The airfield around him was a rubbish tip of warfare, a mass of rusting barbed wire and blackened concrete bunkers. The wreckage of German aircraft littered the airfield.

Adam's two guards led him to the airport lounge and handed him over to two Americans. One was a smart, dapper lieutenant who introduced himself as James Bradford, who was to defend Adam in a forthcoming trial. The other American was detailed to guard him. His name was Private Lewis Grindleford and he was scared of the prisoner, who he had decided was a dangerous war criminal to be kept at arm's length.

They drove through the French sector to Spandau prison, where Adam was formally identified and locked in a cell, Bradford promising to visit his client early the next day.

The walls had been painted green and a dull cream which at least, was a facelift from its Gestapo days. A bunk bed in one of the corners lay on two iron angle brackets. A straw palliasse and a pillow lay on it. Blankets were issued only at night and the prisoners were watched through small sliding hatches. It was already well known to the Americans that some of their prisoners would rather commit suicide than face trial. The chemical toilet was in full view of the guards.

A bare wooden table stood in the centre of the cell, with two chairs. On it were two fountain pens and a supply of paper. Adam threw his briefcase onto the table and set to work. He was certain he could exonerate his company from all blame. He began a list of witnesses for the defence, beginning with Father McDade.

After a while the day caught up with him and he felt his eyes closing. He replaced his pen and knocked on the cell door. Lewis Grindleford threw him two blankets and slammed the door. Adam slept deeply for nine hours. He awoke refreshed and sure of himself and looked forward to Lieutenant Bradford's first visit.

When the lieutenant arrived he seemed cheerful and optimistic having done some research into the behaviour of the Hohenstaufen division and found their record blameless. Adam presented his defence and immediately Bradford wished to see the material relating to the Arnhem battle. To Adam's surprise, Bradford didn't seem interested in the Russian or Normandy campaigns, which puzzled Adam. "I personally am interested in your experiences in Russia and Normandy, but it appears that the authorities who are to try you are not," said Bradford.

Adam looked perplexed. "I too am surprised," said Bradford. "And I must reveal something else. I received this letter from our American authorities today. It ordered me to cooperate with the new German police force. I have been ordered to present my findings to the German Commissioner of Police in Spandau." He paused. "Does that concern you in any way?" he asked.

Adam began to sweat, having assumed that no one would be interested in the fate of Schneider and Rademacher now that the Gestapo itself had been declared a criminal organisation. Adam had conveniently forgotten the fate of the other man in the police car, Jurgen Kammler. He lied and said he had no concerns about those two days.

Adam had already suggested to Bradford he should contact Father Frank McDade as a witness for the defence when they met at Gatow airport, and Bradford did so immediately. The Catholic Church had suffered enough because of the deal between Hitler and Pius XII before the war and the priest was instructed not to help a German officer on trial for war crimes. Neither of them would ever know that the Cardinal had received a letter from the new German Commissioner of Police in Spandau, Heinz Kammler, warning that McDade might be asked to testify.

On a personal level, James Bradford became friendly with Adam. His fluent English helped put the lawyer at ease, and both enjoyed music. Bradford revealed he was a capable pianist and promised Adam a chance to perform when the trial was over. The lawyer even suggested there might not be a trial at all after they had examined Adam's record. He continued blindly, unaware of a clever ambush that had been set by Commissioner Kammler. Neither Adam nor Bradford realised the significance of the failure of Father McDade to testify, and their complacency continued.

"Your first formal interview is in the morning," said the lawyer. Before he left Adam, he said reflectively, "Are you sure you have nothing to be afraid of, Captain?" Adam smiled and shook his head.

Adam's patience with his American guard had become exhausted. He refused to stand by the far wall, to Grindleford's dismay, and pulled rank over the bewildered American. It worked and Adam was able to enjoy a relaxed breakfast.

When Bradford arrived, twenty minutes late, he informed Adam that the German police in the building were responsible for the delay, which the lawyer couldn't explain. He led the way to the interview hall and a military policeman in white helmet and spats followed. All the doors to the Interview Hall were guarded by American Military Police and it appeared they had complete charge of events. One of them opened a door for Adam and cast a critical glance at his SS tunic.

The hall was filled with evenly-spaced wooden tables, each with three chairs. All were occupied except one in the centre, to which Adam was directed. Nothing happened for ten minutes, allowing Adam to take in his surroundings. Most of the uniformed men present were either American or British.

Just before Adam's interview began, three men appeared in a uniform not familiar to him. From a distance they could have been mistaken for regular German soldiers except for their white police armbands. Two stood by the doors and the other, carrying a briefcase, approached Adam.

CHAPTER THIRTY

"You are Captain Adam von Saloman of the Ninth SS Panzer Division Hohenstaufen?" he began. Adam nodded. "Please give me your papers," he said, briefly scrutinizing them. He returned them, turned round and made a gesture to one of his colleagues by the door.

Lieutenant Bradford was ignored until the German policeman remembered his manners and shook hands. Bradford had been caught off guard, as he had expected an American interrogator.

"I am Inspector Topf of the new German Criminal Police," said the German policeman.

"Excuse me. I expected an American interrogator Inspector," interrupted James Bradford. "Then I must tell you that you have been misled," said Topf with some condescension. "We will begin," he stated, laying a sheaf of papers on the table.

Bradford prompted Adam to produce his defence. Topf smiled and seemed uninterested. "I may examine those later," he said, waving his hand in a dismissive fashion. Then Topf asked Adam sharply, "Do you know why you are here, Captain?"

"Of course," replied Adam. "I would like to explain as clearly as I can my involvement and that of my company in the late war," he continued hopefully.

Topf sat back in his chair and crossed his hands. "You are acquainted with Sergeants Thaelmann and Stamm I believe," he said. At that moment, Adam realised he had been trapped and the Americans had been led to believe Adam would have to answer for the deaths of Allied soldiers, not for the deaths of Germans. His blood ran cold. He was at Topf's mercy and the policeman knew it. James Bradford began to feel uncomfortable.

"Do you remember a visit paid to you by the Gestapo on 23rd September after you withdrew from the Battle of Arnhem?" Topf asked.

Bradford interrupted. "No mention of this has been made to me or to my client," he said.

"But of course not, Lieutenant," said Topf. "I will demonstrate now to you that your client would have been highly unlikely to mention it." A note of vindictiveness had now entered his voice. "May I remind you your own occupation authorities have sanctioned this interview Lieutenant." Bradford fell silent.

"Those men did not return to Osnabruck as planned Captain, which I'm sure you will know. Their bodies were discovered by the Dutch police buried near the Arnhem to Apeldoorn road." He began to turn the screw. "It seems our friends in the Dutch police and the Arnhem Gestapo knew of an intended meeting between your sergeants and Kriminalrat Schneider and his party. Was the arrangement known to you, Captain?"

"Of course," answered Adam. "My sergeants were to form an escort in a dangerous area at night."

"Perhaps not so dangerous," said Topf with a half smile, "in an area occupied by two SS Panzer Divisions."

Adam's mind worked swiftly as he manoeuvred, trying to avoid responsibility for the murders. Bradford was furiously scribbling. "We do know the reason for Schneider's visit, Captain, not something I think amenable to you perhaps?"

Adam realised Topf possessed only circumstantial evidence and began to relax. But Topf hadn't finished. "You see, Captain von Saloman," continued the German policeman, "we are not concerned today with the fate of Jews and communists. Our friends in the United States and England will take care of that." He paused and added. "Neither are we too concerned with the fate of Schneider and Rademacher." Adam grew more attentive.

"The third occupant of the car was not Gestapo, Captain. His name was Jurgen Kammler and he had no interest in your friends' ashes. He was killed nevertheless," he continued, closing the jaws of the trap. "You may have noticed an observer at the back of the hall, Captain. He is Police Commissioner Kammler and he is very concerned we catch his son's killers."

Topf stared at Adam enjoying the effects of his last statement. Then he carefully packed his papers into a briefcase. He stood up and said, "It would seem that the new Germany can expect very little from the old aristocracy, Captain. I will leave you to consider your position and we will meet in one week's time."

He walked towards Commissioner Kammler and said a few words to him. Kammler seemed pleased. Before they left, Topf gave Adam's papers to an impassive-looking sergeant at the door. Adam wished to keep track of his documents and looked hard at the sergeant. His face was partly obscured by a large peaked cap. Meanwhile Adam returned to his cell with James Bradford.

His lawyer said nothing until Grindleford's hands were on the cell door.

He seemed to take a deep breath before he spoke. "I feel you have not been entirely honest with me, Captain," he began. "I'm afraid it's my intention to resign your brief. I will try to find a replacement." He shook hands and strode down the corridor, leaving Adam entirely alone.

He followed Topf's advice and considered his position. He had failed his sergeants, who must be wanted men. They were his closest comrades and he wondered what they now thought of him. Adam's evidence was now a stack of useless paper, a shallow attempt at self-justification.

Between them Adam, Hans and Franz had been responsible for the murder of an entirely innocent man, and it was a bottomless source of shame for Adam. He had betrayed his family and couldn't bear the thought of facing Frieda again.

As the days went by, he tried to discover what had gone wrong and began to believe he was nothing without Bruno. Adam refused food and began to lose weight dramatically. The prison authorities thought they would have to deal with a possible suicide.

Frieda, Greta, Helga and Manfred now lived on the first floor of Die Schwanen. Colonel Malek had allocated them the whole of the eastern first-floor wing.

On 30th June 1945, a knock came on Frieda's door. It was the Colonel at his genial best. He announced that Soviet troops would leave the house in the morning and he invited everyone to a farewell party which would double as a celebration of Stalin's birthday. He said it would be both a sad and a joyful occasion. The party would begin at eight o'clock that evening.

Nearly fifty Russian soldiers sat at the tables. A soldier stood behind each reserved place and invited a guest to sit. Another trooper clapped his hands for silence. He wore what seemed like white lace trousers and began a slow rhythmic progress round the lawn. He suddenly rounded on Helga and dragged her onto the grass. Manfred ran after her and tried to pull her back. Alfred restrained him and said everything was all right.

Colonel Malek explained what was happening. The dancer in the white trousers began to sing to Helga in a Georgian dialect. "He has desired her for years and she has refused him," explained the Colonel. "But tonight she will give in to him." Greta was in a terrible state, convinced her daughter was about to be ravished.

"Herr Rust, please join us here," called Colonel Malek, clapping him on the back and producing a bottle of pink vodka. He handed Alfred a small glass full to the brim. "That glass has stood in the cold waters of the lake," he informed Alfred. "And now, like a good Socialist, you must join us."

Helga's dance partner fled to join the drinking bout. One hour later, Alfred passed out.

At nine-thirty a motorcycle and sidecar roared up the gravel driveway. The man in the sidecar produced a camera, the driver a notepad. The reporters belonged to a new German newspaper under strict Russian control. They were to show how well the Russians were treating the Berliners. They decided to ignore the drunken soldiers.

Colonel Malek called for silence. "A toast to our hosts," he began. He turned to Frieda, who had survived an evening of genial boorishness quite well. "To Comrade Stalin and the soldiers who have fought the Great Patriotic War," he bellowed across the lawn. A great cheer went up. "And last of all to our American friends who will be here tomorrow," shouted the Colonel. This toast was not greeted quite so enthusiastically, as rifts had already appeared in the Allied ranks. A captain and two soldiers pulled out the telephone wires running from the house. "We don't want our American friends listening in to any of our conversations," he explained to Frieda.

Alfred was the first to rise on a bright sunny morning and the house was silent. Every sign the Russians had been there had gone. Frieda took her silver-topped walking cane and toured the grounds. Alfred caught up with her. "Please bring pen and paper, Alfred. We must make a note of what must be done to restore the house," said Frieda.

Alfred faithfully followed Frieda round the premises. "Please note the roof. It is in need of repair Alfred," she said. He scribbled furiously. "And we must try to find Stephan. The garden is not beyond restoration. Oh, and we must repair Gustav's workshop and the teahouse," she continued.

Alfred allowed her to bask in her unreality for a short while before reminding her that the Americans would be arriving soon. "We had better welcome them Alfred I suppose," she said in a resigned fashion. "The repairs will have to wait. We will welcome guests in the way we have always done."

CHAPTER THIRTY

Alfred took up station on the road outside. Within minutes he was running towards the house, waving frantically.

A Jeep, flying the American flag, drove slowly down the drive, followed by two six-wheeled trucks packed with soldiers. The convoy stopped at the foot of the house steps, to be confronted by Frieda and the welcoming committee. A stocky figure with a round red face and rimless spectacles jumped out of the front passenger seat. He stood staring at Frieda and the damaged roof in turn with his hands on his hips.

The welcoming committee was much smaller now, but it still managed to look as if the Americans were intruders. The big American behaved as if they weren't there. A junior officer jumped out of the back seat and joined him. "What do you think Frank?" asked the big man. Helga and Alfred shifted nervously.

"Colonel, I think this lady is important. Remember the latest communiqué. Don't forget protocol," whispered the passenger.

"OK Frank, get the men to fall in," said the Colonel. "Let's get it over with."

Forty men formed two lines, standing at ease. The senior American was joined by an interpreter and he mounted the steps.

"To whom am I speaking ma'am?" he asked impatiently.

"I am Frau von Saloman and I am the owner of this house," replied Frieda haughtily.

"Major Aubrey Macey, United States Third Army ma'am, and this is Lieutenant Frank Stephenson." He clicked his fingers at the lieutenant, who produced a copy of a German document headed by the Eagle and swastika. He had already made a legal search with the help of a Lieutenant James Bradford and found that the house belonged to the defeated German government. He handed the document to Frieda, who saw her signature at the foot of the page. "I think that says the ownership is in some doubt, ma'am," said Macey.

"Colonel," said Lieutenant Stephenson, reminding his senior officer of his manners. Macey became polite and businesslike, while Frank Stephenson began to lose concentration. He was distracted by the most beautiful woman he had ever seen and was not discouraged by the little boy standing beside her.

"Ma'am," began the Colonel. "I must tell you this property has been temporarily made over to the United States occupation forces. My men and I are to be billeted here by order of the Allied Control Commission. You must realise that we must have the pick of the rooms and have no obligation to feed you. Do you understand?" he said.

Frank Stephenson intervened, horrified by Macey's attitude. "May I speak with you alone Major?"

"OK Frank, spit it out," was Macey's reply.

"Have you seen the Russian occupation newsletters, Major?" asked the Lieutenant.

Macey said he hadn't and Stephenson produced one from his briefcase. The photograph on the front page showed Frieda and company drinking a toast to Stalin. Macey produced a large cigar and lit it. "That makes me feel like throwing them out," he retorted.

"Major, if we don't treat these people well, the Russians will be seen as one up on us," insisted Stephenson. Macey drew on his cigar and Frieda began to look annoyed.

"As usual Frank, you're right. Ask the old lady where they lived and let 'em stay there."

Major Macey grinned. "Maybe that means Kaminski, Fazola and Timms'll have to camp out on the grass." Macey knew that Frank usually had nothing but problems with these three.

"There's one other thing Frank," said Macey. "Was your advice motivated by anything else?"

Frank Stephenson looked puzzled. "It's a little early to start fraternising with the enemy, Frank," said Macey.

Frieda had to give up one room on the first floor and move to an adjoining one with a leaking ceiling from the damaged roof. Within twenty-four hours, Private First Class Walter Timms and his friends had repaired it. Helga had to move to the ground floor for two days. Aubrey Macey mischievously suggested Frank should help.

Frank was shy and studious and if it hadn't been for Helga's ambitions, he would have made no progress at all. Manfred stared at Frank suspiciously. The American knelt down to his level and offered to shake hands. He drew away, but Helga told him to offer his hand. Frank made signs to ask Manfred to carry some smaller articles. He brightened up and Helga was struck by Frank's patience. He chided himself for his ignorance of German. The only thing he could manage was to say how beautiful the lake was. Frank was genuinely smitten, and resolved to learn to speak German.

Frieda invited Major Macey for morning coffee. He accepted because he was fascinated by the survival of the old German aristocracy. Frieda was anxious to re-establish her ownership of the house, and making a friend and ally of Aubrey Macey would be a good start. Frieda stared at him indulgently, expecting him to make the running in the conversation and placing him at a disadvantage. It was bad enough for the American, who knew only slightly more German than his Lieutenant. Greta served them German ersatz coffee with an apologetic look. Aubrey Macey smiled and produced some of his own, equally apologetically. The relationship had got off to a good start.

Aubrey Macey couldn't help but notice the photographs of Adam and Bruno in SS uniforms and remembered Frank's advice. "Two fine looking young men," he said.

"This is my grandson," Frieda began, holding Adam's photograph. "He was to inherit this house, but now that will not happen. They were both killed at Arnhem. All my family have gone now Major."

"I am sorry ma'am," said Macey. He held Adam's photo and noted the jaunty angle of the cap, the smartness and the Knight's Cross. He committed the striking features to memory. Frieda could not possibly know the problems this would cause.

Private Timms reminded the others of the favours Frank Stephenson had done them, but they were not impressed. "We've kept him alive," retorted Kaminski. "We're quits." "Cut the cards," he said to Jonny Fazola, who offered the pack in turn to the other two. "Aces are high," Kaminski reminded them. "Winner gets the blonde Nazi."

"I think the Lieutenant beat us all to it. Look you guys," Timms said pointing towards the lake shore. Frank Stephenson was walking down to the lakeside, holding Manfred's hand.

Helga had begun to take stock of her prospects. One afternoon she walked with Manfred on the shingle beach watching the pleasure steamers sail once more. She looked at the battered rowing boat and decided it was a symbol of a lost past. Adam was presumed dead and Bruno was gone. The future belonged to Manfred and herself.

She was distracted by Kaminski and his friends swimming in the lake. They had converted Gustav's shed to a temporary bathing hut and were diving into the water from the rocky outcrop. Kaminski hadn't given up. He shouted to Helga. His head disappeared several times and he waved his legs in the air. Helga enjoyed the attention and Manfred laughed.

Helga was still trying to pretend she wasn't interested when Manfred tugged her hand and pointed. A solitary figure stood on the edge of the forest, gazing out on to the lake. A bicycle was propped against a tree quite near him. His head was shaven, almost bare, and he wore a grey suit which seemed too big for him.

He carried a rucksack over one shoulder and cast a few glances in Helga's direction, the last one lingering, as if he recognised her. She felt compelled to walk along the shingle beach towards him. Manfred pulled her back, but she pulled him along him in the direction of the stranger. The figure turned, as if startled, mounted the cycle and disappeared into the forest.

Frank sat at a table in the tea house, dictating a letter. He smiled and waved to Helga. It was a hot day and he pointed to the water, suggesting they might go for a swim. Helga waved back but wouldn't consider it while Kaminski and his friends were in the water.

Frank wondered if he was making advances too soon. He crunched his way down the shingle beach and joined them.

"Good afternoon Frank," she said brightly. "Perhaps it is a little too soon to swim together don't you think?" Frank was ashamed at his clumsiness but didn't give up.

"There is one other thing, ma'am," Frank said, remembering a more innocent ploy. "I would like to join the United States Education Corps here in Berlin. I know my teaching experience would help, but I've been told I have to know German." She looked puzzled.

"Would you teach me?" he asked.

Helga tried to hide her delight. She said she would, on condition Greta and Frieda approved, which was calculated to make Frank sweat a little more.

CHAPTER THIRTY

Within twenty-four hours approval was forthcoming and Frank's German lessons began. After the first few, Manfred was left with Greta and Frank noticed Helga beginning to pay extra attention to her appearance. After three weeks she appeared one day in a lace top and a stunning blue dress. Her plaits had gone and her long hair fell on her shoulders. Frank had never wanted to make love so much, and found it hard to concentrate on the lessons.

At first for Helga, it was pure opportunism, but now it turned into something else. She'd had reservations about all the men she'd met except Adam, but considered Frank to be the most decent one she had ever met. Helga began to fall for him.

She wondered how long she could keep Frank waiting. She needn't have worried. He understood her concerns and moved carefully, cultivating a friendship with Greta and the nearest thing possible with Frieda.

Helga had to be sure and she tested him in a subtle way. He asked about the old rowing boat. Helga said she had been rowed by her now dead husband and his closest friend who was to inherit the house. The stories left Frank in no doubt that she had been very fond of both of them. She produced a photograph of them just before their summons to the Waffen SS in Hitler Youth uniform.

"And you had a choice of these guys?" he asked wide-eyed. He was hugely impressed and not a little flattered that Helga wanted to spend time with him. Helga thought it was a good start, but she didn't tell him about the photographs of the two friends in Waffen SS uniforms which stood on Frieda's dressing table. She thought that might have worried Frank.

"Would you like to go out in the boat again, Helga?" he asked, thinking it might be a potent symbol if she agreed. Helga said she would and Frank said he could rebuild it. His father owned a boatbuilding business in Tarpon Springs, Florida, and had taught his son some of his skills. He said he might consider leaving the teaching profession and joining his father's business. None of this was lost on Helga.

Frank rebuilt the boat with tools and timber acquired by Kaminski's friends from United States Army Stores. Sometimes Frank rowed Helga and Manfred. At other times Manfred stayed with Greta, but always Frank allowed Helga to decide who would be rowed. Occasionally he took her to the American Officers' Club in nearby Wilmersdorf. She had never met so many charming people, but she resisted all attempts to prise her away from Frank. As the summer progressed Frank realised he was hopelessly in love, and Helga realised she couldn't deny him much longer.

Each time they drove back in the borrowed army Jeep, she allowed Frank to kiss her lightly. Helga remembered that Bruno could never have stood for a delay like this. One September evening, Frank drove to the foot of the house steps, still unsure of Helga's feelings. "Let's go for a boat ride," he suggested. She allowed her fingers to travel gently over his face and agreed. Within minutes Frank had launched the boat. He rowed her without any intention of going far.

He shipped the oars. "Thank you for today," she whispered. Her fingers extended up his wrist and she moved carefully to sit beside him. The boat nearly capsized and Frank caught her. She kissed him fiercely and he responded.

"Come to me tonight," she whispered in his ear. "Come at ten o'clock."

Frank rowed as he had never rowed before. The boat grounded roughly and they both leapt out. He kissed her again and lifted her off the sand before she could put her shoes back on. She ran back to the house, stopped at the kitchen door and waved to him. She planned to put Manfred to bed before ten o'clock.

Manfred demanded his favourite story, in which the pleasure steamers sailed across the lake to a land where the passengers turned into knights and woodland fairies. Helga told the story, trying to suppress her excitement. Greta came in to say goodnight and Helga's patience began to wear thin. Greta hadn't failed to notice the progress in her daughter's relationship. When the little boy was asleep Greta whispered to her, "I think you need to relax yourself my darling, before you sleep. Be careful how you do it."

Manfred opened one eye as Helga kissed him and said, "Papa isn't here, is he Mutti," and his eyes closed.

Helga had left herself ten minutes. She went to her room and renewed her makeup. At ten o'clock there was a gentle knock at the door. Helga drew Frank in and locked the door and he kissed her passionately. She laughed and broke away, leading him to the bed, still determined to keep the initiative. She unbuttoned his tunic and hung it on the back of the door, pretending to brush it, quietly singing to herself, and throwing off her shoes.

She unbuttoned her blouse. Then she took his hand and laid it on her left breast, allowing him to feel her erect nipple. Frank knelt on the floor and removed her skirt. She lifted him up and her hand fell to his waist and below, moving up and down on his erection. He let his trousers slide to the floor. Within seconds he had lifted her on to the bed and knelt between her legs. She whispered, "I want your child."

Helga controlled his movements almost clinically and only abandoned her control just before Frank ejaculated. They slept the soundest sleep imaginable, but in the morning, after Frank tried to get to the Major's office before anyone appeared on the stairs, Helga's fears took hold of her. She still believed she might be abandoned, and Greta didn't help when they met at the top of the stairs.

"You've made your decision, my darling," she said, as if it was a dubious one.

Helga saw the chance to escape a lifetime of service. Greta promised, "Of course, I will say nothing to Madam. And it's possible you've made a good choice."

Helga didn't allow Frank to make love to her again until she was certain of his plans. At the end of their final German lesson, he showed Helga the letter turning down his application for the Education Corps. She was stunned into silence and thought for a moment that she was to become another victim of a short relationship with a foreign soldier, but Frank had other ideas.

"Will you return to the United States with me as my wife?" he asked. She looked at him open-mouthed, then recovered and clung to him. "Why yes, of course," she answered.

They walked on the shingle beach arm in arm. Frank told her what it was like in Tarpon Springs and Helga said it must be the boatbuilding capital of the world. From that moment, the initiative passed to Frank, and he felt he could now make an enquiry. He glanced towards the Grunewald.

"Do you know that guy by the edge of the lake?" he asked. Helga was caught by surprise, as she hadn't seen him this time. The stranger limped away and disappeared.

Chapter 31

In August 1945, bombers used the power of the sun to obliterate two Japanese cities. Military ambulances rescued some of the survivors trudging away from the ruins with terrible burns. Some were fortunate enough to arrive at a specially-prepared ward in a Tokyo Hospital. The doctor in charge was an expert in war wounds, and he was not Japanese. The small, portly dark-haired European had been transferred from internment in Osaka in the hope that his expertise could be of some help. All Dr Jacob Meissner could do was administer treatment for severe burns. He looked on helplessly for days on end as the injuries refused to heal.

In late August of 1945, the American battleship *Missouri* sailed into Tokyo Bay. Occupying American troops discovered Jacob Meissner, and given his Jewish ancestry they were surprised he had survived. Jacob said the worst that had happened was being insulted by visiting German SS officers on a train. He had enjoyed the protection of senior Japanese officers who believed they were descended from the lost tribe of Israel. That, said Jacob, explained his preferential treatment.

Within days he had boarded an American warship bound for San Francisco. The international reputation he had built before the war guaranteed him a welcome in the United States, where he became a respected medical practitioner and lecturer. He retired in the early 1970s to a house and garden in the district of Sausalito, overlooking the Golden Gate Bridge. He was fiercely protected by his manservant and companion Stephen. "Our great country has given you a wonderful retirement, sir," remarked Stephen.

"Indeed it has," answered Jacob thoughtfully.

"You mean you wish to qualify that, sir?" asked Stephen.

"No, certainly not," answered the doctor. "It's just that there will always be something which will never be resolved, Stephen. I would not be here were it not for a remarkable young man I met in China who saved my life."

"The authorities are quite sure he died in Arnhem in September 1944, sir," replied Stephen.

"Yes I know, but there is always hope," sighed Jacob.

As Adam slid into a deep decline, he still felt unable to justify the deaths of Schneider and Rademacher, let alone Jurgen Kammler. He decided he would admit the whole thing to Topf at the next interview. He wrote a letter to his American captors asking them not to publish details of his death, so that the von Saloman name should not be sullied. Adam was sure Topf's inquiries would end with his execution.

Inspector Topf was satisfied with the inquiries he had made. He felt it would only be a matter of time before Sergeant's Thaelmann and Stamm were arrested.

Late one night he received a visit from two unannounced callers who refused to identify themselves. "Who the hell are you?" asked Topf.

"That is no concern of yours," the leader announced. "We're here to tell you it's important that von Saloman survives, Herr Kriminalrat. His unit fought bravely and was not guilty of any so-called war crimes. I'm sure you'll understand Germany will need its heroes in the future."

"Matters have gone too far," replied Topf. "We are close to the accused's accomplices."

"These are the accomplices," said the man producing a photograph of two charred bodies. "They are buried in their family cemeteries, which are here." He produced details of two cemeteries, both in Hamburg.

"But what of my colleagues Schneider and Kammler? Surely they deserve justice," retorted Topf.

His visitor became menacing. "If necessary, they will be taken care of," he said, implying that Topf might face a similar fate if he pursued his enquiries.

Adam's cell cleaner was a small dark-haired man who never lifted his head or spoke. Lewis Grindleford had just failed once again to persuade Adam to take food when the cleaner arrived.

"You gotta eat," the guard implored Adam. "It's a big day today. You gotta be on top form." Lewis Grindleford had grown close to Adam, but his words fell on deaf ears. Grindleford left and locked the door, leaving his prisoner with the cleaner.

The cleaner lifted his head. He produced a piece of paper from inside his overall and briefly waved it at Adam. On it was printed in large letters, "SAY NOTHING". He slipped it back into his overall, finished cleaning the cell, and left.

As soon as he had gone, two military policemen arrived to escort Adam to the interview hall.

"Prisoner 146 von Saloman, stand to attention," one of them barked. A tired, dispirited Adam complied. There had been no heating in the cell and he began to shiver uncontrollably. He was handcuffed yet again and led to the interview hall in silence.

When they reached the hall, Adam's handcuffs were removed and he was led inside. It was almost empty. Adam glanced from side to side, but there was no sign of Inspector Kammler. The only occupant of the hall was the mysterious German police sergeant who had been present at Adam's first interview.

The door behind the sergeant opened. An American colonel walked in and the sergeant fell in behind him. They stopped at Adam's table. "Please sit down," said the Colonel.

It was the first time the German sergeant had approached Adam. He looked the prisoner full in the face and Adam felt his nerves grow taut. It was Julius Kolb. Adam's old sergeant stood perfectly still with his arms behind his back.

"I am Colonel John Cresswell of the Allied Control Commission," announced the American. "I am here today to offer an apology for the treatment you have received." There was a pause and Kolb shifted slightly.

"The American and British authorities have mistaken your identity. This became clear when Sergeant Kolb delivered your papers to my office," he said. "Sergeant, please, the Lieutenant's papers."

Kolb gave Adam the old look and it had an electrifying effect. Adam remembered the fatigues handed out for poor turnout. This time, Kolb would have been justified in giving him another. Adam mentally snapped to attention, and Kolb laid a set of identity papers in front of him. Adam's eyebrows rose. They belonged to a Lieutenant Kurt Vietinghoff of the Fifteenth Army.

CHAPTER THIRTY ONE

"Thank you Colonel. Thank you Sergeant," said Adam, saluting the Colonel instinctively.

"That will be all Sergeant," said Cresswell, and Julius Kolb left the interview hall. Adam remembered the cleaner's advice and joined in the charade.

"Do you have a family we might contact, Lieutenant?" the Colonel asked warmly. Adam quickly collected his thoughts. "I am not married, Colonel and have no surviving family," answered Adam.

"Would you mind waiting for a few minutes?" asked Colonel Cresswell. He disappeared into a glass cubicle at the end of the hall to pick up a telephone. He seemed excited and agitated as he spoke. Then he relaxed, smiled and replaced the receiver.

"May I enquire, Lieutenant, what educational qualifications you have?"

Adam was a member of an aristocratic family, yet he possessed nothing beyond his abitur examination. Even that meant little to the outside world now, because standards had dropped alarmingly under the National Socialists, but he put a brave face on it.

"I have a good knowledge of mathematics, science, music and languages," he said proudly, beginning to recover some of his old confidence and humour. "And I have a good knowledge of military science."

Cresswell was not amused and cut him short impatiently. The American became businesslike. "Yes, yes Lieutenant. That's OK. I have a proposition to make to you." Adam showed little interest at first. "The Allied forces have a difficult task in Berlin," continued Cresswell. "I am part of a team which will re-establish free and open education in Germany." He paused and leaned forward. "I have just received authorisation to offer you the post of Chief Librarian for the area of Wilmersdorf. Could you, at least, give me a conditional acceptance?" he asked.

Adam again raised his eyebrows. "You are prepared to see an ex-soldier of the Reich become a librarian here?" he asked.

Cresswell seemed to know more about Adam than he had revealed. "Your career as a professional soldier is over, Lieutenant," remarked Cresswell. "It could be that compliance might now be your best course of action."

Adam glanced over Cresswell's shoulder. Julius Kolb was watching the proceedings as impassively as ever. He behaved as if he was in a supervisory role, and Adam reacted accordingly. He crossed his hands and leaned forwards. "Yes Colonel, I accept the post," he replied. Kolb nodded approval.

"Your assistant is Heidi Graebner. She may frighten you a little, Lieutenant. She has an interesting background and should be a great help to you. Your accommodation is ready for you now in the United States Military Campus and transport is waiting outside."

Cresswell hadn't finished. He reached under the table and handed Adam a briefcase. "Today is Thursday," he began. "You will open the library doors on Monday. I will expect a report on the library's progress within thirty days."

"Of course Colonel," replied Adam, reacting as he would always have done to a senior officer.

" I leave you in the capable hands of Sergeant Kolb," said Cresswell.

"We will meet soon, and by the way, there were no other applicants for your job," he added with a conspiratorial grin. He left hurriedly with a nod to Kolb, who marched towards Adam in the old swaggering way. "There's no time to lose," he said. "Follow me."

They returned to Adam's cell and Kolb slammed the door shut. "Welcome back to Germany, Hauptsturmführer," said Kolb, giving the SS salute which Adam returned briskly. "Please listen carefully," he said perusing Adam's new identity papers. "You have seen now how we look after our people. There are supporting documents in old army files which are not yet in American hands which confirm you are Lieutenant Vietinghoff of an Engineer Battalion in the Fifteenth Army. You worked on the Atlantic wall and there are drawings for you to study in the briefcase." Kolb almost smiled. "Cresswell knows they're there," he added. "All documents relating to your old identity have been removed from Topf's office and destroyed."

"Do you have any news of my comrades, Sergeant?" Adam asked. Kolb was pleased he had enquired.

"Thaelmann and Stamm are alive and well. Both survived the Ardennes attack at Christmas under their old names, but like you, they now have new identities." The urgency in his voice grew. "Don't try to contact them. It's too dangerous. You have enemies here and you must begin your new life as soon as possible." He became deferential. "I have followed your career closely. It's a matter of regret I was unable to serve under you, Hauptsturmführer." he said. They exchanged salutes. "My deep regret at Grabowsky's passing. You'll all miss him," Kolb added with one hand on the door.

CHAPTER THIRTY ONE

"I wasn't too hard on you was I, Hauptsturmführer?" he asked with the half-smile which involved a slight movement of his bushy eyebrows.

Adam laughed for the first time in a long time. "You surely don't expect an answer to that, sergeant," he replied. Kolb nodded and was gone.

Lewis Grindleford conducted Adam to a waiting Jeep. The American farm boy would miss the German officer he respected so much.

Adam's new quarters were basic. He found two grey suits in the wardrobe and several sets of underwear in a battered chest of drawers. There was a desk with pens, paper and a typewriter. On the desk was a bottle of schnapps and a note from Julius Kolb which said, "Best wishes, Kolb." Adam's old sergeant had made him snap out of his mental torpor. The mindless discipline of the training camp at Braunschweig had saved him. Without Kolb's presence Adam thought he might have rejected Cresswell's offer. He was exhausted. He sank down on the bed and slept for several hours.

He was awakened by an American soldier who asked if there was anything he needed. The guard took him down to the mess hall, where Adam ate heartily and began to feel ashamed of his self-pity.

When he returned to his room, he looked at himself in the mirror. He was pale, hollow-cheeked and unshaven and his hair was as long as it had been in China. His eyes were red from lack of sleep. Even if his family were alive, they would surely never recognise him.

There was a knock at the door. Colonel Cresswell was about to present a different image. He was a man under pressure and surprised Adam yet again.

"A lot of people have taken risks for you, von Saloman," he began. "Don't let us down. You won't get another chance. Nine o'clock sharp in the morning and for Christ's sake visit the barber downstairs." He left as if he would rather not be recognised.

Perhaps Cresswell's contempt was greater for Inspector Kammler and his colleagues, or he had a sneaking regard for aristocrats. Then Adam realised that the Colonel would do anything to start the library, to please his seniors.

Kolb's impact went far beyond Adam's decision to become a librarian, and he began to think once again of Gabrielle and their daughter. He remembered the day his father had bought him a bicycle and Bruno and Helga's merriment as he attempted to ride it. He announced to a group of American soldiers that he needed one and within thirty minutes, they found one. Now Adam was mobile.

He resolved to cycle to his old school. It was sure to be a ruin and the staff long gone or dead. Perhaps someone in the vicinity would know where the staff had gone, in particular a certain substitute maths teacher. He decided to treat the whole affair as a fantasy he could revisit from time to time and abandoned his scheme.

The following morning Adam heard the revving of a Jeep engine. Cresswell, in the front passenger seat, was irritated and kept looking at his watch. The other passenger in the rear seat was Adam's new assistant. She got out of the Jeep to introduce herself, as Adam approached. Heidi Graebner was smart and in her early fifties. Her face was thin and her expression alert.

"Please don't worry," she assured him. "I have already been to the church hall to make arrangements. I hope they meet with your approval."

Her eyebrows rose a little at Adam's reply. "Thank you Frau Graebner. I shall examine what has been done, but I'm sure you have started well." Cresswell wanted them both to be compliant, but he realised he might be disappointed.

The Jeep tore off at breakneck speed to Wilmersdorf. It appeared the Colonel was making a point. Most of the craters in the Brandenburgische Strasse had been filled in, but the Jeep was forced to stop for a team of volunteer female labourers. Adam and Heidi watched the women gathering undamaged bricks and carefully stacking them for reconstruction. Adam nodded to them and to his consternation, one of them waved back. It was Hanni Dirksen's sister from another apartment block in Charlottenbrunnestrasse. He was relieved when the Jeep tore off once more and turned into Charlottenbrunnestrasse, towards the church hall.

The splintered trees in the park were gone. Some elderly people, nearly all women, sat in the sunshine on restored benches. The Jeep slowed as a bulldozer crossed the street in front of Frieda's old apartment. Adam gazed at the ruins, which didn't surprise Cresswell for he had done his homework well. "Forget it," he said to Adam without turning his head.

Adam thought of enquiring what he meant and realised that Cresswell was not about to make further revelations.

CHAPTER THIRTY ONE

A six-wheeled American army truck, guarded by two soldiers, stood outside the front door. Another group was unloading timber and office equipment to the sound of curses. All went quiet when one of them spotted the Colonel.

The Jeep party waited while several sealed wooden crates were carried into the hall. Two soldiers were ripping out the old stage, while others were already banging and sawing, building lines of new bookshelves. As fast as they were built, painters got to work. Two new desks were put in place of the stage and the bigger of the two had a telephone line. Cresswell picked up a crowbar and handed it to his new librarian.

"Try opening the crates, Lieutenant," he suggested. "You have a line direct to my office. I'll leave you to do some cataloguing maybe. I'll pick both of you up at four o'clock sharp."

"How will the people know about the library?" asked Adam. Cresswell pointed to a loudhailer in the front of the Jeep. "You'll hear me telling them in the next hour," he assured Adam, "and it tells them in the new newspaper. Don't let me down. I'll see you at four o'clock."

He had a last word with the guards on the door, pointing to Adam and Heidi, and was gone. They heard the Colonel in the distance, informing the people of Wilmersdorf in bad German of the new library. A few gaunt and apathetic figures emerged from the ruins to stare after the Jeep. Reading books, it seemed, was not one of their priorities.

An American sergeant asked Heidi for instructions. She pointed out that Adam was now in charge. Adam examined the new shelves and gave the impression that he was an expert. He startled Heidi.

"May I ask you, Frau Graebner, what are your qualifications for this post?" he enquired. Adam had meant it as an innocent enquiry, but the tone he adopted put Heidi on her guard and she seemed distressed.

"Herr Vietinghoff," she began, her voice shaking with emotion, "I have run a particular type of library for several years. I am a Doctor of Philosophy and was forced to resign after insisting that the views of Jewish philosophers should also be considered. I spent a great deal of the war in a special archive as a punishment. I was forced to collate and make available for borrowers as many anti-semitic tracts as could be found. So you see Herr Vietinghoff, I can organise a library."

Adam gave her a little bow and apologised. "I am in your capable hands," he announced. "Now Heidi, I must demonstrate my skill with a crowbar." He cracked open the top crate and out fell a few musical biographies. He had read one or two of them and found a biography of Felix Mendelssohn. Both agreed it would be interesting to see what would happen to a book about a Jewish musician. It was one of the first to be borrowed, and a week later was found torn to pieces in the park. Adam and Heidi never saw the borrower again. Clearly things were not going to change in Germany overnight.

Heidi was excited by a crate full of books on western philosophy. She hurried to catalogue them, but found that Adam didn't have the same urgency. She found him turning the pages of Sigmund Freud, remembering that Jacob Meissner had mentioned his work. He broke open a crate full of American Westerns and books on the American film industry. He found a biography of Rudolf Valentino and Heidi was curious when he asked her to catalogue and then reserve it. A mere suggestion of Adam's was like a command. He could not tell Heidi that he hoped his grandmother, a Rudolph Valentino fan, would pop by and borrow it. Both agreed that books on the American Constitution should be displayed prominently out of politeness to Colonel Cresswell.

Heidi grew more and more curious about her new boss. Cresswell had told her most of the responsibility would be hers, but Adam grew more dominant and his old condescension began to re-emerge. His imperious attitude began to irritate Heidi, and he seemed to sense this. He modified his attitude, returning to his old charm. The light appeared once again in his piercing blue eyes and she believed she had never met anyone with so much charisma.

On a few occasions he did not immediately respond to his name, and he signed documents slowly and deliberately. These were small matters, but they aroused Heidi's suspicions and she decided to make enquiries.

Colonel Cresswell always took Heidi home at the end of each day. One evening she was met at her apartment door by a young German policeman. He bowed politely and asked for a few minutes of her time.

"There are some who do not favour the opening of the new library, Frau Graebner," he began. "The safety of you and your colleague is of great concern to us. You are easy to track, unlike your colleague. We would like you to inform us of his movements from day to day. This, of course, must be kept secret."

CHAPTER THIRTY ONE

Heidi instinctively felt protective towards Adam. "You could surely do that yourselves," she suggested. The policeman had been told not to push the matter by his Chief in Police Intelligence. "Perhaps you are right Frau Graebner," he said and retired politely to report to his superior, Inspector Rolf Schneider. She became more and more protective towards her new boss.

The time for the first report to Colonel Cresswell drew near. He paid an unannounced visit and found Adam supervising the building of a private study area. Cresswell was annoyed by this side project, which he felt might delay the opening, but left the two librarians alone after Heidi had assured him it was essential to the running of the library. Many of its clients would have agreed, but only because it was warmer there than in the ruins.

"I will have to telephone the Colonel, Kurt," said Heidi. "We have received an incorrect delivery and he may be blamed for it."

On the side of a crate just delivered, it read, 'University of Berlin Dahlem'. Painted on the top of the crates were several Chinese characters. Adam reached for the telephone and then changed his mind. He was completely preoccupied by the crate and almost ignored the sergeant, who asked, "How many guys do you want to seat back here?"

Adam shouted to a number back to the Sergeant while he toyed with the crowbar. "We must not touch the crate," warned Heidi. "The university is so important." Adam ignored her and broke it open. Nearly all the books they had received so far were reprints but not these; they were old leather-bound books. He picked up one from the top. "How can this be useful to us?" she asked.

Adam had suddenly become quite serene. "This is a book of Chinese medicine," he explained, reading a few lines to her. Now she believed he would reveal himself.

He turned some more of the pages. "Give me your hand Heidi," he said. "If you have a headache I can relieve it for you by pressing this and this." She withdrew her hand, as if offended. "This won't go down well in Germany now," laughed Adam. He had picked up *The Art of War* by Sun Tzu.

Adam found himself transported to a life he thought had gone forever. He found another volume of the sayings of Confucius, which he had torn apart. He read a section to Heidi and was excited. "This means so much to me," he explained, holding the book to his chest, the veil of mystery falling from his face.

"We have to send them on to Dahlem," insisted Heidi.

"These books are not going anywhere. I will personally catalogue them myself," he said assertively." He added quietly, "I will deal with Cresswell if it becomes necessary."

Heidi Graebner knew then that Adam had lived another life. She liked and respected him and agreed to conspire together to keep the books. She jolted him back to reality by telling him about the police request, yet he continued to take risks by exploring the area on his bicycle. He cycled to the old sports stadium in the Grünewald and then down the forest paths to the old changing huts from his schooldays. Then he plucked up more courage and cycled to the end of the shingle beach near the house.

Every day Adam took home one or more of the books, and there were no enquiries as to their whereabouts. He kept them in the most inaccessible places, and was even tempted to hide the ladders the American soldiers had made.

Heidi noticed pieces of paper protruding from one of the books. She thought they were bookmarks, until she gave them a second look. They were crammed with pencilled comments. She thought most of them naïve, but some had flashes of insight. She realised her new boss had written them, and confronted him.

"Try reading these," she said, giving him several books by philosophers from other countries. He said he would try, and within a few days, he was excited by one particular volume. It was by Henry David Thoreau, the American natural philosopher. He returned it to Heidi with the comment, "These Americans live in a different world." Heidi was disappointed but patient. She talked with him the next day about the American philosopher.

"Patience, Kurt, it's the same world as yours and mine. It's another contribution, like all the others you've read," she advised.

To Heidi's surprise he began to treat her like a respected tutor. He scratched his chin and replied. "Of course you're right. How stupid of me," displaying humility she didn't think possible. Adam took Thoreau's work home again and within two days was sorry he had done so. Thoreau's words rang in his head. "A man cannot escape his wrongdoing. It is like leaving footprints in the snow."

He began to disregard Cresswell's instructions on security more and more. He began to use the park after hours as an area for private study, carefully avoiding any familiar faces. He relaxed his guard when he saw Hanni Dirksen's sister again. She behaved as if she'd seen a ghost, but recovered enough to tell Adam that all trace of Frieda and Greta was gone. They had been officially posted missing.

"Perhaps now, you have no one. I'll meet you here and talk with you if you wish," she offered. Adam accepted gratefully, but had exposed himself to danger. The young policeman who had spoken to Heidi watched from a distance. He made a note for his superior that Adam used the park regularly after the American guards had gone back to barracks.

One evening Hanni's sister Ulrika sent a message to say she couldn't be there that day. Adam lingered in the park and turned to one of his books, watched from the park entrance by the young policeman walking up and down as if he was on patrol.

Adam glanced in the direction of Frieda's old apartment and closed the book, consumed by curiosity. He left the park, passing the policeman. He passed Berger and Schöler's old offices, now a bomb crater.

He slowed as he approached No.1 Charlottenbrunnestrasse. It was too risky, he thought. Albert Hartmann would be there. They had been close, but in these days, who could you call a friend?

Adam carried on walking, then stopped at the front steps, peering cautiously through the front doors towards Albert's office. The door was wide open and hung partly off its hinges, and Albert was clearly long gone. He walked to the rear of the building, to the spot where he believed his mother had died. He remembered there had been an agreement not to remove the charred timbers and collapsed stonework during the period of mourning, but it had now been cleared.

Adam turned to go, paused at the front of the building and peered in. The remains of the stairwell were still there, with a large red notice forbidding entry. Adam looked at his watch. Cresswell didn't like to be kept waiting, but perhaps there was just time to look at the remains of his old room.

He stood in the middle of Frieda's old lounge and remembered Gabrielle putting her empty cup on the table and turning to be introduced. The far wall still showed the outlines of family pictures, but this family treasure trove was now gone.

He glanced towards the wreckage of his old room. Charred timbers and rubble remained where his chest of drawers and tall cupboard had been. He lifted some collapsed stonework and it seemed safe. He examined the chest of drawers, but each one was empty, as if it had been looted. He moved a metal joist and a few more stones. There was an ominous rumble and he started back.

The cupboard was still there, intact even though the latch had rusted solid. Adam hit it with a stone. It broke and the door creaked open slightly. He pulled it open and stood back. There, still in its scabbard, was the Warlord's broadsword.

Adam lovingly removed it. He drew the sword and laid it across both his palms. Then he walked into the garden at the rear and faced the sun as he had done on the rock at the Si-Kiang house. He stood at the ready, waiting for an enemy to strike, holding the sword with both hands, feeling an elation he had not felt for many years, and standing stock still for as long as he could. He felt the blood coursing through his veins as life began to return. He lowered the sword and replaced it in its scabbard, turning to leave.

"Put your hands in the air," said a voice behind him. "Hände hoch!" Adam turned slowly without obeying the command. Facing him was an American soldier. "Hände hoch!" called out the soldier again, thrusting his rifle forward.

"I speak English, private," said Adam quietly, as if he were speaking to a subordinate.

"I am arresting you on behalf of the United States Occupation Forces," announced the soldier. "You are guilty of looting and you will now come with me." Adam stood firm. "I am retrieving my own property," he said.

"Show me your papers," said the American sharply. Adam handed them over. "I have retrieved my property and intend to return to my place of work which is under the care of your Occupation Forces," he announced, walking past the soldier as if he were an irrelevance.

"Halt!" shouted the American. Adam heard the rifle bolt drawn back. He quickened his pace towards the library. "I have been ordered to shoot looters," shouted the American. Adam carried on at an even pace.

If the man fired, he would have done his duty and Adam would never again have to face the consequences of his former life. He had just reached the beginning of the next apartment block when a shot rang out. The bullet removed chips of stone from a wall above Adam's head.

He stopped and turned to face the soldier.

CHAPTER THIRTY ONE

If it were to end, it must not come from a shot in the back. He stared at the American, who levelled his rifle. "What the hell's going on?" shouted a breathless Cresswell as he ran up to Adam's side.

The soldier was embarrassed and ashamed when he discovered that Adam's story was true. Cresswell threatened to report him to his superior officer, assuring him Adam was officially indispensable. When the soldier had been dismissed, a puzzled Cresswell turned to Adam. "What the hell were you playing at?" he said. Adam had no answer other than to hold up the sword. The Colonel shook his head, deciding to take the matter no further. He reached into the back of the Jeep, producing a bottle of bourbon and three glasses. "Let's go and drink a toast to the library opening day," he said. "I've an announcement to make."

He marched into the library and banged the bottle and glasses down on the table. "Come out from behind those shelves, Frau Graebner. We have some serious drinking to do. The principal of the local school knows we're in business. She wants to inspect the library and will be here within the week."

"That's wonderful news," replied Adam. He hadn't thought for one minute that the school could have reopened, but clung to the possibility that Gabrielle was still there. Cresswell insisted Heidi drink a full class of bourbon. "To your boss, who nearly got shot today," he said.

Heidi could hardly breathe for coughing and spluttering, but the Colonel noticed the speed at which Adam despatched his toast. In other circumstances, he thought, he might make a good drinking partner.

"It's time you locked up, Kurt," said Cresswell collecting the empty bottle and glasses. He left, but the others did not want to follow. Adam was seized by missionary fervour. "We must have a list of the teachers' names and inform them of appropriate books for each of them," he announced. He disappeared behind the shelves and called out, "We don't seem to have anything on mathematics".

Heidi wondered why he should express such a concern. "I think the School Principal will do all that for the staff," Heidi advised. "She might be upset if you did it all for her."

Adam agreed and the library was locked up. "Our American boss didn't say who the Principal was," remarked Heidi.

"Does that surprise you?" replied Adam.

As he cycled away, the young policeman signalled a vehicle to emerge from behind a corner in the park. It carried police markings and was driven as slowly as possible at a distance from Adam. When he reached the American campus, it stopped and turned away. At the wheel was Rolf Schneider's father.

Chapter 32

Major Aubrey Macey was a member of a prominent Philadelphia family and it was therefore no surprise that he drew closer and closer to Frieda. Despite a busy schedule, he took morning coffee with her each day.

He became embarrassed by the American presence at Die Schwanen, which he was convinced belonged to Frieda. Most of the meetings had not gone beyond small talk and the natural good humour that both possessed. Then one morning, Aubrey brought his briefcase with him and surprised her. "Would you mind examining this list of names?" he asked.

Frieda's eyesight was beginning to fail and she refused to use spectacles, depending on Greta for reading. "It's my duty to choose solicitors with a good record to help revive this community," said Macey. "Do you recognise any names here?"

Greta read out the names, which included Karl Berger and Edmund Schöler. "Berger and Schöler say they know you and enjoyed your trust," said Aubrey.

"Indeed they do," answered Frieda. "They are our family lawyers and as you will see, can verify my ownership of this house."

Aubrey Macey was embarrassed. "I must tell you that they face charges of illegal transfer of property to the Nazi Government," he informed her.

Frieda was indignant. "That cannot be so," she replied. "They are men of great courage and integrity." Major Macey could feel the chill in Frieda's manner. "I regret the charges, ma'am," replied Macey. "They are not yet proven of course." He felt sympathy for anyone connected with Frieda.

An American staff car drove down the gravel path to the house. The driver got out and opened the door for two men dressed in old suits. A military policeman also got out and released the two men from their handcuffs. They shivered in open-necked shirts in the cool breeze as they climbed the steps wearily. One of them smiled. "Have we brought all the documents?" he asked. The anxious one was Karl Berger, his reassuring partner Edmund Schöler, who stopped on the steps, smiled and tapped the briefcase.

The two lawyers were ushered into Frieda's presence. They smiled, and formality was forgotten. The war had done much to relax Frieda and she embraced the two men, who shed tears.

"Well?" said Aubrey, anxious to begin.

"We have the documents madam," said Edmund Schöler, brandishing the briefcase.

He briefly told the story of how the bombers had failed to touch the safe in the underground cellar and how American soldiers had cleared the entrance. Aubrey Macey examined the documents, particularly the depositions where witnesses stated that the transfer of the house had been carried out under duress and that the property had been bequeathed to Adam.

Within a short time Berger and Schöler had set up a temporary office in the south wing of Die Schwanen and all charges against them had been dropped. All that remained, it seemed, was to draw up a new will, which took some time, as everything had to be approved by the Allied Control Commission.

When Berger and Schöler presented the new will, everything reverted to Frieda, now that Adam was presumed dead. It was to be witnessed and signed in the presence of Aubrey Macey.

Frieda had not decided who would inherit the house after her death. Greta and Helga were to live there as long as they wished, but the section referring to the main beneficiary was left blank and Macey was impatient. He had a suggestion. Perhaps the house could be bequeathed in trust to the United States Government, who would maintain it and use it as a cultural centre when Helga and Greta were no longer there.

Aubrey handed Frieda the pen. She was about to sign when a hand fell on hers and gently lifted it away from the document. Frieda looked up and saw Helga gently shaking her head. She was astounded.

"What is your interest in this?" Macey demanded, not wishing anything to get in the way of a major coup for his country.

Frieda sat back and realised that Helga understood the world better than most people. She forgave the impertinence and laid the pen down. "It will be left open for now," she said. Helga felt a lump in her throat as she thought of the mysterious stranger on the shore.

For the moment Frieda's freedom of action depended on American generosity. Aubrey Macey gave her every reason to believe that his men would shortly leave, and Frieda began to make arrangements. Alfred Rust thought he had overstayed his welcome, but Frieda didn't agree and insisted he stayed.

Time and again she listened to his accounts of Adam's and Bruno's victories at school. Alfred was full of praise for Gabrielle's achievements in the school and Frieda wanted to meet her again, because she was an important link with the past.

She had been very fond of Martha Reymann, and hadn't forgotten the effect the young teacher trainee had had on Adam. She surprised Alfred by insisting that Gabrielle come to dinner at the house and wrote a letter to the School Principal extending the invitation. After a week there was still no reply, and Alfred could give no explanation.

The late summer and early autumn of 1946 gave no hint of the terrible winter to come. Frank and Helga passed the time planning their future in the United States. Everyone in the house was insulated from the sufferings of the people of Berlin.

Occasionally Frank and Helga asked Aubrey Macey to join them and he insisted on describing the advantages of living in the United States at great length. Helga did her best to listen but kept glancing towards the shore.

Aubrey said he was tired, made his apologies and left, Frank waiting until he was well out of earshot. "You know that man on the shore Helga?" said Frank. Helga shook her head but Frank was not satisfied, convinced he might be dealing with a rival. "No secrets honey, please," he said quietly and pretended to forget the whole thing.

The following morning, Greta and Helga cleaned the tea house together. Greta was usually talkative, but not on this occasion. "What's the matter, Mother?" asked Helga, convinced her mother had doubts about the new relationship.

"Have you been watching the shore?" asked Greta. Helga admitted she'd seen the stranger. "Madam's told us what was in the letter, Mother. It can't be him."

Now two people were losing sleep thinking about the stranger. "Are you sure it's not possible, my darling?" she asked her daughter. "I don't know mother," answered Helga.

The following day was bright but showery, and Manfred had a new toy to show his mother. While Helga was organizing Major Macey's Office, Kaminski and friends were putting the finishing touches to a wooden horse on wheels, a metre high. They presented it to Manfred, who couldn't wait to show it to his mother. The rain had stopped conveniently at the beginning of Helga's lunch break and she took Manfred and the horse down to the shingle beach. It kept falling over on the bigger stones as he pulled it along.

The wind suddenly blew more strongly and a mass of black cloud made its way towards them. It began to rain heavily and Helga pulled Manfred and the horse underneath a large spreading oak tree. She dusted the rain from his clothes. The little boy looked past his mother and started back, grasping her hand.

"Hello Helga," said a voice. She turned to face the stranger, staring at him in shock.

"It's me. Why are you surprised? Surely you must have suspected?" said Adam.

Helga didn't know what to do with herself at first. He had lost so much weight and he was dressed in unfamiliar clothes which were too big for him. She half-bowed to Adam, then suddenly felt ridiculous. She threw herself into his arms and kissed him on the cheek, just missing his lips. She grasped his hand, determined not to let go, stroking his face and inviting him to kiss her, abandoning any thoughts of Frank. Adam kissed her on the cheek and pointedly looked towards Manfred. Helga had forgotten herself and turned a bright red.

"Stay with your American," he whispered. "I have watched you together. He's good for you and Manfred." She released his hand, letting go of him and of her wildest dreams. "Of course you're right," she said.

"I said confession to a captured padre, Helga. I believe he pulled me out of the Rhine as a reward," Adam explained. He knelt down to shake hands with Manfred, who turned away shyly.

CHAPTER THIRTY TWO

"We're wasting time, Herr Adam," said Helga, changing her mood. "Your grandmother and my mother are here and well. Your old teacher Alfred Rust lives with us. Frau von Saloman makes him tell stories about you and Bruno."

"I've been watching you all," he admitted. He had discovered that Frieda was alive and felt elated and relieved. His work as the local librarian was a diversion, but he knew he would have to face her with the truth. Lying to her would be the ultimate sin.

"You take Uncle Adam's other hand and we'll take him to see everyone, Manfred," she said, blissfully unaware.

"Wait," said Adam sharply, "I can't go to the house just yet." Helga was puzzled and disappointed. She wanted to be the one to announce the heir to the house was alive and well.

They sat on a wooden seat on the public trackway. Manfred tugged his horse up and down the path. "As far as you are all concerned," Adam began, "Captain von Saloman drowned in the Rhine. I have a new identity. I am now Lieutenant Kurt Vietinghoff, newly released from captivity in Scotland. It is important that the Americans at the house accept the story."

He held Helga's hands. "You and I are close and I need someone to manage my presentation at the house. Will you do it, Helga?" he asked earnestly. "I know it will be difficult and I am asking you to deceive family and friends. But we have no choice. What do you say?" asked Adam.

Helga had become schooled in the art of deception at Kreuzberg. "Of course I will, Herr Adam," she said kissing him on the cheek.

"This is the story," he began. "I am an old family friend missing, believed killed, during the Allied landings in Normandy. Tell them I am reluctant to see them with an amputated leg for the moment. They must believe I am a very proud man who has fallen on hard times. My survival is at stake and it has nothing to do with the war crimes trials beginning in Nuremberg."

He waited for it to register, and then smiled. "I am now a librarian in the old church hall in Wilmersdorf, a step up from the Hitler Youth don't you think Helga?"

She stared at him and laughed. "You're serious aren't you?"

"Please tell the story first to your American. If he is convinced, the others will be. Please tell Frau von Saloman I have never ceased to think about her and can't wait to see her again. Give my love to Greta and my best wishes to

Alfred Rust. I have to go now, or the United States Army will be very worried." He kissed her on the mouth, forgetting his own advice. At that moment he was not revisiting any fantasies about Gabrielle.

Helga was treated to the rare spectacle of the heir to Die Schwanen limping through the trees, struggling to mount an old bicycle and disappearing, soaking wet, into the forest. The rain had begun to penetrate the branches of the old oak tree and Helga was beginning to feel cold. She picked up the wooden horse. "Run as fast as you can to the house, my darling," she said to Manfred.

At the house, Frank was waiting. He took the horse from her. He had watched Adam and Helga embrace. "Who the heck is that guy, honey?" he asked sharply.

"Frank please, we must go inside," replied Helga.

"This is as far as you go. Please answer my question," he retorted angrily. Greta and Manfred were watching through the kitchen window. Helga glared at them and they retreated into the house and she composed herself.

"I will only ever tell one person outside my old circle, Frank, and that's you. You must promise me now you will tell no one," she demanded.

"You know I can't do that Helga," he said. "I have my duty as an American soldier. He's a wanted man isn't he?" asked Frank.

She became cold and imperious and her sudden distance frightened him. "Then there's no future for us together Frank," said Helga. She had just made a huge gamble, threatening her whole future. But she knew Frank had just written to his parents outlining his plans and spent every waking moment thinking of her.

She had calculated well. "I have no choice then," he said glumly. Helga kissed him on the mouth, once quickly, the second time lingeringly.

"Who is he honey?" asked Frank, more concerned that Adam might be a rival.

Helga held on to Frank's hands but stood back proudly. "He is Captain Adam von Saloman of the Hohenstaufen Division of the Waffen SS. He holds the Knight's Cross and is one of the finest men I have ever known," she said. Frank felt the blood drain from his face. He knew the SS had been declared an illegal organisation and as an American officer was badly compromised. She waited for a reaction.

"I have to trust you, honey," said Frank.

CHAPTER THIRTY TWO

"Are you busy for the next hour, Lieutenant?" asked Helga. Frank grinned and shook his head. She led him through the kitchen to the foot of the stairs past several soldiers including Timms. She led Frank to her room and pushed him onto the bed. She let her hair out, leaned over him and let it cover his face. Then she began to undress him.

Helga was always punctual. Exactly one hour later, they reappeared at the foot of the stairs, both flushed. Frank might quietly and privately express doubts about Adam, but he never took it further.

At seven o'clock that evening Kaminski stood at the driver's door of the staff car. Frank briefed him on the mission. "You treat this lady right Kaminski, or we'll have hell to pay from Colonel Cresswell," warned Frank.

Kaminski's mission was to chauffeur Gabrielle to the house, and he lost his way for a short while. He was anxious and flustered when he reached what he thought might be a habitable dwelling. When Gabrielle emerged, Kaminski began to wish he hadn't wasted his time lusting after Helga. Frieda's guest believed she should dress with some restraint, but that didn't stop her wearing her finest evening wear. She had, after all, to maintain the image of an important local figure.

The American had always been tempted to treat German women as members of a defeated people. This time it was different. Gabrielle behaved as if she belonged in the great house, and Kaminski was duly deferential.

On the way to the house, she thought that nothing but good could come of the evening's invitation. An aristocratic connection could be useful, as well as contact with Colonel Cresswell's colleague, Aubrey Macey. Her mind rarely strayed far from her career, and besides she hadn't enjoyed a good night out for as long as she could remember.

Frieda was anxious to rebuild a new social circle. She had made a good start with Major Macey and looked forward to meeting the highly respected Principal of the Martin Luther School.

"What is this?" asked Macey as he was regimented into position at the top of the front steps.

"We always greet are guests like this," Frieda informed him. "You are a resident and must therefore join us." Aubrey Macey did as he was told.

The car drew slowly up at the foot of the steps and Kaminski opened the door for his passenger. Frieda's eyesight was failing, but she recognised Gabrielle immediately and greeted her warmly. Gabrielle offered her condolences on Adam's supposed death.

Adam had been modest enough not to describe his victories in school to her, so Gabrielle listened politely while Alfred Rust related some of the stories yet again. She was just as interested in Bruno's contribution to Adam's early life.

For the first time, Helga was a guest, and Frank noticed his wife-to-be was not at ease. Then he noticed her glaring at Gabrielle. He began to think Helga had told him almost nothing.

Aubrey Macey thought that if Frank could improve German-American relations, he could do the same, and was very attentive to Gabrielle. Alfred Rust was the self-appointed protector of his School Principal and he interrupted Aubrey and Gabrielle whenever he could. Helga made her contribution by quietly reminding Aubrey that Frieda wished to spend some time with the main guest. The ageing matriarch was beginning to depend on Helga more and more.

Aubrey kissed Gabrielle's hand and invited her to join him one evening at the American Officers' Club. She politely declined, although sorely tempted. It left her worried that any rejection of the American might affect her educational prospects.

Frieda came to the rescue after their guests had left. They sat down together in the entrance hall. "She's a wonderful girl," said Frieda. Aubrey agreed. "I think you might find it difficult to behave yourself Major, if you met Fräulein Hintzel again," she said with a half-smile. "It would be a good time to write to your wife I think."

Gabrielle left in complete ignorance of Adam's survival. Helga knew the story of Adam and Gabrielle's first meeting and all the tales of lost love that went with it. Her passion for Adam had never died, and she did not want them to meet again.

"I could achieve more if these damn bureaucrats from the Control Commission would leave us alone, Elisabeth," Gabrielle said to her secretary.

"They see National Socialists everywhere," suggested Elisabeth, "but they do give us food, money and books."

CHAPTER THIRTY TWO

"You're right," replied Gabrielle. "Will you please tell Herr Rust our truancy conference must begin."

While Gabrielle and Alfred walked the school corridors, two visitors drove quietly up the school drive on a motorcycle and joined a party of parents attending an open day. Neither of the American guards noticed that the bigger of the two men carried a parcel.

He glanced warily around while the smaller man walked quickly to Elisabeth's office and knocked smartly on the door.

"Visitors must make appointments," she said, barely lifting her head, well aware of Colonel Cresswell's security arrangements. She had one hand on the telephone.

"Please, dear lady," began the visitor, "we are harmless and to prove it we brought your Principal Gabrielle a present." He handed over the parcel.

"I'm not sure you're harmless," said Elisabeth. "Will you leave your name please?"

"That's not possible. I must leave immediately. She will come to no harm when the package is opened." Then he grinned broadly. "But she won't be the same ever again," he added. The messenger climbed onto the pillion of the motorcycle and the two men drove off at high speed, disappearing into the ruined streets.

Gabrielle and Alfred were chatting with Bobi Richter by the school war memorial in the entrance. Elisabeth came out of the office and waved the package.

"Did you see those two men?" asked Elisabeth when Gabrielle returned to her office. "It was those two again. They've brought something for you and they used your first name."

Elisabeth closed Gabrielle's office door behind them. "They didn't introduce themselves," she said, handing over the package. "I was afraid at first, but the man who came into the office was pleasant and amusing. He knew your name."

Gabrielle knew who they were and expected her grief to be compounded. She didn't want to open the package. Elisabeth had shared nearly all her boss' problems, but she saw this one was not to be shared.

"Shall I say you're unavailable for the next few minutes? I'll ask Herr Rust to deal with the immediate problems," she suggested.

Gabrielle opened the package to find two more inside it. She opened the first. She recognised the bundle of letters written on personalised paper immediately. She had written them, and they were addressed to Adam. He had tied them together with the blue ribbon she had worn in her hair at the Bavarian hotel. She opened one or two, reading her declarations of love for him.

The most recent, she thought, would be on the top of the bundle. She opened it. Inside was a photograph of herself with Katerina by the lakeside. She placed her head in her hands and sobbed, thinking how callous the messenger was.

Then she opened the second package. It contained Adam's identification papers, and she remembered Eva's words, "How can they be sure if they haven't found his papers?" They seemed to be the final confirmation of Adam's death. She prepared to face the day, but just then a piece of paper fell out and fluttered to the floor. She picked it up. "Destroy these papers IMMEDIATELY, signed well-wishers," it read. At that moment, Gabrielle knew that Adam was alive.

Alfred knocked at the door and she tried to compose herself. "Is it a bad time?" he asked. "For you Alfred, it's never a bad time. Do come in and tell me what's happened out there," she answered.

As they began their progress to morning assembly, the telephone rang in Gabrielle's office. "It's urgent," said Elisabeth. Alfred began the assembly.

"John Cresswell here," began the caller. "How are you, Gabrielle? My congratulations on your performance at the von Saloman house." Gabrielle realised that Aubrey Macey had been in touch with the Colonel. "Did those guys from the Control Commission pressure you to go to the new library?" he asked. Gabrielle said they had. "I fixed up a meeting for you there Monday next. Herr Vietinghoff will expect you at nine-thirty. I know you're busy just now, but there's just one thing." He paused so that his next words would register. "Be sure to take the package you've just received with you. You'll have a slight advantage. He doesn't know you're the Principal. Goodbye and good luck, Gabrielle." Down went the telephone at the other end.

She joined Alfred Rust in the morning assembly in time to read the daily notices and walked on air for the rest of the day. Gabrielle always remained behind after school, but did no work on this occasion. She locked her door and floated round the room, imitating the waltz she had done with Adam at the hotel.

CHAPTER THIRTY TWO

Just south of the Landwehr Canal near the Lützowstrasse, a survivor returned to his little fashion shop in a small square. The few survivors of Berlin's Jewish community had fled to Israel, but this one had returned for a special reason. One day when the German Republic had been about to collapse, the young son of a diplomat had intervened to defend him against boys from the Hitler Youth. On such a flimsy basis did the old man try to resume his former life.

He used his remaining strength to crowbar the wooden boards from his shop window and wipe away the yellow star. He wondered if anyone could be remotely interested in any of the dusty items remaining in the shop window, none of which had seen daylight for many years. Still hanging there was the centrepiece of the display, a dignified ladies' morning dress from the old imperial days.

He wondered at the wisdom of returning and sat in his old rocking chair at the rear of the shop. He rewound his Swiss clock hanging on the wall and regained his seat to listen to its reassuring ticking.

The front door opened and the bells rang above his head. He stepped cautiously into the shop. The visitors were a Russian and an American soldier and a tall blonde girl in her late twenties, who seemed familiar. The girl seemed to be with the American.

"These people have a pass for the Russian Zone," announced the Soviet Lieutenant. "They wish to purchase the morning dress."

"I am sorry," began Julius. "I am keeping it for an old patron."

"And who would that be?" asked the blonde girl rather rudely. Her American companion seemed surprised by her attitude.

"My patron is Frau Frieda von Saloman of Die Schwanen, and you, young lady, are I think Fräulein Helga Hoffman, her assistant housekeeper."

Old Julius had not mistaken the look of contempt on Helga's face, but now he had no reason to look at the floor. The American lieutenant intervened.

"We wish to buy the dress for Frieda von Saloman," he said. The old man was delighted and deeply moved. Frieda could now receive her grandson in style.

Adam's mind was in turmoil as he was driven to Die Schwanen. His thoughts returned time and again to Colonel Cresswell's insistence that he be chauffeur driven to the house because he was central to the success of the local educational project. Adam was certain Cresswell didn't like him and couldn't understand the American's determination to reunite him with his grandmother. A charade bordering on the ridiculous was about to take place. The whole story of Adam's background was so flimsy that Aubrey Macey and Frank would see through it, he believed. Helga had taken care of Frank, but Macey remained a problem.

All American officers had been briefed to watch for war criminals, and Adam was afraid that Aubrey Macey would use his rank to persuade Frank to reveal the details. Berger and Schöler could have assured Adam that Frieda could practise deception, but that was not the young aristocrat's main concern. Sooner or later, Frieda would have to know of the murders in Holland.

Adam sighed with relief when he saw there was no welcoming committee. Frieda had realised it might prompt too many awkward questions. He had never climbed so many steps with his prosthetic foot. He stumbled on the fourth step, and his driver rushed forward to help, Adam steadying himself on his walking stick.

He reached the top of the steps and surveyed his lost heritage. Three American soldiers stood outside a tent on the main lawn and one of them gave a lazy wave. Adam nodded in acknowledgement and nearly lifted his hand in response. He still felt comfortable in the company of soldiers.

Two military policemen guarded the front door. One of them demanded Adam's papers and turned to pick up the telephone by the door. "It's Herr Vietinghoff, sir," he announced. Aubrey Macey appeared, extended his hand and the polite inquiries began.

"You say you were a Lieutenant Engineer, Herr Vietinghoff, on the Atlantic Wall I believe?" he asked. "Please forgive the impoliteness. I have to ask."

"Indeed I was," answered Adam. "I helped to prepare the gun emplacements on the Pointe Du Hoc.

"OK," said Aubrey. "I came ashore on Utah Beach just underneath those batteries, Lieutenant."

"Then thankfully they were not too effective," said Adam, forcing a smile.

He couldn't remember ever telling a deliberate lie and now he had to face the prospect of doing so on a regular basis. He glanced round the entrance hall. The chaise longue was still there outside Frieda's main reception room.

He could see that much of the panelling had been restored and guessed that the resident Americans were responsible. He reminded himself to stop looking. He felt all eyes were on him and he must not reveal any familiarity with the house.

Lieutenant Frank Simpson emerged from Macey's office and a sergeant asked him something. "Tell the Russians politely to go to hell," said an annoyed Frank. "Nice to meet you, Herr Vietinghoff," he said to Adam. "We'll get together later."

Helga had rehearsed her role well. "Herr Vietinghoff, it's wonderful to see you. Madam is not quite ready to receive you. But you know you always liked to steal into the kitchen when you were younger," Helga suggested. She led Adam to the kitchen, gently pushed him inside and closed the door. Greta threw her arms around his neck, sobbing, and he cradled her head. She stood back, holding his hands.

"You're so thin. We must do something about that," she said.

"Don't worry Greta," Adam replied. "Our American friends feed me well."

"You must be careful, Mother," warned Helga. "Here, dry your eyes. Remember Herr Adam is supposed to be a family friend, he mustn't stay here any longer. Come," she said to Adam, "we'll go to Madam now. Please stay here mother." They left Greta wringing her hands.

Helga tried to calm Adam, trying desperately not to take his hand. "She has aged much in the last few years and her eyesight is not what it was," she warned. "Major Macey does exactly as he is told," she assured Adam, who nearly laughed out loud.

He stopped and peered into Käthe's bedroom, and it looked as if nothing had been disturbed. The lanterns she had bought at the Qing Ping market in Canton were still hanging on either side of the bed. It was an excuse for Helga to take Adam's hand and lead him away. She was pleasantly surprised when he returned the pressure.

She knocked gently on Frieda's door and a tiny voice invited them in. Helga gently pushed Adam into his grandmother's presence.

Frieda sat on a high-backed red leather chair, her right hand rested on her silver-headed cane. She wore the elegant morning dress recently bought for her by Helga. "Is it really you, my dearest boy?" Frieda asked, trying to get up. She had contracted arthritis during her time sealed in Gustav's old refuge and grimaced with pain. Adam helped her to stand, and the old formality was forgotten. She clung to him and reached up to stroke his face, as if to reassure herself it was really her Adam.

She led him to a window seat and they sat down together. "How times have changed," she remarked, looking Adam up and down and turning her nose up at his demobilisation suit.

"I am at the mercy of our American friends and their tastes, Grandmama," he explained.

"We all depend on them now," agreed Frieda. "I haven't seen you out of uniform for many years. Civilian dress hardly seems German any longer. You haven't looked after yourself, have you? Will I ever discover why not?" she asked. Adam smiled and dodged the question. "You must tell me your story and leave nothing out. How did you finish in the clutches of my old gymnastics teacher?" he joked.

He looked concerned when she described the Russian stay at the house. Adam assured her she and the others were fortunate to have been treated so well.

Then it was Adam's turn. He had not been home on leave since the end of his Russian experience and Frieda expected a long and detailed story. It all sounded like the evasive letters he had written after his training had started. "I think you must have lost many good comrades and friends," said Frieda, who suddenly realised that this included Bruno. "You know everyone here loved him," she said quietly. Adam nodded.

"There is something I must ask before either of us can live a normal life again," she said, staring at him intently in her old authoritative way. The atmosphere suddenly became tense. "Why does a von Saloman bear another name?" she asked, fearing the worst, now that the SS had been declared an illegal organisation.

"It's not what you think, Grandmama," he answered, telling her as much as he knew about the whole affair. His spirits sank to their lowest level as he waited for her reaction. "I have brought shame on all of us," Adam said. "What is worse, I have used and betrayed trusted comrades."

Frieda looked at Adam in amazement. "Adam, some of the worst elements in National Socialist Germany dishonoured your friend and his comrades. Why should you feel so guilty?"

"You don't understand, Grandmama," replied Adam impatiently. "I know we shouldn't grieve for Schneider and Rademacher but Kammler was entirely innocent. There was no excuse for his murder."

Adam stared at Frieda as if she had intruded on his guilt, but she didn't give up. "Isn't it obvious to you Adam that Schneider and Rademacher must bear the guilt for implicating an innocent man in a dreadful act of spite?" she argued.

"Perhaps you're right," answered Adam, unconvinced by Frieda's argument. He decided not to challenge her any further but to find his own solutions.

She moved on to lighter matters. "Do you still play?" asked Frieda pointing to an old upright piano in the corner of the room. Adam was glad of the diversion. "Please play me something," she asked. Adam lifted the cover and began to press the yellowing keys with his right index finger. For the moment the events of the war were forgotten, and the mood lightened.

"I believe there is a very stimulating library opening on Monday," said Adam as he lowered the cover of the piano keyboard.

"Indeed," answered Frieda. "Can we expect the librarian to be a puppet of the Americans?"

"You certainly can," answered Adam, "although he has broken the rules and reserved books for himself and his family." He leaned forward. "I believe he has carefully hidden a new biography of Rudolf Valentino," Adam whispered.

"Then we shall all be there for the opening," promised Frieda.

Frank Stephenson knocked on the door. "For security reasons I must ask you to terminate your visit, Herr Vietinghoff. I have to remind you that this house is still officially United States territory."

This was the man Helga wanted to marry, and he wanted Adam off the premises as soon as possible. He followed rather than accompanied Adam down the stairs. "Tell me about your war," said Frank mischievously as they approached the front door. Adam told Frank the well-rehearsed story, which amused him.

"You don't seem anything like a man who would have anything to do with concrete," commented Frank.

"Surprising indeed," replied Adam. "And what of your war, Lieutenant?" he asked condescendingly. Adam insisted on shaking hands as they parted. As Frank passed the Major's office, he was intercepted by Aubrey Macey.

"Come in and sit down, Frank" said Aubrey. Frank knew he was in for a grilling. "You know Colonel Cresswell?" began Aubrey. Frank nodded. "Are you two hatching something here I don't know about?" he asked.

Frank was genuinely puzzled. "You know a bit more about this Vietinghoff guy than you're letting on," said Macey. "I know it Frank, and do you know how I know? It's because you're always one step ahead of me, and I don't like that."

"Please Major, ask me again at the next reunion, say in twenty years' time," pleaded Frank.

"I could order you to tell me, but I think your new lady would be very unhappy. Am I right, Frank? OK, we'll leave it for now."

Aubrey had begun to see Helga as a conspiratorial figure with a lot of influence in the house. "Have you bitten off more than you can chew?" he asked. Frank did not answer "There's just one more thing," Frank said thoughtfully. "Have you seen the resemblance between our visitor and the old lady?"

Frank nodded in agreement. Aubrey was getting nowhere, but he resolved to watch Helga more closely in the future.

"The sooner you get the hell out of this mess and take your new lady back to Florida, the better," said Aubrey Macey. "OK Helga, you're off for today," he called from his office.

Once again she had organised his work schedule for the following day. She had been given permission to take calls for Major Macey, and it was useful for her to know the movements of senior American officers in the district.

Chapter 33

Pale, underfed figures emerged from the ruins of Wilmersdorf and watched the new library from a discreet distance. They wondered why the library needed armed guards, and thought it was one more thing imposed on them by the occupiers.

A Jeep drew up outside and two German policemen got out and replaced the American guards. Some of the observers in the ruins believed the change meant the building was more approachable, but no one crossed the street.

Adam and Heidi waited patiently behind their newly-painted and polished desks. Any moment now they expected to hear the anxious voice of Colonel Cresswell. As expected, he arrived after the opening time and nervously paced the library floor. He went into the street, looked up and down and shook his head.

The library had been open since ten o'clock and it was now eleven. Cresswell put his hands on his hips, facing Adam and Heidi. "What the hell do we have to do to get the people here moving?" he asked. Heidi counselled patience, but he wasn't impressed.

A car drew up outside. A hopeful look crossed Cresswell's face and he strode to the door, just in time to see the rear doors of an American staff car being opened. Aubrey Macey emerged from the front passenger seat carrying an umbrella, which he hoisted over the head of the lady who had occupied one of the rear seats. Macey's passengers were Frieda and Alfred, and Cresswell was not amused, because he had not been informed. He was sure Adam had invited her and was determined to lecture him on the subject of security. He didn't like Adam and was amazed his protégé was ready to destroy the web of deception the Colonel had helped to weave round his librarian.

"Good morning, Colonel," said Macey cheerfully. He looked inside and saw only Adam and Heidi. "You're having a slow start. This should get things going."

Adam and his assistant stood up and bowed to their first clients. Aubrey introduced them. "May I assist you, Frau von Saloman?" Adam asked.

"I do hope so," answered Frieda. "Do you have any volumes on the Old Imperial Families?"

Colonel Cresswell listened carefully to Adam's reply, notebook at the ready. "I must apologise for the absence of such books for the moment," Adam replied. "I think the authorities believe the German people are not yet ready for them." He was determined not to show too much subservience to the Americans in front of his grandmother.

Cresswell glared at Adam and Heidi tried to hide a mischievous smile. "However, we do have something which may interest you, if you would follow me," said Adam, leading Frieda to Rudolph Valentino's biography.

Alfred approached Heidi as Adam and Frieda disappeared behind the bookshelves. "Do you have any Western novels?" he enquired. Cresswell's face lit up and he quickly made a note that an important client, a schoolteacher, was interested in American culture. Alfred selected two books and had begun to read one of them before he reached the Librarian's desk.

Nothing happened for twenty minutes after the visitors left and John Cresswell's new confidence began to evaporate. Then there was a quiet knock on the open doors of the library and a pale elderly lady wearing a headscarf and a threadbare black coat stepped inside. She peeped round the door and smiled at Adam. "Franz, come in. I think it's all right," she said to her husband, who joined her inside the building. He wore a Homburg hat and had a well-trimmed pointed beard.

"May we help you?" asked Heidi. They both reached inside their coats for their identity papers. "That will not be necessary," she said.

"There are more of us," said the old man tentatively and gestured that Adam and Heidi should look outside. Standing at a safe distance from the police guard were nearly thirty people of retirement age. Among them was a bespectacled young man who had lost an arm. He stepped forward as if he had been volunteered as a spokesman. "What must we do?" he asked politely.

Adam was taken aback and took a short while to compose a reply with Cresswell standing behind him.

"This library does not belong to our American friends or the National

Socialists," Adam began. Then he paused, clearing his throat. "Ladies and gentlemen, it is my pleasure to announce that it belongs to you all."

He waited for his words to take effect and watched the apathy caused by years of subjugation and recent starvation begin to melt away. Adam held up one hand. "The policeman is here to protect you my friends. You choose a book, sign your name and return it within one week. That's all you have to do," he assured them.

The group disappeared among the bookshelves and there was an excited buzz of conversation. None of them reappeared for at least thirty minutes. The first to approach the desk was the young man, who volunteered a short speech.

"My name is Johann Leidner, Herr Chief Librarian," he said to Adam. "I would like to say that today I have selected a book by a Jewish philosopher which will enable me to finish a thesis I began in 1933. Do you know what that means?" he asked.

Heidi was in tears. Most of the rest of the group gathered round Adam's desk. "I would like to say it is a privilege to be here at this moment," Adam said, and the group applauded. "We'll be quiet next time," Johann Leidner promised.

John Cresswell returned to his headquarters a happy man. His superiors would be happy as they would see him as an important figure at the beginning of de-nazification. He was working, he believed, with the better sort of German, which only just included Adam von Saloman. He would never be the personal friend of this man because he had tainted his background by becoming an SS man. Cresswell had no intention of sharing his carefully-acquired knowledge with anyone else and certainly not with his superiors. His background in intelligence had proved useful.

Frieda van Saloman was another matter. Cresswell felt at one with her as he surveyed his own family tree pinned on the wall behind his chair by his desk. It showed that Cresswell had not been the family name for more than two generations and that the Colonel was descended from German immigrants to the United States in the time of the Iron Chancellor Bismarck.

Every evening in his flat, Adam read obsessively. He clung to the Chinese material, despite appeals from the New University of Berlin to return it. Heidi gave him Rousseau, Thoreau and Hume and made him read them in their original language.

She was amazed at his ability and asked about the origin of his language skills. He showed her the photographs of Käthe and explained how she was beginning to triumph, even in death. Heidi never ceased to be curious about his background. She knew he must have adopted an alias, but couldn't prove it. She was giving him a future, and his excitement built with his successes. She set him a succession of essay titles. His initial naivety vanished and she recognised that she had discovered an original and incisive mind.

Heidi made excuses to work late on many occasions to allow her time to type several of his essays. She sent them to the new university with a promise that the Chinese material would follow shortly. She needn't have worried, because the essays were returned with an offer to publish, and Adam received a letter inviting him to attend the new university for an informal chat. Heidi was delighted.

Chapter 34

Gabrielle's thoughts were concentrated on the library, but not on its relevance to the school curriculum. The two men who had delivered the letters must have been Hans Thaelmann and Franz Stamm. Of that, she was sure.

Silence reigned in the school corridors. She reread one of the letters to Adam and his reply. The words displayed a gnawing desperation to see her again. She took the photograph of him wearing his new captain's uniform from her purse and stood it against an inkstand. She laughed to herself as she looked at the jaunty angle of his cap.

She tried to remember every detail of their meeting in the Bavarian hotel. She walked regally to the centre of the room and held out her arms as if she were once again beginning the Viennese waltz. She heard the music in her head and recalled the conspiracy they had hatched together against the dull authoritarians responsible for the project.

Gabrielle had nearly completed two circuits of the room when Eva's head appeared round the door. "Isn't it about time we went home, or are you in the middle of something important?" she asked mischievously, spotting Adam's photograph.

Gabrielle turned bright red and let her hands fall to her sides.

"Now you see your friend and Principal in all her wretchedness," she said.

"I'm so sorry," said Eva embracing her. "Are you sure it's him?"

"Oh yes," replied Gabrielle, "and at this moment I couldn't care less about the library and the school curriculum."

"Thank God for that," Eva said. "I was beginning to wonder if you were human."

At nine o'clock on the Sunday evening before the expedition to the library, there was a sharp knock on their apartment door. Both were afraid to answer at that time of night. "It's John Cresswell," called out the Colonel. Eva opened the door to see him flanked by two soldiers. "Wait in the Jeep," he said to them and invited himself in.

"I'll not keep you long," he announced. "Tomorrow is very important for both of us. I've called to remind you to look your best, Fräulein Hintzel. Much depends on this meeting tomorrow."

Gabrielle didn't sleep well that night. She lay awake for several hours planning Adam's day. She had already asked Alfred Rust to run the school for several hours.

"How do I look?" asked Gabrielle, emerging from her room to display her outfit. She wore a tight-fitting white polo-neck sweater, a black skirt, high heels and a leather jacket.

"Fine," answered Eva. "Be careful not to walk up and down outside the library."

"Perhaps I should wear smaller heels, do you think Eva?" asked Gabrielle.

Her friend thought that an irrelevant detail. "The sweater on its own should reduce him to a shambles," Eva promised.

At nine-thirty as promised, Cresswell's Jeep roared to a halt outside the apartment. When he saw Gabrielle, his eyebrows rose. "Good morning Fräulein Hintzel. I see you're dressed suitably," he said. "Try to remember our educational project. Please may I have a word with you in private, if you would excuse us Fräulein Knopke?" he asked, looking grave. "You may be going into danger," he began. There are members of the New German Police Force who wish you and the librarian nothing but ill-will. Stay as close as you can to American soldiers and tell Herr Vietinghoff," he warned.

Twenty minutes later Gabrielle and Cresswell pulled up outside the library.

For the second time Aubrey Macey tried to upstage John Cresswell. A staff car arrived at the same time and a genial Macey stepped out with two German civilians. "Please allow me to introduce Herr Frank and Herr Friedman, John," he said. "I have some great news for you. They're here to offer your boy a new career." Cresswell was dumbstruck. "Heidi's done all the work John. Maybe you'll be able to run for the Senate after this! Your boy's the toast of the new University."

CHAPTER THIRTY FOUR

Cresswell recovered and pulled rank. "Aubrey, you have twenty minutes to get these guys in and out, beginning now," he ordered. Cresswell was true to his word and the two German academics were ejected after twenty minutes, but not before they had offered a trial readership to Adam. Heidi wondered if she'd done the right thing, because Adam was stunned and Cresswell was furious. As far as he was concerned the whole day was to have been built around Gabrielle's visit. Heidi was furious with Cresswell because of the rude treatment of the academics.

Adam recovered enough to support Heidi and assure Cresswell that the School Principal's visit would pass off without a hitch. He disappeared behind some bookshelves. "Please tell me when the Principal arrives," he instructed her.

An American staff car drew up noiselessly outside the Library and Cresswell opened the door for Gabrielle. He heard Heidi call out to Adam. "Where's Vietinghoff?" the Colonel asked irritably.

There was a tremendous crash at the end of one of the shelves and Adam found himself under a pile of timber and books. Johann Leidner had just chosen a book and rushed to help. Some of the new members pushed the wreckage of the shelves to one side. "Are you all right, Herr Vietinghoff?" enquired Johann.

Cresswell was beside himself. He wanted everyone to leave except the staff and the guests. Adam brushed himself down and announced that he was uninjured. He remained behind the shelves, worried that some of the books had been damaged.

"Hello, Field Marshall," said Gabrielle, fixing Adam with the warmest smile she could muster. They threw themselves into each other's arms and kissed fiercely. He pulled her behind the remaining bookshelves and he gazed at her hardly believing in the miracle. He continued to kiss her and they clung to each other. He was afraid he'd bruised her, and now held her face in both hands and kissed her tenderly. He let out a long breath and issued a torrent of questions.

"How did you know I was here? No one is supposed to know who I really am," he said.

"My love, anyone of any importance knows who you are. Germany's future is your future," she replied. She kissed him on the end of the nose. "I have spoken to Colonel Cresswell. You are to become Germany's future one-man army. No weapons though! I'm sorry to be irritating, but we have to keep Cresswell at bay and do my schoolwork."

Adam couldn't keep his hands off her. "To hell with the curriculum," he said, but she fended him off.

"Wait, wait, business first. After that we have the whole afternoon to ourselves. I've planned it all, my love," she assured him.

They emerged disheveled from behind the bookshelves and Heidi looked very disapproving. Adam nearly apologised. Colonel Cresswell had stayed well out of sight. "I'll wait in the car," he shouted.

Gabrielle now became businesslike, to a degree that both impressed and frightened Adam. She seemed capable of forgetting everything that had just happened and concentrating on her mission. She opened her briefcase and presented Heidi with a list of priorities. Cresswell didn't wish to miss anything and rejoined them. This was his project, and no one was to be allowed to do anything else behind his back. He sat down and tried to look like a chairman.

Gabrielle asked if her list could be matched with the library's contents. Adam asked Heidi to take over and he and Cresswell watched while the two women worked together. By ten o'clock they had finished and invitations to members of the staff to attend the library had been issued. Cresswell left, and Heidi offered to look after the library. "Will it be for the rest of the day?" she asked. Gabrielle kissed her on the cheek, and the couple fled from the library.

"First, we shall go to the American Servicemen's café for lunch, my love," said Gabrielle. "We can stay there as long as you like, or we may spend the remaining three hours or so at my flat before I'm due back at school."

"It will be the shortest lunch in history," Adam promised.

They walked arm in arm through the park like a couple who had been together for years, revelling in their new freedom and advertising their love for each other each time they walked past someone. They greeted the first watching policeman they saw, holding hands and introducing themselves. "I am Gabrielle Hintzel and this is Kurt," she said to the man. "Come my dear, we shall take a bow." They left the officer deeply puzzled and wondering why he had been ordered to spy on them.

During the short ride down the Brandenburgischestrasse to the American café, they were bursting with questions for each other. Both knew they had to make love first, and they said very little. They could not have sat any closer.

CHAPTER THIRTY FOUR

The café was used mainly by officers and even among the ruins it had an air of exclusivity. A mixture of curious and disapproving looks met the couple as they sat down. A young Lieutenant asked to see Adam's papers.

Adam heard footsteps on the pavement and a voice said "Hello you two." It was Frank Stephenson, with Helga on his arm. Adam and Gabrielle could not refuse Frank's offer of coffee. They left after thirty minutes, at Helga's insistence, realising that their reunion would not be without its problems.

Gabrielle wanted one answer before they left. "Why the alias, my darling?" she asked. Adam's face drained of colour and he played nervously with his cup and saucer. "Please never ask, ever," he said with an air of finality. He looked at her pleadingly. She leaned forward and took both his hands, desperate for an answer. "It has nothing to do with war crimes," he said. "I can't tell you. I could never tell you."

She had never seen him like this before. Now she was surprised by the vulnerability of this man among men and was attracted by it. Adam didn't sense it and was afraid of rejection.

"Am I different, Gabrielle?" he asked anxiously. "Do I seem in any way repellent to you?" She saw his glance fall to his left leg and she smiled mischievously. "That might be a small challenge, my love, but I'm sure it will make our lovemaking even more interesting." She leaned forward and kissed him full on the lips, to the amazement of a few of the American officers. "In or out of uniform, you're just the same my darling," she assured him. She didn't press him again on the subject of his new name.

"How is our daughter?" he asked. It was his first real chance to ask.

"She is wonderful," replied Gabrielle.

"What colour are her eyes? Does she laugh a lot?" Gabrielle began to describe their daughter.

"Is she obedient to her foster parents?" he asked seriously.

"Oh you would ask that, Captain von Saloman. Well of course she is," she answered. "You haven't asked who she resembles."

"She looks like me, of course," retorted Adam. "Except for her hair, which is you."

"Would you like to discuss our daughter somewhere else?" she asked, letting her hand fall to his left knee. Adam paid the waitress and hurried

Gabrielle to the nearest tram stop. She gazed out of the tram windows, and for a few moments they pretended to be uninterested in each other.

The steps to the basement flats were concealed by a pile of rubble. Gabrielle produced a large key and tripped down the steps. She closed the door behind them and bolted it.

Inside, she lit the paraffin lamps in the living space and the bedroom. The air was heavy with the smell of fuel. She pulled Adam's US Army greatcoat over his shoulders, then seized his jacket lapels and pulled him into the bedroom. She tried to help him off with his jacket and accidentally pulled hard on one of his braces. It twanged back into place, and they both chuckled.

She threw off her sweater and Adam removed her bra. He knelt down and kissed her breasts until he felt the nipples harden. Gabrielle moaned with pleasure as his tongue stimulated her.

"Wait," she said. He sat down beside her on the edge of the bed and she touched the scar on his cheek. "Who was responsible?" she asked.

"The Russians," he said as his hand lifted her skirt and found the softness between her legs.

She broke away from him to remove his trousers. She took away his shorts and gloried in his erection. She kissed him longingly on the mouth, then traced her tongue down his manhood. He could bear it no longer and pulled her towards him. She guided him inside and began to move slowly. He slowly withdrew, and she lay on the bed, arms outstretched. Then he knelt between her legs and penetrated her again, moving faster and faster. She gasped with pleasure, gripping his sides with her legs. Her hands grasped his hips and signalled him to move faster. He couldn't bear the pleasure and ejaculated with a shout, expelling all the air from his body.

The passions of the moment he had dreamt of for such a long time still kept him erect. Gabrielle lifted her legs as high as she could to allow him to penetrate her more deeply, and his furious movement brought her quickly to a climax. They lay exhausted and laughed at each other.

"What the hell's this?" said Adam, as he crawled under the sheets. He had unearthed a bedraggled old teddy bear. One of its ears was missing and its left arm bore a swastika armband.

"Oh, that's poor Adolf," explained Gabrielle. "Eva and I amuse ourselves by hurling insults at him. We leave him in peace now."

"He let my men down," retorted Adam. "We're not sharing the bed with him." He hurled the bear towards a wooden chair. It landed squarely on the seat, staring back at them both. Gabrielle jumped out of bed and placed a towel over its head. Then she leapt back onto the bed and kissed Adam repeatedly. She threw back the bedclothes and mounted him, stopping when she saw his face twisted with pain. "I'm so sorry, my love," she said, remembering his left leg.

"I'll be all right in a few minutes," he said.

"That assistant you have is useful," commented Gabrielle, tempted to tease him. "I don't know how she manages without you."

"I can assure you I work hard in the library," said Adam.

"Of course you do my love, of course you do," she said, stroking his nose. It was time for Adam to re-establish his old eminence in the company of the woman he loved the most.

"I am to become a university teacher," he said self-importantly.

"Can the world of education cope with both of us?" Gabrielle asked. He relaxed and laughed. "How often do you see Katerina?" he asked.

"Quite often," answered Gabrielle. "Her nurse takes her to the Grünewald once a week and by chance we meet." Her expression became pained. "I masquerade as her aunt and we spend one hour together. It's hard to leave her. I want to hold her but I can't. Her adoptive parents love her so much. Do you know Adam, I sometimes feel like kidnapping her and hiding down here in the flat."

They became aware of the damp air, and wrapped blankets round each other. "What do you do when you're with her?" asked Adam.

"You know all the peaceful little inlets near Die Schwanen. We go there, hold hands and paddle in the lake. I give her American candy and we feed the ducks and swans. I gave her a special toy. It's a little cloth elephant we call Effy."

Gabrielle let out a sob and Adam cradled her head. "I would like so much to be there," he said.

Gabrielle dried her eyes and reached for her bag. She withdrew a photograph of Katerina and her nurse. "Do you recognise her?" she asked.

Adam's mouth opened. "Can it be the woman who brought us together?" he asked.

"We're her project, my love, but she has had to change her mind about the adoptive parents. She protects them and Katerina's feelings for them. I have to follow all her directions. Perhaps we can never reveal ourselves to our child." She was hardly able to speak the words.

"But the war is over my love. You could tell her who you are," Adam said.

"I have been warned that there are people who will stop even that," Gabrielle replied tearfully. He held her tightly. Adam didn't tell Gabrielle that because of the events in Northern Holland he could never tell their daughter he was her father. She stared at the bedroom wall with her lips pursed.

"There is something you haven't told me," he said, and she nodded. "Our child is healthy and energetic, but she has difficulties. She is a very slow learner, my love. It has just been diagnosed by an American Army doctor," Gabrielle admitted.

To her delight, Adam suddenly adopted a look of missionary fervor. "Everything that can be done will be done," he said decisively. "She must have suitable tuition and we will find it, if necessary. Please inform the nurse."

"This isn't the Waffen SS, my darling. We'll have to tread carefully," Gabrielle reminded him.

Karl and Celia Lindemann did not fare so well in peacetime and couldn't afford the fees for their adopted daughter's special education. As tactfully as she could, Nurse Agnes Felsen told Karl Lindemann that she knew of benefactors who might help. Celia Lindemann insisted that they make an approach to these people.

"They already work in education and manage a trust for these cases," lied Agnes.

The contacts were made. There was no 'trust', of course. Specially-headed letters were devised by Gabrielle and Adam which showed the passage of funds from a bogus account. Slowly, very slowly, little Katerina made progress, but even by the age of ten she was staring mystified at the world.

It was time for Gabrielle to return to school. Before they parted, Adam's hand mischievously pulled open a small drawer on his side of his bed; he had assumed the bedside cabinet belonged to Gabrielle.

"Wait," she said. "That's Eva's." But Adam had already produced a photograph of Eva, arm in arm with Bruno.

"It was a short fling," Gabrielle assured Adam, who didn't seem disapproving. He laughed and replaced it. "I'm not going to school," she announced, throwing on her blouse and marching to the kitchen to make coffee. There were no sounds for a few minutes except the sound of a spoon stirring thick black liquid.

CHAPTER THIRTY FOUR

"I've been to Die Schwanen," Gabrielle announced, "more than once."

"You haven't been wasting your time then," he joked.

"Do you know why I went?" she asked Adam as if he was thoroughly naïve. He wasn't as slow as she thought.

"She likes you, of course," said Adam, smiling condescendingly.

"Of course," replied Gabrielle. "I never believed you were dead." She handed him his coffee, which he drained quickly. He would have been surprised and disappointed if she had not tried to advance her career in any way she could.

He made Gabrielle put hers down and they began to make love again.

There was a discreet knock at the door. "Is it safe to come in?" called Eva from outside.

Gabrielle picked up a two-way radio lent to her by Colonel Cresswell. In a few seconds, she had arranged a lift for Adam back to the American campus, but not before she had warned him of danger.

"I have been told that there are several National Socialists who wish to preserve the worst secrets of Hitler's rule," she said. "You and I were part of the Lebensborn Project, and I've been worried that both of us might be silenced."

"I can't believe that," replied Adam. "What could they possibly gain?"

Gabrielle grasped his arm. "Do the names Schneider and Kammler mean anything to you?" The black look on his face told her they did. "Whatever this is all about, you are in deadly danger from these men," she warned him.

"Where are these people?" Adam asked, at last prepared to listen.

"They are all members of the New German Police Force, Adam, and there is every reason to believe that they have ordered ordinary service coppers to watch you as a dangerous suspect." Gabrielle kissed him lightly. "One of them asked me to watch you," she warned. "The one we met in the Park."

"What must we do?" he asked.

"As soon as we can, we'll leave the district. Cresswell will help us, I know it. You have some strange influence over him. Be prepared for a quick exit."

An American Jeep drove round the corner with two armed men in the rear seat. She grasped his arm and they kissed passionately. "Be careful, my darling. I'll be in touch soon and I'll make some plans."

The light was failing and there were no street lights. "We can't hang around here too long, Herr Vietinghoff," shouted the driver impatiently.

"I'm coming gentlemen," he said, releasing Gabrielle. He glanced across the street and saw furtive movements in the buildings opposite.

"Remember your friends," she reminded him before they parted. "Who kept reminding you of me after Käthe's death?"

Adam's eyebrows rose. "You mean Bruno of course."

"He ordered one of your men to watch your back at the beginning of the Normandy battles. But you didn't know that Adam, did you?" Adam realised that she must mean Michael Kaspar.

"Hold fast my love, soon we'll be safe," she said and Adam roared off into the night.

Gabrielle continued to meet her daughter in the Grünewald. Another meeting took place within sight of Die Schwanen. They were watched by Adam, careful to keep out of sight. He watched his daughter play with her cloth elephant and ached to join her. When he returned to his flat, tears were running down his cheeks.

Erwin Schneider and Lothar Kammler sat round a table in Kammler's apartment in a cloud of cigarette smoke. Arranged on the table was the evidence pointing to Adam's involvement in the deaths of their two sons. Kammler stubbed out a cigarette and swallowed a mouthful of black coffee.

"We know the Arnhem police have stated that Thaelmann and Stamm were to meet them near the Hohenstaufen camp. Here is the deposition."

"Then are we to assume the two sergeants are our main targets?" asked his surprised companion.

"I think not," said Kammler. "It would be difficult to find them, let alone arrest them, and we know they have powerful friends."

"And we are sure of von Saloman's part in all this?" added Schneider.

"Oh I think so. The key to it all was his best friend Grabowsky, and we know why our Gestapo comrades were there," he added grimly. He lit another cigarette and drew on it. "And we know where that swine von Saloman is, my friend."

"If we arrest him for murder, are you seriously thinking that the Americans will allow the conviction of someone who is a key figure in their local plans?" asked Erwin Schneider.

CHAPTER THIRTY FOUR

"I agree with you," answered Kammler. "But I think the Americans might not care greatly about the fate of three Gestapo men." He produced a Walther pistol and laid it on the table. "I therefore suggest we deal with the swine in the old traditional way."

Schneider laid his pistol alongside Kammler's. "Then we are agreed," he said.

"I will make all the necessary arrangements," promised Kammler. "Some of our men are already in place." He opened an illegally-acquired bottle of Scotch and the two men drank a toast to their revenge.

Heidi's escort climbed into their Jeep. One of them triumphantly held aloft a Western novel. "Thanks Heidi," he called out. She didn't wish to keep them waiting and ran out to the Jeep, which then disappeared down Charlottenbrunnestrasse.

Adam remained behind, because a number of books had not been returned. One of them belonged to his Chinese library and he was most anxious to get it back. His delay gave a young man in the uniform of the New German Police just enough time.

Adam's bicycle was padlocked to a lamp-post. The policeman produced wire cutters and cut it free, then wheeled it away and left it leaning against a tree stump just inside the park gates, in full view of the library entrance, as he had been instructed.

The phone on Adam's desk rang. "Cresswell here, everything OK Kurt? We'll come and get you if you wish."

"The bicycle's a symbol of my independence," joked Adam. It was lost on Colonel Cresswell.

Adam cleared his desk. He glanced upwards and decided to reset the clock on the far wall. He pulled on his military greatcoat, went outside and closed the double doors, pulling on the two padlocks to test them. "Damn," he said to himself glancing to his right. The cycle had gone and he chided himself for not bringing it indoors. He took the keys to the library from his pocket. He had decided to take up the Colonel's offer, but then he changed his mind. These days his leg was better. He would walk to the Brandenburgischestrasse and catch a tram.

He crossed the street towards the park and noticed it was very quiet, which was unusual on such a nice evening. "That's good," he muttered to himself as he noticed the park gates had been repainted. He prepared to walk on.

"Your bicycle is here, von Saloman," said a voice from somewhere along the central path. Adam looked in the direction of the voice and saw two men emerge from the bushes. One of them produced his bicycle. "Please come and reclaim your property," said the other man. He didn't recognise either of them.

Adam was no longer capable of running and had no choice but to walk slowly towards them. Both stood in the shade of an oak tree and he couldn't distinguish their features. "Do you recognise us?" asked Erwin Schneider. As he drew closer Adam recognised the beat policeman. He knew Kammler from the several occasions he had seen him in the interview hall.

"A fitting place for our meeting don't you think?" suggested Schneider menacingly. "The place where you humiliated and crippled my son."

"What do you want of me?" asked Adam.

"It's quite simple," said the ex-beat policemen. "We intend to exact revenge for the murder of our sons. Now don't you think that sounds reasonable?" He drew his pistol.

Kammler had also drawn a pistol and he now stood behind Adam. "There'll be no help for you, von Saloman" he said. "Our men have taken care of that. We'll deal with you first and then that disloyal bitch of yours, in the old National Socialist way."

"On your knees!" snapped Schneider. Adam simply stared at him. "On your knees, you swine," barked Kammler. He hit Adam on the side of his head with the butt of his pistol and blood spurted from behind his right ear.

Dazed, Adam sank to his knees and heard Kammler engage the magazine of his pistol. He felt the muzzle of the gun in the back of his neck. Kammler waited a few seconds in the hope that Adam would beg for his life, but his intended victim made no sound.

Two shots rang out and Kammler and Schneider fell lifeless to the ground. Kammler's blood covered Adam's clothing. He stood up and gazed at the two dead policemen in horror. He had seen violence countless times on the battlefield, but this was cold and clinical.

Two masked men in leather jackets appeared from the bushes carrying rifles. "Are you all right, Hauptstürmführer?" asked one of them, examining Adam's wound and ignoring the two bodies. "Yes, yes," stuttered Adam.

The second man looked Adam straight in the eye. "It's as well you're easy to follow, Hauptstürmführer," he said with a satisfied smile. Half of his face was visible and Adam recognised Michael Kaspar immediately. "We haven't much time," he said. "We'll take care of these two. Go quickly through the far gate." He gave the Waffen SS salute, which Adam returned weakly. He went to mount his cycle.

"Have a long and happy life," said the other man. "Sergeant Kolb sends his regards."

Adam knew the other man was Martin Schroder. Two more men appeared and the bodies were carried away before Adam had left the park.

He stopped at the gate and looked back at the killing ground. He felt no gratitude, only disgust at the murders that had been committed on his behalf. Either side of the gates were two more bodies, beat policeman who had stood guard for Schneider and Kammler. Both had Waffen SS bayonets protruding from their backs. Their only crime had been to do as they were told. Adam stopped in his tracks and was physically sick.

He could hardly feel his legs as he pedalled home. The American guard saluted respectfully, and for the first time Adam ignored him. He went straight to his room without calling Cresswell's office. He locked his door securely and opened a bottle of schnapps, drinking himself into oblivion and collapsing on to the floor. He dragged himself to his bed in the early hours.

He awoke the next morning with a blinding headache and had to force himself to take breakfast with his American hosts. He recalled the murdered men with the bayonets protruding from their backs. Kaspar and Schroeder had advertised their brutality, and they were his devotees.

In the following days, Adam came to an almost unbearable decision. He was sure now that he would never reveal who he was to Katerina. Instead, he would watch her grow from a discreet distance without ever heaping the stain of his past on her.

One week later Colonel John Cresswell ordered Private First Class Lewis Grindleford to drive a special guest to the American campus, without Adam's knowledge. He opened his door to be confronted by Helga.

"We need to talk, Herr Adam," she announced. She knew Adam had been reunited with Gabrielle and her attitude was brisk and businesslike. She showed no deference.

Adam couldn't help staring at her. She looked utterly beautiful. "I believe it is nearly impossible for you to tell a lie, Herr Adam. Mistress Käthe made sure of that," she remarked.

"Go on," Adam said.

"Madam has drawn up a will and up till now has not named a special beneficiary. Of course Herr Adam, you are dead! It can't be you. So instead, she has decided to leave it all to Herr Kurt Vietinghoff, a close family friend, who she is sure will promise to recognise the interests of those who live in the house. So you see, you will have to continue the great lie, if only in the interests of Die Schwanen's other occupants."

Helga relaxed and adopted the expression she had used when she had kissed Adam as a teenager. "Would you like to make me a coffee? We have much to talk about," she said.

Karl Berger and Edmund Schöler drew up the new will in their temporary office. Helga offered to act as a witness. Adam sat by his grandmother. She held his hand, as this time no Americans were watching.

"I'm sure you would agree," said Karl Berger, "that it would not be wise to inform our American friends of the new arrangement." Frieda agreed. "I'll take care of Frank," promised Helga, and Adam did not doubt the word of this formidable lady.

"So you have your doubts about our librarian, Lieutenant," said Colonel Cresswell to Frank, who had decided to make his own inquiries without telling his wife-to-be. "He's whiter than white," the Colonel assured Frank, showing him the German army service record of Lieutenant Kurt Vietinghoff of an engineer battalion.

"He's OK, but you were right to ask," added Cresswell, staring intently at Frank.

Lieutenant Frank Stephenson had been told indirectly to make no further enquiries. He built up a working relationship with the new librarian and tried to sound as pleased as Helga when Vietinghoff became a university teacher.

They survived the dreadful winter of 1947 and the Soviet blockade of Berlin. Frank reapplied for a position in the Education Corps and was successful. He was a much happier man, far happier than Colonel John Cresswell, who had been asked to investigate the mysterious disappearance of two leading figures from the New German Police, Erwin Schneider and Lothar Kammler.

As soon as the Soviet blockade was lifted, Gabrielle and Adam moved to West Germany, as far away from Berlin as they could.

Epilogue – Part I

There was an air of expectancy in the lecture theatre as a host of distinguished academics took their seats. It was a warm Californian summer day and the more elderly were glad of the air conditioning. One of them, Dr Jacob Meissner, took a seat near the rear, helped by his manservant and companion Stephen. The retired doctor would have preferred a seat near the front of the auditorium, but he could not face the steep descent. Despite his severe arthritis, he was still alert and as gregarious as ever, exchanging greetings with friends and colleagues.

"Who've we got today, Jacob?" asked one of them.

"Still not organised, Fred," Jacob said to the man seated next to him. "Here, borrow my leaflet."

Jacob's friend read the name of the visiting speaker aloud. He made sure the entire row knew it was a German professor of oriental studies, one Kurt Vietinghoff.

"You could tell this guy a few things," remarked Fred.

"Maybe, we shall see," answered Jacob. It was now 1980, but Jacob's memories of China had never faded. He thought today's lecture could be interesting.

The guest speaker entered the auditorium and the buzz of chatter at the rear was drowned by the welcoming applause. The speaker stopped on his way to the podium, as if surprised by the welcome, and bowed politely. Jacob noticed the slight limp.

The speaker's aide offered a seat, which was impatiently refused. His full mouth, pale complexion and piercing blue eyes were crowned by a shock of wavy gray hair which showed little sign of thinning. He surveyed his audience from back to front and half-smiled as if in approval. Fred turned to Jacob and nodded positively. This time, he probably wouldn't fall asleep.

EPILOGUE – PART I

The speaker quietly arranged some notes on the podium. He stepped clear of it and stood on the edge of the stage to deliver his lecture. He thanked his hosts for the invitation to speak, mentioning the debt of gratitude he owed to his American friends. The audience was flattered and became more attentive.

They heard the Professor describe how American soldiers had given him a new career when so many Germans had lost their way at the end of the war. Other Americans had helped him, he said. He would always remember a volunteer captain in the Chinese Nationalist Forces who had once been a smuggler in the city of Canton in the twenties.

Jacob's mouth opened. He had been leaning forward on his walking cane. Now he dropped it and the noise reverberated round the auditorium. The speaker looked in Jacob's direction with a kindly smile. "I am delighted to see my talk has caused such a stir at such an early stage," he said. There was a ripple of polite laughter.

The professor described his early development, mentioning his close friends on the Pearl River and how they had directed him to his first taste of Chinese philosophy because of the injury he had sustained in a communist guerrilla attack.

Fred began to say something. "Quiet Fred," snapped Jacob, who had suddenly developed an interest in the speaker's limp.

"How old do you think he is?" asked Jacob, without moving his gaze from the speaker.

"Maybe sixty," suggested his companion.

The hour's lecture seemed like thirty minutes to Jacob. The speaker concluded with an appeal to the audience to consider the benefits of Chinese philosophy and culture. He invited questions, and Jacob became very agitated. "Stephen, we must get down the steps and speak to this man," he demanded.

"Take it easy Jacob," said Fred. "It's a long way down there."

Jacob ignored him and hauled himself up. He began to breathe heavily and sweat profusely. "First aid, please," called Stephen to an attendant at the rear and help arrived.

Adam looked up anxiously. The host rushed on stage to assure Adam everything was all right. The question time was cancelled and Adam left the stage. Jacob lifted his arm in a forlorn attempt to gain his attention.

"What's the matter sir?" asked Stephen. Jacob's eyes filled with tears. "It's him Stephen, it's him, and I'll never see him again."

Jacob decided to try to forget the whole incident. By the following morning he had recovered and was sitting in his favourite deckchair in the sunshine reading the newspapers, staring gratefully at the Golden Gate Bridge in the distance. Few people, he reflected, had been so fortunate as he.

Stephen brought an ice-cold orange juice and he sipped it, spilling half of it on to the newspaper. He chided himself for his clumsiness and Stephen brought more juice.

"Stephen, would you find out for me how that speaker can be contacted? I'm sure Vietinghoff wasn't always his name," asked Jacob.

Alarm bells rang in the manservant's head. "Do you think that would be wise sir? There are many Germans of his generation who have much to hide. He spoke of Germans losing their way."

Jacob agreed, and after a light lunch he dozed off in the afternoon sun. Stephen saw an opportunity and began to apply paint to metal railings at the front of the house. He had just begun when a black Cadillac drew up. The driver opened the rear passenger door to reveal the visiting professor.

"May I help you sir?" he said.

"Is this the house of Dr Jacob Meissner?" asked the visitor. Stephen confirmed it was.

"May I speak with him?"

Stephen, as ever, was protective. "Dr Meissner is very tired just now and usually sees people only by appointment," he explained.

"I understand," said Adam. "My main reason for visiting America was to see this one man, probably for the last time. Is this not now possible?"

Jacob had behaved as if meeting his benefactor was the most important thing left for him to do. Stephen relented. "Come this way sir," he said, leading Adam through a long entrance hall to the rear of the house. On the way Adam stopped to examine a sepia photograph, smiling to himself.

"Do you know these people sir?" enquired Stephen.

"This is my father and this is my mother," said Adam. He pointed to the little boy in the battered straw hat with a serious expression. "And this is me, with my Uncle Jacob."

"The doctor would never forgive me if I didn't invite you through," said Stephen.

As they stepped onto the lawn at the rear of the house, they could hear

Jacob snoring. His experience had given him an effective alarm system which told him someone other than Stephen was there, and he stirred slightly.

Stephen whispered, "we have a visitor sir." The old man mumbled and peered into the sun and the heat haze. He easily distinguished Stephen but not the visitor.

"Hello Uncle Jacob," said Adam.

The old doctor was so excited that Stephen thought he was in danger of a seizure. "I knew it was you Adam. I knew it was you!" he said, trying to struggle to his feet and falling back. Stephen helped him to stand up. He held both of Adam's hands and embraced him. Jacob stood back.

"Stephen, this is the young man who saved my life all those years ago," he announced proudly. He grasped Adam's arm, showing him off.

"I'm pleased to meet you sir," said Stephen, "but I don't think you will be needing me at the moment." He disappeared into the house.

"And dear Käthe and Peter?" asked Jacob.

"The Gestapo killed my father and English bombers my mother," said Adam bitterly.

"Oh, I'm so sorry. I loved them both, but you know that Adam," he replied.

"I thought Yuxiang had healed your leg," remarked Jacob. "What happened?"

"English machine-gun bullets, Uncle Jacob, at Arnhem in 1944," said Adam. Jacob held out his arms in a helpless gesture, hardly daring to ask his next question, his face darkening a little.

"I must ask Adam, because I was your friend and teacher. Why the alias?"

"It has nothing to do with anything the Allies would describe as war crimes," said Adam. "It is something I cannot bear to think about, let alone discuss."

"Then we will not do so," said Jacob decisively.

They spent the next two hours swapping stories and photographs, with Stephen having to spend a great deal of time searching old hiding places for mementos. Then Adam's chauffeur appeared to remind him that the aircraft would leave in two hours' time. "You know Adam, when we die, people will really miss us don't you think?" said Jacob. A shadow fell on the meeting as Adam replied, "Perhaps they'll not remember an imposter, Uncle Jacob."

"Don't be ridiculous," said Jacob. "Even under an assumed name you have done remarkable things."

In other circumstances Adam would have been impatient at such a reply, but this was very different. As they walked past the photograph in the hallway, Jacob grasped Adam's arm and pointed to the picture of the heroic little boy. "You'll always be a man among men to me," he assured him.

They promised to keep in touch, but both knew another meeting was unlikely.

"God bless you, Adam von Saloman," said Jacob.

"And may he protect you, Uncle Jacob," replied Adam.

Jacob waved his walking stick until long after the car was gone. Two months later, Jacob Meissner died peacefully in his sleep.

"Katy's on the line, Celia," announced Karl Lindemann. "She wants to tell us something and she wants us both to listen." Celia rushed excitedly to the phone. "What is it dear, what is it?" asked an excited Celia.

"I'm going to marry Arno Kreuzfeld," said a distant voice. Celia let out a delighted squeal. "And this will please you both," added Katerina. "Wait for it. The wedding will take place in Berlin!" Another delighted squeal. "Where? Where?" asked Celia.

"Wait Mama, first things first," said Katerina. "I'll tell you more shortly. I can't seem to find Agnes in. Could you contact her for me? Tell her everything and say I'll speak with her soon."

"Now listen to this, both of you. Are you standing by a chair? Because you'll need it!" announced Katerina. "You know I told you Kurt probably hadn't left a will?"

"Yes, yes," said Celia.

"Well he did, Mama. He's left nearly everything to me."

She waited for the effect, but there was silence as Karl and Celia stared at each other. "I must go now," said Katerina. "I'll speak you both soon. I need a hand with the arrangements."

Karl replaced the phone. "Only Agnes knows. She would never betray us, Celia," he assured his wife.

"This man Vietinghoff, do you think he was Katy's father Karl?" asked Celia anxiously.

"I can't say my love," he answered."We must assume he was and that Katy might find out. There is one other thing," said Karl gravely. "We have always taken Katy's benefactors for granted. I have checked up on the organisation that pays. It doesn't exist. Maybe we'll never know who paid for Katy's education."

Celia sank into the nearest chair. "What shall we do?" she asked helplessly. "We've lived a lie Karl. Will we now pay for it?"

"We mustn't panic," he advised. "We have to trust Agnes."

Karl was almost afraid to phone Agnes Felsen. He tried several times, with no success. "Try Ulrika next door," suggested Celia. He rang Agnes' neighbour. "One moment while I check on her," answered Ulrika. She was away for less than a minute. "Herr Lindemann, come quickly, it's Agnes. I've sent for an ambulance," she said breathlessly.

The Lindemanns were just in time to see Agnes being carried to the ambulance, semi-conscious on a stretcher. Celia asked to stay with her in the ambulance. The medical team reluctantly agreed and Karl followed in his car.

On the way Agnes suffered a heart attack, the second, in the opinion of the paramedics. Celia was left outside the hospital to wait for Karl, while Agnes was taken to intensive care. The Lindemanns were allowed to see her only through a small window.

Agnes made a partial recovery, but knew she did not have much time left. She had seen the stranger in the Grünewald watching Gabrielle and Katerina, and she drew her own conclusions. She decided to embark on the course of action most dreaded by Karl and Celia. Her life had been dedicated to the creation of a family, albeit in the framework of the obscenity of the Lebensborn project. Now Agnes had decided to bring them together, despite the probable consequences.

She asked that the Lindemanns should not be allowed to see her for twenty-four hours. The Chief Consultant refused to agree. She insisted that she wanted to spend what time was left to her with whoever she wished, even though it hurt her to say it. Finally the consultant agreed.

Celia had devoted her life to Katerina, and she now faced the prospect of losing her. She locked herself in their bedroom and sobbed bitterly for hours on end. The telephone rang and she rushed downstairs to hear Karl speaking in hushed tones. He replaced the receiver; it would be possible to see Agnes the next day. Katerina's old nurse made two telephone calls.

Katerina was already driving through the night to Berlin, unaware that she was being followed by a black Mercedes saloon, driven by the person who had received the second call. Both of them spent the night in a small hotel, in complete ignorance of each other's presence in the city. Katerina was instructed to see Agnes at 11 am and the driver of the Mercedes at 11.45. Agnes had treated it like a military operation.

Katerina's taxi drew up outside the Charlottenburg Hospital at 10.30 am. The black Mercedes slid into the visitors' car park and the driver waited patiently for the appointed time.

The Chief Consultant met Katerina at the reception desk. "I must tell you I believe Fräulein Felsen should be left in peace," he began. "She is in danger of suffering a stroke. I must also tell you she insists on seeing you. I therefore leave the decision to you." He hoped Katerina would decide not to see Agnes, but he was to be disappointed. He did not know that Agnes' phone call was a demand that Katerina be there at all costs.

The flowers and a small bag Katerina carried almost slipped from her hands as she tried to decide. "I must see her," said Katerina to the doctor. "She wishes it and I've always followed her wishes."

"Please conduct Fräulein Lindemann to the patient's room, nurse," the doctor said.

The nurse stopped by the window at the end of a corridor. She opened the door quietly and ushered Katerina in. "Half an hour only, Fräulein," she said.

Agnes turned her head and forced a smile as Katerina closed the door quietly behind her. Katerina was shocked by her old nurse's appearance. She looked drawn and pale and was barely able to lift her hand as she bent down to kiss her.

Katerina took her bag from her shoulders, unzipped it and took out a tattered grey cloth elephant with one eye missing. "I had to bring Effy," Katerina explained, placing her favourite toy in front of Agnes. "How are you, my dearest Agnes?"

"My health is not the most important thing now Katy, for I feel I've not long to live." She stroked Katerina's face. "No tears, my dear. I have much to say and little time to say it. I believe you are to marry a nice young man. But you can tell me more later." Agnes paused, and a worried frown crossed her face as she began the most difficult thing she'd ever had to do.

"Your mother and father have been devoted to you Katy. But I think you know that," she continued.

"Why yes, of course I do," answered Katerina.

"My darling, I have been the bearer of terrible secrets in my past life. I am tired of the suffering my behaviour has caused and I'm going to give you a difficult choice." She paused and took Katerina's hand. "Do you want me to go on?" Agnes knew Katerina could not say no.

"You were told you were an orphan, and that your parents died in a bombing raid in 1941," she said. At the back of her mind was Karl Lindemann's behaviour at the outset. He had used the privileges of his Nazi Party Membership to acquire a child.

"I believe it is your right to know the truth, Katy," said Agnes.

"Go on," said Katerina, perplexed. Agnes could not turn back now.

"Your generation knows little of the National Socialist state," she continued. "I will tell you something of a dark period in our history." Agnes seemed to gain strength. "In 1941 twenty young men and women met, in secret, deep in the Bavarian Forest. Their purpose was to produce racially-pure children who would one day rule Germany. The children were to be raised by specially trained SS nurses in special cribs and then fostered out to selected couples. I was one of those nurses. I was assigned to a young lady who I was sure didn't want to be there. I liked her because of her air of detachment. From that moment on it became a matter of urgency to find a partner who might be worthy of her.

"The last young man to sit down was a Waffen SS trooper. He too seemed detached and uncomfortable." Agnes squeezed Katerina's hand. "But oh Katy, he was so handsome, with piercing blue eyes. I wondered if I would be punished for using my initiative. But then in a moment, I saw them exchange glances and I knew they must know each other.

"I summoned up all my courage and took her hand. I whispered to her, 'this is your best chance,' pointing to the young trooper. I dragged her over and informed him this young lady was to be his partner. He gave me a withering look, but then he coloured a deep red. He stood up and bowed and I left them for the moment.

"They quarrelled bitterly behind closed doors and then saw the light. That night they conceived you Katy, and that was the beginning of my lifelong project. They have watched your every move and cared for you. Karl and Celia know nothing of this."

Katerina stared at the floor. "Who are they?" she asked quietly. "Are they still alive?"

Agnes was finding it difficult to breathe and grasped Katerina's hand. "Your father died recently, my darling. He was a highly decorated war hero, much respected by everyone around him, including you." Katerina's eyes opened wide and her lower lip dropped slightly. "Ever since he returned from captivity in Scotland, he has followed your every move. He decided never to reveal himself to you because of a dark secret which might disturb your family life. You knew him as Kurt Vietinghoff."

Katerina was stunned into silence. She had allowed herself to fall in love with her own father. Yet suddenly everything righted itself, and she felt no shame. She realised that only her father could have done the things he had done for her. She missed him now more than ever.

Agnes waited for a reaction, but Katerina hardly moved a muscle. Agnes was badly short of breath and lay back. The nurse reappeared and suggested Katerina should leave, but Agnes reminded her that she was still in charge of her own life. The nurse left them, having made Katerina promise she would not pressure the patient. Agnes took a deep breath.

"His grandmother still lives in the great old house, Katy. Her name is Frieda von Saloman," continued Agnes. "Oh yes my darling Katy, your father was an aristocrat, although for his own reasons, he lived under another name. You have noble blood in you. What do you think of that?" she asked.

Katerina was more interested in Kurt's assumed name than she was in her aristocratic forbears. "Why the false name?" she asked quietly, unsure whether or not Agnes might be too distressed by the question.

"No one knows," answered Agnes, looking at the clock on the wall. It was 11.45. The bed curtains parted and Gabrielle joined them.

"Hello Katerina," said Gabrielle. She bent down and kissed Agnes, who managed to place one arm round her visitor's neck. She sat down and stared at Agnes, waiting for permission to speak. Katerina was pleased to see her old School Principal and was anxious for her to say something. Gabrielle shook her head and gestured towards Agnes.

Agnes forced a smile and took Katerina's hand. "Not even your mother knows the reasons, my darling," she said, sinking back into her pillows, waiting for the reaction of the other two. Gabrielle looked at her daughter as if she was pleading for forgiveness. She expected Katerina to guess the truth.

"You can ask her now if you wish," said Agnes.

The years fell away from Katerina. She became a little girl again and her eyes filled with tears. She turned towards the bed and slowly picked up her cloth elephant, holding it tightly to her chest for a few moments. Gabrielle put her hand to her mouth.

Katerina extended her arms, the elephant in her left hand. They embraced and clung on to each other desperately, the tears flowing freely. They broke free of each other, still holding on, and began to laugh. Katerina stroked her mother's hair, still laughing.

"I should have guessed," she said.

"Now you can enjoy each other," Agnes said weakly, her eyes closing. Gabrielle tore back the curtains and shouted for a nurse. Katerina held Agnes' hand. She felt it go cold and watched the images on the monitor. It had flatlined.

Agnes had fulfilled her life's work; she was gone. Gabrielle and Katerina both stared helplessly at her. Their main support was gone, and they did not know what to do.

"Please," said the nurse "I'll take care of everything. May I ask you who I should inform?"

"There is no one," replied Gabrielle, "except for her employers, the Lindemanns. They will be here shortly."

"Shall we wait for Karl and Celia?" asked Gabrielle. They had been Katerina's loving foster parents, but she did not want to see them; she did not know why. "I think it's better if we leave," she replied.

"Would you like a lift back to Bonn?" asked her mother. Katerina smiled as if she was relieved, and accepted the offer. There was so much to talk about.

Karl and Celia reached the hospital entrance as Katerina and Gabrielle reached her car. Celia saw them embrace. Celia faced Karl tearfully. "Is it possible Frau Ackerman is her mother?" she asked.

Katerina and Gabrielle said very little for nearly thirty minutes as they sped down the autobahn, Gabrielle narrowly missing a large lorry. "This may sound harsh my darling, but it was a merciful release. She had been very ill for some time," said Gabrielle. There was a further silence, which worried Gabrielle. Perhaps she had just said the wrong thing. But to her relief, Katerina then began asking questions.

"What shall I call you?" she asked.

"What would you prefer?" replied Gabrielle.

"Not Mutti surely," said Katerina. "That's for kids!"

"How about Gabby?" suggested her mother.

"Yes, all right," replied her daughter.

Once again they lapsed into silence until Katerina asked her mother, "Do you think Agnes was ever happy and contented?"

"Perhaps she had a different idea of happiness from the rest of us," answered Gabrielle.

"It's possible you kept her alive, Katy," suggested her mother.

"I'll understand if you don't want to talk at the moment," said Katerina.

"It's all right," replied her mother. "Please carry on."

"Did you and Daddy pay for my special education?" she asked. "One of you saw me nearly every day when I moved to Bonn, didn't you?" Gabrielle smiled again, as if she and Adam had been found out.

"Did you know my best friend, Philomena Gabby?" asked Katerina.

"Only slightly," said Gabrielle.

"You all told me to go for those jobs didn't you?" said Katerina, the last person on earth to wish to be manipulated.

"It was only a series of gentle suggestions, my dear," replied Gabrielle, now on the defensive.

Katerina pressed home her advantage. "I don't suppose you arranged my marriage to Arno did you?" she said.

"Oh come now," replied her mother. "He was offered only the slightest encouragement. Your father had his doubts at first, you know but he felt more certain when Arno developed some ambition." Katerina stared through the windscreen open-mouthed.

"I think we'd better pull in at the next rest area, Katy," said Gabrielle. "I have a nice flask of coffee and more things to show you." She was trying to pretend that the things she just said had had no effect.

The car drew into the next rest area and Gabrielle poured coffee into two retractable cups and sipped her drink with a satisfied smile on her face.

"Have I done *anything* on my own?" asked a slightly annoyed Katerina.

"Of course you did," replied her mother. "You ran your father's department." Katerina felt better, until Gabrielle slyly added,"And you said yes to Arno."

Katerina needed to take the initiative. "You're to be a grandmother in five months' time," she said.

"That's wonderful news!" said Gabrielle, replacing her cup and kissing her daughter.

"You've given me a new project, my darling."

"Mama!"

"Of course," said Gabrielle. "I solemnly promise not to organise your child's life." She reached into the glove compartment and withdrew a magazine. "You called me Mama," she remarked.

"I may never do so again, and certainly not in company," joked Katerina.

They resumed their journey after Gabrielle had given her a society magazine. Katerina laid the magazine across her knees. "Take a look at page twenty-five," said her mother. Katerina stared at the full-page photograph of a distinguished-looking elderly lady seated in a high chair, flanked by a square-jawed lady companion. The caption read 'The last of the von Salomans'.

"Read on," said Gabrielle. The article said that in the absence of an heir, the old lady had bequeathed the house to a family friend some years ago. There had even been talk of the house, Die Schwanen, on the Berlin lakes, reverting to the care of the state. And there was a photograph of the house.

Katerina reached in her bag for her photograph of Die Schwanen. "Stop the car, Gabby," she said sharply, and they pulled into another rest area. Katerina was speechless.

"Frieda von Saloman knew very well that she was not the last of the von Salomans, my darling," said Gabrielle, withdrawing a photograph from her bag. It was Adam, in captain's uniform. Katerina recognised her father immediately.

"This, my darling, is Captain Adam von Saloman of the Ninth SS Panzer

Division, the Hohenstaufen," said Gabrielle, her eyes filling with tears. "I'm so damn proud of him," she said.

"I'm not surprised you fell for him," remarked Katerina.

"I had some help my darling, from the wonderful Bruno," said her mother.

Katerina remembered the name on the gravestone and wanted to know more.

"Bruno was his only real friend," added Gabrielle. He changed your daddy from an overbearing, pompous individual into the man you knew."

"Carry on being open and honest, Gabby. I love it!" commented Katerina.

Gabrielle placed her hand on her daughter's. "If it's any consolation my darling, we planned to marry. I think he would have done it," she said.

"Agnes mentioned a dark secret, Mama. Do you know it?" asked Katerina.

"Only that it stopped him revealing himself to you," she answered, her face darkening. Katerina thought she knew more, but didn't press for an answer. Gabrielle's face brightened and she resumed her businesslike cheerfulness.

"You have a duty to perform, my dear," she began. "You must telephone the redoubtable Frieda and introduce yourself. You must, of course, tell her that there is to be another von Saloman," she added. Katerina seemed reluctant. "You'll have to do it sooner or later," said Gabrielle.

"How can it be a problem for someone who had Chinese diplomats eating out of her hand?" asked Katerina.

"If her housekeeper and friend Greta answers, she can sound as if you're an intruder. Give her a few seconds. She's very helpful and caring. If Frank Stephenson answers, he'll do anything to help but you might have a problem with that minx of a wife of his. Perhaps you remember the blonde woman at the funeral?"

"Mama!" said Katerina sharply. "You taught us never to refer to people like that." Then she chuckled to herself. "Was she by any chance attracted to Daddy?" Gabrielle became a school Principal for a few seconds. "Mind your own business, young lady," she retorted, and turned to the subject of wedding guests.

As Gabrielle drove them the remaining distance at high speed, Katerina wondered how Arno would react to the news. She hadn't considered his reaction until they were within a few kilometres of Bonn, and her mother began to obey the speed limits.

EPILOGUE – PART I

The car glided into Katerina's underground parking reservation. Gabrielle switched off the engine and they looked hard at each other.

"Perhaps this won't be so easy for you," said Gabrielle. "May I suggest you take a lighthearted approach?" Her daughter nodded in agreement.

Epilogue – Part II

The more Katerina thought about her mother's suggestion, the more she thought it was a good idea. "Very well Mama," she said as they stepped into the lift. "We'll enjoy this, but not at Arno's expense."

When Arno saw Gabrielle, his jaw dropped. He quickly kissed Katerina and turned to her companion. "Dr Ackerman, what a pleasant surprise," he said. "Katerina should have telephoned ahead to tell me." He was trying to behave as comfortably as he could in the presence of the School Principal, who had ridden roughshod over at least two interview boards he could remember. He had also known for some time, through Katerina, that Gabrielle had been his boss' mistress. Arno was ill at ease, to say the least. He retreated to the kitchen to catch his breath and looked for refreshment. "Frau Klugman's brought us some more cakes Katy, shall I bring them out with the coffee?" he called out.

"Of course my darling," answered Katerina, who saw that her mother was enjoying herself. Arno appeared with the coffee and cakes.

"Well," began Arno. "To what do we owe the pleasure of your company, Dr Ackerman?"

"Arno, my love," said Katerina, placing her cup and saucer down on the table, "I know you have worked hard on the wedding list, but please could you make one change?" Arno smiled obligingly. "I would like Gabrielle to be the guest of honour at our wedding," she said and waited for the request to have some effect.

Arno was puzzled, and Katerina took a deep breath. "Arno," she continued with some difficulty, "May I present my mother."

The cup of coffee in Arno's left hand tilted slightly and some spilled into the saucer. He put it down, but continued to hold the spoon rigidly in his right hand. Gabrielle flushed a deep red, and before Arno had time to recover,

Katerina announced that the man they had known as Kurt Vietinghoff had been her father. "Do you mind, my love?" she asked. She reached into her handbag and produced the photograph of Adam in his captain's uniform. She handed it proudly to Arno, who placed his cup on the table and slumped backwards into his chair. He looked at Gabrielle and began to splutter with laughter.

"These interviews all those years ago," he began. "They were all fixed, weren't they? Oh, I'm so sorry," he added apologetically. "That must sound very rude."

"It's a lovely evening," said Katerina. "Shall we take a walk in the park before dinner?"

They walked slowly by a stream which emptied into a lake. "We can go to our favourite seat by the lake, Arno," suggested Katerina. He let go of her hand and took Gabrielle's. She walked between them, arm in arm with both. At that moment, Katerina realised she was about to marry a quite exceptional man.

An elderly man reached the seat before them and settled down, holding his walking stick in front of him, until he saw them approaching. They changed course to pretend they hadn't intended to occupy the seat, but the old man had guessed their intention.

"I'm terribly sorry," he said. "Please sit down."

"No please," said Katerina.

"You must have the seat," insisted the man. He stood up and produced food for the ducks. "I have important work to do here," he said, looking intently at Gabrielle and Katerina. "Mother and daughter I think," he remarked. "Lots to talk about. You probably haven't seen each other for a few weeks. I'll bid you good evening."

By the time they had enjoyed a hearty meal at a restaurant a few blocks away from the apartment, Arno and Gabrielle had become the best of friends and she had accepted an invitation to stay the night. Once again Agnes was the subject of conversation, and Gabrielle watched her daughter's mood change dramatically. Arno desperately wanted to discuss his fiancée's problems with her mother, but guessed that Katerina didn't wish her mother to know.

Arno suggested meeting again to acquaint Gabrielle with the wedding arrangements. Before that Katerina had to face Agnes' funeral. She had to telephone her adoptive parents first. Celia felt cheated, because Agnes had died before she could see her, and she chided Katerina for not telephoning sooner with the details. There was a distinct atmosphere at the funeral, and Katerina felt she could not have got through it without Arno. The Lindemanns said they looked forward to the wedding, but they did not go back to Katerina's apartment after the funeral, Karl mentioning a business appointment in Berlin.

Katerina made the dreaded phone call to Die Schwanen from her office at the university. Her knees were weak as the phone rang four times before it was answered.

"The von Saloman residence, Helga Stephenson speaking," said a flat, formal voice.

Katerina felt even worse to hear the voice of the fearsome Helga, but she could not have been more helpful and friendly.

"We are delighted to hear from you, Katerina," she began. "We have all looked forward so much to your call."

Katerina remembered her mother's dislike of Helga and was amused. "I must apologise for not properly introducing myself at the funeral," continued Helga. "Herr Adam asked that we should not do so until after the will reading. Herr Berger and Herr Schöler have alerted Madam to receive your call, Katerina. I will transfer to you to her room. Please wait a moment."

Katerina began to tremble once more as she heard the receiver picked up. Frieda spoke slowly and tremulously. "Good morning my dear Katerina," she began. "I despaired of ever having a great grandchild, but here you are and you have made us all happy. Please accept my condolences on the loss of your dear nurse and my congratulations on your engagement." She sounded like a revered international figure speaking on the radio.

She made a suggestion that sounded like a command from a great lady. "Have you finalised the plans for your wedding, my dear?" she asked, and Katerina sensed that an invitation was about to be made. She wisely said that the arrangements were only provisional.

"We would be honoured if you would hold the reception here at Die Schwanen," said Frieda. "We have a small family chapel of our own here."

Not only the reception but the service too would be held at Die Schwanen. "This is like listening to my father," Katerina thought. "I would be honoured to accept your invitation," said Katerina, and Frieda ended the conversation as if only so much time had been allocated to it.

Frieda asked Helga to keep in touch with Katerina. But the responsibility for the success of the wedding day was transferred to Frank Stephenson, who was gently terrorised by Helga into getting everything right.

Katerina wanted to tease as much information as she could about her father from her mother. Arno had noticed his bride-to-be's anxiety on the subject and offered to cook a Chinese banquet for the three of them, based on He Quiao Gu's recipes, which he had found in Adam's room at the university. Arno excelled himself and cooked a succession of simple but tasty dishes, washed down by large quantities of hock.

Arno suggested they examine the objects they had found in Adam's room, which they assumed Gabrielle had seen. They began with several photographs.

"This is the lady who made all this wonderful food possible," said Arno. Gabrielle looked puzzled and slightly hurt, because she had not seen any of the photographs. When she told the others, they were equally puzzled. "He kept all these things here and not at his flat," said Arno, "as if he didn't wish to share them with anyone."

One of the pictures was a group photograph which showed Adam aged ten with Yuxiang's family. "See how comfortable your father looks among them, Katy," remarked Arno. "Notice how the master of the house places his hands on his shoulders. That's a true mark of acceptance. Look again. These three men are of a lower class. Yet they appear in the same photograph as the master of the house. I can assure you that would have been unheard of," he said, sounding puzzled.

"Do you think it's something to do with Daddy?" Katerina asked. "How could he have so much influence?" Both Gabrielle and Arno thought it was. "Perhaps we all know a little of the answer," remarked Gabrielle.

"When he talked about China, he didn't seem excited, only at peace," said Gabrielle. "It was as if he was having a conversation with himself."

"Why do you think he joined the Waffen SS, Gabrielle?" asked Arno. Katerina waited for her mother's reply anxiously, thinking of the Lebensborn project. Gabrielle laid a reassuring hand on her arm.

"He wanted to be like one of Marshall Blucher's Black Guards," she said "You can see them in grandfather Gustav's battle scene at the house."

Katerina's face lit up. She quickly went to her bedroom and unlocked a cupboard, returning with the model soldier which had been left at the memorial stone, holding it up for all to see. Gabrielle became excited. "Gustav made that for Adam and there were others," she said. "I know he gave one each to the sons of Huang Yuxiang. They were like brothers to him."

"Then that must have been one of them by the graveside," said Katerina. The others nodded in agreement.

Gabrielle reached inside her handbag, produced Adam's old leather wallet and kissed it. "This has been for a swim in the Rhine," she said, pretending to hesitate on seeing her daughters' impatience.

"Show us Mama, please," begged Katerina. Gabrielle hesitated before producing photos of the three main women in Adam's life. Katerina gazed at the photo of her mother in admiration. "You look amazing Mama," she remarked.

"What a distinguished-looking lady," remarked Arno when he saw Frieda's photograph.

"That's the lady at the centre of the wreath," said Katerina. "Oh look, this must be Käthe," she added. "She looks beautiful, but so distant and unhappy."

"Welcome to the family of secrets," said Gabrielle. "I don't suppose we'll ever know Käthe's."

"Knowing Papa, he probably knew it," said Katerina, and Arno laughed.

"I believe Frieda was his conscience," said Gabrielle. " But he derived a great deal of his strength from Käthe in his early years." She paused to watch the impact of her next remark. "I believe he was a little in love with his mother." Neither Arno nor Katerina showed any surprise.

"I can't wait for you to meet Frieda," continued Gabrielle. "She'll see into your soul with a glance!"

"Like Papa," said Katerina.

"Oh yes, my dear, just like him," said Gabrielle. "She loved Käthe like a daughter. If you give her the chance, she'll talk all night about her."

Gabrielle produced another photograph of Adam and Bruno, taken at the Martin Luther School. Katerina was intrigued by Bruno, who seemed to be leaning towards the photographer, who, it turned out, was Gabrielle.

"Why did Daddy look so different with Bruno, Mama?" asked Katerina, who had noticed that Adam seemed more relaxed and less formal.

"I'll tell you more about the wonderful Bruno later," promised her mother. "He's worth a book on his own."

Arno nodded to his wife-to-be to prompt the inevitable nagging question which had upset Katerina so much. She had to know the reason for Adam's failure to reveal himself to her. "What happened, Mama?" she asked simply.

Gabrielle could see that her daughter believed she should take some of the blame, and the atmosphere changed. Arno sat beside Katerina and took her hand. "I wish I knew my darling," Gabrielle answered, hoping against hope she would be believed. "He was devastated by his mother's death, although I believe that had little to do with his decision. You'll meet his two sergeants very soon. They're both sure it had something to do with Bruno's death. Both know more than they care to reveal, and they don't like questions. One of them, Franz Stamm, revealed something to me, and I warn you it may not be palatable to any of you. Stamm told me that Adam's last patrol was a deliberate attempt to commit suicide."

Katerina's face reddened. "That is ridiculous!" she exclaimed. "Daddy would never have done such a thing."

Gabrielle placed her hand on her daughter's arm. "I'm as revolted by the thought as you are, my darling," she said. "We are just beginning to discover that so many German officers sacrificed themselves. Your father may have used the cloak of an ancient tradition to cover such an attempt. We are at the mercy of the two men who knew him best. I should tell you they live under assumed names, so I would guess they won't tell us."

"Was it something to do with his oath to Hitler?" asked Katerina. Arno quickly replied, "I believe it was not." He held up of a photograph of Huang Yuxiang. "We all know the famous quotation of St Ignatius, 'Give me the child until he is six and I'll give you the man.' I would like to remind you that when other young Germans were strutting up and down pretending that Hitler was a surrogate father, Adam was under the influence of this man." He held up the group photograph. "I know he loved and respected this Chinese landowner and his family. They would never have counselled suicide." He held up Adam's battered copy of Confucius. "This was his Bible. There are no thoughts of suicide in here, only clever compromises."

"Perhaps you have the answer, Gabrielle," suggested Arno. "You knew him on his return to Germany."

"It is true that for a while he was a shadow of what he once had been, but I don't know why," she answered.

"Perhaps he was like the great Odysseus who met his downfall and yet recovered," said Arno.

"He was a little heroic, you know," said Gabrielle. "He seemed to stand apart from other men. There were times even in my company when he behaved like a distant stranger."

"What's this?" asked Arno, holding up a battle-scarred yellow pennant.

"It used to belong to Bruno. Stamm said they rallied round it and touched it before they went into battle. They were sure that helped them to survive," Gabrielle explained.

"Go on," said Arno.

"I believe he wanted his men to be devoted to him. Stamm said he commanded loyalty from almost anyone," Gabrielle said.

"All the graves in Holland have the Three Lions," remarked Katerina. I believe that was the reason why I took his remains to Holland."

"The power of comradeship in war is beyond our understanding," added Arno.

By now Katerina had placed her dead father on a pedestal, thinking him incapable of doing anything repugnant. "Could he have been a Prime Minister or a President in the Bundesrepublik, do you think?" she enquired.

Gabrielle smiled at Arno. "I have it on very good authority he was being considered as a future Ambassador to the People's Republic of China," said Arno.

"But didn't he hate the Communists?" asked Katerina.

Arno laughed politely. "Your father could change like a chameleon. Please don't take that the wrong way. You'll find his reasons in Confucius' writings."

Arno scratched his chin, as he always did before making a telling remark. "Try reading Confucius on the family," he said. "I would suggest the only suicidal thing he risked was his determination to pursue you at great risk to himself and his career during the war, Katerina. He was desperate for family life but believed he didn't deserve to enjoy it, for some reason."

Gabrielle announced that she had made arrangements to meet Hans Thaelmann and Franz Stamm. "I'll find the reason somehow," she said.

"This is for you two only, I think," suggested Arno.

On a bright spring day, the train pulled into Arnhem. The two women fell silent as they entered the theatre of Adam's last days as a soldier. The station echoed with announcements over the public address system and the sound of hurrying feet.

"That must be them," said Katerina. Stamm smiled broadly when he was fifty metres away but Hans Thaelmann was hesitant and shy. Stamm behaved as if he was taking his companion for a walk.

"Welcome to Holland," said Stamm, wreathed in smiles. "You're both wonderful and beautiful. What an improvement on talking on the phone."

To him, Katerina was aristocracy. He shook hands, bowed and suggested the ladies take some refreshment. "It's not far from here," he promised. "You look like the boss," Stamm said to Katerina.

Stamm drove them to the oldest part of town. In one corner of a tiny square was a small café. The waitress knew the two men and seated the visitors.

"Champagne, Renée, if you please," said Stamm. "And whatever you want to give him," he added, pointing at Hans. She kissed Hans on the forehead affectionately. "The flowers are ready," she said and went behind the bar for a bottle of champagne. "Renée was his girlfriend before the war." Said Stamm

"I can speak for myself, Franz," said Hans.

"Before you ask," said Stamm, "there is no longer any need for false identities. We'll explain later, away from all this. And I'm sorry we seemed rude to you Fräulein when you brought the boss here for the last time."

"Why are the men of my father's company all here?" asked Katerina. "Did they all die here in the battle?"

"No Fräulein," answered Hans. "You will remember Karl Eberhardt's grave, the first you saw? We brought him back from Normandy and had his remains transferred from a military cemetery." Hans knew his friend wanted to do most of the talking.

"They are all here because Bruno Grabowsky is here," Franz explained. "And Bruno is here also because his fatherland rejected him." Franz glanced towards the florist's shop. "I think the wreaths are ready," he announced. "I'll drive."

They passed the crossed-out sign for Oosterbeek. "It feels so different now and so right, I think," said Katerina. "Then the fog and the rain cloaked us and it felt wrong," she added.

They left the town and Stamm turned into a small side track. "It's time to tell them, Hans," he said to his old comrade. Thaelmann produced two long envelopes, each emblazoned with the eagle of the Bundesrepublik. "Each of these contains a pardon for Franz and myself," he announced turning to face the women in the rear seats. "There is another for our captain," he said, giving Gabrielle an envelope. "Please open it," he said quietly and firmly.

Gabrielle opened the letter. It announced a pardon for Captain Adam von Saloman and detailed that in the case of the deaths of Rademacher, Schneider and Kammler, there was no case to answer.

"Speak frankly, for their sakes," Franz reminded his friend.

"The three men were not war casualties," said Hans. "They were German policemen, and we killed them because they wished to dishonour Bruno, our friend." He gave the briefest possible account of what happened. "I have a terrible temper and it cost the life of an innocent young man," admitted Hans.

"And Daddy?" asked Katerina.

"He suggested we do it," said Stamm, who realised his friend couldn't say it.

"His grandmother knows," added Hans Thaelmann, as if somehow that could exonerate them.

The two men sat with heads bowed. They thought the silence was a judgment, and it was no more than they expected.

"He did it for the wonderful Bruno," remarked Gabrielle. Their relief was tangible. "Adam never stopped talking about you two and Bruno. Nothing he told me will change. You're our new friends forever."

She expected Katerina to underwrite everything she had said, and she was not disappointed. "I've never had a chance to disagree with my mother and I don't intend to start now," said Katerina. "Please take us to Daddy's resting place." Gabrielle squeezed her arm.

Katerina remembered the crunching of car tyres on the gravel track that chilly October day in 1985. Now she could see for miles across the endless agricultural landscape, broken only by a small copse in the near distance. The track ran out and the car stopped behind another car. Katerina thought this was a re-run of past events. This time, the oaks were thick with leaves and the picket fence had been painted white out of respect for local feeling.

Piet Kuyt, the ageing landowner, met them at the gate.

"Is everything prepared Piet?" asked Franz Stamm. The Dutchman led them to the centre of the shrine to Adam's Company. Gabrielle placed her hand on the new gravestone and read it proudly to her daughter. "HAUPTSTURMFUHRER ADAM VON SALOMAN 9TH SS. PANZER DIVISION. HOHENSTAUFEN 1985."

Gabrielle and her daughter each laid a wreath and Thaelmann and Stamm snapped to attention. They turned to the other guardian of these men from another life. Gabrielle laid the third wreath on Bruno's grave.

"Thank you for everything," she said, blowing a kiss to him.

"Thank God for Bruno," said Katerina, bursting into tears. "He made Daddy chase you, Mama."

Katerina presented the pennant to the two sergeants and Hans Thaelmann draped it over Adam's grave. "It must never be moved Piet," he instructed the landowner, "so that these two men are bonded together." He patted Bruno's grave.

"All the men who served under the Lions will be buried here," added Franz.

"Where is Michael Kaspar?" asked Gabrielle.

"Kaspar is serving a prison sentence for murder and armed robbery. The prison authorities have agreed to bring him here when he dies. He served honourably with us and will be rewarded. His place is here beside the Captain."

Katerina had instructed her mother not to arrive at Die Schwanen before eleven o'clock on the wedding day. Eva Knopke had insisted she chauffeur her old friend on this momentous day.

The car emerged from the trees near the gates and was bathed in the sunlight of a bright summer's day. Eva slowed almost to a stop. "Did you ever see anything like that?" she asked her friend, staring at the gathering on the steps of the house.

Old Stephan ran towards the car to direct it to its parking space. The car window slid noisily down. "Hello my old friend," said Gabrielle to the breathless old retainer.

Nearly two hundred people were waiting at the front of the house. Katerina and Arno were at the top of the steps, flanked by Frieda, Greta, Frank, Helga and Alfred. Frank was not the only guest in uniform. On his left stood Manfred, wearing the uniform of a tank commander in the Bundeswehr. Helga nudged him as a reminder to behave himself.

Katerina wore a long white dress and a garland of flowers in her hair. No one had ever seen Arno dressed so immaculately. Frieda, now in a wheelchair, stared into the distance, as her eyesight was failing. The faithful Greta stood behind her, one hand on the chair, the other on the walking stick with Alfred watching over them.

Stephan offered his arm to Gabrielle and the four of them walked slowly towards the gathering. Eva whispered. "My God, they're waiting specially for you Gabby."

Everyone looked in Gabrielle's direction. Helga invited her forward with a movement of her index finger. Gabrielle climbed the steps and apologised for her lateness in a small voice which was lost in the expanse of the garden and the noise of the birdsong.

"No my dear Gabrielle, you are exactly on time. Everyone has gathered here so that they may greet you," Frieda reassured her. The guests broke into applause and tears streamed down Gabrielle's face. Frank and his American friends gave three cheers.

Frieda tried to struggle to her feet, but Helga restrained her.

"No," said the head of the family. "Please help me to my feet. I will receive my Gabrielle standing." Frank and Helga supported her as she formally greeted Gabrielle.

"You are the guest of honour Gabrielle," she announced. "All the arrangements have been made." She collapsed back into the wheelchair.

"I will look after you two today," Alfred announced to Gabrielle and Eva. The guests made their way to the ceremony in the family chapel at the western end of the house.

Five months later, Katerina and Arno had a son, Adam Arno. Two weeks later the family doctor, Werner Petersen, telephoned Greta and Helga and asked if he might see them both. Greta had usually taken Frieda on outings into the Grünewald, sometimes as far as the pier where her mistress and friend enjoyed watching the sightseers boarding the pleasure steamers.

It now fell to Helga to take Frieda, and she guessed why Dr Petersen wished to see them. "I have spoken with Dr Petersen," said Frieda. "I shall be interested in any suggestions he has to make." She turned to a small pile of society magazines, picked them up and dropped them on the floor, no longer able to read them. "I will not be offended if you see the doctor without me to begin with," she said. "He would not say anything which would surprise me."

Helga showed Dr Petersen into the first reception room. "This room has had a colourful career," he remarked, knowing it had been used as an office by Colonel Malek and Major Macey. "You ladies have devoted a great deal of your lives to the care of your mistress. It is now my belief that she is in need of twenty-four hour care. I suggested as much when I spoke with her yesterday."

Greta began to shake her head. "Dear Greta," he continued. "You are both in need of help and your mistress needs assistance neither of you can provide." Helga grasped her mother's arm, because it was Greta who needed to be persuaded. "What do you suggest doctor?" she asked.

"I have taken the liberty of speaking to the Mother Superior at the Convent. Your priest has also paid her a visit," continued the doctor. "We have found excellent accommodation for Frau von Saloman. It is a beautiful room looking out on to a courtyard garden. You'll be welcome to visit whenever you wish. I have made an appointment for you to see the Mother Superior, but we must first, of course, secure the approval of your mistress Greta."

"But who will care for her?" asked the desperately worried housekeeper.

"Ah," continued the doctor "I have found not only specialist help but a suitable companion for your mistress, although I'm sure she'll never replace you, dear Greta," he added.

Frieda rejected all Greta's arguments in favour of private care at the house, saying the constant worry would intrude far too much into Katerina and Arno's new lives. Nothing they said could change her mind. Frieda's chief concern was the care of Greta, and she knew her daughter was devoted to her.

Frieda had one last wish; she asked Katerina to turn Gustav's war room into a family museum. Katerina enthusiastically agreed.

A private ambulance arrived for Frieda. Frank and Alfred carried her down the steps in her wheelchair. Before she mounted the ramp at the rear of the ambulance, she said with an air of finality to Greta, "I will never return to the house. Please do not try to change my mind." Greta was unable to say anything.

The ambulance began to move slowly down the drive, with Greta seated beside her old friend. The rest followed in Alfred's car and Gabrielle was to meet them all at the Convent. Frieda's last memory of Die Schwanen was a blurred image of the old chestnut tree in the centre of the lawn. She couldn't see the two little wooden crosses, the graves of Hansl and Gretl at the foot of the tree, but she remembered them. She thought of Adam and wept.

"I will tell you a little about Frau von Saloman's new companion before they're introduced," said the Mother Superior. "She was the Chief Children's Nurse here from March 1944 onwards and studied hard to become a doctor." She rang a bell and they waited. Frieda began to fidget nervously and none of the visitors took heed of the date she had mentioned. They heard no footsteps, but saw the handle of the door turn.

A Carmelite nun entered the room slowly, her head bowed. Frieda strained what remained of her eyesight to try and gain some impression of her companion. The nun lifted her head to reveal a pale handsome face with deep brown eyes. Helga gripped her mother's arm. Greta's body tensed, and the nun smiled humbly at them all.

"May I introduce Sister Michael?" said Dr Petersen.